WANTING EVERYTHING

ALSO BY GLADYS HINDMARCH

*A Birth Account*
*The Peter Stories*
*The Watery Part of the World*

# WANTING EVERYTHING

THE COLLECTED WORKS

OF

# Gladys Hindmarch

EDITED BY DEANNA FONG AND KARIS SHEARER

TALONBOOKS

© 2020 Gladys Hindmarch
Introduction © 2020 Deanna Fong and Karis Shearer

All rights reserved. No part of this book may be reproduced, stored in a retrieval system, or transmitted, in any form or by any means, without the prior written consent of the publisher or a licence from Access Copyright (The Canadian Copyright Licensing Agency). For a copyright licence, visit accesscopyright.ca or call toll-free 1-800-893-5777.

Talonbooks
9259 Shaughnessy Street, Vancouver, British Columbia, Canada V6P 6R4
talonbooks.com

Talonbooks is located on xʷməθkʷəy̓əm, Sḵwx̱wú7mesh, and səl̓ilwətaʔɬ Lands.

First printing: 2020

Typeset in Arno
Printed and bound in Canada on 100% post-consumer recycled paper

Interior and cover design by Typesmith
On the cover: *Convergence (The Bridge)*, 1964, by Roy Kiyooka. Aquatec on canvas, 85½″ × 59″. Reproduced with the kind permission of the estate of Roy Kiyooka.

Talonbooks acknowledges the financial support of the Canada Council for the Arts, the Government of Canada through the Canada Book Fund, and the Province of British Columbia through the British Columbia Arts Council and the Book Publishing Tax Credit.

LIBRARY AND ARCHIVES CANADA CATALOGUING IN PUBLICATION

Title: Wanting everything : the collected works / Gladys Hindmarch ; edited by Deanna Fong and Karis Shearer.

Other titles: Works

Names: Hindmarch, Gladys, 1940– author. | Fong, Deanna, editor. | Shearer, Karis, 1980– editor.

Description: Includes bibliographic references.

Identifiers: Canadiana 20190229225 | ISBN 9781772012705 (HARDCOVER) | ISBN 9781772012484 (SOFTCOVER)

Classification: LCC PS8565.I6 2020 | DDC C813/.54,—dc23

# Contents

xiii    Introduction
         by Deanna Fong and Karis Shearer

## Book-Length Works

### The Peter Stories (1976)
- 3    One
- 6    Two
- 9    Three
- 12    Four
- 14    Five

### A Birth Account (1976)
- 19    Introductory Note
- 21    Pregnant
- 32    Pregnant with Lars
- 47    Birth

### The Watery Part of the World (1988)
- 79    1. The Hall
- 84    2. The *Nootka*
- 90    3. Callback
- 96    4. Faraway Places
- 102    5. Some Trip This Is Going to Be
- 111    6. Nothing Is Simple
- 116    7. Ucluelet
- 124    8. A Single Scrambled
- 126    9. Tulips
- 130    10. How It Feels
- 133    11. I Gotta Get Outta Here
- 138    12. Tahsis
- 142    13. Zeballos
- 147    14. Just Because These Words

| | |
|---|---|
| 153 | 15. Boat Drill |
| 156 | 16. Three in the Afternoon |
| 161 | 17. Just a Moment |
| 162 | 18. King of the Jerks |
| 168 | 19. Underwear |
| 173 | 20. I Got *My* Work to Do |
| 177 | 21. The Watery Part of the World |

# Short Prose/Sketches

| | |
|---|---|
| 185 | A Short Short Story (1962) |

## Improsements (1989–1991)

| | |
|---|---|
| 186 | Improsement 1 |
| 189 | Improsement 2 |
| 191 | Improsement 3 |

# Journals

## From the Vancouver Poetry Conference Journal

| | |
|---|---|
| 195 | A Walk about Campus |
| 197 | July 26, 1963 |
| 198 | July 27, 1963 |
| 199 | August 4, 1963 |
| 200 | August 6, 1963 |
| 202 | August 8, 1963 |
| 202 | August 11, 1963: Aboard the Island Princess |

## From the Blue Notebook, 1975

| | |
|---|---|
| 206 | April 26, 1975: Sunday Afternoon |
| 206 | April 29, 1975 |
| 207 | May 1, 1975: 11:32 am |
| 208 | May 2, 1975 |
| 208 | May 4, 1975: On Virginia Woolf |
| 209 | May 16, 1975: Lars Dressed Himself Today |
| 210 | Left, Right |
| 211 | March 16, 1976 |
| 211 | The Biggest Day of His Life |
| 212 | Late March or April 1 weekend |

### From the Wine and Blue Notebook

- 214    February 24, 1980
- 214    March 23, 1980
- 215    April 13, 1980
- 215    May 2, 1980: 3–4 a.m.
- 216    October 3, 1980
- 216    November 28, 1980

### From the Buff Notebook

- 217    June 3, 1981
- 218    June 24, 1981

### From the Blue Notebook, 1982

- 219    June 24, 1982: Saint-Jean-Baptiste Day
- 219    June 29, 1982: Tuesday, Saturna Island
- 220    July, 1982: Joe's Cappuccino Bar
- 220    July 6, 1982
- 221    July 15, 1982
- 221    July 23, 1982
- 221    August 3, 1982
- 223    July 4, 1983

### From the Silver Notebook

- 224    Undated, 1984
- 226    June 27, 1984: Two Dogs, Three Fights

# Letters

- 231    To Fred Wah, undated, *circa* April/May 1966
- 235    To Stan Persky, September 28, 1969
- 238    To Stan Persky, undated, *circa* 1970
- 240    To Henry Alan Lawless and Prime Minister Trudeau, 1970
- 242    To Daphne Marlatt, October 6, 1970
- 244    To Daphne Marlatt, undated, *circa* 1970
- 247    To George and Angela Bowering, April 26, 1971
- 249    To bpNichol, January 18, 1973
- 252    To the Editor, *Vancouver Sun*: "Writers Forgotten," undated, *circa* 1970
- 255    To the Editor, *Vancouver Sun*: "Cradles as coffins, coffins as cradles, a womb is sometimes both," July 7, 1981

## Essays and Reviews

- 259  So You Ask Me – An Essay in Jazz (1959)
- 262  Review of *blewointment* 1 (1963)
- 265  What Can I Do? Germaine Greer Smashes Myths (1971)
- 268  HERmione, H.D. (1982)
- 271  Review of Sharon Thesen's *The Beginning of the Long Dash* (1987)

## Oral Histories, Recordings, Conversations

- 283  Westcoast with Gladys: Conversation between Gladys Hindmarch and Warren Tallman (1969)
- 297  Before *TISH*: from *Oral History of Vancouver* (interview by Brad Robinson, 1971–1972)
- 305  Jack Spicer Interview with Gladys Hindmarch by Terry Ludwar (1991)
- 311  Always Talking: Interview with Gladys Hindmarch by Deanna Fong and Karis Shearer (2018)

## Occasional Writings

- 349  Women and Words Workshop: Writing and the Erotic (1983)
- 352  For Warren (1987)
- 354  Pauline and Fred: Friends, Parties, Community (2004)
- 363  For George (2005)
- 364  For Sharon (2008)
- 366  Hey, Pierre (2012)
- 369  Untitled, for George Woodcock (2012)
- 374  Kitsilano (1963–1969) (2018–2019)

## Unpublished Prose

### From Third Person Singular

- 381  She Was a Talky Child
- 384  Sentences
- 386  Face It, Mom
- 387  Write Woman
- 387  A Mother's Form
- 388  She Knows
- 388  Listen
- 389  Eyes Tired

| | |
|---|---|
| 389 | Today She Is on Strike |
| 389 | Scrolling Amber |
| 390 | Name Me a Truly Monogamous Man |
| 390 | the day before |
| 391 | Image of a Corner |

## From Swimming with Cancer

| | |
|---|---|
| 392 | Imaginary Valentines |
| 393 | Signs |
| 394 | Lost Girl |
| 394 | Locum |
| 395 | Where Can Taimi Live? |
| 396 | Screening Mammography |
| 396 | Dr. A Examines Me |
| 397 | To Victoria |
| 397 | No Diagnosis Today |
| 398 | No Swim Today |
| 399 | No Results |
| 399 | A Flip-Flop |
| 399 | Dr. C Stalls for Time |
| 400 | Teach Mark Teach |
| 401 | Punch Biopsy |
| 401 | Running Close to Empty |
| 402 | This Is It |
| 402 | A Piece of Glass or Sheet of Ice |
| 403 | No More Waiting |
| 404 | Before I Knew and Now |
| 406 | First Visit to the Vancouver Cancer Agency |
| 411 | MUGA |
| 412 | Core Needle Biopsy |
| 415 | Visit with Dr. D the Afternoon Before First Chemo |
| 417 | Chemo Hats and a Kind Stranger |
| 418 | First Chemo |
| 424 | Heading Home |
| 426 | Itchy Head |
| 426 | Who's There? |
| 426 | What's That? |
| 427 | Buzz Off |
| 427 | Electric |
| 427 | Getting Ready for Second Chemo |

| | |
|---|---|
| 428 | Bloodwork and Bruising |
| 428 | Yew Amulets |
| 428 | Visit to Nurse and Doctor Prior to Second Chemo |
| 430 | Second Chemo |
| 434 | First Few Days after Second Chemo |
| 434 | I Stumble |
| 434 | Strolling in a Storm |
| 435 | I Want to Swim |
| 436 | Swimming Again |
| 436 | And Again |
| 436 | Damn Blister |
| 437 | A Visit with My GP |
| 438 | I Practice Saying Goodbye to My Breast |
| 438 | Love All |
| 439 | Last Acts before Surgery |
| 439 | Surgery Thursday |
| 442 | Discharged Friday |
| 443 | Bad News |
| 445 | First Radiation |
| 449 | What's My Prognosis Now? |

# Postprose

| | |
|---|---|
| 453 | Postprose (1991) |

| | |
|---|---|
| 455 | Bibliography: Works by Gladys Hindmarch |
| 457 | Acknowledgments |
| 458–460 | Biographies |

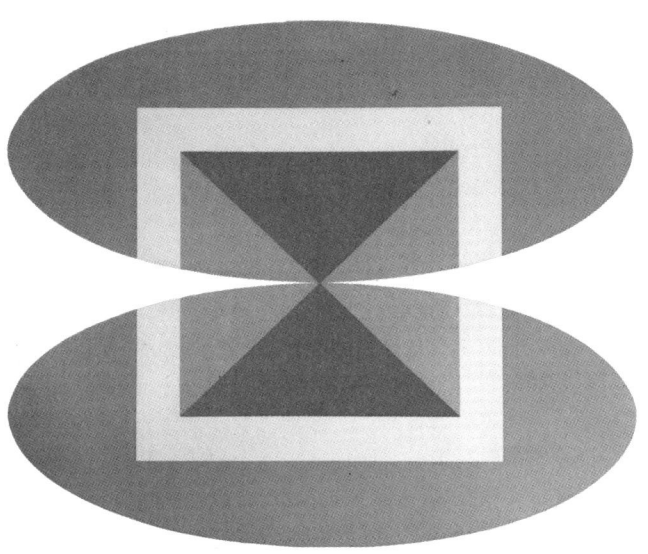

# Introduction

BY DEANNA FONG AND KARIS SHEARER

*She is a contradiction, both passive at times almost sleeping and then move move move wanting to talk wanting to love wanting to eat wanting to write wanting to have everything in a day of her life.*

—GLADYS HINDMARCH
*Third Person Singular*

Gladys Hindmarch's singular practice as an author centres on writing not as a product but as a *process* – one deeply engaged in dialogue with others, and shaped by processes of revisitation and return. As Pauline Butling writes, in Hindmarch's prose "there is a feeling of everything being present at once." In exploring the varied genres represented in this collection – fiction, criticism, journals, correspondence, and interviews – we witness instances of telling and retelling: a redoubling of writing *around* writing. This unique feature of Hindmarch's work speaks to her acuity as an observing subject who wants to bring the world around her into her writing. In "Image of a Corner" from her short-prose series *Third Person Singular*, the speaker describes revising a short story written nineteen summers earlier, hoping to "stick with the image" that stands out in her mind: "She tries to convey the perception of an unbalanced corner accurately while keeping the language precise and rhythmical" (391). The speaker describes a *desire* – a want – to transmit the impressions of her own senses with truth and precision, while at the same time admitting the limitations of that possibility: "She spends more than two hours trying to get this image right and it is still not accurate" (391). Language fails. And yet, the multiple and concentric efforts to *get at* the object of memory through language bring us into its orbit.

This impulse toward documentary precision also marks a deeply ethical desire to represent the subjects of her writing – friends, contemporaries, and strangers, as well as places, relationships, and feelings – with respect and care. Part of "wanting everything" means wanting to bring the real relations of everyday life into writing while doing justice to their specificity and import. Like Jack Spicer, who in his *After Lorca*, wishes for the "lemon to be a lemon that the reader could cut or squeeze or taste – a real lemon" (unpag.), Hindmarch desires a documentary reality that pushes beyond the limits of language, while fully acknowledging that language as a medium to represent the past is inherently flawed. The stories that comprise a body of "writing writing" (as Hindmarch refers to it in *Third Person Singular*) interweave with another kind of writing, one that pulls back the curtain on the writing process itself to interrogate how representation takes place, and how certain details become salient while others fade into the background.

This "other" kind of writing blurs the boundaries that we tend to imagine between "the literary" and everyday life in a way that resonates not only with the aesthetics of time (in the 1960s, aligning with Fluxus and the Brechtian event score), but also with the conversations taking place among Hindmarch's contemporaries. Roy Kiyooka, Hindmarch's longtime friend and writing contemporary (whose painting graces the cover of this book and who makes an appearance in *Third Person Singular*), writes in his unpublished manuscript *Laughter*: "Every occasion is its own artifact. It doesn't need to go through an artifice to become something" (quoted in Fong, 45). Kiyooka's *transcanada letters* (Talonbooks, 1975; reprinted NeWest Press, 2005) similarly blurred the lines between the documentary and the fictive by including correspondence and journal fragments alongside poetry and other forms of innovative writing. Hindmarch's work, however, approaches the divide between art and life differently, not seeking their complete and seamless integration, but rather paying careful attention to the places where they run aground. For example, there is her ongoing struggle to keep up with the demands of motherhood and domestic life alongside full-time college teaching, all while trying to adhere to a regular writing practice. Although art and life are in close proximity in her work, Hindmarch reminds us that "our most realistic fiction scarcely includes housework" (387) and that behind a romantic desire for the integration of art and everyday life there is a tension between art and labour that articulates itself differently for different subjects based on their position in social structures.

Thus, as our title suggests, "wanting everything" refers to a kind of largeness, a desire to push against the constraints of language, time, and competing forms of labour to document, to connect, and to love, without sacrifice or hierarchy. In this sense, "want" rubs against the grain of its usual sense as a desire for material objects. Instead, it signals at a most fundamental level the desire to transform everyday relations for the better and dispense with the default structures that make uneven rules for different people depending on their gender, class, race, and sexuality. "Wanting everything" means wanting to be a writer *and* a professor; to be a lover *and* a mother; to be a critic *and* a confidante. In Hindmarch's work there is an *appetitiousness* that wants to bring everything into its ambit without compromise, and it is from this sense of appetite that its feminist politics radiate – an additive ethos that invites solidarity, generosity, and openness.

## Gender and Labour

Hindmarch's work approaches everyday life from an *embodied perspective*, interweaving gendered experience with the intricacies of labour. Her most substantial work of fiction, *The Watery Part of the World* (first published[1] by Douglas & McIntyre in 1988), follows Jan through a six-day shift as a mess girl on a coastal freighter that travels from Vancouver harbour out to the west coast of Vancouver Island, to such places as Ucluelet, Nootka Island, and Zeballos, before returning to Vancouver. Yet the narrative is propelled less by the geographical journey than by Jan's first-person experience of the phenomenal world around her. Among those experiences is the way in which labour on the boat is gendered, sometimes implicitly, often overtly. Having quit working on the ferries between the British Columbia mainland and Vancouver Island because of pay inequity, Jan is told "a fine girl like [her] has no business on ships" (81). Jan physically and mentally manoeuvres through a work environment that casts her as an outsider because of her sex, her age, and her class.

In moving between the events on the ship and Jan's own diaegetic world, we get a sense of how an economy of social and labour relations coheres around subjects reading themselves and others. She remarks upon the disparity of gendered labour as it plays out in the social microcosm of the boat: "I had often seen men not working, pretending to be doing something in order to cover the nothing they were doing, but somehow these were not *men doing men's* work" (130). There are a number of occasions when she feels the sting of her own labour being subordinated to, and devalued by, a patriarchal hierarchy. For example, when she is finally assigned to a freighter, she is shown the crew's mess by Jock, who tells her it is "where you get to serve us" (85).

Jan is at once critical of these inequalities, and yet still moved by her own internalized feelings of not belonging, of being an imposter in this male-dominated, working-class world. Her focus on her own emotions, doubts, fears, and indignations shows the complicated interface between structures and the individual that navigates them. A careful observer, Jan makes work the stuff of proprioceptive experience: "Of course it makes sense," she thinks, "as the sun and salt air seem to sink through the cells of my skin; everything does when I focus on it" (130). *The Watery Part of the World* reminds us that the personal is political – a surging refrain of the identity politics that mark the era in which it is set. However, it does so in such a way that foregrounds the complexity and difficulty of squaring personal experience with political aims, when desire and affect act as unruly agitators to our conscious intentions.

In all of Hindmarch's works over the decades, and particularly those in non-fiction genres such as journal entries, letters, and interviews, another form of labour becomes apparent: the *affective labour* that is central to the constitution of households and communities alike. Closely related to the practices of "kin work" and "care work," affective labour is the complex of activities that relate to human contact and interaction, which engender states of well-being, satisfaction, and care. Writing on the topic, Michael Hardt insists that, rather than producing commodities, practices of affective labour "produce collective subjectivities, produce sociality, and ultimately produce society itself" (89). Affective labour forms the core of our relations with others, shaping the ways we interact with one another as subjects, at once undergirding and undermining systems of power. In the household, affective labour is a crucial component of what Silvia Federici terms reproduction, which means "servicing the wage earners physically, emotionally, sexually, getting them ready for work day after day" (31) through practices such as housework, cooking, child- and eldercare, and emotional and psychological support. In the broader community, affective labour serves an equally reproductive function by establishing and sustaining social ties. It is visible in the practices of hosting social gatherings, assembling and preserving community histories and spaces, liaising between community members and institutions, and caring for community members when they are ill or in crisis.

Importantly, communities, much like households, do not organize themselves. Both are the products of labouring practices, however immaterial, that keep those social spaces operative. However, too often, affective labour becomes naturalized as a voluntary offering through the management of affects themselves: those who shoulder these labouring practices undertake them as "labours of love," which ought to be compensation enough in itself. The result is that affective labour is concealed *as labour*, so that it is not subject to social (or economic) reform, despite its primary position within social spheres. It is important to note, too, that affective labour is unevenly distributed along gendered lines, with women, femme, and nonbinary subjects shouldering a disproportionate share. In the household, traditionally this has taken the form of naturalizing affective and reproductive labour as women's work; in the community, there has been a deference to default (i.e., gendered) labour practices owing to a lack of deliberated roles and structures.

Recognizing the way affective labour operates within literary communities helps us make sense of Hindmarch's influence in *and* erasure from the well-known TISH and Vancouver writing scenes of the time.[2] At the height of TISH's writing activity and retrospectively, Hindmarch's contemporaries unequivocally place her at the core of the West-Coast writing communities that emerged in the late 1950s and early 1960s. In his 1974 essay "Wonder Merchants," for instance, Warren Tallman declares her "near the centre of [TISH's] energy vortex"; in a 1991 letter, Daphne Marlatt writes to Hindmarch: "i have always felt that you were central" to TISH; reflecting in a 2012 interview, George Bowering locates her at "the centre of the Vancouver writing scene" (SpokenWeb). And yet in literary criticism and historiography which have so often focused on the DIY production, the technology, and the editorial work that produced the first nineteen issues of *TISH: a poetry newsletter*, Hindmarch's contributions have been hard for critics to place. Often Hindmarch is, as Marlatt has suggested, overlooked by "the filter of history," despite having been "involved right from the very beginning" and having "continued to write, continued to publish" ("Between," 102). Despite being immersed in the community from the beginning, Hindmarch was curiously absent from one of the moments that galvanized the TISH group: the student reading that followed Robert Duncan's July 1961 series of three lectures delivered in the Tallmans' Vancouver living room. Held at the UBC's Buchanan Building penthouse, the gathering featured poetry readings by Fred Wah, George Bowering, Jamie Reid, David Dawson, and Frank Davey.[3] Hindmarch, a woman and a prose writer, was not invited. When asked several years later why she wasn't selected to read, a then-twenty-nine-year-old Hindmarch commented: "I guess I'm the wrong sex."[4] Further, despite her engagement with the proprioceptive poetics that was so central to the work of the TISH group, Hindmarch was not involved in producing the actual newsletter; she is not on the masthead as an editor in the first phase, nor, as an experimental prose writer, was she published in it.

What, then, makes her so central? Warren Tallman aptly declares Hindmarch "a seventh, unnamed 'editor'" of *TISH*. "When she said 'no' to a poem, or went silent, the other editors tended to put that poem aside" (77). He also points to the many social activities she undertook to bring the group together, such as reading others' writing, acting as both an auditor and a critic who pushed works to find their fullest expression:

> Possessing such marked extra-sensory powers, working entirely by intuition, she provided endless hours of direct personal response to the lives and poems of the other editors. Because her being was so volatile at that time, she became for all of the others whatever image of the feminine they happened to need: mother, sister, muse, lover, consolation, inspiration, sounding-board, scold, conscience, mover of leaves on poet's trees. (77)

This description of Hindmarch puts her activities and practices in the community in close proximity with a number of feminine archetypes – mother, lover, muse, scold – in the process subtly conflating what she *does* with who she *is*.[5] However, while Tallman's rhetoric naturalizes her work as gendered feminine, he nevertheless names, if not quite in these terms, the affective labour Hindmarch performs and recognizes it as essential to the community. As Hindmarch herself recalls, "every time I went into the cafeteria (at UBC) I would join in a discussion or argument about some poem that was being submitted to *TISH*. By the time the next issue came out, I had seen at least half of it" (in Butling 1990, 63). That the work Hindmarch performs isn't tied to a literary product bearing her name as editor or author has, to date, made it invisible within almost every critical context. Yet, that affective labour – the countless hours of discussing, arguing, listening – contributes to the reproduction of the TISH community as we know it, both the publication and the constellation of individuals behind it.

Hindmarch was also a key figure in organizing and hosting the social events that took place around the more public-facing literary events of the 1960s in Vancouver, including the 1963 Vancouver Poetry Conference.[6] In our interview with Hindmarch that appears in this collection, she talks about her role, and the role of other women in the community, in crafting the social events that made the literary scene of this era so memorable, in large part giving them their irreverent, countercultural flavour so appreciated by subsequent generations. It is the effects and affects of this labour that are probably referred to more often than are the actual poems published in *TISH*. With a gesture to Olson in an essay that makes Pauline Butling's labour especially visible, Hindmarch theorizes community, which, as she writes, is grounded in

> communication, the giving and exchanging of information, ideas, messages, signals, feelings. Communities have centres both formal (school, town hall, community centre) and informal (someone's kitchen, the general store, a garage, a café). Here the *real* exchanges of the day take place and sometimes the most important decisions are made before they are put into motion. This is how polis works: several eyes, I & I & I & I become a we through exchanges leading to common ground and hopefully consensus. ("Pauline and Fred," 355)

Hindmarch's involvement in the Vancouver writing communities, unsurprisingly, preceded and exceeded TISH even in the late 1950s and early 1960s. During her undergraduate years at UBC, she was a "prime mover" and one of several women, including Betty Lambert, Judith Copithorne, and Carol Johnson, in the Writers Workshop (Wigod 59). Significantly, she also bridged the divide between the so-called TISH and "downtown poets,"[7] living at one point in the same building as bill bissett and Martina Clinton, reviewing the first issue of *blewointment*, included in this volume, and, soon after, publishing work in bissett's magazine. Her communities have always been multiple and broaden in scope as time passes: in our interview, Hindmarch speaks of her involvement in a women's discussion group in the 1970s that included Sheila Day and Judy Williams Fraser in its members, and a prose-writing workshop with Will Goode and Bill Schermbrucker called "stretchers" – so named for stretching a tale. Her centrality to these diverse groups speaks not only to the flexibility of her writing, attuned as it is to poetics, rhythm, language, documentation, and critique, but also to her contributions to the social forms that enfold communities of production – forms that are represented within her writing as much as they exist outside of it.

The 1969 recorded conversation between Hindmarch and Warren Tallman, an excerpt of which is transcribed in this volume as "Conversation between Warren Tallman and Gladys Hindmarch,"[8] reflects on the same period and stands as an example of how sound recording can remap the literary history by citing and siting gendered affective labour as an important foundation to collectivity and community. Here, we discover a different material map of the era's literary history, which, to date, has mostly relied upon first-person testimony in the form of memoirs, formal interviews, and critical studies.[9] This recording inscribes the second of two lengthy discussions that were intended to be grounds for Tallman's book on West Coast Canadian poetry.[10] Hindmarch enters the conversation as community historian, feminist cultural worker, theorist, and, occasionally, provocatrice. That Tallman would wish to test out his arguments and confirm details with Hindmarch, is unsurprising, for, as Daphne Marlatt writes in a letter to Hindmarch: "you, of everyone, have the memory of a historian, no, not of a historian, that sounds too abstract, but the kind of memory that remembers how it all was, how it *felt*" (1991). Throughout the conversation, Hindmarch not only relays dates and details but also revises Tallman's accounts of the writing scene by adding the names of women back into the story. "There's Claudia Irving and Diane Grant, who's got a play on in Montreal" (286), she adds to Tallman's account of the legacy of TISH. This referential network of women marks a citational practice that Hindmarch, Marlatt, and Butling in particular would continue to practice throughout their careers, writing and speaking each other back into the historical record. For example, in "A Tishstory," Marlatt cites Hindmarch's importance to the historical narrative (102); Butling notes that "in the published accounts of the *TISH* group formation, only Gladys [Maria] Hindmarch mentioned [my] name" ("Who is she?" 149). It is worth noting that these citational practices all happen in recorded conversations that are then transcribed and published in print, a feminist practice of mutual acknowledgment and reciprocity carried out by this group of writers well beyond the 1960s in the form of reviews, criticism, and feedback about each other's work.

Letters, however sporadic they would become, from 1964 through to the 1990s reveal a strong affection between Marlatt and Hindmarch as they think through community, gender, motherhood, writing, and relationships in conversation with each other. Each woman engages with the other's writing, offering critique that is specific and honest, with evident familiarity and care. In doing so, they push each other to draw out the best qualities of their respective writing – in Hindmarch's case a physicality that Marlatt has come to expect in her friend's writing, what she refers to as a "Closeness." "Which brings me back," Marlatt writes in a 1970 letter to Hindmarch,

> to the physical & what I was going to say to you about that, how I missed it in Boat Story #15 compared to say the #2 in Writing 5. & despite your talk of the feel of Hal's jacket on your body, That's there, yes, – but what I guess I've come to expect of you, that body moving with such fantastic consciousness of its spatial relations to people & things around it. (Dec. 8, 1970)

> You are much more (beautifully) realistic than you think you are, but more on that & the story, when I see you. (Dec. 17, 1970)

A careful reader of Hindmarch's "Boat Stories," Marlatt offers both encouragement and critique, much as Hindmarch does for her only a few months earlier when Marlatt sends a draft of her *Vancouver Poems* manuscript with the note "to Glady, or as they now stand / June 1, 1970." Hindmarch, in her response included in this volume, provides a close reading of the poems and pushes Marlatt "go further":

> I see this work as breaking out of the cupboards, the card house, the glass jars, the broom closets: where to? no one knows, you're moving on the edge of it, go further, balance on a bridge that may snap at any second: there aint no safe way to write. (246)

We find a similar reciprocity inflected with a sense of writerly professionalism in Hindmarch's friendship with poet Sharon Thesen. In "For Sharon," included in this volume, she recalls that when she couldn't face "retyping *The Peter Stories* for bpNichol at Coach House, Sharon did it for me. In 1987, after Coach House published *The Beginning of the Long Dash*, I wrote a review that was published in *Brick* ... and she wrote a comment on my *Watery Part of the World*. Neither of us read what the other had written until it was in print (365).

Hindmarch's writing attests to the vast amount of labour that goes into building and maintaining communities, recognizing that they are intertwined not just with the professional spaces of the academic institution but with the domestic spaces of the home and its surroundings. "Kitsilano 1963–'69" is a retrospective poem written in the early 1990s for the artist Judy Williams that serves as a meditation on the community of the 1960s, the ties that maintained it, and the ways in which community shifts over time. Figures come and go in "Kitsilano" but are held together in temporal friezes that are layered gently, one upon the other, and drawn together by the cadenced passage of the poem through the intimate spaces of the apartment and the building into the public spaces of the surrounding streets.

## Gender and the Body

Originally published in 1976 by New Star Books, *A Birth Account* engages with a different kind of labour. The narrator describes her experience with two pregnancies: the first resulting in a "missed abortion" after the fetus stopped growing at eleven weeks, and the second culminating in the birth of her son, Lars. The account not only details the intimacies of the female body in pregnancy and childbirth, it also engages with domestic labour in a communal setting: the coordination of comings and goings, meals and housework, and the mental load of managing a household. The narrator notes, "the other day I made a list of seventeen items: brandy, diaper pins, toothbrush, bank, buy material for nook, etc. Seven remain. And only one (the sewing of a curtain) has to be done by me, yet even that, one of my men could do if he had to" (45). The body works – internally, creating biological life, and externally, making everyday life as we know it, and we are privy to the speaker's fluctuating attention between inside and outside. The narrative is structured by these two worlds, trying to reconcile the exceptional events of conception, pregnancy and childbirth with everyday rhythms and activities. How do these two separate modes of being coexist simultaneously? How can sensations so deeply rooted in the body be externalized and communicated to others, but through language?

Interspersed with the narrator's internal observations – the baby's movements inside her womb and, later, the cresting sensations of contractions – are passages describing her interactions with doctors and other health-care professionals, passages in which the gendered power dynamics of the medical profession are laid bare and scrutinized. Hindmarch's narrators have a keen sense not only of their own internal worlds, putting into language the elusive experience of emotion and physical sensation, but also that of the entities that surround them and the ways that these different discourses connect, or fail to connect. The narrator plainly remarks, "all I know is how the Braxton-Hicks (named after a man, all these things so close to women named after men) contractions I have almost daily feel: a push about fist-size which surfaces for ten or fifteen seconds, is hard, then disappears" (43). On the one hand, a name. On the other, a feeling in the body that can only be translated through likeness ("about fist-size"). This is one of many observations that throw physical sensation into sharp relief against the ways that these sensations are read, coded, and interpreted by others. Magazines, birthing books, husbands, lovers, and doctors read the female body as hysterical, as psychodramatic, as transgressive. While these acts of reading are imagined to be self-evident and inscrutable by those who perform them, Hindmarch shows how interpreting the body is never neutral or without the inflection of power. The normalization of these readings is itself the product of a kind of cultural work that must be repeated over and over to maintain its self-effacing sense of normalcy.

Thus, a *Ladies Home Journal* article titled "How People You Love Keep You Fat" connects to the same patriarchal apparatus that allows the narrator's obstetrician to dismiss her physical and emotional concerns about her pregnant body: women are taught to trust others' readings of their bodies even when those readings are at odds with their self-perception. The narrator acknowledges the impassable contradiction between these two readings of self, one coming from an intimate knowledge of her own body and the other from an internalized sense of patriarchal value that conflicts with that knowledge. Regarding the women's magazines, she writes, "I do read them and they always ... make me feel uncertain, hungry, out of it, not a woman in their sense, and I know they play on me, play on feelings I do and dont know I have, use them, turn them around, but fuck it, like, the impulse to have them to read most of that crap ... is strong: locked in, they lock me in, cut me off from myself" (27). Hindmarch keenly shows how there is a contradiction at the core of every instance of self-knowledge – a struggle to become oneself against what one *ought to be* in the eyes of the other. Her writing is not prescriptive, seeking to resolve these tensions, but rather offers much needed reflective space to feel, examine, and work through these contradictions at an emotional and intellectual level.

Appearing here for the first time in print, Hindmarch's *Swimming with Cancer* offers a terse yet intimate account of the speaker's experience with breast cancer – its discovery, diagnosis, and treatment, culminating in a mastectomy. The piece opens with a description of the speaker swimming in a pool, an image that is at once from her perspective, yet also seen as though from a bird's eye view: "my arms shoot straight forward forming the point of an imaginary valentine" (392). This split, a doubling of perspective, marks her experience throughout the narrative. Cancer is a complex of physical sensations, emotions, interactions with others, and imaginative forays into the past and future. It is at once deeply felt within the body while also remaining outside, seen as though from a distance. It makes the body not-self, alienating the self from itself.

Because of this split, the experience of cancer is an *event* in the most fundamental sense: it marks a temporal rift not only between a before and an after, but between potential and actual worlds. After finally receiving the diagnosis of inflammatory breast cancer after four months' delay, the speaker says, in a strange turn of temporality, "I want the weekend to be what I thought it would be this morning" (404). She mourns not only what is, but what might have been – even if it's just a peaceful summer free from the daily tasks of her job as a college instructor. The cancer event not only changes how we view the present, it also retroactively changes how we interpret the past. The section "Signs" at the beginning of the narrative attests to this fact as, in retrospect, the speaker realizes *what will have been* the symptoms of cancer all along – pain, puckered skin, flashes of swelling and redness. Thus, while the account unfolds in a fairly straightforward, chronological manner with many sections arranged by date, it poignantly gives a sense of how all major life events disrupt us to our very core, uncannily meshing the present with the past before it and the future that is yet to unfold.

*Swimming with Cancer* moves deftly through these different temporalities, showing their effects on the speaker, who is subject to their vagaries. While the text is in many ways written with a plainly objective gaze, cataloguing a litany of drug names, doctors, and briefly passing characters, there is profound meditation in and through these details on selfhood, its meaning and purpose. Swimming in the pool, the speaker affirms with each stroke: "I am" (392), calling in the subtlest of gestures to the *cogito* and the philosophical problem of mind–body duality. Being, much like the spidery cancer on the core needle biopsy screen, flashes into our view only briefly before slipping away. It resides in the body in ways that are both within and outside the speaker's control – the movement of her arms in the swimming pool, the involuntary opening and closing of the valves of her heart "like inside an open barnacle" (412). Yet it also resides in her mind and, particularly, the language she uses to articulate her subjectivity. Language, like the body, is simultaneously within and outside her control. In addition to demonstrating its descriptive particularity, the narrative also shows us moments where language fails (returning, again, to an underlying want), or eludes the speaker's control: involuntarily, the street names *Terminal* and *Ash* wave like red flags as the speaker drives to the hospital. In the wake of an event, *Swimming with Cancer* responds to the question "What does it mean to be?" in ways that are *multiple*: every assertion of "I am" is also undercut with its opposite, "I am not (only)" playing out the subjective drama of mind–body duality on the most concrete set.

As in all of Hindmarch's work, *Swimming with Cancer* also articulates selfhood as connected to, and nourished by, social ties. The events of the speaker's diagnosis and treatment are interwoven with her work teaching at Capilano College in North Vancouver – the daily ins and outs of grading, invigilating exams, and administrative work. We get a sense that in addition to the speaker's vacillating existence in her mind and body, she also views herself as existing through her connections to others and the impact that she has on the world around her. Moments after her diagnosis, she drives to the college where she teaches and discovers a letter from a former student in her mailbox, in which he writes, "my writing has been my strength and has, for the most part, got me where I am. I have always felt like I owed it all to you" (405). At a moment when her sense of self is reeling from the blow of the cancer diagnosis, this connection is felt as life-affirming and anchoring: "His spirit calls out to my spirit and I feel grateful" (405). Indeed, the narrative is filled with moments of connection with others that contour the social situation of being *together*. Doctors visits and chemotherapy treatments take place in the company of named others: Sharon, Penny, Renee, and Leni. Their tenderness and care show the radical potential of affective labour to support individuals within a community in ways that are nourishing and generative – particularly friendships between women that fall outside the nuclear family paradigm. In these scenarios, language fails yet again – fails to conjure the right words to express the gravity of the situation, the weight of hopes and fears – but there is love and comfort taken in that lack, expressed in the silences between small talk.

In the final lines of the story, the narrator's lover asks her, "Are you sure you are okay to be alone?" (450) – meaning that he is about to part ways with her for the day. She replies, "I am," echoing the affirmation from the beginning of the story. The space between these two declarations is minute yet momentous. It seems as though an entire world has shifted between them. We share with the speaker the knowledge that she is never quite *alone,* knowing how deeply her ties to the community run. Being pronounces itself in these little articulations to others, as well as in the minutiae of everyday life: returning home, taking a nap.

## A New Form

*One perception must immediately and directly lead to a further perception.*

—CHARLES OLSON
  Projective Verse

The short piece "Sentences" expresses Hindmarch's frustration at being a writer of fiction in a community of poets:

> She is sitting at her table in East Vancouver drinking coffee and trying to think of something, *any*thing, to write for the David Thompson University Centre reading at the Western Front eleven days from now. As a fiction writer, a ten or seven or five minute limit is so ridiculous that, well, why *not* read a third of a story? or two pages, or one fat paragraph? One sentence: that's it, a reading where the whole audience gets to read and each person can read only one sentence from any source – that would cut the crap, wouldn't it?

On the one hand, her location among poets is obvious. Hindmarch's work embodies the notion of proprioception that was so central to the poetics of the TISH group and other experimental writing in the West Coast tradition. In her writing, "sensibility within the organism" is revisited as a feminist stance that connects the experience of the body – moving through space, breathing, labouring, connecting with others – with a keen observational reading of situations, the self, and others, played out in sentences as carefully constructed and as rhythmic as verse. As Sharon Thesen puts it, like Marlatt's, "Hindmarch's writing explored the experience of childbirth, marriage, and sexuality in lines that were long, crowded, prosy. Lines that ran around quite a bit and wore 'holey slips' and had 'moley knees'" (4). In *The Peter Stories* (originally published by Coach House Press in 1976), we find lines like:

> Long leg stretches to burnt-out stump up dirt bank hand tree roots up weeds up cliff touching holding stopping kissing, and then down skipping through a no-pathed forest to the apple-smelling hooked-rag thick-quilted cottage. (13)

Here, not only does Hindmarch's writing dance through playful rhythms and cadences, it is also grounded in a chain of proprioceptive images in which language, subject, and exterior world become inextricable from one another. Her work engages and performs a poetics, even when it is lineated as prose. However, Hindmarch's work isn't included in contemporary publications such as *TISH* because it's written in sentences and not lines. It demands more space in print and more time at readings, contributing to its marginalization in the productive and receptive communities at the time of its publication.

The struggle to find a form that *fits* her ambitious writing is a theme that recurs throughout Hindmarch's work. At times new forms come slowly and are even resisted. In her June 27, 1984 journal entry, for example, she remembers Warren Tallman advising her, a writer and mother of a three-year-old, to "invent a new form, one that allows for interruptions." Hindmarch remarks: "I didnt want a new form then. I only wanted two or three uninterrupted hours every day." One form of writing often points to another; journal entries, for instance, invoke the absence of another more desired form: "Writing sentences like this one is easy, but the form or shape I want needs more of this – i.e. to warm up, to become easy with a sentence so I do not think about it just as I am here by not ending this one earlier. So, I do it. But. But still this isn't writing, is it?" "Third Person Singular" emerges out of a determination to make "writing writing" a regular practice even and *especially* when it is in tension with the demands of single motherhood, teaching, housework, and other responsibilities. This series of short prose pieces make writing within those constraints one of its main subjects. That commitment to "writing writing" and its being at odds with other wants within the household is evident in "Face It, Mom" where her son's wish to go to a motocross race finally takes priority over her attempt to produce a manuscript for a contest:

> He runs upstairs to his mom's study every hour. He reads what she has written. "Face it, Mom, face it: you'll never make it. Eight pages in six hours, you have to do fifty a day for the 3-Day Novel Contest, and *you* can't even *type* that fast!"
>
> She knows this is so, but she is in the middle of writing. She wants to go on. But her desire is not as strong as his insistence. She tells him she will take him, but she wants to write for just one more hour. (387)

Especially remarkable is the speaker's determination to "go on," to write "for just one more hour" in the face of seeming despair, knowing it is impossible to write fast enough. Here again this writing marks the absence of another form (the novel) but becomes itself, perhaps, more satisfying and true to the conditions of writing. As Hindmarch writes in "A Mother's Prose," when she did manage to "write graceful sentences in shapely paragraphs making stories that had structures which weren't immediately perceived," that writing "held the present out."

Hindmarch prefaces *A Birth Account* with the lines, "Please read my work aloud. The rhythm, the sound, the breathing are all part of what it is. When you come to the third section of this book, breathe the breaths" (20). More than providing a concrete notation for the sake of accurate documentation, this text actualizes the tenets of Olson's *Projective Verse* by joining the breath and the line indivisibly, making one the content of the other. The non-objective gesture of this notation – crafting a poetic line that does not seek to represent in the usual descriptive sense – anticipates conceptual work in the decades that follow, as an interest in the materiality of language surges. Hindmarch's breath line is rooted in the labouring female body, bringing avant-garde poetics into alignment with material feminism, grounding aesthetic experimentalism in personal, concrete experience.

# Coda: Reflections on Editing as Community

## KARIS

The grounds for this book and for the collaboration that led to it were laid many years ago. In 2013, the fiftieth anniversary of the Vancouver Poetry Conference, I organized a summer event called "Poetry Off the Page" where I work at UBC Okanagan. Not long before that moment, I'd received a box of audio tapes from my colleague and friend Jodey Castricano, who had received them from Warren Tallman; the box contained his copies of the Vancouver Poetry Conference tapes, plus many others. The idea for the event was to invite writers who had some relationship to these literary audio artifacts, to analog tape recording, and the poetry scene of the 1960s/1970s in Vancouver. In organizing "Poetry Off the Page," I invited George Bowering, Frank Davey, Daphne Marlatt, Sharon Thesen, Fred Wah, and Phyllis Webb to participate in a reading and roundtable. Frank Davey and Sharon Thesen suggested I invite Maria Hindmarch, with whose work I was only slightly familiar at the time. I did, and we exchanged emails though, in the end, Maria wasn't able to make it, for a happy reason: her dragon-boat team had won four gold medals in the breast-cancer division and was going to nationals. Although we were not destined to meet on that occasion, the cardboard box of tapes was magnetic, in more ways than one.

In that box, I found the 1969 conversations Warren Tallman and Gladys Hindmarch recorded on "DHL 100 tape," and the voices were so compelling that I listened to them over and over. They sent me back to read Maria's work more closely and begin rethinking her place in Canadian avant-garde historiography.

## DEANNA

I first met Gladys Hindmarch in the spring of 2017 when I interviewed her for my dissertation work on Roy Kiyooka's audio archive – yet another place where her voice features prominently. She welcomed me into her home on Parker Street that is the setting for so much of her writing, and served me a cup of strong tea and a slice of banana bread. Our first conversation, in fact, was about our respective approaches to that versatile loaf: White sugar or brown? Half or full cup? Nuts or chocolate chips or neither? It was my first interview for my doctoral work and I was nervous, but Maria put me at ease, with her quick laugh and confidence driving the conversation. We talked expansively about her family of origin, about growing up in Ladysmith, her arrival at UBC and all the connections she made there – the chance encounters that would become the stuff of West Coast literary history. I returned for many follow-up visits where we would talk for hours, sometimes on the record and sometimes off. She read me pages from the books she was reading and gave me a tour of the artwork that hangs in her home, each piece with a story behind it.

Around the same time, Karis and I began realizing the deep affinities in our academic work. In the AMP Lab at UBCO, she and her team had begun work on the SoundBox Collection, whose audiotapes[11] capture the candid, spontaneous dialogue that we make a case for in this collection and elsewhere. We had ongoing conversations about the literary import of these kinds of artifacts, the ethics involved in working with them, and the skills that we would need to bring them to the public in a literary-critical context.

**KARIS**

Deanna and I continued to cross paths. Encouraged by Jason Camlot at Concordia University in Montréal, we shared our interest in Hindmarch's writing and cultural work with each other. In the winter of 2017, while I was on sabbatical in Montréal, we closed ourselves a small room to listen to the "DHL 100 tape" and, through a practice we've subsequently called "feminist close listening," began mapping the way women's – and particularly Maria's – labour figured in these recordings.

**DEANNA**

We listened to tapes together and transcribed them, at cafés when we were in the same city and over Skype when we were apart. So much of my current thinking has been crucially shaped by working with these two women.

**KARIS**

Soon, the idea of a book that would assemble over fifty years of Hindmarch's work was born. Deanna arranged a phone call on January 2, 2018, and as the three of us talked I remember being amazed at how easy the conversation felt.

## DEANNA

When we first approached Maria about doing the collection, she was hesitant, saying she wasn't sure she had published enough material to put together a collected works. However, when we gathered around her dining room table for the first time to work on the project in February of 2018, she produced several document boxes titled by decade, each packed with writing – some handwritten, some typed or stenographed, some inkjet-printed. We sat around the table sifting through work, occasionally asking Maria to read things out loud, laughing and chatting together as we relished her keen observations and sense of humour.

## KARIS

In the months that followed, Deanna and I visited Maria regularly in Vancouver – sometimes together, sometimes separately – to continue these conversations, some of which have been recorded as oral histories. They've been important ways by which we've oriented ourselves within such an expansive body of writing, and have been full of lessons: I've learned much from Deanna's generous, responsive way of engaging as an interlocutor; from Maria I've learned a certain frankness and openness.

Sounding and listening have been foundational to the making of *Wanting Everything*. Sitting in Maria's living room one evening, we listened to the tapes she hadn't heard in nearly fifty years – an intimate practice we would repeat many times over. On other occasions, Maria and I walked through the Kitsilano neighbourhood where she lived in the 1960s, her recalling aloud the way the houses used to look, the people who lived in them, what took place where; my listening to her voice connecting us to a particular past and place. This was my orientation to Vancouver: an experience of listening that was both visceral and relational. Sounding her texts aloud has been as essential to Maria's revision and composition process as listening has been to our work as editors. In tandem, those practices have guided the shaping of this book. Near the end of this project, I sat on the floor of Maria's study sifting through her box of journals, checking each one against our manuscript, when I saw an unfamiliar brown spiral notebook. I flipped through it. They were her Vancouver Poetry Conference journals, written when she was twenty-three years old. Late into the evening she read them aloud, both of us occasionally laughing at turns of phrase, but also marvelling at this powerful, assertive young woman's words. The writing is, to my mind, among the most insightful about the Poetry Conference that exists.

## DEANNA

This collection seems a record – an archive of sorts – not only of our work together, but of our truly impactful collaboration and friendship, which has now unfolded across years. In the last two years, our collaboration has been punctuated by life moments through which we've drawn on each other's support: tenure (Karis); knee surgery (Maria); dissertation defence and childbirth (Deanna). It has been incredible to live the kind of connection and support that we see throughout Maria's writing practice.

## DEANNA AND KARIS

Ultimately, that cardboard box which held tapes bearing the records of community was itself community-building through the exchange and engagement with its objects, the friendships that formed around it, and the writing that emerged from it. This book bears all these traces: Gladys Hindmarch not just as a writer crucial to the West Coast tradition of innovative writing dating from the 1960s, but Maria Hindmarch, a writer emerging across time and community, her words opening to new and future readers.

# Endnotes

1. Many of "The Boat Stories" that make up *The Watery Part of the World* were published individually over fourteen years in such venues as *The Georgia Straight, Iron,* and *The Capilano Review*. For a complete bibliography of "The Boat Stories," see Butling 1986.
2. The TISH scene included George Bowering, Frank Davey, Fred Wah, Lionel Kearns, David Dawson, Daphne Marlatt, Jamie Reid, Carol Bolt, Robert Hogg, Ginni Smith, and David Cull, among others.
3. See Davey, 113.
4. In the same interview, Hindmarch refers to the reading as the one "I wasn't invited to," recalling those invited to read at the UBC "bubbledome" were "not all of the people involved" but "the ones [Duncan] selected." To suggest Hindmarch wasn't invited because as a prose writer she would have nothing to read overlooks that she would not have been the only one in this position. In the same 1969 interview, Hindmarch notes that "Fred wrote a poem in order to have a poem to read, and David [Dawson] also." "West Coast with Stan and Gladys" in the SoundBox Collection, UBC Okanagan.
5. See Davey's critique of Tallman's "unconscious sexism" and romanticization of Hindmarch in *When TISH Happens*, 120–21.
6. Ellen Tallman and Pauline Butling also performed significant affective labour. See Tallman's "My Stories with Robert Duncan" in *Robert Duncan and Denise Levertov: The Poetry of Politics, the Politics of Poetry,* and Butling's "Who Is She? Inside/Outside Literary Communities" in *Writing in Our Time: Canada's Radical Poetries in English (1957–2003)*. Butling writes, for example: "I have spent thousands of hours doing volunteer work in literary communities: I have organized poetry readings, hosted visiting writers, helped plan workshops and conferences, cooked party meals and cleaned up party wine spills, made posters, written press releases, helped with magazine production – all the while taking part in the ongoing dialogue, gossip, debate, and argument that is the lifeblood of any community" (141).
7. The TISH poets affiliated with UBC and the "downtown" group of poets and artists (bill bissett, Martina Clinton, Judith Copithorne, Maxine Gadd, Gerry Gilbert, John Newlove, and others) are often presented in contrast to one another. This divide obscures the connections between the two communities. In addition to Hindmarch's involvement in both, Copithorne was part of the Writers Workshop; in 1959 bill bissett was a student at UBC in Warren Tallman's poetry course with Frank Davey, Gladys Hindmarch, and Lionel Kearns (Davey, 145).
8. SoundBox Collection, UBC Okanagan.

9   See Davey 2011, Wah 2014, and Niechoda and Hunter 1991.

10   The book never came to fruition, but there is a strong affinity between "Wonder Merchants" and this tape.

11   The SoundBox Collection contains over 160 audio tapes, including tapes from Robert Hogg, Sharon Thesen, George Bowering, and those Warren Tallman gave to Jodey Castricano. The collection's catalogue and a selection of recordings can be found online: https://soundbox.ok.ubc.ca/.

# Works Cited

Bowering, George. "An Interview with George Bowering." *SpokenWeb*. October 12, 2012. https://montreal.spokenweb.ca/oral-literary-history/george-bowering-oct-12-2012/.

Butling, Pauline. "Gladys Hindmarch: Pointillist Prose." *Essays on Canadian Writing* 32 (Summer 1986): 70–91.

———. "'Hall of Fame Blocks Women' Re/Righting Literary History." *Open Letter* 7.8 (Summer 1990): 60–76.

———. "Who is She? Inside/Outside Literary Communities." In *Writing in Our Time: Canada's Radical Poetries in English (1957–2003)*. Edited by Pauline Butling and Susan Rudy. Waterloo, ON: Wilfrid Laurier University Press, 2005. 141–160.

Davey, Frank. *When TISH Happens: The Unlikely Story of Canada's "Most Influential Literary Magazine."* Toronto: ECW, 2011.

Federici, Silvia. *Revolution at Point Zero: Housework, Reproduction, and Feminist Struggle.* Common Notions series. Oakland: PM Press, 2012.

Fong, Deanna. "'I love you is a vocal variable': Everyday Life and Collective Self-Articulation in the Roy Kiyooka Audio Archive." In *Pictura: Essays on the Work of Roy Kiyooka.* Edited by Juliana Pivato. Essential Writers series. Toronto: Guernica, forthcoming. 33–56.

Hardt, Michael. "Affective Labor." *boundary 2* 26, no. 2 (Summer 1999): 89–100.

Marlatt, Daphne. "Between Continuity and Difference." Interview with Brenda Carr. In *Beyond TISH*. Edited by Douglas Barbour. Edmonton: NeWest Press, 1991. 99–112.

———. Letter to Gladys Hindmarch. 1991. Simon Fraser Special Collections.

Niechoda, Irene, and Tim Hunter. "A Tishstory." Interview. In *Beyond TISH*. Edited by Douglas Barbour. Edmonton: NeWest Press, 1991. 83–98.

Spicer, Jack. *After Lorca*. San Francisco: White Rabbit Press, 1957.

Tallman, Ellen. "My Stories with Robert Duncan." In *Robert Duncan and Denise Levertov: The Poetry of Politics, the Politics of Poetry.* Edited by Albert Gelpi and Robert Bertholf. Stanford: Stanford University Press, 2006. 63–70.

Tallman, Warren. "Wonder Merchants." *boundary 2* 3, no. 1 (Autumn 1974): 57–90.

Thesen, Sharon. "Writing the Continuing Story: Gladys Hindmarch's *The Watery Part of the World*." In *Beyond TISH*. Edited by Douglas Barbour. Edmonton: NeWest Press, 1991. 166–170.

Wah, Fred. *Permissions: TISH Poetics 1963 Thereafter—*. Garnett Sedgewick Memorial Lecture. Toronto: Ronsdale Press, 2014.

Wigod, Rebecca. *He Speaks Volumes: A Biography of George Bowering*. Vancouver, B.C.: Talonbooks, 2018.

# Book-Length Works

# The Peter Stories

COACH HOUSE PRESS, 1976

*This book is for Warren Tallman*

### The Pumpkineater

**Peter, Peter, pumpkin eater
Had a wife and couldn't keep her;
He put her in a pumpkin shell,
And there he kept her very well.**

**Peter, Peter, pumpkin eater
Had another, and didn't love her;
Peter learned to read and spell
And then he loved her very well.**

## One

There was a man whose name was Peter. He had a wife who ran around quite a bit. Peter would come home at night tired from logging and find no supper on the table. Then he would go into the bedroom and find that the bed had not been made. He would look at the refrigerator – here a piece of toast, at the kitchen counter – there a bite of cookie, at the table – here a paper, there a magazine, everywhere a clutter clutter. Then he would go out into the backyard to look for her: up the alley, through the pumpkin patch, around and around the woodpile. But still he could not find his wife.

Peter would go back into the kitchen and open the refrigerator and get some beer to take outside to drink in his pumpkin patch. His pumpkin patch was the largest most orangest most prickly-stemmed in all the town. He would sit on the tallest pumpkin, watching the rowboats of the harbour, watching the coloured cars of the street, eating pumpkin drinking beer – waiting for his wife to come home.

He got to know how often the people below had tomatoes for supper, who packed groceries in a little pink bag, who came from a dry-goods-store job to a nobody-there house and left quite soon to an empty-yet bowling alley – waiting for his wife to come home.

After he had drunk three or four beers, and after he had left his pumpkin patch to the night moths and rats, and after he had watched a western a sea hunt tale and a court story on TV, and after he had fixed himself some cold pork beets and pumpkin pie from the fridge, he went to bed – waiting for his wife to come home. And sometimes somehow in the middle of the night she did. She did with her thin legs and short hair and holey slip. She did with her sloped bottom and scrunched shoulders and moley knees. She did licking and touching and sliding and holding. She did and it didnt seem right to bawl her out now and there wasnt time because it was morning so she got up and made him breakfast and things seemed almost right as he went off to work.

And after work it was as he had done before: waiting in the pumpkin patch, walking up the alley, opening beer, closing gates, sitting, anything to stay out of that house to keep away from her carrot bites, pepperoni sticks, dusty flowerpots, from her splotchy-duster, unmade-bed, scattered magazine box. He threw beer caps between the leaves, saw tomatoes being plucked, watched garbage coming out, and left. Left to the pub where one man he knew was, left to a poker game with four teenage hoods, left to a bowling alley with five local girls, but all of this was no good. So he went home, picked the duster off the chair, and sat and rocked and ate baked pumpkin slices and waited for his wife.

But again she did not come. And again he went to bed. And again she came in: curling legs around above his hips, sliding arms fullways along his back, dropping fingers all over lightly, loosely touching, then letting go; down his front, past his thighs, over his kneecaps and ankles and toe cracks; then up a bit firmer in longer touching presses lightly and starting with her mouth. And again he turned to her, jagged tongued and heavy knuckled: squeezing her bottom up, jerking her front down, blowing her legs out, circling her breasts in, twisting her waist, smoothing her top, stroking and hugging and licking all over.

But not again did he just leave her and let her be as she was. The next morning he took her and bound her. Bound her with sheets and belts and neckties. He wrapped an orange felt blanket round her and left her there moaning ready to cry. He fried his eggs, caught his crummy, sat with his pail being driven to work. Up to Second Lake, "I hear they're clearing the canyon"; up a tree rigging; down, over, to limb another; down again and then back. "There was an accident on First. A young kid was killed." "Yeah, he set chokers I think" – on the way back from work.

"Who's for a beer?" and caulk boots on pavement and kids eating popsicles and hard hats all sweaty – on the way back from work.

And when he got home his wife was there. Crying and screeching, she was still tied to the bed. "It's you ... what are you doing this to me for ... what have I done ... you've had other women, havent you ... get me out of here, wont you ... cant you even loosen the back ones a little ... the least you could have done was turn on the radio."

"I hate you ... what do you mean you dont know ... you know, dont kid yourself ... what does it matter? it matters a lot ... am I going to sit here night after night waiting ... am I meant to ..."

"Yes, you are. You are you are you are."

"No, I'm not."

"You're nothing but a ..."

"Go ahead, say it."

"You're nothing but a ..."

"Havent got any words, have you?"

"Bastard ... bugger ... goddamn stinking fiddilly fidgety."

"Doesnt mean a thing, does it. Doesnt mean a thing."

"No. I guess not."

He sat by her back and started to untie her, dropped a finger between two belts and touched.

"Dont touch me. What do you want to touch me now for?"

"I do. That's all. And that's that."

"You're an odd one Peter. You know you're really odd."

And after she was loose and they had made love and eaten supper, he took her outside into the pumpkin patch. He sat her down on the biggest pumpkin and with a breadknife and a hammer and his caulk boots, he squashed and sliced and banged and cut, he stamped and tore and busted every pumpkin in the patch except that one. He spread the walk with newspaper and slung the pulpy chunky juicy seedy hard stuff on it. He rolled it up with the tips of his boots; but the paper kept breaking so he left little heaps lying all over the walk. Then he lifted his wife off the only pumpkin and plunked her down on one of the heaps.

He cut into the big pumpkin and pulled fistfuls of fibre out of its bulk. He sucked it and chewed it and spat. He ate it all and his stomach swelled, pushed through his pants out; and the sky pulsed, shrunk through its skin down; and the fence boards squished, pressed through their veins in; and the walk and the pumpkin leaves just lay there flat, doing nothing; and his wife just sat there numb, looking stupid. He yanked her off the paper and dropped her into the empty pumpkin belly. He cut out an eye and made her eat it. Cut out another and made her eat that. Put on the lid and sat and stared. Listened to her scream and holler and pound. Looked at her wiggling and bouncing and pushing, trying to roll it to bust it open, trying to bite the eyes out with her mouth. But she couldnt, couldnt move freely, couldnt get the noise out through the eyes, couldnt roll it over or bust it open, couldnt gouge it or do anything at all. And so it was there, during the days, that Peter kept her, and kept her very well.

## Two

For the first week that Peter kept his wife in the pumpkin shell, he was very happy. And for the next two weeks after that, he was quite happy. But one night during the fourth week after he had watched her scurry about the kitchen cleaning, plunge her hands into great gobs of dough kneading, pull feather after feather off a chicken plucking, he left the house and went outside. He walked on the patch where his pumpkins used to be, squished the earth in with his boots, kicked a buried bottle-cap high into the dark, stood by the gate, and wondered: wondered what he was doing and why.

And as he wondered, he looked inside the house and through the curtained window he saw his wife's form bending, ironing, hanging shirts up. Now she's always busy, always doing something, and has no time for me. She's either baking a fish dusting a shelf starching the curtains or bleaching the bathtub; she's either scrubbing carrots mixing cookies sewing shirts or washing her hair; she's either wiping the stove waxing the floor stuffing a chicken or hemming a tablecloth. She never is as she was before – never sloppy or silly or lazy or cuddly, never jumpy or fighty or lovey or free floating. Now she just works about the house all night, stays in the pumpkin all day, and does nothing except housework unless I tell her to.

As day bumped into day and week fell into week, Peter grew bored with his too-passive wife. He'd become restless and get mad at her.

"Stop doing housework for a minute, stop I said." And she would stop. "Get into something, we're going to the Travellers'." And she would squeeze into a skirt and they would go. "Smile once in a while... speak to Tom... dont eat so much... be nicer to Mary... come here." And so she'd do what he said when he said how he said but did nothing that was her own.

When the day came that the pumpkin shell had rotted, there was no need for Peter to make something else. His wife wanted nothing, only to sit coated, scarved near the pumpkin remains each day and to swing about the house cleaning, eating each night. But he knew he had to do something, had to be more than the order-giver stay-out-of-the-house-as-much-as-he-can person he now was. One evening after work when he was sitting on the steps of the back porch, he got up and left.

Left to another town fifty miles north. Left with only his boots and his kit and plaid jacket. Left with his thumb and the clothes he had on from work in a beat-up Chev driven by some young insurance-selling kid who didnt like it but was doing it anyway for he wouldnt have to stay in it long, just enough to get himself set up in a garage. Left to a blue room with gauze curtains with a beer parlour below and a dance somewhere around the corner and no one here now but himself.

And he liked it very much. He met a woman and had some beers, took her to a dance and swirled, pivoted, cut, dipped about the floor. He met other people, went to a party, sat on a rug, stood on a couch, sang with the group, brushed women's bottoms, talked with some men in the kitchen about logging, shouted on the porch with some men about circuses, yelled in the hall with everyone about old songs leaving accidents movies better beer new equipment. "Why my coat now, it's still going on, everything, nothing must stop, no not ever, woodpiles are as they are, why arent we; milk bottles can sit, why cant we?" And Peter went on and on until everyone had passed coated hatted rubber-shoed and the hostess had gone nightgowned and there was nothing but himself and one cat and empty record jackets, so he left.

Left running shouting down an alley, yelling anything. "Are the children in their beds... who gets up in the morning, who gets up in the morning... who has a hole in his bloody head... hey hey where's that Johnson Rag, yuh yuh diddle do yum de yah... you dont say, you cant mean that I tell you let's put it this way... up there again and again... what do you mean you dont know, what do you mean you dont know ... limb it once more and once more and once more." Left kicking wood pieces off the roadside, knocking gravel to where it belonged, lifting a slug up with his fingers, rolling a bottle to the edge of the street with one knee. Left – feet up hotel stairs and body passed radiators and finger pressing the middle of all the door knobs – to his room, to bed.

When he got home the next day, his wife was not there. The house was warm, there were loaves of bread on the cooling racks, the floor was shiny, the bed was made, everything was in place where it should be. He called for his wife, rang up a neighbour, stood at a window and watched the rain hit the fence. He decided that maybe she was at her mother's the way she used to be and made himself some coffee and went outside.

His wife was sitting on a box in the patch where the big pumpkin had once been.

"I'm back," Peter said.

"So what," she answered.

"Just wanted to tell you, that's all."

She looked to the roof gutter and then to her skirt.

"It's raining," Peter said.

"I know."

"Well then what's the matter, are you stupid ... why do you keep doing this, why dont you do something, why dont we go somewhere, why is night after night like this, dont you want to do anything ... you didnt used to be this way, you know."

"What's wrong now."

"What's wrong now she says, what's wrong now. You wont talk, you wont say anything, just what do you expect me to do?"

"Nothing."

"Nothing is it? Then nothing it'll be ..."

He went back into the house and waited in bed. And his wife stayed out there most of the night. Early in the morning when the grape vines banged the window he turned over under the quilt and shouted, "Stop your bloody noise!" And later in the morning when the snow made the room brighter he got up to light the fire and said, "Who the hell's been here?" Then later in the daylight he walked outside to the pumpkin patch and back to the cellar to the pantry and the attic stairs. What is she doing now, he thought, just what could she possibly be doing this time? And so it was that no one anywhere for a number of days nor weeks nor years saw Peter Pumpkineater's wife.

## Three

One snowy morning on his way to the beer parlour, Peter Pumpkineater met Miss Contrary. A potato had fallen out of a grocery bag as she bent over her car door trying to get it open. He picked up the potato, "Here I'll take this," and held her bag. She nodded a look that seemed to say, "I know something you dont," and then slid into her car and took off. That afternoon as he came out of the beer parlour her car passed him, then stopped and backed up. "I'll give you a ride if you want," she yelled through the snow. And so it was that they met.

One night two weeks later, Peter walked down to Mary Contrary's place and asked her if she'd like to go to a show. "Sit here till I finish this will you... there's hot tea on the stove and some coffee biscuit in the breadbox... I'd love to go, certainly, I was wondering if you'd ask me out." She gave him a fast nod that was open and full, then went to her table to work some more. He smiled at her through his bottom lip then turned to the sink and rinsed off a mug, moved to the chimney and there to one side was a small calendar stapled with little paper pumpkins that were coloured in waxes of yellows and greens.

"What are these doing here?" Peter asked.

"What? Oh, those. My pumpkins."

"How did you get them?"

"Peter, I shrank them and tinted them and hung them to dry. I pulled one out of a gravel pit and another from the sky and another from a little bottle found on a delta stuck to a log. What do you think?" She looked at his nose and said, "What do you think... I'll get ready to go."

He watched her move to the bathroom to the bedroom and thought I dont know and noticed her pert bottom and muscly legs and snappy walk and saw how she grabbed her purse from the bed and her coat from the pantry – as if she owned them completely and they were all hers.

Peter listened to her talk as they walked up the thick treed road, poked in a question here, ducked away with a half comment there. He watched her as they ran down the flakey highway into town into a theatre into a pub and then back. When they were going down her road, a branch of snow slid in front of them.

"I did that," she said.

"You couldnt have," he answered.

"What makes you think so?" she said. And he had nothing to say. When they reached her door she said, "You're coming in for tea."

And Peter said, "No ... I'm not." Then he brushed the front of her coated breasts lightly, and said, "Thanks for the evening, good night."

The next time Peter went there her body seemed flatter and more alive. "Come on in, I thought you'd come, but I expected you earlier and not tonight of all nights." She was edgy and in a full skirt that folded as she moved to the chimney to the dining living working room to the sink (snatching a pumpkin off the calendar, switching a record halfway through a piece, rinsing the dirty dishes one by one) to the porch to the window to the stove.

"Do you ever do what people ask, Peter, do you ever feel that you must? Have you ever gone on for no reason but all reasons just because? Do you ever wish there was more than just this?"

Peter looked at her waist and small breasts and thin neck, then his eyes fell upwards to hers and he said, "Yes, yes you are."

And Mary kept moving, "I didnt mean ... but that's nothing either ... what I meant was ... oh, why be bothered ... what I started to say was ..."

"Come here," Peter said.

"What?"

"Come here."

They made love in her soft single bed, then on her hard hook-rugged floor. The first time it was serious, a getting this straight. Then between it was all fun: throwing pillows and books and things about the rafters and light bulbs, kissing fast and slapping about the house naked; jumping on table tops; stepping on window sills; standing with a broom in a corner; skipping with a tape measure in the living-dining-everything room then rolling on the rug and loving and semi-fighting all at the same time.

Peter slept there that night which was windy and wide awake, which was close to the sea and alive. Mary lay next to him silent, small bodied, not waiting, in a thick I've-had-it-all sleep. And early in the morning he dipped out of bed to go to work where everything he did, all the men he knew, even the ride he had taken day after day year after year seemed important and not what it had been before. After work he went back to his own home and wandered out to his own garden to look to decide where his pumpkins and tomatoes and bean stalks would go. Then, just before dark, he walked down to Mary Contrary's once more.

"Hi Peter before you do anything I'm saying now that I wont marry you until you're able to talk to listen to me ... I ... that is I know who you are, and dont think I dont, because I do, and that's so ... does this make sense because if it doesnt then ..." And they slept together another night.

The following morning Peter noticed that several of the pumpkins had fallen off the calendar and were lying curled on the floor. As he bent to pick them up, Mary came out of the bedroom, and said, "No ... no," and the muscles of his back became smaller, would not move. She twirled, naked, circling in front of him, said, "No," quickly, and he fell to the floor. "I should have told you not to try that, not to touch those, but I didnt so I must say now that you'll do as I say until the time comes that – sit up." And Peter did. He did everything that Mary told him how she told him when she told him: this to wear that to eat, this fence to patch that wood to chop, fill this hole kill that rooster kiss me let's go to town. They went over the railway tracks up an alley along a street to an old wooden building to the second floor and there within a few minutes they were married.

But Peter could not love his wife. Anything else, Mary could make him do: to go to work in the morning, to be as he always was with other people, to tease her to fight her to sleep with her to stroke her. But it was not what it had been or how it should be. Their life became a pattern of you do this and I'll do that. They didnt fight, there was nothing to say, they moved about the same house, drank together with the others, worked, went to bed, got up, ate, and started all over.

The one thing that Peter did on his own was go to the ball game, and that, too, was part of the pattern: Thursdays and Sundays meet the boys there, go to somebody's place or the beer parlour after, come home reasonably late, bed; up; work; and on and on and on. Then, one night at the game he heard the umpire backcatcher people on the stands yelling he didnt know what about he hadnt seen he couldnt figure he joined it anyway and the game started again right after one ball one strike they yelled, "Get under it Bill now, here we go now, here we go, you can make it," and Peter whispered, "Get 'er Pete now, get 'er Pete now." And the town was behind, six to two, seventh inning, and didnt have a chance what with all its poor batters coming up; but they yelled and he yelled; and they clapped and he clapped; and they stamped, and he stamped; and last frame, last inning, one two three four five runs in a row. And they all went and had beer and played the game over, and played it over, during which time for Peter things seemed clearer and freer than they had been for a long time.

He sang the way home, he tore tips off fir branches, kicked Mary's flowers that were all in a row. Instead of sleeping inside, he stayed out on the porch. Suddenly he was in a pumpkin belly trying to dig his way out and his feet were rooster's claws. The harder he scratched the thicker the pumpkin bottom grew and then grew and then burst. He fell down onto an endless field that was covered in high rows up to the sky rows of vines, and on the bottom of the vines were little pumpkins which he plucked off with his mouth, upwards, sideways, on top of. He squatted on somebody's chimney made of leaves like shellac that peeled off, and he dropped again, on to one that crumbled. Peter stood up and walked into the house and snatched the little pumpkins off the calendar and ate every last one and then went to bed.

The next day Mary told him to get up, but he didnt. She was surprised. She jumped on top of the covers and rolled all over him. Peter simply lay there and said, "Stop it will you." And she did. "I'm tired of your bossing ... get me some coffee." And she did.

"Who do you think you are?" she said when she came back into the room.

"I'm me," he said. "Peter."

He said, "Who are you ... you're not Mary ... you're a cat." And her body scrunched down and leapt up to the bed to between his legs. He looked directly into her eyes, "You're a pumpkin seed." And her body curled up. "You're a seagull." And her shoulders lifted and her head rose and her breasts rubbed through covers along his chest. Peter touched his finger on a bone of her neck and said, "No, you're not, you're just my wife." And she popped inside the bed. Then they made love and did so very well.

## Four

Peter the Pumpkineater and Mary Contrary lived, for the most part, an unsettled (close for three weeks here, I dont care enough to care for three weeks there) hectic (up all night sleep all Sunday work all Monday miss the crummy Tuesday dont speak Wednesday Thursday Friday) life. Mary, at times, was bitchy and most contrary. She would run out to her garden and stand on top of a rubbish pile and squeal away to herself absolutely oblivious of Peter or who he was or what his needs were. She would place pebbles in a row, would scatter dry seaweed in the wind, would bury the remains of yesterday's supper beneath cockleshells and sing in a high many-angled odd-toned jerky-rhythmed voice. Or she'd climb a tree and not come down.

Let him walk back and forth underneath and not tell him she was there. Then after it was over she'd say, "I must be sometime each day by myself or else I'm totally not anyone at all." To which he would agree, within limits, and argue that at most times this was simply an excuse, a knowing she did not want to be with him and had there been any person else she might be with that one.

But each time Peter let her go until it passed a certain point where he stepped in and simply did. Did what? Took over. "You're not that way really ... dont be silly, come here ..." And then slowly would follow her whole person self. His Mary but not his, he Peter but not him. He never could and never tried to figure the whole thing out. Only knew that he must act, must bring her to be with her-himself, for many moments at least, and then they could move apart about skitter skatter past the porch, down a bushy trail dancing, along the sea edge from log to log from boulder to boulder leaping. Long leg stretches to burnt-out stump up dirt bank hand tree roots up weeds up cliff touching holding stopping kissing, and then down skipping through a no-pathed forest to the apple-smelling hooked-rag thick-quilted cottage.

Very late one night Peter's first wife, the one he had put into the pumpkin shell, came tapping lightly to their door. He, undressed, left the bedroom to see what it was, thinking it was maybe a large bug caught inside, or a raccoon on the porch, or perhaps a nightbird flapping on the screen. His former wife stood there, large, in a green woolen scarf and a big many-patterned coat made of oranges and yellows and deep browns and golds. What to say. What to do.

"Come in, wait, I must get dressed, sit anywhere, what are you *doing* here? ... Wait." And Peter returned in work pants, without a top, an unbuckled belt at the waist.

"I dont know why I'm here either," she said simply, "it is this ... what are you doing and how are you and it's useless to say but I had to see for myself and wanted you to see too but maybe I'd better go for there's nothing, but how could there be, but there is."

"I wouldnt say that," he said. But he knew it too. Perhaps Mary had changed him, or he her, or both each other. This woman in front of him her large coat he could fall into, but herself and her body so resigned and look what you did to me, which he didnt, and he had been with her or to her many times past and they had gone through a lot together but even then, no knowing, and now, "What have you been doing?" he said.

"I dont want to talk about that," she leaned forward. And at this moment Mary drifted into the room.

His first wife looked up and saw Mary and said "Hello" without looking at her although she was in the other woman's house. Mary thought, no I wont, wont have that, and made coffee and cut cake and suddenly wanted Peter for herself as she had not before, not since a long time ago. The woman ate and she ate without tasting anything. Stuck her fingers round the plate edge and took all the crumbs too. And the three sat and they sat without saying anything.

Finally, Peter was the one to go. Out for a walk. Let the women settle it themselves. He went to the beach to an old boatshed and sat on the edge thinking hoping Mary would work things out. Later he climbed up the bank to the back of the house to his garden and walked slowly between the night tomatoes and squashes. He sat at one end and looked over at Mary's little pebbles, empty shells uncluttered all in a row. Then he went indoors.

The women were still there. His former wife did nothing. Mary scowled through the dark room then smiled to bring him over to a chair. The large woman made motions to move but didnt, how could she, she wanted to be here, settled until finally Peter asked her where she lived now saying nothing of where she had gone or been these many years. And she said simply, "Nowhere. Up on a hill somewhere. Under the earth anywhere. I cant tell anymore. Dont take me, I'll go myself, and someday come back. I must. I will. Goodnight." And left.

## Five

One night, after several years of not seeing her at all, Peter Pumpkineater met his first wife. He wasnt sure how it happened. He was driving along a moonlit logging road and turned a corner. The moon the air the long black shadows shifted from spring to snow. The branches and the road and the windshield were suddenly white. He leaned forward to see through the thickness. The road curved. It shouldnt at least it didnt when he was here last but he stayed with it. And then a sharp left. He turned the wheel hard, and the car just made it, just managed to keep on the ridge. A huge white boulder blocked his way. He slammed on his brakes. What could he do? The car skidded. He let go. Then the car floated right up to the edge of it and crunched to a stop. Peter leaned over the wheel for a moment or so. "What's happened? ... I'm alright ... where am I? ... I'm alright ... I'm right here."

He got out of the car and walked around it and stood on the edge of the road. He looked down: hundreds of feet below, water ran in the valley. He looked around: several giant fir trees started to shake with the weight of their whiteness. He felt a lightness and clarity come up from the soles of his feet – as if all that was out there was coming in and up and through. His body shook to the rhythm of the trees. And his brain cells felt as if they were being kissed by snowflakes. He loved it here, he wanted to stay. He knew he had a choice. I can go back or try to, to the world, to home, to Mary, if I can figure how to get out. Or I can stay here in this forever.

As pleasant as the clarity and lightness was (everything was pearly and angular as if nothing had substance except air which was particles of light) he chose to tackle the difficulties. Yet he knew he would return someday and perhaps this was what death is. He knew he would no longer be afraid of dying, he felt so beautiful and loose and weightless. But for now he chose doing, to move out and down there to the world. Peter looked about for a hunk of wood to pry the boulder. He knew that even if he found one, the boulder was too large and too heavy for one man to move or to break. But he would try anyway. He saw a lump in the snow which looked like part of a log. He scrambled to the edge of it and scooped the snow backwards through his legs.

She seemed distant now, Mary Contrary, his present wife and present life; she and it seemed part of the other and far far away. Why work to return there? As soon as he thought that, his body scrunched into a somersault. He floated above the log and the car and the huge (it seemed to be growing, now it was as wide as a house and as tall) boulder. He looked down, drifted close above it, just missed the jagged top, and saw, to his utter amazement, his first wife. There at the wheel of the car. He swam back to see her. Her hair sparkled at the tips, silver speckles surrounded each strand. She didnt seem to see him, to know he was there. He was overtaken by a memory of her eyes as they were making love. At the edge of coming each eye fell into and opened up to each. His hand moved to touch her. She didnt see or feel. The windshield wiper was still going. Very slowly. Narrowed by snow. His finger fell from the sky to open the slit more.

She looked out. He reached the glass. Suddenly the car started to slide sideways as if completing its former motion. She didnt seem to see his hand, him, at all. He felt his whole head right up there trying to swim in. His finger was holding the wiper and his whole body was in it or his finger now had the faculty of sight. He could see out of it into her who was moving slowly, impossibly slowly, sideways over the edge of the road. That's no way, he thought. Cant you see? I am here. I am here. I can help you. He could not hold the weight any longer but he knew he would be able to if she would only open and ask for help and see him and give her energies too. Together they could. But she didnt want to. Or couldnt. Or wouldnt. The car rolled over the edge, over the cliff.

Her mouth opened. Her hair floated. She looked like she was drowning in air. In that instant before it tumbled, at the edge, she recognized him. Peter's body stayed where it was on the road but he glided to her. The vehicle turned over and they merged: he was her, she was him, she was behind the wheel, he was. Turning, and events of their lives came together, like branches of hair. They could see through the eyes of the other and self. Simple moments turned over: he saw her at their door when he came home from work, the light of the kitchen outlined her body; he became she opening out to him who was her muscles tired from logging yet full and happy to greet; she saw him gardening, talking with his plants, she became him digging the earth and pulling out weeds, and he became her watching him an instant before coming together to eat.

They fell over and over: kneading bread, hammering a spice shelf, holding hands as they walked up a hill, soaping each other's backs, making love in the forest; and never being there, tying her to the bed, gouging out the pumpkin shell, being locked in that mold that goo day after day after day. The good and the bad and the anger and the love but always the deep: ordinary seconds and looks which are so feelingful that they are the real. The blurs, the moping throughs, the indecisions, these were nothing, transparencies without shape, drifting without feeling: these, they cast off and stayed with, as they turned through that forest, the simple the direct the full. They landed on the blue roof on the snow above running water. Peter's head, her head, crumpled. He felt his brain wrench into and around bone, pieces, corners, curves.

Suddenly he moved up backwards through the moments of coming and going and being and tumbling to the present. "My god, help." He could see her, down below there. "It's not too late," he knew that. It was not too late. She lay on the bottom of the vehicle facing the sky and him. He peered over the ridge and saw her arm flop. Not long, it wouldnt be long now, he *had* to get help. She was on her back, her mouth was open, her body covered in white gossamer which unfolded and folded with the air. But how could he get down? *There was no way*. He would have to go back along the road he had been coming on which was long and winding and far away from anyone, or he would have to get over the boulder or around it and move forward along the road which he thought he knew up until a week ago but had no sense of now.

He chose the unfamiliar. He tried to scale the boulder. It was icy and hard and slippery but his fingers were strong and his caulk boots dug in, got a grip. He almost made it the first time. Slipped. Scraped his entire front. He tried again. Got up beyond the middle. And fell again. He'd have to work his way round. It would take a long time, too long. He edged himself between the boulder and the bottom snowy branches. He tried to scramble through and up white fir steps. He held his breath and wedged against the boulder, crawled up through the snow, let go, got it again. If he could keep against the boulder he knew he'd make it; he just had to get higher to stay up there to keep his breath. He slid and he pushed and he pulled then he dove through the snow over branches and he crawled out on the other side.

There she was. Motionless. Inside ice. Deep beneath the surface of the opaque boulder, her skin, creamy and rose, shone like porcelain; her dress, blue and patterned, fell like silk about her body. Peter's belly smiled, all his cells all his nerves were pulling forward reaching out. And his tongue, his mind, wanted to say all he had thought at once: I want you, I love you, I've always loved you, I loved her too but it was other, another form of love somehow, my need and hers but willed, and now I know two cannot will anything (or one) yet they can and they do and they will, I feel more open than that, I felt so loose with you at first, we sure got stuck in a mudpie such a gooey mudpie of children playing grownups and grownups playing what we had learned to be, I didnt mean to hurt you, I never *meant* to hurt you, but I did, you did, and we did, I feel out of that, I want out of that forever, do you? Do you? He thought what felt like everything in less than a moment as he crawled toward her who was so beautiful and glowy and static inside the boulder of ice.

He opened his mouth to speak. He stretched out his arms to touch the surface. And his tongue, his tongue grew solid in air. Blue crystals froze it and his nostrils and his eyelashes and his lips and all his skin. He tried to go forward, to crack through, but couldnt; to wiggle backwards, to shake loose, but couldnt; to wedge sideways, to get free, but no, no, he couldnt get out by himself. He saw her through the crystals, could still make out her features which fell apart and floated at odd depths. He tried to pull them together. The choice would be hers, he knew that, they could die here in this or live there in that. He wanted so much to shout to her, to sing out, to talk, to be. But she would have to choose, to say yes to herself. He couldnt hold any longer. He could scarcely see at all.

He and she stayed there for a long long while, just a small distance apart, on the boundary, solid but not solid, seeing but not seeing, feeling but not feeling. Snow swirled down and covered the ice which covered them. A white soft sky above and around and beyond. Peter's veins turned slushy then hard, his nerves spiralled into his spine, his brain throbbed then numbed then closed to the centre. All that was left was his slow slow heart. "Love yourself," his heart beat. "Love yourself," his heart whispered. "Love yourself woman then you might choose love and me and he and she and we." Its whisper, its beat, its song, cracked through the ice to her. Her heart heard his heart and began to beat. "Is that you?," it whispered, "Peter, are you there?" Her sound broke a corridor through the blue crystals and turned fragments of ice into tiny rainbows. "Where are you?" her heart sang. "Where are we?" Peter was surrounded in light and ice. She floated through the melting tunnel toward him. "Peter, Peter Pumpkineater." She gently brushed off the snow and frost and ice with her arms and tears. From her skin into his. From her eyes into his. Eye into eye. Open. And so it was.

# A Birth Account

NEW STAR, 1976

*for Lars and Cliff*

## Introductory Note

There are three parts to this book. The first, a group of sketches, begins in January 1970 when I was pregnant and ends in June 1970 when a doctor performed a D&C to scrape out the remains of what later was termed a "missed abortion." The second, more sketches, starts in September 1970 when I was again pregnant but not certain that I was; it finishes on the last day of April 1971 just hours before labour began. The third, an account of birth, begins and ends on May 1, 1971. I wrote the first few pages of the birth account between contractions during the early stage of labour. The rest I wrote between mid-June and mid-August of 1971 – I'd get up at five to nurse and change Lars and then write (whenever he slept) between feedings, cleanings, answering the phone, etc., until noon.

I wrote the birth account to share my experience with others and to see if I could as closely as possible record what happened. In *no* way is it meant to be a guide for someone giving birth for the first time; as I say in the text, "for every woman it is so different that any description is only a trace of what is." You, reader, will know no more than I did what was occurring, e.g., I did not know that Lars was slipping up and down the birth canal, but I did know I saw his head on one contraction and it was several contractions later before he was helped out. At moments my confusions are articulately conveyed, at other moments they are not – I record as well as I can the state of consciousness, the images that came to me, and the feeling of just wanting to go home and to come back tomorrow to have it.

Please read my work aloud. The rhythm, the sound, the breathing are all part of what it is. When you come to the third section of this book, breathe the breaths:

> > > > > > > > > <h <h <h <h <h <h <h <h <h

in through your nose (a deep abdominal breath) out through your mouth

> > > <h <h <h

in through your mouth (a chest level breath) out through your mouth

<h t    <h t    <h t
say, very quietly, out    out    out
(pronounce the t: this is an extremely shallow breath)

You may find your consciousness alters. I am convinced (after reading portions of the whole of this account to groups and experiencing states similar to those of labour) that part of the reason I was dissociated from sensations and why I perceived as I did was directly related to how I had learned (from the Childbirth Association of Vancouver classes) to breathe.

# *Pregnant*

There are three: Cliff, Daigen, and me. Daigen is a dachshund, he lies on the wood floor in the February sun. Cliff is a man, a student of economics, he walks down a treey hill to a vacant lot which has thirty or more motorbikes on it, he puts on his white helmet and starts his yellow Yamaha to drive home. I hesitate, it is not home, or is it because we live here: a house on Old Middleton Road on the edge of Madison, Wisconsin, across the road a railway track, beyond it a lumberyard, near us pines and elms: home is Vancouver, British Columbia.

I am a West Coast woman, born on the forty-ninth parallel at Ladysmith on Vancouver Island. Cliff is a Maritimer, born on the Saint John River at Fredericton, New Brunswick. We first saw each other in a high-ceilinged classroom five years ago this September: Cliff near a door at the back, I near a blackboard at the front, he must have said something, I forget what, but the next night his was the only name out of seventy I knew, Mr. Andstein – that blond smiley (I thought) married man who sat with a clutch of (I thought) married men on the left at the back.

Daigen's paws press my thigh (jean-covered) and he squeaks cuz the sun has gone. He doesnt know that I can do nothing about it, he leaves me now and runs (nails on bare floor) to the top of the couch to look out the window and see Cliff. The bike has just come in the driveway. Now he's at the door, locked, I left it locked, I dont get up but write. "Hello Daigen, weiner, you dont want to go out there, it's all wet, yeah, eh, eh, HEY," he yells. "Wait a sec," I say. "You hungry, you hungry Daigy?" Daigen bounces on Cliff's leg as they come over to me: three.

―――――

Three o'clock is mug-up time on the boats: the roast is in the oven and the cook sits in the mess with the men. Three o'clock and I'm in bed chewing cinnamon gum, just a moment ago I ate a hermit which is a soft cookie made of brown sugar dates raisins nutmeg and cinnamon. I had such a yen an hour ago (stopped by a sentence,

Pound's: "it seems unlikely that any man of cabinet rank in England or the USA has, during the past twenty years, committed any act that cd. in any way however slight or remote conduce to support or fostering of art or letters"*) that I turned on the oven and stood there feeling the taste of the cookie the spices crumbling in teeth touching hot dates and said to myself, you know if you can taste this well without having one you dont need one you should get to work, but my body-me got out a bowl and quickly mixed half a batch up and soon they were there: brown-goldy hermits, crunchy on the edges, soft inside.

I feel a bit guilty and slightly indulgent, but wow, what fun: lying here like Proust (but not working: I am stuck on a story and should be focusing on that), Daigen cuddling my foot, tummy just slightly hungry, and no classes to teach no papers to mark no rush (as it is with supper on the boats) about to start: I just chew gum and look out the window at the cedar boughs dancing and hear Daigen snore, cars drive by, and the air in the registers causes the metal to click: not high sounds, but fairly low, like large drops of water.

———  ———

In September we will be four. Shinwa (her/his name till birth) is just a couple of inches now and is unreal to Cliff and me except that I fart and burp a lot. And the other morning when we were fucking the gas moved up and down my bum tickling slightly: where Cliff's cock pressed thru my vagina the air wasnt, as it moved the gas followed: this wasnt the least bit like having a finger in and fucking at the same time, no tightness, the air-gas moved exactly as his cock did, kinda floaty, groovy, I laughed, and he didnt know why till I told him then he giggled a bit too.

———  ———

I hear the garbage truck stop outside and seeing the plastic bag full mostly of paper (we are killing the trees I said to Cliff last night) I think of what Paul Ehrlich said here a week ago: a baby born in the States uses three hundred times as much of the world's resources as a baby born in Indonesia. Three hundred times, I think, what is it, medical care, water to wash to wash with soap, soap too, and those

---

\*     Ezra Pound, *Guide to Kulchur* (New York: New Directions, 1968), 256.

hundreds of jars (cant return them) and cans (takes ten years for a can to break down) of baby food, plus all the diapers and towels and woollens, etc., and the objects, so many objects, and every couple buying new.

———  ———

It is cold this afternoon and we are in March now. I print (cant write: never could very well: have printed since grade seven) small. Why? Depressed? Inward? When I squinch up I dwell too much in the self. But misty/foggy, it is not a day to move outward, even the snow shrinks in and down. And the reason it is cold in here, and it is not so very cold, is simple: the furnace is broken, the motor will have to be replaced. The repairman, Vern (I know his name because it is sewn on his coveralls) and Cliff are down there now. Scraping sounds, like someone shaking a cutlery drawer, come up to me. And they talk every so often, a warmth in their voices.

The mist is not like a West Coast fog. But I cant see the lumber warehouse just across the road so it is a fog. And the sky has a peculiar lightness to it, that is it is round still, there's that height, and I have the sense that the sun is beyond it. On the Coast in fog there is no sky, looking up at a large tree you cannot see the top, but the air is water and through it comes the beeeeooooop of foghorns: alone, low sounds, which are snuggly if you're inside especially if with someone if only for an evening; but if you are alone and outside you feel enclosed somehow, the air comforts, the ocean is near, and the earth also, and the lights in the buildings do not scream at you but have a warmth which you need not enter, not cuz you cannot, which may be so, but cuz you choose not, which is different.

———  ———

I drink jasmine tea and smoke a five-cent cigar as I write. The early March sun sinks through Cliff's T-shirt into my back, the muscles loosen, open to the warmth, and I undo the fly of my jeans so I can bend forward and breathe easily. Have had energy these past few days (for about four weeks there I was asleep) from the earth and sun feeling of gotta do something, move.

Last night going to a Fidel movie I felt a beautiful long-haired boy from about a block away. As we walked toward each other our presences were ahead, they met just before we passed, totally happy. Then inside the theatre I felt connections with all sorts of people and sat next to Cliff and his fingers squeezed my nipple and I was with him but also the others – not the whole audience – but waves, vibrations, presences of energy throughout, they were coming into me through my back my arms my chest my head.

Another form this energy is taking is a desire to sew (and shit like I made one dress last year still not hemmed and absolutely nothing for five years before that) to get ready a wardrobe: bought a blue-green quilted skirt second-hand for fifty cents, bought two maternity pouches, am cutting and pinning and getting ready to use a friend's machine, am removing the dye from an ugly-patterned nice-lined smock and a pair of coloured jeans which Cliff splashed bleach on: in other words I'm preparing to do something I normally do not have the patience for, in fact I am doing it, and it's as if I'm receiving forces/motions/energies from without, they flow through me.

———  ———

Yens: banana-cream graham-cracker crust pie, last week; fresh rhubarb-crisp, the week before; brownies with mocha icing, over the weekend; oatmeal – from the round Quaker box recipe – cookies, two nights ago; raspberry sherbet with honey and walnuts, last night; and for about a month now, strawberries and strawberry ice cream. Yumm-mmm-mmm.

———  ———

Damn didilly damn damn: pants that wont stay up, sup-hose that's too long, elastic that's too tight, panty-garters that get pulled down mid-thigh: damn. Wake up hungry, gotta pee gotta pee, Cliff cuddled about me chair fashion, I hang there several moments then gotta eat gotta pee but first, yes first, before the right leg touches the floor, I have to put on these damn sup-hose so the veins, varicose, of my lower right leg, dont fill. The bed squeaks and wiggles and Daigen, who never misses a noise for food or going out, stretches on the rug and starts *his* squeaking which is light at first but louder as I pull the top of the panty sup-hose up or hook the fourth garter on to the sup-nylon. So feet outta bed, into slippers, and I pass the bathroom go to the kitchen and let the little-bouncing-tail-wagging fucker out the backdoor. And so to the can and so my day starts.

But after breakfast (orange juice, an egg, toast or pancakes, and sometimes bacon or sausage or bratwurst) on come the jeans, the wine ones I dyed or the patterned ones I put a pouch in, and on top of them something long to hide the pouches which are kinda low cuz I didnt know what I was doing when I sewed them in. Then it starts: I pull them up, put on a jacket, we go for a walk and I stop to pull them up from the back, maybe twice, maybe three times, maybe four I dont count. We return and every time I stand up from sitting down I hitch them up, up, the elastic of the panty sup-hose pulls the crotch down, the elastic of the regular sup-hose pulls the panty-garter crotch down, and the crotch of whatever I'm wearing pulls the jeans down, down: damn didilly damn damn.

―――― ――

It is April now and I've been homesick (daffodils are almost over, said Leni on the phone, I have a sunburn on my nose) but it isnt homesick, I think it's just my mood, and what a generalized one it is: a few nights ago Cliff and I started talking about what I dont like in women's lib, i.e., I said I thought the articles I read missed the fact that several women work because they feel useful, that yes the money is very important in terms of this consuming-buying-consuming society but they want to work with people and however boring their jobs might be that need is not filled by clubs-coffees-charities-liberal-organizations-etc.-etc.; and he stopped me, what *was* I saying, I didnt know what I was talking about, and soon – after mentions of women I know who work out of economic necessity but they, I thought, would be turned off by women's lib's romanticizing of the worker – I was crying.

Okay, *I* feel useless then. I feel needed when I'm teaching, sure, sure I get tired of papers and so much energy in bringing people out, to themselves, in, in, and the not moving the slowness of it all at times, but yes, I miss teaching, and that sense of me I have when I am. But your writing, Cliff said, it's work. I'm so alone, I said and ran to the bathroom for toilet paper, I'm lonely, teaching is public, I dont know, I just feel useless, and writing is useless. I cried and let myself cry (it's okay, I said, let me, I have to) then changed to a nightie, made cocoa of skim milk, brought out a blanket for my legs which were cold and we sat on the couch and spoke about it and slowly the muscles of my back and arms and legs loosened and gradually Cliff was able to get me to at least recognize that whether I like it or not there are two things I do which are not alienating even if alone activities: I cook and I write. But, another part of me kept saying or doing, but, and I'd start to cry again, come out of it, then start again.

Okay. Two mornings later I wake up and we have pancakes and bacon and eggs and we go along the railway tracks for a walk to an abandoned field which is nearby, and throughout the walk I keep hitching up my wine jeans and suddenly I'm mad at them: I have to have a pair that stays up, that's large enough in the legs that I can sit tailor-fashion (a pre-natal necessity) right this morning, today, as soon as we get home. We left Daigen in the house and got on the motorbike (car in the garage being fixed) and drove to a super-duper American shopping centre and went into a small store, eee-gads, the groovy black and white striped pair was too big, but the saleslady was a-selling a-selling and the colours were dismal, so we went to another store and I got a pair of six-dollar-wide-wide-leg-baggy-baggy-middled (but no panel so I can wear my usual tops) blue Viet Cong type pants. There's no reason this should make me cranky but yes it did: maybe they should be smaller (only ones left in shop), maybe I should have tried harder to find material to make some (so far the pouches, the fifty-cent skirt, and two long tops I can wear anytime are all I've bought), maybe I was just caught into this buy-buy-buy impulse, maybe, maybe.

Now the third. On Sunday we drove to some friends to see the Stanley Cup preview (we dont have TV, the announcer was selling hockey like it was cars but not as slick, more like a local dealer with a special on) and a NET special on Pinter (the gaps between sentences are longer now, he said). Lying on their coffee table was a *Ladies Home Journal* which had on the cover, "HOW PEOPLE YOU LOVE KEEP YOU FAT." Now I've been just a little plump to definitely overweight all my life (Gladys, my mom told me in grade four after the doctor had said something to her, you should try to have just one chocolate bar a week) and if there is anything I love to do when I am not gaining weight it is to talk or read about overeating. So I read it. And so when I was about to leave the house I asked our friend, Sue, if I could borrow a couple of magazines (a former occupant didnt have her subscription sent on to wherever she is now and that's how Sue gets them) and of course she said sure. Well, these damn magazines, I do read them and they always (like *Cosmopolitan* which I've bought maybe nine times in the past three years) make me feel uncertain, hungry, out of it, not a woman in their sense, and I know they play on me, play on feelings I do and dont know I have, use them, turn them around, but fuck it, like, the impulse to have them to read most of that crap (Ruben's diet article is not shit, it makes sense but is slicked up in spots) is strong: locked in, they lock me in, cut me off from myself.

WOMEN ETC.

THE NEW YORK LIFE
LIFE OF JACKIE KENNEDY ONASSIS
HER APT
WHERE SHE SHOPS
WOMEN WHO LOOK YOUNGER THAN THEY ARE
ETC.

WOMENWOMENWOMENWOMEN
SHOP     SHOP     SHOP     SHOP
WOMEN LOOK YOUNGER
WOMEN LOOK YOUNGER
SHOP ETC.
SHOP ETC.
THEY ARE ETC.
THEY ARE ETC.
WOMEN THEY ARE ETC.
WOMEN THEY ARE ETC.
WOMEN ETC.
WO ... MEN ... ETC.
WOO ... ... ... MEN ... ... ... ET ... CET ... ER ... AH

―――――

Shinwa hasnt kicked yet and (s)he is about nineteen weeks old. I spoke to my doctor the other night cuz I was bleeding slightly and he asked, among other things, you've been feeling life havent you? No, I said, cuz in his office he told me if it would be a definite kick. But flutters? he said; yes, I said, I guess so. But now I wonder. A friend was over on Sunday and tapped three fingers lightly on the back of my hand: that's what it feels like, she said, that's how it feels. I'm waiting for that feeling or an equivalent to it, waiting. And I guess once it comes then I'll know Shinwa's there, really know; cuz except for that February four weeks of burping farting and sleeping – once a minute I either burped or farted – I in some ways dont know, I'm conscious of it at moments (like I dont really want to bend down to fasten my sandals) but I dont really know.

———

I am lying on a child's bed in Milwaukee. Tired, I couldnt sleep well, a cramp, quick, only a second, then it goes, images of floating wave-like over soft apple fields as I drifted off, and now, this room, Christie Weigner's, a giant stuffed turtle on the floor, a painting by her on the wall. A few moments ago some clots came out: little dark pieces of liver-like tissue. I dont want to think about it, I'm writing so I wont think, but writing always brings me to what I am thinking even if I dont know I'm thinking it. And it's Cliff I see/want, wish he were here, not yet seven, nothing to do but wait. I look at the felt-batik of fish, a family, lions, an elephant, an owl, grey clouds.

What can I do? Become a cloud? No, the red in the yellow-green-red swirly painting by Christie, just three and a half, stands out. I like this room, it isnt an adult version of what a girl might like, but is *her* room, I know she's here even though she's with her father in his apartment, and a white rabbit lies under the bed, and a white rabbit poster behind my head and – another cramp – if I'm losing Shinwa, I'm losing her/him, (s)he may be dead already, the doctor said yesterday that my womb is small, that it isnt growing, that if the baby doesnt kick in the next two weeks and nothing else has happened (meaning a miscarriage: he asked about cramps and said the fact I hadnt had any was encouraging) he'll run another pregnancy test to see if I still am.

Am I? Are you? The blood last night and clots this morning say no, no, but I still want to say yes, hello there, yes.

———

Not knowing is worse than knowing. Yesterday I felt a thing like fingers moving *in* rapidly, it stopped, then much later little jumps like my belly jumping fast, not rolls, jerks. And now today I feel many motions as I lie here in the sun next to Lake Mendota which is bigger but similar to English Bay of Vancouver. Shinwa's alive, but I dont sense (s)he is, maybe, perhaps, but it is not the same as knowing, really knowing.

I know now Shinwa is dead. Phoned the doctor last night cuz my whole body was jerking, fast all-over jerks, they slowed down when I went into the childbirth-class relaxing position, but continued, my whole body jumped from its centre. He told me it was tension and to come see him in the morning which I did. After he looked inside with that cold shoe-horn-like instrument and felt my belly with his fingers pressing hard, he told me I would miscarry, when he couldnt say, but I certainly wouldnt let you go six months, the longer we wait the smaller the uterus becomes and the easier it is, for him, for me, I didnt get that straight, all I could do was cry. And now I cry in spurts then stop, do things, make a nightie, sweep the floor, listen to music, write this. And at least that pull of yes (s)he is alive, I think so, no (s)he isnt, am I making this up, is this real, is gone.

I feel awful, but not as awful as I did that year I was emotionally disturbed like the shrink said which is a euphemism (funny how many euphemisms there are) for what? I dont know, that year I was out of it I would say sometimes and people jump but it aint that way, no words to describe, and that was not as bad as being physically alive moving but dead in the head dead in feelings, not there, not here, not anywhere: that year merely broke the old patterns, the blockings-in, up. Outside now the leaves are yellow-green and the sky is blue and Cliff is at the university where the cops are and the National Guard are waiting, and last night after we saw Charlie Olson in a film (big Charles, a trifle drunk, arms flinging, Apollo, Zeus, Vulcan, who are they? there is earth and heaven) we had a beer then stepped outside into the tear-gassed air.

---

Crazy. The world's so crazy. And beautiful. When we walk I love the weeds and chipmunks and squirrels and worms (can hear them in the park at night chewing oak leaves: sounds like light rain hitting the dark brown dryness) and Daigen digging holes or running after rabbits or trying to climb a tree which a squirrel has just scurried up. But when I see the police in their goggles and gas masks and with tape over the windows of their cars, I dont hate, I havent come to that yet, but almost, almost, just how can those men not recognize what it is that they do, who they support.

Shit, I feel like I gotta shit. And for twenty-four hours now I've been having cramps, not full muscle-really-there cramps, but sharp fast low down warmths. Warmths? Yes. But only some have quality like a rush of blood which quickly goes back to wherever it came from; others are like pieces of string an inch or so under my skin, taut, pulled fast.

---

May 16, 1970. And now we are two. Daigen died today, was killed, no intention, he ran across the road for a piss, probably thought he saw a rabbit or squirrel or bird there, and cars coming fast turned back, was hit, not her the driver's fault at all nothing she could do, an oncoming car also, but Cliff saw it and I was already out there to get him back not knowing, and as I turned toward the road there he was lying on the edge of the tarmac his tail just coming down, and another car stopped, why I thought, go, but I went between two stopped cars and picked him up and called Cliff who had seen it but I didnt know, was getting his clothes on and then we were three but two but three, Daigen's spirit, joy, tail up cuz so happy here, why didnt we not let him out? No, no, that protection that, no.

I cuddled him and he died in my arms – perhaps was dead already – but let loose, slackened, as we drove to the vet's. And then moments later Cliff wrapped him in his dauxie towel started toward the car and the blood splattered on the cement – so we wont stare at it and remember – and I went to the bathroom above to wash my legs, all bloody, and from my pussy fresh oxygen blood, Cliff, I called, it's happening, but it wasnt, our blood there, Daigen's and mine mixed, his dark and tacky, hard to get off.

The three of us walked along the railway tracks for the last time, Daigen in Cliff's arms wrapped in the dauxie towel Leni gave me long before I knew either of them cuz she knew I loved dachshunds but, but, Cliff ahead for the first time, and it started to rain, just like Vancouver but soft, yellow-green air cuz the plants the land so alive now, and we didnt stop at the trail for his pisses or along the edge cuz some rodent (perhaps a chipmunk) has a tunnel there, just two nights ago he was so excited, no stops, no waits, we crossed up the hill and went through the bushes to a hole he dug a few weeks ago which was almost his size then.

Cliff dug the hole deeper as Daigie lay across my thighs and a bird just two yards off sang like mad. Then Cliff lifted him from me and opened the towel just enough to kiss him goodbye me first then him and he placed him in mother earth, in a dauxie Valhalla of squirrels and rabbits, no Daigie bark now, no squeaks, only a racket of birds and squirrels as the rain came down. Cliff packed the earth with live worms down and placed two live plants in deep then more earth then dead oak leaves but I wanted a live blossom and there was an apple tree there, wild perhaps, but I wouldn't kill the seeds, and I saw violets (am always careful not to step on them) and one anyway to place on Daigen's grave which he largely dug himself.

———  ———

June 2, 1970. I'm propped up in a hospital bed in Madison watching the green elm branches bend and dip. Five weeks ago today I started bleeding and now, finally, they'll scrape me out. The drug from the hypo is in my blood, I am starting to feel loose and kinda nice, women talk, the sounds of hair being brushed in the room and metal utensils just outside the room touch my ears. Groggy, forehead slightly heavy, I just phoned Cliff and we talked, Cliff my man, we move together so well yet we are very separate, a one and one, I love him so. Stomach is funnyish, voices are distant, I can make out the emphasis on syllables, like they're bigger than usual, yet I cant tell what the words are.

## *Pregnant with Lars*

Yellow-green plants grow: one is rooted in my belly, one in my ass, others form a row between. I touch their spongy bodies a second as I float up into Cliff. His fingers fondle my cunt and the thick plants with whitish warts disappear.

―― ――

I am flying toward a cloud and my mother is talking. I fall upright into water, see her on the dock holding a brown paper bag. And there are others, all adults, talking. The camera is heavy, hangs from my neck; black, big, it and my winter coat pull me down.

―― ――

Feel wretched but wont go to a doctor to see if I'm pregnant in case I'm not but that's stupid. Period four weeks late. Already think if I am I wont believe it till it is kicking. Silly not to phone. Shouldnt hold it in in a way I didnt when all that other was happening.

―― ――

I will be going to see Dr. Herstein, a specialist, this afternoon. He'll probably poke and smile and say everything's normal you've nothing to worry about. And I'll ask him if Cliff can be with me throughout, can help the birth. But birth, as soon as the word came (I hear words as I write, usually three or four ahead) no, it may not be, dont think, focus on the now. I wont. I cry. I see Daigen that last moment alive. I should tell him of this, try to stay here, now.

I dry my eyes on the blue-green towel which is wrapped around my wet hair. I take deep breaths and watch the woman across the alley sweep the little parking lot with a broom. Blow my nose. Sip mint tea. I must try to be more here and not think of what might happen, but maybe that protects you from it, no I dont think that's possible, it clogs you, thwarts you (fucking plastic pen cracks cuz I press so hard) from being all you.

Dont dream. Dont dream. Worry. Worry. Worry. Worry. At nine weeks fingerprints are formed. Dont think. For about a month now I've had supper aversions: the tomatoes are peeking out at me, I said one night; the rice looks like rain-covered pinworms; oil slurped over pale lettuce, did I ever eat that guck? Suddenly, two days ago, the night not wanting to eat this and that stopped. It's not growing, I think, can even my thinking make it so? Dont. Dont think. I cant stop. There's no way of telling. Breathe low, loosen your muscles, breathe.

Sun on the mountains, belly hungry, tomatoes and apples ripen in the backyard. A girl goes down the alley on her bicycle, red, I love red, and roundness. On my windowsill sits a vase of a dozen pink rosebuds, who they came from I dont know. On either side of them, stones: one a thunder-egg, blue icy crystals, Jack gave it to Cliff; the other is pink, hard, from Slocan. Next to it, a picture of Cliff in a funky brass frame, and beside it a wooden fish float from my father and a sperm-whale tooth from a man in Coal Harbour, the whaling station on the west coast of Vancouver Island. Then three objects just there: a buckle, a hide-a-key box, and a razor to scrape paint off the window. Ocean, deep earth, man, mammal, plant, things manufactured, made, given, taken, all here.

Eleven weeks, October, the leaves crackle in the wind, and inside, what happens, do you grow or not grow? I have been waiting for this time cuz I have a picture by Lennart Nilsson of an eleven-week embryo: so human, thumbs up to its mouth, ankles crossed, ribs formed, head huge, the little being floats in a background of blue with little white specks like stars. This picture is more real to me than you are. I stare at the small hands and pretend you are here, in me, but somehow I cant.

Fresh snow on the mountains. A woman in a blue-striped dress leans out the window across the lane and talks to her cat in a tree. A seagull glides by. And the noon whistles and horns blow.

In an hour I'll go to see Dr. Herstein: dont give me any of that psychodrama, he said the first time, as far as I'm concerned it's simple, boy meets girl, boy makes love, girl gets pregnant, but even though he said/insisted on this he talked with me and the nightmares stopped.

The next time I saw him he seemed to indicate everything's normal and an intelligent girl like me shouldnt worry so much, that's just the problem I said I cant help but. The phone rang, women waited, he really cant predict anything at this stage, he came back from answering it (his receptionist wasnt there) and I gave him two William Carlos Williams books and a bottle of piss.

Today I'm slightly calmer, but I still dont know. Cliff and I walked on the beach before breakfast (poached eggs, homemade-bread toast, orange juice, coffee) then I sat down to write this: not as focused as I can be at other moments.

———  ———

A red heart made of a bread tie sits on my typewriter. It encloses the letters GH. My initials. Cliff. Tied. Thin hairs reach out, he kissed my legs and cunt and bum so gently last night, firm, there, light, his beard stubbles are gruff but his lips are not. My hairs mix with his, reach, stand, wave like cilia, what's the word? Those long speary bendy things in the tubes which bring the ovum down, down into womb.

When he kissed my belly I felt he was kissing both me and you, little one, inside, his love to you direct. That instant I thought you moved to him and I felt you there for the first time, he more with you than I am, how can that be, now I feel you are here, there, I was more afraid of love than he. All three of us are tied in this heart, this belly.

———  ———

Again. A red heart made of a bread tie sits on my typewriter. Cliff made it. Cliff, so ungruff and reaching out, I, so held in and inward till this moment and that, last night, he kissed you through my belly. I felt you there reaching up to him, you little four-incher, red cells growing oxygen blood ears organs hands feet, miniature of what you will be, laid out already. You are him, and me, yet it took his motion his love for you to feel mine, any. I've been so locked in myself, so unwanting to feel anything but pain, but the loss of Shinwa of Daigen, and worry and worry, not for you but for me. Have you known that, felt? Is your world large enough for you? You, I hope the fuck you got your dad's stamina, love, outwardness. I feel better realizing you are not only from me you have his qualities too, your own also, you are you, you cut through toughness, feel what is here.

---

Swimming breaststroke today I saw my fingers stretched, blurred, boneless. Light through the rafters reflected off the bottom. The fingers – six? twelve? – moved out there in green water unformed. Are yours like that?

---

There is a white almost-square building in front of me: in one apartment window is a globe of the world with a venetian blind about to hit it. There are mountains beyond the apartment tops, white scars of snow. There are white paper blinds in the building just slightly to my right, a white parking line on the tarmac in front of me, and two white flowerpots beyond it. They, full and scalloped, are the only outside roundness I can see.

I'm in black today. Black and soft brown. Brown. I see the garage, the brown bricks on the corner of the right apartment, the brown-gold of the telephone pole: feel chestnutty. A woman in a cream coat with brown boots and purse appears, walks into the white building. I'm a big round chestnut. My skin is shiny. I lie in the sun. Take me. Hold me if you can. Crack me open (watery warm cream cells) and eat if you dare. But if you start, your size will reveal itself. You must be large also, or one bite and you'll shrink, disappear.

---

You kick now. At first there were nudges like a knuckle through a feather quilt: these came after supper, little knocks, I wasnt sure it was you. Then one morning after breakfast you poked in an inch-and-a-half radius near my belly button: five or six times in two minutes, and, within an hour, riding in downtown traffic on Granville just three days before Christmas, eleven or more pokes. I laughed and ate an orange. Now, two weeks later, I feel you mainly when it's dark out; an hour or so after supper and in the morning before dawn. You wake me. At least I think you do cuz I'm not sweaty or just out of a nightmare but drifty, pleasant, about to turn over. Then you kick.

I swam forty-five lengths today. Came home to Cliff mouth frozen from the dentist. He followed me, too close, to the bathroom and I kicked his empty moccasin at the door. You havent eaten yet, have you, he snapped.

Then I'm in the kitchen, he's on the other side of the little work table. I grab a loaf of bread out of the drawer, throw it at him. He slings it back, knocks over a glass. Within a minute he leaves the house and I try to cut bread for toast: crooked, raggled.

I start to cry. What the fuck. I dont know what this is about. I shouldnt eat now. I'm not hungry. Yes I am. I make half a chicken sandwich, slap coleslaw on a plate, fill the teapot, and come to our room to eat on the bed. So grumpy.

---

Starlings land on the snow-covered compost heap. Through the slit between two apartments, through the thick brown branches of a snow-edged tree near the water, a green barge moves. You kick within: light thumps move out slightly in tiny waves. Where you knock doesnt hurt, is slightly like a blood spurt in one spot of a large vein. I smile. Feel soft. The barge moves slowly through the upper half of the tree. A chunk of snow falls off a telephone wire. I listen to the noon horns and a dog and a typewriter. And maybe, just maybe, in Herstein's office this afternoon, I'll hear your heart.

---

There are five of us: Lanny Beckman, Brian DeBeck, Stan Persky, Cliff, and me. We live in a wooden house in Kitsilano at 2249 York. Our dining room (wooden panels, oak table, a long buffet with windows above) feels like a warm ice palace, a comfy brown-gold place to be in, looking out, surrounded by thick icicles which grow longer and fatter.

Somehow two is not enough after four years. Patterns and habits of being and talk become settled, not set exactly: student or reindeer herder? Cliff, just back from the snow-filled street, asks Bri: But what new is there to say? To learn? In a growing sense, I mean, not gossip or what I did today or an item just read. We moved so well in so many ways together we could have stayed in that pleasantness months, maybe years, more. That was the known.

I hear Bri fry eggs in the kitchen and the foghorns beeeeooooop across the bay. The tree in the park is blurred by the mist: only the trunk, the centre, is identifiable. Many couples we know are so bound in circles and roles and dependencies that they cant be together, except at moments. One or both are caught in, thwarted, unable to move out. Is this inevitable? does the mode mould, set up daily-domestic-emotional-buying-learning patterns which one doesnt choose, but simply is in?

The noon whistles blow: first a light one, then three, now or now a chorus. We didnt know it but we werent choosing as much as accepting what is as what is. Hey Glad. Call Bri. Are you stuck? Yeah. I call Brian and he gets his jacket and boots on to go out to the car in the white alley of snow.

―――  ―――

Stan peels potatoes: ttcch-ttcch, ttcch-ttcch, ttcch-ttcch. Cliff writes in the study above. A yellow barge slips quickly through the brown branches of the tree. And Bri runs water for a bath.

I look at the azalea on my windowsill: deep pink blossoms reach out, so many, how many, I lean over to count my pretties: one two three four five six seven eight nine ... fifteen, sixteen, seventeen, eighteen, nineteen, twenty. YIPPEE. That's Cliff. FINISHED IT. Twenty-four, twenty-five, twenty-six, twenty-seven. His thesis. It's done.

He comes in. We kiss. A warm smack. His blond hair falls on my brown. The blue of his denim shirt remains in my eyes as I write this. The pork chops sizzle. Where did I come from? says Stan to Ralph Maud who is out there. You kick, little kicks, low, just above my clitoris. And twenty-seven doesnt count the buds (mostly in threes) about to open.

―――  ―――

I'm on the top deck of a ferry boat, Queen of Saanich, heading for the island, Vancouver Island, to go to Ladysmith where I was born. No land is visible. We're enclosed in grey mist. The red bottom of the maple leaf is stuck on a grey searchlight. Seagulls, about fifty, ride on the rails and wait for slops. Two on a lifeboat just out my window seem to stare at me, their heads are sideways, their beaks are yellow with red dots.

I had to get away from city noises so few trees and my men for a while. My daily rhythms are all disrupted: I cant sleep full, you press/hurt my right ribs, dogs howl and wake me, cat too, in heat, the toilet being flushed, sirens of night, I feel shattered, phone calls of the day. I need to get out, to go where I came from. Now a seaman hoses my window and the two gulls fly, glide off. He has a reddish beard just a little lighter than Cliff's. He soaps the thick glass with a long-handled yellow brush.

Oval bubbles slide slowly down the edge of my left eye. I think of you and Cliff: you are really here, yet I cant imagine or see you; he is not here, yet I see him everywhere, yet I dont know him, only sense. How can that be, after five years, strangers? I know not what he thinks or feels, just is. I love the sounds here: vibration of boat, clacking of cards, chatter-laughter of two men several seats back. Can you roll? asks one of them. I turn and watch him (he is blond does every man remind me of) walk over to a woman who smiles like mad, she'll show him how.

The soap is hosed off and the flag loosed and my gulls come back. Our relationship is what, so much sensing, not what the other thinks, is. I would like to be able to say more but I cant. Or wont. Cant. Will try. We arent in love with an image of the other, we never were, we arent disappointed cuz we're not what we thought either would be. But what are we? We arent whole as ones either. Arent. Arent. Both of us are growing/changing. We may always be together. We may not. That scares me. Now it doesnt. We simply arent in love the way we see others love: definitely two who are not one yet two who arent complete as selves.

Okay, see you later. The blond guy leaves the woman. Mine fell out at the end, he says to his buddy. I still cant get at it, the quality. Balance, ease, the gulls are flying, simplicity. These words are not enough. Too heady. A joining. We join across a room. And cuddle in bed. Like the last time we met at a party, I had come in from outside, I felt his waves/energies reaching out from the living room. Mine came from my belly as his brought me in there.

Three black stones stick out of grey water. We near Departure Bay. All the gulls are gone. The flag is wrapped about the pole. The chatter has stopped. The card playing also. Men and women get up to leave. And I wonder if, if ever, I'll be able to say how it is.

─────

Forced air rushes. Am I inside a sawdust truck or behind a warming airplane? No. Outside of whatever it is is a ticky sound, uneven crackles. I'm on my bed. And there's a motor below. I'm being crushed by air, what, a giant vacuum cleaner, no, I gotta get up, out.

Lan – what's that sound? I shout from my pillow. He comes to stand at our door, white shaving-cream face, just one strip of skin. The fire? No. The furnace? Uhh-uhh. The only other thing is water.

That's it. He goes back to the bathroom which is right next to our bedroom and I, not awake yet enough to feel easier, slip down to near sleep. His razor scrapes skin as if it were two inches from my ear.

─────

Four pale-yellow rectangles on the side of a grey house: light reflected off of apartment building windows. I'm sitting in the living room and Stan is reading a letter to me. And Lanny walks above me singing. And Bri is on his bicycle pedalling through snow toward the reindeer. And Cliff is in our bed under the quilt asleep. Your kick has changed. More of you pushes more of me. It's less distinct and fuller. Sometimes you turn and float without coming to touch my belly surface. I feel big, like my middle is a room of water. The ceiling is my stomach, the bottom of one wall my rectum which you bounce against, the centre of the floor my cervix, a small circle which tilts as you press it like a coin on a firm surface. You occasionally roll to the inside of my bottom front, touch my bladder, but when you do, so far, you give only light rapid pokes. The rectangles have slid down. The two on the right have merged. And the most left is only half the width it was. It gets lost in a cream-coloured drainpipe.

─────

A wrinkled dauxie pup, five weeks old, sleeps in a box near my feet. His forehead and arms and nose are all goldy black folds, little waves.

You thump. You may still be covered in hair, lanugo it's called, maybe yours is like his or perhaps more a blondy-red like Cliff's.

I am almost every moment aware of your presence. Before it was only when you kicked or I tilted or someone asked me how I felt, but now – this is thirty weeks – the top of your/our womb pushes my right rib so hard it hurts. I sometimes squat like a cat, arch my spine, try to jiggle you over.

I am seldom aware of your coming. Do I avoid? I've read two books which have at the back accounts of first births, have decided to take breathing classes, but I have not thought of how I'll feel and be as you are being born. I've also not looked at, bought, or picked up one item of clothing or furniture (a crib, a bassinette, a carriage) which I've been offered.

Am I afraid you will be dead? It's as if getting or fixing or making just one item says you will be here. You will be, I say now, just as he is. He is about your present size: fifteen inches, four pounds. He jumps onto the bed and pushes a pillow up to create a tunnel for himself. Goldy-black disappears inside mustard corduroy.

―― ――

The mountains are again scarred with snow. They are soft. Their peaks touch, are in, cloud. The ocean (through the slit between the two apartments) is a dull greenish-grey, bursts up from under in high waves, white foam. Rain splishes on my window. I am not fully awake. Feel cuddly like the air. My cells could dissipate out: it, me; I, it.

―― ――

In a few minutes I'll be swimming in Crystal Pool. Breaststroke is my favourite: arms out, back to the side, together like a heart: breathe, pull, kick, glide. You weigh almost nothing, salt water holds you up, two salt waters, the one you're in, and the one I'm in. When we're at the pool-ends, I turn slowly, if I dont, you slam my side. Wednesday, one hundred turns, fifty lengths in one hour.

―― ――

Blazer lies on my thighs. Rain drizzles. You are due in seven weeks. I cant focus as well as I usually do or I do but not for long. The birds came into my breast this morning as I brushed my teeth. The new leaves on my azalea reached out to me as I lay in bed. And last night when we ate strawberry Jell-O with fresh berries in it, I felt all four of us (Cliff was in Nanaimo talking Waffle\*) were at a birthday party. We were under ten, and this space-time-moment only. Then we became who we are now and how we know each other and I was aware of the limitations of that.

———  ———

I saw Dr. Herstein yesterday. He punched his hands into my lower womb about a hardness, you, then poked his fingers in the top: six weeks, he said, the head is down. We talked, in and out of the blood pressure, de Beauvoir, Trudeau, bisexuality, he listens to your heart, I want to be sure Cliff can be with me.

Yes yes, he says, I'd do anything to please you. You want a rock band too? No, I say, I wouldnt mind a camera. My son plays drums. Cliff would like to take pictures. You're going to have it for life and you want a picture? What for? I cant do it, he says, there just isnt enough room in there. He presses my swollen legs and pulls my tit to show me how to nurse.

Now, anything else? he asks me. I am still on the table. He is on a little metal stool at my feet. The only thing I worry about at this point is the enema. Dont have one, he says. What? I'll give you a note and you wont have to have one. But, I thought, I thought … the books say it's easier if that's empty. Then I can give you a prescription for a suppository, he says.

But, but what if I start shitting? Look, he says, for thousand of years women have been giving birth, do you think they all had enemas? It wont be the first time even if you do, you worried? I'll stop the worry, what more do you want? I leave his office with the prescription inside *The Prime of Life*. I'll just slip this thing in and shit half an hour later at home, here, 2249 York.

---

\*   From 1969 to 1972, the Waffle was a radical wing of the New Democratic Party (NDP). The group existed as an independent political party from 1972 to 1974.

―― ――

A plump red ladybug and a brown-gold beetle lie on my window sill. The ladybug has full white dots on her fat back, a thick gold stripe down its centre. Her face is black, her eyes gold, she sees the world through black moony crescents. She is happy, has no thoughts, is just bodyfeeling as much as can be. The beetle, a glowy brown, is slender but not skinny, his eyes are white with black circle centres, they are much smaller than hers and closer together. He has a closed mouth, a pucky look: his happiness is other, he is closer to earth and enclosed and secretive. She could float over our brown garage. He'd have to crawl but could get to the mossy fence or the top of the apple tree or even the telephone wire. She would go first. No decision. Just go.

―― ――

My azalea is growing and dying at the same time. There are fifteen pink flowers left, most with one or two brown-edged petals. But it has three large new shoots, more than two inches long each, and over (I stop to count) eighty new light-green leaves. The new ones (the largest is three-quarters of an inch long) face up. The old, a dark green, droop toward the soil.

―― ――

After fucking last night (which is weird, I get excited but it's not sustained, one second I'm all clitoris, no sensation elsewhere at all, and it's so contained, then we are jumping and bumping around with you between, and I forget, and then I'm a big funny belly with muscles at my back which Cliff bounces on and about), I felt a thin band cross my middle about an inch under the surface. It's like a thin chain which jumped lower, shot across, and pulled down again. Perhaps this is our first contraction.

―― ――

Breakfast is my favourite meal. Two fried eggs over easy, homemade or sour-french or light rye toast, two bacon, orange juice, milk, and mocha-java coffee. Or scrambled eggs. Or three buckwheat pancakes with an egg on top of one. Or Cliff's cornmeal pancakes with an egg on one. Or the buttermilk recipe I used to make on the boat with an egg on one. But I enjoy lunch too.

The last day of winter and it is not yet seven. Blazer snuggles in my lap, his head is under my blue-green paisley gown. The birds sing in the apple trees. The whole house (except for our cat Puck and me) sleeps. I hear pigeons, not ours, but on some roof over, cooo cooo. My legs are swollen, are up on a pillow and a broken stool. And now my belly (I've been up since five with little Blaze who shits and pees everywhere and wants to play so I do) is hungry. I've had only a cup of cocoa. And so is Puck. I'll put Blazer down and feed her. Me too.

———  ———

What do you think a contraction feels like? asked Ruth, our birth instructor, last night. I dont know, I thought, I've read four books now, and I dont know. No one said anything. She waited. Well, what do you imagine? The two women who have had a child dont speak. Like a band I thought thinking of the first one. Like a fast shoot across the belly? I said. She didnt respond. Then moments later I said like a lump, a tightening. She smiles. But maybe that isnt it. All I know is how the Braxton Hicks (named after a man, all these things so close to women named after men) contractions I have almost daily feel: a push about fist-size which surfaces for ten or fifteen seconds, is hard, then disappears.

———  ———

It's the twenty-first of April. A sailboat is in the tree branches. My womb contracts about once an hour. It hardens, pushes out, stays firm for over a minute. At times I'm giggly. Like last night, I came home from women's lib and Cliff was watching a Bergman movie on TV, I ate a piece of date loaf, was still hungry, made toast with strawberry jam. When I bit it, the crust made such a crackle neither of us could hear the dubbed-in words. I started to laugh and chew and snort. My womb, my whole body bounced. I finally got up off the couch and fell into bed where I laughed till tears fell.

At other times I'm weepy. Cliff diapered Ruth's baby in childbirth class. The others oohed and aahed as he picked up her little bottom so fast and moved the diaper into place like he had done it many times before which he hadnt, this was his first diaper ever, but seeing him, hands holding those tiny ankles, I cried. And cried coming down the North Shore hill and crossing the Lions Gate Bridge too. Cried cuz you are here, and cried for Daigen also, but it was mainly a happy cry, I'm getting excited about your birth.

The sailboat slips behind the apartment. I breathe deeply cuz your pool contracts: what does that feel like? what happens to your water? I have no idea. You havent hiccupped or punched or kicked or pressed for an hour. Your head is sometimes so hard on my lower right side that about three inches of my inner thigh seizes. I have to stop walking until the muscle loosens.

―――――

My azalea grows and grows. I can hardly see the old leaves cuz the new are so big and upright and out. I put my fingers in. Yes, they are still there, a third the size of the new, and dark, but no longer droopy, green.

―――――

Tastes of chocolate cake and mocha icing on the edges of my mouth. I lie on my left side, a pillow under my right leg, in bed. The hockey game is over, Lan bangs dishes, Cliff talks politics over the phone. No nap today. No nap any day. Aretha Franklin, "Do Right Woman, Do Right Man," crashes through the walls. A birthday present for Bri.

You push my womb so hard in a four-inch spot near the right top that I feel the skin cant possibly stretch anymore. This lump is lower now than it was yesterday and your leg (I supposed it is, but it seems more bum-size) presses in the same position it has for the past two weeks, only it has slipped further down my outer skin.

―――――

Driving hurts when I park and unpark. You dont move but my torso must. Cooking (about once a week) is slower: not at the start but near the finish of each item. Yesterday after I swam I made potato salad and the last three strokes were so heavy I could hardly get through. Doing anything is longer, elongated, that's a good word: getting up, rinsing a bra, walking down to Paul's Meat Market (just half a block down to York and half more down Yew) taking bottles down to the basement, wiping an ashtray with a serviette is extended not slower in a clock sense but my rhythms are different, elongated.

―― ――

Everything is almost done. The other day I made a list of seventeen items: brandy, diaper pins, toothbrush, bank, buy material for nook, etc. Seven remain. And only one (the sewing of a curtain) has to be done by me, yet even that one of my men could do if he had to.

What I resent in these books I've read on childbirth is that the woman as she is becoming a mother is already placed in the mommy-role to her husband: get his food, you can stock your freezer with three to five meals; think of him, take a book or magazine along for him to read while you're being prepped; and when you come home, dont neglect him, pick up his clothes like you usually do cuz a man likes a tidy house, arrange your work so you'll be fresh and look good when he comes home so he'll know he still has the woman he married. Do, do, do, and dont complain. And somehow accept who you are in the centre of this?

Another thing I resent is that the baby is always referred to as he. I know it is simpler since the mother is she to call the child, male or female, he. Yet it pisses me off. I am a woman, I was once a girl, I was once an infant, she. Our language does not have the word: little being, little person, it (it's certainly not an it), one (that's awkward), so that for a child there arent these his-her-hims, he, he, he.

―― ――

Will today be the day? Every night when I wake to turn will I say, will today be the day? Once I hear the gulls or starlings or robins call, I usually feel, no, not today but (cuz my womb is contracting and occasionally I get these little shoot-like things travelling up my vagina-cervix) tomorrow. Then when I wake more, I think soon, soon, two or three days, a week, maybe two, certainly by the seventeenth of May. Yet today there is still that thought/possibility, will today be the day?

―― ――

Saw Dr. Herstein yesterday and he stuck his finger up, diddled my cervix, put his other hand down hard about your head. You're a natural, he said, you and your husband going to go up to the bush for this baby? No chance. He pulled out his hand and showed me his finger, it is thicker than most men's, I hadnt noticed before. You are more dilated than this. You might just be one of those women who dilates – he spread his thumb and middle finger about an inch and a half apart – this much before you even go into labour. Great, I thought. What's your guess now? Within a week, within a week, but I wont promise anything.

# Birth

May 1. Two to four in the morning. Are you beginning to begin to come out? I awoke moments ago, felt a nook in the top of my womb, took a slow deep breath and felt with my hand to see if, yes, I was having a contraction. Exactly the same as these hardenings I've been having except earlier this evening I noticed what I call my Viet-Cong jeans were wet about the crotch. So I waited a few moments more, felt this dip in at both sides, almost six inches down from the womb's tip. Again. Fuck it, I better get up and pee. Stepped into the bathroom and white spermy looking stuff dripped onto a blue square of the linoleum. Yes, it may be, just may be, you, beginning to begin to come out.

―― ――

Red Jell-O into white bowl. The pup hears the fridge door shut and comes skittering into our kitchen. Hi, Blaze, no, it's not morning yet, hey, no, little Blaze, it's too early. Water into red bowl.

I come into the living room to eat and write this. He is on my lap trying to chew the wire coil of this book. I roll a skinny cigarette. Is this at all like having a period? Slightly, so slightly a mild pressure down below.

We'd love you to come today. May 1. International Solidarity Day. Hiphiphurray. I better get out of this giddiness and back into bed.

4:20    Another crook. It is a contraction. Hard enough to feel without my hand on my nightie. But very mild. I should get back to bed.

4:24    You'll know, you'll know, the books and Ruth said. I am on the can. I wipe myself. Just a dabble of blood: the bloody show? The feeling at my entrance is much lighter than a non-pill period beginning.

4:30    Hardening again. Should I take the suppository? An hour before you come to the hospital, Herstein said. It's much too soon. I'll lie down and try to sleep.

5:05

```
> > > > > > > > <h <h <h <h <h <h <h <h <h
> > > > > > > > <h <h <h <h <h <h <h <h <h
      > > > <h <h <h         > > > <h <h <h
      > > > <h <h <h         > > > <h <h <h
      > > > <h <h <h         > > > <h <h <h
> > > > > > > > <h <h <h <h <h <h <h <h <h
```

Cliff turns over cuz light is on. I havent told him yet. I dont want to wake him or Ellen. I'm supposed to phone Ellen as soon as I know but it's too early to know.

Blazer comes to my side, puts his paws up on the wood. Go back to bed. He whines. Okay, okay, I'll pick you up little Blaze. He warms the bottom of our womb.

5:11    The first birds chirp. Seems like five at once. And Blazer snuggles my belly. I wonder about that fucking suppository. Could feel your head on rectum, even thought I felt your nose, during the last. I dont want to hold in. The birds are light, magical. They reach out to me.

5:18    contraction

5:25

```
> > > > > > > > <h <h <h <h <h <h <h <h <h
> > > > > > > > <h <h <h <h <h <h <h <h <h
      > > > <h <h <h         > > > <h <h <h
      > > > <h <h <h         > > > <h <h <h
> > > > > > > > <h <h <h <h <h <h <h <h <h
```

Did it. Got up after I wrote about the birds chirping, opened suppository package which was in the cooler behind the apple juice, stuck it in: a tiny wax bomb. Then hurried down to the basement to see if I could find a sanitary pad cuz I'm bleeding and I didnt think to buy any and havent needed any but after the operation in Madison I had some and they were there in the suitcase in among the cement and cardboard boxes ... made it back up the stairs to the living room to the rocking chair in to meet the contraction with loose muscles and deep breath. I wish Stan and Bri were here. They're up in Selkirk. Will be back tonight. I think of Cliff. Yesterday he wanted to take my picture in the red slacks and red-orange top I wear so much. Crumpled on the closet floor. I didnt want a big crumply picture.

5:30

\> \> \> \> \> \> \> \> \> < h  < h  < h  < h  < h  < h  < h  < h  < h
\> \> \> \> < h  < h  < h  < h : is this suppository speeding it up?
\> \> \> \> < h  < h  < h  < h : an enema would be better  \> \> \>
< h  < h  < h  \> \> \> < h  < h  < h  < h t  < h t  < h t  < h t  < h t :
is that your head or more shit?   < h t  < h t  < h t  < h t  < h t  < h t :
my hand presses my lower spine   bones against bones  < h t  < h t
< h t  < h t  < h t  < h t : as soon as the pressure is equal it's easier:
\> \> \> < h  < h  < h : there cant be anymore shit, there just cant be:
\> \> \> \> \> \> \> \> \> < h  < h  < h  < h  < h  < h  < h  < h  < h

5:39     I look out at the poplar through the open window and flow with the leaves, my arms, my chest, my head and neck. Then branches draw back. Little birds, you seem distant. I'm with me, here, in this house on this wooden seat. And you, little one, I know now, you are going to breathe air today.

We lie apart: bum to bum. Cliff's scrunched to the wall facing Roy's painting. I'm facing an orange window.

5:47     Press my back, Cliff. **CLIFF, PRESS MY BACK.** He does. My hand pulls/pushes his hand down further, in harder. My bones on his on mine on yours: thin layers of tissue in between. Tight. All tight.

5:52     Nothing's together. I flip up. My mouth opens: < h t  like a fish: < h t  < h t  < h t. **Slow down**, I hear from behind, **SLOW DOWN**, Cliff's voice next to my ear: < h t       < h t       < h t. I try to catch the beat. Cant. Half my time: < h t  < h t  < h t. Then I turn a high corner. Start falling down: < h t       < h t. I slip near his rhythm, that's easier: < h t       < h t. Right on. Just one. But I'm down further
\> \> \> \> \> \> \> \> \> < h  < h  < h  < h  < h  < h  < h  < h  < h
Over.

Fuck, I think, and I really dont want to think, are we about to start fighting now? I dont think so, but I just did, I dont want to, cuz I'm so busy just breathing.

I turn to see him, hairy-chested Cliff, sitting up in bed not yet awake. Our eyes meet as his head curves over to see me. You (his voice sounds entirely different, firm but not picky) were panting (I'll listen, you may not be right, but I'll listen) it's like this, eh?:
\> \> \> <h <h <h      \> \> \><h <h <h.
I know with my head that he's right and he knows that I know but I'm still pissed off so there's that too.

Then we smile. Both so excited. You're going to come today. Mayday. He crawls over my legs and gets out of bed.

5:56    Starting now. He's dressed and sitting at my desk. He jots down the time and comes to press. Over my hip, under the blanket. I pull my hand out as soon as his is there. Push him down slightly:
\> \> \> <h <h <h \> \> \> <h <h <h      <ht      <ht      <ht:
got it, breaths together, muscles all working, liquid, like a fish, with a weight on my tail just where it joins my body:
<ht      <ht      <ht: my head is loose my spine is stuck:
<ht      <ht      <ht.

In between he rushes: gives me a pillow from off the desk, gets part of the living room couch for my back, I try to turn, I'm too awkward, too big, cant. I lean forward, he places the pillows in, then pulls a rolled-up foam mattress from under the bed, slips it under my knees, so I can sit with my legs open without using energy to sit. He goes to the kitchen to feed Blazer to make toast and coffee and eggs.

My muscles are loose, easy. I think many things but none for long: Wreck Beach, August sun, you starting to grow but we didnt know, log limbs static, our bodies stretch, roll over. Gotta phone Bri and Stan. I'm chilly. Should get them here. Do I have to shit? It may be quite a while: ten, twelve? eight? how long is it? They wouldnt have to stop like we did every hour, I cant remember, eight? We should phone. We gotta phone up there, I shout. It's too early, Cliff answers. It is, I think as I get cold, is it?

**6:04**   All shivery. I pull the covers up. Back tightens. I write the time. Breathe low:
> > > > > > > > ><h <h <h <h <h <h <h <h <h
Hands between pillows: > > >  <h  <h  <h. Pressing. Pressing as hard as I can. As soon as I get it, I'm up, shooting upward: <ht       <ht      <ht. I shouldnt have stuck that thing in. That's okay. Is it your nose? Not more shit. Your nose? Impossible. We turn. Down. Muscles loosening. I dont loosen the press to see what it would feel like without:
> > >  <h  <h  <h> > >  <h  <h  <h. Orange juice? No, I say in that fraction there is between breathing out and in:
> > > > > > > > >  <h  <h  <h  <h  <h  <h  <h  <h  <h. My whole upper body lifts. Just coffee?

Yeah, hon. In a moment Cliff brings me a Japanese mug full of fresh mocha-java, places it on the bedside table. The toast pops and he goes there. I sip: ugh, it's awful. Another cold wave coming. Jesus, am I getting the flu? Warren's?

**6:12**   I glance at the clock: 6:02. Up. Floating up. Everything is moving away, out, the books in the bookcase seem to be where the kitchen sink normally is. Cliff has Pauline? <ht      <ht      <ht. I cant hear: > > >  <h  <h  <h. I see him hang the black object:
> > > > > > > > >  <h  <h  <h  <h  <h  <h  <h  <h  <h. I'm down. He floats into our room. I'm not.

Pauline says to go back to sleep. No way, I think. Maybe she's right. I feel connected, she's had kids, I trust her. But I trust me too. I write the time. It cant be. I try to focus the clock, put my eyes almost in its hands, not 6:02 but 6:12. A hot flash fills my skin. Sweaty. I'm all sweat.

**6:20**          **6:25**          **6:33**          **6:39**

**6:46**          **6:53**          **6:59**

Hot flashes. Cold waves. Pauses between. I can always tell when a contraction's coming cuz the coldness comes first. And what do they feel like? This is what I've always wanted to know and havent known and havent asked and now I know that for every woman it is so different that any description is only a trace of what is. Going up an apple branch, a brass pole in the Ladysmith Fire Hall, or half the drainpipe of the white three-storey apartment across the way. Up fast as it tightens, then a liquid loop at the top, then, sliding down, fast, much faster than going up. No panic. No thoughts. No images. The only thing outside me is Cliff's hand on my spine. It takes about two breaths till the pressure is exact, equal, balanced.

7:06        7:12        7:18        7:26

In between we talk. And in between Cliff asks, when did the doctor say to call? When they get regular, I say. How long do they have to be regular before they're regular, eh? I dont know and I dont remember and maybe I didnt even ask. Probably an hour, I say. This might even be false labour, I think, but I dont think it is.

7:33        7:40        7:46

I think I'll take a bath. I dont think I'll want to later and I dont really want to now. I get up. Wobble. Turn on the tap. The tub looks unreal. The toilet seat. Wood. Circular. I turn to sit.

7:50    Starting now. The sink. I lean my head into it. Press my back. And stare. The stains run: > > > < h < h < h > > > < h < h < h. I see like I do when I have the flu: > > > < h < h < h. Soap cake cracks. I could fall into. I'm out.

That was easy. Real easy. No need for the next level. I shouldnt have been lying down. That was so much easier.

The water looks strange. Just a few inches in the bottom. A yellow-white cloth floating. I'm not going to wait. Going to get in before the next starts.

7:57    Starting now, I shout to Cliff. I lean forward, hand through water on flesh. But it doesnt come. Or, is this on? It's so weak. Yes, it is/was but so light and fast.

I lie in water which should be hot since I added no cold but it's neither warm nor cool. I splash it over you. Where you are. And you shift over. Belly looks different now. Longer. No. Shorter. Looser somehow.

Instead of it all being up near the front so over my tits I see a firm roundness, it seems longer and looser on the side where you arent.

I wash but I dont need to wash cuz I just washed a few hours ago. My arms and legs have almost no feeling. Should I get out before it? No, stay here, there might not be time.

**8:05**   Starting now, I shout. Hair droops, hand presses, muscles tighten but not hard or as hard as before.

I lean over to get out, I dont call, lately I've called Cliff to help but I know I can get out myself this time. You fall toward the bottom. I'm on all fours. My right hand grabs the tub edge, grips, left leg and arm push first, then right, then weight shifts to my right and my left side steps out.

Big orange towel surrounds me. No slow cuddle. Drying is what I do, is not the long stroked pleasure it usually is. On goes the talcum but I dont smell it or feel the fluffy puff on my belly. No lingering. None at all.

I look at the bed and look at the floor and look at the bed and look at the floor. Down or get dressed. Lie down or stay up. I hold my panties. I gotta be careful. I get one foot up and in then the other. And my slacks. All this leaning and pulling and balancing. And my bra. And my top. Shoes. Shoes? Shoes? Cliff can put them on but I'll have to lean over later to pull the fuckers off. No shoes.

**8:12**   Starting now. He comes to push my back. My arms lean on the unmade bed. His hand in on you. You push out to him. I breathe above, breathe, breathe: > > > <h <h <h    > > > <h <h <h. I dont know what's happening. That seemed awfully weak. The last three have been awfully weak. Maybe it is false, I think as I put my feet into moccasins.

**8:18**   So weak. But I dont take my hand off my back to find out what it is like without. And I breathe. I dont even think of trying one contraction without breathing or pressing. I can truly say it is not pain, not like pain. I once had an infected cyst which was so painful I only knew when I came out of it and was about to go back in how painful it was. I dreaded the going back in, wished I'd never come out till it was over, over, all the doctor had to do was cut it open and the puss would gush out and then the pain was over. He did this twice. The cut didnt hurt cuz all I could feel was the bigger hurt, the pressure there, a large egg between my legs, unending waves of pressure. But this, this is different. These muscles all work together. And my lungs move in the same rhythm they do. And not once between do I think: what is to come? I cant stand it, what is to come? But I do think: this must be one-fifth of what will be and I know I can handle that, that is one thing I know now.

I should eat. I feel nauseous. I should eat. There's nothing I want. I havent eaten since six last night and I'm in labour and I dont want to eat but I should eat. Canned salmon? Oily pink stinky salmon. No. Jell-O? There's nothing in it. I need meat. I'll need meat. Why didnt I eat meat? Guuuuuh. Toast. That should do. I stick a piece of Elsie's bread in the toaster. Down it slips.

**8:23** I lean over, press my back. Get it on the second breath. Exact pressure. This is more like it. But it's not as strong as any in bed. Nose almost on enamel stove. No need for the next level, this is right, maybe I should go down cuz it might be a long time yet, fuck no, this is so easy, try the lowest anyway: > > > > > > > > <h <h <h <h <h <h <h <h <h : it's alright too. I finish the last full-lunged breath as the toast pops up.

I butter it fast, stick a bottom corner in my mouth. Gkgkuuuk. Puuuh. I spit it into my hand. Throw it in the garbage. Drink a mouthful of water. Water. Even water tastes dreadful.

**8:27** It's starting. I press. This time I dont have time to write the time. Cliff leaves me at the table to walk Blazer. Why is he out there? I know why. To walk Blazer. Down to the point? Is he going to Kits Point? I see him and Daigen on the point, yellow-green trees, all sun. No, Blazer. He's out walking Blazer. And I'm staring at grains of oak, the table. And why is he away? How long, how long will he be away? Not long, I think as I turn to come down, not long, but why, why did he go away? Now I remember, he's out walking Blazer.

I cross out the six and put down seven. It was seven. That's odd. He hasnt been long at all. And there he is, I see them through the window, there

they are, he's coming back, good, coming back, my two goldy animals
slip behind green cedar. And I notice the time and start breathing.

8:32            8:37              8:40

8:44
> > > > > > > > > <h <h <h <h <h <h <h <h <h
> > > > > > > > > <h <h <h <h <h <h <h <h <h
> > > <h <h <h         exactly            exactly on
> > > <h <h <h         > > > <h <h <h         I can feel
my cervix opening         opening with each breath
> > > <h <h <h         I think that's what's happening
a huge circle lifting       coming back           lifting
in tune to the very motion of air        > > > <h <h <h
am I imagining this?        maybe I should go down
> > > <h <h <h        liquid tissue opening
closing slightly       opening more           now slightly lower
opening more                  now lower
> > > > > > > > > <h <h <h <h <h <h <h <h <h
> > > > > > > > > <h <h <h <h <h <h <h <h <h
Done. Beautiful. Cliff, Cliff. It's perfect, I can feel it moving, it's just
perfect. He looks at me but I dont understand his expression. I felt
it moving. My breathing is right with it. It was breathing with the
breath, right with the breath.

8:47            8:50

And when did the doctor say to call? When they're regular, five to
six minutes apart. They've been regular for about an hour now, eh?,
they're three minutes apart. You better call Herstein. His home or
office? I dont care, his home, he wont be in, it's Saturday. They're
both the same, he says and I start to breathe.

8:53
> > > > > > > > > <h <h <h <h <h <h <h <h <h
> > > > <h <h <h <h        > > > > <h <h <h <h
he has an answering service        > > > > <h <h <h <h
I dont hear what he says even though he's right next to me
> > > <h <h <h        I shake my head no        I cant talk
on the phone        > > > <h <h <h        She's having a

contraction            >  >  >  <h  <h  <h         his voice is calm,
that's all I hear, he sounds like he knows what he's doing
>  >  >  <h  <h  <h              he'll call us Cliff says
>  >  >  >  <h  <h  <h  <h          >  >  >  <h  <h  <h  <h
>  >  >  >  >  >  >  >  >  <h  <h  <h  <h  <h  <h  <h  <h  <h
how long, I think, how long.

She's having a contraction. That's right ... right ... really well. Cliff nods and I breathe and Herstein speaks. Cliff gives me the phone when it's over. Well kid ... it's a propitious day ... a bit misty out ... I have to go to the hospital for an emergency ... how are they? ... you might want to stay with Cliff this morning and come in this afternoon ... tell you what, I'll call you from there just to check.

**8:56          9:01          9:04          9:07**

Each contraction lasts about a minute. In the two minutes between Cliff rushes about. He gets me a book from upstairs in Lanny's room. He brings me lipstick and comb and shaving mirror from the bathroom. He phones the hospital to say I'll be coming in sometime today. Almost always he is here to press but when he isnt I do.

**9:10          9:17          9:20**

My face is dry. Underneath I see a fifteen-year-old me. That's what I expect to see. I comb my hair and smile. A so happy so excited young me.

**9:23          9:26          9:29**

There's a green and white sucker in the paper bag in the bamboo basket beside me. I'd like to open you, big sucker, to suck, but I'll probably want you more later so I'll wait. I can wait. I can wait for anything now. Cliff, when he calls back tell him I want to go. Tell him I'd feel safer there.

**9:33**

Cliff, when Herstein calls tell him I want to come in. I'd feel safer.

**9:36**

Cliff, when he phones tell him ... I know, he says, I will, I know.

**9:39**

How are they? I dont know, mild I guess. Since it's your first, you dont really have a measure. We laugh. Mild to medium, I say. I want to come in. I'd feel much safer. Tell you what, he says, you come in and I'll check you then we'll decide what you want to do. Okay? Yes. Good. Okay ... Hey, Cliff we can go.

**9:42** I wrap myself in the multicoloured afghan Cliff's mom made and lean over the table and press and breathe:
\> > > > <h <h <h <h        > > > >    <h <h <h <h
when I first started classes this was the breath I couldnt get:
\> > > <h <h <h     > > > <h <h <h      but now it's easy
so easy           > > > <h <h <h <h <h
as long as I can equalize the pressure with his hand or my hand
it's easy      > > > <h <h <h <h <h <h      going down
\> > > > > > > > <h <h <h <h <h <h <h <h <h
done

Cliff is on the phone trying to get Ellen. You're not wearing that, he says. Yes I am. No answer. Line busy. He goes to the bedroom and gets my poncho. If I'm hot, if I'm cold, I want to stay with the blanket. He pulls it off. Puts the brown-black poncho over my head, gently, flips my hair. No sense arguing now. No sense arguing now at all at all.

We'll have to time it, I say, we'll have to make it in between. I stand at the glass door. He's on the phone to Ellen. Busy. Still busy. I do this one upright. Mild, quick. And then, right after, we run.

But not quite a run cuz Cliff's hand is on my arm to help me down stairs I havent seen for almost a month now. I see the ones way ahead, but not ever the one I'm on. My hair brushes a cedar branch and then we're out, out to the sidewalk. Green door opens and I flop in, into the car we know so well. There's Lanny. Lanny's at his attic window, pulling it up or out. I try to wind mine down but cant or do slightly, and he's smiling, tousled, unawake, he leans out. I smile but am contracting, want to be able to see him for the last time with you inside and do but dont, his black curly hair, his smile, only for a portion of an instant an eye connection. Just as we pull out. The contraction is over as soon as we're in the street. I wish we were leaving this second and not that.

We turn left. Up Vine. We're on our way, on our way, to have a baby today. Today. Mayday. I see an apartment where late in summer huge sunflowers grow. And now I'm in, inside.

My lower back goes out to the seat, my right hand on the springs or whatever metal is there, bones, metal, bones, all pressing as hard as hard as we can. The rest of me is leaning forward toward the dash and floor. I breathe, breathe: > > > <h <h <h        > > > <h <h <h:     then come up for regular air.

We're going down 3rd to avoid a red light on 4th and I see trees which usually come out to me flow, wave away as we come closer, they are going away. We're out on 4th passing Kidd's Honey place and the Natural Food Shop. I see these store fronts but they are away, all the edges of all the buildings could flop onto the street and they'd still be away. We'd glide over. As we cross Burrard, I lean forward, push back, press, breathe.

I come out and up under the curls of the Granville Street bridge. Thick, thick, cement thighs. I'm happy to see you. And happy to be with Cliff. He takes the curve smoothly, these past four months he seems to do nothing but jerk and brake too late, I've been afraid we're about to crash, but now I'm not, we curve with the road and slip out onto 6th.

I lean forward, push back, press, and breathe. I want the sucker in my bamboo basket. I want a lick right now. Fuck. Wait. Turning to the back to get it, pulling it out, unwrapping, particularly unwrapping, would be so much energy. Wait. I can have it in the hospital when I'm waiting and waiting. But I want a suck just a little suck right now.

The buildings on my left are fat. The city is there beyond False Creek just as it always is but further away, no individual buildings, away, all one.

We turn up a hill. I lean forward, bend, press, breathe:
> > > < h < h < h      > > > < h < h < h       my whole body is breathing this car/container is carrying us up Heather
> > > < h < h < h      > > > < h < h < h
and it's hard to lean forward with everything tilting back
> > > < h < h < h      > > > > < h < h < h      so I fall back and breathe      > > > < h < h < h      it's just as easy
> > > > > < h < h < h < h < h      I think I'll try effleurage
> > > < h < h < h < h      fingers across lower womb, lightly, it's horrible, prickles, I stop      > > > > < h < h < h < h      but it is easier leaning back cuz I had to use muscles to hold forward:
> > > > > > > > < h < h < h < h < h < h < h < h < h

We stop at the ticket booth and I'm leaning back, pressing, I know this is the hospital yet I dont know, the bricks could fall at any moment, the lines on the pavement are simply paint, could be washed off in a second.

Lots of space, Cliff mutters as he whips in close to the entrance. RESERVED FOR DOCTORS, I read. He pulls it into reverse, we arc backwards then to the left, only one car there, Saturday morning, just one car.

We're parked. He's getting out. Why didnt he wait? Strong, this one is strong. I press as hard as I can against the seat back, I bend toward the floor, am breathing:      > > > < h < h < h
> > > < h < h < h      am pushing with my hand
> > > < h < h < h      need his also      > > > < h < h < h
cant speak      > > > < h < h < h      door is open he is here
> > > < h < h < h      waiting      > > > < h < h < h
we'll both just have to wait. It's over. Still no pain, but the tightening and pressure is stronger than any of the past two hours, all in that one base-of-spine spot, less than the size of my hand, my hand covers it all.

Cliff helps me out. I focus on the entrance just a few yards away, it's so big and I'm so small, I whip past the one man in the waiting room. Cliff is behind me. I look at the slow-moving girl near the typewriter. She turns, I try to meet her eyes through glasses but cant. Mrs. Andstein, I say. I called about an hour ago, Cliff says from behind, he's so far behind. Yes, she says, and your doctor? Doctor Herstein, I say.

I see a wooden chair, plop down. She's fiddling in a file, turns as if absolutely nothing is happening and starts to ask me a stupid question. Ask my husband, I say, my voice is certain, I mean it, and she knows it. I have no idea what happens as I lean over her desk and breathe and press and breathe and press.

When I look up there is a blonde woman with glasses telling me to come in. We walk past yellow curtains. Shit smell. Someone is having an enema. The blonde nurse starts telling me what she'll have to do, an enema and a shave: it's not necessary, I had it at home. Everything is distorted. I'm trying to tell her, she's trying to get me to, to undress, yes, I can, she helps, or does she? Nothing is clear.

My arms move out to get the white nightie on. Press my back, I say. I lean over onto the high cot. Her hand rolls, presses, rolls, professional, she really knows how to massage, but, no, here, I say in that partial second after letting out air. My right hand goes on hers, slaps it down, to the exact spot. And it is my bones against hers against mine against yours: thin thin muscles in between, all pressing with all strength, the utmost there is. As soon as it's over she helps me up onto the table. When was your last bowel movement? she asks.

There were three, I say, one at 5:20 and the others, I cant, am rattled, I cant remember, cant really speak but I know normally I'd be able to, I'd be able to tell you, I dont say anything to her but she seems to understand. I'm going to shave you, she says. I open my legs as she goes to get whatever she'll need. Herstein's voice beyond the door. I hear him.

Dr. Herstein, I call out to the curtains, to beyond the curtains, I'm here. Dr. Herstein. And in a second he's here, at the cot end, smiling. And I'm happy he's here. I know he knows exactly what he's doing and somehow this is important to know your doctor without thought knows through the muscles of his arms and fingers exactly what to do.

Hi kid, he says to me. Seven and a half, to her. I'm going to examine you on your next contraction, he says. She gives him an amber glove from out of the cupboard. I see his left hand up, the light hitting his thumb. This may hurt, he says. My legs which are apart flop even more apart.

Starting now:        > > > <h <h <h        > > > <h <h <h
I am breathing        am completely open        he is stepping
toward my cunt        > > > <h <h <h        his fingers slip in
> > > <h <h <h        but I dont feel them in
> > > <h <h <h        his touch is not like any I've had before
> > > <h <h <h        the closest is a dentist in a totally
frozen wide-open mouth        > > > <h <h <h
in my head I know he's in, and only through my head can I feel
> > > <h <h <h        he is smiling, a full-faced smile
> > > <h <h <h        good god, he says his hand slips out
I feel it at the outer edge only        > > > <h <h <h
fully dilated, I hear his voice beyond my breath
> > > <h <h <h        case room        > > > <h <h <h
no labour, I'm through the first stage, I didnt even know it, through
> > > <h <h <h        he is giving her commands and leaving
> > > <h <h <h        the cot rolls next to me and I'm still
> > > <h <h <h        > > > <h <h <h
> > > <h <h <h        > > > >

I know I'll have to get over, dont want to, want to stay where I am, this is the way it's going to be. One container to another to another between. In the pause between. My hand slips on the sheet. I have to turn over. This is the difficulty, my whole body nothing but belly to turn onto from wobbly metal. My head does it, makes the connections for me, tells my legs and arms to move. How to. Learning again. Like a doorknob for the first time. Only it's my head telling, not someone else. Rest, rest between, going to delivery, rest.

Voices above. Sides being snapped. Rolling. A large metal wall opens and I turn slightly to get my back free, it is so tight. I dont need to press if I can only get free. A huge bump below. We float in, in …

Doctor Herstein. What's he doing here? And Cliff. What a surprise. They are both here with me. The motion of Cliff's voice pulls me up. I feel his sounds, their sounds, on my outer edge, slapping. I cant pull the syllables together. Dont bother. Try to. He's been gone so long. My ear reaches out: Finnish peasant woman, he says smiling. That's all I get, am being swung, pulled, back, down, inside. I leave their smiles and sink backwards into the rickety barge.

A wrought iron gate. Swaying. Swinging. Walls turn. Suddenly I know exactly where I am. Being wheeled along a hospital corridor. One woman beyond a glass door is screaming. Another, closer, grunts.

We turn into a small room. Cliff drops off. Isnt let through. A door opens. A woman comes (the light behind her) to me. Mrs Campbell from Ladysmith? No, but I want her (a nurse), am disappointed when I realize she isnt cuz I thought she was, yet my head tells me I am here, in Vancouver, not Ladysmith.

She pulls me into the delivery room and I see the table, large metal stirrups, mirror on the end wall. Neither friendly nor cold. Her skin needs sun, hair is dead, works too much, all's never done. Herstein's telling her what to do or get but I cant make out what and I dont care.

Sit in the sun. They are both so distant. Tired-happy. Dont rush. There's time. The blonde woman curves into my eye edge. Hey, I know who you are, you're from down below. She must go. I want to say, stay. But I know she must go.

I watch/hear the Mrs. Campbell nurse open a cellophane package above my cunt. Just tell me when you're about to contract and I'll stop. A job to do, firm yet tired. One quick stroke. No pulling. Now.

She comes to my left side as I breathe while sitting up and holding, trying to hold, the air. Picks me up with her right arm under my right armpit, her left under my knees. I stare at her muscles, feel that base-of-spine spot but dont need to press: it's so different, so mild, and there's a funny little ripple on the front. Her arm isnt soft, it has loose skin at the bottom, like the muscle was big once but isnt anymore.

Push, she says as I let out to take in a second breath. Cant get the air right, not enough room, and my muscles arent moving with me or my lungs with them. A big ball, no feeling under, little ripples across the top under outer skin but not far under. I can push now? I say when it's over. Yes, she says as if she has said it many many times before, push.

I lie down so she can shave my under-cunt. Is she pissed-off she has to do it? Is she worried about something else? Are there too many today? I fall back into myself ... you are coming, you are going to come: floats above me, at the top of my head, below it I almost sleep.

I'm jerked into the cot into the room by a tightening of my entire middle. Gotta get up. Fast. She's here. With me. The air's no good. Try another. With her. Her mouth and mine open together. Take in. Hold. Push, she says angrily. I am, damn it, I am. Yet I cant somehow. Cant locate muscles to push with. Her head and mine together. But bottom just isnt with us. Tip of bum on cot. I need a floor. I want to stand. No wobbles. Wood, steel, cement, hard earth. No cloth.

Dr. Herstein, brown jacket gone, covered in loose green, comes up from the room end. I know it is a small room but it seems so long and he walks so slow yet I also know he doesnt walk slow. Gladys, he says, this wont hurt, I'm just going to break your waters. Sure, I think, and I just want to drift. To sleep. To be cared for. I cant now. I want to know what's happening. I cant be bothered to try to remember to forget to remember I'll just close my eyes.

Cool liquid splashed on naked skin. Feels good. His hand touches the outer lips. Know he or it (the instrument) is inside but feel nothing. A liquid, warm, gushes on my thighs. Not much. Your pool, broken. Doesnt seem like much.

She rolls me over to the table with a fat cylinder base. Not again, fuck it, I dont want to move again. Know why I gotta, but I really dont wanta, move again. Fuck it, it's so much trouble. Have to sit up first. I see a bit of blood on the wet green. Have to turn over. I do. But I dont know how to get there. I've forgotten how to get there, how I did it before. Can you tell me how to get there? I ask. Crawl, she says (and her voice is changed has no edge she wants to help), like a crab. I dont want to but I know I have to, have to think how, it's so slow, my head to my arm to my leg, like a crab, scatter over. You hang above the cot a second. Now. Heave. Leaving. Leaving. Come on, I say or think, left arm and left leg drag, uncertain. The weight is here. Let them go. Yes go. And they come. And I'm here. And you're here. Finally. Seemed like forever. But another part of me knows it was only seconds, probably even faster than I would be without a baby inside.

My front turns over, comes up under happy faces: Herstein's, two nurses', a dark haired man's. *Prima,* Herstein is boasting (?) to the other, and she arrived fully dilated. I look at him looking at the older him and know that the younger him is a resident. About my age or younger. Brown eyes smile down, reach out. My outer or upper me, not my gut, answers. Head, face, eyes smile. He and I meet an instant and my body pulls back. Pulls in. Womb, huge ball, hardens. The men step toward my legs. The older woman lifts my back as I pull up. The men squeeze my knees toward my tits as I grab the air to push, much harder than the hardest shit, my head makes me do it, my head, cant feel any of my middle or lower muscles, womb takes them all, can scarcely feel the contraction, just a numb tightening, lowering, tightening. Then they let loose, fast, not like the coming down of the others, just a moment, a loosening out.

What's that? My asshole in the mirror. Grey. Huge. Beneath a shaven cream cunt. Piles. Wow. Cant believe they're so big. Triple-layered. A wet stone sculpture. Alive. Beneath flesh I've hardly ever seen.

My head. The long hair. Happy face underneath concentrated skin. That's me who I've been with all my life. I watch the nurses arrange my legs in the metal troughs. Those limbs are parts of me yet arent. My back, the same base-of-spine place, hurts. I press it against the table. Not enough pressure. I start to put my hand in. Wait, says Herstein. The nurses move out, he in. He jerks the metal up so my knees are closer to my tits. Bare limbs. Mine yet not mine. How does that feel? he asks. Okay, I say, but they were okay before too. It's my back, I cant get to my back.

I dont care anyway. I want Cliff. Where's my husband? I ask. Odd, I've hardly ever called Cliff husband. It's an odd word. He's just outside, says Dr. Herstein, we have to get everything set up first. But he is going to be here? He nods yes. Is he mad? His expression gives me a what-do-you-think-I-am-a-liar feeling. I did, for a moment, yes. He isnt mad. Cliff is going to come. I dont have to think about it anymore. I sink back, the whole top of my body, back to pillows.

My womb pulls down in the top of the front, and I pull up, and the men come over and lift my legs out of the stirrups (why are they there then?) and push my thighs toward my chest. The women lift my back. I hold air and push with it, weak, but with the contraction. I let out, grab another breath fast, try to come down on top of it again, cant. Cant find the rhythm, have to do it with my head. My head tells me what to do. My head tells my hands to hold the metal grips after Herstein tells my ears which tell my mind which tell my arms which tell my hands to do it. So much to do. At once. And every outside thing takes me away. Takes energy away. Every look or word I try to follow. Every being. Every object like the ridges on the steel handles. Just seeing takes energy out.

I lie back to rest to not think. Eyes close. Cliff. He'll be coming. Soon. Dont have to think about anything. Just sleep. Arms and legs and chest and neck and head so warm, heavy, flowing down and out. (Herstein's voice comes through my back: give her twenty minutes, it'll catch up.) Good. The contractions will come. Going to sleep in between.

I just want to ask you a few questions. The resident. A clipboard. A form. He doesnt say it but he knows I know he knows this is idiotic. A form: and when did labour begin? and when was your last period? and what operations have you had? and when did you first menstruate? and when did the pain get stronger? and when did they come five minutes apart? have you been pregnant before? what happened? how many days is your cycle? at six when I woke him, at four I got up, let me think, fourteen, no thirteen, in '48 my appendix, I was eight, last year a miscarriage, no a missed abortion, in a letter but I didnt know then, nineteen weeks, in Madison in Wisconsin, in the letter the doctor said eleven weeks, I forgot the cyst, '65, a Bartholin, Herstein did it here, O-positive, I think it was around eight-thirty, it's hard to, usually I could tell you, I cant remember now, ask Cliff, Cliff has it written down just out there, ask Cliff.

Numbers and dates criss-cross. He leaves. It's so crazy to ask in labour. Anyone could give the wrong blood type. They have that type they have that information so many times. They have my history here in this hospital twice already. I cant get mad at hospitals now. I cant. But I am. But it's over. I just want Cliff.

My womb pulls down, in, I pull, am pulled, by the nurse, up. The older one pushes my legs in. I push my lower womb down. Bowels out. Cliff is outside the door. I want want him in. You are inside. I want you out. But I cant get my top to move with the contraction. It's above where you are, no sensation where you are, I try to feel you, cant, try to move the muscles about the birth canal open, down, out, but cant cant feel them at all. I couldnt feel that, I say to the young nurse when it's over. But she doesnt respond. I close my eyes and just lie, lie and wait.

Your husband's here. I turn to to look up, under, beside. All green. I see his blue eyes through glasses. Smiling. Cliff. He touches me at the side of my right breast. But I cant feel as I usually do. Know he is here. That's enough. I'm not here, am away from him, from everyone, even you. I start to sit up on the pillows. Cliff and the older nurse put their arms in under my arms to lift, put their arms under my knees to pull, as I block the air. Hold it. Push. I feel in that bottom-of-spine place I was feeling before and little ripples in the front outer edges of my womb. I try to roll onto it, roll the muscles at the top down, the ones at the bottom out, cant, cant get with it. I feel the other two pushing, use part of their energies through my head, all heads, to do it. The contraction loosens fast, no fading out, just a second, over.

If you hurry up, Cliff says, I'll be able to make the demonstration, I'll be able to tell them. Wall and Redekop. Sharon and Michael and Peter. Lanny and Georgia. Eleven o'clock. Just around the corner. Others. Everyone will be there. Everyone but Stan and Bri. I wonder where they are now. Keremeos? Not yet. I see them on Anarchist Mountain before Osoyoos coming down, coming down through green.

I see a clock: 10:27 on a fat round clock. Mayday, I think as I go into a contraction, see Lan lying in bed even though I've never seen Lan lying in bed. Morning baby, I think as the womb ripples down. Slow. Mild ripple. Weak pullings, tightening as. Not nearly as strong as any in bed at home. But it's going to catch up, it'll catch up Herstein said, and I can wait, I believe him, they just havent started yet. Water gone. But the walls of the womb/birth canal just havent got their message yet. Dont know.

I lie back onto the pillows. Cliff smiles and rubs my arm. The older nurse leans with telephone operator knobs sticking in her ears. Compass-sized stethoscope. Black circle in loose white flesh. 120. The other nurse writes it down? This has nothing to do with me. Nothing at all. She is going to leave, the older one, she is giving instructions? I see the two talking beyond the foot of the bed. And she is doing most of the talking, like leaving home for an hour with something in the oven and dusting or sweeping to be done and phone messages to give or take. Short phrases cuz the other understands, nods.

I look out through the window at the far right corner of the room. Grey-bricky air. See placards, people standing on a corner in twos and threes, trees, breathing. He might make it for the end. I wouldnt mind being there. Out in the air. No pine forest, no sidewalk corner, no grey round sky, just there.

A contraction starts and I come into the bed. Lower this time, the top is lower. The young nurse and Cliff lift me up, push me in. I see my scarlet face in the mirror: expressionless, concentrated. Breath held. I let it out, pull in another, fast. In each contraction I get two breaths, the second always firmer than the first but not as much air. If I could only suck in the whole room I could blow you out, blow. Suck in from both ends and you'd float. But I cant. Can only push.

I cant do it, I say, I cant do it right. The nurse comes to me. Gauzed mouth moves close. I cant hear her. I cant hear you, I say. She mumbles something about how to hold the breath and to push. She is polite. She's not really mumbling. I simply cant hear or hold onto what she was or is saying. I close my eyes to sleep. Feel the lightness of the compass but not the temperature. Then can tell my blood pressure's being taken but there's no tightening of the upper arm like in the doctor's office when it feels full of air.

Up I come again and up they lift again and down I push again. And I cant get with those ripples again. And I take a second breath again and through my head/my will tell those muscles what to do: loosen, press out. Tell. Tell. Nothing of their own. When they're ready, they'll work. We'll just have to wait: me, you, you Cliff, you nurse, you Herstein way down the hall, you resident wherever you are, wait.

**10:36** So slow. Going to be here forever. Yet I'm not. At that edge of falling off. Cliff here like my mother. I hang on, it's light out, hang on just that wonderful moment so (s)he cant leave the room, not yet.

I open my eyes to Herstein's voice at the wall and far away. Talking. To the resident. With the nurse. 115. Parts in a slow movie. They are conferring. Herstein's hand moves to his head, his forehead rests on his hand.

Contracting. Cliff lifts me as they pull to the table as my womb pushes out. Herstein grabs one leg. The resident the other. He pushes twice as hard as the resident does. It's really hard. Put your hands on the grips, he says. I'd forgotten. Everything is hard. Remembering. And muscles. My womb my lungs my legs my head all my centre outside muscles, hard. PUSH, he is saying, PUSH. That's hard. That's outside to grab but I am. So hard.

It's no good, I say when it's over, I'm not pushing hard enough. Is he getting pissed off? I dont care. I dont care about anything anymore… wish I could go home… might as well go home… come back later… when it's, when I'm, ready.

So thirsty. I try to swallow but cant. Cracks at back of throat. Try to wet my tongue but cant. I'm thirsty, I say. My voice goes out after. The words separate from me. Reach Herstein. He moves fast to the sink on the left edge of the room. I can drink. He'll let me. I see his hand turn beneath running water. In it. I want to be in water. A forest. Inside. Cool earth. He hands me the white terry cloth. I slap it to my mouth. Suck. So good. I taste the water touching my mouth skin all the way back. (My mother, fevers, coming in a shaded room, placing the cloth on my lips, then folding it on my forehead.) Slurp till I want no more. Cliff takes the cloth, wipes my face, tender all-over Cliff.

The ball tightens. Herstein and the older nurse push my feet/legs. Cliff and the other lift my back. I pull in air and my top comes down on top of it hard. Like a bowel movement, one says, like a big movement. Push all around but not with. It seems separate from all other muscles or all the others immediately around are so numb I cant feel them. I'm totally inside my skin, as if my head is where my throat is, shoulders on top of womb.

Good, someone says, good. I hear the voice up there through air through ear. Know the others are close yet really so distant. It loosens. I float up to my outside head. See my face (scarlet) far away in the mirror.

Lie back. It's just not right. Can push as much as I want through my head but it's just not what it should be, overwhelming urge, any urge, not at all like what I read or heard, could be home, come back later, maybe I should have had that sucker, so little energy, veins and muscles should be full, I have so little. 120, says the nurse. And Herstein leaves, might as well leave, will come back when something's happening. For sure nothing is happening. Cliff wipes my face and asks if I want more. No more. Not now. I dont want anything anymore.

Cliff and the nurse pull me up, push me in, for another contraction. With all the head I have I push but nothing is changing. I can grab the air more easily, can hold more easily, can feel little ripples on the outer edges, but everything is so slow and drifty and the same.
I drift out between.     Come up for another. Maybe this'll be better. Maybe if I just push as hard as hard as I possibly can ... something's wrong, I'm going to be here forever. I just know it, forever and a day. Today. It's going to be born today. Maybe quite a while but it will be born today. That doesnt excite me.

The rag dries on the bedsheet. Leaves a wet large mark. Cliff gets more. I see him bend. Then come to me. And I suck. And we smile. So far apart. Eyes touching, hands touching, but I'm so far away. And he wont get to the demonstration today. And Herstein wont get away early today. And I wont go home today. And you? I've forgotten you're even in there, I dont think about you at all. I have to think to remember why I'm even here. But when I do remember, it's okay, everything's okay, I just have to wait.

I sit up for a weak contraction. No drugs but – except for that faintness in the base-of-spine spot and light ripples across the front – I feel nothing. Thought I'd feel/know where it is, have clarity, not at all. It takes such concentration just to breathe and push, to push down without any pull, to centre my energy onto the outer edges of the ball, to keep the pelvic floor muscles loose, going out. PUSH, Herstein's voice gruff, PUSH. I am. PUSH. What the shit.

**10:50**   Only ten to. Less than an hour. Unreal. Time. Criss-crossing. An hour in grade two was no longer. Measure. That other world. They are all moving. Cant hear them. Cliff is of them. But he's beside me, not moving, not speaking. The nurse leaves. I feel her quickness on my right side.

Something is happening. To do with me. I see Herstein come up to my right foot. Tone changes from the command. His voice, forced warmth, talks down and not across: well kid, we're going to have to do something to help you; we're going to put in a drip to make your contractions stronger.

Great, I think. That's okay, I say with my tone reacting to his. All this is going on inside but that other me still responds. Thank god, I think. My head is back, my eyes are closed, it takes seeing-outer energy to keep them open. Make them strong, fill me up. I should have had that sucker, I need sugar in my veins.

The nature of the contractions changes (I remember from my reading), hard to tell what they are, the rhythm, but it is anyway, those were first-stage accounts, this is second, maybe if I had eaten at midnight, no way to tell now.

That urge. Induced. Will come. Just wait. Will come. I touch Herstein's cloth arm, firm muscles there, as we wait for the bottle to arrive. Need more air. Breath's in already. Didnt take enough. Hold it, Herstein says. But I need more. Too hurried. Too empty. Push with it anyway. Let out. Herstein's mouth moves with mine to grab the second. Much better. Hands on chrome handles. Am down on top of hard ball. Feel at my back. Muscles about the big intestines. Slightly. Out beyond them at that base it's tight. Cant catch the rhythm of the hardening. Cant feel that. Move those muscles I can feel, down, out.

Wire rickety stand. Coat hooks made of hangers. Plastic tubes. One bottle. Two. She – the young nurse – could do it. But he does it. Sticks the needle into my arm. Little pile up of flesh for the indent. Dont feel it coming in. Numb. Absolutely no sensation at all. Piggyback, he says. She doesnt know how? He steps close again, helps, does, maybe she just isnt fast enough for him. Twelve a minute, he says. She fiddles with the dial. Isnt sure? The older nurse checks. It's right. You hold her arm, he says, dont let her jerk it out. Her, not me. Not Gladys. Nothing to do with me. All happening to parts of me. When I bring myself up to the outside (my head is outside too), I remember why I'm here, but it takes energy even to remember why I'm here. Forget it. Wait. They will come. It will hit.

I sink back. Almost sleep. Come out to come up. Fast glide to surface. Everyone's here. I'm pleased (that outer/upper) everyone's here. Light ripples on top of ball tightening and from my head pushing and from their heads pushing. Out there is my arm with the intravenous, limp, being held. I can feel all parts and people except the very parts, pushing. I try to get it out, get it out. A little more room. More middle to push with on the second breath. Head, hair even, top of shoulders, lungs, abdomen, all down on top of it. No sensation in the birth canal. But that will come. They will come. They will come. They will.

I cant seem to push hard enough, I say or think. It's lost. I'm alone. They are all here. But they cant hear. Maybe the next will be different, it probably takes a couple of minutes to work, it's going to be, gotta be, maybe not next but the next after next.

Up for another. Thighs against tits. You fucking muscles, you buggers, work. So what I cant find you. I got all the ones on the edges, whole middle from outside in and top down. Those, they, push. Head there too on top of womb.

Ears and mouth way way above. A grunt. I come out of it happy. Know who I am. I'm Gladys, pushing, trying to get it out. Herstein says, it's going in the tissue. He's exasperated. I flip up to the bottom edge of what's happening out there. I see a green and white movie from underneath: he and the older nurse fiddle with plastic veins, the younger holds the bottles, the object is to not tangle. Herstein pulls the needle out. From another time, Madison, I expect it to hurt. But that limb that white flesh is part of the flick. Metal goes into long-fingered hand. White adhesive is put on top of it. Clear bottles are hooked onto the wire. They are as much me as any hand is which is not me.

Up for another. Whole centre moving down. Everyone on me. Still cant feel those under-muscles or the baby in the canal or an actual contraction – would like to know that – but can see: their eyes, pushing with me, my arm limp, the other holding the chrome, and my face in the mirror, scarlet, far away. We're all together. Working, together. Breathing, down. That's it, keep going, that's it. I come out-up happy then flip-lie back for a moment then my eyes reach out to the clock: 11:03. The demonstration's starting, I say to Cliff.

Twenty, Herstein says to the nurse who changes the dial on the drip. Cliff doesnt mind. He says he didnt want to be there anyway. Is he just saying? No he means it, of course he means it. Bri and Stan are still coming down. Manning Park? Too early. Wont they be surprised. They're riding, thinking of me at 2249 or here, but not here in delivery, in labour, down the hall, but they dont know the hall, I cant hold it, thought I'd be so clear without chemicals, just aint true.

A hundred and ten, says the nurse. Now. I pull up for another. Light ripples seem to be disappearing. Just the curve of non-ball tip or top tightening. More space. More space both at back of it and around the front, just a little but it seems even a quarter of an inch of gut is a lot. All I can do is bear down with what is there, cant feel the rest or the rhythm, use all the edges of what I can.

As it loosens I look in the mirror: breathing wet piles, above them cream skin with what looks like two small lemons under. Bulging. Starting to bulge. I lie back excited but havent the energy to move any of how I feel over/out/up to the others and dont care anyway. Am glad they're here, that's enough, cant jump that far away or up to talk to say glad you're here, I like you pushing too, other times I'd like to talk with you.

Another. They pull in to me. My womb's a heart which pulls us all in. They do their job. I do mine. Down and out. Down and out. They are all about. Down. In. Out. The bulge is bigger. It curves in above the grey sculpture. Ceramic. Flaps. Above stone. Alive.

Is she still here? asks the resident. Of course I'm still here. What does he mean. It's evident. I'm here. Thought it would be out. Well it's not out. He looks at me smiling. Simply expected ... so did I ... so did they. I close my eyes. Push his words tumbling up on top there away. Sink in. Below. Green. Stillness. Can stay in this. So loose. Wait without waiting. All of me loose.

Tightening. The centre tightening. Gotta get the rest of me up. Fast. Huge gulp of air down on top of womb. Air, muscles, blood, bottom ribs even, all push/pull down and along, down and along. Curve crumbles. Isnt there. Or is but not much. Whatever is where it was has no feeling no sensation at all.

Upper muscles let air out, pull the next in fast, so fast that if there were feeling in the low centre, there'd be no time to feel it anyway. My whole self is centred against the top and around the edges of where it is. Skeleton is not a part of me. Neither are limbs. I'm fluid moving against liquid hardness.

No trouble with air. Plenty of air above. The lump loosens suddenly. My mind moves up. Slides up backbone into my head.

Cream bulge bulgier. Wet stony asshole smaller than before or further in cuz it's further out. I see old Finnish-northern-Slavic-mother-me face in mirror, peaceful, white starting to surface as red goes under. Bulge is smaller than it was? Less firm?

I'm going to freeze you, says Dr. Herstein. I dont understand. Why. Will it hurt coming through? I'm not feeling anything anyway. It's the first time I think of hurt. But I dont push him. Havent the outside energy to understand what he's trying to say. Or he's saying it without trying. It's me who has to try to follow: ten minutes to work...same as the dentist...a local...you'll still do everything. I dont understand. Why. He told me already. He said something.

What. Episiotomy? That I understand. But the drugs are to stitch up. Is there something else? He turns his back.

Ninety, says the nurse. What. What is it. Ninety okay? I breathe deep through-nose-out-mouth breaths. A huge looseness. My whole body is huge and loose. Mind also. Floating. Beautiful non-thought thought. Clear nothing. Just the looping of air.

Way in, below belly button, it tightens, presses out. Gets, snaps, me-them up to push in, down. Down, down, around. Down, down from the top, around. A pulling. A pulling from the bottom. Is it starting to work? Not that urge I heard about. But it's starting. Seems somehow to move with. But it isnt moving that much. Loosen the floor. Keep it open, loose. Cant feel but know I am. Uhh. Outside. My clit. A pushing under on it. Not like fucking. Numb. Closer under, a pleasant unkeyed tautness.

I float up seeing the flap-encased bulge. Your head. But I cant see it. That close. Just under skin. Unreal. In moments. Cant feel you. Thought so much I'd be able to feel you. Where you are. As I look you recede. Do you? Does it? Diminish?

Herstein comes with the needle. I close my eyes. Somehow he gets in, I feel just ever so lightly his hand on outer lips. Can feel the needle also touching what seems like about four inches up inside. Where are you? Does he go around you? Your head? Doesnt seem to. Cant feel the liquid coming in. Just the push of needle through thick spongy skin. He comes out. Goes in my other, right, side.

Loose. I feel so loose. Like the body I'm in is a log sunk in sand. Dissipating, disappearing, becoming grains in the sun. But you – I dont think of you as you – it is the centre coming up, curling through. The rest is still. Invisible. It moves.

Pull along. Along to what's attached. Guts, me, my head (down there) comes in, floats up, to push. As hard as I can, can, can. My whole self is where you moments ago were. Mind there way below air-hard lungs. All centred behind you. Those people above and around are talking. So are throat muscles. Mine. But there's no energy in my ears to hear. They are parts of the other and far away. But lungs need more air so my head has to come up to bring it in. And it's Herstein who crashes through as my mouth goes to grab: come on, I can see it, there it is, (I'm already sinking back down with air above), come on now, push, push, PUSH.

It stops. Your hair. I can see a slit. Your hair. There. Wow. You're really real. A slit. About a quarter inch of wet hair. As I look, it goes. Flaps enclose.

They chatter. They wait. I cant stay out there with them. Or up in my skull. That's all energy. Too much. Slip down to tummy to top of it. Warm large flesh all around. Peaceful. Still. Can stay here. Do. Or go. Go up. Out. Down. We all come down. Gotta get it out. IT OUT. All muscles about. GET IT OUT. They are all here trying to get it out. I am here, in middle, skull too, knowing what it is to do, with a pull pulling and every cell else pushing, down and around, down, lungs shoulders way above moving with, middle tight, loosening slightly, tight, with, against, with, against, all down, the loosening is only sideways, and so light, but I can move with it, pulling to the down.

I float out feeling good. Cant reach where they are. Their smiles seem to drift to me but are caught about two-thirds between by air. That's me there, in the mirror, and your hair, being covered by skin. Slowly, gone.

He's going to cut. I close my eyes. Cant sink down as far as I did. Feel it open and then a nick: I can feel that, I say. A fast hurt. Cant explain now. It's over. Sink into where I was. But it's not peaceful anymore. I dont want to stay.

They are all – the two doctors mainly – talking about something. Way out. Way beyond. Back of the room seems over the road beyond the trees. I look at them, something to do with time, too long in? Cant get any of the words. Cliff seems to know. The energy of the room is all there where they are. I lie below. Feel it sweep above. Sometimes from them coming over to me, sometimes from Cliff and the nurse going over me/you to them.

I fold in. My womb from the bottom or front seems to pull in, from the top or back hardens out. I sit above, along it, pushing the back and top. It collapses in, hardens out, in, hardens out. Got the motion: down, then not as down even though I push down, down along, it's hard against my hard then it's hard not as hard, then it against/with, then it pulling up (not out, but up) forward.

I come up to my mouth to let out/pull in air. See them from eyes above. Talking. Telling me to push. Talking about the push. Excited. But so far away. I flip back down: it's hard against/with my hard then it's hard not as hard, then it's hard pulling up pulling my hard down so the push although it's using all the energy/focus I have isnt pushing all itself cuz it gets pulled along, pulled in, too. The bulge is getting huger as I push, am pulled, push. My mouth grunts. I cant hear. But I feel it grunt. As the contraction stops, I hear way down sow sounds. That didnt hurt, I say to them. They tilt, laugh. Dont know why. Had to tell. They dont know. They smile. I'm out there smiling with them for a second or so but there isnt a total with.

White flaps enclose hair. Solid. Less solid? Not as out. Firm flesh sculpture curving in. Wet breathing piles moving out.

Herstein cuts the seeing. Leans toward me to say: I'm just going to hold it. He's going to hold, my ears tell my mind. To keep it from slipping. Slipping? Back. I dont understand. You're going to do all the work, he says. I dont get how. He's lying? I'm going to push, he's going to pull? Does my mouth say this: I'll push you'll pull. (?) He repeats: I'm just going to hold it to keep it from slipping back. I dont see how that's possible. Forceps. That I know. Everyone else is with him. They understand. So it's me. Takes so much head energy to see. But it is me. I cant hold words long enough even if I can get them in and that is hard to haul them in, I cant hold/pull a sequence together.

Feel alone. Not knowing. I see his back at the table at the end of the room. Know I'm not by myself, know Cliff and he and everyone else is here. Yet alone. Metal comes out of cloth. Green.

A pull. My under-body front. Not from behind at all. Bulging out. A hard tightening as I come down, up, on it from under, what feeling there is is all where your head is, I dont think of it as you, only what's under that beautiful curve. Everyone is out there down on me squeezing in. I'm under, in, pushing along, and up, along with the tightening and up with the loosening. A long the tight, up the loose. A long, long up. THAT'S IT, they chatter, THAT'S IT. Wont have to do. Good. THAT'S IT. C'MON NOW. I float up under excited faces. Herstein opens one flap to slide a forcep in. Seems to slip in around. Opens the other flap, circle seems to tighten, quite tight, yet so easy, it just slides into/onto your head. GOT IT.

I'll push, you'll pull: I say or think as we go into it. Every bit of me is down on top of the back of the moving. I close my eyes to get it out. Down. Up. Out. Circle tightens. I can feel it opening, tightening, opening, tightening, opening. Up, out there. I'm down, around, down, around, down, around.

Even the tightness seems far away. I'm squinched into one space with muscles and looseness behind/around, hardness above, air. Long, moving long, so tight yet big, long moving long up. Open. Open.

Open. There is a hard yet vast looseness immediately above where I am. I flip up past it to get more air to come down and under.

Circle is taut. About to: DONT PUSH, shouts Dr. Herstein. Pant, Cliff says. He breathes with me: >h> &lt;h &lt;h    >h> &lt;h &lt;h
>h> &lt;h &lt;h    >h> &lt;h &lt;h    >h> &lt;h &lt;h
Out, your head's out, but I dont feel your head out, cant see, dont, just:     YOU CAN PUSH. Push.     Am all muscle. Dont feel. Dont know at all. Am muscle moving up and out.

Blue thin legs. Curve of balls. Poppy-pod size. Light from behind. A BOY. Suspended there. A BOY. Swinging. Being swung by Herstein. Over and up so I can see. White covered. Wet. Unalive. Unhuman. Twisted firm white cord. He snips? I dont see. IT IS YOU. Your first breath. A cry. So light. Arms swim gracefully in air upside down. Long-limbed motions. Un-erratic. Stroking out. Through air. With ease. I see the cord hanging in the mirror. White, blue.

**11:33**   Fat round clock. Cliff smiling. Crinkly. His whole body through his wet eyes. He's with you, with me, with you, with me. Herstein explains what he's going to do, stitch, but I cant listen, am so high, just want to see you, him, you. HOLD HER HAND, he says. Cliff leans, all glowy, over me where you moments ago were. His hand scrunches mine tight against sheet. He's changing colour, he says, watch him change. I turn to you. Cant see colour. Only arms moving, oval head, wet hair. Bones defined. Unfleshy. Warbly half-lip smile. Not startled at all by the world.

Maria Hindmarch, photo by George Bowering

# The Watery Part of the World

DOUGLAS AND McINTYRE, 1988

*"... having little or no money in my purse, and nothing in particular to interest me on shore, I thought I would sail about a little and see the watery part of the world."*

—HERMAN MELVILLE
*Moby-Dick*

## 1. The Hall

I've decided to ship out on a coastal freighter, if I can find one that takes women and if they'll have me. I walk up the curved, granite steps of the SIU hall on the corner of Cordova and Main. The Seafarers' International Union Hall is actually a bank built of stone – so different from the wooden Chinese newsstand or dusty pawnshop or concrete Public Safety Building that also shape the intersection. I pass Ionic columns, which seem out of place on the West Coast, and note the AD 1910 chipped in stone above the modern glass door. Despite a Members Only sign Scotch-taped on the door, I open it and enter.

Inside, at the far end where a bank vault might once have been, is a coffee bar surrounded by thick pillars: a fat woman is pulling used mugs toward her with a stick. She gives an impression of slowness but there is no wasted motion. On my immediate left is a curved red counter which starts from just inside the door and goes the entire width of the room: behind it, at a modern desk, a thin woman of thirty is typing; on the counter (probably oak underneath), a white-haired man fills out forms. I walk toward him and he slowly looks up.

You used to be on Black Ball, he says. No ... but I have my shipping book cuz I worked on the ferries. That's odd. I could have sworn I saw you here before – just come back, from the Lakes? No ... I, I asked you about a job in May and ... Do you want to re-gis-ter? He doesn't understand. I'm not a union member, I say. Are you a-vail-able for work? He speaks slowly and deliberately, introduces himself as Albert, asks a few more questions, then opens a brown scribbler and carefully writes my name, Jan Henderson, and my telephone number in pencil. I notice the book is two-thirds full, but dont ask him about that. Something might come up soon, you should pack your gear and be ready to sail, but if a member wants the job, she gets it; if she isnt in the hall and cant be located, she doesn't. An hour's notice might be all you'd get – can you do it? Yes, I say, and thank him.

I walk past two men playing checkers at a table and an older man who is rolling himself a cigarette and has a piece of toilet paper over a spot on his nose. I go up to the counter and introduce myself to the woman behind it, Bea. Are you shipping out? she asks. I dont know yet, I answer. Come down here before ten and three every day, she says, we're shorthanded ... good girls are hard to get. She gives me a coffee and smiles, you a student? I nod, is it that obvious? Her whole body seems to smile, to be open. I didnt go past grade eight myself ... didnt see no necessity to those days ... all right, all right, Johnny, she says to a man who I cant see because he's on the other side of a pillar. You must have built-in antennae or something ... every time I get talking, you come a-running .... Bea has an easiness of self and motion. I'd like to ask her questions, to listen to her, to find out what I'd have to do, but Johnny swings around the pillar and sits on the stool next to me and introduces himself.

The rest is a blur of tan and blue eyes, of walking up an alley, of some beer at the Empress. The place is dark, as all pubs are after walking in from outside on even a dull summer day. The place is crowded, compared with others, and the people are more talky even if they dont know you. Are you shipping out, kid? What would I do? Where do they go? Is it hard? You never been on the outside? Why, it gets rough; why, I've seen some real sailors who wouldn't even ... Dont listen to him – it's nothing.

I go to the can and an old woman asks for a cigarette, so I give her one. Dont do that again, honey, she'll be after you, you know. She sits here day after day begging, you know. You're new to this part of town, ain't you? Well, stay away, your kind dont belong here: cracked tiles, brandy, paper all over the can. You sure you dont want some, sweetie? It's free ... it'll warm you up ... what's wrong? ... I ain't got germs. No towels, only toilet paper, one sink is plugged with hair.

What took you so long? Get lost in the hole? Shut up will you, she's mine: a plump belly, a yellow T-shirt, three tattooed arms on the table. You know a fine girl like you has no business on ships, why dont you get a nice job typing or something: cardboard circles, peanuts, beer glasses all over the table.

I cant see being cooped in one spot doing the same thing over and over again, I say. Maybe you should teach... No... I think you'd make a good nurse. Women shouldn't ship out, period, not even as passengers: Cheezies, pastrami, cigarettes, more beer. Take one for yerself. Thanks.

We already have three university nuts around... that young yahoo without the shoes... you know who I mean... that big monkey. You mean the one who played drums on the oil cans when we were unloading in Tahsis and read poetry when he was operating the tow-motor? The one who says he's studying brain impulses or something? Name's Ken. That's him... Ken Douglas... do you know him? I dont want to say I do because I dont want to be connected with him and I dont want to say I dont in case I see him around the hall. So I say, I've heard of him, and let it go at that cuz they dont really expect me to know Ken anyway, and with so many boats that dont ship women, I dont expect to see him either. In fact, he's my ex-boyfriend, if you can call a lover a boy. At twenty-one, he was not my idea of a man and not really a friend.

C'mon, I'll give you a lift home, says Johnny. You're not going to take her away from us already, are you? says Whitey, a huge-bellied man, who signals for another round. The bartender laughs at some jibe a guy at another table makes and a captain arrives from the alley entrance, hugs Johnny, old boy, howya doing? slaps Whitey, you crazy shit, still on the old tub – whatza matter with you, taking up homesteading? He falls backwards as Johnny says this is Thor, tips a table full of beer and knocks someone's money off: money, cigarette butts, beer, legs on the floor.

Well ain't that just. Someone punches Thor. Then Hal from our table hits that someone and it isnt like the movies or TV at all where it goes on for minutes with insults and grimaces and dodges and sounds: just two hits, like that, that fast. A broken nose without any seeing. Just a sense of motion after, not during.

C'mon, kid, let's get out of here, quick. Johnny shoves me past other tables where people arent the least bit concerned, out the alley where the cop station is, almost to the street.

But he's hurt, I say, arent you going to ... look, I'm in enough trouble as it is without getting involved in a ... Whitey knows him, he's got friends, he'll be looked after. Water in an eye, a drop of blood coming out, legs straddled.

As we get to the curb, Johnny lets go of my arm and says, if you want to go back, go ... I'm crossing the street and if you dont want to come it makes no difference to me. He walks across and I stay. Blue eyes. I cant think. I cant help it. The light itself's bothering me. I wish Ken were here. Johnny might be right, I shouldn't get ... I am going back to see. He doesn't even know what's happened to him. S'long kid, Johnny shouts, s'long.

# WEDNESDAY

## Callback Time

All members of the unlicensed personnel shall be aboard the vessel in a sober condition at least one (1) hour before notified sailing time in the port of Vancouver and one-half (½) hour before notified sailing time in upcoast ports.

## Dumping Garbage

Unlicensed personnel of the Deck Department shall not be required to handle galley garbage.

## Ship's Delegate

The ship's delegate shall be a member of the crew selected by a majority vote of the unlicensed personnel of the vessel ... In no case shall the ship's delegate interfere or threaten to interfere with the conduct of the ship, the authority of the officers, or the discipline of the crew ...

## 2. The *Nootka*

Ken is painting the outside of the wheelhouse. I can see him as I come up the *Nootka*'s gangplank. I'm wearing high heels I should have had enough sense not to put on cuz she's a coastal freighter with slits between the greasy planks. There he is, Ken, painting the outside of the wheelhouse. I dont believe it. What a coincidence. He turns and smiles in that loose shambly way of his, *Miss* Henderson, how *do* you *do*? What am I supposed to say? Pleased to see you here? How *are you* doing? Who's your lover now? He blocks the end of the gangplank. I put my suitcase down in between us. He comes closer, chest near my eye close. His wet paintbrush almost touches my nose. I simply say, hi Ken, I didnt know you were on *this* boat.

C'mon you big monkey, let the lass go, says a round-bellied man whose face I cant see cuz he's behind Ken. Some of us has manners, the round man says, some of us knows when we're not wanted. But you dont *know* Jan, says Ken as he steps aside. He waves his brush near my ear then turns toward his paint bucket, which I'd love to dump over his head. I look down at a sixty-year-old, coveralled man, who's three or four inches shorter than I am, who introduces himself as Jock. A deep voice from inside the wheelhouse shouts, you gotta watch out for that dirty old man. Dont listen to Beebo, says Jock, he's just jealous.

Jock grabs my suitcase and goes ahead of me down a ladder made of metal pipe which is smooth and slippery beneath my shoes. You sailed before? he asks. I wonder if he's referring to my high heels or to Ken. Just on the ferries, I answer. Which one? The *Princess of Vancouver*. We pass behind the winch that takes up more than half the width of the main deck. Did you like that? he asks. Sure, I say, relieved he isnt asking me about Ken, but I quit cuz the women were getting substantially less than men for doing identical work. That's a company union, he says, there's not a one anywhere that's any good.

As you can gather for yourself, says Jock as he opens a door, this ain't the CPR. Yeah, I can sure see that! It certainly isnt: grey dirty paper covers the deck, rags hang on a railing, a broken chair lies legs up. This here's the passengers' lounge, he says, such as it is, and that's where the officers eat. I look at a two-by-three foot table covered with a tea towel, an empty Crisco tin, and dirty mugs. No fancy silver or white linen for these officers, that's for sure. Just beyond it, covered in plastic and canvas bundles of laundry, is a longer table.

We move into the galley, which is about the size of a large bathroom, as warm as a sauna, and noisier than a print shop or small mill. Jock takes me through it to a little room off the left where he puts my suitcase down near the wall and under a blackboard. This here's the crew's mess, Jock shouts, where you get to serve us. The room is no more than eight feet long, no wider than seven, and is dominated by a pale-green built-in table that has a red built-in bench behind it, a chair on the end closest to the galley, and two chairs on the side next to me. Pour yourself a coffee, lass, Jock shouts over the racket, I'll fetch Coco or Puppi for you. Thanks, I say down into faded blue eyes, and he winks then steps out the door that is near the attached end of the table.

Damn luck. I'm happy to be here but not happy to be on the same boat as Ken. He just has to smile and I fall right into whatever it is that makes whatever we were so impossible. If I had sailed on a coastal freighter before, it might be different; but, as it is, good god, almost a week on this tub with him. Certainly seems like a warm, almost spicy place. I glance at the table and guess the men's eating habits from it: chutney, HP, Tabasco, and Worcestershire sauces, open newspapers, ketchup and Colman's mustard and scrunched serviettes, ginger marmalade, honey, and canned Pacific milk and coffee stains, used toothpicks in dirty ashtrays. I glance at the blackboard:

Four different hands. 1300 that's 12 and 1 so 1:00 o'clock and it must be about 11:30 by now. I lean over to pick up the newspapers and am folding one when I hear a voice behind me.

You the new mess girl? asks a woman of around thirty who has entered the mess from the door Jock left by. I'm Coco, she says, what do you go by? I'm Jan. Are you the cook? Yeah (bright red lips/laughing voice), try to be but that isnt easy around here. Coco's hair is dark and wavy and swept up into a soft, full roll. She has a large white rag around her middle like a butcher's apron. I smile and dont know what to say but know I'll like her. She steps around my suitcase and I step aside so she can pass me. She tries the tap. *No water*, she says, and *I've got my lunch cooking.* How are we supposed to clean up, serve coffee and tea for fifteen to twenty men, without water? I dont know, I say and laugh a stupid laugh. It was supposed to be back on soon, two hours ago, she shouts. Do you want some of this old coffee? Sure, I shout. She rinses out two mugs from the sink with water from the kettle and wipes them with a clean pillowcase from the wire that runs above the old black stove and stainless steel sink. Back on *soon*, she repeats. Wish I could say that for our regular skipper. She pours herself coffee then turns to me, her red lips smiling but her eyes all wet. Let's sit in the mess, she says.

We sit down on the two side chairs and she offers me a Craven A, which I refuse. You're relieving Betty, she says, but she's in no condition to walk yet. She's drunk as can be and is in her cabin, which will be yours, and we want her to stay there till she can walk, then the crew will help her off. Her lipstick goes round the filter tip of her cigarette and I can see her deciding whether to say more or not. Something else wrong? I ask. Certainly is, she says. The company has suspended the skipper cuz Betty was caught naked this morning crawling up to his cabin even after some of the guys had packed her down to her own. He might never be allowed back. That sounds awful, I say. Not as bad as things might get, she says, with him gone. Her expression goes soft for a moment, and I wonder if she has ever slept with him.

Got different shoes? she says to me. I nod. Best to put them on now before you hurt yourself. I open the suitcase, which takes up all the deck space there is between the wall and chair, and pull my unwhitened, worn nurses shoes out, then sit down next to Coco to put them on as she tells me what my duties are.

You serve the crew, she says, here in what we call the boys' mess – Puppi, our stewardess, serves the officers and passengers on the other side. You do all the dishes except the silver for officers and passengers. You prepare all the vegetables and make salads for supper. You scrub the decks here and in the galley at least twice a day, usually after breakfast and supper. At the end of the trip, you do a big cleanup and scrub down all the bulkheads and the boys' cooler and at the beginning, like this afternoon, you help me unload the stores. You also take the garbage out and dump it overboard as long as we're not in port or harbour, and then you clean the buckets with a special brush which we keep outside for that purpose. There are all sorts of other things, making toast and bundling dirty linen, she says, but I'll fill you in as we go along. Thanks, I say as I put my stupid high heels in my suitcase, I know I'm going to need help, but I'll do the best I can.

Coco picks up her ashtray and is about to go to the galley when I ask her to tell me where I might iron a uniform. We use the galley counter, she says, not much room but the only flat space we got where there's an outlet. Direct current, though. You can borrow my iron. I examine mine, AC/DC, I guess this will work, I say, but thanks for the offer ... can I do it now? If you're quick, she says, the guys will be in as soon as the water is on. I take out a wrinkled uniform, one of the ones I wore on the ferry before I quit and went to summer school to complete my B.A.: rolled after a wash seven weeks ago. I am just setting up when a little man-woman comes running into the galley from the passenger-officer side screeching that's my space at me. Outta my way, she screeches, outta my way. She pushes aside the towel I'm trying to iron on and swears in German at Coco then runs past the stove back out of the room cawing about The Chief, the boiler, and greenhorns. All I can see as she goes are hairy ankles, turquoise vinyl slippers, a white uniform covering an almost straight little body, a shaved neck – shaved way up just like men's used to be.

That's *our* Puppi, says Coco, turning to me, she's all upset because of what's going on and because she cant scrub the captain's quarters because there's no water. By the time Puppi returns, I'm halfway through. She opens a huge walk-in cooler which is next to the sink, brings out two pounds of butter, gives Coco a nasty look, which Coco ignores, then starts cutting butter about six inches from my towel edge. It's *scheisse* union this and *scheisse* union that and training new help who dont stick with it. Are you going to stay with it? she says for me but not to me. No, she answers. You wont stay with it. Puppi will show you, ask Puppi, Puppi will tell you. Well, Puppi wont. Puppi's sick of training help. Puppi wont show *anyone* how to do *anything* anymore.

She slams butter into round fruit dishes and says *you*'ll have to get *your* own. I just look down at her. The boys'll be in, Puppi warns. I still look. If Betty doesn't set up, you have to. She flies out of the galley to the officer-passenger side.

Dont pay attention to her, says Coco, she can drive you crazy but she has a heart of gold. I seem to be ironing more creases in than wrinkles out and have just decided to leave it when: I need milk, Puppi announces to the two of us with her gnarly hands on her little hips. Get your own, says Coco, I'm busy. Puppi marches up to me, eyebrows rippling, get me some milk? she says childishly. Why not? I think, if it's so important, but why cant she? and where? I go toward the walk-in cooler without saying anything. She tugs my blouse: not there, the boys' fridge. She points me to the mess then stands at the doorsill, feet in galley, body leaning over to see and direct. I open the little cooler that is above the bench and also behind the end chair. I pull out a glass jug. Not that one, the enamel, she screeches. So I move jars of water and cans of juices out of the way and pull out the jug she wants. She nods yes. But when I get it over to her she snatches it, no thank you, no smile, just a cold grab. Coco takes no notice, keeps her back turned, fills the kettle. I wait till Puppi's out of the galley to ask what that was all about. She's not allowed in the mess, says Coco, it has something to do with Betty and the crew and whose jug is whose. Just ignore it.

Two stew to follow, one bean up, the crow caws from the other side. Two stew, one bean, repeats Coco. I wait for Coco to dish out the beans before I ask where I can change: Puppi runs in, elbows Coco over, ladles soup into two bowls, then takes all three dishes out at once. Coco, where can I: see, she doesn't have to do that. We both speak at once and laugh and then I cross my legs and keep laughing and look at the iron which seems so silly and she looks at the tap and we both look at each other and keep laughing. And a curly-headed young man walks in carrying a pail of water and laughs at us laughing at him looking at: two beans no dogs, Puppi caws. C'mon you two magpies, get the food on, he (bass voice) says between laughs. He gives the pail to Coco then picks up my uniform which is still on the counter. First tripper? he says to me laughing as I follow him/it laughing into the mess and giggle yes as he throws it on the back of a chair. I'm Beebo, he says, and I laugh at his voice as he starts cleaning off the table. What a funny name. As I put jars away in their little wooden stand at the end of the table, he takes mugs to the galley and comes back with a clean cloth, which he places around my middle. He yanks the tie ends in, makes a knot. He gives me a damp dishrag to wipe the table with and puts silver down right after me. I spill the toothpicks from a saltshaker and keep right on laughing.

And he says, shake a leg, c'mon, c'mon. We get glasses out of the cooler, water jugs, two half-empty, bread from the walk-in cooler placed on a saucer, heel up; butter, cut some butter, he says, we're covering for Betty, cant let her get canned, too; crackers, in the cupboard past the stove on the right, get some more honey while you're there, he says. Ho-ot, ho-ot, Puppi caws as I run back past her and we touch. Be more careful, she screeches, on a ship you gotta be careful. I get the crackers and honey to Beebo, and two other men walk into the mess.

Hal, whom I met last week in the Empress, is one of them, and the other, who is cocky and has black black hair, whistles: whirrrip-whirrroo. Get a load of that, he says to Hal and Beebo, some run this is going to be. Jan, this is Lefty, says Hal. Hal looks at me direct, right in. I want to ask him about the fight and the guy who was hurt but dont because something tells me not to right now. They sit down, quite quickly, Hal on the outside near the door, Lefty on the inside on the bench taking up half the table, Beebo on the end chair with his back to the cooler.

Lefty bangs his elbows. Where's my food? he roars. What will you have? I ask. Give me some beans – at least she cant ruin them. Before I go into the galley, I take the other orders, which somehow perturbs him, but I can easily remember three orders at once: soup please, says Beebo, packaged isnt it? Yes. Okay, I'll take it. Tea only please, says Hal. When I bring back the over-boiled beans and murky chicken-noodle soup, Lefty asks the table at large, where's Betty? I hand Lefty his plate and, while he sniffs it, Beebo answers: Piss-eyed, excuse my language Jan, the lady is sleeping it off in her cabin.

I go out to make Hal's tea, and when I return he's making himself a peanut-butter sandwich. Where are all the ashtrays? asks Lefty. They're dirty, I say, as soon as there's water, I'll clean you one. When I come back from the waterless tap, Beebo says in a helpful tone, Jan, love, when you make tea check to see the kettle's boiling, will you? See that? I go over and look in Hal's mug: the water is a light green; around the bag it's slightly brown. I'm sorry, I say to him, I'll make you another. But Hal says, never mind, I didnt want it anyway. So Beebo reaches back without leaving his chair and opens the cooler and brings out the milk for Hal and himself. Jan, says Lefty, that's not our jug – ours is the enamel. What's the difference? says Hal.

There's a few seconds of no talk before Jock arrives, sits on the chair next to Hal, orders soup me love, and then Beebo asks me for more bread, and Hal passes the salt shaker full of toothpicks to Lefty who says he didnt know anyone could do that to beans. Then it's why dont you sit down and rest your legs, you're entitled to a half-hour lunch and just because these other women dont take it is no reason for you not to: it's in the contract, one half hour, thirty minutes, c'mon now there's nothing you can do till we're finished eating. They seem to want me to, so I ask Coco who tells me there's not much I can do till the water comes on and that she'll join us as soon as she's served the shore crew. I slide behind Beebo and onto the bench next to Lefty and place my feet on Beebo's chair rungs. So while Coco stands over her hot stove and Puppi runs back and forth through the galley slapping instant pudding into fruit dishes, I sit with the men and drink apple juice.

Hal offers me a Player's, which I refuse. I know I should be working yet there's nothing I can do. I feel stupid. I dont belong here. I'd feel better in the galley just talking with Coco, but I'd be in Puppi's way. I wait till Lefty finishes telling them about something funny he saw on shore then excuse myself. Lefty grabs me by the end of the cloth about my waist and pulls. I push his arm: it's hard, harder than any man's I've felt before. I try not to hit the porthole with my head. Duck. Push Lefty forcefully. Right then Ken walks in. He smiles over as I knee Lefty in the thigh. Dont bother getting up for me, he says, I can get my own food. Dont bother, that's just like him, dont bother with anything but Ken. Ken, I say. He's in the galley talking with Coco. Finally, Lefty lets me go. I stick out my arm to catch my balance and Hal, Hal looks at me as if he has something figured out.

## 3. Callback

Nobody is moving quickly because when they do move quickly they only have to wait, so why move quickly? Two longshoremen on the dock catch the slings, slowly place the narrow pipes into the sides of a wooden flat that is loaded with crates of Molson. The men steady the wires as the winch driver hauls the load up, then swings it above the wharf, across the water, to the *Nootka*. The two men just stand there and wait and talk. The Molson sways a moment as the winch driver moves to another handle, then it jerks as he centres the load, then down it goes into our dark hold. I've been standing near the winch watching men work and wait. Men weave tow-motors back and forth around the dock, in and out of the warehouse carrying stacks of empty flats and full loads of McGavin's bread, potatoes, 7 Up, lettuce, bales of wire, everything imaginable – even a motorboat. Nobody seems particularly happy or unhappy; they just know what they're doing and when to do it.

How come you're not at the Princeton? the winch driver asks me as he waits for the men in the hold to unload. I dont answer, just smile at him: is that difficult? Nah, wanta try it? he says as he steps out from the gears. I look at all the metal sticks and huge green wheels of wire cable, shake my head. One of the men on the dock hollers, c'mon, c'mon, and I leave.

I climb up the ladder and walk past the freshly painted wheelhouse and go down another ladder to the poop deck then around the corner to just outside my cabin. I lean on the railing next to empty boxes, full garbage buckets, and wooden crates covered in lettuce leaves and crumpled brown paper. I watch the oil on the water, the night city neon just starting. I think of Ken. The boat keeps shifting, we do also, changing, not fast enough, wonder where he:

Whistling, not too far off but so lonely.

A body flops over me ... tight. I cant ... a rough chin scrapes my neck ... breathe. Hands glom onto/into my tits. What are (I try to duck down) you? Just seeing if they're real, Lefty says. Lefty, you're *not* seeing, I say as both my hands circle his left wrist. You're (I pull that hand away), you're (nothing – no words – too shocked to think). He gently slides his other hand out as if I had let him touch me, and he just stands there with that cocky grin. Scared ya? he says. No, you, you didnt. (But you did, you bastard, and I'm not going to show it.) Come have a mug-up. I dont want one. Come have one anyway. We go through the hot mess to the hotter galley. He pours boiling water into a green square pot, swirls it around. See this? It's mine. You dont use it for anyone but me. OcTOPus QuINtON in white paint, mixed upper-lower case. I wouldn't think of it. Not even when I'm not here, he says. I wont.

I rinse out a mug and pour myself a cup of coffee. Cut me a slice of onion, he says. (I cant see any onion.) Where are they? In the fridge, where'dya expect? I cant remember seeing any there when we stowed the stores this afternoon, but I go into the walk-in anyway, which is jammed with supplies, and I look around at the packages of meat wrapped in brown paper, pounds and pounds of butter, huge hunks of cheese, heads of lettuce, celery, *green* onions but not ... The door slams shut from the outside and the light turns off. Let me out, Lefty. Lefty, I cant see! He laughs a dirty gut laugh. Betty always has onion peeled, on the deck, in a can. (Absolutely no light. Surrounded by vegetable smells. My fingers feel for a handle all over the cool metal door: none.) Let me out!

The cooler opens. I almost trip on the sill as I duck under his arm. My head just misses the mugs, which are in a long white case on the wail. I straighten up (limbs awkward – my breasts still feeling his fingers), dont look at him. I lift my coffee from the wooden counter and take it into the mess where I find the canned milk beneath the *Vancouver Sun*. He's soon next to me, Spanish onion in his mouth, one arm on the table, the other hand holding his tea, which he puts down. He takes the huge onion out and says, how d'ya like boat life? I dont know, yet, I answer. I ... Do you like men? Sure, I say, stirring the coffee much too much (which he notices). What type appeal to ya? Well I ...

How 'bout me? I look at him, medium built and loose-legged, brown eyes that dare me, biting his onion as if he knows who I am and how he is. He sees me taking in the whole, looks proud, slowly slurps a bite down. Do you like to suck? My god, what do you answer to that? I don't.

I just walk out of the mess to the poop deck. Lefty follows me. Hal's there, leaning on the railing; and Jock, sitting on a wooden box that he gets up from, then gives to me. Didnt mean to frighten you ... you dont mind, do you? says Lefty so all three of us can hear. He then passes me and sits on the after-peak.

I look at Hal; he whistles:

and at Jock: he's not impressed; and at Lefty: his legs spread apart, waiting but not waiting for me to say something but I don't. He finishes his onion, licks a cigar, lights it with a wooden match struck on his thumbnail. Hal looks at the sky:

and I do also. I feel more with him than anyone else.

Going to be a good run, says Lefty, looking at the sky and looking at the three of us. No one says anything. The *Nootka* keeps shifting as she's being loaded. I steady myself by bracing my foot on rope and pressing my hand, fingers spread, on the bulkhead as the boat moves the other way. Finally, Lefty tries to make conversation with Jock who's right beside me: how much more to go? They're loading Zeballos last again, Jock answers, those hotshot supervisors you cant tell them anything – they dont even know their ass from a hole in the ground. (Hal and Lefty nod agreeing.) Excuse me, Jan, but the longshoremen here are putting our next-to-last load in last, so we have to keep moving Zeballos's cargo every time we unload at twenty other ports. Alphabetically? I suggest. No excuse, no reason, nothing but stupidity.

I watch the car lights moving down the hills on the North Shore as the men chat about overtime they'll get because of this mistake. Where's Ken? a tall man shouts from between passengers on the upper deck. Dont know, says Jock, this here's our new mess girl, Jan; Jan, that's Buck. Buck gives me a crinkly smile, waves, and disappears. You seen the young monkey? asks Jock. I shake my head up at his belly. Not since noon. Supposed to start watch, Jock says. And Beebo? he asks Lefty. With his wo-man, he answers.

Hal passes between Lefty and me, goes into the crew's wash-space or fidley, which is just off the deck:

On the upper deck are some passengers, mainly old people; sloped bellies and knotted necks and heavy heels move close to the railing. The passengers look at us a moment or so and, getting no particular response, drift off. I watch the flag fold in and out and think of the flag at UBC with the sound of metal clips hitting the metal pole and carrying right into my bedroom in the dorms at night.

Jan, says Jock, tell Lefty why you quit the CPR. Lefty looks at me questioningly and, for the first time since he asked me that other question, I look him in the eyes. C'mon, Jan, tell us your story. It was nothing, I say. Let us decide, he says. (Why not? He's going to push me no matter what I do.) Well, at the beginning of this summer, I worked on the *Vancouver* for six weeks without a paycheque. When we got ours, they were only two-thirds of what the male coffee room attendants got, and they had the same job we did. When I asked one of the seamen about the cut, he told me who my union rep was.

I'm your delegate here, says Lefty. If you got a beef, you come to me. Even if it's about you? I ask. Sure, he says, why not? I dont know about that, I say, double jeopardy. Tell your story, he says, you just found out who represents you.

Was I surprised! Here I had worked all last summer and just assumed that the man who always wore a dark suit was an officer or supervisor cuz he only came on at noon and always spent his entire time drinking coffee and eating pie with the Chief or Second Steward...

Beebo swings down the ladder from the upper deck. I'm not here, he says to us, drops down the ladder inside the fidley to the crew's quarters, is gone.

Jock winks at me and signals with his head to look up. Beeeebo, a plump blonde calls from above. Beeeebo, she repeats as she stands above the ladder. You seen Beebo? she yells at Lefty. Not yet, he answers. Jock nudges over next to me and shrugs. Happens all the time, lass. I know he's around here somewhere, she says, I know cuz I seen him. Over his shoulder Jock calls up to her, Why dont you check the wheelhouse, lass, or ask the mate? I look up at her swelled-out belly, droopy breasts, formless waist, but cant quite make out her features because the light's between her and us. He's down with you, isnt he? Isnt he? she yells right at me or I take it that way. I shake my head toward her. I'm coming down, she says, I'm coming. And she does.

Her red skirt blows up, blocks the light, but I can see her, no underpants, round rump, rolly thighs, little tuft of hair. Embarrassed, I turn my head and look at a rope wound round the bit. So little hair, I could see her folds, *everything*, I cant believe it. All right, where is he? I can smell rye and lavender perfume. She pinches my arm above the elbow, pulls it, hard, are you going to tell me or.... I *really* dont know, I say. I can feel little blood pricks float to the surface of my face and back.

Lay off the kid, Beebo says as he runs out of the fidley, then jumps over the bit, rounds the corner of the superstructure. She follows him as fast as she can run, which is pretty fast: my money – I'm not leaving, ya bohunk...

Lefty laughs at me. I rub my arm and look down. You ain't seen pussy before? I dont look up or over. They're not all the same, you know. (I know. I wish you'd shut up. I know. I wish I hadn't looked. I know. I feel like an intruder.) Watch your mouth, Lefty, says Jock. I look at the creosote piles and smile over at him.

Well, what happened? says Lefty. What happened? I repeat. With your union rep? Oh... that. (I can hardly think. Her naked labia. The pinch.) Well he told me that during the winter at a meeting where no women were present, the men voted to lower the female CRAs' wages in order to keep the males' the same. He also told me that there wouldn't be a meeting until September when all of us would be back in school. So I said, I quit. You cant quit, said the Chief. Just watch me, I said, I'll work the weekend and that's all.

Jock gives me a big grin. Things are better here, says Lefty, the cook gets the highest wage of the crew – even higher than me. That so? I say. Yes, Jock says, but Lefty packs in the overtime as do the rest of us, so the crew does take home more.

Hal steps out of the fidley as Ken comes down the ladder: where you been, lad? says Jock as Ken says, turn-to in five.

Motherfucker, we hear the woman shout. I turn toward the mess, the galley. Beebo laughs as he runs like it's all a big joke. Cocksucker, she yells as she passes the canned-goods cupboard. Beebo nudges my leg as he passes, almost stumbles on the bit as Hal and Ken get out of the way so he can make it up the ladder. Her head is large, hair blown out, eyes small, almost a double squint. She pauses above Lefty, gives him a nasty look, spits on his jeans. Then she passes and stands at the bottom of the ladder and looks at all of us as she wheezes and snorts and tries to catch her breath. Lefty knocks the gob of spit off his jeans with the side of a wooden match in one slow stroke. And she doesn't say anything and neither do we. Then slowly, heavily, she climbs the narrow ladder.

Ken moves next to my shoulder, laughs down at me. Enjoying yourself? I turn up and we both smile, too much happening to tell. He brings his thigh close to my arm as Hal goes up the ladder:

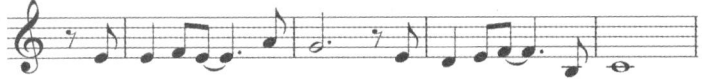

See you later? Ken asks me. Lefty gets up as Jock goes to the side to start to do something with the ropes. I move my shoulder to Ken's thigh. I dont want to talk about us or anyone we know, I say quietly. That's up to you, he says, I'm on the eight to twelve. He's supposed to be. Same old Ken, always. Here, he says, in half an hour.

You better get going you big monkey, shouts Jock. Ken nudges me with his leg then quickly swings up the ladder wearing thongs of all things, smiles at me (big round head, cauliflower ears) from above, takes off. I watch Jock for a minute then go toward my cabin to straighten myself, but the engine noise gets louder, faster, and I look at the piles, the lights, the edge of the green gangway being pulled in from above. And there the blonde whore is, on the dock, waving and screaming as we start to move out, arms high, curved, a weird sorta dance to the fucking bastard and fucking ship. We back out past her and she stays there, solid, the same place. We start to turn. Her legs are apart, arms fluid, mouth screaming, and we're out, and cant hear her any more.

## 4. Faraway Places

I stand on the deck watching the granaries, huge cylinder shadows each connected, and the piers, some dark blobs and others partially lit, pass by. It seems that the *Nootka* is not moving but the city is backing up: slowly, steadily, the hollows that are the streets, which score the hills with even rows of light, pull over; in the hollows, scattered pairs of yellow lights and red lights drift; beyond them, the night mountains of the Coast Range sleep. I watch a thin, scrappy cloud move between the dipper and me, and then I look at the deck. The galley buckets are squished full of garbage, enough to feed ... why think of that? I light a cigarette and watch the edge of the seafoam where it curls into the black water. I can feel the air through my uniform, filtered by cotton, on my arm, more direct, neither cool nor warm.

Thinking about your boyfriend, Hal says. I turn around. He's just behind me; his eyes seem black, like an animal's, flat, near the surface, yet deep. I could go way in. As a matter of fact, I ... Do you mind if I spin a yarn with you? Spin a yarn?

Gab, he says, you know, talk. That's too much. Spin a yarn. He's putting me on. He almost smiles but not quite. Sure, I say. He grabs a wooden box and puts it on the poop deck, then gets a rag from just inside the fidley, shakes it out, lays it down.

Dont want you getting cable dressing all over that uniform. Thank you, I say as he sits on the after-peak. Hope you brought some old clothes to put on when you're not working. Just a skirt and shorts, I say, my jeans were filthy and Albert told me to get here right away. Rain gear? No. You can borrow mine, I got extra. I look at him. We *are* about the same size. Will I need it? You might if you want to walk when we're in Ucluelet or Tahsis or Zeballos.

Faraway places with strange sounding names – not far, just the West Coast. I look at the Lions Gate Bridge as we start to pass under it – huge cement thighs; even with the engine noise I can hear the traffic whir above. Have one? Hal says as he leans over with a Player's. Such small limbs compared to Ken's or Lefty's, his body so compact, so quick. He cups the match with his dark hand, and I watch the edge of a bridge pillar. Ken your boyfriend? he asks. Used to be, I say, smiling at him and his black hair falling over his face. He moves his head up and away, flips it, so straight, so firm. We smile at each other for a moment. You haven't smoked long, he remarks. No, how can you tell that? He blows a circle which drifts toward me, just misses my forehead. The way you draw and the way you hold it like it doesn't belong. I cant see him sharply because I'm blocking the running light, but I know he's slightly pleased with himself and I can very much, too much, feel his presence.

What happened to Thor? I say, trying to shift the mood/subject/emphasis/whatever but also wanting to find out because I'm curious and sense he wont talk when other people are around. You know that's a funny thing. He just went to the head and came out sober, dead sober, never seen a man who can do that like he does – the tapman even offered him one on the house. How do you like that, and they *barred* me. He looks so different when he talks, so … they what? Barred me for a month, and Thor said if you wont serve my buddy, you wont get none of my business till you do, so we went up to Whitey's. Can they do that? Sure, I cant go into the Grandview or the Marble Arch either. Disturbing influence, one of them called me. I never *start* a fight. I've never done *that, never*. I cant quite believe him, but maybe it's so; he certainly didnt start the one I saw in the Empress. Behind him, far to the right, there is a sharp rock, one craggy tree on it: all black, a silhouette against the softness of the night park. I dont see why you shipped out, he says. And I come back to him and the deck after thoughts of Pauline Johnson, "As Red Men Die," chocolates. I, well I, I dont like school and I need some money and I dont like static situations – you know, offices and such, and I guess I just prefer working with some men or around them to working entirely with women or inside. You're going to get hooked, he says. What? If you dont hit the beach and stay there when we get back to port, you're going to get hooked. I dont see why, I say. You haven't been around long enough. I say to myself, you're twenty-two years old, and you have been around. No you haven't; you have a bit and more than most girls, but you haven't really been around long enough as he says.

You seen the men on this boat? Most of the crew. They cant stick to a shore job, none of them. They all tried it sometime or other, several times, you ask. Ask Lefty how many he's had. They just cant do the eight to five race or even stick to the bush for two months. You know how long I lasted last time? No. Three days, not even three days, I told them to shove it. I cant imagine Hal in the city delivering milk or repairing refrigerators, digging ditches or driving cab, certainly not selling, certainly not in a store, certainly not in an office. What did you do? Steeplejacking, he says, but the foreman thought he could tell me what to do. That's it, he doesn't like to be told, in fact he wont be told, that's what …

You're called, Ken shouts from the deck above. We look up at him. (Six-two, thick-thighed, well proportioned: so much larger than Hal who's around five-six.) He goes back to the wheelhouse; then neither of us speaks for a moment. We watch the lights on the North Shore, so many high-rises now, huge cuffs about the sea edge.

Feel like talking about it? he asks. No, not yet that is, I say. I'll relieve him now. You dont have to do that. Just waiting anyway, he says as he gets up. You know that's what gets you about boat life, you work, you sleep, you wait, you eat – that's all there's to it. He smiles then slips up the ladder. I try to pin up the back of my hair. It wont stay put. I should get it … damn it I dont know … cut, if I, I dont want to see him, yes I …

Hi, says Ken from the ladder, just have to take a leak. He looks so, so boyish, overgrown crewcut, so, tear halfway up his shirt, he could afford, floppy thongs, I dont remember him looking sloppy, it's funny what six months can do, but I just saw him less than a month ago, it's not the time, it's other men who make the, I dont want to think about it, I hope I look, Jamie said he dropped chemistry because he was playing around too much, playing …

A mop next to my eye, wet, through the porthole from the fidley, twirling. I get up, move to the side, stand next to the railing and watch, without saying anything. The mop moves to the side, quickly, back to the other side, then up and down, more slowly, retreating, a small circle, then in. Less than a moment later, he jumps onto the bit, puts his arms up, sways. You curling bastard. Same old Ken. He springs onto the peak, then steps onto the deck edge, next to me. I move away a few inches. I dont know what ... he shouldn't be this close ... it isnt ...

You're looking good, he says. So are you. Nice of Hal to let you off early like that. I've got to think of something to say so he doesn't take over. Not about us. We dont know what happened. We tried it before and it just gets nowhere. Huge circles and loops that seldom, if ever, coincide. He's a good head, Ken says, but you know why he did it, dont you? What do you mean? Come off it, Jan, you know as well as I do. I guess so, I say (at least I know what you're insinuating).

What have you been doing lately, that is, what are you getting into now? That's safe. Last time I saw him it was the brain and how it works. He knows or should know I dont mean women, and he usually moves around in one enthusiasm for two or three months before.... He talks about the mind and ideas he has on chemical reactions and response to light. I dont ask him why he dropped chemistry – he might not tell me anyway – it obviously wasn't going where he was at the moment. Hypnosis. Neurosurgery. (His father's a neurosurgeon.) Tantras. He talks in huge, looping phrases I scarcely follow. I listen to a phrase or two and take off, come back in a minute or so, go into/onto another tangent – mostly about myself – nothing intellectual going for me right now, not quite, but other people are the centre on which I depend too much. Less than five hours a day is all the body ... I slept so much before we did break up, sixteen hours sometimes, and then, then I couldn't take the fact that we had ... but it was so senseless as it was, but he always does/did have something that ... always someone too ... listening. He doesn't even notice I'm not. Maybe that's part of what went wrong – he never listens. A habit, habits are such traps. Me listening, he talking, me taking in, in the beginning anyway.

The light from the lighthouse at Point Atkinson turns. We've seen it together from so many city/mountain/water/angles at so many past, now present, times. Oh, I say, that's interesting. And he continues. So careless the way he uses the language and his observations about people are so ... Ambivalent's the word, he breaks in. What? I say, sorry, I was thinking about something else. I just hate her sometimes, then we argue and fight, and she makes me see things but I dont admit it right away. Well, I certainly didnt do that. She's so logical. She went around with a philosopher before she met me. (And you're going to undo it.) She's younger; she doesn't reach the same levels you do. Maybe that's what you need, I say, someone you can show things to and... (I want to get out of this.) Ken leans his head against one of the pipe-posts that's between our deck and the upper one. His thick long neck deliberately scratches, loosely caresses the white metal.

You know you shouldn't tell me about your girlfriend, I say. I dont want to hear about her. He stops rubbing, looks hurt, like he doesn't understand – a little boy puzzled. He cant be as insensitive or unfeeling as... Cant we at least be friends? he asks. (You idiot – it wont work.) Okay, let's try it, I say, but I better turn in now cuz I get up at six. I try to smile, but... Want a hand with the garbage? he asks as he snatches a small cardboard box from the heap next to him, chucks it over. Am I supposed to do that? Sure, as soon as she's out of harbour – see Point Atkinson and Point Grey? I look at the lighthouse on the North Shore and then at the towers of the university and well-spaced, large buildings with just a few lights on. They're the boundaries, he says. I dont really believe it's my job, but we do it anyway – sling and throw and drop huge and small and medium-sized bags/boxes/crates into the dark rolls/folds of the sea. No sounds as they enter cuz the engine noises block them off. Only the three buckets left. I try one, but it's too heavy for me to lift. He heaves another. Then he grabs mine, then the other, and I smile as he puts the last one down and he smiles too. It's kind of fun, not the doing we used to do, but fun to be doing together again.

THURSDAY

*Safe Working Conditions*

The Company shall take every
reasonable precaution to provide
safe working conditions at all times.

Crew members will not be required
to work aloft on masts, derricks,
or king-posts, while winches or
cargo gear are being worked.

Unlicensed personnel shall not be
required to ride ship's gear except in
an emergency.

## 5. Some Trip This Is Going to Be

The afternoon is supposed to be my time off, but that doesn't mean it's my time off. Because I'm slow, I couldn't get the potatoes peeled for supper before nine in the morning when I had to scrub the mess and galley so the decks would be dry by the time the men came in for early mug-up at quarter to ten. And because that took me longer than it should (simply cuz I didnt know how to wring the mop out properly even after Coco showed me how, and I kept hitting my leg with the wooden squeegeemidoogle), Coco got behind but not noticeably cuz she can do anything fast, but she did get "behind" in terms of her baking which she says is usually in the oven when the boys come in for mug-up (so at lunch today they didnt have pies but tapioca pudding or fisheyes as they call it). And the guys insisted we have morning mug-up with them (it's your right, they said, you gotta do it), so Coco and I did, and after that I washed their dishes and filled the honey jar and peeled carrots and onions and washed out the galley buckets and made bread crumbs and fetched cans of peas, tomatoes, and corn for Coco, and set up for lunch.

During lunch I couldn't peel, and then I had to do the dishes again. And when they were finished, I ate with Coco and Puppi who were talking about Roy, half the crew, and about Thor, their regular skipper, the one I met in the Empress, who was suspended because of Betty crawling around naked in port (that's why she's off now, said Coco, she knows Roy will watch every move she makes, just one wrong one and that's it, game over). So, anyway, here I am now on the poop deck of a rolly ship with a bucket of small, unpeeled, eye-studded potatoes between my legs, and a large cake tin on my lap for the peelings that every so often I dump over the side. On my right is an enamel bucket (which has a few peeled potatoes on the bottom) and is two-thirds full of water. I drop a white nicked peeled spud in it, pick up an unpeeled one and wonder how long it'll take me to get enough done for supper.

We are entering a wide bay, a huge curve in the sea's edge. There is a small clearing, far off. The light and land is golden surrounded by dark-green-Douglas-Fir-West-Coast-rainforest. The *Nootka* begins slowing down, and I get up to empty the peelings. The sea behind us turns white as the engine reverses, creating yards and yards of foam on huge (at least twenty feet high) slate green waves. Quite a way off is a long, open boat right on top of a wave. It slides down the wave, is hidden. Then something yellow, a blotch of red, and a bright green triangle disappear. The dot of yellow comes up first, then the large green and the smaller red. They seem to float above a wave for a moment or so, then they slide down, disappear again. In a few seconds they slowly come up a wave that is thirty maybe forty feet high. I cant quite figure it out – the yellow is above the other two, a toque or something? I really should be finishing these potatoes. I'm stalling, that's all I'm doing, putting off. I know what I'll do: I'll race to get them done before *they* get here. I pick up the box (knocked over by the ship's movements) and sit down on it to peel into the empty cake pan, faster, faster than before, but not fast enough. Wish they'd peel themselves.

Lefty comes out of the mess, stands over me, complains I didnt watch the kettle. If you're up, he says, you gotta keep checking the kettle. That's my job too? Sure, he says, it's everyone's – there wasn't enough water to make coffee. He chomps a raw onion sandwich made of raisin bread, butter, onion, HP Sauce. Where are we? I say suddenly. Near Clo-oose, gonna pick up a couple of Interports. A couple of what? Interport passengers. They'll get off at Bamfield. Well, I say hesitantly, why arent we moving? cuz it's too shallow – there's no dock – cant you see that? Oh, of course. He leaves and I peel several more potatoes. When I get up to dump the peelings, I see the cabinless, grey boat. It doesn't seem any closer. I think there is a kid in the middle, standing up of all things. I wonder what for. The yellow's more muted now, blunter. It's funny how sharp the light is on the coast, how suddenly it switches. I leave the railing and look in the enamel bucket – there's at least eight inches of the buggers ready – and I sit down and peel even faster than a few moments ago, yet I dont seem to be getting any more done because I keep missing spots. But finally, I finish and look over the side again. The boat's much closer – there *is* a kid standing wearing a yellow toque and there's a dog and a woman in a red sweater holding something and a man in a green jacket sitting near the motor steering the boat. The yellow and green against the green of the waves against the distant yellow and green of the land are like a Cézanne, but the sky is like a Carr.

I race into the galley to put the potatoes, etc. away, so I can go forward and stand near the winch to watch them come aboard. But as I turn into the passenger-officer lounge where the air smells of bleach and the chairs are all up on a bench ... Dont walk, I just washed it, screeches Puppi. I can barely see her head peeping out from the table end. Go above, go around. Okay, I say and turn back. Such a caw and such button eyes. I pass through the galley. Wonder why she's working on her time off. Pass through the mess out onto the deck and then up the ladder. Maybe it's the only time she can do it. Pass the sooty flag and the captain's quarters (hasn't come down to eat yet, said Puppi at lunch). Pass the back corner of the dark green wheelhouse. Then the front, all glass. Hal nods out at me from behind the huge wheel and a lanky, almost blond man smiles at me then quickly looks down at his clipboard. He opens the wheelhouse door, quietly introduces himself as Don, and when I ask him what he is, he tells me he's First Mate. He puts on a navy-blue cap and leaves to go down the ladder to the main deck.

I move to the corner and brace myself by holding onto the gritty pipes and keeping my legs apart, but my uniform rides/blows up; so while I support myself with one hand, I pull my skirt down and in between my legs with the other. Feet now together, I notice the men below have no trouble standing, and they arent even holding onto anything. Beebo and Jock are waiting by a stack of lumber near the edge of the hold and are talking. Lefty is leaning on part of the winch and is smoking a cigar. There's something different about them. I cant identify it, but I can see it in the way they are talking and the way Lefty's leaning – less belligerent, slightly subdued.

The boat is just a few yards off. The boy, around eight, is still standing even though the water's rough; the woman, slightly squat, sits, holds her baby. The three are Nuu-chah-nulth, strong high cheekbones, beautiful; they look proud and quite different from the Coast Salish People I grew up around. In front of the man are three cardboard boxes. He steers the craft alongside, tries to steady it and maintain position, but a wave smacks the side and the boat almost tips over. The kid doesn't move, just stands, looking ahead. The next wave looks like it's going to swamp them, but the man is able to turn the prow in time to face into it.

He shouts a word or two to Jock and Beebo, waves to Lefty and Don who tells Lefty something. Lefty starts the winch, winds the slings (two sets of wires with pipe bases like long, narrow seats of swings except that the wires all come together at the top) over to Jock and Beebo. Can you get on these, lass? Jock shouts. The woman looks up at him, says nothing. Jock then grabs both pairs of wires in separate hands and stands on the pipes. Lefty lifts him to show her how. Jock's arms are out in a high, loose, U-formation. He lets go of one set, does a fat little dance. I giggle at the jig, but the woman doesn't think it's funny and neither would I if I had to get on the slings. She talks excitedly to the man who can do nothing because he has to do everything he can just to keep his vessel upright and in the same position. She wont come, he shouts, she says she wont come.

Jock jumps onto the deck. He and Beebo quickly place a wooden loading flat between the metal pipes. Then Lefty winds the flat up, over the side, then very quickly jerks/drops it down. The loading flat (about five feet by four feet by six inches) swings over toward their boat and almost hits them. The boy falls, holding the dog's head down. The woman and man duck. Then it swings back over them again. When it comes toward them for the third time, the kid grabs it. Lefty tries to lower the flat to a position where they can step onto it, but a wave hits it from underneath. The man gestures with his head for the woman to get on. She wont. It's just not possible. I dont blame her. It isnt safe at all. She clutches her baby and stares stony-faced at her boy.

Then the boy grips one of the four wires. He swings/leaps up. Down. He's on. He scrambles to get near the centre of the flat, but another wave hits it and one side tips into the water. He holds onto a board. Goes down. Under. His little yellow toque floats on the green water, but he's still holding – I can see his finger – now his lower arm and shoulder. Finally (it must be all of six seconds but seems like minutes) Lefty manages to get the pipe on the other side loose. The loading flat then splashes into the water and floats. The boy pulls himself up onto it.

Beebo and Jock are yelling, keep down, keep down. The other pipe loosens itself as the flat floats away from it. The kid just lies there on the grey boards as the narrow pipe moves over him. Then the flat pushed up by a wave moves toward the *Nootka*. In a second or so, it smashes our side. Then it bobs back toward their little grey boat.

Hold on, shouts Beebo, dont panic, stay put. Lefty winds the empty slings up to Beebo who jumps onto them. Then Lefty winds them and Beebo up, over the railing, and down over the side. Down in the direction of the boy. The slings jerk as Lefty tries to position them right above the flat. Beebo swings above the kneeling boy once, then twice. Finally, with one hand holding onto the flat, the kid grabs the pipes near Beebo's foot. Beebo lets go of one set of wires and squats, reaches the boy and grabs him under the arm. He pulls and the kid scrambles from the boards onto the slings.

Beebo moves out of his crouch simultaneously trying to balance the slings, and the kid almost slips into a wave but doesn't. He moves to the end holding the wires in one hand and clutching Beebo's arm with the other while Beebo (maybe a hundred and sixty pounds or so) tries to redistribute his weight and change the almost-forty-degree angle of the pipes back to one hundred and eighty. Once the pipes are almost parallel to the ocean, Lefty slowly, very slowly, begins to wind the slings up. I look at the woman with the baby. She has almost no expression – she must be too frightened to show anything – I would be.

Finally, after what feels like five minutes, they clear the railing. Jock helps them, steadies the slings, then down they step onto the deck. The kid stands there, all wet, all smiles, listens to what Beebo and Jock say to him, looks over the side to his room or the woman I take to be his mom, and motions her to do what he did. She looks scared. The man keeps moving the boat back and forth, trying to keep it out from the *Nootka*, but close. The loading flat has drifted away.

The woman, the woman, what can they do? She sits there and waits as Beebo gets onto the slings again, is raised again, clears the side, comes down toward her. She looks at him, expressionless, doesn't move, doesn't say a thing. The man says something to her; she shakes her head. Beebo says something; the man translates. Still sitting, she clutches one set of wires, then, very reluctantly, leans forward to lift the blanketed baby up to Beebo who cradles it in one arm while he balances the slings and tries to steady them with his legs. She lets go and turns in the tossing craft. Beebo swings the pipes right under her bum. She grabs the wires with one hand, the pipes with the other, and sits on them. A wave strikes her feet as the slings swing out from the little boat. Two waves away, a much larger one is coming toward her. Beebo is trying to get the slings balanced and parallel for hoisting. The first smaller wave arrives, goes under her, then the next. Just two seconds before the large one is about to hit, Beebo manages to balance the pipes. Immediately, Lefty begins to hoist them up.

Red sweater. Frightened face. Arms rigidly clutching metal. She looks tiny against the sky and water, yet there is something powerful about her. Beebo, who also seems small, cuddles her infant. His leg/her shoulder press and brace against each other. The three are higher than the deck railing when a male voice close to me shouts, What do you think you're doing? Crew members *only* are to ride the gear. He's mad. That has to be the Skipper and he's really mad, but I dont have to look to tell that. Even though I've done nothing wrong, I disappear across the upper deck, down the ladder, along the side deck. He has a huge wart on his ear. A pug nose. A voice like my grade-four teacher's when he blew up at our class. Not a large man. I walk past where I was peeling potatoes, which seems like forever ago. He means it. Never again. Pass Coco's cabin. Mine. I dont go in. How does such an ordinary afternoon turn into this? I pass the canned-goods cupboard and engine-room entrance and step into the warm mess.

Coco's sitting there, legs upon the red bench, a white mug of coffee on the green table. What's happening? she says without removing her cigarette from her mouth. I ... the Captain's mad ... the guys tried to get the Interports on using a loading flat, but it got smashed by a wave ... this little boy crawled on it and almost drowned but he clung on and ... Slow down, she says, you're talking too fast. Relax, I'll get you a coffee. I follow her to the galley and hang there at the entrance. Dont want to leave or be left. I unpin my wet long hair as she bends over the black stove to pour fresh coffee into a mug. I feel like a little girl who's run home to Mommy. He means it. Never again. I knew, Coco says, *something* had happened when I saw the guys missed their mug-up – bet the old man had his finger in that. I guess so, I splutter (all I can see is the Captain's jaw and the woman's terror ... but now I know *why* Lefty was fussing about the kettle, the men wanted a mug-up while they were waiting for the boat). Coco, you should have seen the mother get on the slings. She had to stand up in their boat which was tilting back and forth with each wave almost rolling it over and she had to lean over and reach up to give Beebo her baby then she had to turn around with the boat going like this (my hands and fingers are stretched out as high and wide as they will go – it's as if I'm tossing a giant ball from arm to arm) and get the slings under her bum without even seeing them and ...

*He's here* at the galley entrance holding a little, black book. But Coco doesn't see him because she's watching my arms. I look directly beyond her shoulder at his squinty eyes. Coco, he says harshly. She turns to him with her mouth open. I stare at a pot of potatoes on the steel counter near the stove. Did you authorize the crew to exchange coffee for salmon? Yes, she says. He writes a note in his little book. (Now Coco's going to get it? My insides tremble and I look from the pot to her, not frightened or defensive, just standing like she always does in her galley.) That's not a regular procedure, he says. On this ship it is, sir. Bartering is not allowed, he says. But Captain, she explains, the salmon we get from the company's chandler is frozen and is never chinook or coho. Company policy, he says. We get the best here, she interrupts, and each pound of coffee is exchanged for three to four pounds of salmon. From now on, there's to be no exchange of ship's supplies for anything without my prior permission. Is that understood? Yes, sir, she says, but ... And it is only to happen when we are out of provisions, not as a normal procedure. Have I made myself clear? You have sir, she says. Do you have anything else to say? he asks. (I'd answer no if I were her but it's not my jurisdiction that's being questioned.) Yes, she says. What? Perhaps, Captain, when you've had some from the chandler you'll understand that for the company it's cheaper and for us much better to barter for the fresh. We're going by the book, he says, I understand Thor didnt and that led to difficulties. She doesn't say anything. He waits a moment for no answer and then leaves.

Just as Coco puts my coffee down on the mess table, we hear a voice behind us from the galley. Lady? We turn around: it's the Nuu-chah-nulth boy. Could I have some water for my mother please, lady? he says to me. Sure, I say and look at him, soaking wet, all muscle. Would she like coffee? Or tea? Just water, he says. And you? I ask. Nothing, he says, nothing now.

After I return to the mess, neither Coco nor I speak for a minute. She lights a Craven A and inhales. I sip hot coffee, my fingers enjoying the warmth of the mug. Could I get the Interports some towels and blankets? I ask. No, she says, that's Puppi's job – you start doing that and *you'll* be in trouble – not just with her but with *him*. I dont say anything for a second or so. Ray frightens me, I tell her, but I like the way you stood up to him. Thanks, she says, he's only doing a job. (I'm puzzled: she just accepts that?) He's got orders to clean up this ship, and he's going to use every rule and policy he can find to do it. Do you know what that means for us? she asks. No, I say. We just do *our* jobs – we dont let him control our time or ask us questions that are *none* of *his* business. That's why you didnt answer him? I ask. He's not going to hear any remark from me about Thor, *any*, and he wont hear anything from the crew either. If he asks me to pour him coffee? I say. He'll fetch his own, she says, flicking her ashes, that's our "regular procedure." We laugh lightly.

Did I do enough potatoes? I ask her. Plenty, she answers, I'll use what's left in the chowder tomorrow, but no sense wasting your time peeling them when they're under three inches. Now she tells me. I dont say anything. I didnt want to disturb her or wake her up to find out. The *Nootka* used to be a happy ship, she says. What did you hear about us around the union hall? Nothing, I say, but I was only there once. The *fun* ship, she says, but it seems some people dont like others having too much fun at work, you know what I mean? Yes, I say, but what happened out there just now wouldn't have been fun no matter who was here.

Sitting on your ass again, says Beebo, you women sure got a soft touch. He tousles my hair as he passes. Some trip this is going to be, hey kid, some first run for you. I cant believe it. Here I expected him to be grumpy and roaring around like Papa Bear, and here he is whistling in the galley as he pours himself coffee. I raise my eyebrows to Coco, who shrugs. Then Jock steps in, thumbs in suspenders which he snaps as he passes; he's not at all like an old man who's been told off by someone younger. Coco and I exchange a what's-going-on look (I-cant-guess; can you?) Lefty steps in packing a cardboard box which he holds down so Coco and I can see inside: a large salmon, silver-speckled on smoky-grey, rounded firm flesh with eyes that look alive/caught in a gesture. Twenty-five pounds, Lefty says as he opens it: white-orangy-coral, the most salmony salmon I've ever seen. A spring, Coco says, just beautiful. Her whole face glows, and Lefty struts into the galley to place the salmon on the stainless steel counter.

Beebo comes out, puts his mug down next to mine, flips out the end chair between Coco and me, and sits down with the back of the chair leaning against the table. What's up? Coco says. That son of a bitch thinks he knows what to do ... so we've decided to fix him ... we'll just do exactly what he says. What happened? says Coco. He's ordered us to use the gangplank no matter what. But how could anyone get on? I ask, how could *they* get on? They couldn't, Beebo says, you saw what happened to the flat when we tried. Jock comes in with a pot of tea, an empty mug, buttered bread. He has to squeeze behind Beebo in order to sit on the bench next to Coco, who has to slide over to Lefty's usual place to make room. There's no roads, Jock explains to me, the old lifesaving trail's through a rainforest and is no good for the sick; seaplanes cant land cuz it's too rough; small craft cant come in unless the swell is down.

She could die, says Beebo, as long as he follows his book. How is she? I ask. Sick, says Beebo, any fool can tell she's in pain, but there's a doctor comes to Bamfield, and they'll bring in a seaplane to get her to a city hospital if need be. He pours honey into his coffee and stirs it. I think she's going to make it, he says, but only cuz she's getting out in time.

Thought the big one slipped away, did you? shouts Lefty to Coco. He's standing at the galley entrance eating a sausage leftover from breakfast. I did, says Coco. Got to meet the Old Man when he came in here to tell me not to let you guys exchange provisions for salmon. Figured as much, says Lefty, Jack *gave* it to us after Ray left to check with you. You got a take on him? asks Lefty. Too early to tell, says Coco, sounds to me like he's from Nova Scotia. Maybe a plate of salmon will soften his heart?

Nothing will soften him, says Beebo, but we'll pack in the overtime if he insists on following every rule. Why? I ask, cuz I dont understand. It's this way, says Beebo, if he dont give us our mug-up when we're supposed to have it, we cant help it if a job takes longer than it should, can we? I nod yes, shake no. He could have let us have it early while we were waiting, Beebo says, then the company wouldn't have to pay extra. I'm still confused. The job didnt take us an hour, Jock says, but when we've missed the break we're entitled to we're already into overtime, and then when finishing up goes even five minutes into the next hour, we get another half-hour overtime, understand? Uh-huh? I say. Stick around, he says, you will.

You're wrong, says Lefty, the way I figure it is we usually mug-up around 2:30 but the contract says 3:00, so when we work straight through and we get it late, the only thing that's broken is our normal procedure. If he or the mate had waited till just before 4:00 then knocked us off, we wouldn't be getting any overtime for this afternoon at all. Bullshit, says Beebo, he's got to learn how we do things and that he cant order us to miss a break. Even Jan can see that we should have had the break while we were waiting.

While they're arguing, I lean over the table to get Coco's mug and then stand to fetch us more coffee. Grab us the contract, Jan, says Lefty. *In* the desk, lass, says Jock. I put down our mugs and open the drawer of the little wooden cabinet: an orange scribbler, an airmail-letter pad, a black book, a purple one, two seabooks, one *Sports Illustrated*, beneath them some white paper, stapled. This? I say as I pull it out and shove the others back. Yeah, says Beebo reaching his arm out to mine, that's it. He smiles. I give it to him. He holds it between his thumb and fingers. It's our Bible, by god, and the only one we got.

## 6. Nothing Is Simple

Setting up for supper is not nearly so slow as setting up for lunch or breakfast because by now I've learned how and dont make as many trips back and forth because I carry more into the mess and remember, for instance, to bring the ashtrays out before taking the butter there. It is really so simple, but then nothing is simple until you can do it, and what is not obvious to me might be obvious to someone else immediately, and what I can do, like making a tossed salad, someone else might find more difficult than, for instance, drying utensils, which Puppi says I do the hard way, and I must, because even though we have the same silver and she has twice as many people to dry for, hers is shinier and she's faster. Not that way, she said at lunch, dont even touch the handles, pick them up with the towel, like this, see? No, dont switch hands, the fewer motions the better.

Wow. I've got to get to the john and Coco has to, too; every five minutes or so one of us runs down below to check. Someone or two or three must be having a shower; or if it's a shit, they should give up; or, if people keep switching, we should have numbers like they do in the bakery on 41st, so at least one of us could get in. Not that I'd use the officers', but I would the male passengers' if it were free, but I'd really prefer the women's even though with six female passengers and three crew it's almost impossible to get in. I'm going to try again, says Coco, would you stir the gravy in a couple of minutes?

Sure, I say, as I place tomatoes about the edge of a full salad bowl, be glad to. The red on the deep green looks so good. I feel pleased, as if somehow I had something to do with the fact that the tomatoes are not watery and so red red. I complete three salads and put them away in the walk-in, one on top of a twenty-pound round of cheese with a clean cloth between it and a gallon of pickles used as a wedge, and two in the green box itself, held in by cabbages and celery. I remember, without being reminded. Dont assume anything will stay put, Coco said yesterday, even a mug on a counter in port can slip. I go to the gravy pot which is held in by metal bars which criss-cross the stove so that the pots wont slide off. The gravy has just started to scum; my sense of timing must be off, slower than it usually is. I skim then stir it with a whisk that is about five times as big as any I've seen in homes.

Lady. I turn around. It's the Nuu-chah-nulth boy wearing dry jeans. Could we have more water please, lady? Sure, I say and look directly at him. Are you sure your mother doesn't want tea or juice? Milk? Anything? Just water, he says. And yourself? I say as I shuffle the gravy pot to another section of the stove. Nothing, he says. What's wrong with your mom? We dont know; the doctor doesn't say. She's seen a doctor? Last year, lady. He sees my expression (last year! she's been sick for a year?) which I try to hide. I grab a plastic glass and run the cold water. She doesn't want to go to Bamfield, he says, she's afraid she'll have to fly to the city. That's too bad, I say, wishing I had more adequate words. I hope the doctor can help her there, but you tell her for me that flying in a seaplane will be much simpler than getting on this boat was. Sure, he says, lady, I'll do that. Hi, Coco says to him, I heard you had quite a scare getting on. No, he says to her, I wasn't scared at all, lady. You're courageous, I say, as I hand the water down to him, and so is your mother. Thank you, he says, excuse me.

What a nice kid, says Coco. Yes, I say, thinking damn it who taught him to say lady that way – just like ma'am, a European manner that doesn't belong here. Coco, do you think we can do anything for his mother? I dont know, she says as she begins to reshuffle the pots, check with Puppi first; hey, you better scoot down there before it's full again. Okay, I say, where is she? Must be in the women's, Jan.

I leave through the boys' mess, going outside even though it'd be quicker to go inside through the lounge. I have to run almost as we go up a wave. And then, when we slide down, I take tiny steps so I dont slip. Cape Beale lighthouse up ahead, Graveyard of the Pacific underneath. That enormous bluff might be the Execution Rock I've read about where invaders hurled locals hundreds of feet to the ocean below. As the air rushes past me, I imagine falling through it (limbs askew) toward the cold water and huge rocks.

I climb down the steep stairs and knock on the closed door: it's busy, Puppi shouts, use the men's. Puppi, it's me, can I come in? Wait a minute, she says, wait a minute. She opens the door and lays a piece of grey paper out on the deck for me to step on. *Sheisse* passengers, I just got the shithouse cleaned up and one of them had to get sick. Puppi is on her knees on the deck, wiping it with a rag. I step about her cuz I really have to go, and we talk while I pee. Cant even take a shower, she says, I cant even take a shower. Were *you* in here? I ask. No, she says, I use the men's you cant even get in here with all those passengers. Was it the Nuu-chah-nulth woman? I ask. No, no, she'd clean up her own, she'd do it herself. I just came out of the shower and this *lady* says to me, Puppi, Puppi, there's a mess in the washroom.

They shouldn't come on here if they cant hold their food, if you ask me. They come down here thinking it's an ocean liner or something; they shouldn't let them on; this isnt the *Queen Mary*.

I try to flush the toilet. Cant. The water in the bowl is on a slant. I stand there a few seconds then shout out, Puppi, it wont flush. I'll get it, she says, you go ahead. I come out, wait while she rinses a rag in the hand basin. Puppi, I say, do you know the Nuu-chah-nulth woman's sick? Yuh, yuh, I know, she says, there's nothing I can do. I told her when she arrived she could use my cabin. Wouldn't she? Oh no, she's too proud, her boy explained to her, she understood, but she wont put anyone out. She's not like some of these passengers with their airs. And she *is* sick, you can see for yourself she's sick. I wash my hands and there's nothing to dry them on so I use my apron. Anything I can do to help you? I ask Puppi. No – but – you can cut my butter, she says, if you have the time. I'll be there as soon as I change. Dont you worry about me, Puppi always gets her work done, Puppi always ... she looks up and smiles, understands that I only wanted to help. Okay, Poops, see you up there. And I leave.

I go up the dark stairs and glance at the Cape Beale lighthouse, step through the hatch into the lounge, pass the long table to my right, the metal cabinet on my left, see half the woman at the other end, her head erect, lips clenched; the other half is blocked by bulkhead. I'd like to go ask her if there's anything I can do, but what would I say? How are you feeling, that would be silly! What *could* I do? Nothing, I guess. I go into the galley and Coco says, you about ready? Almost, I say, I'm going to cut Puppi's butter, and, and, oh the boys' salad. There it is on top of the clean draining board with a damp rag under it. I forgot to put a rag there so it wouldn't slip. Coco's done it for me. You finish the salad, she says, I'll cut the butter, then we'll have a mug-up. Thanks, I say, I'm sorry I didnt think about ... It's okay, she says, you're doing really well, you're catching on. Thanks, I say, pleased.

I slice two large tomatoes while she fetches butter, then I place them about the edge of the bowl in a circle. Looks delish, she says as I pass her to put it away in the boys' fridge, I think I'll have some later. Thanks, I say, flushed with pride as I open the little door, place it on top of the grapefruit-juice cans, wedge it in with the water and milk jugs. Ready? Coco shouts from the galley; sure, I answer as I return, but I think I'm going to ask her if she wants more water first. Offer her anything, Coco says, as she pours a second mug of coffee, I'll be in the boys' mess.

I pass the stove and turn left toward the woman. She's sitting on one of the padded seats; her baby is lying, sleeping, across her thighs. She doesn't know I'm coming to her until I'm close; then she looks at me, and I can see she has no front teeth. Her eyes look itchy like the surface could be blown away almost, but her hair, her bones, the way she wears her flesh, beautiful, so composed. Would you like more water, I say, or cold juice? She turns her head, the muscles so proud, and her son who is outside must sense it, comes in from the deck. Can I bring your mother anything? I say. He turns to her, asks, she looks up at me and says very quietly, no. She just wants to be left alone, he says, but thank you, lady, thank you. Okay, I say, when you want anything, just come ask. I will, lady, thank you. I smile at him, so certain of himself, and at her, and leave.

In the galley Puppi, a cracker in her mouth, is getting side plates and cups and saucers out for supper. (They use cups on her side even if the officers prefer mugs.) I step around her and notice how she packs so much at once, and she notices me noticing and smiles. In the mess, Coco's sitting on the bench with her legs up on a chair. She didnt want anything, she says, I didnt think she would. I sit and have just one sip of coffee before we hear the men on the deck above us. Coco scrambles out and I quickly put the crew's milk, water, and salad out on top of green rubber mesh so they wont slip. Where's my salads? shouts Puppi from the galley, you made me salad, didnt you? Yes, I say and go to the walk-in. I couldn't see them, she says as she stands right behind me, Betty always puts ... Here you are, I say (Betty, Betty) and pass the two from the cabbage-celery box out. Ahh, she says, pret-ty, but that's too much. It is? I didnt know how much to make. That's all right, you never can tell. Puppi takes them. The officers dont eat any, she says, except for The Chief. I dont say anything about having a fourth large one ready. I just stand near the sink and Coco hands me the kettle to fill. Dont worry about it, says Coco, we'll just heave what's left over. Over, I think as the water splashes into the kettle top, but you never can tell. How do *we* get some service around here? shouts Lefty.

Be right there, I say, as I pass Coco the kettle. I tighten my apron as I step into the mess. Beef and beef, he says, what type of menu is that? Huh. Is the roast rare? I dont think so. You know it isnt, he says. Are the sausages burned? I dont think so, I say. But you dont know, he answers. Uuh. Tell you what, he says, slice me some bologna and cut pepper and onion for Buck and me. Okay, I answer. And a plate, he says. Of course, I say. Well, you dont think I'm going to eat on that? he says pointing to his side plate. No, I say, but dont you want any, any vegetables? You kidding? he says, I'm eating that salad.

I leave him and go to the walk-in, bring out the bologna, three onions from a SunRype can, one pepper, then start cutting on the wooden counter edge which faces the mess (Beebo's just come in), but I'm slow and it's so misshapen and ... what's Lefty having? says Coco. I guess it's a cold plate, I answer, he ... five beef, hold the corn on two, no spuds on one, shouts Puppi. Five beef, two no corn, one no spuds. I get the meat cut and go into the mess because by now Hal and Buck are there also. Here you are, I say to Lefty, I'll get the rest ... I just want a plate, says Beebo, and some cheese. Roast, potatoes, and gravy, says Hal (as Lefty holds a ragged piece of bologna up) and could I have tea please? Yes, I say, giggling about the bologna, and you? Two sausages with nothing else and tea, says Buck. Nothing for Beebo, I say to Coco, roast with potatoes and gravy for Hal, two plain sausages for Buck. Beef no veg, she says, small order sausages only. I slice the pepper and onions, arrange them on a plate, pick up the two orders, and take them in.

What's the holdup? says Beebo, could you bring me a plate please? Sure, I say. That's not enough onion, says Lefty. I run back out, grab a plate for Beebo. Two sausage the works, says Puppi; two sausage, answers Coco, I take Beebo his plate and am slicing more onions when Jock comes in, but I finish first and take them out before ... any more salad, me love, shouts Jock. What? (I look – just half a cup left) sure, I say, pleased as can be, I have another one. Single slice of beef, he says, potato, no gravy, nothing else. Yes, I say, and run to the galley. I haven't got Beebo's cheese yet and the tea. A single slice of beef for Jock, I say, no gravy, nothing else. Beef only, she answers, small portion. I open the walk-in, hook it open to the bulkhead, lift what was to be Puppi's salad (even though she didnt know about it) and the block of cheese, put them on the wooden counter, unhitch the door, shut it, and take the salad to the men.

You forgot something, says Jock. Oh, I say, I'm sorry, and Coco *had* put his beef on the counter right next to the salad. I step into the galley, grab it off the counter, and hand it to him. Then, finally, back to the cheese. But I have to wash the knife because of the onions and ... More salad, says Puppi, I ran out of salad. Oh, I say, both pleased and flustered, I can make you some once I get the men served, but ... No rush, she says, the rest haven't come yet, but I'm out – this *never* happens with Betty's.

Quickly, I try to slice cheese from the block and it keeps breaking when I do it too thin but the knife gets stuck when I do it thick. I show you, see? says Puppi. She holds the top of the knife with both hands, uses her red-nylon-aproned middle to steady the cheese on the counter (I cant do that with all the guck on my apron), and cuts a slice that is well over a quarter of an inch thick. She wipes the knife, does another, and then another. Poops, someone's waiting, says Coco. I just stand there watching. Puppi cuts the three into fours. See? Yes, I say, thank you, thanks Poops.

I take the cheese in, and Jock wants more milk and Beebo some plums and Lefty coffee, and I still haven't made the tea. Then with Puppi filling the milk jug from the ten-gallon can and giving me plums she has dished out in advance, and with Coco pouring coffee, and I making tea, everything in some way gets done. And I start to make another large salad, able, at least, to do that, simply, on my own, but not fast.

## 7. Ucluelet

Dont get lost, says Lefty as I step up onto the gangplank to get off at Ucluelet. I wont, I say. Are you sure, he says, we dont want you getting picked up by a fisherman. Sure, I'm sure, I say and keep going. Jan, bring us back a couple of cold ones will you? says Beebo as I step off the gangplank. I'm not going to the pub, I answer. Make that one for me too, eh? shouts Ken, yummy-bodied Ken, who is standing, one jean ripped at the knee, just a few feet down the dock. You have to pass it, says Beebo, if you're going to go anywhere.

As Beebo talks, a load is swinging down from above and Hal is steering the empty towmotor over. I step out of the way of both. Hal jerks the machine, fast. It halts right next to me. For a second I'm startled but come to quickly, laughing slightly, and Hal catches my look, smiles; we're together a moment, and then I watch Ken and Beebo stretching up to touch the underside of the loaded flats. I can see all of Ken at first, his eyes dazed almost (like sometimes in bed) there but not there, his long chest and shoulder muscles pressing out from under a many-coloured T-shirt. He and Beebo grab the boards and slowly Ken's outstretched arms and face disappear behind the load, then his shoulders, his chest, a four inch strip of tanned skin between his shirt bottom and belt, his hips; boxes of canned pears, sacks of potatoes, bales of wire come between us, and then suddenly, on top, I see his overgrown crewcut and blue eyes.

How about it? shouts Ken over the load. I dont feel like it, I answer as Hal shifts gears then centres the prongs and jerks them in, under, through the flats. C'mon Jan, says Beebo. I glance into his curliness, turn up to Hal who half smiles. He backs the towmotor, fast, turns it, heads toward the edge of the wooden shed which is part of the dock and the green Ford truck there. Everyone will be too busy to notice, says Beebo as Ken wanders over to me. Why not? Ken asks. I'm afraid. Of what? he says, getting caught by the skipper? I dont look at him, feel my face tighten, look over to Beebo. Forget it, Beebo says, we were only teasing.

I walk toward the ramp feeling their eyes follow me, not just Ken's and Beebo's, but Hal's also, and those of the Second Mate, Chuckles, and the three men from town who are loading a Ford truck. I try to ignore them, notice my work shoes, feel the boards of the dock almost slap my feet cuz they dont move like the *Nootka* does. Only a few yards more, but getting there, like walking through a corridor in high school, takes so long. And even when they're not looking, I feel the weight particularly of Hal's eyes, so centred, so certain, and Ken's, lighter, but knowing me in a way I dont like to be known. Because he has made love with me, he can make me feel awkward, not consciously, but he does it without thinking and in some ways that's worse, damn him.

I kick the damp dirt that covers the long, wooden ramp and glance up at the shining village: a curved slope which slants down; the crest, all covered in bush, is almost directly up from where I am; the buildings, their tops, some of the sides standing out through the green, are either over and down to the left or over and slightly down to the right; and the wet street, its blackness, runs at an angle from the ramp. I feel like I'd like to slide up over it, to fly through the cut it makes, to touch the fir tips, the unpainted fence, even the shaggy poles as I pass. Just as I start to run, a guy behind me on the dock shouts: watch out for the bears! The what? I say as I turn to the men beside the truck. The bears, says the Nordic one in an open green shirt, the woods are full of them. Okay, I shout back, I was going to stick to the road anyway.

I turn and again start to walk up the ramp. Bears, he's gotta be kidding, that's the type of thing my Uncle Andy used to say, only it was cougars. The village seems more distant now and on a clearing high up to the right, the last of the sun makes a side window of a tin-roofed shack shine gold; but since it wont be dark for another half-hour or so, I've nothing to worry about, and besides that I've never been afraid of the dark or woods anyway.

I stop and lean on the railing for a moment, pick off a wet splinter, stick it in my mouth. I glance up at the gold window again and wonder about the people who live there, then turn to the water, the fishboats, a bobbing Coke tin. The boats, a few yards down the bank, are mostly white on top. Their poles form almost a forest as they sway, well over a hundred, above their bodies, the ships, the floats. The forest of white seems almost suspended there, the reflection, the extension of it, nonexistent because the land forest and hill cut off the light, create a water/earth/tree darkness of their own. I pull the splinter out from between two back teeth but part of it sticks so I poke it with a piece of fingernail as I watch two men fixing an engine in one of the boats. Then, I make out five guys drinking/yakking/listening to a radio. One of them whistles up and they all look or shout or say something, but I cant hear what because of the distance and the *Nootka*'s noise, so I smile and start going again.

Ahead, on the right, there's a general store and old vine-covered house; then there's a curve in the land and everything else is the woods as far as I can see. I take a deep breath of salt-fish-boat-motor air and start to run. The first thing I notice when I step off the ramp onto the paved road or main street is how hard it seems; it feels as though the blacktop comes up to smack my feet rather than feet going down to meet it. I take four steps just to feel the hard surface then move off onto the dirt shoulder, past the library, which is new, just like any stucco building in Vancouver, but it has orange and yellow flowers growing haphazardly in its garden, and the grass hasn't been cut recently so in that way it's better even though the windows are aluminum-framed and not nearly as attractive as the high criss-cross ones of the general store on my right. The store needs paint, but the light on what used to be is perfect; the store has a slow not-too-many-people-go-to-it-anymore look, but obviously, at one time, it was the main building in town. Maybe that's why the library garden looks okay – they didnt take it up and redo it all in rows – they must have just taken down a house and built the library on the land.

I pull out a piece of couch grass, suck the yellow-green tip, wonder what it was Hal said about rows. I guess he didnt, I just thought he did when he was talking about the guys not being able to keep a shore job, and I saw the city then all in straight lines and rectangles, the people moving evenly on the surface of its streets, no ragged indents, like here. Ahead, a little monument of some sort stands on my right, covered in salal and alder, and on my left, just ahead, the government liquor store, recessed back, not in line. It's closed, of course; it's past six. I step up onto the cement sidewalk; the Ucluelet Lodge, a two-storey ochre-coloured building, is flush against it.

The smell of French fries and coffee comes into my nose as I pass the beauty parlour at the bottom end. White sheets cover the chairs. And next, the café, licensed; several men (the only woman in it is the waitress) are eating and drinking and two teenage boys, more dressed up than the others, are leaning on the jukebox smoking cigarettes. They're not really dressed up; they both have on tight jeans, their shirts are ironed carefully, tucked in just so, and their hair has been combed toward the centre with parts on both sides like it didnt take just a minute to do it and definitely there was a mirror. I scurry past the windows of the empty lobby to the corner where the men's entrance to the pub is, look up at the hill, want to get out somehow, up there – the tip's only a block and a bushy half away – but dont for some reason. I turn, look down the angled road. I cant see the dock, just the edge of the ramp and the lights. I find myself going left, walking rapidly, not thinking about the men or the beer or Ken or anything at all.

Between the chunks of gravel there's a piece of coloured glass. I stoop, pick it up, roll the blueness in my palm. After a moment or so, I come out of the stoop and am right in front of a half-wooden, half-glass door. I step up to it, look through the thick-filmed glass; a big-bellied man is leaning over, doing something to someone who's sitting there; walls which arent walls, I cant figure it out. I turn the brass knob. Open it slowly. Walk in. The men dont look up. The two of them, one a barber, seem to hang there in a cubicle near the front on the right, while in the back, far to the left, pool balls bump each other. There's a closed Coke machine a few feet in front of me and stacks of empty pop cases and beer cartons form almost a wall to my immediate right. I watch the big-bellied barber, whom I guess collects the empties to sell later, slowly shave the old man with one of those long straight razors.

I step toward the pop cooler while looking at the two of them, and neither notices me. The barber dips his razor in an oval enamel bowl; he wipes it with a cloth, then holds the old man's head as he shaves. I glance to the counter on the left; behind it is a wall with one shelf covered in stuff: dice, cards, Oh Henrys, Jersey Milks, Player's tobacco, and three bags of stale popcorn stapled to a card which originally held twenty or more. To the sound of the balls, I open the pop machine and no one says anything – the barber keeps shaving and the men in the back move. Rather than see any of them, I look down into the metally water: ginger beer, 7 Up, Mandalay Punch, Coca-Cola, ginger ale, Orange Crush. I cant decide. Maybe I'm not supposed to be in here at all.

I look up at the beam in front of me. On a poster for a dance last month, there's a girl I recognize from high school who looks tougher now. I look down again, cant get over it, here, her, and one of the guys I used to play in a dance band with. I pick up the ginger ale – he must be no more than twenty-one and it's his band now – not Canada Dry but Nanaimo Bottling Works, much browner, the taste more full, I used to love it, but I hesitate, see that no one's watching, put it back, pick up the Orange, maybe this place *is* for men only, not Orange Crush but Mission, better than Crush; I place it on the metal opener but just before I open it, I stop, hold it, the cold wetness, dont know what the rule is if there is one about pool halls, see the lime rickey, not the green stuff but the ouzo white which came out first. My god, they got every choice here, three I really want.

I look up at the barber. Maybe I'm taking too long. I assume he's the owner. He hasn't got on a white frock but a blue shirt with little red hairs coming through the splits where the buttons just hold over his belly. He's shaven the right side of the wrinkly brown face of the old man and is just beginning the left; probably doesn't even know I'm here yet, or, if he does, he's in no hurry. Well, the whole place is in no rush for that matter, kinda nice, so unlike the city. I can almost see the whole front section of the poolroom; after a man hits the ball, he picks up another stick, chalks it, and the other stand around while he takes another shot. I start to open the orange again, but don't, put it back, pull out the lime rickey and open it. No one, not one person, has said one word.

I begin to go toward the barber but don't. Instead, I swallow sharp lemony-lime and delicate other tastes, I wander to the counter to the sound of bumping billiards and stand there, looking: chuckwagon stew, just two cans; handkerchiefs in dusty cellophane; rabbits' feet, four left on a faded card, a light brown. I drink my pop, look at the green metal light shade over the billiard table. The young kid is now shooting, is that what they call it, I dont know, anyway he has the cue and after he hits the balls with one ball the other men stand away while he gets ready for another shot. A skinny-legged spider skitters over nail clippers to one of the wooden crib-boards that lean upright from the shelf to the wall. I finish drinking and put the bottle down on the counter, wander over to the window, look at the dead flies on the sill, try to see out, there's nothing, turn slowly, and the barber smiles, comes over to me, belly jiggling, and I place silver in his wet hand which has a dab of foam on the index finger. He takes the money, puts it in his big-flied pant pocket, and I say thank you and leave. The old man is still in the chair and still has not moved one bit. Mine were the only words spoken during this entire time.

I close the door softly and run in the darkness, where to, I dont know, along a dirt road, down a dirt lane. Bushes, grass, trees on the side. The *Nootka*'s engine and winch throb and whine louder and louder; wherever I am, I am getting closer to her, can hear her. The branches and leaves are shaking/trembling. Funny I feel no breeze, only the motion past my body, and ahead, through the darkness, there's a gulley, a clearing, maybe water moving. I come out of the bush the lane must have led to and there is a small opening; that is, the trees stop and there's a trail ahead where they start again. I'm too far to the right, that's it, over there up the dip must be the library, but if I just keep going, surely this will lead me to it, the water, at least a moment ago I thought I saw it, and once I get there I can always get out, follow the shoreline that is. So I take the trail through the trees, which again leads down, fast, it's sharp, I hold onto the salal, drop, catch my balance, lead more carefully this time with my right foot, get the feel of the rock first, then come down to it by clutching the wet roots and letting go once my foot knows where it is.

My left foot feels out through the dark wetness and again my hand clutches salal. I slide, land, and here I am surrounded by bush, and the ship's racket is loud, very close, but no light in this dense foliage. I grope out with my hands, touch wet prickly branches which drip on my skin, stoop, feel for an opening. And there is one, a thin slit, which I crawl through, not far, but scratchy. Stairs, there are stairs. I stand at the top of them for a moment just breathing as my hands do my long hair up. Then I start to walk down, to go toward the engine throb. No railings and my leg, my skirt are caught in thorns, a blackberry branch. I try to lift it to disentangle, step closer, as my right hand holds the thick branch, my left pulls the skirt out thorn by thorn. I slowly move it with both hands, pass it, take two steps, let it fall back and suddenly, below me, I hear other branches and water.

The branches are getting louder. For a moment, I just stand there. The best thing to do, my dad always said, is stay put, dont move at all. I do, try to, my blood swoops to my centre, and I try not to make noise as I gasp, gulp the air.

In a moment, I realize it is someone not something on the steps: thank god. Whoever it is, is coming up. I try to say, hi there. But I cant because nothing comes out. In a moment, there he is, a cowboy-belted young man just three steps away. Whatya doin' here? he asks. I just look down at him and he stops, waits for my answer: I, I, I'm trying to get over there. I point. Wanta have a drink? he says, I'll show ya. No, I say, can you, can you tell me how to get to the dock? I wont try anything, he says, I promise. I, I got lost, I say as I turn around then start to lift the blackberry vine again. Let me do that, he says as he brushes against my bum and back. I step down and he gets the branch while I still feel his touch and the motion through me. We dont have to be alone, he says as I come up to him, I'll get my buddies so we're not alone, you dont have to worry about that. No, I say as he lets me pass, you dont understand, it's nothing to do with you at all. I look at the step. I, I just have to get back. You sure got in the wrong place, he says as he lets the branch go. It makes a heavy crashing sound with light whips as the leaves cut through the air.

I know that, I think as I step off the last stair. Just go that way, he says as he comes up from behind me, it'll take you there. Uuh, thank you, I say as I turn and sorta smile but not really cuz I'm scared and gotta get going. Thank you, I say again and just leave him there standing on the top stair as I head back. Sure you dont want me to come with you, he says. No, I say, I'm all right, I know where I am now, but thanks, I say as I step over a log, thanks a lot, I say to his outline, the face non-distinct, the body masked. And I turn/run along the narrow path, tall couch grass on its sides, no lights yet but the alder's getting thinner. The library, ahead I can see the library. I dont think (a light, a clouded light through the trees) I'd want to (it's at the end of the ramp) do that again. Suddenly, the trees stop and above the shed there's the *Nootka*'s light. I pause on the widening path, the *Nootka*, her light, my ship.

FRIDAY

*Washrooms*

Adequate washrooms and lavatories shall be made available for the unlicensed personnel of each division, washrooms to be equipped with a sufficient number of shower baths which shall be adequately equipped with hot and cold water. A sufficient number of buckets shall be supplied for washing clothes.

# 8. A Single Scrambled

Short stack with sausage, Puppi calls; short stack with sausage, Coco answers, right up. Two in the water, five minutes; two in the water for five. Bacon and over easy; bacon and over easy. I'm not quite awake yet, but then I never am awake until two or so hours after I get up. Somehow, dont ask me how, I've managed to get the overnight dishes washed with a minimum of confusion by doing them the easy way as Puppi calls it, that is stacking all similar things such as dinner plates and doing them in a pile right in the washing sink, lifting that pile to the rinsing sink, taking it out, placing a bowl on the long steel counter with its damp, but not too wet, terry towel on it so the crockery wont slip off and alternating the pile of plates – one plate slightly left, one slightly right, and so on – so they dry by themselves. Poached on two; poached on two. There isnt even a real sink plug, just a copper pipe that I place a rag over the end of and stick in the hole. Single sunny side and; single sunny side and. Puppi's feeding the passengers early and the officers as they come; but there's no boys, as Coco calls them, because it's the second day out and they still have hangovers or portovers and wont, she says, feel like much, just coffee and toast.

Single scrambled. Single what? Single scrambled – single scrambled, for Chuckles. I cant scramble a single egg. Single scrambled, Puppi retorts as she struts into the galley, hands on flat hips, stands behind Coco. I know *you* cant, but the Second Mate wants a single scrambled, Puppi caws. She turns, butters two pieces of toast on the wooden counter, slices them rapidly, leaves. Bastard, Coco says, and cracks two eggs into a soup bowl, adds water from the tap. *Whoever heard of a single scrambled?* she says loudly enough for everyone on the other side of the bulkhead to hear. Did you? she asks me, then takes a drag from her cigarette, which sits on a glass ashtray between the vanilla and salt. I dont answer because she doesn't expect me to. As Coco pours the eggs into a light frypan that she grabs from beneath the rinsing sink, I see a gapped-tooth sour-looking man come up behind her. I have, Chuckles roars, my wife has, every idiot except you has. *I want a single scrambled egg.* Coco slams the pan onto the stove without turning to him. And that is what you'll get, she says, now look what you've made me do: a little glob of egg slowly solidifies on the grill.

I'm supposed to be peeling a potato, not a potato, but a bucket full of potatoes; anyway, I get back to the particular one that has deep eyes all over it. I try not to look at Chuckles whose thighs are only a few inches from Coco's uniform-covered bum or at Coco who is scraping the egg off the stovetop with exaggerated energy. I put the finished potato (what's left of it) into an enamel bucket half-full of cold water, pick up another spud. He hasn't moved. She flips pancakes. Stack with bacon; stack with bacon. Bacon and over easy; bacon and over easy. How come it's not cooking? he roars. It'll cook when it cooks, Coco answers.

Jan, pass us two coffee will you? Who's that? I hold onto the half-peeled potato and look at Chuckles. Then I go to the mess entrance – no one's here. One black, one with both. I heard that voice at supper last night. Chuckles looks at me as if to indicate I'm just as stupid in my way as Coco is in hers; then he flicks his head just slightly toward the ceiling. Above the centre of the galley is a hatch which lets in the light. I move toward the stove so I can look up and see whoever it is because he's standing on the mess side of it and what with the angle and such I have to lean against the steel counter. Outta my way, outta my way, shouts Puppi. Sorry Poops, I wasn't thinking. She whizzes past me from behind. Chuckles leaves. I should know better than to back up without looking. Through the hatch, I see a bald head fringed in black hair framed by the white hatch made sharper by a rippling plaid shirt – it's Buck, the guy on the four-to-eight watch. Okay, I say, I didnt know where you were. I go to the mess entrance where the mugs are behind wooden slats (so the crockery doesn't get broken) and there's Puppi again, coming out of the walk-in this time. I press to the wall so she can pass and then Coco pulls herself closer to the stove so Puppi can pass, out, out of the galley.

I hold onto both mugs as Coco pours and gives me a Puppi's-in-one-of-her-moods look. I shout up to Buck, what do you want in them? Black and both. Just a minute, I shout – of course, he did tell me, funny I forgot. Hurry on the scrambled, will you? shouts Chuckles as I pour cream into one mug. Puppi runs in to pick up three orders and Coco says, Puppi, when you go out will you tell that man for me that I cant cook it any faster, tell him *I am not the stove*. Too much cream. I pass the black one up first. A long-fingered hand with a gold and jade ring takes it. Then I pass the white. Part of it spills as I hand it to him. Thanks, Buck says, see you at eight. Who's the other one for? I ask. The Skipper. Are you just behind the wheelhouse? Yes.

Eeeruh-eeeruuuhhhh, dirty, dirty! screeches Puppi. She jumps away from the coffee spots as if they're a disease or something and points her thin muscly arm at them – dirty. I grab a roll of paper towel and simply wipe them up. Such a production. When she comes back in, I look at her. Her eyebrows go right from her nose through all the folds right into her hairline. She squiggles them. I smirk and that aggravates her eyebrows/her whole body more.

*Ready on the scrambled*, Coco says, Puppi, *His Highness's egg's ready*. Puppi picks up the dinner plate with the egg and leaves with it without toast. Coco says, Jan, do you want to eat this? Yellow-gold-brown scrambled half the portion, still in the pan.

## 9. Tulips

Slow. Everything is so slow. I dampen the rag to put under the just-cleaned galley bucket which is actually an oil tin and wring the old shirt out slowly as my body sways, as the ship does, gradually to the right. Then, at the base of the wave, as we start to roll back, I move my left foot, which is holding the bucket in the corner, grab the handle to pick it up, and with my leg muscles pulling/pushing to hold me there, as quickly as I can, which is not very fast, I lay the rag out so that the empty bucket will stay put. The *Nootka* lurches as she starts up the wave, jerks against it, jabs. I brace myself by holding the sink edge and, finally, we're there. She seems to stay steady just a moment at the top of it, then she and I roll to the right, smoothly, no jerks, slowly, we slide down. The cardboard (from a McGavin's bread box) behind the bucket is dirty, has peas and mush and gravy and fat all over it. The stomach inside me is bloated; chunks of egg and pancake seem to float in a watery world of their own. The air around me is heavy, is led with smells: clam chowder, coffee, and diesel oil.

As we roll to the left, I bend to pick up the cardboard in order to switch it around. We lurch. A mushy pea almost hits my eye and my head swings over as I breathe the disinfectant I used to clean the bucket. Clams, there are so many clams. A clump of hair falls down my wet uniformed back and sticks there as, finally, I do turn the cardboard around. There arent any more clean pieces cuz Ken and I threw them all over as garbage the first night out. And the way I feel I dont really care, but I guess I do care or I wouldn't have thought about it. I turn toward the mess with my right hand on the walk-in door for support. If only, if only I could breathe without smelling. My damn stomach wants to take over as if I'm just a part of it. I take a step toward the mess, hold on to the white wood that the cups are behind, and my belly which is so tight and huge seems to press up, up to my lungs.

I nip, gulp the air with my mouth so I wont have to smell.

There are runny footprints all over the mess deck. It's as wet as I am: it, because I just washed it a few minutes ago and some damn fool must have come through; and I, because it's raining and I took the garbage buckets out to clean them with the hot scrubbing water (and disinfectant and a toilet brush), which took me longer than I thought it would because of the lurching and rolling. I wouldn't have washed the deck if I had known. Christ, that's easy to say. But just who would walk on a clean wet deck? I watch a footprint close to me spread into a grey puddle. Then I step into/onto it myself, and Jock's there in the corner smiling with a mug in his hand.

You feel okay, lassie? he says. I'm all right, I say as my hand grabs for the blackboard, I just gotta get (the ship rolls and I slide to the table) used to it. He looks at me. Even though I want to say something, I cant. I feel very conscious of my wet scattered hair, and I'm concentrating to keep my stomach down. My guts swirl as I look at a skin graft and an indent on his forehead. Smooth, the skin's so smooth and unreal. I move from the deadness. I'll be right back, I say as I edge myself along the table and chair, as soon as I get changed. Dont drink anything, he says, that's the worst thing you can do if you feel sickly. Okay, I say as I turn to the door and almost fall as the *Nootka* rolls, just as I step out into the wind/rain. Jock starts whistling "When You Wore a Tulip," and I shut the door on that.

Tulip. I cant imagine ever having seen one in my life. That black acrid earthiness comes to me as I step along the deck holding the wet white bulkhead which has nothing sticking out for support, but even so it feels safer than nothing and it's just three slippery steps to my cabin which is first on the left, but the ship's jerking the other way, and the door's hooked open. If only I can ... I do reach/clutch it as the *Nootka* jabs her way up to the top of the damn wave. I remember taking the heads off of tulips once. I dont know how old, less than four, on a Sunday morning in a neighbour's yard before anyone was up to stop me. I played in my pajamas. Someone with thick legs took me home, and later there were several other legs – several voice talked and laughed in a small room that smelled of biscuits. My mother didnt laugh. She kept saying, but she tore every tulip.

Finally, the *Nootka* starts righting herself, and I step into my cabin in that second (that only second of stillness) that there is both at the top and then at the bottom of a wave. Diesel fumes and sweaty nylons come into me as I forget to breathe through my mouth, and my tits are soaked, are hard, hurt as they tighten even more than they were, two solids above the huge one, my stomach. My hip hits the sink as I go to grab the towel. Damnit. I just cant get used to the motion. The towel is coarse and thin and splotched with lipstick. Even the big one is smaller than any I have at home. Prickly cloth around my neck. Nothing soft here. I take out the hairpins which are hardly holding anything and flick my hair down in front of me into the sink. Nothing like flower petals. I wrap the towel around my head and my belly floats up as the ship does. The chunks, I can feel those chunks. Damn. I see poached yolks Jock had for breakfast, hard little pale things with only scraps of white cuz they cooked too fast.

   I move my head, which is heavy, solid, up and make a turban, each fold tight, and breathe (if only I could) deeply, but the air so surrounds, doesn't want to go in, the diesel/foot/leather smells so distinct, each so here, and besides that my tits hurt, no matter what I do they hurt. With my feet as solid as they can be on the deck, I slowly start to unbutton my uniform. My feet, my breast, my leg muscles, my stomach, my head, even my fingers are all parts of me, I know it, yet they all seem so separate, have feelings and motions of their own even while caught in the larger overall motions of my body and the ship. My fingers are down to the third button and all the front, except right under my bust, is wet through, the white not white as the brown-pinkness of my skin sticks to it. Then, down my top dips as my swirly insides meet my midriff. My head drifts up, surfaces. What can I do with my wet uniform? Where can I hang it? Pieces of egg seem to float through the room, sulphur. I burp, not vomit, just burp.

   I dont really know, and I wish this were over and I dont really care and I ... What a pretty-plump bum, Ken says. Is it, I turn still holding the limp material on my right arm as if I were a hanger, *him*? The ship lurches and my left foot doesn't hold so the other foot skitters/falls quickly to the cabin door where he isnt in the slit it leaves when hooked open. Am I hearing things? My head turns and seems to pull up, up, itself pulling/surfacing to bunk level. My shoulders emerge and my eyes open out of a dive. And Ken *is* there, head through the open porthole like a stuffed moose cut off from me and framed by the circular green metal. His eyes are motionless, glass-like, blue petals. They see but dont see as I seem to swim over and up to him.

   How are you making out? his voice says. His eyes enlarge, tulips opening. I, okay, I answer as we start to fall down a wave, and I try to cover my tits with the uniform but cant because I cant brace myself in since we're listing the other way. Okay, I say. A lot better, I think, if you'd just bugger off and not scare me. Jan, he says, Jan. I hold onto the top bunk and back up from him. Would you please go? I say. He smiles in that little-boy-caught way of his. See you at mug-up he says. Then the air is there. The big moose gone. Empty water moving on the pane. I feel giddy all of a sudden. Naked. As we start to move up the wave, I throw myself onto the bottom bunk, curl, hold the pillow in one hand and the wooden bunk edge in the other, laugh almost cry, see his eyes so liquid, floating alone. Our lips kiss as we stand on an open green above the water in Stanley Park near dawn, and the lookout man high on the centre of the Lions Gate Bridge whistles. Then suddenly we're in Ken's apartment above False Creek and he's standing in his shorts holding a coffee pot full of red tulips. I giggle, open my eyes, stare at the white folds, the mountain and indents of my pillow.

Just what is made up? I run my finger through a white cavern. Nothing, I laugh as I flatten it out, nothing at all. That was real and this is real. I pull on a pair of dry panties. I put my tits into the bra cups. I get a clean uniform, just ironed last night, from the cupboard and try to pull it on with one hand as my other holds the sink as my leg muscles pull and push to hold me here. On. I look in the mirror: all white except my eyes and lips. I'm all white and in white, and I'm me who went out with Ken not long ago but it seems long ago. I undo the turban and my brown hair falls out, hair that grew while I was going with, going with, oh shit how could you ever go with, well you did.

I sit down and dry my hair with tips of it touching my thighs. I feel my stomach contracting, in, in, and my god, up to my throat comes, I lift my head, swallow, food, mostly liquid. I stand and it's better, but I cant balance enough. Have to get in the corner to have both hands free and it just isnt comfortable. I go back to the bunk and press my legs against the wall (the cabin's that narrow) to brace myself in a sitting position. I wish this were over. How I wish this were over. Rover, rover, coming over, I repeat and repeat. I put on lipstick. I hold onto the bunk edge near the door till we're up on top of a wave then I open it, shut it, run through the rain toward the mess. I grab the round latch and wait for that second of stillness at the top of the next wave. I breathe clean salt air through my nose then carefully I step into the grey-floored, green-walled, men-smoking mess. No tulips.

## 10. How It Feels

The sun on closed eyes makes everything red. To my left, I can hear a chain hitting metal; long lines and beads shoot and criss-cross in and out. I know the water is out there but feel it as a huge earth swelling yet solid. No line is solid or, if it is, only for a fraction of a second. The lines move and loop to a rhythm punctuated by the chain. The chain is held by one of the men who rubs it on the railing in order to chip the paint off slowly. I asked them why they worked so slowly when I came up from the john after peeling potatoes and having a shower after the lunch dishes were done and again it was supposed to be my time off. Why hurry, said Beebo as I twiddled my towel, we'd only have to do something else, anyway. Well, that makes sense, I said, and left him and Jock: one chaining, the other standing and looking out at the sea.

But I had never thought of work that way, work *men* get paid for that is, for I had often seen men not working, pretending to be doing something in order to cover the nothing they were doing, but somehow these were not *men doing men's work*. Of course it makes sense, I think, as the sun and salt air seem to sink through the cells of my skin; everything does when I focus on it. The reds switch to swirly purples which are cut off by a shadow then reappear as I hear Hal whistle on top of the chain-roughing; his whistling becomes louder as I move into the shadow again, then it passes and floats off, each note distinct.

I imagine seeing Hal's back naked. Black hair full to the neck. Tanned skin. All muscles alive, fluid in motion. No flab at all. Not chiselled. Not hard in a bodybuilder's way. My hand touches his ankle and fingers move slowly over curled hairs upwards, no veins standing out, and stop at the back of his knee. I trace a circle then a heart and kiss, a long kiss, just wet, my tongue lightly brushing the two indents twice each.

Jan, shouts Beebo, look over there! What? I squint as he walks over and I get the motion, stand seeing him, loose belly covered in denim blue and the eyes blue also against the sea and sky. And I walk toward his weight till I'm near him, then there's a distance, and my belly presses against the just-chipped railing and we look out to where his arm points. Five great black logs rolling, but not logs but... whales, he says, baleen I think. They go up and down as the waves do and only a black curve makes them look unlike logs. Sometimes,

Beebo says as his arm comes down close to mine, you can see them play. Oh, I say, and they are moving, turning, or *we're* turning, what do they do? They jump, he says, leap, right out, smack, all eighty foot of them, out of the water. *Eighty feet*, I say. Sure, he says, some of them are ninety, even a hundred; I guess those are about seventy though.

I keep my arm which is trembling next to his and ... see him blow, Beebo says, and the farthest away does, a huge spray, up, up, but we've turned completely as they glide; black arcs on grey water, away. You'll be able to see some in Coal Harbour, he says. I look into his eyes, a recognition, but we break it, that's where the whaling station is, where they take them. They, they kill them? I say as I watch the tops roll. What for? Fertilizer, he says, and they ship the meat to Japan; it's a delicacy there, whale steaks, you know. No I don't, I think, and I step back from his belly and from them away way off.

Fertilizer, I think as I lean against a pipe, *fertilizer*! 'Course we might not go to Coal Harbour, says Beebo as he pushes his arms out and leans against the railing, his back to the sea, it depends on whether they call or not. You mean the boat doesn't always go to the same places? I ask. No, he says, if they've been busy then we go in and load up whale meat, but if they've had a bad week we don't. Oh, I say and I watch his cheek, the thickness when he smiles. I feel it in my belly but not like before cuz mainly what I'm thinking of is being a whale surrounded by water, how it feels, that much surface, that much flesh, outer edges stretched against the cold and only once in a while to jump into the air, the difference then, but it's not cold, the water, cuz I'd always be in it. Mug-up time, says Beebo, you going to share a cup of tea with us, Jan? Uh, I say, oh no thanks, I think I'll just stay out here.

I move back to my box as Beebo and Jock joke about something then go into the fidley to wash up. I can feel the two behind me: Jock, his huge belly in coveralls, and Beebo's cheek, the skin firmed by salt air and rain and wind on the outside and by flesh pressing up from within. I wanted to touch it when he smiled; it's not tight, the gristles are heavy though and the skin so alive, to kiss it, lightly, and slide to his lips, thicker than mine, wet, his kiss is a slight holding back, not pressy, not too tight, but very much there all over, not centred in the jaw as some men are and not a tongue so soon, but *in* the lips. As we break it, my eyes see Jock watching us and I float over to him, over pails and cans, and I kiss him on the forehead where his scar is and he, belly in the way, hugs me, hard, squeezes, too much, my arms go backwards to Beebo, back, back, they grow, extend, curl about him.

Suddenly his woman is trying to say something to me. She is standing on an island, legs apart as she was on the dock, green salal between them and she shouts over the water a yi yi I lean toward, reach over the railings, cant hear but lip-reading it's a yi yi yi and suddenly her weight drops as she stretches, her hair curls, her hips and great breasts reform, assume Sarah's shape, Ken's girl, Sarah, who we double-dated with once, and she smiles in that fraction of a second it takes me to know who she is, waves as I turn, turn from her into a huge white mattress ... but I didnt cry, I think as I open my eyes on the white bulkhead, not at all, I, shit, why think of that, why. I trace the edge of white chip with my finger, an indent painted over, the whole bulkhead is covered in painted-over indents, some several layers deep and some just a layer or so like this, and I feel sorry for it a moment, feel ... I brought you a coffee, a voice says from behind me.

I turn toward it/Hal. My left arm leads me and my hand stops just below his knee which is covered in loose denim. I look up past the thick belt, up, and his eyes meet mine there at his side. I thought you might like one, Hal says as he lets go of the handle and turns the mug with his fingers. Thanks, I say as I take it with my left hand. Somehow my right is scrunched down on my thigh and it's too awkward to disentangle my body; how simple, yet I'm all limbs and blushy and ... I, I just saw some whales, I hear me say as I try not to think of his look and how to move my arm. I've forgotten how to move my fucking arm; it just stays there with the coffee shaking on the end of it. Whales, he says, first time? Yes, I say and look up at him and hope he doesn't notice what's going on, but just then, in that instant that I see into his wet eyes, my arm jerks. Then it moves over my right thigh and belly and left thigh and puts the coffee on the deck. I feel Hal leave – only two steps to the railing but such a distance in terms of my side – the skin near the edge loosens, then the centre and the whole front of my body.

I lean back onto the bulkhead and smile shyly, and Hal smiles. Well, well look at this, says Beebo to Jock who's just behind him. She wouldn't take tea with me, would she, oh no, but a married man. You're not quick enough, lad, says Jock and he winks. I catch the wink and pull my legs in so the men can pass and think of how Jock isnt like I imagined him a few moments ago and how Beebo is shorter. Then I dont look up. I just dont look up to where Hal is. You're blushing, he says. Not cuz of what Beebo said. Yes, I say and dont mean it.

How do I say that's not it; no, I hear my voice say, and I look at my feet close to his, his boots and my dirty shoes, alone there, the four of them making a pattern and space that has nothing to do with us.

## 11. I Gotta Get Outta Here

Damn. Goddamn bucket, fucking water. *Shit.* I'll never get through. Spilled greasy water spreads around chair and table legs and moves along the baseboard of a bench. *Shit.* I'll have to mop it up. I've already washed the galley deck twice cuz the tomato can hitched to the drain of the stove got too full of steak fat so when Coco went to empty it, it spilled. And when I mopped the deck the first time, I didnt get it all; in fact, I spread grease all over cuz I didnt use enough hot water. So *then* I filled the bucket almost to the top and changed the water three times just to make sure I'd get the grease off. And now, I've spilled the bucket over the clean deck and have to mop it over again.

Slowly. I'm so fucking slow cuz I cant wring the mop out dry enough. I roll it through the squeegee. Grey water squishes out of plastic foam spaghetti noodles, I stare at them, wet and green, slop them down to sponge up. I wring them through the rollers, wring them again. I pull out a chair to get under the table, and the fucking rag about my middle catches on a chair rung. I tug away. It tears. What the shit. What the fuck am I doing this for? I slam the chair back to the wall. Cuz I am. Cuz I am. I shove the next chair back, bend under the table to mop, and get out then up to wring; bend under to mop, get out and up to wring; bend and mop, out and up to wring. And now I've put a film of soap on the bench paint. I should wipe it too. Fuck that. I gotta get outta here. But I do it; I get a clean rag and a pail of clean water and wipe it before I finish scrubbing and mopping the deck.

Okay. I'm through. Again. This time I leave the pail inside. I step out, turn around, grab the mop and brush with my left hand, pick up the bucket with my right, put it down and close the door. Why the fuck didnt I *think* about what I was doing *before* instead of trying to do it all at once? It is so simple if I think, yet it isnt, and that's the difficulty – to think about something I haven't done *before* I do it, especially when I've not done it before and am tired and thinking of something else *while* I am doing it. I have to tell myself, look, this is what you're doing now, see what it is, figure it out, and then you *can* do whatever it is you want to do – if you have the energy left to do it that is. I lean the brush and mop in the corner against the canned goods cupboard. The air. At last.

I take a full breath: diesel fumes, salt, low tide. Creosote pilings, that's all I can see of wherever we are, pilings which hold the wharf up. I lean over the railing and see the leg of a man on the edge of the dock, a tatty bottom of a jacket. I stare at the piles driven into the ocean floor – barnacles and fine, yellow-green seaweed grown on their bodies. If I were a log, I'd like to break away from the boom and just drift; but if I couldn't do that, I think I'd be happy as part of a dock. I walk along the deck. Beyond the freshly painted redness and the water is a logged mountain, naked where it's been scraped off, some slash left, but empty contrasted to the green of the ridge. I hate all that cutting. Mountains and mountains of forest. The kind of work men do to live. I wish they could cut it where no one would see. That's silly. If you cant see, it doesn't happen?

I lean over to dump the water. A school of fish swims back and forth in a definite ellipse between two of the piles. What makes them do it? Over and over and not one in front but six or seven, and they turn so close to the pile the seaweed wiggles; the ones behind look like they'll hit but don't. A body without arms or legs is so less awkward. Only the tails stick out. They are so solidly whole. They loop and loop. The same motion over without thought, just eat and swim and eat and swim. Beneath them, two larger fish loll. I cant dump here. They break, scatter, several float to the surface; others reform and continue the ellipse in the opposite direction. The two larger ones swim further under the dock, away.

Gotta get moving, gotta get off. I walk to the stern and dump the bucket. Grey water into dark green. Early evening light touches the surface of everything. I want to get off, to walk in the edges of the forest or to follow the road and see where it goes.

After I put the bucket away, I walk around the deck to go below to shower off the grease and sweat. I climb down the ladder to the narrow corridor with rope carpeting. I wait at the closed door. Knock. No one answers. Knock again. Wait. Open. No one's here. Funny, I assumed someone was. I close the door and lock it and unlace my sweaty shoes. Deck's cold. I stand on a piece of paper towel, pull off my nylons, my dirty uniform, throw everything in the tiny corner beside the wash basin. Damn. Forgot clean clothes. How could I? Towels too. Shampoo. Everything. Stupid me. I dont care. I'm not getting dressed to get them. I just want to be clean. I step into the shower – a blue galvanized box. Turn on the tap. Not warm enough. Fuck it. Too strong. Nothing I can do: either no water at all or cold water with too much pressure. Pellets. Some Friday night this is going to be. Going out nowhere. Everything's wrong. What am I doing here? Should be swimming in the ocean rather than inside this piece of tin. No. It's so cold even good swimmers dont last thirty minutes, and I'd have to shower the salt off anyway. Cool water surrounds my toes, reaches my ankles, I dont want to wash or swim or do anything. Hair's all tangled and knotted. I cant see. Tinny smell. Diesel oil. Skin aching from the assault. I lean against the side of the shower and cry. And cry.

    I should try to get out. Dont want to. My whole body is below the ocean if all this metal weren't in the way. Maybe I could sink and touch the ocean floor and just become part of it. I slide and sit on the bottom. Head on my knees. Spine curled. And cry and cry. Nothing is worthwhile. Nothing. Everything moves round and round on the surface. No matter where I am, it's going to be the same. No matter what I do, it's going to be the same. I have to change somehow, change, change …

    I see a wet green plastic sheet in front of me and blue metal between my bent legs. On bottom. Shivering. Dont know how long I've been here but it feels like forever. Ten minutes? An hour? Doesn't seem to matter. I want to get out. Why? I gotta get up. How? Grab the ledge. I just want to stay. My fingers reach out to the metal which holds the water in. Don't, says part of me. Grab, say my fingers. Balance, answer my thighs/my feet. That's it. My fingers hold and one foot pushes against the side. Together my limbs pull the rest of me up, and the water coming down is warmer now, hits different edges of skin, hurts, is hot. I stand up into it. Hair in my way. Cant see the soap. Forget that. Turn it off. Turn the tap off. Right arm/hand cant do it. Slips. Use both. I do. It stops. I stare at the empty nozzle a second, step away, out.

    Out of the blue coffin into a white metal room. No towel. Use the linen hand one. I do. Then I pull on dirty clothes which stick to my skin. Out into the dark corridor of paint and diesel smells. If I can just keep going, I'll soon be off. Up the ladder. Ocean air comes down and through my greasy uniform, slaps my face, neck, arms, chest, my belly as I near the opening. The salt air touches/surrounds all of me as I step out into it. I breathe deeply. Salt air in as ribs move out. I float at the bottom of this heavy ocean, glide along the blood-red floor. I want to merge with the real ocean, yellow and green, to fall into it. That's too easy. Not at all. Stay here in air. The ocean with the sun on top only seems to be lighter, is dark and cold and once you fell in you'd try to get out. Maybe not. Maybe not. I turn out of the shadow. Suddenly, all of the water is speckled with gold light, twinkles. How I wonder what you are, out and over, over there. I want to touch you somehow. Cant.

SATURDAY

*Night Lunch and Coffee Time*

When unlicensed personnel are required to work after 5:00 p.m., they shall be entitled to a coffee break as closely as possible after two (2) hours' work and a meal break as closely as possible after four (4) hours' work.

## 12. Tahsis

This is the land I'm from, Vancouver Island where I was born on the eastern side. We live on the edges of it, one huge green hill pressed up from the sea, mountains and mountains of timber on its top, the bottom joined to the mainland under the straits of Juan de Fuca, Georgia, Johnstone, Queen Charlotte; the edges defined by blue and grey water, pockets of lakes, scratches of rivers.

I breathe the cut forest air as I walk between stacks of lumber at Tahsis. These creamy stacks are shorter than whales but were originally longer, giant Douglas firs, just a few weeks ago standing upright with their branches out, needles, green short needles pointing, surrounded by air, feeling the sun and rain. And now they are planks, horizontal, lying on each other; only the bottom ones touch earth. My head turns to the grey sky. It's so low that I feel if three firs were placed on top of each other I could climb them and touch it. I skip through the maze of the largest lumberyard I've ever been in as I feel Hal's navy-blue jacket on my arms, his shape around me. I love it, so soft.

For the first time in my life, except for Port Alberni and Point No Point, I'm on the western side of the island, blocked by an island, Nootka Island, held in by an inlet, Tahsis Inlet, but it's the West Coast I've been on these last three days, not the east of the west but the west of the west. Nothing out there but water between us and Japan, Coco said to me yesterday. I see myself crawling miles and miles holding my breath to Japan. I stop. Rest a moment. Place my hand flat against two pieces of thick wood. Will you be used for a house or to hold cement in for an ugly apartment? Become part of a dock, a huge shipping container? Stay in British Columbia or go to Asia? Be taken by train hauled through the Coast Range the Cascades the Kootenays and Rockies to Saskatchewan? Or be carried on a Norwegian-flagged Greek-crewed vessel of an American-owned Danish company to Europe? Will you be the same one piece of that much larger tree even one month from now or further cut, further cut, maybe one end will be a toy boat and an edge of you burned, thrown into a furnace to give heat and return to the earth and sky? A pulp mill: some of the cells that once joined these may already be paper. I lean over and touch my lips to one of the boards, then run.

In my ears, I feel the salt/forest air and hear machines: the winch and engine throb of the *Nootka*, the whines and shrill turnings of metal from inside the mill, and other ships, freighters, deep sea, just down the harbour, loading, huge winches, loading, taking lumber away, and lighter sounds from stilted-yellow-empty-in-the-middle machines which move piles of lumber in their middles and make a swishing sound through the puddles. Men at work. All men. They are taking and carrying and bringing and lifting and driving and maintaining or repairing too, I suppose, because no lumber is being cut on Saturdays. Cleaning chains. Young men get work cleaning chains. I used to wish when I was defrosting a fridge and doing weekend chores that I were a boy, that I'd grow up to be a trucker or maybe be, like Smitty next door, a high rigger, or maybe a parachute tester, or maybe a fisherman – not a sports fisherman, but a fisherman fisherman. But I dont kill. I couldn't fish unless I was willing to kill and to gut.

I stop. I cant decide which way to go – to stay here among the lumber stacks just smelling fir and cedar or to go left along the paved road. I hesitate a few seconds, look at the unpainted mill to my right and the high rows of lumber piles in front of me and the about-to-rain sky above, then turn left. The edge of the yard is enclosed by a high metal net fence to stop stealing, I guess, but it seems silly: *metal poles* bent inward at the top, metal poles freighted here by the *Nootka* to hold in pieces of dead forest which once belonged to all or did until there was a licence on a piece of paper from Victoria, a piece of paper made perhaps from pulp from this very land, and that piece of paper says, what does it say, I dont know, I've never seen one, yet it exists and gives title to companies, a right to cut. Then the men of British Columbia work: cruisers and riggers and whistlepunks and fallers, buckers and chokermen and cat drivers and boom men, barkers and sawyers and tailers and greenchainers. And that's why lumber costs so much, or so the companies say, it's the labour, but my dad knows of a guy in Chemainus who got a percentage discount because he worked at the mill and it turned out cheaper for him to buy wood – cut in Chemainus and maybe even loaded by him – through the catalogue, Eaton's or Sears of Edmonton or Calgary, and to pay the freight costs to bring it back from the prairies to build his home five miles from the Chemainus mill. He saved $120 by doing so; that I dont understand; that makes no sense to me.

I pass a V-roofed-attached-to-a-shed structure. There are cards in wooden slits: time cards, check-in and check-out. I cross the road which must be the main street cuz there is a general store and a post office up and over there. There arent any houses along it, just a rectangular building up the hill almost straight in front of me; and over and up a larger hill to my left there is a *pink* church with a cross and a few recently built houses. The store must be closed. Or, here it is, Saturday afternoon, and no one except for a red-haired man is standing on the wooden platform, and there are no cars or trucks or station wagons in front of it. Odd. No cars or trucks on the road either, not like Ladysmith or Chemainus Saturdays with teenage boys in secondhand cars gunning up and down the main drag circling, slowing down, teasing, trying to pick up girls. The man waves at me and I wave vaguely back and decide not to go there but to stick closer to the waterfront and visit one of the deep sea freighters if they'll let me.

The first one, Japanese, doesn't. The second, Norwegian, does. The officer, about my height and around thirty, speaks English. After I tell him I work on the *Nootka*, that little freighter right over there, we walk up a spotless gangplank that seems longer than our ship is wide, and he gives me a tour of the wheelhouse (all sorts of instruments), the galley (stainless steel – two complete stoves and a separate grill), and a huge freezer stocked with full sides of pork, lamb, beef. Wow. Enough to live for weeks. He opens an empty cabin on the upper deck. I cant believe it: so light, clean, wooden, with a little desk and bookshelf and a bathroom. Are the crew's quarters like this? Almost the same, he says, but below deck; this is, how do you say, spare crew? Extra? More than you need? No, he says, the radio operator flew home because her father died and another will arrive to ... Replace or relieve her, I say, to take over. Yes, he says, relieve, replace. You have women operators? I ask. Certainly, he says, is it not so in Canada? Not so, I say, at least not on the West Coast where the officers handle the radio calls. Women, he says, make excellent operators – why not in Canada? Why not? I say, I dont know why – maybe that will change soon – there just arent many positions. Maybe it is because before you become an officer of any sort you must belong to a union where many men are already out of work. Why is that so? he asks. I dont fully know, I say, but Canada used to have a large deep-sea fleet which was disbanded, broken up, after the war or during the battles between unions, and now those boats sail under the flags of other countries and use cheaper labour. That is too bad, he says, the situation is comp-li-cated? Complicated is right, I say, complex too. But women do not have the same opportunities as men? he says. Yes, I say, you understand English very well. He smiles with pride.

He takes me to a dining room where there are polished wooden tables all attached solidly to the wooden deck. On each, there is a basket of fresh bread and a carafe of wine. This is beautiful, I say, so airy and spacious. This is not like your *Nootka*? he asks, it is not the same? Not the same at all, I say, but I've been in Vancouver restaurants that arent as uncluttered or well-designed as this. He takes the compliment personally. You would enjoy a glass of wine? he asks. I'd enjoy it, I say, but no thanks, I must go soon. Coffee? No thank you.

Your vessel, he says as I look out a large porthole toward her, it used to be a fish packer? A fish packer? I do not understand. He laughs slightly at my not understanding an English word. We built several like that in Norway, he says, I think it was o-rig-inally – is that how you say it? – built in Norway as a boat that takes the fish from the grounds to the canneries, like a mother ship. I dont know, I say, I'll find out. Find out? I will ask those aboard and perhaps one of them will tell me. Find out is an idiom? he asks. I guess so, I say, uum, I find out from you that the *Nootka* may have previously been a Norwegian fish packer. I found out from you that radio operators are sometimes women. Discover. Learn. Come to know. Good phrase, he says, I find out that our dining room gives pleasure to our guest. That is right, I say. I found out that she likes our ship. Yes, I say. What other languages do you speak? he asks. Just English. Only English? No French or Spanish? I took French in high school and two years of Russian at university, but I cant say more than hello and goodbye and yes and no in either. Why not? We dont get to use them, I say, we didnt even speak in the classes – mostly grammar drills and not even the most frequently used phrases. English grammar is most difficult, he says, but I am amazed, you rarely speak in class, why? Our classes were too big and most of us did not learn much. Everyone in Norway, he says, learns some English and Danish; they are needed for commerce and travel. I could travel for a thousand miles north, east, and south, I say, and the main language would still be English. You should come to Europe, he says, see countries smaller than your province. Different peoples and cultures, they are exciting, no?

Yes, I say, I suppose. I've always been in school or working to earn money to go back to school. No holidays? Once across Canada to Montréal and Toronto and New York with my parents, I say, and to California with my professor and his family. A custom? he says. No, no, not a custom, I say, but many people my age have not seen our country. Not so in Europe, he says, but you work on the *Nootka*, why not here? On a Norwegian vessel? I ask. You would like to? I might... is that possible? Not impossible, he says. How? You would go to see the Norwegian consulate in Vancouver and arrange an interview. If a master agrees and you have a passport and the right papers, you might join as a cabin girl or officers' mess girl. Really? I say. Really, he answers in my intonation and we both laugh.

It might take several months, he says; the consulate has to know you are of good character and have references. The master has to need to replace (I smile at the word) someone. Thank you, I say, I really must go now. You are in Tahsis this evening? he says, you could return and meet our officers? No, I say, we go on. On? Sail, move to another port called Zeballos. It is a shame, he says, we could all practise our English and maybe you could begin Norwegian? I would love to, I say, but not by myself. It is much better with native speakers, he says, I find out, or I found out? You have found out, I answer, and thank you for everything. It has been my pleasure, he says.

## 13. Zeballos

I walk through the pale greenness of the mess to the white galley and pluck a piece of lemon-icinged cake from the pan on the counter. Turn the corner, about to bite, but dont cuz I see Ray see me in that second before his eyes fall to his cup. Hello, I say. He nods from the jaw (a funny man from Newfoundland, alone, alone), and I pass him. It hurts him to move to an edge of politeness or acknowledgment even that much. I step through the open door. What a creep. Also sad.

I step outside and bite into the sponge-sugar-lemony cake and watch the men work: muscles moving, always moving. Beebo stretches his arms to grab the slings, and Hal zooms over on the towmotor to stab under the boards to lift the load. I enjoy the tastes of lemon and egg and vanilla, the textures of the icing and cake. I watch Hal scoot the load over to the shed which is on the dock, and I look around for the Third Mate, Marty, for his soft pear-like shape. Cant see him. But the Second Mate, Chuckles, is near the mustard-coloured shed with ZEBALLOS painted in black. I walk up the gangplank and jump off it to go toward him, but the towmotor in reverse zips toward me.

Dusty tires turning. Yellow metal speeding. Jan ... here, shouts Beebo. My body moves sideways out of the way. You were fine where you were, says Hal, I would have missed you. Not by much, I think as I fluster and stare at the planks I was standing on. My eyes drift slowly up to him. He's smiling. No laugh or tease, at least I dont feel it, just a full wet look which waves way in. My eyes float back, guts too, hit a centre, then I loosen, out, me to him, not as far in as he to me. We stay there a second then I feel the squished cake in/through my fingers. My hand comes up and I put the whole glob in. A glump. Sticky. Too much at once. I can scarcely swallow. I walk toward the side of the load, to get away, to get out, to go around it to where Beebo is. The empty slings swing up. Hal then jabs the forklift under the loaded boards. I look down so as not to look at him. He knows I'd like to make love, and I know he knows I know.

My eyes come up Beebo to his belt, the edge of flesh there, to his chin. I lick my fingers one by one. Beebo grins. Will you fetch me a chocolate bar, Jan? Sure, I say smiling. He makes me feel cuddly. I look at Hal lifting the load which he does without looking at what he does cuz he knows what he's doing so well. Do you want me to get anything? I shout. All three of us exchange a teasy look. No Jan, Hal says, and takes the load away. I follow his motion with my whole body then turn to Beebo who laughs with me. What kind? Doesn't matter, whatever they have. We stay in the ease. Something chewy or with nuts. Eat-More? Oh Henry? I want to hug him. Burnt Almond? Crispy Crunch? He gives me money from his back pocket; get one for yourself, too. Thanks, I say. Our eyes part. Candy lovers.

I leave him but am still connected somehow and go over to Chuckles who's checking off the transfer of goods, bills of lading, on his clipboard. I wait beside him while he checks the entire load. I glance at a black pile of slag, taller than a three-storey house, tailings left over from mining. How can I help you? Chuckles asks. Garlic air shoots through gapped teeth. What time do I have to be back? I ask. I have to give you permission to go off, he says. What if I don't? Shit. I request permission to go for a walk, I say. You have it, he says, laughing. His laugh feels like bullets just missing my shoulders. Be back by nine-thirty, he says, just to make sure. Will the night lunch be at ten? I ask. That's up to Marty. But he's not here. Why should he be? He's not on till eight. Do you know where he is? I ask. Am I my brother's keeper? he says. Forget it, I say, tell him I'll be back by nine-thirty. Please? he says. Pull-ease. He laughs again and I leave.

Behind me I hear the men and the winch and the towmotor and a truck and the boat engine: metal, throbbings, windings, chatter. I am on the edge of a circle which is spreading backwards. Take it away, that's it, here, over here. Sounds touch my back, my ears, the edges of my arms as salt air filters through my skirt and I walk up a wharf above water then mud flats, a wharf longer than the long side of a city block.

Bet Beebo is not a bad lover, I think as I feel his money in one pocket and my own in the other. He would enclose me, but I'd still be me since he wouldn't take over the way Hal might. We would laugh and hug and kiss all over. Why he *pays* for sex, I dont know. There must be hundreds of women in Vancouver who would like to make it with him. Maybe a bit slobbery. Those thick lips always wet. But such a good body. Maybe he just doesn't get to meet women wherever he goes when he's ashore. A shame. What a waste. And he looks delicious when he's just had a shower and his curly blond hair is all wet and his work clothes all clean.

Zeballos looks like someone took a jackknife and scraped it out of the jagged valley. The buildings look plunked down. Firs and alders could take over at any moment. The mud flats ahead on my right are full of drift logs; yellow-green weeds press up between. I imagine Hal and I would be quite slow. I cant see a bed. I cant imagine a where. Our limbs kiss. Muscles full. Well matched. Skin cant contain us. He'd control me ... Would he? Shit. I'd probably come right away. His whole body, like his black eyes, pulses in and out. Slow waves. I stop walking. My body seems to float ahead a step. Then it comes back to where I am at the ramp's end. I close my eyes and can feel the mountains, smell them, darkness sinking in from above, giving out from within. Cool dark green needle branches. I step onto earth. I could hold off if I really wanted to, and Hal could keep me there on the edge of coming. How do you know? I just do, that's all.

I walk up to the first building. A white sun porch with white curtains. No lights on. Whoever lives here sees the whole inlet. Too small. Almost a cabin. I'd like more space, more colour. Perhaps it isnt too small to live alone in. I'd read and look out and swim and bake cookies. Why, the porch is just the side of a larger building that from where I am on the road looks like a child's stick drawing of a house. The sign says it's a Mine-Registry-Standard Oil-Justice-of-the-Peace-Coroner-Marriage-Death-Birth-Harbour-Agent-for-Zeballos-Trading-Company Ltd. office. It's dark inside! George Nicholson, deputy mining recorder, agent, justice, agent, etc. is out. Probably down on the dock receiving goods. But where's everyone else? I see no one on the dirt street. No cars either, no signs, no poles, only the front steps of stores and wooden fences of houses. Steps, which almost form a boardwalk like on a western-movie set, must be for mud (rainforest rain). I skip across the road to the other side. Corn and potatoes and green beans grow in front of a little, unpainted house. I could live here. I see me pulling weeds, baking muffins, reading on the porch, washing the floor. Waiting. For what? I dont think it's a man. Must be if you dont think that. It's so vague. I lean down to touch an orange nasturtium outside the fence. The petal is fluid inside yet soft out. I look up through the fence slats through the dark window and see a woman there watching me. She has a *cigar* in her mouth. Her hands rest on thick hips, I stand up slowly. Wave. It's her garden. Her house. I wasn't going to pick it. She's so solid. Perhaps she doesn't see me. She does. She speaks through the screen door, what do you want? Nothing, I say. Go away then.

Gravel knocks gravel. You'd think she'd be happy to see someone. Scat. Bugger off. Did she think I was going to hurt her nasturtiums? Eat them? I wouldn't want to be a crab like her. I pass a two-storey wooden building, probably a bunkhouse, many windows, all narrow... vacant remnant of gold-mining days. A naked lightbulb is the only sign I can see of anyone having ever been inside. Hi, I feel like shouting but don't. A flapping noise slowly crackles in my ears. I hear the *Nootka*'s engine and gulls crying and dogs barking beyond. But the flapping is loud and getting louder. Now I see a structure of translucent plastic, a light inside, two-by-four frame. No shadows or bodies move. But the plastic sheets do, as the air does, in large slow flaps and bumps. I glide past, then turn about, walk through long couch grass to look inside. It's a cookhouse with a light on. No one's in it. I turn away.

A few yards up the road is TED'S CLIP JOINT. A guy with dark curly hair slouches in the barber's chair reading a paperback. Stacks of comics fill the wall behind him to within a foot of the ceiling. He doesn't seem to be absorbed in his book. He doesn't seem to belong where he is. There's no light on inside, yet it's dusk out. His head lifts and I feel his eyes press out to the edge of me. What do you want? he asks. Is there a café here? I ask. Ted stands and takes two steps. I stay where I am outside the doorsill. The room is less than six feet wide. I can almost touch him. We look at each other, and I understand that he probably hasn't been with a woman for quite a while and doesn't, yet does, know what to do. His eyes, squinched at the edges, loosen, assume a pose. A few doors up, he drawls.

I step back from him. They may be out, he says, they usually are. Are you Ted? I ask. Yup. Do you get enough to live on here just cutting hair? I can see him decide to answer that. I fix trucks and cars, he says proudly, you might say I own the garage. I look up and down the road; I dont see any garage. A field back there, he says nodding his head, I get along all right. How about you? I'm the mess girl on the *Nootka*, I say, just off for a walk. Do you want to have a beer? he asks. No, I say, thanks anyway.

A dogfight, between two large dogs, has just begun in the middle of the street between the agent's building and the woman's house. We can just make out their shapes through the swelling dust and twilight. A yowl cuts through my ear. Suddenly, men are running out of a hotel just up the street from us, and a kid in a Cowichan sweater appears from nowhere. Then a car swirls in from the dock. I cant move. I feel like I'm on a frontier set. One of the dogs will surely die unless someone does something. Sure you dont want to go for a beer? says Ted. How can he say that now? My mouth opens through a film. No thanks. A guy jumps out of the Chev. Four men conglomerate near the two animals. They shout. They go into the dust swirl and pull apart the dogs by their haunches. A yowl flattens to a whine. The other dog barks until it is struck three or four times and then it, too, whines. Then all the men begin to head back to the hotel, one of them with the dog that was hit following him several feet behind. Maybe you'll have that beer next time? asks Ted. Maybe, I say.

I start along the street past unpainted, unused, tin-roof buildings. Strange to see such an abandoned town. I pass the café-hotel-pub. The café is empty, closed; licensed premises, checkered-cloth-covered tables sit with salt and pepper shakers waiting, waiting for that time they'll be surrounded by people. The men laugh and banter as they come up the road behind me. Up ahead are two cars from the late forties or early fifties. Three women unload driftwood, take it into a yard through an open gate and place it on the porch of an unpainted house. Hello, I say and one greets me and we exchange a happy look. She probably has had a tough life, always working and using her body (she has on ankle socks and a house dress, the muscles of her calves are hard) while managing (they most likely all have to) on very little. We all exchange greetings and one of them tells me to say hello to Coco for her, and then I head toward the little café Ted spoke of.

"It's a Sin to Tell a Lie" comes out onto the street. The words pull me in. I am surrounded by men except for the teenage waitress who is wearing curlers and leaning on the counter. The men wear open plaid shirts, clean jeans, and some of their faces are clean shaven for

Saturday night while others have beards. *Be sure it's true when you say I love you.* Their energy surrounds me, presses the ceiling, the windows. Naked arms. I step up to the counter, watch the waitress wipe a low shelf. The record stops. They shut up. I feel their eyes on my back, through my skirt. No one gets up to put another record on. The waitress's birdy head turns. Yeah? she says.

Her father (they have the same darkish hair and peaky bone structure) hearing the silence comes out from the poolroom to see what it is about. I'd like to have a cone, I say to her, if you have any. We don't, she says. Her father stands behind her, small-hipped and worn looking, white rag about his waist. Hank Snow comes on the jukebox. I tell him I want two Crispy Crunch. His daughter continues wiping the shelf. The ice cream is on the *Nootka*, he says as he gives me my change, you can have one tomorrow. No thanks, I say, and suddenly everyone is talking again.

## 14. Just Because These Words

It's past three in the morning and I cant sleep. I have to cuz I gotta be up by six-thirty. I keep trying. Cant. The metal sounds of the engine go on and on, over and under and through me. Cant stop thinking. Cant not worry. Cant be easy. *Be sure it's true.* Damn. I try to shake the words off, to float under the tune. Images come: Ken's blue eyes swim in and out of focus; the jukebox grows large and the neon colours of its edges take over and spill into Zeballos's only street – Mae West Avenue, that's what they call it, said Beebo when I got back, what a handle, eh Jan? The dogs have enormous tails and teeth; their teeth come toward me through the dust. I stretch out my arms to shove them off and find myself floating, floating up to, no, the song, again. I cant get rid of it.

*I'm between the devil and the deep blue sea.* I wish it would stop. I wish I would stop. What am I doing thinking about this sweet-talking bastard who made out and made promises and is afraid to tell the preacher he was drunk? What about her? How does she feel? I wonder if she believed him, I wouldn't, maybe I would want to, maybe everyone wants to, what the shit. *Cross my heart and hope to die.* White lies, black lies, what the fuck. I sit up and watch the shadows on the metal bulkhead next to me. And I throw off my white cotton cover cuz I'm hot. I'm next to the boiler and over the engine. What a racket! They're too cheap to fix the muffler, Puppi said, the *U-Chuck*'s got the same engine and you can hardly hear it.

I turn over on my belly, spread out my legs and arms, and try to think of nothing. Cant. Ken again. He comes drifting toward me over mud puddles and grins like a five- or six-year-old who's just learned how to do something. I wish we could go back, I say. He doesn't hear me. I wish we could go back to that moment when we weren't what we were before and talk about us. He splashes mud all over. I slide away. I never said I love you because I believe in love somehow and whatever we were wasn't whatever it was I thought or think love is. But what was it? Puppy love? Puppies? Where'd they come from? Bobby Williams, dark curly hair and blue eyes, almost exactly the same blue as Ken's; it's just puppy love, Mom explained. Just. Just?

What nonsense. Seven years old and in love. I gotta do something. I gotta get out of this. I move further to the edge of... blackness, I dont want to, I'm afraid of... I slip back and turn over and look at the shadows. They seem to dance toward each other. Some merge then they break the rhythm and fold off, off like clouds into a larger whole. I feel swept up by rhythms larger than self: the engine, the ocean, coincidences, so many coincidences. If I hadn't taken the buses to go downtown and got off at Main Street and entered the hall exactly when I did, I might not be here. If I hadn't been in the dorm when Albert phoned instead of at the caf, if Ken were on any ship but this, if Betty hadn't crawled up to the skipper's cabin naked for the second time, if, if. Okay. I say I dont believe in fate yet moments of my life and moments of others seem to have been meant to coincide and collide. I cant imagine anything happening other than what has occurred, but I guess that's true for everyone. The past is what did take place and at certain moments of the present we select a focus on it and try to make a pattern.

Coincide and collide. Coincide and collide. I turn onto my belly and say these words. I move my arms out, breaststroke, and try to swim to the ledge of falling into, smoothly falling, gliding into *coooinnnciiiiiide* and *collliiiiiide, coooooinnnnnnnciiiiiiiiiide* and *coooollllllllliiiiiiiiiiiide*. The dogs. Far below me. They collide. They are pulled together by smells by heat by rhythms that can be almost seen. Lines, neon-coloured lines, move in and out. The dogs turn. One jumps through them up onto me. I am being pushed over by him, his thick paws, his furry brown chest. Hair in my nostrils. He scrunches me into gravel. He is huge. Teeth, teeth on my throat. I cry out. I wake up crying but I'm not awake. I hear my aunt laugh. He was only being friendly, she says. And I wake again. But, but I am afraid, I shout to her. She laughs.

She just stands up the sunlit alley with her hands out toward me and laughs. I wake again.

I cant breathe. My face is scrunched, is covered in cloth. My arms are ... loosen them, loosen your fucking arms/hands; they are your hands, let go, that's it, more, that's it. My fingers very slowly untighten but still clutch the edges of my pillow. My hands hold the case taut. I raise my head and slowly lift myself off. It is only a pillow with a pillowcase, only a pillow. But that dog, that moment in the alley when I was three, keeps coming to me. I'm afraid. What of? My fingers trace circles in the pillow, incomplete, open at the centre where they might meet. Okay ... I'm afraid of being lonely. Okay ... I'm afraid I'll never love. That's not true. That's nonsense. You will someday. I cant imagine it. There's more ... more? I'm afraid I'll never grow up. But you are grown up. No I'm not, not yet. I've wasted so much time already. I'm afraid there's no me. Sometimes I'm like water, the shadows, I reflect what's around, react, but I'm not anything solid inside. You know that's not true.

*Be sure it's true.* But I just keep reacting and reacting and reacting. *When you say I love you, say I love you.* I haven't lied about that, not yet. Cant imagine what it's really like. When I make love, I sometimes go out, way way out and away, and when I come back the clutter is gone. But this isnt love, this is just sex. I use men to go elsewhere, to where I'm no longer me at all. It certainly isnt whatever it is I imagine love to be, or if it is I can "love" almost every man, almost every man here I "love" in some way and the only one I knew before was Ken. He's certainly not the one. Will there ever be one? Just one? That's what the song says, that's what my room says, you will know it, it will happen, it's like chemistry almost. *Chemistry?* That cant be *it*. I just wish it were over. I wish it were decided for me. I wish I grew up in another era or place where they arranged it all. What crap. You want to believe it will happen, the love of your life, and you're just afraid it wont, that's all.

My high-school friends, almost all of them, are married and both my university roommates, married, a home, children. They are needed. My god. Is that where you are? You want to be needed? Yes. But you're needed here. Not in the same way. I get paid for it. And I can leave. And no one would miss me, would need me, really need *me*. I'm going to have to decide what I'm going to do even though I dont know what it is. Even if I got married *that* wouldn't change. If I had kids it would, and I want to, yet I'm not ready and besides that there isnt anyone. Isnt anyone. Isnt anyone. I've got to get to sleep. I've got to focus on nothing, make everything clear, empty. A map. Just put a pin on a map of possibilities, my mom suggested, and say this is where I'll go, this is what I'll do. I cant. I cant do that! What *are* they? I cant continue this way. There's almost no connection between then, the closer then, and now.

I simply must stop and get to sleep. I lie flat and stare at the ceiling. One shadow looks like an island covered in forest. Think of it, the tree tops, the sun in the day, rain in needles, the moon at night. Be a branch at the top swaying, moving gently (I spread out ray arms) with the currents, the wind. *When the wind blows the cradle will rock, when the bough breaks the cradle will fall, and down will come baby* ... what? Down? I open my eyes and the island disappears into a chasm. Shit. Nothing works. *Cradle and all.* Cradle and all?

I know what. I'll think of everything I like to do and put each in order, then put each of the eaches in order: dancing, cooking, eating, making love, walking, swimming, talking, listening. I start with things I like to eat: asparagus, turkey, Dad's potato stuffing, wild-blackberry pie, strawberry shortcake, lake trout. But images from here disrupt: black beef sausages, oily salmon skin, grey scummy cream corn. I boil like the corn, fat heavy bubbles plop; yuk, I see closeups of broken eggshells covered in coffee grounds with cigarette ashes sprinkled on top; and the slop bucket, fat, bacon fat sausage fat steak fat chop fat everywhere. Damn it. It's covering everything. This isnt going to work at all.

I know what. I'll think of everyone I've ever had a crush on (there's a funny word, crush, crush my heart and I hope to die) and at least three things about each and maybe I'll sleep before I get to ... I start with Bobby Williams in grades one, two, three, until he moved, and Ronny Wilson and Brian Grant, also in three, and then in four ... right up to Ken. I visualize each and remember moments, games we played and things we swapped, and places we had forts. I can see the general outline of each, their features; their faces arent distinct, but their eyes are. I put each in order by grades as if the report cards of my life were dropping, dropping as the rain does into the ocean away. Shit on this. I turn over, curl into a ball, and watch the shadows again.

Backstroke. Sidestroke. Front crawl, dog-paddle. Floating. Breaststroke like a heart, floating. Millions of hearts have been broken. Hearts everywhere, but they cant be broken unless they've loved. They beat away, pumping, bodyless, pumping. I see them in the ocean, in the alleys, on the street, in the garbage, in the tree tops. Baby and all. Not again. It's not going to work. The words were spoken. It cant be because of words? Maybe if they were said and not meant, that's it, to say something and not mean it, but yet it becomes real because we expect… that's the difficulty. But we cant or I cant get away from expecting because we learn so early what we do, what we see, what surrounds us. I'll never get away from that. Damn it. I cant get to sleep like this. Just an hour or so left. Left over till I work again. I better get up. Get out of this. I'll make some cocoa, that's what I'll do. And then maybe, maybe.

## SUNDAY

*Drills*

Lifeboat and other emergency drills shall be held on weekdays between the hours of eight (8:00) a.m. and four-thirty (4:30) p.m.

Preparations for drills such as stretching out firehoses and hoisting or swinging out boats shall not be done prior to signal for such drills, and after drill is over all hands shall secure boats and gear and replace firehoses in safe custody.

One-half (½) hour's notice shall be given prior to all lifeboat and emergency drills.

## 15. Boat Drill

Open those, eh? Coco says referring to two large cans of tomatoes sitting by the can opener. She chops onions as she talks while I try to get the can into the right position so when I slam down the big wooden handle I wont hit the can rim but get the triangular metal stabber just inside it. I tell you, Jan, I'd much rather sail with Thor than Ray; as much as I've seen Thor drunk, I *know* he's safe. I huddle the can toward my waist and hold it in, brace it, lift the heavy handle again. He took chances, she says, we all know that, but he *knew* the coast, every current. (I got it. I got the stupid metal punch in.) I just dont know about this one, she says, guess we'll find out *if* he lasts till winter. He's experienced mind you. (Coco has chopped five onions in the time it has taken me to open one can.) I dont know, she continues, I wish they had chosen the mate instead – Don doesn't take risks, but at least he knows these waters. Why didnt they? I ask as I start on my second can. Not tough enough, she says, and she laughs. Besides that, he was here already. She keeps laughing. You think they'd let him be skipper knowing he couldn't stop the way we were? He's respected, mind you, it's certainly not that. They just saw a chance to change us and took it.

So they stuck Ray on here to do dirty work? I ask as I (finally) open the can. Yeah, she says as she dumps the tomatoes onto the meat. You see? You see how one stupid action can spoil it for everyone? Sure, I say. He's going to be watching Betty like a hawk, one wrong move and that's it, game over for her. She sprinkles chopped onion and green pepper on top of the tomatoes. There might be a steady job opening sooner than you think, she says, just hang around the hall. She salts and peppers the sauce and I step over to open the oven for her, so she wont have to put the full pan down in order to do it.

The handle is in my hand when the horn blasts. I jump. Coco almost trips forward. It blasts again. Right above us. The sauce sloshes over the meat and some spills on the deck. It blasts again. Boat drill, she shouts. It blasts again. The pan seems to pull her as she slides it into the oven. It blasts again. Wet me a rag, she shouts. The horn lets go a steady, high-pitched blare. I dampen a rag for her and wring it out while she turns the pan in the oven around to wipe the sides. Boat drill, like the CPR? He inspects our cabins? Damn man, she shouts, *you'd think he'd warn us.* The horn blares/pierces almost; it does not stop at all. I throw her a clean rag and she throws me the dirty one;

then she bends down to wipe the deck while I rinse the rag. Leave that till later, she shouts, you get up there, I'll be right behind you.

I run through the mess. Turn the siren *off*, you bugger, we know, we're coming, turn it off. My right foot almost trips on the goddamn sill; then my left foot starts to slip on water on oil on deck next to the engine-room entrance, but my arm glides out and grabs the bulkhead and I manage, somehow, to maintain balance. Slow down, I say to myself, slow down. A firehall, the siren running, worse: I wont have any ears left. Turn it off. I stop at my cabin to hide underwear and nylons in case *he* comes in here. When I step out, I cant get the stupid door hook to hook open the way it usually does. The hook simply will not slide into the brass eye, and that's what I'm fiddling with when Coco comes out. C'mon, she says, we're supposed to be there. I slam the damn thing shut and follow her past her cabin and the men's wash space to the poop deck.

Boat drill, screeches Puppi who is at the bottom of the ladder waiting for Jock to move up further. She looks mad. Her arms are filthy. *This* is interrupting *her* work. She sticks out her jaw to indicate to Coco to follow Jock. But Coco touches Puppi's shoulder (all knobby) to tell her that she's next. Hairy legs. Purple ballet slippers. She's a fool, Puppi mutters. Red nylon undies. Stupid man. Puppi glares back at Coco who begins climbing, and I look up into the faces of several curious passengers who are looking down at us.

When I get to the upper deck, almost everyone is there: Jock, Buck, Hal, Lefty, Marty, Beebo, Don, The Chief, and Ray. Lefty is beside the crank that is used to lower the port lifeboat down, and Hal is behind him, and Ray's beside him with a watch. Get outta the way, Puppi mutters at the passengers who then scrunch up toward the starboard side to let us through. Ray glowers at his watch. And Coco and I both plug our ears as we step toward him. He waits until we are assembled before he gives the signal to Don who is next to the wheelhouse to indicate to whoever's inside to turn it off which he (finally) does, thank god. I glance at Ray staring at his round watch then look away. I'm so relieved that the sound has stopped that I dont feel anything else yet. I know he's upset, but I dont feel anything.

I look at Beebo; we are slow, very *slow*. He gives me a smile. We are, everyone else is, waiting for Ray to say or do something. I look at the others; everyone seems to be seeing Ray although no one seems to be looking at him. He pulls out a yellow pencil and marks the time down in a black, wire-coil book. HUUUUMPH, is all he sounds. Ray takes a step toward us and then says in a voice that conveys almost no tone, no feeling: stand back, let the women do it. What goes through my head is, we'll show you, I've lowered a lifeboat before and it was a bigger one than that. Puppi and I step over toward the handle as Lefty and Hal move back, and Ken emerges from the wheelhouse. Ray glowers at me and notes the time.

I feel myself fluster. I grab the handle. He's not going to make fools of us. Puppi is as mad as can be: *he*, this man, he is telling *her* to do *this* on *her* boat. She grabs the handle from the other side. She pulls and I pull. No Poops, I say, *this* way. Her eyebrows scrunch but something in the way I say it makes her realize she should listen and she lets go. I keep pulling but nothing happens. I can just hear what they'll say around the hall about this – two crazy dames trying to lower a boat by pulling against each other.

I move around to her side: push, I mutter. Everyone seems to be standing back. I swear they'd be laughing their heads off if it weren't for Ray. The thought makes me put even more force into the push. But we are not together. Puppi springs onto the handle. It doesn't move. We stop. One, two, three, push, she mutters. We push and it wont budge. We try again. It wont move at all. Coco steps over to help us. She gets on the side I was on and prepares to pull. We bend our legs and push and pull. It wont budge. It wont budge at all. The three of us look at each other and try once more. Puppi isnt with us. We cant do it. I'm pissed off. I use all my body on the next push. I even spring onto it and so does Puppi. It wont move.

I feel them all looking. Fools. Fools. Are they laughing? I cant tell. I know my skirt is almost up. I can feel the air. I can see Ray's bottom jaw. We're going to try once more. Just one more try and we're *going* to do it. We try. All our force. It gives a bit? Not at all. I stand back. Hurt. Humiliated. Puppi and Coco are both red in the face. They try this time without me. I see white and muscle – Puppi's spider-muscly arm. I want to laugh. What kind of joke is this?

That's enough, says Ray. I am really mad. I stand back and see the men. They are smiling. I stand next to Beebo who whispers, no sweat, kid. I could almost kill him. The men will do it. We'll see. Lefty grabs the handle and starts. No sweat all right. I glance at the passengers who seem to be peeking around the captain's cabin and pretending not to notice what's happening. Lefty cant get it. (Well, big boy, having trouble?) I hate to be shown up. I hate to be weak. I know I'm not as strong as a man, but I just hate to be shown as physically weaker. Jock steps up to join Lefty who's still smiling. (Smile away.) They try. More force this time. Good. It doesn't move. They try again. I'm about to giggle. The men are not smiling. Neither is Jock nor Lefty. I look at Coco who is like a serious mother warning me not to laugh when she really wants to laugh herself. The men cant do it. I'm glad they cant.

They try once more. It doesn't work. The goddamn thing doesn't work at all. Ray steps close. He must be mad. He's still not going to show it. How long has that been like that? he asks Lefty. I dont know, sir, Lefty says in a more polite and subdued tone than I've heard him utter a word in all trip, it must be jammed, sir. Ray shakes his head. I start to wonder what would have happened *if* we had needed it. We would have sunk by now. It's been at least fifteen minutes. Ray mutters something to Don who isnt responding. Get over and lower the other one, Ray says to Lefty and Beebo. We get the message: it *better* work.

We follow the men around to the starboard boat. The passengers scatter forward and aft and to where we were. I stand against the captain's cabin near Coco and Puppi who are shivering in the breeze. I got *my* work to do, Puppi says. Wait, says Coco, it wont be long now. *What if it doesn't work?* I whisper. It Jesus well better, Coco says, or someone is going to fry and it wont be us.

Some of the men look pissed off, some amused. Beebo, who is closest to it, grabs the handle. He smiles. We all wait. He rolls the lifeboat out in three easy turns, and then it starts to go down toward the water. That's enough, says Ray, that's far enough. He notes the time in his little black book.

## 16. Three in the Afternoon

A white bedspread. A green ceiling. Shadows. I lie naked and clean on my bunk and try to nap. I roll slowly with the *Nootka* and listen to her engine sounds/throbs: some deep, some high, most in a mid-low range. I watch shadows dance/change shape and think about what happened at lunch when the men argued in the mess.

Hal and Beebo told Lefty: You're our delegate; it's in the contract, boat drills on weekdays with a half-hour's notice; we gotta make him stick to it or we lose our rights. Lefty wanted to let it go: give the old man a chance, will yuh? – we know why he did it; we stalled so's the women would get an extra night lunch and he wanted to get back – that's all there's to it. Horsefeathers, said Beebo, I dont care why – he's breaking the contract and we cant let him get away with that. You're our delegate, said Hal, whose side you on? Give him time to learn, said Lefty, give him a break fer godsakes. No, said Hal, he's gotta start his learning now. If he doesn't read it now, if he doesn't respect it now, then who knows what he'll try to shove at us? C'mon, said Lefty, *that* was shoving? Ray could get Thor on *that one* if he wanted. Cant you see the report? Eight minutes for ship's crew to amass on deck. Port raft nonfunctional. Twenty-five minutes to clear the ship, *twenty-five*. If he puts that in writing, Thor might never sail again. I hear you, said Beebo. When is the last time that bugger worked? They all laughed. No one knew for sure. A summer ago. Two winters ago. Last Easter. No one knew for sure.

    I turn onto my tummy. My back muscles are stiff from trying to get the lifeboat down. I cant get comfortable, cant find the right position. Coco and I weren't taking that drill seriously at first, but in some ways we were: she sure as hell wouldn't want someone slipping in the galley breaking a neck cuz she didnt wipe spilled sauce up, and I didnt want him or the mate in here looking at my underwear drying all over. I had no way of knowing no one would come. We had no way of knowing the port boat was jammed. What *would* happen if we had to use it? Would they cut the cable with an axe? Would there be an axe to chop it with? Would there even be time to get up to it? I've never thought of it. Hal and Beebo dont want anyone stepping on their rights, but if death is the potential, what good are rights? I was always told it's safer to stay with an overturned boat or parts of it than it is to swim. What was it? What did I hear? If it's over half a mile, dont try? Even though I swim well, I bet I couldn't last an hour in that water cuz it's too cold, even in summer, life jacket or no life jacket.

    Death by drowning. One time I dove too deep and stayed down just above the bullwhip kelp too long. As I surfaced, or thought I did, the surface wasn't there. I lay back and looked up at it: a thin line, like a telephone wire, way up. I realized I could stay there forever in that warmth/that ease. Then a very small part of me told the rest of me to keep moving, to go up to the next surface, and the next. No fright after. No recognition. Nothing except that it felt nice and warm down there, enclosed yet free. I almost returned. No. This would not be that. I'd be cold. I'd wait. I'd hope. How far away would I have to swim from the *Nootka* to not get caught in her suction? I dont know. I dont even know who knows. If I couldn't get in the lifeboat, if we had no chance, I would swim and try to find something floating to hang on to, that's what I'd do.

I see dying fishermen: one clutches a log, two are stranded on an overturned boat, another tries to reach an oar held out by a buddy, but he cant make it cuz he cant swim. They are freezing, hypothermia, they are freezing to death. Green arms reach out to me. Skulls with thin skin stretched taut. Gasps. Wheezes. Gurgles. Open jaws. Bloated bellies. Eyes that knew something. Eye sockets where gulls were. Caked blood. No blood. Expressions of horror. Hideous. Empty. Arms that clutch. Clutch to wood. Purple-black skin. A little piece of green seaweed hugs rotting flesh, hugs bone.

I roll over and wake up partially. I scrunch into a fetal position and hug my clean, sore self. Feels good just to be here. I choose to concentrate on something comfortable. A coffee mug is all I see, a white mug with a blue lady on it, a bonnet on her head, a tulip in her hand. I feel the warmth of her hair. Then I walk in from playing late outdoors and warm golden air touches my skin. My mother lifts a glass casserole of macaroni and cheese out of a black and white oven. My flesh is surrounded by its smell and there's a lot of crust – goldenbrown crunchy – for me, no one else, just me.

Gulls cry. Shadows dance. *Jump. It isnt far. Jump.* The down side? Or the up? Grey, fifteen-foot waves. Where do I go over? I dont know. The salt cuts my eyes. There's no time now. Get off. I cant see. I hear shouts and screams. A fat red shirt slides backwards down the deck toward me. The man's feet slip out over the narrow metal edge. His enormous thighs get caught between it and the bottom railing. He screams. He broke a bone? Help, he says to me, please, I'm afraid of water. I grab under his fat wet arm with my right one and grasp his suspender and shirt neck with my left hand and tug. The water rises. Meat vomit sticks between his teeth. I cant let him drown on deck, but I haven't the strength to pull him out.

Mommy, Daddy, he whimpers. Let him go, Beebo shouts to me, save yourself. The man is so scared, he faints. Metal screeches/scrunches – our keel is caught on a reef? This is stupid – we're not going to last here. I try to hold his lopsided head up so he doesn't drown and his tongue down so he doesn't choke. Passengers scream, crawl, scramble. Beebo inches toward us. The ship shutters and cracks again. Jump, says Beebo, Jan, jump.

I step through the just-painted railing, my foot touching the man. Salt spray cuts my eyes and nostrils. I cant see anything but water.

People shout: I cant swim, Mommy, Mommy, god, oh, god. Their voices are far away. Metal gives out from under. I jump over, out, into a large grey wave. The inside of my head is red. I see nothing but red. My brain coils in away from cold skull. Little planets of white start to appear in the red as I try to swim, to swim against the current away from the boat. Thighs lift, arms thrust, legs kick, and I move slowly, so slowly away from it all. Stroke: kick, kick, kick. Stroke: kick, kick, kick. Breathe. Stroke: kick, kick, kick. Stroke: kick, kick, kick. Breathe. Stroke: kick, kick, kick. Stroke: kick, kick, kick. Breathe. Stroke. *Jan. Jan. Jan!*

Dad? I feel a large lump near my thighs. Fingers touch my spine? I cant turn. I have to keep going. Voices. No engines. Angel voices? Thick thighs kick. Ankles balance like fins? Red and white splotches. There is white cloth all around me. Is it part of me? I try to lift my head to see what it is. But I cant cuz I have to breathe, have to concentrate to not take in water. Have to get further out of her way. Have to get far, far away. Have to get warm … it's warmer here. Keep breathing, that's the main thing, that's it. Make your head into a prow and breathe air from the tiny trough, that's it.

*Jan.* That voice again. He's not here. He cant be here. Where am I? *Jan.* He is here. Where am I? Get back to the warm spot. Float. The lump on top of my legs grows. Do I have to carry it and swim for it too? I breathe, stroke, kick, and float: breathe, stroke, kick, and float. Cant get rid of it. It doesn't cling but presses. *Jan.* A seal? A giant jellyfish? Firm flesh slides up and down my spine.

*Jan, it's Ken. Jan, wake up*! I turn over into white and particles of his voice filter through air. *He is there.* Ken, I say, Ken, what are you, what a, what a. You were shouting in your sleep, Jan, he says as he moves his arm around me to untangle the cover. (I cant believe I'm here. I'm really here and he's here and the cabin's here and the boat is floating and we're on it and everyone else is on it too? It didnt happen. It didnt happen?) I heard you through the port as I was passing by, he says, you sounded scared. He kisses the top of my head. (I cant feel him. I can see him touching me, but I cant feel a thing. He shouldn't be here. It must have been a dream, but it feels more real than this, so this is the dream?) I tried to wake you up, he says. (I can see my breast and arm, but they dont feel like parts of me.) What happened? he asks, do you feel all right? I dont answer. (I hear you, Ken, but I cant get my throat muscles to work. I'm afraid I might wake up and swallow water.) After what feels like moments – his eyes blurry, blue, close to mine – I hear my voice blurt: we are, we were sinking, the boat drill, and I, and I …

What a fiasco, he says into my neck. Slow down, Jan, breathe deeply, that's better. I move back into him while he starts to talk about the boat drill: no one's going to complain, you know, cuz there's wrong everywhere ... the Mate's wrong, the Old Man's wrong, the winchman should have checked, Thor should have checked, even the daycrew could have checked the davit. The words swirl. They are like large building blocks. I cant piece them together. I can only feel his muscles starting to give their heat/their energy to my skin/my flesh. His smell – diesel and dirty clothes and rancid sweat combined with his particular, almost cedar-edge – surrounds me. Everything will work out, he says as he turns me over and slides under the cover, everything's going to be all right, Jan.

Our eyes meet/almost hook above the pillow. His smell floats right into me. Belly almost touches belly. Only trying to help, he says as his fingers slide first onto then slowly off my hipbone toward my cunt. Don't, I say and our eyes merge, unmerge, unhook. (My insides just crumple. I cant stand how I feel. I cant stand it when he looks hurt either.) C'mon, he says, tilting his head back slightly. Warm little waves circle out from his fingers as he brushes the top of my cunt. You better go now, I say. Why? he says, letting go and moving his jean-covered cock against my belly, you like this. Not now, I say, not here. Just a quickie? he says. (A quickie? I dont want a quickie.) He fingers me inside hard. Not now, I say, no Ken. He wont stop. I grab his wrist and pull his hand away. (Bone. Muscle. Bone.) Okay, he says with a little-boy-cant-get-his-way-hurt look. (That wont work on me; that wont work anymore.) I'll go to the mess, he says, *will you join me there?* Yes, I say. He tugs me. Yes, I say.

He smiles like he's still not sure, like I still might change my mind. He gets off my bunk slowly. My cunt prickles/burns. I watch his silhouette against the green shadows. Sure? he says gruffly as he opens the door. I'm sure, I say. He turns his back quickly. He shuts the cabin door hard. (Pissed off.) I'll join you, I shout through the closed door, in a minute.

Blurry blue, so blurry blue, I smell your smell and I love you. I get up and pull my nylons on. Yet I hate you too, you self-centred prick. You dont understand. I dont want a quickie here or anywhere. I breathe the warm air and suddenly realize I am really here; everything is beginning to look good. Even the gummy soap looks good. My shoes. My uniform washed yesterday like the guys do their jeans – soaked in a bucket for hours, then plunged with a toilet plunger. Nice to have clean things to put on. Nice to brush clean hair. Nice to get ready to go talk with Ken. Just talk. Maybe not about what just happened. Maybe not about us. I brush and I brush. He probably doesn't even know what he's doing. I bet. I bet he knows exactly how to look that way and exactly how helpless it makes me feel. Nah. He's probably just unaware like so many other men. I take one last long stroke. Bastard.

## 17. Just a Moment

Wet. West Coast rain comes down so hard that in just four steps from my cabin to the mess entrance, I'm all wet. As I turn the brass latch and step inside, a chunk of wet hair falls over my left eye and cheekbone. I flick it back and see Ken sprawled on the bench. Hi, he says as if he hasn't seen me for a day or two. Hi, I say as if he weren't in my cabin moments ago. I flick my head again then shake it.

Poured you coffee, he says, pointing to the white mug on the end of the green table. Thanks, I say as I stand there combing my hair with my fingers. This isnt the way I want to look. This isnt the way I want to feel. I pull the sticky uniform from my shoulders and then my thighs. Ken just lies there facing the galley and me with his legs spread apart and his mouth grinning. I glance at the slit of red leatherette bench between his legs and at his crotch. Then I step toward the cooler, open it, fetch the milk for my coffee.

You going to stay like that? I ask before I put the milk jug back. The latch clicks. He doesn't answer till I sit down. Like what? he says teasingly. You know, I say. No, I don't, he says and gives me his little boy blue look. We each see into the other but not very far. I look down at the pale green oilcloth to avoid our look and a drop of water falls onto the table. And then another. My fingers bring the two drops together and more drops fall off me. I feel stupid. He's teasing me and he knows I know he's teasing me. I make a star of water and then a circle. I cant stand this avoidance. My eyes drift up his legs to his knees, thighs, cock, there, on his left next to the zipper.

Why dont you sit up? I say. Why, he says, I enjoy this. So do I, I say and I lean back in Buck's chair which isnt really Buck's chair, but he usually gets to sit here which means he usually has to move every time anyone wants in or out of the bench or the cooler. I look from Ken's jean-covered cock to his red-covered chest to his blue, blue eyes. *He is enjoying this.* I look back to his crotch. Ken waits a moment then lifts his right knee up to block my stare.

That's better, I say. What's better? he says. You know, I say, why do you always make things so hard? He laughs. Who's making things hard? C'mon Ken, I say, but laugh too. You know, I say, you'd make love with me with anyone passing by and it wouldn't bother you, would it? He nods and grins. You wouldn't care about any of them? Or me? Or Sarah? His whole body grins. Just cuz you feel like it? That's all? That's all it is?

He doesn't say anything. I go back to making water stars and crosses on the green oilcloth. I, I want to know something, I say, without looking at him. Shoot, he says. Dont laugh. Promise. I want to know if you want *me*, or is it just a moment? Could I be any woman? You *could* be any woman, he says, but you certainly are not. My wet eyes stare at his denim thigh. Ken doesn't say anything. You would take me here, wouldn't you? I say looking directly at him. Sure, he laughs totally confident. On the table? He keeps laughing but sits up.

*Do it*, I say.

His face whitens. His laughing stops. His mouth opens.

## 18. King of the Jerks

Just as I finish scrubbing the deck Sunday night after a big turkey dinner, Lefty comes stomping through the mess from the galley with his OcTOPus QuINtON pot. He stops to put honey in his mug (leaving the jar all gooey), pours in the tea (the pot stains the just-wiped table) and stirs it (the spoon leans on the pot and drips). I stand at the doorsill watching while I wait for him to finish, so I can wipe his footprints off the deck. Couldn't wait any longer, he says as he passes me, Betty's usually done before this. No fooling, I say.

I quickly wipe up his footprints with the spaghetti-noodle-like foam mop. When I go out to the railing to dump the scrubwater, he's standing there waiting; I have to go further aft to throw it over. You better put in enough overtime, he shouts. Jesus F., I shout back. Whad'ya say? he says stepping closer. You heard me, I shout with my back to him. He comes up to me and places his right arm next to my bent elbow. When I finish dumping, I turn. He holds his mug in a lean, brown hand just four inches from my nose. I back against the railing with the bucket in front of me and between us. I cant see anything but him (wet, black curls, light brown eyes, sassy expression). I dont like to hear women swear, he says, it doesn't suit them. I'm not *a* them, I shout. Oh yeah? he retorts. Yeah. Bet you dont do your overtime the way we tell you, he says. I haven't done it yet, I say. You wont – you'll just do like the other women do.

I'll do what's fair, I say, after I discuss it with Coco. My back presses the railing. I want to get out and away, but I'm pinned in by him and the gear on the deck. What's a matter, you dont trust us? he says. It's not a matter of trust, I say, but my eyes are on, almost in, his hot tea which could spill. It's confusing, I say as I push the bucket with my leg onto his leg. The contract says I get so much for each thing and then sometimes there's a lot more to do because I'm learning and I shouldn't get paid for that, but then sometimes I'm going to get paid for work that wasn't as long as it says like that second night lunch last night. So you figure you'll just follow Coco and do what she says, he says. Yes, I say, what's wrong with that? That's a mistake, he says. He moves his mug to his lips and my neck loosens just a little. You got to learn to look out for yerself right from the beginning, he says after he takes a sip, and then you can help your sister understand too, eh? Perhaps, I say, but I'm new to this. You're new all right, babe, he says. I'm not your babe, I say, now let me go.

Just one question, he says. Okay, one. I notice you shave your legs. What of it? Do you shave your pussy? *You're dis-gus-ting*, I say. C'mon, he says, you want me sweetie. *I don't*, I shout. *C'mon*, he says as I knock the pail into him. *Fuck off*, I shout. He looks slightly shocked and stands back. Suddenly, Jock's there on the deck. I duck out so Lefty's between the two of us. Suuccccccch, suucccccccch, suuccccccccch: Lefty sucks air in through thick lips. I feel him laughing at me although I know I hurt him (and my leg will be all bruised). I move further away and stare into his eyes. He's just sucking and acting like he's won. What a fool. From behind, Jock pulls Lefty's arm. But Lefty and I keep up the stare, him daring me to do something, anything. This man, this jerk in front of me cant stand hearing a woman swear but it's perfectly okay, perfectly okay, to tell me to open my legs for him or to ask me if I shave my pussy. What a jerk. C'mon you monkey, says Jock, got something to show you below. Jerk, I hear myself mumble. Whad'ya say? retorts Lefty breaking our stare. Speak up, he says, I cant hear you. Who do you think you are – King of the Jerks? I shout. He looks really proud. Slurpy proud. He's got me. It doesn't matter that I just won our stare, I cant help smiling about it. It's an honour to be called King of the Jerks: *to him it's an honour*. And what's more, he's got Jock as witness. You're not wanted, Jock says to Lefty. They leave and so do I.

Half an hour later, after I've had a shower and slipped into Hal's jeans and white cotton T-shirt, I enter the mess. Green walls. Men and smoke. They have their overtime sheets in front of them. Everyone, except Ken who is on watch, is present: Beebo on the chair near the door, Hal on the one next to him, then Buck at the end in front of the cooler, with Jock and Lefty each taking half the bench. Whrrrrrrrrip-whirrrrroooo, the king whistles. I ignore him/it and go into the galley to make myself a sandwich for the supper I couldn't eat.

Put down one and a half at Clo-oose, says Beebo, that way we're consistent. Aye, Jock says. Hell no, I hear Lefty say as I carve leftover turkey, one, only one. Chickenshit, says Beebo. I explained it at Clo-oose, says Lefty. While they bicker, I slap the cranberry sauce onto my sandwich for which I need mayonnaise from the boys' fridge (boys all right), so I enter the mess. The contract's clear, lad, says Jock. Here it is, says Hal, section 6a: *Dayworkers covered by this agreement shall be entitled to a twenty-minute break for coffee at 10 a.m. and 3 p.m., but such coffee break may be varied up to one half-hour either way.* As Hal reads, Buck, whose back almost touches the cooler handle, moves out and Jock over just so I can get Miracle Whip. We didnt break till nearly four, says Beebo. The way I understand it we should get the overtime for the break just as we would if we had to work through part of the supper hour. Aye, says Jock, find the section about meal hours, Hal: *In all cases if one unbroken hour is not given, the men involved shall receive one hour's overtime in lieu thereof. This overtime shall be in addition to the actual overtime worked during the meal hour, but sufficient time to eat shall be allowed at first opportunity which shall not be deducted from the overtime period if work is continuous.* Trouble is, says Buck settling in his chair as I lean over Hal trying to see the contract myself, you have to be a lawyer to figure it out. Cocklepot, says Jock, we weren't given the mug-up during the stated time and he's got to learn he cant push us around on this or anything. Agreed, says Hal.

Bullshit, says Lefty, we get one hour for the few minutes we worked after our shift, and I'll remind the skipper that if he had allowed us to break early, then there'd be none. *You working for the company?* says Beebo, *or are you representing us?* Everyone stares at Lefty whose face whitens: us, he says (eyes shift slightly), but some thanks I get. I slip back into the galley to finish making my sandwich – wily man, tells me to go for more and argues with them for less, pushes me, bullies. Bullying doesn't always work, does it, jerk? If he disputes it, are you going to stand up for us? asks Jock. Hell yes, says Lefty, I might even put down the half so the dayworkers are together, and when he disputes it maybe we can settle some of the other items by giving this up. I dont want to give up, says Beebo. It's the principle, says Jock. Well, says Lefty, trying too rapidly to explain or cover, he wont interfere with an early mug-up ever again. No one says anything. The unmuffled engine racket is all I hear as I pour myself a coffee.

With my sandwich on a plate in one hand and my mug in the other, I stand near the little wooden cabinet and roll as the ship does. I suppose you want to sit down, says Lefty inviting me as distraction. There's no room, I say, I'll just stand here. You heard us, Jan, says Beebo. Yes, I say. Members' ears only, he says (letting me know I am not to say anything to anyone about this which I wont), but tell us what you think. (Lefty, nonplussed, looks like he doesn't believe this; this is certainly not my business; overhearing members argue is one thing, speaking another.) About the issue? What else? Let me read the contract, I say, putting my coffee and sandwich down between him and Hal. Tell you what, Lefty says, I'll give you a thrill – come sit next to me. There's not much I can do. I can stand and try to read and eat while the ship lists and sways, or I can go back to my cabin and eat alone sitting on my bunk with my head bent over because there's so little space between it and the upper and between the upper and the ceiling, or I can sit next to the jerk. Great choice.

I look at Buck whose whole forehead wrinkles as he shrugs. He slowly starts to get up again so he can step out again so I can move in again. Jock squishes toward the corner but he is so roly-poly that he cant get his right leg over as far as the table end without standing to get out, so I have to slide over it/him. And then my leg gets squished between his leg (thick coveralled thigh) and the table. Dont excite him, says Lefty as I'm moving slowly over Jock's lap, he hasn't had it up since Noah's ark. Wise guy, I say, but we all laugh and it breaks the mood/shifts the focus. Lefty's sure raunchy, I whisper to Jock just in case he's a trifle hurt which (even though he's laughing loudly) I can tell he is. What's that you say? says Lefty, What's that?

Nothing, I say turning to him, but it's good you're getting home tomorrow. He gives me a wet, sexy look which I turn from and ignore as Hal passes me my coffee, sandwich, and the contract. As I read the contract, they continue checking their overtime: three and a half for Ucluelet, three and a half; one at Gold River, one; one at Tahsis, one; eight at Zeballos, eight. Well? says Beebo. We're waiting, says Buck.

There's no question, I say, that you missed the break at the normal time, and that when you miss part of a meal hour you get an hour's overtime, *and* you eat, *and* the overtime you get for working continues *if* the work continues. Am I right that that's what those two sections mean? Yes, says Beebo, you got it. Agreed, says Lefty. Okay, I say, then *if* the same principle that applies to meal hours *does* apply to coffee breaks then Beebo, Jock, and Lefty should be entitled to twenty minutes overtime in lieu of the break *plus* the break *plus* the overtime for the work after regular hours, and Hal should get overtime for the break he missed while on watch. We dont have twenty minute overtimes, says Beebo, it's one hour for the first hour and then in half-hour units after that. If that's the case; then the way I understand this Jock and Beebo are right – one and a half each for the dayworkers and one for Hal. See, says Jock grinning, Jan understands it, Lefty, do you?

Lefty, just slightly chagrined, adds the half-hour to his sheet. He's annoyed cuz he's lost yet pleased cuz he's got a reasonable argument, even if it did come from a woman and a non-union member at that.

MONDAY

*Linen*

The following items shall be supplied for the use of the unlicensed personnel:

1. Two (2) white sheets, one (1) spread, and one (1) pillow slip, which shall be changed weekly.
2. A suitable number of blankets which shall be laundered and changed every three (3) months.
3. One (1) face towel and one (1) bath towel which shall be changed twice weekly.
4. Sufficient suitable face and laundry soap and soap powder and safety matches.

## 19. Underwear

I'm through now, Coco says, you can start cleaning the galley. Okay, I say. Jan, she shouts from the mess, the guys will be in for early mug-up in half an hour. Okay, I say. And if you smell my pies burning, she says, will you turn the heat down? Okay, I say. I'll be back, she says, to pull them out. Okay, I say. I pick up a full pail of water and Mr. Clean. It's cold. I empty half, fill it with kettle water, fill the kettle with cold water, and place it on the stove. Half an hour, I better do the ceiling first. I take off my shoes and stand on paper on the wooden counter. First I dampen and wring the rag. I wish I had brought gloves; my hands are flaky already from the Fels-Naptha and they sting from Mr. Clean and I'm just starting. Just starting.

I wipe the hatch which is just behind the wheelhouse: soot, thousands of grains of fine soot. The *Nootka* rolls gently through smooth water and grey air. Monday morning. No sun. Just mist or close grey cloud. Water runs down my arms. I rinse and wipe, rinse and wipe. I move the paper over with my feet and start the other hatch. I'm a rinser, I'm a wiper, I'm a rinser, I'm a wiper: that's what I am and that's what I'll be. I wipe the top of the slatted shelf that holds all the plates and bowls. I'll do the insides later.

*You are my sunshine*, I start to sing, and keep singing. My pail is dirty. I do one final long swipe across the top of two white pipes and am squatting to get down when something lands inside my collar. Aaaacccch, I scream. My shoulders tighten about it. I see Ken's feet through the hatch. Bastard. I pick out the scrunched piece of paper and throw it up at him. Not hard enough to counteract the breeze. It twirls around and lands in my bucket. Pass me a coffee, eh Jan? Come down and get your own, I say. C'mon, he says, just one little favour for an old friend? I cant refuse him. I blush. I scramble down and step over to the stove. I feel shaky at all my edges. I hold my bum in. I straighten my shoulders. I try to pretend he means nothing to me at all. I bring the full mug to the counter. You still take both? I shout. Sure, he says, double everything. He pushes his hand down and I stretch mine out and up, up to those beautiful just slightly stubby fingers. Thanks, he says, see you later.

I check the kettle and fill it and put it on. I empty my bucket in one sink and fill it in the other and dump in more Mr. Clean. What next? The slatted shelves. Do I have to take everything out? I wont get through this and the galley walls and the whole mess in an hour if I do. I wont. I'll leave them until lunch when we're using most of the dishes and then it'll be easy to lift the rest out and do the insides. Nothing is sooty; there's just a thin layer of grease that cant be seen but is here. Here. I stroke down to wash, wring out the rag, up to rinse, and occasionally swirl where fingers, oily male fingers, have touched. Down one slat, down the other, swish at the bottom, rinse the rag, wring, then up one slat and down the other. One ... two ... three ... four ... five ... done. Then the whole of the under. I stand on the deck and tackle it like I'm in a contest: who can ... who can clean this board the fastest? I can, I can the fastest, I am the only one here. I empty the bucket again and do the slats over on the other side of the mess entrance where the mugs are. Do the under. And then over the top of the walk-in and down that wall or bulkhead toward the galley bucket.

*Shit*, it's full. Well I dont want to stop to empty it now. I pull it out in front of the sink so I can get in behind. I lift the gucky cardboard and lean it on the walk-in door. The wall is filthy. A brush. Use a brush. No. S.O.S. I grab the S.O.S. The first one gunks up. I use more, more, more: all soapy, all gooey, but the crud is coming off. Come off, I say, beans, egg yolk, sausage fat, off, off, off. Talking to yourself, eh? says Beebo. What? I say. I cant get this stupid junk off. Dont worry about it, he says. No, it's got to come off, I say. He looks at me and laughs. It's very important, I shout to him, it's gotta come off. You're serious about dirt, eh Jan? Yes, I say very definitely and loudly, it's gotta come off.

Beebo picks up the cardboard, shoves it under where the mugs are, and goes into the walk-in while I rub and rub. He comes out with bread, onions, tomatoes, and a cucumber and drops them on the counter. We're going to be having mug-up, he says, you wanna come sit down with us? I cant, I say as a piece of paint comes off with the yolk, I want to get this done. You know what they say, he says, all work and no play makes ... how does it go? I look up at him from my corner and see the gucky cardboard against the wall I just cleaned. It has "dull" in it, I say. He empties the coffee grounds in the bucket next to my bum. You wanna sandwich? he says, I'll make you a special sandwich, Jan. No thanks, I shout to the wall, *shit*, the paint's coming off. Take it easy, he says. I turn round to him and look straight up and over into his eyes. You look good when you get mad, Jan, yeah, you look good. I dont care how I look, I say. Oh yeah? he answers.

He makes coffee and I throw the S.O.S pad into the bucket. I empty the cleaning pail in the sink. You shouldn't do that there, says Lefty from behind me. Why? I turn around and shout to him. He comes right up to me and touches my bust with his chest. cuz you'll clog it, sweetheart. *I'm not your sweetheart*, I say as my back digs into the metal of the sink, *and stop feeling me*. My, my, he says, boy are you hot. And I'm not a boy either, I shout as I shove him. Getting horny, eh? he says holding both my wrists. Not for you, I say into his mouth. C'mon lad, says Jock to Lefty, cant you see you're not wanted? Lefty lets go of me and snatches an onion from off the counter and starts to bite it. I turn from them to finish rinsing the narrow (it's only about two feet wide) bulkhead as the three of them make toast and sandwiches.

I haul the galley bucket back into its space and pick up the cardboard that Beebo got for me at Tahsis after he realized I really didnt have any because Ken and I threw them all over the first night out. I put it (all splattered and greasy on both sides) back to protect the bulkhead from more junk, more fat, more leftovers. Sure you wont change your mind, Jan? says Beebo as he slaps HP sauce on a sandwich of sausage, cheese, onion, mustard, lettuce, tomato, cucumber, pickle, and god knows what else – there's no way that's going to hold together. No, I hesitate. C'mon, says Lefty, I poured you a coffee. *Lefty poured me coffee?* He is standing next to the stove, two mugs in one hand and an onion-green-pepper-leftover-bacon sandwich in the other. You promise you wont bother me? I say. Do *I* bother you? he says and laughs. You know what I mean, I shout back. I know, he says, what do you take me for? Just what you are, I shout, and Beebo and Jock laugh. I walk out and he says something and they laugh at that.

Laughing, they pass me while I just stand there inside the mess waiting for them to sit down. What did you say? I say to Lefty. Just teasing, he says. I know, I say with my hands on my hips. Sit down then, he says. I'm not sitting Lefty Quinton until I find out where *you're* sitting. *Jesus F. Christ,* he says and slams my coffee down on the end, then he slides along the bench to the far end. Jock sits on the bench between us, I sit in Buck's place, and Beebo's next to me on my left. Well, how do you like boat life? Beebo asks me. I just snicker. That's no answer, he says, we want to know. Everyone's arms are in the centre grabbing cream and sugar and honey. We're waiting, lass, says Jock. It's a lotta work, I say, that's for sure ... uuh ... how come Ken's not here? Washing up, says Beebo. Eh, lass, says Jock, you didnt answer.

I like it, I say. You like us? says Lefty. Sure I do, I say, especially when there's someone between us. The others smile. We were wondering, says Beebo, what you did at university. My god, how do I answer that? Not much, I say, it's kinda hard to describe in just a couple of minutes. Try, Beebo says. It's, well it's, it's, it's different than school and way different from here. They're all looking at me as they chomp their sandwiches and I feel funny. I almost say I didnt like it at all, but that's not entirely true. I read stuff I'd never have read if I hadn't gone there, I say, and I went to lectures and plays and poetry readings. You read poetry? says Lefty. Sure, I say. They look incredulous. Someone they know reads poetry? I like it, I say, I go to readings where poets read their own works aloud. You mean people pay to listen to some "guy" recite about flowers and bees and love and all that stuff? says Beebo. Sure, I say, but it's usually free; it's good you know, it's not, well it's not about flowers and bees and it's not like what you think poetry is, it's, well it's real. They laugh but with a type of curiosity. Give us some, says Beebo. Now? Why not?

Let's see, I say, uuuhhh. (The first lines that come are Gregory Corso's, "Should I get married, Should I be good? / Astound the girl next door with my velvet suit and faustus hood?" Velvet? Faustus hood? They'd laugh. I think of Williams's "The Red Wheelbarrow," god no, and Ginsberg's *Howl*.) I know, I dont know much of it, just three or four lines. Say them, says Beebo. There's a man named Charles Olson who's a big, big guy and lives in Gloucester, Massachusetts, who wrote this:

> to dream takes no effort
>  to think is easy
>   to act is more difficult
> but for a man to act after he has taken thought, this!
>  is the most difficult thing of all

*That's poetry?* says Lefty. Yeah, I say. I like that, says Beebo, do it again, why dont you? You mean it? Yeah. And I do, more certain this time, and just as I get to "for a man to act," Ken steps in. I hesitate. Dont stop, Jan, says Beebo. "But for a man to act after he has taken thought, this! / is the most difficult thing of all." Ken smiles at me and goes into the galley. What are they like? asks Lefty suspiciously. The poets? I say. He nods. They're just like everyone else, I say, but I know that isnt true and it isnt what he's asking. They talk a lot, I say, and I know that's true but doesn't say much to him. You wouldn't be able to pick one out on the street or in the pub, I say, they're tall, they're small, they're attractive, they're gangly, some are gay, if that's what you mean, but I bet you wouldn't be able to tell. I can always tell that, Lefty says in a mocking-queer tone. I know at least one you couldn't, I say, he's a bit bigger than you and works in a warehouse for the ILWU. Really? says Beebo. Sure, I say, poets are doctors and millworkers and insurance salesmen and teachers and carpenters and pea pickers and almost everything cuz nobody or hardly anybody can live off writing. That so? says Beebo. Yeah, I say. Any seamen? he asks.

I think Olson fished, I say, and Jack Kerouac worked in the merchant marine, but I know ... he's not a poet but he wrote all sorts of good fiction ... you ever heard of Joseph Conrad? No one has. Well, you might like him. He wrote *Heart of Darkness* and *Typhoon* and *Lord Jim* and many more. What's going on here? says Ken, leaning against the mess entrance. Jan's giving us a lesson, says Beebo. No I'm not, I say, but shut up. Ken comes and sits on the chair next to Beebo's. Did you ever go to one of these here poetry readings? asks Beebo. Sure, he says. He doesn't look embarrassed or anything. What do you do there, lad? asks Jock. I listen, he says, everyone listens. That's not my idea of fun, says Lefty. Poems *can* be funny, says Ken, like Ferlinghetti's. You ever read about him? No one has. He's got a poem, says Ken, that'd make you split your gut. It's about a dog pissing and walking his way around San Francisco; he's got another one about underwear that ... Underwear, interrupts Beebo, poets write about underwear?

It's not *just* underwear, is it Jan? it's about ... you might say, the underwear symbolizes everything, Ken says. I dont like his tone when he says "symbolizes" cuz I think of it as a way/a word that belongs to university, but I also dont like it cuz he's asking for help by looking straight at me. It starts off like this, I say:

> I didnt get much sleep last night
> thinking about underwear.

But then he brings all sorts of things in, the pope, the underground movements and Lady Macbeth and Castro and everyone wears underwear and it's, I dont know *how* to describe it, but it's funny and serious at the same time. Underwear, says Lefty, what a subject; I bet I could tell that poet a thing or two about underwear he's never heard of.

I betcha could, I say and get up and leave.

## 20. I Got *My* Work to Do

Gold on blue. White on blue. Green, West Coast rainforest and undergrowth green, floating on/in blue. The flag scarcely moves. The green island slowly, ever so slowly, slips by. Salt air and sun on/in skin. Stalling. I am stalling because I dont want to go below to sort linen. I watch the island (both it and its full reflection in the calm water) slowly pass, and then I descend the metal ladder. Diesel fumes enter me. The smell of sweat mixed with paint mixed with damp laundry hits my nostrils/my throat. Daylight disappears. Near the bottom of the ladder, I see it: a pile almost my height and wide enough to almost block the little passageway. I keep on the ladder cuz there's nowhere else to stand except on the linen pile, and I lift the top item with the tips of my fingers so my palms dont touch it – a grey (even in the dimness I can see that it can *not* be just *one* week dirty) sheet. But what can I do with it? There's nowhere to toss it but behind me and behind the ladder toward The Chief's cabin. So, I throw it there.

No, no, caws Puppi. I straighten and turn toward where her voice came from: a passenger's cabin (at the end of the little corridor which is only about five feet long). A white uniform struts toward me through weak, artificial light. I show you how, see? She tosses towels into the ladies' room and throws pillowcases behind her into a corner of the passageway. That's what I was going to do, likes to likes. Let me do that, I say. Puppi looks up at me (still on the ladder) and kicks the whole pile over with her legs (hairy legs surrounded by damp cloth). I step onto it and kick too: towels, sheets, blankets, spreads. Where can I sort? I ask. Anywhere, she says, use the corridor in front of the passengers' cabins, that's what *I* do. But I'll have to block some, I say. This isnt the *Queen Mary*, she shouts, the passengers will have to wait.

Puppi leaves to continue cleaning a cabin. I stand near the pile making it smaller as I make the smaller piles bigger. And I notice that some pieces are still white, and others are grey and even spotted black, black as cable dressing, black as creosote. I pick up a sheet that smells of Coco's powder or soap just like her cabin and toss washcloths, handcloths, towels, pillowcases, rags (aprons), blankets, bedspreads into their own piles.

Puppi comes toward me dragging a worn, canvas bag and muttering something about the big bag is mine, I used it, it's mine. Sure, I say, what's the difference? Use this, she says with a peculiar expression, it's yours. (Shit. I got it. Puppi's using Betty's bag just like she used the enamel jug till Lefty insisted and took it back. It means nothing to me, nothing, except for her delight in the deception.) What do I do when I'm finished this? Count a pile, record the number (she sticks out a card at me), then stuff the linen in the bag before you count the next one. I take the card issued by KEEFER LAUNDRY LTD. She hands me a red pencil stub. Thanks, I say.

The only space in the corridor to repile the piles to do the count is a small gap where the big pile used to be. I go into the ladies' and start throwing bath towels backwards toward it: eleven, twelve, thirteen? Thirteen, there should be eighteen less mine which I forgot to bring down, seventeen. I retoss the towels into the entrance of the ladies'. Thirteen. Take the card and pencil from my pocket and write thirteen in red in the towel column and place the whole pile (some wet, some greasy) into the bottom of the bag which I put where the towels moments ago were. No, screeches Puppi, big things go first. But there isnt room, I shout, I'm counting the smaller piles first and then I wont have to take up the passageway in front of the cabins. No, she says, shaking her head not at where I'm piling but at how I'm doing it. Big things first, she screeches, you're supposed to put! ... What difference does it make? I shout, they take up the same space no matter what order I or you put them in. UUUUUUUUUUUUUUUUUUUUUUHHHHHHHHHHHHH HHHHHHHHHHH, she screeches. She struts over to me. You *must* push down to fit them in, she shouts up to me, sheets or spreads or blankets go first. I look down at her and say in a calm voice, I cant see the difference, Puppi. You see? she says. No, I say.

Puppi jumps right into the canvas bag and pulls it up around her neck. You see? she says. No, I say. She pulls the rope cord tight and ties it; the top ruffles around her shoulders and neck like a clown's collar. You see? she says. No, I say. She bounces up and down. Canvas to her chin. Grey blob bouncing. Greasy man-head nodding. Eyebrows painted right into hairline wiggling. You see? I laugh. Her head ducks, disappears. The bag is about to roll over. My arm reaches out to steady it and she laughs. The top of her head, partially bald, clumps of fine hair held down by sticky stuff, emerges. She is laughing, laughing like she does when she crosses her legs to keep from wetting, which she is probably doing. I hold her/it in both my arms and prop them near the entrance to the ladies'. *I got my* work to do, I say down to her like she usually does over to me. She just keeps on giggling. *I got my* work to do, I say again in her inflection, and laugh. Then we both say it in unison: *I got my work to do.*

She/it jumps up and down, knocks over a pile of dirty sheets and then a pile of pillowcases. I grab her/it and almost lift/steer her the five feet to the longer corridor where she zigzags the entire length past all the passengers' cabins while I just lean against the bulkhead giggling. She bounces and zigzags back to me then steps out of the bag and without a word trots down the passageway back to the cabin she was cleaning.

I count sheets, cases, rags, spreads, etc. and stuff them into the bag till it's full then bundle what's left into one bedspread, two, three, and tie knots with corners; untie the first one, tie it again as tight as I can. I drag the bundles to behind the ladder so they wont block the bottom steps and the entrance to the ladies'. Then I haul the canvas bag to the corner of the corridor, but now there's hardly space for anyone over a hundred pounds to pass or for the passenger who has the corner cabin to get in or out. What am I supposed to do?

No, Puppi caws, no. What now? I say to myself – it's as if those moments of giggling and bouncing hadn't happened at all. Not here, she says. Where? I shout. She points to her cabin at the end of the passageway: number nine, she says, put it in nine. I drag the bag behind me down the corridor and haul it over the sill into a cabin which contains three fat bags that take up almost all the deck. I get my skinny one in by wedging it between all of hers and her bunk; now her deck is totally covered and she wont be able to use her cabin at all, and no room for other bundles except on top of them. Well, that's her business – gotta go get the rest.

I take a bundle and drag it by the knot which gets looser and looser as I pull. No, she screeches, you cant do that. She stares at the bundle that is opening. What *can* I do? I say. She looks mad again. There's nothing else to put them in? I say. They wont take bundles, she mutters. Garbage bags? I say. No. Puppi will take care of it, she mutters. I'll do it, I say, just tell me where there's another bag or show me how. *I'll* do it, she says in an I-told-you-so tone. But I know she cant stuff them all in the skinny one. She just cant. *Leave me alone, leave.* Okay, I say. I dont want to leave her to do my work, but I know from that tone I better get out; arguing will do *no* good. I bet she is going to repack one of her bags and wants me out of her way to do so, or she has more bags and was hoarding them and cant let me know. Leave it right there, she says. And I do. Right in the middle of the dingy passageway sits a bundle with facecloths and apron rags hanging out. *Nein, nein*, she mutters as she bends over my dirty linen. *Nein*. There's two more behind the ladder, I say. Leave them, Puppi shouts, go.

Okay. All right. I'm getting out of this dark, stuffy hole. I'm getting out of *her* way. I climb the ladder above the bundles toward daylight. Ocean-island air hits my forehead/nostrils/throat. When I get near the deck, light hits my face. My eyes squint. I see splotches of blue, white, green, and red as I walk toward the poop deck. Hi Jan, says Beebo. He is holding a scrubpail with hot soapy water in his hand and is standing inside the fidley. Hi, what's the time? Ten of eleven, he says. Can you let me know just before it's eleven? I ask. Anything for you, Jan, he says, sure. He leans back into the fidley to scrub the washspace and I sit on a wooden box and notice the buckets full of jeans and coloured shirts all soaking – for centuries seamen must have done their clothing this way in containers made of other materials – clay? What? What did they have that was unbreakable?

· I squint out at the sea then close my eyes and feel the sun on my skin and through my muscles. Muscles, I've got muscles that are beginning to be muscles again, like they were at twelve or thirteen growing almost daily. They're stiff from the boat drill, and my arms are almost hard from packing garbage buckets and tossing the slop over, and my legs firm from just standing and walking with/against the motion. I'd much rather be cleaning buckets and wiping greasy finger marks off paint and getting outside like this to sit on the deck for a couple of minutes smelling the ocean than sitting in a classroom or an office or a house. I wish I could stay here, now, forever.

Jan, Beebo shouts, look ... no ... over here! I stand and turn and see an island. Douglas fir and cedar: there's not a house or shack or a boat to be seen anywhere. Then, between the island and us, I see what Beebo's shouting about: a black, shiny, almost triangular fin of a killer whale. As I run to the railing, I see more, more curved, black, erect dorsals cutting through the water. We lean on the metal railing and point and count ten. On the deck above us, passengers lean and shout, whales ... come see them ... look ... look at that! Two leap almost directly out from where we stand: shiny white bellies, white ellipses above their eyes, soft-yet-strong-looking smooth skin. I shiver. Wish I could be one of them cavorting in air and sea. The two loop, turn, squeal high squeals and clicks, then slide into the Pacific, smack and slap their tails. That big one probably weighs four tons, maybe even five, says Beebo, big for a killer.

Three now leap where the pair did. Not even ten seconds after the duo, the trio reach a point at which they are almost vertical, as if they are about to balance there, twenty to twenty-five feet of squeally, black and white, shiny flesh. Then they arc and turn/slide into the same tilt-angle as the first pair before making almost identical, graceful entries and loud smacks. Choreographed orca, I shout to Beebo through their whistles and cries and squeals which go way way up further than our engine sounds: a blend of over a hundred notes both mammal and metal at once. I dont even see the next trio break the surface because I'm watching the first trio enter. They, then, repeat the same movements, a synchronized killer whale dance.

What a display, Beebo says to me as he slings his arm over my shoulder, and I slide mine around him just above the belt. We smile into each other like two five-year-old kids with full bags of candy. The last duo emerge and do their aerial acrobatics as the trio ahead sing their trilly whistle-songs as they all make percussion clicks. Together we watch the pod, which has the whole Pacific to play in, glide away. I wish.

## 21. The Watery Part of the World

We reach Point Atkinson in the late afternoon. I've just dished myself a bowl of potato salad when I see the shiny-white, red-roofed lighthouse through a porthole in the mess. I step on grey paper I put down moments ago to protect the mess deck from whatever might happen in port. They dont care, Puppi said, shore mechanics dont care if they tramp oil in or not, it's not their boat. I turn the brass knob. But before I step outside, I glance at the clean walls and ceiling, the shiny green table, the clear honey pot and chutney jar and sauce bottles, sparkling ashtrays, a blackboard that is really *black*. Nothing's going to stay this way long, but the clean order makes me feel good. I step outside to see the lighthouse which I saw perhaps before I could even speak, then again and again as a little girl and young woman on ferries to Vancouver.

I walk along the red deck and sit in the sun on a wooden box just outside the fidley. I take a bite of creamy, new potato salad, which tastes so good. West Vancouver homes and North Shore mountains on one side, distant university towers and green trees and huge sandbanks on the other. Everything is clear and sharp. Have a wee beer with that, lass? asks Jock from just behind me. I turn left and Jock's not there.

I stand up and shout into the dark fidley to the pails, mops, and sinks: You in there? Aye, he says. But I, caught by the glare of white paint and sun, cant see where he is. His hand, then his upper body, comes out of the darkness holding a plastic glass of beer. Thought drinking was against *all* rules, I say into his slightly red, close-shaven face. It's only apple juice, Jan, Jock says as he steps out of the fidley and I step back to my box. I sit down in the sun. Thanks, I say. I feel the fluted ridges of the glass then take a swallow of warm beer. Best juice I ever had, I say. It's only half a one, Jock says, not to worry. I look up at his stubble-less face, so much younger without the grey. I imagine passing him on an escalator in Woodward's, wondering about him, about his energy, about what he does. I look at his dungaree shirt and *clean* coveralls and imagine him at thirty.

You off now? I ask. Not yet, lass, he says, but there's nothing to do till we dock. I take a sip of beer: my skin and hair all clean and warm in the sun, the potato salad and beer so good, the lighthouse beautiful (white so white, red so red); everything seems perfect. And what are you going to do when you get in? I ask Jock as he leans on the ladder. Go to the Legion with Mabel, he says, maybe quarrel a bit. Must be nice to have *two* nights off, I say, trying to ignore what he just said. Not the way the wife blathers, he says, been together forty years now and mostly we just fight. What about? I ask, what do you fight about after forty years? Nothing, he says, canna even remember what started the last one or what it was about – never do – they're always the same. I look at him. He's gotta be kidding. We drink, he says, dance (I imagine a fat lady shorter than Jock and the two of them foxtrotting belly to belly), quarrel a wee bit, more than a *wee* bit, love a little. You have any kids? I ask. No, he says, never had any, dont regret that either.

I want kids, I say, someday, not many, maybe two. Enjoy yourself first, he says, no sense rushing into marriage when most of them dont work out. I dont say anything more. I look out at Spanish Banks and the sea and the little sailboats gliding through muddy green water. I see the sand of the beach and cars moving between willow trees along the Spanish Banks Road. We slowly pass a yellow barge full of gravel heading in and a green barge full of wood chips heading out. Even without getting up, I can see streams in the water: wide bands of browny-green fanning out from the Fraser River among bluer, non-river strips of ocean water. I love that, I say to Jock, ever since I was a kid I've loved seeing that Fraser mud in the ocean. Sometimes I've seen it halfway to Nanaimo. One time I flew and I could see it even further. Jan, he says, you love many things. You should go around the world before you settle. Never can tell what might happen or who you'll meet. Go to Piraeus. Sail the Greek islands. The ocean is so clear you can see down a mile or more, and visit Egypt and Australia and Hong Kong. There is nothing, nothing like the smell and noise of sailing into Hong Kong. I might, I say, I just might ship out on a Norwegian freighter. I met a mate in Tahsis, you know, he said it's not impossible for me to get on. That so? he says.

After we chat about the possibility for a few moments, Jock leaves me to go into the galley. I stand at the rail and dream; I could sail on a Norwegian freighter and my travel and food would be free, or I could work here every run they give me and save up for a year. I love being right where I am now. The sun, when there is no barge in the way, reflects off the *Nootka* and ocean floor in such a manner that rays come up from below creating broken strips of light in the murky brown-green. I haven't seen enough of British Columbia to leave it. The mud here, good soil, is washed down from the interior, from places like Osoyoos and Summerland and Kamloops, brought down by the Thompson and Similkameen to flow into the Fraser to form part of the delta or to settle in the inlet or to drift out to sea.

I feel like it's part of me and I want to merge with it, to swim among the particles in the ocean of ever-changing water and light. We pass a green and grey freighter which is wider than we are long, a hundred and sixty-five feet according to Beebo. Six or eight of us wouldn't make one of her: Japanese? Russian? Greek? German? I cant see her name. She is floating high (without cargo) and is waiting, waiting for what? Grain? Salmon? Lumber? Sulphur? She's out on the edge of English Bay and Kitsilano Beach cuz there's not room in the inner harbour for more than the freighters that are already loading or unloading or just waiting to load.

I think about Hong Kong and Bombay and Port Said; I'd love to see Cairo, Athens, Singapore, Rio de Janeiro. I look up at the centre of the Lions Gate Bridge coming toward us, not the actual centre but the centre of where we are which looks like the real centre coming out faster than the edges, and I hear the traffic whirring away and look straight up as we float under tons and tons of vehicles and steel. And I can smell them, or I can smell it, the city and Stanley Park; maybe it's all the people and all the fumes and all the trees and dust combined, but it's a smell I haven't had for days, a wonderful, particular, Vancouver smell. I am surrounded by it. I enjoy several breaths and then try to imagine the smell of other city-ports I've been in like New York or Montréal or Seattle or San Francisco. Cant. But I've always come from the land. I bet Jock and all of the men know the smell of each city, could recognize each with their nose.

Coming up on the north are triangular piles of yellow sulphur which were loaded in the gas fields of southwest Alberta and northern B.C., a by-product that's become a product for something, loaded into railway cars in small towns and unloaded into piles here, piles that are larger than three-storey buildings, piles that are brighter yellow than anything else in the harbour, piles that will be loaded into ships' holds as cargo to be carried to where? ... to be unloaded by more men to be used for what?

What are you dreaming about? says Hal. Loading, I say. I didnt hear him come. I didnt know he was here leaning over the rail just a few feet from me. He, like Jock, is clean-shaven and just-showered. Loading, he laughs with a mug of tea in his hand, loading? Sure, I say (he looks like a darker, slightly smaller James Dean wearing a green plaid shirt), why not? I thought you'd think of other things, he says. Like what? I reply looking right at him, right at the *married man*, Beebo said, *married man*. Like how you're going to spend your paycheque, Hal says, or what you're going to do when you get off. I look away from his wet lips. Kissy lips. Just-showered body in clean clothes. I dont have any plans, but I certainly wont tell him that. I stare at the sulphur piles and the boxcars from all over North America. There must be tons of sulphur – thousands of thousands of tons – in that huge bright pile, and the air doesn't smell of it at all.

Hal, I say. Uuh-huh? Do you have any idea where that stuff goes to? The sulphur? Yeah. I think it's used for chemicals to make plastics, he says, much of it goes to Europe for that. Then we buy it back, I say, in coffee grinders and kitchenware and such. I guess so, he says, but someone told me it's also used for fertilizers and explosives and pharmaceuticals. We smile. Well, that's one of the things I was thinking about, I say, about how the whole province, about how the workers of the prairies and us are just growing and loading and unloading and cutting trees and killing fish and harvesting grain and loading then unloading, always moving cargo elsewhere, waiting to do it or doing it, but all this energy, and for what? So we can buy a pill made in England or a car from Japan? Or sugar from Cuba? Sure, he says, what's wrong with that? Keeps us all working, doesn't it? Yes, I say, if you look at it that way. I do, he says.

He smiles. He takes a drag of his cigarette and broods. I'd love to touch his arms through his shirt which I am looking at in order to avoid his eyes. You didnt answer me before, he says. I dont know what I'm going to do, I say as I cover what I'm feeling. Hal, let's go over there. He follows me starboard as we pass Pier A where the *Princess of Vancouver* always docks. I glance at it and Piers B and C where hundreds of immigrants who built the railway who farmed the delta who fished the ocean began their Canadian lives: more loading and unloading, beginning and beginning again. You know, I say to him, that's where we always docked when I was a child. I can see and smell the inside of that building even now. I remember how exciting it was to get outside of it, to be on the mainland and in the city. He smiles. Island girl in the big city.

Hal, I say, I think I'm going to ship out again. He flicks his cigarette butt into the bay. You know what I think about that, he says (black eyes into blue, I cant think at all, can you?), you should throw away your shipping book and forget this, just forget it. (I would love to run my tongue under the edge there, under the edge where the ribbing of his white undershirt touches his neck.) We both look right into each other. I wish, I wish life were more settled for me than it is. We both laugh a little. I was only trying to find out if you're coming for a beer with us, he says. Does everyone? I ask. Usually.

I want to hug him but don't. I look at the brick sugar refinery again, old bricks in a city that's mostly built of wood and concrete. What are you thinking about? he asks. I dont say you, I love the way you look. Sugar and golden syrup and bricks, I say, then hesitate, I was thinking about my uncle who has worked in that factory there for thirty years (we both look at the refinery as if my Uncle Frank is at this very moment looking out at us). I cant imagine what that feels like, I say, thirty years, but you couldn't last a month? No, I couldn't, he says. Wet kissy lips say.

Well? he says. Well? I say. We can see the company building, a cream-and-red warehouse sitting in the sun on a dock covered with crates and boxes of cargo. Well? he says, will you be coming for a beer? Sure, I say, thinking this is not the end, we'll be on land together before we part, all of us sitting around a beer table instead of a mess table, sure. At the Princeton, he says, want me to sign for your cheque? It's ready? Of course, he says, the Old Man radios the information in to the company office. I'm fetching everyone else's ... how about yours? Sure, I say, totally pleased that I'll get it so soon, sure. You're in for a sweet surprise, he says as the *Nootka*'s engine stops. Huh? You'll probably earn more here in five days than you did on the CPR in two weeks. No kidding. Would I *kid* you? Hal says and chuckles. Not about that, I say. Gotta go, he says, I have to jump off the moment we tie up cuz it's closing time at the office already. See you at the Princeton, I shout at Hal's back.

As the *Nootka* drifts into dock and Jock stands ready to throw the line, I breathe air full of fresh salmon and look up at the lush North Shore mountains. Then I glance down into the swirls in the harbour waters.

# Short Prose/Sketches

# A Short Short Story

*MOTION* 6, DECEMBER 25, 1962

I woke up in the darkness hearing a slapping noise as if a piece of canvas was loose and banging the lifeboat in the wind. As it kept hitting, I slowly seemed to realize that it was not outside somewhere but in my cabin. Rather than turn on the light to see where the noise was from, which would have been the sensible thing to do, I ducked my head under the sheet and faced the wall. After a moment I slung my feet over the bunkside and saw some type of small bird caught in a pipe which was just inside my door. Being too afraid to do anything about it to go look to know what was the matter, I didnt twist the lightbulb or get close – I only grabbed a duster and edged out of the cabin onto the deck. There I stood trying to think about what I should do – "something, you know you should; help it, dont let it suffer" – and I finally moved over the damp deck up the slippery ladder to the upper deck along the wet surface to the wheelhouse where the second mate and the watchman didnt seem to understand what I wanted quickly enough but stood there smiling at the woman me in short pink pajamas, duster, wet hair, not listening to the person me about this bird that had to be killed right away because it was hurt but even before I had stated it clearly enough the second mate, who is usually snarly and acts tough if he isnt really so, stepped out of that green-radar-lighted-nothing-else-except-two-men-the-wheel-and-a-couple-of-tables-with-instruments cabin and walked in front of me across the windy rainy deck down to where it was. I watched his dark small head and narrow shoulders turn into my room then stood in the early-morning darkness on the back of the lower deck waiting for it to be over, looking at the redness of the edge of the ship at the point where it falls off to the black large-swelled sea, thinking that it was stupid of me and I shouldn't have waited making someone else do it and if it happened again I would have to when he came back and said "look here" holding it in his hands. I couldn't. "It's all right," he said as I moved over to where he was and he laughed lightly and shoved it up into the dark air then said "Haven't you seen that before?" I moved my head. "Sea pigeon, we get lots of them out here."

# Improsements

## Improsement 1

Beginning and beginning: writing is always (all ways) be(com)ing and be(ginn)ing in the wor(l)d. Once upon a time, she thought she'd write a beautiful book. She thought she was writing about here for (t)here. She though, thinks almost everything was/is a possibility in writing. Here includes her as does hear which includes ear; she includes he as the (or thee) includes he. Letters and words are presents/present, presences. Sentences: shapes or structures which depend on who the writer is and how she feels when she writes which also depends on how much she loves sentences and what she's been doing with them recently.

Recently, she's been marking finals and critical essays. She doesn't ever think of writing a beautiful book or beginning a story. She marks down her time to keep her going. When she notices she's too slow, she walks the dog or washes the car so, when she returns, she can grade more quickly. She looks forward to minor amusements such as the student who wrote improsement meaning imprisonment and the one who wrote thoughs instead of those, but she had added a "t" for thoughts before she reread his sentence. One student, trying to get the title of an Ondaatje poem, wrote cinanum, cinimen, cannamen, cinnimen, cinniman, cinnamin. Another wrote, this exert from *In the Skin of a Lion* focuses on the workforce. Exert force. Another said of bpNichol, he's talking about politics in general, that people must react, be aggressive, make changes, rather than stand back and watch as passifiers do. She imagined the whole Peace March, which was marching through Vancouver as she read that, sucking plastic pacifiers and thought that this student has no idea that pacifists make active choices.

### CLAUSES

Three years ago, she was in a composition class trying to explain, as one of her students put it, the mysteries of the semicolon. She was joking away about independent and dependent clauses when a young man near the window said, I dont understand – what does the first cause have to do with the second? She looked over his shoulder and saw a male teacher named P. walking toward what was supposed to be a temporary building. I'm glad I didnt sleep with you then, she thought. Oh no, she said laughing lightly, you're thinking of *cause*, but I mean (in a very teacherly voice) *clause*.

    A clause has a subject and a verb that might be surrounded by a number of other words but can, without these words, if it is independent, stand alone and make sense. Birds sing. Jack jumps. Jill wins. Each of those is a bare sentence with a subject – birds, Jack, Jill – and a verb. Each stands alone. Each is also an independent or main or principal clause. But look what happens if we add a word that makes them dependent or subordinate: when birds sing, if Jack jumps, because Jill wins. They dont stand alone anymore. Jack jumps over the candlestick – that stands alone and is what type of clause? Independent. Right. When Jack jumped over the candlestick – does that stand alone? No. Right. It's what now? Dependent. Right. While, because, since, which, that, who, when, where, after, if – all sorts of words make independent clauses dependent or sometimes called subordinate. Excuse me, said a student, why cant they just give one name to these things? Because there isnt really a they, she said; I know it would be easier if all teachers used the same terminology, but we don't.

## INDEPENDENT

When the class was over, she went to her office. She thought about the teacher she had seen and how, in the context of a class, she hadn't missed a beat, but she had thought of that one night several years ago when she first went out with him and how horrible she felt when he kissed her. He was between his first and second marriages then; she was still recovering from her first. He reminded her too much of her ex-husband or, given the fact that she had truly enjoyed the evening, she was afraid because when she relaxed she wanted what was over and wasn't ready to begin again. Displaced loyalties. An urgent kiss. A pushing away. Nothing soft. A desperation. She wanted a man, but not that man. He wanted a woman, almost any woman. Maybe not. Maybe he really wanted her then. She'd never know. Just another mystery with a semicolon.

    Within days, he visited her in her office. Semicolon. His second marriage was over. Semicolon. They talked. Semicolon. Can we talk again? Same time next week, she said. (One of the few things she hates about her work is how long it takes to arrange meetings of any sort, so if two people are available one week at a particular time then...) The next work day, he came to her office door and said, what I really meant was, if I asked you out, would you go out with me? He was standing in the open doorway. She was sitting at her desk. Independent. In minutes, she was going to see the man she was then seeing but who was pissing her off with his self-centredness as much as she loved his particular use of language, e.g., the lower intestines of Burnaby. Yes, yes I would.

Within weeks, she and he were in bed together. But we're so different, she'd say. They were different. They are different. They are also different than they were then different – then, back then, and then, three years ago. She discovered that he only kisses when he wants to make love. She loves making love, but she also likes to kiss kiss not butterfly kiss at other times. Compromise contains promise. Promise contains prose. Prose contains most of the letters of poetry, but means to turn forward, straightforward, the ordinary language of men in speaking and writing. To her, the turning forward is more the essence than the straightness (or men). To her, a sentence both improses and opens possibilities.

She loves turning, crookedness, circles, flexibility. Ability. The form of a sentence is so elastic that when she is not teaching others how to write sentences that are supposed to be straightforward she thinks she can do almost anything she wants within the confines of its structure. Sentences do make sense of the world. Ondaatje wrote *In the Skin of a Lion* in structures which, one of her students delighted in pointing out, are sometimes fragments, are sometimes run-on sentences, contain comma splices, etc. But, but, she said. Laurence uses fragments too, and there arent any quotation marks, and she uses you when she doesn't mean the reader. Yet, yet she said. Wah wrote whole paragraphs without punctuation in *Waiting for Saskatchewan*. Yes, she said. Wah's paragraphs cohere. Laurence's lack of quotation marks makes sense. Ondaatje's lines are written in the cleanest way they could possibly be. Naked prose. Speech rhythms. Everything fits. They begin and end in exactly the right place. What more is there?

# Improsement 2

### EXITS EXIST

She sits at her computer on a grey August afternoon trying to think of some(any)thing to write, takes a sip of coffee out of a blue-and-grey mug, looks out through Japanese cherry branches to where the mountains usually are – nothing but mist. There's only a few days before the new term begins. Sounds like a sentence. Feels like a sentence: 120 or so new students. Some will be getting excited, exit, *x* it – in a newspaper the other day the word excites instead of exists caught her attention. Further down the page was exits instead of exists. She thought about spellcheckers, how they cant catch mistakes like that; she thought about saving the article and writing a letter to the editor, but she threw it out because she's on vacation and every time she turns on the TV or reads the paper there are misused apostrophes, it's or its' instead of its, subjects that dont agree with verbs, etc. – an unpaid language cop she is not.

When she was in grade five, she went to the Diamond Elementary School which had three outhouses at the foot of the field and a pot-bellied stove at the back of the classroom on which all the grade fives and sixes melted their rat-tail combs and plastic rulers. They had to write with straight pens on foolscap, a lined unsmooth and unbleached paper with flecks of brown pulp in it. Her fingers were always blue with washable ink. She made big blots. She jabbed holes in the paper. Her grade-five teacher, Mr. Wilson, told her many times that her work was too messy. She broke nibs so frequently that her grade-six teacher, Mr. Winter, told her once she had to try to write with just half of one. Impossible.

One day she spelled lawyer without the "w" and then put the layer in parentheses and spelled lawyer right. Mr. Winter marked it wrong and, when she began to argue, he sent her out to the hallway where there was a red fire EXIT sign. She worried, waited, and began to cry. She tried to stop by pressing her fingers into her eyes. The tears rolled down her dirty arms, and whenever she opened her fingers she saw EXIT in red. She didnt want him to see her crying. Maybe she should run away or go home. She waited. She heard his feet walking down the aisle along the coal-oiled floor.

Finally, he opened the door. Mr. Winter did not carry the strap. He did not look mad. He quietly explained that she was supposed to cross mistakes clearly with one or even more neat lines – exactly what Mr. Wilson told the class not to do – and that lawyer was wrong no matter how much "fuss" she made. He was accusing her of deliberately crying? She cried more. He ordered her to go to the washroom, meaning the outhouse, and not come back until she was "better." Writing now (words simply appear on screen), she sees that messy foolscap and muddy yard and remembers the smell of the girls' outhouse at the Diamond Elementary School where she threw that spelling test away.

## X IT

X it: in London, at Somerset House, people can look up records of births, marriages, and deaths. When she was in England, she went there, at her mother's request, to look up some information on her father's grandmother. Within less than twenty minutes, she had located her great-grandmother's marriage certificate, not a Xerox copy but the actual certificate, signed with a large X. The lines were extremely zigzaggy, much like those a two- or three-year-old creates. She felt strangely connected with this great-grandmother she had never seen nor heard anything about. She imagined she had large hands and wore a long dress and had not held a pen until her wedding day. Perhaps she had had to focus really hard to get the two wiggly lines to intersect which they did way off centre. She imagined her, excited, exiting the church on a hill which overlooked a coal-mining town in the north of England: moments ago, she was single, but now with that X, married.

# Improsement 3

May 1, 1948. *I thought I would write you sooner but you know how you think you will write tomorrow and by the time it is tomorrow you leave it to the next day.*

Yes, she knows that feeling and so do many other writers know that feeling, but she didnt know she knew it then when she was eight years old and living at the Diamond, named the Diamond because two sets of railway tracks – one for Comox Logging, one owned by the Esquimalt and Nanaimo Railway Company – cross, forming a diamond in the centre. She reads the letter that she wrote to her cousin that already shows her voice forming, her style, and contains concrete details of her family's day such as, *Leni bought a watering can and now that we are home she is watering the garden.* Her mother kept it along with another:

Dear Mom

There was'nt enuogh grain to feed any of the chickens I thought that daddy or you could feed them. But since it is my day I will give who ever feeds chickens a dime. ~~I will take a banana from the warming closet.~~ I am going to Lael's and will be back soon.

Love
Gladys

Those sentences improse/open particulars for her. She smells wet chicken coops in February and sees a 1920s enamel electric stove (bought by her grandfather in Nanaimo), shaped like old woodstoves with a warming cupboard on top of the oven and a shelf above the elements. It had high curved legs: Leni used to crawl underneath the stove and hide. The warming cupboard was only warm when the oven was on for an hour, so that's where her mother hid the bananas which were something very special in the 1940s and the price may have been the same as it is now. Did she put the banana back because she had already had her share? Did she think her parents would be mad at her because they forgot to buy grain? She remembers a path through the Douglas firs, a shortcut to Lael's house, and almost chokes at the feathery-shitty-dusty closeness of chicken coops she hated cleaning or even entering. She always felt relief when she didnt have to scare hens off nests so she could collect eggs. She hated plucking dead chickens. But she loved little chicks and the feel of a warm egg in her palm, especially in February. The sentences and words in these notes improse/open memories for her: warm eggs from the Diamond on a winter afternoon.

# Journals

FROM

# The Vancouver Poetry Conference Journals

1963

## A Walk about Campus

Start with the sound of fog horns, of lunch bags being opened, of rain on a window. Move to one of the army huts along the East or West Malls – they're gradually being squished out by the glass concrete buildings – but still there in winter is a smell of damp clothing and overheated radiators and coal-oil floors. A girl sitting in a bloated armchair watches a narrow-hipped boy walking to the front of the room. A young teacher moves in, settles his effects, and talks to three students before starting the class.

Go into one of the new, much-plastered, thinly painted plywood corridors. One-thirty. A place full of bodies – crewcut, puffy-haired, raincoats over the arms, suit-covered, unanimated except for the going somewhere which is a room anywhere with a number whatever nailed to the door. Move up the stairs and many brush you, slow dull pressings but no one seems to notice for there are so many and this has to be and why expect more except one "hi" slung out from the crowd going down or an occasional mixing of eyes.

Upstairs in one of the seminar rooms, a tall balding-headed professor speaks quietly, definitely, while a seagull swoops up past the window. Outside, the mountains beyond the salt water are covered in fog and the horns bee-oop through the class making that part of it too. Students in the class sometimes fiddle with watch bands, scratch thoughts down on book covers, lie with their heads on the table; students out of class sometimes dawdle with each other, talk about what just was, ask the professor and other pupils questions as if this shouldn't have been cut off by a loud, too-long-ringing buzzer and next week will be too late for then there will be some thought/feeling else and this should by right be found out/talked out now.

From there to the caf if you haven't got a class – and that if you have two in a row sometimes gives you seven minutes to pick up and put on a coat, get down a muddled staircase, open your umbrella, go across (trying to hold lunches, books, gym strip, everything) gravel, paths, slippery pavement, cement, sidewalks, soggy grass, one quarter of a mile to another building to unload, take off coat, set up notebooks and texts again – where the tables are full of books, paper, leather cases, cups, and seats are covered with coloured blobs of sweatered people. It depends on who you are as to what type of conversation you'll get into that in part depends on where you sit. It's hard for a first-year student to walk up to a front poet-theatre-library-writing table and say something.

But then for anyone to say anything is difficult so for the most part it is a loud chit-chat of where I wents, what we dids, how the party or the movie or the dance was, how to get to and from someone's place or a laundry or a second-hand bookstore, how much a fifty Ford is selling for, where and who from what high school got which mark on what midterm and which professor is known as a soft marker on the essays but a stiff one on the finals. Sometimes thoughts get bantered back and forth but rarely do they seem connected with the people who are saying them – words skitter on the surface and it all becomes a game. The game is in a basement, ceiling held up by pillars, a bright red floor.

Leave the plastic sticks for spoons wonderful clean-up man caf and head for the library. Black umbrellas open in the air, yellow wires block off areas of the grass. Two inches of water cover the cement by the pool and this must be walked around or sloshed through depending on what's covering your feet. The wrought iron gates near the door are open but on Sundays and at night are closed and then look insubstantial, from another time, as if they could hold nothing of the large building in. Two fat staircases lead up to the main floor – usually there aren't too many people on them but almost always the tables and desks are crowded. A sign says you can't reserve places by leaving books open but most people do.

A number of people studying in the library aren't working at all: a short-haired girl sits pulling Scotch mints out of a package with one hand, thumbing through a Spanish dictionary with the other while waiting for her friend to come back from the stacks so they can talk about what's been happening to the people they know; a horn-rimmed-glasses medical student studies an anatomy book by filling out white cards and falls asleep; a crew-cut, probably-taking-freshman-English-for-the-second-time fellow skims a poem, turns the page to see if there's any more of it, watches a girl opposite him who seems to be copying notes furiously, seems to know what she's doing, then turns back to himself: many students don't know what to do and hide this by activity which is wasteful, others become sleepy and sludgey and unaware of anything.

Drift back to the Buchanan building, late afternoon. People are standing watching bulletin boards, putting in time, looking for some answer there? A janitor walks by wheeling a grey metal cart to fill up with paper – he at least knows where to go. And a secretary from one of the offices whips in the door packing plastic cups full of coffee – does she think what she does has meaning, or does that even concern her at all? Right now there's a smile, a break from the work. Then to the outside onto the cemented-in-a-box flowers and sculptures that sit there and a bicycle that leans next to a wall. The workmen are closing their lunch kits, putting their tools in rectangular metal boxes, coming down from the opened-piped cement wooden structures. And the roads are filling up with two lights, two lights, four six eight ten, gradually a thousand – as everybody gets ready and leaves it all.

## July 26, 1963

One hour I was watching a Norwegian tow-motor driver picking up flats of whale meal and the next hour I was hearing Robert Creeley talk about the spongyness of paper. The remark he made that most interested me was how Olson in a letter would want to put one thing here

    another here

        **yet another here**

and show how no matter what their resemblances were they were far apart or could only in so many ways be this much closer yet in the other ways would have to stay where they were. The whale meal driver has it easy, he picks up his load at the same place each time and takes it to where he stacked the one before or starts a new pile right next to it if the last one is finished. He knows what's expected of him and does it. Creeley has it hard. He doesn't know quite where to start so it sounds as if he has picked up on the last thing that has happened or was said before he came into the hall. He finds it even more difficult to close off because he thinks he hasn't done enough.

Ginsberg started out by saying, "I don't even know what I'm doing here." He didn't seem interested in Creeley's conversation of paper sizes and textures of typewriters and background music of people around interrupting, yet the whole thing had to begin somewhere and he had no way of getting to it other than telling the students to feel free and do their journals as they wish.

The situation itself – seventy people, faces pulled in from the front, many who know each other from times past – seems strange.

## July 27, 1963

I walked into the no-windows classroom expecting I didn't know what – a thought already growing; seven people leaning in and adding to it taking away with a no that's not it, a what I really meant was; everyone equal but many not quite understanding – what would happen might be partially understood by most, completely by some for the moment but if these same some were there three years or seven hours later they might not get it all this time because it would be something else again showing another implication, another opening, another side-thought-area.

It was a beginning a starting out time. Creeley talked about the physical aspect of writing – how a paper longer than the size he was used to would bug him at the bottom because he was ready to write on the new one yet the old one had not been completed; how the type of paper had to have a certain texture, a spongyness and feeling; how a typewriter had to be not another's but his own because the unfamiliarity of where the marks were and the spacing might distract him yet using another's typewriter who he liked (as wearing another's jacket at times) could be pleasant; how people coming in and out or even just the thought that they might interrupt his thought and broke up the writing; how he liked to have music there to fall back into, it was something solid outside himself yet had variations inside itself.

Ginsberg started with "I don't know what I'm doing here." No one else did either. He tried to make us relax into ourselves. He told us how our journals should be free-floating forms of anything of interest but was brought to his notebooks by Creeley, what type do you keep? A large and a small that I can carry in my pocket; you can write anywhere in a room with people going on, in a subway, at a coffee counter? Yes, but that's me. Ginsberg is a rich warm man with curls on his neck and brown heavy eyes. His voice touches my breasts. I would like to bury my head in his middle.

In the course of the lecture, three disruptions took place that are now just as real as what was said itself. Two men in suits walked in, whispered a couple of phrases to Tallman and sat down. Later, they walked out as if politely they had been there to see if officially it was going on and finding it not too controversial as their curiosity had partially expected not anything they were interested in they walked out and probably went back to their work. A pixie-headed girl asked a question as to the form the course itself would take if continued to be shaped by the room we were in. Ginsberg failed to understand what she meant but Creeley did which surprised me because I would have guessed it would be the other way round. She became nervous in not connecting, not being able to say clearly her feelings about the university grey-heads squinched forward in a dead room. And the third, a bearded fellow who talked quite a bit. Many reacted against him, wanted him to shut up. He interrupted questions from the class directed to the speakers to answer them himself. Ginsberg interrupted him on one of the interruption tangles to say "I know what's going to happen to you – you'll become a square yet" and many people laughed a nervous laugh that swept up the desks to where I was at the back of the room.

At the end of the period there were so many people present who I had been open with at some past moment or other that I didn't know what to do when they came up. I couldn't be with any. Couldn't talk. There was an unsure-happy-just here-right here-hi-where are you now-what do you do-how do you do *really* do-what did you think of that-what was just this-it's finally happening-New York-Terrace-San Francisco-India-Albuquerque-Portland-Coal Harbour feelings to it all.

## August 4, 1963

Until the afternoon my feelings and personal life were jittery and hung up – any sketch-impressions-thought-record of the course became hung up (tried to say too much) and blocked/stopped also. So now it begins. Thoughts: Herodotus story way of reporting history as contrasted to Thucydides political (logical, objective, the normal words) way – we don't get the history as we don't get the news from what is given us so Allen must see, be there or at part of there himself (in India while Cuba happens, what then) and Williams must comment that "men die miserably every day for lack of what is found there" in the poems which should (depending on where you stand) carry this also. With Duncan if it's there it will come out only in a more general way for the location is more in a world he has made up himself as compared to Olson who starts from an actual and then gets to himself, his awe of the thing. Tides – the artist in his time whether he knows it or not and only after like the ring on the seashore when the tide goes out and can we/anyone see where they (W.C.W., Pound, Eliot, Moore, H.D., Lawrence) had been/are. To Duncan sometimes there is a low, a hanging nothing period (Patchen, Rexroth of this).

Rooms-houses-places are to live in and should be right for some people or they are unable to think-move-be. Jamie's place was good for awhile but now (too many people) he must move. The lecture rooms we first had were (people too close not being able to see) not good or free. Some people can sit closer to you and still you are able to be, but others must have half a room apart in order that you are still be yourself. These (Alan Graves, Helen Davey, Norman Moses, Sam Perry) I don't know how to handle except by trying to get in position that I am away from them.

## August 6, 1963

Duncan gave a lecture last night that showed the wonderful freeness of his mind. He started with three at-random openings in his *Kenkyusha*,* a book of Japanese character with phrases, sentences to illustrate the meaning.

1. Go to the <u>office.</u>
2. He would go to any <u>expense</u> in such matters.
3. Throw a person off his <u>balance</u>, upset, bewilder.

He also wanted to work in the words "work" and "futility." The structure of the thing was to be the poet, how it came about, what he should

---

\*   *Kenkyusha* is an English–Japanese dictionary or reference book used for miltary purposes. Jess Collins (Robert Duncan's lover) picked it up and used it as a kind of oracle. A person flips and lands on a page and their finger is drawn to a word it lands on. Fred Wah names Sum magazine after consulting *Kenkyusha*. Gladys names her dog Daigen and also Shinwa after consulting *Kenkyusha*. It's often referred by this group of writers as though it were a person.

and did do. He was going to show what he thought was the offices of a poet were; how he should use all of himself, his resources; and I don't know how he intended to work in balance. He started before the age that words had meanings, told how they swam about him, how his childhood book of Japanese prints illustrated either letters or words. He at one point thought he might become a poet and sat naked in the night on a rock listening for the sounds. He then went to "work" to light and dark, doing and futility and read some poems. About twenty minutes before the end he started stumbling on how he was going to tie this together – how a poet must work on a poem, how he must go to every expense he has, how little one can enter another person's life-poem-body and somehow he did.

Thinking about what I have just written I realize how very little I was there at all.

• • •

After hearing Duncan on form in the Monday Herodotus lecture, I had wanted to make the journal into a form that worked easily for me. But I couldn't and so things sound like reporting and not wanting that, there's nothing. So I'll do as he did and open the only dictionary I have here and see if something related to the course can happen:

**Phonic** – Of, pert to, or of the nature of sound; specif. of or pert. to vocal sounds, phonetic. b. uttered with vocal tone.

**Echelon** – An arrangement of trooper with units drawn up in parallel lines, but each somewhat to the left or right of the one in the rear, like a series of steps.

**Spelunker** – One who makes a hobby of exploring caves and studying phenomena observable in them.

Phonic to Olson to the nature of not just sound but the word itself. A person can wear them loosely and use the other man's meanings without knowing it. On Monday he got at Sam for using words without defining in himself what he means. Sam spoke of moving on a ladder of steps out into the non-ordered to him chaos world. Olson insisted that it all had order, nature's order. Sam was thinking of all that is not known yet but there to be discovered. I do not know how Olson means anything – cosmos and polis, that's all you need to know. Yet everything in a poem must have that arrangement that inner intensity-connection each word-thing-perception-thought with the other, which comes again to sound and to meaning and to order – someone's order, whose? Nature's? The event itself's? The poet's? The poem's? Spelunker – I read hobby or habit and combined with studying phenomena observable it goes to Levertov seeing a scene and then being fired to get something out of it or to wait there longer really having the scene come to her. She talked of not inducing this faculty but letting it happen and being ready to have it happen by consciously observing. I think that when anything goes straight into a person it cannot help but come out sometime in some form later (reappear – part of it – however briefly).

## August 8, 1963

One thing that I have noticed while taking this course is that ordinary speech bothers me. Yesterday after leaving the morning session we walked to the graduate centre. The men ahead of me in line were having a what's-going-to-be-here-this-year discussion. They so irritated me that I heard myself saying "I can't stand to heat chit-chat any more, I keep reacting to every word." They were naturally startled and shut up until they sat down. Then they kept looking to see what it was that we'd be saying that was so important, which of course was nothing but I can't cut it off. For example, Olson said "monism" in class the other day and I misheard him as "moanism." It went like this – "The trouble with modern society is moanism" – yes, that's true, that's what I like about some of the people on the boats, they don't complain; when you ask "How is she to work with?" the first thing that is said is "She complains a lot" or "Really easy, never complains at all" – to university and being critical where it is easier to complain or whine or moan about something than it is to do or make straight.

So far I have not been pleased with myself in the course. I feel I should be coming across with something and that I am not in it the way others are.

## August 11, 1963: Aboard the Island Princess

I went home this weekend – now, people scattered on seats all around me, rain from thunderstorm on deck above me – and woman in yellow sweater with dog in her arms comes up and introduces self just after

I explain to a bearded man who I once ate clam chowder with on another ferry that I want to try to get something down – and had a talk with my father about the newspaper item above.*

To begin with, "to toe the line," to become average like the rest. My father felt that this is what it meant. I felt that he could see how others lived and was willing to live within this scheme while not necessarily accepting it or any of its values, that he goes along with people as people. The money I saw as the reporter asked him how much he made last year and the year before and the year before then coming to a figure. But on the page it can sound as if he deliberately was trying to live cheaply on $1,500. My father asked, what's Jamie going to do? What does Sam intend to do? Which again circled back to how are they going to earn money. He spoke of the "daily struggle to cope with the demands of rent, housekeeping, savings, and children's bills" as a great straightness and direction-giver yet he said was most happy just before and just after I was born. Forty cents was a lot. I told him that Ginsberg could not help but change if he got married but to say that this is coming to terms with life was wrong; he thought, no, that earning a living and having a child and a wife forced a person to come to some terms. I said just existing did this, that it took a pattern whether one knew it or not but that a person should be able to not accept the habits-pattern as the best for him/her if they weren't, that he/she should be awake to what they are and want to do. "Generous gesture" bothered me because it had the sense of not serious, flippant, not living yet until he did have their daily struggle. I see work not as a trap but a deadener after the repetition sets in of awareness-openness. I think that I learned much from people of people by working and living with them on the boats yet in the end it is simply a matter of that's where I get the money in order to live. The question is more, and how to live? Olson talked of haunts and habits: to have an order, a way of handling things makes one freer in a sense but also closes over sight-hearing-swell-thought off just because one does know the way it is, accepts almost than what is there itself. But without some pattern – to bed at night, marriage for most, class meets at 10:30 MWF – which a number of people however loosely or rigidly accept/believe in/go along with everything (driving where there are no roads) would be too hectic and impossible (stores are not open all the time) to live, be with/at.

---

\* Refers to a newspaper clipping entitled "Marriage is for Ginsberg" that appears pasted in the journals.

Looking at these four men – Allen Ginsberg, Charles Olson, Robert Creeley, Robert Duncan – and two women – Denise Levertov, Margaret Avison (first names here because Olson insists on his, although in thought I think of most without except for Denise Levertov and Margaret Avison), I wonder who I would most like to live like, to have as a model. Before they came, Ginsberg was the one I liked the best. He seemed warm and full, open to colour and place, easy in his feelings, at one with his body. Olson and Duncan were the ones I was with the least. Olson seemed too concerned with style, the way of it, the sound of it, and not enough with sight, feeling, interpretation, present, people. Duncan seemed too made up and unreal like curliques somehow but I realized this was just for me and not other people (ones who got sound). Creeley seemed too inside himself, making problems where none existed, consciously becoming alone by not handling those he did not like by being too polite and so hurting himself more. After they had been there two weeks both in classes and at parties and gatherings, my impressions switched. Ginsberg, because he does not move in terms of conceptions and because talking in lecture rooms almost forces this situation on a person, started coming across as a mind that had limits he did not want but were. Creeley, bugged by personal matters by feeling obligations to produce or show or say, came across as being very nervous and an upsetter to the way that otherwise it might go – he talked obsessively. Olson, willing to not talk and just look about, wait about, until something occurred which sometimes (histology of Herodotus day) he made happen, was much more there. Duncan, who I had not understood one item out of eleven of the last time he was at UBC, was much clearer and more accessible than I had expected – I liked the way he was able to talk freely, how he lived in a world made up on his own. Levertov, who had been a favourite of mine on "The Earthwoman and the Waterwoman," "The 5 Day Rain," "The Peppertrees" was more romantic and prissy than I had thought she would be. For someone to look up to, I started choosing Olson because his structure like Duncan's was large enough for him, which is something that Ginsberg's and Creeley's seem not.

Location is something that interests me. Ginsberg has a strong sense of place: parts of New York, San Francisco, South America, Denver, Seattle come through. He locates himself in it, in the many. Creeley has a very weak sense of yet he moves about a lot. He locates himself in the "I." Very few rooms ("my love was a feather" poem) come into existence or compared to Allen (rose in the closet of empty organ-grinder room). Olson locates himself in one place, Gloucester and makes that real for everyone not through description (Ginsberg) but through action (history). You can hear a name with him and it has no meaning other than the sound of it but later just as the sound of the name of a city some small sentence away in childhood became more real and gradually attuned to the place. Duncan like Creeley has little sense of definite place. He is more in his imagination, what was real to him from his childhood and medieval history. Even his "I" is a more made-up and not primal-he one ("often I am permitted to return to a field [sic]") than Creeley's I-this-self-me-right now is. Levertov, too, connects herself in space (the New York son forgets glasses she rushes down into cold coming up street, the Berkeley drive many-laned gasoline stop poem). Her "I" is closer to Duncan's or compared to Creeley's – less of her close self, more of a cover to make her so she can do what she does ("wear scarlett... don't let me forget" a dress reminding self of self).

My notebook has a mixture in it – mostly one or two words with an occasional sentence. Creeley – "I'm not satisfied with the habits of living that I've created for myself"; on another day. "I wonder if I'm not making myself up." Ginsberg – "If you speak from yourself, you'll be speaking to yourself, which is other selves." Levertov – "People deny themselves the things to which the poem leads them"; on form or a revelation not extension of content and self the thing through which the poem is made, "I'm not talking about my body." Whalen – "Don't worry about the meaning of terms." Olson – "The sentence is the ordering of the universe"; "How do you possess what it is that you do?" "I abhor fiction"; "I believe in an objective standing condition"; on the lateral line: "I ain't got no prejudice against it, I just don't like it." Creeley – "How can you be other than what you are?" Ginsberg – "Words say more than you know."

Words that reoccur – "consciousness," "risk," "intention," "habit," "inscape," "engaged in," "context," "care."

FROM

# The Blue Notebook

1975

## April 26, 1975: Saturday Afternoon

We are two: Lars, a banana-eating cowboy who is almost four, and me, a Player's-smoking mom who is thirty-five. We live in a house owned by Sheridan Cooper in North Vancouver, B.C., on Premier Street, a paved road to the district dump.

I work full-time as an English instructor at Capilano College. Lars goes to daycare at the college from 8 a.m. to 4 p.m. or more or less depending on my day, its ways (class and meeting schedules). I get up at six and Lars usually goes to bed (after a story and a talk and just another cuddle and just one more pee – carry me, Mommy, carry me) by 8 p.m. I, like so many mothers working outside the house or not, have very little time for me.

And who is this now coming toward me? A red-faced, snotty-nosed, wet-jeaned cowboy just a few more days three. Is it nighttime? No, it's nap time. It's getting dark, Lars says, the sky's dark. And so it is. We are in for an afternoon of rain.

## April 29, 1975

Got my grades in yesterday and joined our faculty negotiating team for supper before meeting with the college board and their lawyer-negotiator. As we were waiting for a table on the second floor, I looked out the Coach House Inn window and saw Lars racing a friend on our edge of Premier (our side of the street has no sidewalk – that's where the kids were – cars and trucks race by when it's lights out). I ran out of the room and down curved stairs to the main floor then outside between several parked vehicles and crossed Lillooet Road to bawl Lars out and who began to run ahead of me back home to Mike, the teenager I was paying to look after him.

"When I am fourteen, I can run across the road," Lars shouted.
"Yes," I shouted back, "when you're fourteen, not now."
"Mike, I told you to watch him – don't you ever let him run on the street ever …"

• • •

Talked with a student today who told me her husband thought maybe she should work as a typist or go to school full-time rather than do as she is doing now. This is her first academic course. She has four children, is thirty-seven, and is just starting to feel some confidence in her thoughts and self. Her papers are definite As. She and I know she couldn't manage full-time college without the support of her whole family which she doesn't have yet. Part-time (writing her essays from 10 p.m. till 1 a.m.) is what she needs: time to read, to think, to develop, to mull. And without more pressure: from self or family. "I feel guilty," she said to our whole class, "I enjoy reading so much that in the middle of the night I get up to make muffins because I enjoy reading so much."

## May 1, 1975: 11:32 a.m.

Four years ago, a moment from now, you were born. Lovely boy, pumpkin joy. "It seems to me," you said yesterday when you did not want to eat. "Mommy, it seems to me," you argue, you love, you say, "I'm sorry, I'm having such a bad bad day." You speak directly, not always, but so many times, you say how you actually feel.

You are such a pleasure, Lars, and such trouble – muddy in the morning before we go to school, throwing your scrambled eggs into the bathtub and telling me you ate them all, demanding more this and more that, but also reading and loving books, sharing toys, runny nose and comic looks, giggling, loving, kissing, cuddling, arguing, I love you, little boy.

• • •

In one week what I thought were alders beyond my backyard but now think are a form of poplar have grown leaves which are over two inches long. In another week, I probably will not be able to see the green and white houses beyond them.

White blossoms in the lot across the way. Pink blossoms on some of my blackberry vines. Nothing yet on my big apple tree, but little leaves on the small one. And tulips (supposedly two dozen red) I planted in the fall now grow – one yellow, two white, and a tiny mauve one are opening up. Dandelions – brilliant yellow – are scattered throughout my large back lawn. First full flowers of spring from this cool and wet land.

## May 2, 1975

One red tulip sits on my desk. Little leaves come out of the old apple tree. I plant a garden: onions, carrots, tomatoes, radishes. I answer the phone: Brian Fisher, my painter-lover.

"I'm trying to get the focal point right. If I go in too far too fast, I lose the all-over composition, too much detail, too close. If I stand back, I need the other. Easier. With joy. I need delight, a space where I work fast and on edge and if I lose, it doesn't matter. When I overwork it, I lose it."

What Brian speaks of holds for writing too. We need care, skill, a sense of form, voice, directness, but also looseness, freedom, rhythms which can include the whole but not forced – floating, engaged, and there.

## May 4, 1975: On Virginia Woolf

She is certainly an interesting person whom I can and cannot identify with. Such another time and circumstances: more money than me, servants, no automobiles (till 1925 where I am now) no indoor bathtubs-showers, no children; but yet much is similar – a literary crowd, reviews, incestuous relationships, people who come into and out of their lives but so many return, are in, forever.

I identify with her criticalness, with her awkwardnesses re buying and wearing clothes, with the despair and tensions and dependence on others for support and approval (yet here there are strong differences), with her not writing about the World War going on (again different: but I notice Vietnam is hardly anywhere in my notes) ...

I have obviously been afraid to publish. I most obviously stall on work which is finished to publish. I am pleased when I hear people talk of my quality as a writer. I believe what they say. I know Peter V is a strong story. I know some of the boat stories are. Yet I do not know that of *Sketches* or *A Birth Account* which I still return to as the most positive feeling of doing I had – to NOT care except to get it as close as I could to the actual perceptions of then.

## May 16, 1975: Lars Dresses Himself Today

brown rubber cowboy boots left on right foot right on left
brown denim shorts with a leather cowboy belt
blue T-shirt (yesterday's snotty) inside out
brown leatherette vest
red & blue cowboy shirt (upside down: collar at bum, shirt tails flapping through vest neck)

It is raining hard. "You should probably wear pants."
He is mad at me but pulls the shorts off and puts on a pair of second-hand wide-striped red blue green pants with patches.

When we get to daycare, he proudly pulls his boots off by himself and puts on his plaid slippers. His socks (also yesterday's) were inside out and upside down so the heels were top of his toes.

I'm proud of my independent beautiful clown-cowboy who totally dressed himself today.

• • •

Lars woke up crying at 6 a.m.

> "You wont buy me (sniff sniff sniff) you wouldn't (sniff sniff sniff) get me a round cracker."
> "I can get you two square ones."
> "YOU wont" (sniff sniff sniff).
> "Lars, did you dream this?"
> "In the red store, you wont buy me a round cracker."

At seven at eight at nine, he still wanted and cried because I couldnt give him a round Ritz cracker.

• • •

Another Sunday. This one started with Lars and his friend Miles at 6:30. But now – a spice cake made and iced in chocolate, the window frame at the side of my house painted, the toys and mess of last night picked up (wet toilet paper rolls thrown away – they played boats and bubbles so hard almost everything in our bathroom is soaked), omelets made and eaten, toast and jam too, then hot dogs made and eaten – it's over, it's naptime, and I can sit here for a few moments outside at my picnic table and write.

## Left, Right

"Left – that's right?
That's left, right?"
"Right."

"Right, right?"
"Right."

Shoes are left or right. Leftovers are left. Left behind. Left on. Left in (the cupboard, at home, the car).

Right and wrong.
Right on.

Right and left.
Far right, far left.

Turning left, right?
Yeah, that's right.
We turned left. You got that right.

(Lars and I conversing while going somewhere local in my red '67 Valiant.)

• • •

I have been in or near this city half my life now. The memories of then and presences of now criss-cross my being. Dogs bark and the fear I had as a child is gone if I am inside as I am – but the sense of it, of those large German shepherd paws on shoulders pushing me down, down into gritty gravel, my skin scraped, me crying, is not.

A crow flies by. I am surrounded by birds because we live near the dump. And before, in buildings on corners in Kitsilano (Yew and York, Larch and York, 6th and Vine) close to the sea. And before that, 37th almost at Larch, the Diamond just north of Ladysmith, and Ladysmith itself – not so many, some yes, crows in maples and cherries, occasional robins, starlings, grouse, even pheasants, but never as many birds as here now.

## March 16, 1976*

Four robins in the apple tree. Five starlings in the pear. And the air so very soft and grey is full of song is about to receive more rain o rain o rain.

This morning at eight, Sheridan called to tell me she accepts my offer on this house. Perhaps two years from now I'll be writing in a loft above this ex-utility room where I now press my pen – the rough design is already sketched by Noel Best. Money, money, money not yet but $8,000 is needed: 4 robins, 16 March, $8,000, even. I've so balanced it – what I dont like about here and what I love, what I do, why I'd like to move, why I would not. It will be so different with more light, with more height, and knowing I wont have to move unless I choose to, but teaching and working and wanting to write but not the time I need will remain the same. I think, I hope, in my heart at this moment I know I've made a good decision for me – security. Not this time with a man, but still there is a we.

## The Biggest Day of His Life

"It's a big day, Mommy. It's the biggest day of my life."

Saturday. Cartoons. Breakfast (grapefruit, peanut butter, strawberry jam and whole-wheat toast) in bed. In the afternoon, a bonfire mostly of blackberry vines. A fort. Five kids. Hot dogs. Marshmallows. Fresh pineapple extra sweet. Water and dirt to muck in. Cherry-flavoured apple cider.

No nap. Hide and seek. Roasted apples. Chocolate cake. On and on the fire burned, then one by one their parents come or call to take or send them home.

---

\*   Hindmarch remembers: "I had the gas dryer and the washing machine taken out of the utility room so I could put my desk and bookshelves there. This meant that I chose to drive my laundry to a laundromat once a week – first in Lynn Valley, later in Burnaby. I chose a study over a washer and dryer even though my boy was under six and loved getting dirty as most six-year-olds do." (Email to Fong and Shearer, July 13, 2018)

Bed. Seven o'clock. Exhausted. Happy. Huggy. Biggest day – "the biggest day of my life."

## Late March or April 1 weekend

North Vancouver District used to allow fires and the widow next door to me had a whole backyard of dead vines to clear out so we joined to create a fire to dispose of almost all of hers and mine. By July, new vines grew and blossomed and began to ripen.

• • •

Lars, five years old, naps. He is exhausted from playing with Miles, five also, almost all of yesterday (he slept there overnight) and today – riding bikes. He learned just yesterday at Miles's new place up Lynn Valley where there is pavement without cars-trucks 35-45-50 mph whipping past. When I picked them up, we put both two-wheelers into the trunk. After eating lunch (hot dogs and hamburgers I made at home), we went for out first long ride.

I asked them to ride in front of me and stay close to the sidewalk. I was behind to block traffic and to warn them get in, "get in, that's good, no no stay on the road but closer to the sidewalk" – about three city blocks. Then we drove under a busy bridge and up a dirt hill to ride across another bridge on the sidewalk to go down to where we could cross to a park (cars trucks cars trucks) where we played with no one else there.

No traffic because it's so grey out. We rode round and round the pavement in Bridgman Park. We stopped for a few minutes and threw rocks into Lynn Creek. We swung and twirled on a push-push-push then stand-or-sit-on-it contraption. Then we cycled again on the sidewalk then down and under the bridge.

Popsicles. Drumsticks. Around and around. Several small falls. Home again, home again, jiggity jig. So tired. Yet they wanted to play more.

A fight begins over "Teddy Bears' Picnic."

"Lars, you are tired."

"No, Mommy. It is my room isn't it? It is my record player, right? I get to say what I do."

"No. No. It is your room. It is your player. But Miles is your guest and – and." Tears fall. I sound like my mom. "His choice is first."

The player is broken. No choice at all.
"I don't need rest," says Lars.
So they start to watch TV sitting together and within two minutes, Lars is asleep.

• • •

Two single parents who teach full-time talk on the first day back at work after the summer holiday.

For five years now I haven't lived my life
my house is a mess
I haven't done anything
not one room is comfortable   (says she)

I've had a bad summer
I worked and worked but I didnt finish the book
it got so bad I couldn't sleep
I don't want to be here   (says me)

I know what you mean
I'm postponing
I'm postponing living
and I'm not getting much done

You too? I say
What can we do about it?
I don't want to continue this way

one thesis incomplete
several stories not written
two homes running down

FROM

# The Wine and Blue Notebook

1980

## February 24, 1980

Now that a desk and bookcase (made for this small dormer by a friend of Bri's along with a smaller desk and two cubbies for books and stuff in Lars's room) are here, I sit down for the first time in this study. It's a puffy-white-clouds-and-blue-sky day. I look northwest to enjoy a seagull gliding gracefully over a grey metal roof. So many building tops: houses, stores, a corner garage at Venables and Commercial, a grainery, piles of lumber to be loaded onto freighters on the North Shore and a brilliant yellow sulphur pile close to the Lions Gate Bridge. I see blue, red, grey, and white: white snow splotches on the mountains, white houses on the North Shore, a white and red brick home just opposite me on Parker, and white-silver seagulls gliding through salty air lit up by sunlight.

## March 23, 1980

In a few moments, Roy Kiyooka and I will be driving to our old home – not our – but Lars and mine – to dig out a small hemlock tree to place in my East Vancouver backyard. Cant seem to get my pronouns right. Yes, it is ours. Yes, that cottage on the North Shore was ours. Yes, whatever Roy and I have is ours: for eighteen years or more we have been and are friends. And yes, I love it here. Yes, there Lars and I were. And here I am. And Lars isnt. He is with his dad today. But he is here also. His also. Ours.

Two hours later

Roy dug the tree out while I held branches away from his face. He had to use an axe to chop old cedar-tree roots (the cedar probably cut down in the 1890s – its trunk was six feet wide) to free the hemlock. I pray it will live. I love this tree, little tree just two feet high when Lars and I moved to North Vancouver. Now it is bushy, really full, and seven feet tall. Shouldn't move wild things? I hope that isnt so. I hope with my heart it will take root here at Parker and Commercial.

Roy did all the work. His hands in earth brought from there. His hands pushing down wormy earth already here. When I knocked at what two months ago was my front door, I felt odd. I did not go in. I didnt even look in. I simply greeted the new owner to say we were now here to take that hemlock tree out of the wonderful big backyard with so many trees. We simply as Roy said left a hole there. We filled it up as best we could but left a space, a hole.

## April 13, 1980

Still marking papers. A white sailboat glides between the Lions (a home for seniors) Building and the grainery. And two dead daffodils still sit on the white window ledge. I have to push myself to work whereas I love just looking up at the-tide-is-out north shoreline and the deciduous trees over there not at all green yet but full of that fuzz pressing energy of being alive and about to burst.

I wonder if the low buildings near the water near the bridge are on the reservation; or, if I cant see that well, and they are just piles of lumber. I do not HATE grading. I just dont get much pleasure from most of it. When phrases come through or a whole paper does, right on, I, still, after fifteen years, get excited and somehow one good essay makes it possible for me to move through the marking of the next five essays more easily. That one good one helps me see the better parts of the following five and sometimes seven or eight. On to it. Get onto it. Cant stall like this much longer. Mark.

## May 2, 1980: 3–4 a.m.

Sirens awaken me. I hear winches, a horn, and far off – an ambulance. The sirens – half an hour ago – were interweaving. I can tell I'm not alert by the way I write this – am used to not having a gap between head and fingers and now, this instant, I have it.

After waking more, I began to make a list; but to do that, I needed paper. The back of anything will do – a package of snapshots. In it, Leni and I at seven and at ten on our knees praying. The floor is shiny, our old bedroom, a desk between our beds. We look earnest. That was it, I tried, we tried to be Christians. I kept thinking I was "saved" but always some part of me couldn't believe as totally as I thought, then, others did. I could almost touch us in that snap (Mom must have taken it). Leni and I went to sleep talking almost every night – like last night, here, Leni and I talking – of self, Grandma Grey, our bodies, Mom and Dad.

## October 3, 1980

First Friday of this semester (September 8 to now) I've been able to sit at this desk to do my own (not student not house) work. I want to be able to clear Fridays from repairmen, doctors, dentists, washing, shopping, painting, marking, etc. so that I have this day while Lars is in school as my writing time. A possibility?

I watch a brown-vested man walk across a flat roof. He is checking for leaks. I stare at the blue pipes of the grainery far beyond him – a blue much like the shutters and doors of Greek islands. I notice him kneel and check out the gutter. To me it's strange that anyone would create a flat-roofed building for Vancouver. It hasn't rained for two days now, but that roof is all wet. He opens his vest to the sun. His big, white-T-shirted belly moves slowly out of my vision.

Sunny. Fall. I hear a child's voice. Trucks. A seaplane. A boat. A car horn. Three or four crows. A train. Everything moves along.

## November 28, 1980

Grey no blue at all today. Fred Wah read last night at Capilano College – clear, unpretentious, musical, direct. No crap. He sounded like a dog dreaming one moment, a screeching bird the next, a bullet. I could see logs from which hunters were about to kill. This contrasted with Pauline's voice telling Fred to dig, to dig, to imagine fat red tomatoes. His poems for Jennifer and Erika (his daughters) caused some people to cry. The eye or eyes one I particularly loved; the about to leave one, I must let you go (no longer thirteen) caused the instructor next to me to gasp. Fred had an exceptionally good audience because no one felt they *had* to be there (which sometimes happens when teachers bring a whole class). In Fred's work I felt and feel the unexpected followed by delight in the familiar followed by yet another surprise.

FROM

# The Buff Notebook

1981

## June 3, 1981

I am finding it hard to get started again. Writing sentences like this one is easy, but the form or shape I want needs more of this – i.e., to warm up, to become easy with a sentence so I do not think about it just as I am here by not ending this one earlier. So, I do it. But. But still this isnt writing, is it? And "But still" isnt a sentence in the ordinary sense, yet it is when everything around it is understood. Still.

• • •

I am always doing this. Ever since Cliff left – almost ten years ago now – I've had several incomplete notebooks: little coil ones, large coil ones, hard-covered black ones (one lost at Capilano College: I took it to my creative writing class to read two short entries and left it outside close to a trail to the north campus. Did a student pick it up and take it accidentally? I returned to the hidden-by-brush place we had all been sitting in but could not find it. I checked the lost-and-found for weeks. I asked the class the next time we met too). There are also pads of paper which at times tell stories and at times contain what used to be called free writing.

These two entries from four years ago make as much sense here as this does.

(That lost book was complete. And I think there was one other little black one written immediately after Cliff left which was complete also.) The rain today pours down hard. It feels and sounds more like an October than a June rain. Loud chirps from or inside my roof. Continuity is broken. Pieces/chirps everywhere. Pull in the net. Pull the facts and fantasies together.

## June 24, 1981

You get used to it
the rain
You get used to it
the sound
You get used to
the spongy thickness
damp toes
a drop or two or three
trickling down your neck

Today
I am not used to rain.
Today I feel clean inside and open.
The rain has cleared all the nonsense out.

FROM

# The Blue Notebook

1982

## June 24, 1982:
## Saint-Jean-Baptiste Day,
## the Day Last Year the Rain Finally Stopped

Last night Roy and I talked about many things: H.D., initial impressions of people and how they hold throughout decades, sex, our lovers, what Roy's going to do, his work, my work, and summer. "It's a child's summer," I said, "a child's imagination of it – it goes on and on, everyday I get up and it hasn't gone away, yet." We sat up on my balcony (a 1908 sleeping porch) and watched the sunset and the new moon and the lights of the North Shore for two or three hours – a lovely, satisfying talk. We are yakkers. We like to yak about almost anything, but we both wonder if sometime our talk will run out since we have been talking for nineteen years now maybe once a week throughout times we have lived in the same city which is almost all of the '70s/'80s and '63–'65. Occasionally, we hit some area neither of us knows about the other, but mostly we gossip re self re others re books, music, poetry. An exchange of selves. We are similar in some ways – hold on to relationships, get bored with artificiality, dont take changes gracefully, perfectionists, want to control others in our personal lives. Really, we just want things our way.

## June 29, 1982: Tuesday, Saturna Island

I'm still working on the review of H.D.'s *HERmione*,* and I have just read what I wrote. I dont like it. It does not convey how good her book is. It does not centre on women which are the centre of the book. Lowndes (Ezra Pound) is there, but that relationship, poignant as it is, is a refrain. The pattern is: male poet talks, jokes, wants a muse, and female poet does not speak clearly (the longest conversation

---

\* See p. 268.

she has with him is over water), yet she sees herself as the superior intellect. My sense is that she probably was, but partially because of the roles of the time she did not have the confidence to speak out. Her mother is her reality principle, and for Her to leave her for uncertain financial-sexual circumstances is simply not possible. I'm also reading *On Lies, Secrets, and Silence* by Adrienne Rich. Looks good.

## July, 1982: Joe's Cappuccino Bar

Talk with a red-headed young man re Buddhism, self, bullying (power: male/male), writing (he writes four hours per day), etc. I mainly listen: he is stuck in a way, i.e., will take training "to learn a trade" after ten years of writing. I feel depressed by our talk because I cant help but feel the aloneness of it all and his presumption, i.e., he feels he is a good writer and has lived his life to have writing occur.

I am cautious. Feel so much the opposite/conservative: i.e., full-time job, house, second-hand car, yet know for me all these choices were better than not working full-time and not earning. I love having time in the summer to come to Joe's without rushing, but only feel really good when writing works. Would like eventually to have half-time money job, a partner, and writing. I couldn't live on unemployment or welfare like so many others do for months or years. I do like to accomplish. And do.

## July 6, 1982

Reread H.D. review. It's okay. I get upset writing something like this, i.e., I want to say everything, and somehow I become frustrated because I cant in only so many words. Instead of sticking to one to three main concepts as I ask my students to do, I do not. I've spent three weeks writing that review, four if I count rereading *HERmione* and H.D.'s biography. I should review the biography now while it is still in my mind. I should write the last boat story while I still have holidays. I am excited about the idea that finally it may end. Now, I have to do it. Not simply do it. But do it.

## July 15, 1982

Finally finished the H.D. review last night. Feel much better about it – not exactly what I wanted, but something (am at Lars's allergy testing as I write: patients talk with other patients between testings) clearer in terms of emphasis, and more on women and language than what I now have. Too many interruptions here (now it's pulse taking, nurse talking, other patients chatting) to write.

## July 23, 1982

Boy in red-and-white T-shirt and red shorts cycles down street. An Italian man who lives opposite to me reads his paper in the sun. And I sit out here, slightly chilled, and try to write/think. Yellow potash? sulphur? piles on the North Shore catch my eye. Lars has flown up to Comox to join a friend on Denman Island, and I hope to get the last story done before he returns. I think of Nik – do miss him – haven't phoned him – wonder what happened and why he hasn't called – refuse to call him – but it's unlike him – he hasn't phoned at all – must have his reasons but who knows what except him. Maybe I'll find out someday (passive) and maybe not (pride). I certainly do not like the way this ended at all. Not that I like any ending, for I do not, but at least there's usually some articulation.

## August 3, 1982

Just finished the Charters' biography of Mayakovsky and Lilya Brik: *I Love*.* Having met Yevtushenko, I imagine Mayakovsky quite like him: tall, expressive, emotion all out there constantly. Women obviously are attracted to M., but he feels like a bear and a boy. I assume M was not a good lover, i.e., from L's, T's, and N's rejections. Maybe he never did fully explore a woman's body or learn from her things she likes best. He so wants to possess, but it is all me, me, me.

I met Yevtushenko at a small dinner party held at Robin Blaser's cottage in 1973 when he visited Vancouver, sponsored by the Ministry

---

\* Ann Charters and Samuel Charters, *I Love: The Story of Vladimir Mayakovsky and Lili Brik* (New York: Farrar, Strauss and Giroux, 1979).

of State. RCMP officers were stationed in Blaser's garden and driveway all evening.

Yevtushenko followed me when I left the living room to go to the bathroom and he waited outside the door. He grabbed me when I came out and scooped me into an almost empty room lined with books. "You are the most Russian woman in the room." He kissed me extremely roughly and tried to French kiss, but I didnt want tongue and pulled away. "I just want to talk," he said after he loosened his grip. (I bet.) We did talk a little, but again he came on to me, so I wiggled away from him to the living room and asked Dennis Wheeler to dance with me. I thought Yevtushenko was physically attractive, but I was not attracted to him because he assumed he could have me (or any woman there) and because at that time I was not sleeping with any man. A dance or two later, he muscled his arm between Dennis and me to pull us apart. He flung me around his upper body and twirled me with my legs in the air. I yelled. Others managed to part us when they realized I really did NOT want to be with him. Two or three women pleaded me to go with him, but Robin agreed with me. And Yevtushenko yowled as I imagined Mayakovsky did from Charters's biography.

Certainly M's letters in translation are not distinct at all. But the way the three (Lilya, her husband, M) and then four (Lilya's husband's married mistress) lived their lives, i.e., chose their relationships, was unconventional and still is. Charters's book doesn't focus on this, but it is quite obvious that the Charters are definitely interested in this aspect. Mayakovsky's poems, as translated, lack power and thrust. This is too bad because I sense that his work (hundreds came to hear him) is meaningful and full of humour. The note at the end re translation gives a sense of their complexity, but the excerpts inside the text are clichéd.

Have completed one draft of the into-port story. Must get at it now. Turns out it is not the last.

*Post-note:* Yevtushenko let us know a single book by a poet sells 300,000 copies in Russia. We were amazed. Not one poet but several poets sell this many. He told us he'd get off a boat at an isolated river port and there would be twenty to a hundred people there waiting to hear him and arguing over one word or phrase and asking him who was right.

## July 4, 1983

Women and Words is finally over. My attention for the past two weeks – ever since the Wednesday I "finished" the boat story – has been on Writing and the Erotic, a workshop I gave there and should write up today or tomorrow if I am going to write it up at all.* My heart was going so fast during the conference that (I daydream): the fact is, for three–four nights I scarcely slept at all. The French feminist writing is extremely exciting – I'd like to get hold of some more to read soon.

---

\*   See p. 349.

FROM

# The Silver Notebook

UNDATED, 1984

You has become what one once was.
YOU has become what ONE once was.
You HAS become what one ONCE was.

Spelling

college
knowledge
privilege

Why does one of these have a "d"?

Majid wrote what follows in class in my basic skills course.

    Writhing Essay's

I, Majid, have spend three
hours in English today
October 21
and what have I achived?
tones of spealing mistakes
and have waysted twenty-one
peaces of clean paper
for four pages of nothing
which is called "an essay"
to the eyes of my teacher.

And what have you ocomplished
but wasted your time reading this paper
whill you could have wrote one yourself
or at least tryed to learn something?
It's no fun writhing essay's.

My comment:

Majid –
I enjoy reading your work because you always say what is real.

Gerry Gilbert asked me for a piece for *BC Monthly* and to read it at a benefit for MacLeod's Books.

### Writhing Essay's

It's no fun
writhing essay's
Majid
one of my students
wrote.

Images of Medusa's
hair her power
hair her energy
danced
off the scrawl

Sentences writhed
and paragraphs
composed of/shaped in
fear
disintegrated.

Then out from one of Majid's words
a goddess a graceful
mother of English teachers
walked.

She offered me
a basketful of green pens
that I
who mark 1,200 essays a year
accepted.

Majid
thank you and
forgive me.
I did not want to
green ink
your phrase.

## June 27, 1984:
## Two Dogs, Three Fights

Years ago, when I complained to Warren Tallman that I'd never be able to write again, he said you'll have to invent a new form, one that allows for interruptions. (A neighbourhood Doberman and Boss play as I write this – Boss's neck chain scrapes concrete and their muscly bodies smack.) I didnt want a new form then. I only wanted two or three uninterrupted hours every day – hours when I was clear – but as my notebooks testify with detail on detail of maintenance (car-teeth-orthodontist-gynecologist appointments-window cleaning) juxtaposed with weather and work as an English teacher: this was impossible. Warren was accurate in his perceptions, but I was unable to say yes, yes you are right. Lars was then three.

Lars, now thirteen, has a black swollen eye and a red other eye and little cuts all around his mouth. Yesterday at this very moment, he was fighting in the park. A friend of his phoned a moment after Cliff arrived at the front door as I was beating chocolate fudge about to set. (I get up and take two bowls of water to the dogs. Boss is 125 or so pounds – white and tan long hair is all muddy. The two have squashed all my lettuce plants which an hour ago were so alive.) Cliff who sometimes phones when he'll be an hour or so late was angry that Lars wasn't here with all his motorbike gear at the front door ready to go riding – right now. Lars's friend told me he was hurt and walking home. I scraped the fudge out of the pot as I yelled to tell Cliff who wasn't there. (The fudge is another story. Lars is *not* supposed to make it cuz he hasn't mastered the softball stage yet, and when I went outside to find an ashtray – smoking, I am smoking again – I could see tucked away in our mudroom a pot with its lid on. Inside it was undercooked fudge.) Both dogs bark.

Cliff comes back in from the outside with a picture of Lars on his motorbike taken by a *Sun* reporter who is an old-timer like Cliff (in his early forties) as the boys call them. I am trying to look at it as I hear Lars on the back stairs. His nose is all bloody. There's a bump the size of a large walnut on his cheekbone. His lips are scraped by his braces.

Ice. Soft towels. Warm water. Cliff starts cleaning Lars's nostrils and lips so tenderly. I sit down at my table and watch a couple of moments, but then I have to ask:

"Who?"

"Alex."

"Why?" No answer. Damn machismo ethic.

"Why?" No answer.

"What was it over?" No answer.

"What's his last name?" No answer.

"What does it matter?" says Cliff. "He's in pain."

I want to know what and why, but I stop.

"You told me not to back away," Lars says to Cliff through puffed lips. "I didnt start it, Dad."

"Did you hit him?"

"Yes," Lars said with a wobbly smile.

"The creep," I say as Cliff winces. "Let's go to the living room so you can lie down with your head up."

I can see I am not going to get the story with Cliff here and I might not even if he were not here. Lars does not squeal. I wouldn't want him to. I only want to know why it happened at all. I also dont want a front tooth broken off or an eye damaged for life. Stupid. This is manliness?

Sherry and Rachel, two of Lars's classmates since grade three, arrive at my back door to see how Lars is and I hold Boss (a Great Pyrenees–golden retriever cross), so they could get in, and then push Boss back outside. When I return to the front room, I hear pieces from the hallway. Did the fight have something to do with an autograph book? Does Alex think Lars is a homo? Or did he say that to provoke a fight? Gay lib alright. It's 1984. Gays started organizing in the late '60s and early '70s but not here for males or at least teen males in this East End. Girls' moms can be "lez" as the kids say, but men must, boys must, fight to prove what?

I return to the kitchen where Cliff is and he now does want to know whatever it was about which we really do not know at all.

"Maybe Lars should take karate or tae kwon do," I said.

Cliff snorted at this suggestion. "Boxing. East Hastings."

Am I really going to let Lars learn how to box so this doesn't happen again or so that he learns to hit harder or accurately? Kickbox or box-box, kickbox for me. I dont want him to fight. I dont want him to be beaten up. I dont want him to lose an eye or a tooth. For dogs, like Boss and our neighbour's Doberman, it's a form of play. But for my kid? Your kid?

Men have wars and kill others and make and sell armaments for as little reason as I've yet heard today.

# Letters

TO
# Fred Wah

UNDATED, *CIRCA* APRIL/MAY 1966

Dear Fred,
It is one of those cool indistinct days that we so often get here. The rocks, the tree branches dont stand out, yet arent blurred together. The air moves but not quickly. Seagulls swoop past my window as I write this: slowly, calmly, nothing to it. Kids walk by with transistor radios: I hear them underneath, it neither bothers me nor makes me pleased. All the city I feel in touch with because it is close and out of touch with because each thing and person is its own. People I do and dont know drift into my life – the garage mechanic kids me about my windshield wiper being swiped and I feel toward him as I do toward you now: a distance there/here and yet not.

We are so odd together: we know and dont know who the other is. So often we talk and cant say what we want to say perhaps because we dont know how to say it. And that closeness is there that never comes through in the words:

> yr letter arrives and a new landscape to step into, though I'm so jumpy at the moment that I probably wont be able to keep this up for very long

: we both jump, hop, skip, stall, so frequently – and that's what I'm doing now. Acknowledge and stop and nod and stop again. You here, I on the boat; you in Albuquerque, I in Vancouver; you in Nelson, I in Buffalo; I in Nelson and you also, two days; you in Buffalo, I on the West Coast; then both in Vancouver; two days; you in Nelson again, then here a week, and gone. And the geography of it is like our conversation: both together on same level feeling similar small town and rain senses then miles apart, you stubborn, me flighty.

Okay. So we dont often relate and seldom correspond except through Pauline. Yet I am now writing you soon after a note. Several moments coincide to force this through or over:

1. *Kenkyusha* has been giving me some pictures about the poet from this port.
2. Pauline mentioned Gerry Gilbert's visit – "quiet, articulate compared to all the ranting."
3. Frank was here last week.

This last first although they're each connected but writing isnt like chords in music and only one note, one word, can be played at a time, and so only one theme now because the continuity gets lost quickly enough along the way.

So, Frank. He let me see his new manuscript then we argued for an afternoon. They were phony poems to show a real he emerging; I thought they should be true poems to show a phony he. Didnt get very far, after all it is his and not mine, but I felt like writing you tonight because I dont know how I feel until after I've tried to say it, and then I find out it wasnt what I thought it was after all. You know how fed up we've individually become and you know how we dont say what should be said. I think now we've all been not responsible (sensitive) to/each other and it's a defeating bicker, bicker, bicker process. Never a direct you're lazy, sloppy, preachy, right there, with it comments on the work to the one who writes it, just little snickers and snipes to others who also read. I bawled Frank out for backing away from self; hah, who's the most guilty of that when asked "what do you think?" Last summer and the summer before you read and I said nothing. But clodhopper-feet-on-ground-stalky-Fred, here it is, I'll probably change my mind tomorrow but this is now tonight.

You seem the most collected of the Vancouver poets we grew up with. At times I've thought you obstinate, stubborn, dumb almost. You persist and persist and ask the same question until it's answered. And you never seem to back up or step over even when you must sometimes concede to yourself that there is another way. So, I'm amused by "The October Argument," the last four lines, so much you:

> my love there is no compromise if you will not wait
> while I drag my ass
> in the past.

I've never seen you compromise, so I smile; Paully-bean-bean-bean must have. The dragging your ass, anyone who knows you recognizes: Fred in armchair looking through window at chestnut trees in midst of an unpainted room cluttered with cartons. You are a dreamer so often and very rarely do I see that in your poems. I see you in that mountain snow poem of a girl taking a picture – event is past yet present but the dream of what might have occurred is not there.

In "The October Argument," when she says, you "cling to the past" she is right, you do in a now sense. The what ifs arent there when I speak to you and arent there in the writing. Maybe one is in "Song for Sally"* which is really a song for Pauline who is not on the continent at that moment. You so much want your wife that her sister becomes she. And it's not left out yet the reference is indirect, only those that know you know who you mean:

> hands fumble the smock
> on hips which are not yr own.

Any reader who didnt know you might wonder what you are talking about. And the clues just aint there. When I asked *Kenkyusha* about you and this poem he said "he found himself in a very awkward position." But it rides through without the awkwardnesses right to the seacoast poet and guitar – damn simple. It cant help but make me agree with the charges against TISHites of in-group references. You are not as flagrantly this way, the latest worst I think is George's reference to J (from S.F.) in *Open Letter*. Why did he go as far as naming the initials and place and yet not do the decent thing of naming the Poet? Who is protecting what from whom?

I guess I'm just being literal-minded. I dont agree with the meaning meaning meaning approach of New Criticism because the themes are so repetitive (any one critic seeing the same basic five mostly Christian largely puritan possibilities in any twenty works: the study becomes the critic and not the work itself – okay so they did get away from biography but where have they got to?) and like anything that repeats too often, such a drag. Yet I dont agree with all this quasi-linguistic talk hiding the fact that all these little meanings are dodges and references to and from actual events that must be hidden to be

---

\* The Fred Wah poems quoted in this letter are from his first book, *Lardeau* (Toronto: Island Press, 1965).

recorded. Am I making any sense? I dont know anymore as if I ever did except when I was so uncertain that I became certain. For now, goodnight. A heavy rain has started, not northwestern but an eastern New York summer burst: there are layers of water moving down the street to the sea.

    Love,
    Glady.

TO
# Stan Persky

SEPTEMBER 28, 1969

Dear Stan,
Funny, did I tell you I was trying to get you into that chair of Dennis's (those apostrophes like Gladys's bug me either way -s' or -s's) and cdnt, quite? I think I started the letter twice cuz of that. And one thing I told myself when I wrote the first thing to you is that a letter is a letter and if it comes out all off, okay, accept it, send it, dont start the first one by rewriting or else it might always happen and then if I was stuck in my own writing and got stuck in my letter writing, got to revise revise revise, I'd not do either till unstuck and that's not what-where I should be anyway, that the letter to you each week was/is a break from, a different type of writing than, my boat stories.

Yr letters arrive on Saturday: a wonderful feeling that first morning when I got up and had a shower and got dressed in jeans as usual and thought well it might be, but dont expect, well it might be, and it was (as I opened the yellow flap of the mailbox) there. We have pancakes and bacon and juice and coffee and I read slowly cuz I dont want it to end. Yr story arrived on Monday and I knew I shdnt read it before writing but I did: that huge energy moving so quickly so I-gotta-breathe-but-I-cant.

For me the going-on is in the house. Mr. Milkweed and Miss Puffball and the pancakes and the daisies and the Navajo blanket and the phonograph and the sounds coming through the wall and the beans in plastic in the fridge form a unit. Your anger and Brian's start to come and then they go. The sections with the kid and the woman in red and with you and who? on the bus are the least active. I guess I can figure out who everyone else is and cant here. The Herndons? Rick? (If I didnt know you, Robin, Rick, Brian, Martha, Lanny: how would it sound then? A stupid question, I do.)

It's cathartic as it stands. To move it away from that, I sense you'd have to start in the bedroom (you and Bri lying there abt to get up) and then go to the kitchen. Then, of course, there wdnt be so many relationships so all that would be lost – but six people plus a landlord, that seems quite a bit for eight or ten or twelve pages.

Just had a chocolate-marshmallow cone and went for a walk through a park which is close to here (abt half a mile away) and through a trail: oak trees, acorns all over, several grey squirrels, and in the clearer spaces, grasshoppers. Which reminds me of something we saw a few nights ago which you may have seen before: a whole sky of clouds (altocumulus) moving rapidly, the moon and stars far far up between the holes. We stood, slightly drunk (had gone to our tavern after watching *The Battle of Algiers*), on our back lawn and stared. The clouds in the northwest tend to accumulate so much more.

• • •

Movies here are cheap: $3 for a ten-plus-bonuses series, $2 for six Garbo, $2 for an Italian-French series, 75¢ *Pierrot le Fou* (just been released in the States). We saw *Anna Christie* the other night and I thought Garbo's posture (breasts down, slouched at hips, tummy slightly out) and expressions (uncertain, tough, happy, fed up) and motions (knocking the ashes off her cigarette with one finger, slamming beer on the table, hugging her father and holding back) were great. She feels, is in, her whole body and not just her face or head. (I must go and put the scalloped potatoes on for supper: tonight it's that, flounder, acorn squash, and peas.)

• • •

So potatoes, like your getting up to buy rolls at Elsie's or stamps at the drugstore (by the way did you know you can get them at the counter when the post-office part is closed), are on. And it's Warren-you I wish to talk about: I like his statement "hick being only a word for WEST, uncool like they say, naive as all get out, but naive traces to something like just-born"; and I like what you say, "that deeper thing, my, what, contempt for the poetry here, that I had taken that into account on first hearing, that I was responding to that, which is, simply, the business of taking those people seriously."

When a WOW reaction is a real WOW, that just-born first-breath quality is there. But there aint no WOW to a here-I-go-repeating-my-or-another's-rhythms-or-subjects-or-sense-of-relationships-but-I-dont-really-know-it-do-I, like that's-cuz-I'm-naive and I'm-from-B.C. and it's-okay-sorta-aint-it-to-do-what-I'm-doing (mumble, mumble, mumble) cuz I'm-from-the-woods: it's a drag and you know it and that's why I underline seriously. Like, a real hick doesnt exclude, a real hick doesnt try to put something over on a city boy, he may copy but he (usually) doesnt do this knowingly and besides that there's a beautiful clumsiness to his imitations, an honour of sorts.

I think Vancouver is naive. I think in a sense my writing is, but THAT you take seriously as Jack took Neap seriously. You are both speaking of what's real and it's the fakery we're all arguing against from how we see it. And I see a city that is no longer peopled by nineteen-year-old poets although nineteen-year-old poets (or perhaps writers-to-be, or initiates as you say) will continue to arrive there. And, they will continue to copy others. And, some will learn. And, those that are good will care. They wont hide. They wont stop growing.

And Warren does care. Every single word he writes shows how much he cares. He has that quality of WEST he speaks of, he is taken in at times (I think very seldom) but he doesnt take in, he is not a fake. A fake hick pretends, he learns semi-skills and ways-of-being, he says he's having an apple-dunking party for everyone he's met and has even just heard about (hey why dont you and you and you come over Friday night and invite anyone else who might be interested), but the apples aint real – that's what we're talking about – and he didnt really mean it about anyone: that was just a saying (a city way) he had learned.

Love,
Glady

P.S. I have trouble reading your writing. I type cuz you asked me to.

TO
# Stan Persky

UNDATED, *CIRCA* 1970

Dearest Stan,
Your long teaching letter (rec'd Monday) came across strong for me and I could see you there and feel for you and there's some things Granny-Glad-Teacher (who was out till 5 a.m. last night) is going to say that may or may not be useful. 1. Do not be afraid of silence – if it seems like thirty seconds to you, it's probably ten – quite a few students who are about to say something stop because another question or thought (which may seem too complicated or not on their thought) comes in. 2. Up and down, off and on feelings – the classes I got most high on my first and second year teaching were not the classes that most students remember, I thought they were good because very on, yet sometimes I realized it was only the top four or five who were there – great to do some hours, in fact necessary at moments or certain days. I've also had the feeling "well that certainly was a wasted hour" then two or three weeks later when I'm with a student found out that the question that occurred that day was the one which got him started. 3. Expect them to do the reading if it is not too much – find out where they are by asking questions. But, if it is too much, well I dont know what to say here, I ask very little and imagine that that course asks a lot, perhaps too much for the average first- or second-year student, you might try giving a twenty-page assignment for one seminar and ask them to read it at least three times or else dont come. (I'm afraid I really am an old-maid school teacher – I just tell those who havent read to leave.) 4. Some of your students probably dont know how to read. One day ask them how many people found this week's reading difficult? easy? in between? why? (focus on the why – you'll find all sorts of ways of reading and not reading – some will complain of style-syntax – and what you think is simple just aint – frequently there is a language problem, i.e., the way they read a word is not how the author uses it – and these can be five- and six-letter words, it usually is not what the student thinks it is that is in the way, not always but often enough.) 5. Preparing – after a while you just know what takes roughly an hour and a half or for you two hours but in the beginning

it is better to have too much to do (and then dont do it) than too little: some days you only do one-third of what you thought they'd be able to do but that doesnt matter because you've focused on that one thing. 6. And again, dont be afraid of silence – they might just be thinking. (Sometimes I ask the one who seems most into a thought what he or she is thinking about – if it's a daydream on something else it usually can be tied in, i.e., if the daydream connects however loosely with where you were ten minutes ago – in English they almost always do – the source is close, might not be so in philosophy, but might be.) Well, well. I guess it does depend on how democratic you are. Most teachers are interested in students who are somewhat like themselves e.g., Eliot Gose teaches to the B student who is about to break through – that's his excuse for not being with the really interesting minds that are in the room. I suspect that you want to be with the readers, with the really-intelligent-many-thoughted-open-or-so-close-to-being people. Was interrupted by Mike Liebowitz (for supper) and Cliff. Now it's past ten and I'm filled at my eyes with wine and ears with thunder. I guess I wont mail this tonight so it'll be late – am about to conk out. (Heard Muddy Waters last night – and we do have the new Beatles album: probably listening to some of the same moments as you last weekend: got it with money from Cliff's birthday which was the tenth.

Good night,
Gladys

TO

# Henry Alan Lawless and Prime Minister Pierre Trudeau

1970

Dear Henry Alan Lawless and Prime Minister Trudeau,
I am writing in reply to your letter of May 14 which stated that "the decision as to when an abortion can be made legally is a medical one and, for this purpose, committees are established in accredited hospitals across the country who will consult with the patient and her doctor as to whether or not they can authorize abortion."

I am aware that last year Parliament passed the above amendment to the Criminal Code but the point of my message was that abortion should not be under the Criminal Code at all, that the decision to have an abortion should be up to a woman and her own doctor.

1. Women should have the right to control what happens to their own bodies, no committee should decide this.
2. Many women are <u>injured</u> and some <u>die</u> from illegal and self-induced abortions each year in our country.
3. There should be no unwanted pregnancies in an affluent nation such as ours is: because a child born in Canada uses more of the world's resources than a child born in many other nations; because many unwanted children grow up in circumstances of little or no love which in turn is the cause of many emotional and social and hence economic problems; because no woman who is poorer than another (and sometimes even illiterate so through circumstances may not know what the present law is or may have a doctor who by nature or social or religious training is opposed to abortion) should be denied the right that another has simply because she was born into a higher economic class or because she happened to know someone who knew what the present ruling is.

I realize that Parliament, which is composed almost totally of men, wishes to move slowly and cautiously in this matter. However, I feel that if all the Canadian women of childbearing age were allowed to vote on this matter that abortion would become legal, would be a woman's right instead of a committee's decision.

Yours truly,
(Mrs. Cliff) Maria Andstein

TO

# Daphne Marlatt

OCTOBER 6, 1970

Dear Daphne,
Horrible morning, I've cried twice, tried to write, gone for a sun-misty walk on the beach, written cheques (almost always puts me in a foul mood, brought up to the fact of last $100 again), read part of a women's lib paper, dressed (am at the stage my jeans are too tight but everything else wd be too big, nothing seems warm enough, would like cuddly-coloured smocks or tops), read a letter and it's not yet eleven. I'm stuck on the bottom of the third page of the seventeenth story – usually when I'm blocked the rhythm breaks, in this instance it doesnt, I dont like the content, after seeing a school of fish swim round in ellipses between two piles (wooden of a dock) I see a pile of slag, tailings, I trip out on what is left over, a tail is an intricate part of the fish, the tailings are what's left, as profits are too, and I rattle on, not rattle it's quite okay, but I'm uncertain and dont like the sentence: have been at this same place for a week. Tails. Piles. Waste. Use.

    Saw Bob and Bobbie* on Friday in Bolinas which is about thirty miles from San Francisco. We decided to go there on Wednesday after Stan got a letter saying there was a big reading: Joanne Kyger, Rick Duerden, Ebbe Borregaard, and others you may have heard of – Lewis Warsh Bill Berkson Tom Clark from N.Y., John Thorpe, something Kearney, and someone else, all of whom live in Bolinas except for Rick. Creeley and Thorpe stood out, Bob read a few things written in July, one really good poem, and a few like pieces, Thorpe told a story, literally, just stood there and told a child-dream-lost-eaten-up story, no errs or ands or uhms. Rick and Ebbe I also enjoyed, I dig Duerden's soft intricate rhythms and Ebbe's songs, he sings poems. But the rest, wow, the N.Y. contingent is absolutely flat, not a strong flat the way Spicer can be at moments but a monotone flat, they do something called deep gossip, and it aint deep at all, and Joanne takes lines and plays with them, dramatizes, and it's a bore: Gertrude Stein in any two sentences goes so much further.

---

\*    Robert Creeley and Bobbie Louise Hawkins.

Bob and Bobbie (went there before the reading) look good, relatively relaxed. I'm so in awe of him that I cant speak. He's my favourite. So much would like to sit with him alone for half an hour or an hour sometime. Dont know what I'd say but I sense it would work. In a group it focuses on anecdotes and they're both great at that. Alone, it wouldnt.

You were right about that woman-consciousness piece. I do put myself into giggly situations. The sketches arent meant to entertain but both times you've heard some when other people are there, I've done that. Will probably send that one to *The Pedestal* which is the Vancouver Women's Caucus paper. I was thinking that yr femina piece should be there too – how would you feel about that? So far their paper hasnt had much literature and I'm not certain they'd print either, yet it is also in flux, and it is not hard line. I think that strong women, which both you and I are even with all our hang-ups and hesitancies and giggles and repressed annoyances (I dont hear you giggle, that's me), who have definite senses of language, should make ourselves heard just as much as women who appear to be stronger do.

Let's see, there were other thoughts, on the fishermen, money from labour (wage or individual) is different than money made from other people's labour, and as for the Dominion Trust building, who built it?, the men who built it did, but who had it built and why and where that money comes from is a different question. Somehow you should take me seriously and know when what I say isnt right for you.

I guess I better get back to that story. Dont really want to. Feel defeated. Wont when I work my way out of it. Hope you're writing and that Kit's well and that you have a good time in Montréal.

TO

# Daphne Marlatt

UNDATED, *CIRCA* 1970

Dear Daphne,
I sense I cant get at what I take in and miss in yr Vancouver poems without writing a letter so here it is: I think this work has SIZE both in a geographical and historical sense and since you've worked at that history there are many references which you know that I dont– Olson, Pound too, no criticism, simple fact; I think this work has emotional depths which occasionally you move away from through fear, you're afraid of balancing on the edge, of remaining stranded, out there, so you come back, hands in pocket. The insect-drowze-I-know-only-what-I-can-touch-of-you poem has this tension:

>    The white o the sudden white of your buttocks   2
>    cold moons I pull down, amaze this cloud of green riven thing
>    I am, stranded as water
>                             We wade into
>    the cold again, wilful branches, two, in the crashing
>    wet.

The buttocks-moon image is sudden, there, has depths more than touching (and the green, white, cloud, moon, water lock together). And the "riven thing I am" is descriptive, loses strength, steps back from that edge you went out or down to, whereas "stranded" is not simply descriptive, it creates a pull. In the next line the branches stand out, I see you two as large trees not connecting (but in the same elements).

Maybe I can come closer if I mention a poem where there is no fear of how you (personal) feel (it's all personal but with immigrants and old men you are freer): the fishy public library slimy old man one. I sense this is right on. The birds mean what they cry. You too. Bread wilts in closets. Hubbard figures hump. All the cups, soup, fish, steps are present (not a telling about which is what I mean by descriptive). Then you end with a beautiful line: "I want to know how gulls keep flying."

That line, like the buttocks-moon one, simply came? was dictated?

I'm asking. The good poem is the one that scares the poet, Spicer once said. Those two lines have that quality.

To give you a sense of what I dont like, contrast the first two lines below with the last:

deficiency, yr blood an extraordinary grassgreen night the
mercury vapour lamp pours out, for hope, for glass,
shatters love sometimes.
All the lovers of grass come back, eventually, unload their
cargoes in the chill scream of the sea.

The first two hold their energies in till "hope," the last two maybe I miss the meaning (have this sense, my god I cant criticize if I cant get it), okay, I dont understand what their cargoes are and I dont feel the chill scream of the sea. (I guess I also dont like "Blackball Ferry balling into 'high seas'": **a.** ball balling – but betcha Warren wd like tho **b.** whoever you are quoting reminds me of Levertov's forests which are really parks – i.e., Vancouver Island blocks the possibility of high seas – and I dont think the reference is tidal.)

The you in that poem also bugs me. You who? "There you are, 2 of you, below the sign." Is this Al and who? But the first you is morning? And the YOU at the bottom of the page is Al? Noticed this elsewhere: lagoon poem, I take it that the you who comes home, who brings what, who confirms sailing east, whose lips are caught on the future, is the same you as "yr coin proves nothing," "yr going? a salmon run?" (in this poem the line that is sudden is: their edges are always murmuring: beautiful); femina-you-who-fail poem, is the you who fails the same as the you who is there at the end and is this you historical or is it supposed to be you, Daphne? (I guess in this poem it doesnt matter, it's just that the end is so strong, is the same you throughout? yes).

    You are there
        bristles of the broom are there
The bones of yr face are pinned with autographs.*

---

\*    These seem to be early drafts of *Vancouver Poems* (Toronto: Coach House, 1972). Marlatt read unpublished poems from *Vancouver Poems* at Sir George Williams Reading Series in Montréal on November 3, 1970.

No matter who the you is, that's a great image. (I guess it doesnt matter who the you is either, I feel the fish opens the door.)

When I say this work has SIZE I mean you are taking on a job as large as Joyce, Olson, or Williams; you are not writing a series of poems or a number of individual poems which connect in time-place (moment poems such as Frank does well, Lionel did, Dave Cull, etc.), you are writing a history: fires, docks, Indians, Chinese, suicides, old men, immigrants, stores, streets, squares, buildings, rain, forest, fur, fish, bridges: of city. In the city you tend to focus on lonely individuals (like the great old bird poem: the man whose room is a shell sucked dry and you're in a cupboard of clotted broom bristles) and one couple (yrselfs) and hardly any groups (white lunch, public library, Chinese being shipped east – the exceptions) or movements (my god, Vancouver is almost a city of strikes).

I dont know if you get me: you have a fisherman fishing for profits but you lay off the real shitheads: find out something about canneries rather than that one man, read how Dunsmuir got his start (a scab, was given one thousand acres of coal in Nanaimo cuz he didnt strike), and the land-mineral grants to the CPR, fuck it, its not those few Brits only, in the present-day senses I'm sure you can see how this city itself is a rip-off: I sense you resist my Cliff's present left position, I know you will never lapse into rhetorical screamism, but I think everyone who writes is political and the loneliness of the Indian Chinese Hindu (you havent got, I just thru in) Yugoslavian etc. which you put down on the page (like Robson Street poem) is here, yes, but it can become romantic (which you arent, you fight it). (I see this work as breaking out of the cupboards, the card house, the glass jars, the broom closets: where to? no one knows, you're moving on the edge of it, go further, balance on a bridge that may snap at any second: there aint no safe way to write.)

Courage,
Gladys

TO

# George and Angela Bowering

APRIL 26, 1971

Dear George and Angela,
Just a note to say we do have a chance on that place after all – Vancouver City Savings gave us tentative approval, now they'll send an appraiser out and look the land and house over.

I got the thirty *Sketches*\* just one day after you mailed them, and today, the three extra copies you mailed book-rate the day before that. My head isnt here. I've been in a mescaline-like high for almost two weeks now. Doctor sd on Thurs. that it'd come within two weeks since I'm one finger dilated as it is. Swimming and sitting in the sun seem the easiest things to do. Even making potato salad becomes an effort in the last three strokes. I stop, rub the top of my womb – it takes the pressure off the skin or desensitizes it – and smile. Am going to pop into the bath then smother myself with cold cream and talcum.

                Love,
                Glady

Hello again,
Something is happening but just what is happening I dont know. Last night I woke up as Cliff came into bed, and then an hr or so later when Lan came down for his middle-of-the-night snack: each time to turn over was such an effort, the right side of my womb was hot, it was tight like it frequently (the whole womb but more particularly this one five-inch spot where the doctor thinks a knee might be and I sense the buttocks) is but hot also, a new feeling, a bit like a fourteen-yr-old menstrual cramp except high up.

At times I'm speedy, like now, have put *Sketches* into envelopes, written a note to my parents with Schroeder's column in it (he praises me but has no sense of his sense other than that he likes), soaked a bra, made a list, etc., etc., and it's go go go. The stops are sudden.

---

\*    *Sketches* was the third in George Bowering's Beaver Kosmos Folio series. Twenty-eight pages long in stapled binding, it was produced in Montréal.

No knowing when. I'm giggly and excited about the baby coming. Havent yet reached the wait wait wait it'll never be here stage that several women have spoken of. The girl in our class we give a ride to had hers last Wednesday, she talked with me yesterday and she said she never could have done it without Jim, her husband, and with him, it hurt and was the hardest work she had ever done, but it was so good. Maybe – if you are thinking of taking these classes and you can back out and it doesnt cost anything to register – you should send your names now to:

Vancouver Childbirth Association
1595 West 65th Ave.
Vancouver 14.

Our class (Ruth Babcock the instructor – I recommend her, we had a sub one night who was uptight) has ten couples, there are ten lessons, took me three weeks to get in. Send yr due date. (By the way doctors seem to know fuck-all about due dates so yr experience doesnt surprise me one bit except for the fact that you were pretty well certain you were feeling life). I hope you're feeling happy again, outward, and arent gaining too much weight (I'm now up twenty-six pounds and those last six simply came), that you have colourful things to wear, and are using your marvellous heads, and walking, and doing together.

Much love,
Glady

P.S. Warm responses to *Sketches*. I feel very good about them and thank you once more for getting them out.

TO

# bpNichol

JANUARY 18, 1973

Dear Barrie,
I am here and I heard you. Nothing does fit, there is no explanation, it would be simpler if there was, the desire in us is so strong for that, I loved what you said, I've no effective response left except to care for the living, the within and without, and you show so much, and yesterday one of my jade plant leaves sprouted a little leaf from its dying tip and a root hardly visible and I planted it.

Much has changed since I wrote you last. Shortly after that note I told the commune that I wanted to leave. It was difficult and I had known for a long time that I must but I kept hoping and trying to make the ideas of what was fit the actuality and I couldnt break through personal barriers to say how I felt authentically, to tell them my needs cuz my vision and theirs were/are so discrepant, and at points there was no me left, all the feelings flowing in from outside, perception overflow, emotional jamming, in between so many. Anyway, I found a place, am a caretaker of sorts, picking up rain-filled garbage, phoning carpenters and mouse control, cleaning up when people leave, getting new tenants, sweeping the hall in an old, six-unit, fairly large suites, building at 6th and Vine.

It is hard now, no man in my close life, Lars and me, I teach three nights a week and hate my job but now I admit the hate, I am starting to enjoy it whereas before I didnt have it straight and wasnt there when there much of the time, and Cliff lives with Marianne and just recently has started to take Lars overnights on Wednesday (a teaching time) and Saturday (hopefully a going-out time) plus all day Sunday. And I so needed that, time alone to come to self, to work, to think. But also I need to share emotionally and sexually and intellectually and so much is partial, and it is so damn hard to unlearn ways/modes of being.

I dont know how you can read so open, so many times, so many wheres and be you as I know you, I dont know how you can leave and come and leave and come "without that sense of playing cheap with things you care about" but you do seem to. Do you have to/need to read so much? Deep down do you really want to? It seemed to me that Peggy has hurt herself by doing what she is and is asking why but if either one of you really knew you shouldnt, then why do it?

Home is extremely important to me. My exterior has to be ordered (Lars has made me more flexible and so has the commune but still I need much more explicitness than others) and how I like it for my interior to move easily. I remember your surprise that the commune had moved only months ago cuz you felt the place felt longer but my method my seeing was people were not yet in that place or I wasnt, and in this apartment I am more and more here. I'm painting, planting, cleaning, etc., am so domestic, yet I need to write, to read, to go out for fun, and I'm so fucking serious that the last is extremely rare, and the reading is coming, is when Lars sleeps, but the writing, havent written since Cliff and I separated.

Yet I know I will. And making the home is saying I am here for two years or three. And saying I hate my job has forced me to organize it more so it wont drag me down the way it did in niggly ways so I can clear some decks, but those larger ones, to say verbally how I feel, are slow, slow to change, but recently I have gotten pissed off out loud in the present and damn it it feels good, facades dissipating, now if I could only be a little more casual with men, but it is so hard for me to move up to a lightness, and I've put myself into an almost untenable sexual position by saying I dont want to make love with anyone whose baby I wouldnt want to have in fantasy cuz I feel if I ever did become pregnant again I would have a very difficult time saying yes, I want an abortion. So, except for those very few times with Dennis, I am or have been celibate, and for the first time in my life it has not been hard to say no to men, yet inwardly it is hard cuz I do need and I am attracted and I use much energy in blocking off those attractions which make me feel so good, to be alive inside again. I am bitter, but I am not a bitter person, and the swing moves, and this instant I hear my nephew and sister and niece in the hall.

Bye,
Glad.

• • •

Sunday. It seems speedy yet I didnt feel speedy when I wrote to you. I have been thinking much about that sense of playing cheap with things you are about. When I see people hide their despair and joke about it I feel awful. Yet I dont know how to respond. I dont want to know what is going on in people's inner lives cuz I feel so bruised yet I also want others to know that I do take them seriously. I have no balance. And I cant take responsibility for knowing what to do when I dont. I find even my listening without any probing makes people like Brian (Fawcett – he lives below) think I'm approving of his actions when it is his person I like but sometimes despise his behaviour and I cant explain cuz the explanation is not what is going on. He knows I'm pissed off at him cuz I said so but the feeling isnt out. And I'm so tired of repression. I dont want to hurt others. But I cant let myself be hurt just so I wont hurt. I am strong in some senses, and fragile in ways most others cant see.

TO THE EDITOR:

# "Writers Forgotten"

*VANCOUVER SUN, CIRCA 1970*

On Friday, September 11, in the LEISURE section of THE VANCOUVER SUN, Michael Finlay published an article on who's who among local authors. This letter is in response to Mr. Finlay:

Mr. Finlay's article, "The Authors," is not representative of the Canadian northwest writing scene at all. His bias which is pro-creative-writing-departments and anti-local-revolutionary-classical-and-Black-Mountain, should have been stated clearly rather than covered by sentences such as "these aren't necessarily the best new writers in Vancouver, but they are representative."

He says there are no cliques of writers in Vancouver. This is a distortion. Although I know of no "group" which meets formally, I would suggest that any responsible person who wanted to do a serious survey on local writing should contact:

a. bill bissett who could speak of *BLEWOINTMENT*
b. Gerry Gilbert who could talk of the Intermedia writing scene
c. John Hulcoop who could tell of the UBC non-writing-dept scene
d. Jim Brown who would tell in his words of the TALON and VERY STONE PRESS scene
e. Chuck Carlson who could speak of the UP THE TUBE WITH ONE I OPEN and its writers
f. John Mills who could talk of the non-academic bawdy SFU BALLSOUT writers
g. Brian Fawcett who could talk about the young IRON group
h. George Heyman who could speak of the CIRCULAR CAUSATION cluster
i. Stan Persky who could tell about the *Georgia Straight* WRITING SUPPLEMENT
j. Warren Tallman who is writing a book on Vancouver Poetry 1960–70

The above list is not inclusive because I only know of the writers and magazines I know of, but it should be made evident to the public that

Mr. Finlay speaks from a most limited (UBC creative-writing-dept influenced) stance.

Since many people are unaware of the range of writing in British Columbia, any article which attempts to do a capsule survey of the past few years should state who is being omitted and why. The "accomplished" writers Mr. Finlay leaves out only indicate how unqualified he is "to look briefly at Vancouver literary history in order to place this surge of activity in some kind of perspective." Of my elders who have lived here, not all of them all the time, during the 1960s, I would include: Milton Acorn, Earle Birney, Raymond Hall, Margaret Laurence, Dorothy Livesay, and Phyllis Webb.

And now, to those who started writing in the early sixties; and first, those influenced by Black Mountain writers (Charles Olson, Robert Creeley, Robert Duncan) which Mr. Finlay dismisses by saying, "their poetry was loose, scattered across the page, written without punctuation or capitals." The two main principles of this writing are: FORM IS NEVER MORE THAN AN EXTENSION OF CONTENT, and, ONE PERCEPTION LEADS TO A FURTHER PERCEPTION. The main proponents (most of whom, by the way, took writing courses at UBC and argued with their teachers, which helps explain Mr. Finlay's lack of knowledge and prejudice against something neither he nor those teachers comprehend) formed a group, clustered around a poetry-newsletter called *TISH*. The elders, in their early twenties then, were George Bowering, Frank Davey, David Dawson, Lionel Kearns, Jamie Reid, and Fred Wah; the youngers, David Cull, Robert Hogg, Daphne Marlatt, and Dan McLeod. Some of these people are still here, all have published widely, most have more than two books, etc.: the point is, in terms of Mr. Finlay's article, this group which has had a strong influence on Canadian poetry is the enemy whose name is not mentioned, so his article mentions Black Mountain, which doesn't make any sense to a non-writer or a beginning reader.

At the same time, again in the early sixties but NOT at the university, bill bissett and Gerry Gilbert and John Newlove moved into their own sounds and voices and started publishing their work here (and elsewhere). These three writers – who in no sense form a group – are now well known to all but academics who have stopped ears and cant hear the spirit of a place until fifty years after. bill bissett, who single-handedly started BLEWOINTMENT PRESS (which is still active and ignored by you-know-who), first published many writers such as Maxine Gadd, Judith Copithorne, Al Neil, and myself. Mr. Finlay refers to "the beat and hippie phenomena, printed cheaply, stapled together, and largely unbought." It is true that at times pages of both *TISH* and *BLEWOINTMENT* were physically unreadable, but to dismiss the presence of their writers on monetary terms (the idea is to lay your work open to others, now, not to be printed in slick-university-subsidized publications) is bourgeois stupidity.

Most of the writers I have mentioned so far are "home-grown" Canadians. Many of them had only one true mentor at the university, Warren Tallman, who was born in the northeast just south of the border. Warren Tallman has that rare ability to encourage one to develop his or her own voice, he has consistently stressed be local, write about what it is you know. Besides, most of the people above, he has had over to his house – where many informal talks and parties were held – or taught, along with such others as Pat Lane, Jim Brown, Pierre Coupey, Brad Robinson, Scott Lawrance, Seymour Mayne, George Heyman, Barry McKinnon, etc. Because of his aesthetic and open intelligence, Tallman has never been in favour with the teachers of the UBC writing department; and because he has constantly insisted that poetry is to be heard, is not to be read on the page as a symbol puzzle, that the work of a critic is to be receptive and not make tidy arguments, he has been snuffed at by the academics. Why bring Warren Tallman into this? Because Vancouver already IS one of the literary capitals of North America, and this is largely so because of his energy and insistence which has acted as a catalyst for so many others. Any article on Vancouver writing which says it is "representative" and omits mention of him – for or against – is sneaky and fraudulent.

So far I have still omitted many authors: Robin Blaser, who has had a strong influence on many of the young such as Brian Fawcett from Prince George, Neap Hoover from Vernon, and Colin Stuart from Vancouver; Jane Rule, in her mid-thirties, who has just published her third book of prose; Roy Kiyooka, the well-known artist, who has written three books of poetry in the last seven years; and there are several others such as Joe Rosenblatt, Beverley Simons, David Watmough, and so on. It is possible that I've left out as many writers as I've included, but this letter does not purport to be "representative," it is simply a response.

I think what annoys me most about "The Authors" is the pretense of no cliques, the lack of knowledge of Mr. Finlay, and the similarity of statements. Next time you have someone do an article on the local writing scene, you should have him state his prejudices in the first two paragraphs – if he can't do *that*, he ain't no author.

TO THE EDITOR:

# "Cradles as coffins, coffins as cradles, a womb is sometimes both"

*VANCOUVER SUN*, JULY 7, 1981

Art Perry's review of Judy Williams's recent work misrepresents through omission and through the use of slanted language Williams's art and its purpose.

The caption under the reproductions insinuated that Ms. Williams's "bitterness toward being a mother" is the subject of her show. This is not so: Williams used medical anatomy models from Italy as the basis for her work.

It is precisely because she was so struck by the images of these fetuses which had no chance of survival (almost all were illustrations of unusual birth positions) that she was drawn to paint, rub, scrape, construct in watercolour, pastel, graphite, and cloth these so-very-human forms.

If Williams has any bitterness, it should be directed toward a reviewer who attacks her person rather than comments on her art, e.g., "the images stem from a deep-seated psychological quirk within Williams herself," says Perry.

The headlines of Mr. Perry's review is "Artist Obsessed with Suffering and Woman's Role." To me this implies that suffering and a woman's role are equated and that they are both subjects of the show.

This is not so as anybody with eyes to see with can see by going to the Burnaby Art Gallery and by looking at Williams's paintings and wood-steel-silk-pulp-paper-wax constructions. I find them gentle, repulsive, vulnerable, direct, and tender images of unborn and dying humans: the subject is the cycle of life. Cradles are coffins and coffins are cradles and sometimes a womb is both.

Perry's article among other unclear and biased statements, says that "the viewer becomes William-ized or woman-ized." What does "William-ized" or "woman-ized" mean? And why is an art critic attacking a female artist for not showing enough "universality in her womanly images"?

Has he ever attacked a male artist for not being male-ized or not being macho enough or universal enough in his male images? Has he ever pejoratively added on an "-ize" to a male artist's name? Is Perry, might I ask, a misogynist?

When male representational artists create images of "tortured bodies," they are not criticized on the basis of their maleness, of their fatherhood. If there is not "evidence of pain" in their paintings, they are not attacked for not doing what they did not intend to do.

Perry attempts to review their shows for what the shows are and does not write conclusions about the artist such as "this leaves the viewer wondering about Williams's ability to express his personal traumas through his art."

Perry should keep this Perry-ized column in front of him as a reminder to open his human eyes next time he reviews a female artist's show.

He should criticize and present her work rather than misrepresent the work and attack the woman.

# Essays and Reviews

# So You Ask Me – An Essay in Jazz

*UBYSSEY*, NOVEMBER 20, 1959

What's jazz?
Something.
What's jazz?
Anything.
What's jazz?
Nothing?
Are you nuts?
No.
Well then, what is jazz?
Many things.
A few of them –

Jazz can be a moment. A moment starting deep in an underground stream of nowhere. Notes seep down from the soil above. Through little particles of earth, through larger particles of stone. Hit a base then start long journey upward. Journeys upward at times go downward but always upward. Little bits of water join other little bits of water and together make themselves a route. A pattern conceived.

A pattern to develop. To develop to grow to search for the top. It takes a dip. It takes a similar dip. Soon the dip becomes the pattern. Then a surge toward air. Another pattern. Yet the dip is still there. And so is the base, that's peculiar, so is the base – in a meshily distinct distance. But dip fades and new pattern asserts itself. It rushes, it rushes in a hurry to grapple with air. But a strong sound hits it, clay. Disperses the pieces. Quickly they run and meet together again. This time a more congenial pattern formed. Upward they push. Together, altogether. Heave.

The part below pushes the part above. Then air takes over. Air wants a pattern. She sucks. Thin hilly air pulls, clean hilly water pushes. And makes it. Water makes it. Moment is born.

Moment herself is wonderful, free. Flitting and darting. Kissing one needle of a fir tree, dusting the top of a fern. Up over a log, and down a hill. Then a rest on a cedar bough and a visit to a spider. Wherever she wants: one mountain, two mountains; ten clouds, no clouds. Below her a bluff, through her a whisper. Delightfully free to the finish.

Then she is gone. But the experience of her remains. Maybe just remembered till the next time. Or maybe lingering and relingering by giving the new moments what were the best parts of herself. In them, recreating.

Jazz is sometimes a scene developed. Acadia Camp at breakfast. Seven-thirteen: door opens once, closes once. First person has arrived. Opens again, closes again. Second person has arrived. Opens and closes, opens and closes, forms a pattern, dee dee dah dee dah, dee dee dah dee dah.

A line starts to form. Still nobody talks. Muscles move bodies up lines to grab trays. Muscles move bodies up lines to give cards to get punched. Juice, two eggs, milk and coffee. Go sit down and slowly refuel. All quiet instruments, all non-asserting, all in communion.

Not for long. A dirty sax comes through the door. His feet make a racket. Hear him march to the back of the line. Something's going to happen. It does. Through other door comes a wicked trombone. Copies the same hot footsteps.

"What do you think you're trying to do?" asks sax.

"I can do anything I want. It's a free country," evades trombone.

A loud brashy argument, insults and cuts. No one listens to no one. People suddenly awake and join sides. Everyone shouts. Everyone bellows. You cant hear the door now, but it's still there. You cant feel the communion, but in its way it's there. Underneath, the door; above, noise.

But noise to one isnt noise to another, but it's noise to me so it's noise noise. With dirty sax slicing wicked trombone and trombone slurping cagily all over, winning by outsmarting. Not good, smart, noise.

Eight-thirty: most students have left. A pattern I can follow starts appearing again. The door can be heard faintly in the distance. Finally all students leave. Nine: eight bars of snare as the man with the broom (muscles pushing wood touching floor) sweeps up.

Or jazz can be a nursery rhyme. Two. Mary had a little lamb whose fleece was white as three blind mice in a pressure cooker who didn't really care anyway because they couldn't see, so blind were they chasing after a farmer's wife who wasn't in the pressure cooker, not knowing why they were chasing her but that's not important because it's just the way things are in this arena of an upside-down cake world which is really right side up but we call it upside down anyway this life in this pebbled pineapple sugar sucked earth of cold steel hot damp dry pressure here feet are the only "in contact" part of one and where one's instinct makes rats choose farmers' wives who go around cutting off tails with carving knives off things that should never have any sight in their lives so blinded by little white lambs are they that follow Mary everywhere, everywhere, everywhere, through schools that laugh and play at you so you can become a million dollar baby in a five and sugar soured curdled pineapple store of wet blind mice running and running naked of tails in a pressure cooker, bleeding slowly pineapple squeezed apple red drop by drop perplop perplop did you ever see such a sight in your life as little Mary coming home crying to the three hollow straws in the breeze of the green stream that were plucked by the farmer's wife's palm fingers above pressing down pulling them up, perplop perplop little pineapple red drop by drop they rush rush rush and Mary cries cries cries because wife chops chops chops and Mary has lost lost lost all contact contact contact with the earth earth earth.

Save me dear little mice, save me.

We cant, Mary – the farmer's wife the farmer's wife we love the farmer's wife, here we go round the Mary do you really have a little white lamb whose fleece is as…

So what's jazz you asked me. So what's jazz I didn't answer. Because I cant in words. But I've tried to give you in word-thought somewhat the experience of jazz-thought. So what did I give you? One mountain, two mountains, ten clouds, no clouds.

REVIEW OF

# blewointment 1

TISH 22, 1963

A reaction. Loose, open, free. As an editor, bill bissett says in a sketch-essay-response to a movie made mostly in Vancouver – "there is no great (i'm sure you mean here – significant) control." The poems and stories are chosen loosely are unforced are unacademic. bill is open to seeing to hearing anything for what's there from a failing freshman theme on a wounded grizzly bear – "with three wardens having three rifles and three chances cannot eliminate a creature where and what is being done with the Canadian taxpayers' money which is being allotted to the national park warden training school," to a short story based on a "nursery rhyme middle that doesn't exist," to a mother's poem on her child –

> little miss too good
> trompling down the hall
> cheerful little goodmorning.
> Same to everyone,

to one sentence statements – "what is important in the poem is its high" – "love me baby and you contend with life," to poems that are short and poems that are long, filled with love and secrets and gold staircases and visions and things.

Especially place. The Northwest where we are but do not know it until somebody makes it there with words –

> hillside
> running with molten
> snow
>
> charred stumps stared at
> his shoulders
>
> & the smell of a creek
> filled his ears (Doug Matheson),

dreams of dogteeth and small mashed hearts ... it's raining ... the wind creaks. We would have gone north to Alaska ... Sikh ... RCMP ... steel girders in the bridge / are harsh and hazeless ... salmon river ... the reindeer and the ice skater ... I told them that cold afternoon ... went to a town fifty miles north ... why the birds go south to avoid the cold / is beyond the birds' control / is beyond the birds' control

i come from Halifax
      a city of many churches
i come from Vancouver
      a city of many churches

both cities have trouble
with their visions and the world (bill bissett).

The objects are in a time sense deep, the continent in a place sense here, the images are in a literary sense non-Christian but definitely American-Indo-European so non-Chinese non-Japanese which is a surprise because partially most West Coast rooms are. Castles and prairie wagons and peace pipes and licorice smells, pumpkins and cavalries and great mud pie banquets and deadly grizzly bears, "total vineyards in his nostrils" and "ill tell yu my secrets" and "dragon shadows on the wall," moldy candy aunty said King Alexander 1,293 Arabian caravans little badgers hidden beneath wet holes stopping at inns – "that's certainly tru of him, he wrote 5,000 poems in the basement of his grandfathers castle" – castles and kings and no limpy crosses, porpoises and cummings and no rejected lovers, none of the usual normal boring objects. So I like it.

    But then I don't. Another part of me wants things more finished, more there. The subjects have the energy and then get trampled under by even rhythms and lost by visual on-the-page-not-auditory-in-the-ear forms. One of the poets who least loses is Martina Clinton and yet here too there is a problem in the notation not matching the (I take it that all poems are meant to be heard, that poem on page is a transcription of what sound will be like music in air) auditory form –

im a young girl tonight nipples
pointing belly flat
ill ride hairy goats and

eat grapes thru
the back alleys
nobody else
knows my dreams.

but most the one who talked to me and
                                        made
                            the coffee
—Joy Long

The holy man at the school says
the person you are looking for is
yourself.
—Judy Copithorne

But now at least she knows
her navel's for breathing.
—Lanny Beckman

illusion stands naked
realizing the abstraction of love
—Martin Jensen

a ferris wheel          firewords        and names
 being called out
                        we discovered
            pride of this kind diving for
        each other
    in a soundless but still ocean
—bill bissett

There is an advantage to doing it this way. The subjects the feelings the senses do get out, are made. But there is a disadvantage – not with care, not art. Having one poem out of the way a person makes more and goes on learns on that. He trusts himself enough to try rather than folding under by being critical as so many do.

# What Can I Do? Germaine Greer Slashes Myths

*UBYSSEY*, SEPTEMBER 24, 1971

I know that, I do that, I did, was, am now. That's how I feel as I read *The Female Eunuch*, which pulls into me at moments, and at others I stand outside the past and the present details of a crowded-many-relationshipped life and see.

What I see is we do not happen to be the way we are. Most of us make few choices in our lives, many of us refuse to struggle with the people we live or work or play with because we fear, several of us assume we've failed because we accept the love image which surrounds us since birth.

What I see are dependent women who see themselves as independent because they work or think or buy or believe since they are less dependent than other women they talk with that they themselves are free. I hear the sadness of what-can-I-do, see the loneliness of thwarted non-growing destructive relationships: people who quarrel or blank, nag or martyr, make love with everyone or no one: circling in, circling in.

Greer's contention is that we have been sold a middle-class love-life image (the one and only or many but separately) which castrates our energy, prevents our being. Most women do marry, do lock their men into the capitalist-nuclear-private goods-and-space-consuming-get-get-get system. And most are unhappy.

Stuck. In an apartment or house. A child. Two. Buy, buy, buy. Live alone while the kids are young. Be a mom. A super-mom-wife-lover-serf. Accept isolation and tedium. But most work is tedious. His may be slightly more interesting. At least it's social. Maybe jobs would change women's attitudes, but what, which, low-paying or part-time and not much movement for self.

And what happens to the kids?

Horrible daycare centres with only health facilities, not little beings, children, in mind. Or babysitting. Exploit other women for fifty or seventy-five cents an hour since you don't make much yourself. But the job (unless you're of the elite) ain't any piece of piss either. It doesn't give much satisfaction. What DO you want. What do YOU want? Goods, goods, the answer (for most) is more.

It doesn't work. You. WOMAN, nothing's enough. So bitch, so hate, so drink, so dope, so eat, so clean clean clean, so save money for his boat he can only use on weekends plus two weeks a year, so redecorate the house, so health-food-freak, do anything with this energy (compulsive for some) or lack of (sleepy dopey numb) but question the myth and how we live so alone (among our objects) so separately.

And the buying happy-as-two myth is everywhere: rooted in church in state in law, propagandized by commercials by pop songs (her references are from the fifties: love and marriage go together like a horse and carriage, little things mean a lot, our love will last though years may go) by movies by TV by love-story books and women's magazines and by education starting in kindergarten where many kids are still told/shown how they should behave inside static sex roles.

In her it's-never-happily-ever-after chapter on the middle-class-myth-of-love-and-marriage she says:

> most women who have followed the direction indicated by the myth make an act of faith that despite day-by-day difficulties they are happy, and keep on asserting it in the face of blatant contradiction by the fact, because to confess disappointment is to admit failure and abandon the effort. It never occurs to them to seek the cause of their unhappiness in the myth itself.

And although Greer does throughout her book slash the myth, the question I ask is: How to get out of it? Here Greer is not so good.

Throughout the book she speaks for community and against nuclear monogamous relationships (the deadness) from an individualist single girl's viewpoint. She has no sense of struggle within long-term relationships or groups or state. She is for self-examination (perhaps through books like hers), she is for non-monogamous relationships. That's her solution.

But my god, children. She has some fantasy of a commune in Italy (sounds bourgeois to me) where the father and mother can somehow afford to go several days? weeks? a year and where the housemother and housefather bring up the children. Stem family. And the adults commute from wherever it is they are in the world.

And just what does the intellectual heterosexual woman who is on the left do with her sexuality? She mentions truck drivers, working-class men, dont be hoity toity, maybe you can even spread the revolution or change of consciousness that way. Sounds romantic to me. She simply replaces the mess of what she sees with an individualistic image of change where somehow, magically, joyfully, "women's souls change so that they desire opportunity instead of shrinking from it."

In her fuzzy last chapter she says that:

> the chief means of liberating women is replacing compulsiveness and compulsion by the pleasure principle. Cooking, clothes, beauty, and housekeeping are all compulsive activities in which the anxiety quotient has long since replaced the pleasure or achievement principle.

And that:

> the fear of liberty is strong in us, but the fear itself must be understood to be one of the factors inbuilt in the endurance of the status quo.

And:

> Women's liberation, if it abolishes the patriarchal family, will abolish a necessary substructure of the authoritarian state, and once that withers away Marx will have come true willy-nilly …

It seems to me that the life-as-spontaneous-as-it-can-possibly-be idea with the kids off somewhere in dreamland and the adults all free of crappy love images so meeting when they want to meet and withdrawing when they want to withdraw and the women somehow working for peace by not fucking soldiers is an avoidance of community and change in a larger sense. That is, I get an image of millions of heterosexuals (her bias) making love with absolute freedom and no responsibility except to self. And with no sense of continuity, or actual struggle to change the daily patterns of work, loving, money, playing, buying, and education, in community and state.

# HERmione, H. D.

THE READER 1, NO. 4, 1982

H.D., poet and novelist, fiancée of Ezra Pound, wife of Richard Aldington, lover of D. H. Lawrence, and analysand of Sigmund Freud, wrote *HERmione* in 1927 based on events which occurred twenty years earlier: her failure, particularly in geometry, at Bryn Mawr, her inability to leave home and Pennsylvania, her engagement to and rejection of Ezra Pound, her fascination with a young woman, and a nervous breakdown. Although *HERmione* wasn't published until 1981, twenty years after H.D.'s death, the work has remained fresh because the writing is pared and uncluttered, the phrase/sentence/paragraph rhythms poetic, and the content "prefeminist" and "imagist."

Her, the protagonist, is a twenty-one-year-old Victorian woman whose "mind had been too early sharpened," who "could not then know that her precise reflection, her entire failure to conform to expectations was perhaps some subtle form of courage." She has failed her whole year at university and introduces herself – "Her Gart. I am Her Gart. Nothing held her, she was nothing holding to this thing: I am Hermione Gart, failure." Her vacillates between despair of herself and her future (conveyed through geometric, drowning, black rose, and doll imagery) and pride that she has an excellent mind which can match anyone's, specifically that of George Lowndes (based on Ezra Pound. The two writers first met when she was fifteen and he sixteen.)

> Her thoughts, panther-lean cat, strode up behind George. Her thought was swifter than George's witty, tricky thought. Thought chased thought like two panthers. Her own thought, swifter than the thought of George, was there beyond him. "You'll never catch me."

Hermione's intellect, unlike that of so many women of her time, was encouraged to develop by both her artistic mother and her scientific father. "Her mind, could she have so formulated thought, would have conceded: I have tasted words, I have seen them – words may be my heritage and with words I will prove conic sections a falsity – my mythopoeic mind will disprove science and biological-mathematic definition." It is to her parents she owes this utter confidence in her intellect, but it is also them (particularly her mother) and their place (not the home as much as the forest) she is unable to leave. As a twenty-one-year-old in 1907, she would not have been allowed to travel anywhere alone yet she knew "if she stayed she would be suffocated" and would continue to see herself as she sees others seeing her – "a disappointment to her father, an odd duckling to her mother, an ... unincarnated entity that had no place here."

Into Her's world comes a one-sentence letter from Europe – "I'm coming back to Gawd's own god-damn country." It's from the "only young man who had ever kissed Her," George Lowndes. He is presented as harlequin, Punchinello, a man who wears "patchwork clothes" who speaks "patchwork language" in a voice that makes "circus tent noises." Her is both attracted to and repelled by him. She fights her mother to see him, but when she does is disappointed because he does not conform to her fantasies of a companion-lover-saviour. She wants him to tell her to "get out of this place." She wants him to "correlate for her, life here, there." After they meet and become engaged she asks herself, "Why is it that I can't *love* George Lowndes properly?" and answers herself "George being funny is piglike. His eyes are too small in his face." Also his sexual addresses were not sufficiently forceful:

> George was like a great tawny beast, a sort of sub-lion pawing at her, pawing with great hand [*sic*] at her tousled garments. George had been like a great lion but if he had simply bared teeth, torn away garments with bared fangs, she would have understood, would have put narrow arms about great shoulders, would have yielded to him.

Throughout the book, Her has more interesting conversations with women (her mother, her friend, her mother-in-law to be, the cook, her nurse) than with men (her father, brother, fiancé). It is through one of these conversations – "one conversation of all conversations may retain significance; by one leaf you may judge the contour of a great tree" – she first meets Fayne Rabb. The two form a contentious bond of psyche and will and become so intimate that both move into a blend of each other and lose their identities in the intensity between.

> Her seemed to be dragging beat on beat out of that heart by her very static willpower. I will not have her hurt. I will not have HER hurt. She is Her. I am Her. Her is Fayne. Fayne is Her. I will not let them hurt HER.

With Fayne's mother, George's mother, Her's mother, and George pushing against this relationship, it continues until Fayne collapses, Her breaks down, and George is rejected. H.D. develops the arguments which occur between both mother and daughter and friend and friend in such a way that no one is diminished by the exchange (a contrast to George's remarks such as "you are a poem though your poem's naught"), just as she develops the emotional breakdown without sentimentality or simplification.

Although H.D. did not write *HERmione* as a feminist novel, her choice of the name "Her," her refusal to blame the mother for the breakdown, her development of the female relationships (including Her's jealousy of her sister-in-law), her wit, and her ability to make Her extremely intelligent will help to counterbalance images of women composed by men in the twenties *and* the eighties. The imagism, love of language, and consciousness that inform the book make it a work, now that it has finally been published, worth reading.

# Thesen's Long Dash*

*BRICK* 32, WINTER 1988

One of the minor certainties/continuities in Canada is the ten seconds of silence before the beginning of the long dash, which is broadcast on the CBC at exactly ten Pacific – Standard or Daylight – Time, eleven Mountain, twelve Central, one Eastern, two Atlantic, and two-thirty in Newfoundland. People all over the country hear the National Research Council Official Time Signal at exactly the same moment. As a child, sick in bed and cuddled under a quilt, I would think of other children throughout the North and near the Great Lakes or in Saskatchewan also sick, also waiting for the pause to be over, sometimes I would imagine adults such as a railway engineer, a seaman in a wheelhouse, a farmer in a truck or barn, a janitor at a school resetting the clocks and buzzers, a doctor stopped by a red light while driving to a hospital to deliver a baby, waiting and listening. To me, this fact of our existence was also a type of magic: something exact. As an adult, childhood bedrooms sometimes come back while I wait for the signal; I've also occasionally wondered about the broadcasting of silence; and I sometimes think of particular people in other provinces: is she or he listening right now? What context surrounds her or him?

The contexts that Sharon Thesen's poems create in *The Beginning of the Long Dash* are familiar, urban, female, West Coast, and contemporary. Her fourth book of poetry – not composed as a book but as singular lyrics and runs of poems – catches moments in time, pauses, expectancies, sadnesses, loves, silences. The "I" of the poems extends through time: girl, young wife, mother-to-be, mother of toddler, lover of man/language/beauty, ex-wife, friend of women, urban dweller, neighbour, single parent of teenage boy, new wife in new home. Here are houses and rooms in which the poet once lived, gardens and their smells, nearby streets and sounds. Here a "wandering dog / gilds the landlord's tiger lilies"; there

---

\* Published in *Brick Magazine*, this review was originally titled "L'amour, l'amour," a title Hindmarch never particularly cared for. It has been retitled here.

> the car accidents
> out on Broadway
> so frequent now I rather like
> the sound of a small collision
> & don't bother
> going out to see.

Here she wanders "the yard with a bag of tulip bulbs"; there a

> removable red shoulder pad
> and a paperback dictionary
> side by side on the desk signify the woman
> writer's desire for an exactitude.

*The.* Thesen's work is always specific. In the above lines, I see the orange-black dotted tiger lilies and the golden urine, the tulip bulbs which will become red/purple/yellow tulips; I hear a collision and see the red satin shoulder pad near a dictionary. Without opening the book, I remember a green frisbee gliding through goalposts in a poem called "The Green Wind"; I recall the sky pushing five colours down against the horizon and a woman stretching to pin coloured shirts on a clothesline. There are blue hydrangeas in a September-birthday poem for her son – the leaves and rain and petals and grass impressionistically blur into one; there are roses and peonies of all hues, and red-and-white candy canes in a second-hand store Christmas tree hanging above "toe-sculpted shoes." Always there is the rain which both cleanses and encloses – in one poem her "whole face" is raining; in another, she is constantly crossing over bridges in a car through the rain; in yet others, there are rainy windows and umbrellas which are such a fact of West Coast life. Many of her lines capture neighbourhood rainy moments, but she is so specific that they come alive:

> The Divine Fools
> who live on our corner
> & drive rainbow-coloured vehicles
> will soon see me pass
> with a black umbrella
> over my head & a letter in my hand,
> stamp shining in the upper right corner ...

The "rainbow-coloured" and "shining" here play off against the wet black, the non-coloured intersection, and the non-coloured envelope. "The Divine Fools" are mundane but more at ease in the neighbourhood than the author at that moment feels she is.

*Beginning.* In writing, one begins and begins again. In life also – the beginning of love, the beginning of change, the beginning of life/ of walking/of talking, the beginning of an ending or endings, the beginning days in a new house. There is no attempt at narrative or chronological continuity in Thesen's text which allows these single moments, turning points, angers, acceptances, awarenesses to almost float in the pause before the long dash, float in relation to each other. There is, occasionally, a linking of a smell, image, or event from one poem to the next or a deliberate juxtaposition. For example, one of my favourite poems, "Chrysanthemum Perfume," which contains a flashback to an evening in the sixties, is preceded by "Raid," a prose piece in which an eighties control operator says to the poet, "Raid ... that's not poison. You could take a steak, spray it with a whole can of that stuff, put it on the barbecue and eat it for supper. It's made out of flowers. Chrysanthemums." After thinking about this absolutely clear and almost blunt piece where a stranger comes to the porch of her rented home to rid the place of wasps, I turned the page and entered "Chrysanthemum Perfume" which begins with a "So," followed by "what now." Thesen describes "cats crouching jewel-eyed / under parked cars" in a present summer Kitsilano evening, their eyes "a sharp lime green x-rayed / by streetlights." Right after she says "streetlights" everything changes, and "birds long ago / preparing for the story of night" suggest at once both ancient birds and birds on the corner of a page in a childhood book. The next line, "torch songs," the story of the poet's (cats' too?) present night suggests a thirties songstress whose man has done her wrong, and at the same time the torch leads back to the streetlight and forward to the flowers:

> chrysanthemums
> huge white heads
> blooming thru thin November ice
> against the fence along the path
> home, to Bluebeard
> it was almost that bad –
> through that one particular garden
> we had, 1967 or so & Jamie Reid

> with the collected works of Lenin
> in the basement suite
> & the Narcs parked outside
> in a tan-coloured Buick

The twenty-year-old Thesen is coming home from work and although she does not yet know it ("*almost* that bad"), something is wrong in her marriage, and the police are there about to violate their home, to search unsuccessfully. She goes through the gate which her husband has just repaired the latch on, and the

> bitter scent of chrysanthemums
> grabbing like dry hands at my breath
> as if they knew what I wanted
> to refuse, would light my way

It's as if the flowers know and want to tell her. Note the line break, as if the flowers can read and comfort her, but then there is the acknowledgment that she wanted to refuse what she already was beginning to know. There is a stanza break so the flowers "light" her "way"

> up the porch stairs
> beside wasps asleep
> in hexagons & dark forms
> of the police tilting
> wristwatches to streetlights –
>
> and no mother anywhere –

This poem, brought to presence by a smell, accurately and unsentimentally states the acrid constriction of a particular relationship in which the young poet-to-be was silent. When the poet says "and no mother anywhere," she means it; no mother will come to comfort, to sustain, to ward off the police, the wasps, or Bluebeard.

Another beginning in this book is a beautiful sequence, "Marine Life," a memory of Thesen's son's birth and moments of his early childhood which include the disintegration of a marriage, images of other more substantial mothers, hands on hips, this mother and child swinging in a park, swimming in the ocean, baby's first words and steps. Juxtaposed against images of terror within the marriage such as knives flashing in the kitchen, the poet in bed watching headlights climbing the wall, dinner and breakfast lying on "the table like torn-up telegrams," are lines such as:

> Your parents
> fell in love again
> buying your first shoes.

The young mother becomes "smaller and smaller / inside the nightgown," her elbows "like a sparrow's kneecap." Moments of joy counter-exist with the sadness and emptiness of male indifference and female repressed rage. The sequence ends with a poem on the occasion of her son's fourteenth birthday, which is a curious blend of expectations and surprise cakes from past birthdays and a present acknowledgment of the teenager's "cold self-possession / the colour of TV." This poem, which began with hydrangeas, refers to typical fights with the son, and ends after the father – "This child / is expert. He is his father / when he makes a wish" – goes home. It is both a realistic awareness of the present and a yearning for what was not.

*Of the.* Awarenesses are fragmented. Perceptions come to us, and sometimes we are not ready to receive them, to listen. Sometimes there is silence without, emptiness within, sometimes a sweet sadness, but with Thesen there is always a graceful irony and a reaching for the *of the*, for the turning point, for the explanation, for the perception that will lead to another. Many of the lines I like best reflect this reaching both inside and outside for change/confirmation/signs/explanation/awareness. In "The Landlord's Tiger Lilies":

> For the barren reach
> of modern desire
> there must be better forms
> than this –
> something cool,
> intimate as a restaurant.

Here she asks for another to answer her, to be there, "If I thought you would answer me"; but what we, the readers, are left with is the reaching, the calmness of "cool," the contemporary emptiness and intimacy of a restaurant. In "The Occasions," she refers to "women who wait / for a war to end." These women, in twos, talk over restaurant tables:

>   Their perfume recalls to them
>   a certain gesture in the back seat
>   of a taxi in Toronto that said
>   *I agree to this.*

Her women struggle with her and yet are accepting of the current conditions. She quotes Heraclitus to show that, although particularities may change, little has changed, that most men have always "talked about the world / without paying attention to the world / or their own minds, as if / they were asleep or absent-minded." Heraclitus appears near a contemporary souvlaki stand run by the Pericles Society on Broadway's Greek Day, and he:

>   admonishes the crowd
>   to wake up & share a world
>   as a small plane
>   trailing a river of plastic words
>   progresses round the sky.

I love this plastic river, the contemporary pagan smells of roasting meat, the loud bouzouki bands, mixed with statement – old statement and new – a desire for a sign, for something and someone to make sense of contemporary wars both public and private, both militaristic and sexual, both outer and inner.

In "Byzantium," Thesen, sick and delirious, desires to leave the pause, to move on, to escape her body perhaps as Yeats did in "Sailing to Byzantium." She falls half-asleep "inhaling a fold-out map" of that ancient city. She is outside of current time and describing herself as a "tourist of late Romanticism" she floats and swims "back against history / with everything open." Here, in the *of the* float objects such as suitcases and doors, all open.

>   plenty of places
>   for a fever to lodge. I am not
>   the whole
>   hotel ...

She, fragmented, reaches for wholeness but "lodge" leads to "hotel," a place to rest away from home, to be partial, to be free, to be exactly what the body is at this moment, empty with that clarity that only comes at odd hours when one is out of normal or familiar conditions. The line which completes "hotel" is "I am a lobby." What follows is a contemporary image totally unlike Wieners's *The Hotel Wentley Poems* but like them in her clarity of imagery, cleanness of language, and the cinematic quality of the present. What is in the lobby are red armchairs and a woman traveller, wearing only pajamas and an overcoat, who gets into an argument with the night clerk who refuses to communicate and talks only to a computer screen. The traveller desires to be alone but to be taken care of, to be unencumbered, to have a bed and perhaps food, at least to have a place for the night, and then to awake in a room with "an open window / a pink & yellow sky." Thesen expresses with exactness and without clutter a feeling of being here yet not here, there yet not there, partial, in transition, in transit, waiting for the pause, the rest.

She can imagine herself in "Woman Like Me" running away "with just an address book, / a couple of recent snapshots, / some blue silk pajamas." She is by this time remarried, but knows that – and fantasies of freedom – are just that; she turns to one of her friends and captures here an exchange which feels so accurate:

> In the Japanese restaurant
> she begins to confess
> that sometimes they go
> for more than a week without –
> & a faint sexual odour
> of kelp is on our hands
> as we lean toward a mutual place
> filled with deep-fried tentacles,
> things floating in soup,
> a bit of carrot here & there –
>
> Such elegant meagreness,
> & our big empty shoes
> parked like cabs full of secrets
> outside the shadowy screen
> of our leanings, the turning
> & returning sustenance.

Talking with and being with women creates one of the continuities in her life, but so often the stories told are of "elegant meagreness," and frequently there is a screen, a car, or house window, between what is and what is expected. In this poem, the pauses are as important as what is said. The two women reach out of their silences and give each other an absolutely necessary sustenance.

*Long Dash*. Longings. In the long run. Language. Having a language. Articulations. Signals. Being ready:

> & when the text says jump
> we say How high?

This ten-part poem separated by dots, just as the little dashes are broadcast before the ten seconds of silence, is a marvellous mixture of contemporary and mundane-made-beautiful images with childhood undertones and semiotic overtones. The opening section presents a tacky beauty salon complete with pink hairdryers, old women reading current magazines, a miniature dog with a miniature ribbon in its ponytail. Thesen lovingly details this tawdry paradise; it is near Christmas and the "cotton batten / snow contains miniature lights." But the cash register signals a change and "eviction" onto into the raining street. Following a funny line from a magazine in which the most compelling words in our language are "*sex, free, cure, money,* and *baldness,*" comes an enormous image of a female polar bear:

> What does the body of the polar bear
> inscribe on the ice in the cave
> of her winter residence, months on end
>      in the dark?

The bear is from childhood, but the "inscribe" is semiotic:

> Scraping the ice away
> practically in her sleep –
> the goddess language is
> stretching ...

And Thesen herself stretches in this poem which moves from demons in the woods to paintings to children's choir singing "Daddy, daddy did" in answer to the question, "Who felt you there?" It moves from animals ringing us in our sleep to the acknowledgment that "no one is immune from the condition / of abuse."

There is a freedom in this larger poem which contains inner and outer commentary, images of contemporary Christmas/New Year's mixed with musers and H.D. Once upon a time, the Bible, Fantasy Gardens,* images from television coexist with:

> exactnesses
> like the way you sit on the sofa
> with that book that pen
> and will never again
> in that way, that light, just so
> many grey hairs in your hair as today,
> how many peels it took
> to peel your morning orange.

In one section, Thesen and her husband take a trip across the border where signs of God are everywhere. They want us to "send" our "money now." Thesen's comment is:

> God is a profusion of exactnesses
> inside a phone with bad connections:
> Hello? Hello?

Hell. O. The poem, which makes present a contemporary neighbourhood, also depicts "Hades of an entrepreneurial spirit." The portions I like best are to do with her husband and language which "breakdances / the invisible." I find myself laughing at a green jelly salad, and loving the homage to their Christmas tree along with other trees which are "discarded / like victims in the alleys":

> I spoke to ours, I said Thanks,
> you smelled great, your beauty
> made us happy. Imagine bringing a tree
> in the house to adorn with coloured lights
> and tiny birds and bending angels –
> to offer our anxious gifts to, sacrifices
> of love and obligation.

---

\* Former amusement park in Richmond, B.C., owned by Social Credit Premier Bill Vander Zalm.

One of my favourite poems in the book was published originally on the back of *Brick* 27, "Song of the New House." Thesen begins with the light, how it keeps changing "according to whatever / music is on" and we imagine her in the new rooms seeing familiar objects from new angles. She then looks outside through venetian blinds to house roofs on a hill, a sparkling pale tree and hears the traffic, "a reassuring breath / expelled by systems." The question of the day on *Cross Country Checkup* is: "What do you think / about Chernobyl?" Thesen moves outside her neighbourhood and imagines Ukrainian women and their garments and contexts. She identifies with them, these women who are outside the immediate disaster area who smile as they breathe "a spring-time air fluttering / with pretty streamers." She then describes

> this shallow valley of the
> clean and safe,
> & beloved this one outside
> in the afternoon & beloved that one
> also.

Her husband and son, just as their husbands and children, are safe, but others are not so fortunate. She and her husband on a walk down an alley hear "someone singing *L'amour, l'amour* / from *Carmen* in the tricking sound / of the shower."

Although much that happens in the world is horrible, and although she will not block out consciousness of that, there is her love for her husband and child which makes this day and this spring live:

> in this awakening
> we all stretch & come alive
> slowly, out of the rain.

This song of praise and thankfulness is one that anyone, anywhere, female or male, could identify with. What I so like about it is her particularity, her unpretentious recording of what is inside and outside, her ability to write a political poem that contains no rhetoric, her ability to stay in the *of the*, to be immediate, direct, and above all simple. Thesen's work is never overly simple, but like the long dash it is exact and is heard dearly by any reader who at the particular moment happens to be listening.

# Oral Histories, Recordings, Conversations

# Westcoast with Gladys

## Conversation between Gladys Hindmarch and Warren Tallman

1969, PREVIOUSLY UNPUBLISHED*
Transcribed and edited by Deanna Fong and Karis Shearer

## Introduction

Originally recorded on reel-to-reel tape, this conversation between UBC English professor Warren Tallman and Gladys Hindmarch takes place sometime in 1969 at the house of Warren and Ellen Tallman. It follows (probably very closely) on a previous conversation in which Tallman, having been commissioned by Michael Gnarowski to produce a book on the literary history of West Coast Canadian poetry of the 1960s, has sketched out an initial thesis on the subject and has invited Hindmarch and Stan Persky to discuss the scene with him.

Recording technology, as Tallman describes (however facetiously), is an essential part of his composition process: "so I have to put 150 pages on tape fast (*laughs*) and then type it up" ("West Coast"). As Hindmarch notes, however, composition is not merely dictating into a tape recorder; it's important to have an interlocutor or several – that the composition be a social one. Although a book-length publication never emerged from this project, Tallman's well-known essay "Wonder Merchants" draws very closely on these tapes, and this recording becomes evidence of the degree to which Hindmarch contributed to that essay and the oral history that underpins it. Also important is the role of the sound recording in the consumption and circulation of poetry. Tallman remembers, for instance, that the first time he heard Allen Ginsberg's "Howl" was because "Bob Patchell at CBC went down to San Francisco very early, about '56, and did a

---

\* "DHL 100 Tape" in the Warren Tallman fonds, SoundBox Collection, UBC Okanagan.

tape of all of those people reading. He had Spicer, he had Ginsberg, I think he had Duncan" ("Westcoast with Stan and Gladys," DHL 100 Tape, SoundBox Collection).

In what follows, Tallman and Hindmarch return to review the notes from the first conversation, discussing the shape of the book's narrative arc and the key details of the story. We see Hindmarch acting as community historian, editor, interpreter, and arguably co-author:* She fills in parts of the history that Tallman is unfamiliar with, such as the way the Writers' Workshop was run, and adds the names of women such as Diane Grant and Claudia Irving back into the record. Together, Tallman and Hindmarch parse what constitutes public history (to be put into print) and "inner history" (not fit for print). Unsurprisingly, perhaps, the division is largely gendered; for Tallman, the literary action that takes place in the domestic space of the house, involving Ellen Tallman and Hindmarch, is a kind of private history that doesn't necessarily belong in print or the public record (here coterminous).

## "There Is an Inner History"

**Gladys Hindmarch:** What you were saying about Creeley, I've never thought of that negative-type energy. You're right that Duncan's spirit is a very positive thing in terms of people.

**Warren Tallman:** He gets them writing poems.

**GH:** And Creeley and Robin [Blaser] both are much more critical. They both get people writing in a sense.

**WT:** It's a much tougher world.

**GH:** It's a line. I don't mean a line you hand out but a straight line. They want that verticalness. The person is much more centred. Like, what right do you have to be a poet, too?

**WT:** Let me just move this [microphone] here though.

**GH:** You're going to do the main talking.

**WT:** That way it's between us. Can I have that sheet? You see, just going through this [his notes from the previous recording session], I think the Souster-Birney thing is the right place to start. And the only thing that I wasn't mentioning was that it seems to me

---

* See Deanna Fong and Karis Shearer, "Gender, Affective Labour, and Community-building through Literary Audio Artifacts," *No More Potlucks* 50 (2018), http://nomorepotlucks.org/site/gender-affective-labour-and-community-building-through-literary-audio-artifacts-deanna-fong-and-karis-shearer/.

that there are a cluster of poets, namely Eli Mandel, Doug Jones were both connected with the Souster-Dudek-Layton world very soon. They were the earliest ones to join into that world. But to me, you get kind of a split where you get people like [Al] Purdy and [Leonard] Cohen who went for [Irving] Layton's thing, and people like Jones and Eli who went much more for the poetics. And it shows in their poems, although they're getting a kind of... I don't have any particular sense that... Eli keeps saying he had one of the earliest copies of *The Maximus Poems* and was quite familiar with them. But I don't get the sense that he was really familiar at all. I don't think it made sense to him at the time. He tends to stay in a more kind of conventional poetry, even though he's aware of other possibilities. And the same with Phyllis Webb. I don't think anything began to dawn on Phyllis Webb until she met [Robert] Duncan and actually began to get into what Duncan was doing. Then her poetry began to change.

**GH:** And I think of Dorothy Livesay with Jack Spicer. We had all the readings before that, some of which she'd been to, some of which she hadn't. When she was asking the questions of Jack, a lot of the people in the room thought, "Oh my god, what is this question about 'dance of language'?" But she was really asking that question, and I think it very much shows in her next book. There's this absolute breakthrough. I don't find the stuff she's written previously... What was it, *The Unquiet Bed*?* I've never been the least bit interested.

**WT:** [overlaps] Previously, she was a very conventional poet. A friend of Earle Birney's. And of course after the Spicer lectures when Duncan came up in '66, she had Duncan come to her poetry class. She had him come and give all the evening lectures to the class. In fact, [E.J.] Pratt's imagist poem† had just come out, so Robert used that. So it wasn't a good night. He didn't get too much said. The form didn't work for him somehow.

**GH:** As a side comment on that book, I really don't think teachers should use that book. It's an absolute mistake.

**WT:** Why is that?

**GH:** Because the imagist thing, in no counts is the influence dead. But the imagist poem itself ended about 1918. You have all these

---

\*     Dorothy Livesay, *The Unquiet Bed* (Toronto: Ryerson Press, 1967).
†     Very likely Tallman refers to *Here the Tides Flow* (Toronto: MacMillan, 1962).

people looking at things now as *if* they were rules. That was the description of what they were trying to do, as they didn't like what had previously been done. Then you get teachers who put a Souster or a Layton poem on an exam. It's supposedly an imagist poem and there are so many unnecessary words.

WT: I agree. It can be kind of a trap book if a person takes it literally.

GH: And that's what most teachers do.

WT: Now the things I've jotted down: the whole section of the Souster quote, then the section about Birney, then the section about *Prism*.

GH: There wasn't much on *Prism*. There's not gonna be much, anyway.

WT: No, I'm not too interested. To me, the main thing about *Prism* was why weren't they concerned with what was around them. The reason is obvious: they were always on the make to print certain poets and writers. The only way in which they were at all interested in the local scene was via the creative writing students. But they were writing such uninteresting things that there was no future in the writing that appeared in *Prism*.

GH: There's no relationship in the relationship.

WT: Right. So the only thing was the Vancouver issue. That was the only time that *Prism* acted as though –

GH: That was done by Eliot Gose, too, who –

WT: Eliot did that? –

GH: – he's not one of their main editors.

WT: Now, the Duncan thing makes sense to bring that in. And I'm not too worried about that, because I will have to go back to those tapes and pull some quotes.

GH: But previous to that time you also have the Writers' Workshop and it should have about a two-paragraph mention.

WT: Right, yeah. Because I wasn't conscious of that.

GH: Mainly the people getting together. When you think of the people who did get together, it's amazing how many of them are still writing. George Bowering was there, myself, Daphne Buckle [Marlatt], Bobby Hogg, David Cull, and Frank Davey as the main centre. And there's Claudia Irving, who still writes, and Diane Grant who's got a play on in Montréal. Mainly it was an occasion where people got together regularly to hear what other people had written. They also got high and drunk on sake regularly, too. People felt quite free. The teacher that they had, Tony Friedson, was not acting as the teacher. His capacity was to run the poems off on the machine. Even though there were times he tried very hard to be a teacher in that situation, he just didn't have the authority.

**WT:** But he had the social bubble.

**GH:** There were eight or ten people in the room that had authority. And he was very manic. And I think in the question "How does a city get a writing," that maybe someone who was just sort of manic or totally scattered is just as important as someone who was totally focused, because they're limited sometimes by that focus.

**WT:** I think that what Tony actually enjoyed was the social.

**GH:** Yeah, right, and that's his realm anyway. You see, so it's not a writing world. That made it so that people weren't so lonely. Besides meeting in the caf and showing off all their poems and stories ...

**WT:** How often did that meet? Once a week?

**GH:** No, every second week. On Monday nights, I think. That was regular.

**WT:** The one other thing that's to Tony's credit literarily is that he was the person who discovered Daphne.

**GH:** Right.

**WT:** She was a freshman and he was really taken by her writing. To me, Tony's literary judgment was just appalling usually. He didn't have it. But he certainly clued into Daphne.

**GH:** As soon as Daphne arrives at university, she's at the Writers' Workshop. There's a world that's already started there. That's why that workshop was worth eight creative writing courses put together.

**WT:** I'm glad you brought that up, because it was something that I wasn't particularly conscious of.

**GH:** The meetings would last from 8:30 p.m. to about 12 a.m., then frequently they went on until 2 a.m. or 3 a.m. elsewhere.

**WT:** Was this the kind of workshop where papers were given?

**GH:** No, no papers. Nothing written about.

**WT:** People brought poems and read them?

**GH:** Yeah. If the person had time, which most people had, they had to just give the typed poem to Tony the day before, and he ran it off. So none of this thing of a week in advance. Occasionally, if somebody wrote a poem that day, they'd make about six carbons. They'd type it maybe two or three times. They had maybe six to eight copies and the things were passed around. But you always saw *and* heard. I think it's very important that you don't

WT: just hear, the way you go to a reading. In a workshop you also have to be able to hear the thing four or five times and to be able to read it as a reader.

WT: Now, is this how Frank first met Daphne?

GH: Yeah, Writers' Workshop.

WT: One thing I'm curious about, just as background info, were Frank and Daphne ever lovers?

GH: Oh, no.

WT: Or she strictly didn't see anything in him and he was just overboard?

GH: Daphne at that time had her high-school sweetheart, who is now her husband, but was then in Europe.

WT: And she was focused on him.

GH: Daphne was never particularly taken by Frank. She's become a lot more friendly with Frank two years after her marriage. It was quite a strain because suddenly this big guy, in terms of the writing world, was focused on this freshette. Totally focused on her. And the more she didn't want to be with him, the more he wanted to be with her, because it was like a Gatsby thing, which he has a poem about. "A Jay-walk with Gatsby."* It was his image of her that he was in love with. He created her. And he also unintentionally created her for most of the other people present. That was the "her" that they kept seeing through his eyes. That's where literature is not real. People would see Daphne through his eyes, rather than see Daphne for Daphne. But I would say that Bob Hogg and David Cull saw Daphne through Daphne. The young recognized what was going on. Though the elders were just two years older.

WT: And they're both attending these meetings of the workshop.

GH: Right.

WT: But, as I remember it, they both also went through this stage where they were anti-TISH because they were going to start up a separate magazine, and then gradually realized that TISH wasn't an enemy.

GH: Yeah, you've got to realize that there were several fights in the TISH world, the main TISH poets at that time being Frank Davey, Fred Wah, Lionel Kearns, George Bowering, and Jamie

---

\* Frank Davey, "A Jay-Walk with Gatsby," *D-Day and After* (Pollock Pines, CA: Rattlesnake Press, 1962), 18.

Reid. And even David Dawson was not really in that TISH world. Their sensibilities were such that they could say something and because of the social structure, all these other people would believe them. So that Bobby and Dave and Daphne might want to do something on their own is totally understandable because if Frank didn't like something, everybody knew it. He didn't go around blasting it, he just makes one critical remark and it was repeated five times within two hours. Even though the university had well over ten thousand students at the time, that news travelled. That *was* the news. It could be described as much more close than fraternity.

**WT:** Oddly enough, that was probably part of what kept the scene hopping, that Frank would make these probably outrageous statements off the top of his head, but that people would believe them. That it would then produce a reaction and it would involve people in writing the poetry. Whether they were true or not was a different issue. (*pause*) Okay, so I think I've got that pretty clear. Now, the other thing that Stan got out in the open, which I hadn't thought of in terms of the book, was that whole Ginsberg phase earlier on, that Ginsberg-Kerouac phase, which must have been Spring of '59.

**GH:** Yeah, it was.

**WT:** Of course, I can remember so many times people coming to the house, where it was Ginsberg and Ferlinghetti whom they came to hear via Allen's record or a tape of Allen. Did we have a tape or did we just have a record at that time?

**GH:** I don't remember a tape of Allen.

**WT:** Well, there was a tape. Bob Patchell at CBC went down to San Francisco very early, about '56, and did a tape of all of those people reading. He had Spicer, he had Ginsberg, I think he had Duncan.

**GH:** I don't remember listening to this.

**WT:** No, it wasn't available. Mo Steinberg had an evening at his house where Patchell brought that tape over. That was the first time I heard Ginsberg read "Howl." That was on that tape. That was very early. Patchell just did it on his own, kind of, and evidently played it. I assume it was played over CBC.

**GH:** So you're saying there was a scene here except for the writers weren't writing ...

**WT:** Yeah, and they had no connection with writers that ...

**GH:** Just the way that the sort of Birney-Layton thing does not really connect. Nobody of my age would say that Souster or Dudek were an influence. Like, it wouldn't even occur to us.

**WT:** Right, right, right. I remember when Robert [Duncan] was here in '61 and Birney had Ellen and Robert to lunch out at the Faculty Club, and Birney was talking about Robert as one of those Beat poets. Clearly Birney just had no sense at all of Robert or San Francisco, except for the Beat thing at that time.

**GH:** The people who should not generalize are poets.

**WT:** But, anyway, I thought it might make sense to put in a little bit about Ginsberg. Now that whole Ellen story. I still don't really know how I feel about Stan's proposition that it should be an inner history rather than a public history. There are public events like Duncan comes to town, and you can talk about them. There is an inner history that obviously involves you, involves Ellen, involves myself, involves the house, but I'm not entirely sure that it's possible to convey that because it would involve knowing the people.

**GH:** Is that really how you feel about it?

**WT:** Also that I don't know how – it would be easy to say that Frank, and George, and Lionel, and Fred, and Jamie were involved in a series of upsets with each other that they *then* would go off and talk to you about them.

**GH:** Separately. So they're secret.

**WT:** Right. That undoubtedly was a part of the whole generation of poetry. The way that the poetry was getting written had to do with those. But, golly, I don't know.

**GH:** That seems in some sense egotistical, but in another sense it doesn't. Like when you say that about Ellen, I'd say it should be in, and when you say it about me, I'd say it shouldn't. I'm just wondering if there shouldn't just be a section of *Paterson*-type story, just little paragraphs –

**WT:** Well, you see, I don't see Ellen involved in the actual production of the poetry, just the coming in of it.

**GH:** No, but –

**WT:** You were much more involved, much more inside of the fact that the poetry was being written. In a personal way, you were much more inside that.

**GH:** Well, I'd say you and Ellen are very, very much so, because that's an audience. It's an older audience. What does Warren think, what does Ellen think? That's another side. That's absolutely essential.

**WT:** But you know me, all through that period I was not making value-judgments about those poems.

**GH:** It's much easier for the older ones to argue against or for something, in a sense. Your comments would have been taken as – like, you don't want to be an authority. That's one thing that you've somehow made yourself to not be, where it would be so easy. Maybe someone like Tony Friedson wanted to be an authority, but people had such confidence largely because of you. Like why do I have confidence? Because I had you for first-year English. Suddenly there's a way to see. Not *your* way to see, but my way to see, which is largely created by you. There's a separation there. You are, in a way, similar to Olson. You're not going to show people how to do things the way you do them. You're not a craftsman-of-the-guild type that's going to pass on. To get to yourself.

**WT:** Well, when I was commenting on your papers I was mainly puzzling out what *you* were doing. I remember having suggestions about it but it was mainly to intuit your mode rather than mine that I wanted to impose on you.

**GH:** This would be how I acted for those guys largely, too. Even though there were times –

**WT:** You took that role with them.

**GH:** – that I would prefer to find out what they were thinking they were doing at times than to say quickly what it was I thought. But then within an hour I would say, well, if that's what you're doing then this detail is false. Like you just skimmed over that. That type of confidence comes from you.

## On *TISH* and *blewointment*

**WT:** Okay, then with the Duncan thing, obviously I'm going to have to go through those lectures and pick up what seemed to me to be kind of key statements that will match up with excerpts from *TISH*. Then I also want to use issue fourteen where Robert began to write about the Vancouver poets. Remember that long thing that he wrote?

**GH:** Right, to Frank and George.

**WT:** Because that was a tremendous booster for them. Again, a feeling that they were being defined, because they began writing poems on the basis of that. There's also a thing of Bob [Creeley]'s in that same issue, which is a turn-off thing. It's a much, much more restrained and doubting and not explicitly but implicitly imposing certain restrictions. They're both in the same issue. By the time that comes out, Bob's just about arrived. That's issue fourteen, so that would be October of the year that Bob's teaching [1962]. Oh, yeah, here's one thing that's still out of this. Probably the best thing would just be to get together with bill and talk to bill about it. That is, I want the *blewointment* thing in. Not mingled. I want a Duncan thing, I want a Creeley thing, I want a *TISH* thing, I want a *blewointment* thing. I'm not too worried about how the sequence will go, but I think it would obviously make sense to just have bill come over and start asking him about it.

GH: I think one of the main differences between those two, if they were groups in that sense, is that in the TISH group there's so much competition, and fighting, and seeing who knows what Olson's saying. Who knows what Duncan – did Creeley like what I wrote? Does Gladys like what I wrote? There's a whole thing of little rewards. Among Newlove, and bissett, and Copithorne, and Gerry Gilbert, very little feeling of that. They're people who are writing, so the exchange is not as tight, which is what partially crystallized the whole *TISH* thing. But at the same time, it's much freer.

WT: To me, *blewointment*'s a funny thing. Because for one thing, during the early issues of *blewointment*, I thought "Oh god, there's so much *junk* in this." Anything bill was handed he just put in. And I think partly that was true –

GH: Except bill also – I remember he went around, and when anything of mine was in he just came up and asked for it. And I'm sure he was going and asking people.

WT: The overall impression that I get is that, the more it went along, it really is an example of bill bissett's growth as a poet. That is, you can see where he was in the early stages just by looking at the early ones. bill is doing this on his own. It's very different. As far as I can make out, I had always assumed it was a bill bissett enterprise. He didn't have a large staff of people helping him.

GH: He did not, and he never did. He typed it and ran it off on his own, and stapled it and usually delivered it and collected the money, all at the same time.

WT: He was fantastically persistent. The real message of the whole thing was, one, bill's development, but that in the later issues, by the people that begin to appear, he begins to define the kind of poetry he was interested in. You see, for so many issues it was always his drawings that interested me and not the poetry. I had that feeling about early bill that I had about early Leonard Cohen, that his written work was just dull as hell.

**GH:** Well, bill and I used to have readings. I don't know how it happened, but I think in '63 and '64 – the fall of '63 – I think it started on Sunday afternoons. I think it started as every second week, but there were so many writers that it ended up every week. People would come over and read and I'd make a huge pot of soup and we'd have biscuits later for the people who wanted to stay. Bill and I had a lot of discussions in this period.

**WT:** bill's always trying to invoke spirits, really. In a sense, his most interesting poetry is the one as it becomes more religious, it becomes more interesting. Just by the way he's involved, the fact that he's become a more interesting poet in the last three years than he's been in the previous three or four, is the feeling I get. That he's gotten into it. Kind of like someone who plays the saxophone for four years indifferently and then suddenly gets into the potential of it.

**GH:** No, I'd have to really read bill to say this but I bet you in a larger view, looking back, there are going to be some good poems from every year, that are just as important. Very definitely. It's quantity, right? He writes a lot and sometimes he's just right on.

**WT:** See, he's harder to deal with – *blewointment* is harder to deal with because it doesn't have a poetics, it doesn't have statements. The poetics is kind of implicit but it's not stated, which means I'm going to have to write about it.

**GH:** And this is where the TISH group – a lot of people felt very exclusive and bad because they did have a poetics but it wasn't really as formed but there certainly were pronouncements from on high. And one of the things on high was the fact that there were so many people, like a core of six. Where thirty people were essentially involved with that and a number of people outside of those thirty very aware that there was all this sort of thing going on, not knowing *what* it is but to have said hello to Lionel Kearns today, that's enough of a high for two weeks! You know, and that sense, I don't know if that should be here or not ... like, you know this is the other book, you know.

**WT:** That inner one.

## On the Dispersal of *TISH*

**WT:** I really don't know how to deal with all the breakups. That is, the dispersals, where suddenly Fred's in Albuquerque and Buffalo, and Bobby Hogg's in Buffalo. David Cull is off in Europe and around, Frank is gone.

**GH:** They're absolutely essential. If anyone was going to keep writing, that was essential. Now, the effect of that breakup on all three of those poets has just been a disaster. They actually needed that group and activity and that fight. That gamey fight. Because of a lot of it was a game. It's like when you're four years old and you're playing a game, is it a game or not a game? That *play* was so important. That is the world. And some of those poets have not been –

**WT:** Well, Frank has never recovered from that.

**GH:** I would say Frank and Lionel.

**WT:** Lionel's had great difficulty.

**GH:** George has recovered but there's no audience. That was one of the things about the workshop and having that whole clutch. Suddenly there was an audience.

**WT:** George has done well. George has done so well. He's kept *Imago* going, for one thing. He's done a tremendous amount of writing on his own – more than anybody else.

**GH:** That's why I would just say just the other two, then.

**WT:** I think with George and Frank both in Montréal, that's going to be a very good thing for both of them, because I think it will start up again for them. Because Frank hasn't had anyone to be in touch with since he left Vancouver and that was '63. That was six years ago.

**GH:** I'm not very good at questions.

**WT:** No, no. You see, if I get enough on these tapes, then I can work on a tape by myself. But I was thinking, oh god, if Glady was out of town, then I couldn't get ... Talking to you, I can get it all blocked in. Then my plan is to do another tape by myself, just start doing a type of tape ... then I'll have somebody to talk to, namely the tape – like I'll pretend you're there.

**GH:** You should really have someone here because it does make a difference.

# "The Bob Episode" and the Breakups

**WT:** We were just starting on Bob. You were saying something about…

**GH:** Oh yeah, that I had never thought of that inwardness. I just automatically accepted Creeley's world. I thought, it's right. All this parodying. There's not the inside on a lot of these people. But I think you're right. What he actually did, those conflicts – which were able to be in the person anyway – were brought into focus and out of focus. That whole year that he's here there [was] a series of fights among the writers. So when that breakup finally came, that dispersal, in a sense, most people left were pleased.

**WT:** Were pleased?

**GH:** You can never be romantic and think that group was ever totally happy with each other. There was always a shift of relationship. It was always shifting. But when that dispersal came, Fred couldn't stand using that fucking machine again that was broken down. Frank was blaming Fred for *TISH* not getting out when the machine wasn't working. Fred was mad at Lionel because Lionel's not doing his… But mainly it was anti- or pro-Bowering, you know. I think it was necessary for the breakup to happen.

**WT:** The one thing I always was impressed with was even though they were fighting with each other, they've always been quite *loyal* to each other. Like George has always been quite loyal to Frank, at the same time that they might have cause never to speak to each other. But then that wasn't the reaction.

**GH:** *Publicly* loyal, privately not. When I came off the boat, no matter where I went, I heard a sad tale. That's why you were right about the Creeley thing. When I came here it was always a sad tale about Bob and the writing department – which was true, it was a horrible tale. The energy was going into that tale, that shift… Everybody was alone and complaining about it.

**GH:** But it went off the writing and into the personal. The writing was always personal anyway. But the energy went –

**WT:** Well, I always felt the breakup was too soon. But maybe it was necessary.

**GH:** I think it was necessary, but I don't think at that point – I think at least another year. At least another year together would have been great. Because it never became formed. And I don't mean formed for then you break it up. They needed to move through a couple more stages together before going off on their own. And

what I would say is that they went through one stage together and went through the breakup.
**WT:** See the Black Mountain thing had about six years of a *strong* period when it's at Black Mountain, when it's there. Although they're travelling away, they're coming back at the same time; the place was available. Whereas when this broke up, there wasn't something for them to come back to. They come into town and there was really nothing for them to do, because the other people were all out of town. So that when they came back it was mostly social.
**GH:** But say, when Bobby Hogg came back, that was when there were again readings downstairs in Gordon Payne the painter's studio. That was bill bissett's ex studio and there were seventy-five people.
**WT:** That big a crowd?
**GH:** And that was with no posters. It wasn't like it is at a university where people phone people to try to get them to come out. If ten people come out then great, if more fine … What happened was it was a Saturday and Bob [Hogg] said he'd like to give a reading on Sunday and there were seventy-five people.
**WT:** Which is huge for that kind of thing. Okay, well, I think I've got the Bob episode pretty clear in my mind.

# Before *TISH*: from *Oral History of Vancouver*

## *Interview by Brad Robinson*

OPEN LETTER 2.1, WINTER 1971–1972

**Brad Robinson:** Gladys, how did you come to live with Warren and Ellen Tallman?

**Gladys Hindmarch:** I had Warren as a freshman English teacher ... I was extremely ... I don't think depressed is the word for how a person feels ... at university, if they're sort of below depression. If a person says "I'm depressed," you're at a certain level of consciousness so you know what it is to be not depressed, and I think I was in a state where anyone who really recognized it would have sent me to a shrink. But because I was able to go through the lineups in the cafeteria, went to classes, passed things, I suppose no one thought I should be sent.

The only person I met in the first year of university (UBC) that I could really speak to was Warren, and I talked to him an awful lot and he turned me on to D.H. Lawrence. I was a non-reader, I didn't read for enjoyment, I still seldom do. Only in my last year have I read quite so much. It's my "readingest" year.

The thing that turned me onto Lawrence was not the short stories which Warren gave me to read, but the *Studies in Classic American Literature*, which I bought in the Hudson's Bay Company in Victoria while waiting for my mother to do one of her typically mother things. I began to keep a notebook, which was essentially an argument against many of Lawrence's sketches that I didn't like – mainly lines and phrases – and in the process of this I learned a lot of things and because, not because of the notebook, but because of Warren, he talked me into getting back into university by having me signed up in Creative Writing without having submitted anything. He also managed to get me into second-year English with Eliot Gose ...

Until all this I had thought of joining the armed forces – just like I've got to do something with my life, not my entire life, just my immediate life.

**BR:** This would be around ...

**GH:** It was the end of my freshman year, which was the end of 1958. I was going into my second year, and I met Frank Davey in the writing course I mentioned – the teacher was Jake Zilber.

Frank Davey was a red-headed kid from Abbotsford or Chilliwack – I think it was Abbotsford – I always get the two mixed, probably heard it wrong the first time. Very much a country boy, such as I was a country girl, but Frank had grown up inside the town ... cars the main thing, and cruising after girls, but never very successful ... the beautiful fuck-ups of kids that age ... trying very hard, blushing ... not blushing, you know how it is ... and Frank and I used to sit together in this very large class. I think Jake had twenty-five or thirty people in the class, which is too much for a writing class, just too much really for any type of class where a lot of individual thought and perception is supposed to be going on, because you don't want to block it off. It's pretty hard with that number of people especially if you're used to talking, like Jake was. He would lecture for an hour, and then try and structure it, but even so, it was a pretty successful class.

It was a lot of fun and was certainly a focal point of that year for me – those Friday afternoons were, on the whole, so visible.

I was hurt a fair amount in that class – I don't think I should go into why I felt hurt by Jake, but like one of the things would be Frank who would write parodies. I would get pretty good marks, and I was sort of mark-oriented, in a sense, at that time, not that I'd be pleased when I got good marks and not pleased when I didn't, etc. ... but, in a sense, underneath, I really was, but I wouldn't admit it. Frank also got good marks, but he at one point wrote a parody of something I had written that was put in the *Ubyssey*. Frank got 5 percent more for his parody than I got for my original. Then another parody appeared in the class and I said, sort of jokingly, to Jake that I should get extra marks every time someone writes a parody on something I had written ... sort of like added on to whatever my total thing is.

I've never really liked satire or parody and I don't think I ever will. Partially, I don't really understand it, but my experience I had with it sort of hurt ...

**BR:** I can recall that you had once written a story and it was published in *Mademoiselle* ... some sort of contest?

**GH:** The setup of the course was such that it called for an essay or a description. At that time Warren was writing something on Kerouac, which later became "Kerouac's Sound."

A girl that I knew from high school who happened to be in Victoria wrote me a letter on the same day that Warren had talked to me about jazz, and she wrote quick, quick, I've got a new boyfriend and I'm acting like I know more than I do, so sort of tell me something, and I thought, "What a ridiculous question, like what's jazz, how can you answer that?" Also, I hadn't done any writing for Jake for a week, so I sat down and started writing this essay that was quite rhythmical and very, oh, I don't know if I should describe the essay, but various impressions of various types, as I say, you can't just lump it all together, three types in words, even though these divisions aren't ... just my own ... I don't have any deep impression of jazz ... I used to play sax in a dance band and I have a definite sense of improvisation ... just what it's like to fool around and have fun on an instrument. And Jake really liked this piece and I sort of put it away – you weren't supposed to hand in revisions after a certain length of time and I just wasn't interested in revising what I had written.

There was a fellow in the English department who was going to give a lecture on jazz and literature, and so Jake said to me: "Hand this back."

And so, on the day that I was to hand my piece back, or the night before the day, as I was looking through this sort of folder that I have all sorts of things in, I came across, in front of the jazz thing,* this sheet from *Mademoiselle* which Jake had handed out to all the women in the class. So I typed my piece up, gave Jake a carbon, and sent the original of the new thing, with sort of half the other thing I had written, off to *Mademoiselle* magazine. And, a couple of months later, I heard that I had come in second out of all the people who had sent in things, which meant that I had a relatively strong chance of going to New York if I wanted to.

Also Jake and I – this was sort of getting toward Christmas vacation and we were not getting along, from my point of view, I don't think he felt that – but he really didn't like the nursery

---

\* "So You Ask Me: An Essay in Jazz"; see p. 259.

rhyme things that I was doing, meaning, really, that he gave me 70–75 percent, and I thought this meant that he didn't like me. This is where I don't think they should mark something like creative writing. I don't think you should be marked in English either. It's just so stupid. And because of the contest, I was this sort of smiley girl and I got A marks.

BR: The terms had changed.

GH: Yeah, right.

BR: At this time, had the second issue of *Evergreen Review* appeared?

GH: Gee, I don't know. I was never very aware of *Evergreen*.

BR: I asked because that was the number that sort of classically defined the writing scene of the time. I believe Warren's "Kerouac's Sound" was also printed in that issue.

GH: Oh no, that would be much later. He'd just done "Kerouac's Sound" in November of '58 and that came out in February of '59. I know he showed me the *Evergreen Review*, and as with all other things, I just wasn't interested. I found the things hard to read, and I was feeling pretty low. And I was reading Beckett and that made me feel even lower – not lower, but it just didn't make me feel warm to find someone who was in despair. Yet I would read writers like Hardy who made me feel better.

BR: So at the end of that summer you had established links with Warren and Frank Davey?

GH: I'd come back from New York and went to sit in on one of Jake's summer classes. There was this large teddy-bear kind of figure, a guy with really curly sandy hair and gentle quick smile, who turned around and said: "You don't know me, but I know you." And it was Lionel Kearns. We only talked for about three minutes. But I'd heard from Warren that this guy was a *poet*, like a great writer, and we really had nothing to say to each other at that point. I was a pretty plump girl then – 160 pounds or something like that. Not much chit-chat or razzmatazz.

Moving to the fall of that year, I met George Bowering – I had started going to Writers' Workshop ...

BR: Where was that?

GH: Tony Friedson, who then became a member of the Writing department, had a writer's workshop that ran for three pretty solid years. Actually, I had met George Bowering in my first year ... I had read something of his in *Raven*, the UBC literary magazine. I really liked everything in the magazine, there were things of Barry Hale – but I walked up to George and introduced myself on a rainy day. I remember we didn't have much to say, but I recall sitting there for about ten minutes feeling very warm, and picking up a couple of stones on the parking lot when I went back to the dorms. It was one of those "good" days.

And when I went to this writer's workshop, it was quite crowded. It was down on 4th Avenue or 6th – somewhere in the Kitsilano area. It's hard to tell when you don't drive – I had no sense of the city at that time, other than I didn't like it. I've had senses of Vancouver in earlier times, like when I used to sneak into the PNE under the fence.

At any rate, I sat on a couch next to George Bowering, and we met. So it was pretty rapid, once we hit that sort of time in terms of when you meet people, not sort of what starts happening.

We're now into my third year of university. I took a course from Warren which was then called English 406: An Introduction to Poetry. In that class was Frank Davey, Barry Hale – who later became a writer for the *Toronto Star* and is now an art writer, and Lionel Kearns. Even though I'd met Lionel that summer, it wasn't until after Christmas exams that he came back from the middle of the room. I always tend to sit in the very last row, or second last row, preferably close to the door or window. Anyway, Lionel came down and said, "Can I read your paper?" And I said, "Can I read yours?" And he said, "Well, I don't really want you to see mine." I said, "Why? I'm so shy and I'm showing you mine?" And so we read each other's papers. This was getting into the spring of '60 …

**BR:** What was Warren teaching?

**GH:** Warren's idea was that university students have to read *so* much, and they don't really absorb all the reading, they don't ever have a chance to absorb it and really think. So why not have a course that is relatively light – not light-hearted, but that the reading load is light and has focus.

So I think his idea was that you only teach nine or ten poems in the entire year – for instance, a month on "The Ecstasy" by Donne and a month on "The Garden" by Marvell – and by that spring we got into Hopkins, and Lionel and Frank and I yakked all through the class. Mainly me yakking and them having to listen. But they did sort of talk.

We just didn't pay attention, in a sense, to the rest of the class. It's then that we really got interested in each other.

I really don't know how Warren stands those twirps in the back of the room, draining all this energy, but he does, and that's one of his great advantages as a teacher. He lets all sorts of things just simply happen.

**BR:** By this time you were living at the Tallmans'?

**GH:** Right. Third year was when I moved out of the dorms and into the Tallman house. In the spring of the second year I used to visit there quite a bit. They had a washing machine there and it used to cost fifteen cents to wash your clothes at a laundromat, so I said: "Well, can I use your washing machine and babysit the kids in return?" And I thought this was just great. And then I would stay for supper, which was always better than the dorm food.

So I sort of had this social life centring around food – suppertime – it got so I was always eating there. And the day I won the *Mademoiselle* contest, I mentioned it in the car to Warren – we were driving *out* to supper. Warren had this '48 Chev or something like that, and he steered it off the road.

**BR:** He drove it off the road?

**GH:** Yeah – he couldn't believe it – a little freshman girl going off to the big city!

**BR:** Well, during the time you lived there, that would be '59, early '60, right? Were the younger people starting to come around to Warren's place at that time?

**GH:** I'm not sure. But I do remember Frank Davey, after he had written a new poem, getting so out of his head with excitement, and driving over to Warren's and sitting down. We'd always sit down and read it …

**BR:** Out loud?

**GH:** … always out loud, even previous to our Black Mountain influence – before *The New American Poetry* anthology came out*. This is before any of us got into that.

So I haven't got a clear sense of numbers of people dropping over at that time, cuz mainly the people I was talking to were quite a bit older than myself and were the people I was meeting through the Tallmans.

**BR:** You said after Frank came over there wouldn't be much to talk about. Was that because the poem was bad?

---

\* Donald Allen, ed., *The New American Poetry, 1945–1960*, (New York: Grove Press, 1960).

**GH:** No. Warren would say it was great or something like that, but, in one sense, we had no aesthetic to talk about. And by that I don't mean any definite aesthetic, I just mean any aesthetic other than "the perception is good, the images are strong." No language sense in terms of sound and rhythm that could be of any worth in terms of criticizing or helping – even on lines.

Ellen Tallman's complaint at the time would be like: "This guy's just come in, and you've spent hours together, and you don't say anything, and nothing's happened." So I guess we just talked about our courses, problems, little jokes Frank had written about Pope and whatnot.

When we got into Hopkins that spring, that's where Lionel and I start to argue out a sense of writing. We go around shouting "Holy Moses!," getting drunk with Lionel, George, and Kenny (Tallman) in the car and yelling "Holy Moses! What an escape!"

But the real pickup isn't until we have to skip an entire year – that's when *New American Poetry* comes in.

**BR:** This is 1961?

**GH:** Yeah. And after the spring term. Fred Wah and Pauline Butling were members of Warren's next poetry class. The *New American Poetry* anthology came out and they looked at it. Pauline wrote a piece on Duncan and Fred wrote something on Williams that I was really impressed by – my first meeting with him was over an essay that he wrote.

Warren then arranged a thing where everyone got together on Sundays (this was after the term's over) and we decided to sit down with the *New American* and try to read through it. Well, he just decided to start with Charles Olson, and we had four meetings and we didn't get through the first section of the first poem – there was no sense, we got into big arguments about what "sprawl" was and what not.

I should say that the origins of *TISH* began when Lionel and Fred decided to start a magazine called *Cock* or something like that, and Warren says: "Start a magazine? You don't write enough, you don't know enough to start a magazine." And so this group got together, it was quite large – about twenty–thirty people …

**BR:** All discussing *New American* writers?

**GH:** Yeah. New American poetry. We'd all read "Projective Verse" and were not getting anywhere. It was sort of like out of "Songs of Maximus to Himself": "words, words, words all over everything."

"What does this really mean?" – we kept doing that sort of thing – "What does this really mean?" Warren comes from the New Criticism school and later, after he reads *New American*, he switches. But as a sort of in, we kept getting hung up on content in the sense of the meaning of it. And we eventually had Robert Duncan up – we all had to pay five dollars – and Robert Duncan came up ...

**BR:** How was it that you became aware that Duncan had force ...

**GH:** We'll have to flip back a year. Ellen's father has a heart attack, Ellen flies to San Francisco, and who does she run into but Duncan, who she knew back in 1945–1946 when she went to Berkeley. And he said, "You know, I'd like to come up to Vancouver to read." And they arranged a reading in the Tallmans' basement in December. This was just previous to the *New American* anthology coming out, and he was just fantastic, but "Strawberries Under the Snow" would be the only poem you could make any sense of, and his sense of understanding, it was just this guy doing this huge dance with words, and nothing like anyone had ever heard – sort of a foreign language, but you know it's English.

People like Bobby Hogg came in from Chilliwack or Abbotsford, whichever one it is. Frank brought his old high-school teacher, Alan Dawe. Bobby Hogg was still in grade twelve at that time.

So now let's flip back to the summer. We were going to get Duncan up here to tell us a little bit about Creeley and Olson. But all Dunky talks about is Robert Duncan ... he has such an expansive mind though, just so total in encouraging you to write your way through life. He just lives in the world of life and writing. You get all sorts of charges going, even if we didn't get that far on Charles, we kept hearing about this *huge* man.

And Duncan arranged a reading at the end of that, which, for some reason or other, I didn't go to – I don't think I was asked to – it was just that he asked poets – and David Dawson wrote "Fart in the Snow" for that, and Fred had three poems, and after that reading it was decided they would start *TISH*.

Warren sort of objected to it, and Duncan encouraged it. I think it was sort of a manoeuvre on Warren's part – to object – so that they had to have a certain strength, to pull together and do it – which they did.

# Jack Spicer Interview with Gladys Hindmarch

## *Interview by Terry Ludwar*

1991, PREVIOUSLY UNPUBLISHED

**Terry Ludwar:** This is Monday, July 1, Canada Day … This is Monday, July 1, 1991, at the home of Gladys Hindmarch, and I'm going to first use the questions that Kevin [Killian] has as a framework. Kevin indicates, "I want in general Gladys's impressions of Spicer in the following contexts: at the Vancouver Lectures, at the Berkeley Conference (especially since she was also staying with Warren and Ellen at the house on Tamalpais), and any other sightings she may have had of Spicer either in B.C. or here in the Bay Area." So I'll just let you talk about the time of the Vancouver Lectures which would have been June 1965.

**Gladys Hindmarch:** The first time that Jack [Spicer] came up here was just prior to that, when he and Lew Welch read at UBC.

**TL:** In February –

**GH:** – Of '65. And he just gave an absolutely smashing reading. I've heard many a good reader. I've heard Olson at his very best, and I've heard Ginsberg doing the "Sunflower Sutra" in a way I've never heard on tape or elsewhere. This is just different – Jack was absolutely marvellous. It was as good, or better than – it might have been the best reading I've ever been to in my life. It was a noon-hour reading, and normally at noon-hour readings, there are a lot of people who eat their lunches. Anyone who is in the dorms gets a free lunch, in a lunch bag. There were a lot of brown-baggers, a lot of noise and rattling of papers. And it was absolutely silent. Even when the buzzer went, I don't know, it was like seven minutes before period begins the buzzer goes, and there's like a huge shuffle. But they just stayed silent, let him finish what he was doing. And we stood up and cheered. It was just terrific. And everybody knew they were in the presence of something really magical at that reading.

**TL:** That's the indication I have. It was well attended?

**GH:** I think it even overflowed. That room was just jammed, including the stuff – they have little things where you can hang your coat; the stuff behind that was jammed. So these people – many of them would be really interested in writing, but many would just catch onto the excitement.

**TL:** Many of them had never heard poetry before, and this was their first impression.

**GH:** So it was just great. Then later, he and Robin [Blaser] and Stan [Persky] came up and gave a reading at the New Design Gallery in May. That's run by Gerry Geisler. He lived in the same apartment building that I did in Kitsilano. Anyhow, one morning we went over to get Jack. And I think Robin and Stan were staying with me at that time, I'm not sure, but I think they were staying with me, but whatever it was, the occasion was, I remember getting in the car and going over to get Jack from the Tallmans' to go for this – sort of ride along the North Shore up to Horseshoe Bay, and up to see Judy Copithorne, who then lived with a man by the name of Harry Mann in this really, really small Japanese house on this marvellous scale. Just this little, little house that is meant for one person, or even perhaps two as it was for them, but probably built for one, which to get five people into it was really something, you know? Like it was five hundred square feet, or four hundred square feet or something.

Anyhow, when we were at the Tallmans' we were having coffee. A second pot of coffee was made, and I was pouring the coffee to each of the people present. Jack was talking, and I was trying to serve or find out if people wanted more, or didn't want more, but he just sort of kept talking. So I poured his coffee, too, then put the pot back on the stove. About half a minute later there's this enormous noise, and he stood up and hit the lampshade off the light which was right above the table, absolutely furious at me, because, it turns out, what he had in his coffee cup was brandy, and he didn't want coffee, and I had poured a bunch of hot coffee on top of his brandy. Stan and Robin both sort of went to my defence after the rage was over, because he was still enraged. I actually think he was embarrassed by his own anger at a certain point in it, but he really was mad. Really mad at me, and I felt really quite – I mean, it was just like so sort of alcoholic behaviour, but it was a true mistake!

TL: In terms of various accounts I've heard was that Jack was extremely particular about his person and people coming into his "space," or touching him, or – you know, he had those particularities that caused that – so it's not uncharacteristic, it seems. So in February – the February reading, and I believe he was reading from *The Holy Grail* – was that the first time?

GH: That I heard Jack? Yeah. I may have seen Jack in San Francisco prior to this, but this is what I really recall. Because I go down to Stan in San Francisco before. But since all my feelings about Stan start at this time, too, I really think it must have been the first time, too.

TL: So you knew people in San Francisco and were aware of the writing scene in San Francisco?

GH: Just for a little way. What it was that I would go down – I went down and visited Ellen and Warren in Berkeley a couple times prior to the Berkeley Poetry Conference. I'd be down there just as a visitor.

TL: And the Berkeley Poetry Conference was in '65. That's the summer when people come back. So you were at UBC as a student in the early '60s, and you were studying – ?

GH: I was taking English, Asian studies, classical studies. I took a whole range of courses including linguistics – a great course run by Ron Baker.

TL: Ron Baker was teaching linguistics at – (*earsplitting crash heard on tape*)

GH: We're taping, honey!

TL: (*laughs*) It's all right, it's part of the surround. I'm not aware of when the Tallmans arrived in Vancouver.

GH: They came in '56. I don't know what princely sum Warren got in those days, whether it was $3,000 or $4,500 a year, but it was like a really – I mean, he was really glad to have a position as a lecturer at that point, and I had him the following year. I was really fortunate. Just by sheer coincidence I got him to be my first-year English prof. And I met Ellen – I don't think I met her in my first year, but I certainly met her prior to the second year. Right. Because we invited their family to my parents' place near Ladysmith on Vancouver Island. And they stayed overnight and we – you know – just sort of a brief little visit. The following year, I was in second-year university, staying in a different camp, or dorm, living very close to where they lived, and I would go over there. I ended up actually doing my laundry there – I'd go over there and have a meal, or look after the kids a bit, and talk, and whatnot. So I was there quite a bit in my second year at university.

TL: So by the time of June, the indications that I have are that Jack didn't want Robin and Stan around, so he sort of ordered them, or indicated to them, that they should go back to San Francisco.

GH: Didn't they all come up by bus? I mean, they all came up by bus from San Francisco, didn't they? Wasn't the idea that Jack was afraid to come up here, then he gets there and they gave this great reading at the New Design Gallery. Then he gets confident, that it was really good, yeah, and he has like two great performances in Vancouver, this really big one at UBC, and this other one? He was just a star.

TL: That seemed to be something on his mind, so I mean he was very sensitive to other "stars" around. So he sent Robin – like Robin and Stan weren't around for the Vancouver Lectures?

GH: No, they weren't.

TL: What I have is that he insisted that they go back.

GH: (*laughs*) They probably just had jobs.

TL: Maybe. That would be interesting to try to fill out. At least that's the story I have, that Jack didn't want them around. Robin has actually told me that.

GH: Well, Jack was interested in several of the young men who were around. And one of these would be Dennis Wheeler. Another would be Rick Byrne, and another would be my brother-in-law, Neap Hoover. And Jack was interested, whether the people were heterosexual or homosexual. And he was apparently very attracted particularly to Dennis and to Neap. Dennis was tall, dark-haired and blue-eyed at this time, and thin, quite thin, he was always quite a thin person, as was my brother-in-law, except he was a fair person. It would be something like having sort of like twenty-year-old, nineteen-year-old, twenty- or nineteen-year-old –

TL: Acolytes?

GH: Angels about, having them in and out…

TL: Apparently Dorothy Livesay wrote Jack a letter which indicated that – she cautioned him about, and I don't know exactly on what level she meant that about this, but that he might seduce the young people, either with his poetry or whatever. Jack was quite amused by this.

**GH:** Since he wanted to seduce them! (*laughs*) With his poetry or whatever!

**TL:** I thought that was kind of interesting.

**GH:** Yeah. You see, Dorothy was present at the Vancouver Poetry Lectures, and she asked a number of questions, and she wrote one of her best books right after them. She wrote *The Unquiet Bed* shortly after the Lectures, and she's on almost every tape asking questions – an older female voice. At one point he says something about clearing out; you know, like how do you sort of clear a space, what do you do, you clear a space, sort of as if he was telling her to leave. But there was no way – she asked, she was there. If you hear sort of a somewhat caustic comment after, a middle-aged woman's voice, it's Dorothy Livesay. She really wasn't being given her due by these young poets. Here's all these young poets and nobody's paying any attention to her and they were certainly paying all their attention to Jack. But to give her credit, she came to these, and listened and participated anyway, as a poet there, not as a person who was then going to try to persuade another way. She was just pretty good.

**TL:** The things in terms of Jack's take on poetry as I understand them in the Vancouver Lectures is the idea of dictation and the serial poem. The dictation argument: did that have quite an impact on people? His big thing was against the "Big Lie of the Personal," and his ideas, all the stuff about the Martians and the blocks – did that have a good effect on a lot of the writers who were around?

**GH:** It's hard to argue that it was a good effect, but I think it had a strong effect on a number of writers, and I think you can see that in some of George [Bowering]'s work. A very sort of freeing effect, and George is free anyway so it would be hard to argue what the full impact of Spicer's presence in George's work would be. I'd been working – I'd started on *The Peter Stories*, which was already a serial story, so this is really interesting to me. I just felt that I would just wait till that last story came, but it came a lot later! Funny, it's about thirteen years between the first story and the last one and, I don't know: part of the reason I had fewer problems with that than other people would is that, well, that's the way it's meant to be. You don't know how it's going to come and if it's not, it's not. You can try to guilt yourself into it a bit, but if it doesn't work, you just go with what works. I think you can see his effect more strongly on people like – well, you no longer see it now, but on Brian Fawcett's poetry.

**TL:** That's interesting.

**GH:** And all that. Particularly Brian, I guess: I guess Colin Stuart is more – I guess Brian is the one I think of right now. It certainly was exciting and interesting, and I guess it is hard to know how strongly someone affects your aesthetics as they're developing, because you're still grabbing from – and it surfaces in different ways, but I would say that my stories, the boat stories which became *The Watery Part of the World*, and *The Peter Stories* would be affected by Jack; and then, to some extent, *A Birth Account*, where I just let those things come, in just like moments, and there was no revision (and he's strongly against revision). That would be closer in principle, and then the selection process there as I just didn't type some of them up. So there is – yeah, I'd say he had probably a very healthy and strong effect on much of the writing here, and in Canadian poetry in general. So when people say, "It's all Black Mountain," I say, "No, you have to say Black Mountain and Jack Spicer." And Robin Blaser, too, who came to teach up here.

# Always Talking

## Interview with Gladys Hindmarch by Deanna Fong and Karis Shearer

FEBRUARY 12, 2018, PREVIOUSLY UNPUBLISHED

**Deanna Fong:** It's funny, every time I know I'm about to be recorded, I get a little flutter of nervousness because it's not the same –
**Gladys Hindmarch:** – as just talking.
**DF:** Yeah. Slightly different. (*pause*) So there are a couple things that I wanted to pick up on from the last interview, so maybe I'll refer to the interview and then ask you the question that I had originally hoped to ask you instead of the one that I did ask you. (*laughs*)
**GH:** Okay.
**DF:** So last time we were talking about your relationship with Ellen, and I asked you what your impressions were of her. You said she was at Mills College, a specialty women's college in the Bay area, and so she definitely hung out with [Robin] Blaser and [Robert] Duncan and really liked them. Then you said she had stories to tell about all these characters. Do any of those specific stories come to mind? Did you have impressions of all the people that she knew before you met them?
**GH:** I think I did, but I don't remember what they are. But I'm pretty sure that I had an impression of Duncan, Jack [Spicer], Robin, and Kenneth and Marthe [Whitcomb] Rexroth. Marthe and Ellen were good friends. Kenneth, I had sort of some negative impressions. And positive, but more negative because of Ellen and Marthe, the way they were.
**DF:** Did you have a sense of these people, these poets, as personas? Had you read their work before you heard about them, or did you encounter them through their work first?
**GH:** I think I encountered them through Ellen, through what she was saying about them, and then I would get to meet one. Robert

Duncan lived at Stinson Beach with his pal, his lover, Jess, for a number of years. So they'd be describing who these two were as we'd be driving up to wherever it was that they lived. They had stained glass all over the place, and glass that you find on the beach. Really lovely small place that they were at. But they were not big in my imagination until I met them. Once you met Robert Duncan you'll never forget that you've met Robert Duncan because he takes a lot of space. (*laughs*) He had a big voice. He was not a big man, he was not an imposing man, but he dressed with a big cape and whatnot. I think that you certainly knew that you were in the presence of Robert Duncan. I think of [Robert] Creeley with his, "I could creep into a room, you might not notice." But Duncan could not go across the street and pick up a newspaper without you noticing him. (*laughs*) He liked to be noticed!

**DF:** So, you first met him in '59 when he came out after the study group, right?

**GH:** No, there were two separate occasions. One, he came up to the basement where the Tallmans lived. Bobby [Hogg] was still at high school when that happened. Bobby and his teacher Allen came along with Frank Davey, in from Abbotsford. So there was that time, and then it was a whole year and a half later when we noticed that we're in a lot of trouble meeting every second Sunday and not getting anywhere.* Not even becoming entrenched in any position, any one of us. We just couldn't do it. It was like circles. So that became an obviously good choice: "Oh, why don't we ask Duncan to come up and teach us?" (*laughs*) We didn't realize that he was gonna be teaching us ...

**DF:** Something else. (*laughs*)

**GH:** Cosmology and whatever he was into. But that was the way he was. He would just turn them on, basically. He'd take any small or large group and talk.

**Karis Shearer:** How much was Ellen involved in those conversations?

**GH:** She was there, but I don't recall her interjecting at any point in any of the printed interviews. But she was definitely present, and the beer, or wine, or tea, or whatever, kept coming. She was the hostess.

---

\* Referring to the group that met bi-weekly in the early 1960s to discuss *The New American Poetry* and poetics at the Tallmans' home, focusing on Charles Olson's essay "Projective Verse." See interview with Brad Robinson, pp. 297–304.

**DF:** But it seems she had a really intimate knowledge of his work, too. She had been reading Duncan for a long time.

**GH:** She did, yes, and she was reading it as it was coming out. We got to read some of Creeley when he was here, some of his recent work. So, yes. She was highly involved with him. They were sort of god figures to her.

**DF:** Did you get much opportunity to talk to Duncan one-on-one?

**GH:** No, no. I mean, there must be some times when it was one-on-one, but I can't really recall.

**DF:** So what was the structure of the conversations? Was it just that he was talking and everyone was listening? Or did people talk in smaller groups?

**GH:** Well, it's like if you were in a car and you're going somewhere and Duncan's there, he's talking. (*laughs*) I didn't question about his writing or anything like that. Nor did he ask anything about me. But it just seemed very natural.

**DF:** Okay. So, in that interview with Terry Ludwar about Spicer you talk about Spicer's influence on your own writing. Do you think that meeting Duncan and encountering his poetics also had an impact on your writing?

**GH:** In a sense. Duncan rolls with something and it's sort of that speed. You just sort of get going, and you roll and take it to the next thing, and the next thing. So it's part of the conversation that Angela Bowering, Luoma [her maiden name], had from her childhood – and part of me from my childhood – that you connect out, and connect out. It was something familiar, in a way, but it was more eloquent, more focused on poetics than on a number of other subjects. So, yeah, I think I sort of liked Duncan's looseness in that regard. And certainly the fact that he talked so much about H.D. That's where I hooked into H.D. was through Duncan. It was his leadership. I'm sure this happens with a number of writers, when they're speaking about someone, and someone gets the name and it tweaks something in them, and then they start to really sort of go with it and find it, you know?

**DF:** Yeah. I think of that term "activation," like the whole field being activated, as Warren says in "Wonder Merchants." That there's something in his visit that really activated something in the scene, and activated something in H.D., and activated something in Olson. Not that they're coming out of nowhere, but something is lit up or something like that.

**GH:** Well, Duncan helped us an enormous amount. It just wasn't the help that we thought. The "Projective Verse" part became more minimal and *TISH* was formed, and with all that resistance that Warren put up to it, that resistance helped. People were strongly objecting. But Duncan, he likes to stir things up. So does Stan [Persky]. And Jack. (*laughs*) Agitation. Resistance might clarify things on the other side.

**KS:** When you say resistance on Warren's part, do you mean when he wanted you to wait to start the magazine?

**GH:** Well, yes. He thought it would be smarter to wait until people were slightly more accomplished or established. (*laughs*) But I said you have to write something. You've got your four pages there, or the two pages they each had, and then he had to do something with it. But everybody could object to something, as in George Bowering's "Meat Grinder" poems. (*laughs*) George is always living this one thing down. But it was a very exciting time to be a part of.

**KS:** One of the questions I think we were thinking about is the way that you're often referred to by the other members of TISH as being at the centre of the group.

**GH:** I didn't know that.

**KS:** Yes, as being the core of the group, in a lot of ways. I wonder, how do you think they perceived you as a writer at that point, as you were writing in a slightly different form.

**GH:** I guess the answer is I don't know how they were perceiving me. It seems a few times I'm sort of fighting to just get a word in. You know, "I'm here, too." Perhaps I should've had two pages of *TISH*, but of course, I wasn't writing poetry. So that was where the line seemed to be drawn. Are these things written in lines or are they written in sentences? I like writing sentences. (*laughs*) I didn't think to just sort of twist them a little bit. I like the compression of poetry, and I'm more expansive in sentences than I probably could ever be as a poet. Plus, the fact every time I wrote a poem for the creative writing class, Frank wrote a parody of it and got better marks than I did. (*laughs*) So it was not exactly a happy experience putting your toe out there.

**DF:** Seriously. But it seems to me that you are, in a similar way, or maybe even in a completely different but equally profound way, thinking about poetics.

**KS:** For example, on one of the tapes, you talk a lot about arguing in the sense of providing feedback, and debating things like word choices and line breaks. How would you describe your contribution to the group in that sense?

**GH:** I think that would have been more the Writers' Workshop. If I saw where a work could be improved, I would speak up and say, "Well, what about this word?" or, "What if you just shift it to this side? That's how you're reading it, so why don't you put it there?" So, I probably helped some with notation, but I can't recall particular instance or particular poem. But I think I probably have a pretty good ear, and if rhythm is getting monotonous... You've already discovered that, for me, I don't like hearing these L=A=N=G=U=A=G=E poets who are not focusing on the sound at all. They think language is a type of thing that they're moving. Something hard, or harder objects in a way, instead of a flow and a connectedness. I guess I'm opposed to that.

**DF:** I'd like to go back a bit to the idea that because you're writing prose, that maybe that's a reason that your work's not getting included, at least in *TISH*. But then, you are thinking about poetics and about sound. You're thinking about all the things that go into poetry, so the fact that it's not lineated like a poem seems to me maybe not a good enough reason. (*laughs*) You're thinking about poetics, even if you're not writing poetry.

**GH:** I am, but I don't say I'm a poet, I say I'm a prose writer. And certainly I'm drawn to poetry, because why else would I put up with those guys? (*laughs*) I mean, there's a lovely description somewhere of when Ferlinghetti visits, and I go out to the kitchen, and there's George and Frank, and George is punching his hand into his hand like a baseball glove. And I'm pissed off that they – Okay, they didn't like Snoodgrease* (*laughs*) but what, are you going to sit there and punch all evening or whatever?

**DF:** Why was he doing that?

**GH:** Well, they're like boys, you know. They're being like really young kids, in my opinion. At times I would be frustrated by them.

**DF:** But this is after Ferlinghetti and ... Snoodgrease? Snodgrass? (*laughs*)

**GH:** Was Snodgrass reading with Ferlinghetti? I can't imagine the combination, but he may have been. Hardly anybody wanted to hang around him and learn some things.

---

\*     Play on W.D. Snodgrass, who had recently read in Vancouver.

KS: Recently, there's been a lot of reflection on TISH, and people have pointed out that it was, to a certain extent, a boys' club.*

GH: Well, I mean, Daphne's there. She was there the whole time, and her things would be selected a little bit. We were younger, but we weren't – I wasn't young. I might be three or four years younger than George, but with Frank, I'm actually two or three months older than he is, so we're the same age. But they got to select Daphne. Daphne didn't get to select Daphne. To them, that's the difference.

KS: What would you like critics, let's say of our generation, to recognize about TISH that maybe hasn't been recognized?

GH: That's a good question. I mean, TISH people got a lot of recognition in one way or the other, so I can't really think of what I would like. I often feel that many younger people just wish they had lived in the '60s. (*laughs*) Some of these, they say, "Gee, it sounds all so exciting," but I thought, "Well, isn't your life as exciting as that, in a different way?" I don't know.

DF: When I interviewed Maxine [Gadd], Trudy [Rubenfeld], and Rhoda [Rosenfeld], they all agree that the '60s was the last time that there was this real humanist desire for freedom, for the freedom of self, and that they haven't felt that since.

GH: Yes, there was a big freedom in the '60s and early '70s. There was also a smaller community. A number of us were at the Western Front last week because of Al Neil's death and, again and again, people were harkening back to the fact that the dancers, the singers, the visual artists – photographers, and painters, and sculptors – and poets, and musicians could all be part of the same thing, in a way. I mean that there's not this specialty – there's a lot of cross-fertilization occurring. I imagine that for young people now, there's a fair amount of cross-fertilization with both the internet and a bunch of other ways of connecting, but it may not be as a group or community as much. So when my contemporaries are harkening back, in part that's through a glazed remembrance, but part of it purely was a very exciting time. I mean, we didn't lock our doors, people could just barge

---

\* See Pauline Butling, "'Hall of Fame Blocks Women' Re/Righting Literary History: Women and B.C. Little Magazines," *Open Letter* 7, no. 8 (Summer 1990): 60–76; Pauline Butling and Susan Rudy, *Writing in Our Time: Canada's Radical Poetries in English (1957–2003)* (Waterloo, ON: Wilfrid Laurier University Press, 2005).

in – until police had barged in a number of times and once they did that, we started locking our doors. The police actually felt free to just come in to my place to spy on my neighbour and just to tell us to be quiet, or get out of there, get out of your own place, because they want to sit in my kitchen to look at my neighbour, Gerry Geisler, across the way in his kitchen. It was acceptable for the authorities to do that.

**KS:** Was some of that surveillance directed toward the gay community as well? Or was it strictly to do with drugs?

**GH:** It had more to do with pot and the effects it may have on young people, and that this was gonna cause huge problems out at UBC because this is where people were being trained to be lawyers, and doctors, and nurses, and teachers. They figured this was really going to affect the youth, so they tried to get a hold of those people and throw the ones they could catch with something into jail. One student, she went to jail for six months for, like, one joint, or something like that. You'd have to check out the records, but it really was an "us and them" type thing. And then of course, in Madison, Wisconsin, we had the Vietnam War, so then there's also another, bigger scale of "us and them" with the military. But that's very different. It wasn't individual narcs following individual paths, it was something that different politicians were in favour of or totally against.

**DF:** Right. Madison, Wisconsin. Let's talk about that. So you were talking about meeting Daphne [Marlatt], and in our last interview we talked a little bit about the connection that you had when you were both living in Wisconsin – you said about an hour's drive away from one another.

**GH:** I'm not sure. She said around twenty-five minutes. It felt like quite a substantial drive. Further away than Ladysmith from Nanaimo.

**DF:** I wanted to pick up a little bit on your relationship with Daphne, to ask you how you would characterize your relationship with her, both personally and your relationship with her writing.

**GH:** Well, I like her personally, but it's all through writing that I meet her, really. She comes to the Writers' Workshop and Frank is besmitten right away. (*laughs*) And then she and I, and Sonny Choi, we're all in the same class with Earle Birney, so I got to know her fairly well. But then in Wisconsin, we got to rely on each other more.

**DF:** Would you say you have a pretty close relationship with her writing? Did you talk about your writing practice?

GH: Not very much. If either of us saw something we really liked, something strong, we would say "good going," or something. I think there's some really parallel things, but we're on sort of separate paths.

KS: Can I follow on that and ask who you feel have been the main people who you've workshopped or discussed poetics with? People you feel are the main sounding boards for your work?

GH: I don't think I have any. I mean, the process of assembling this book is just great for me to start looking at these things and realizing there's content there, because it's basically been between me and me, the typewriter and the computer. Others just sort of slipped away. At one point, after retiring, Bill Schermbrucker, Will Goode, and I met for something we called "stretchers," named for stretching a tale. But it quickly expanded to more and more people, and it got to be quite large. For a story, you got about ten minutes or something. That was nice, having an audience and being able to note things, and to have people be able to criticize openly how they could make something better. That was a fairly positive experience. I didn't have that with my contemporaries very much. But I don't imagine George was doing that with Fred [Wah] or Frank, like pointing out things and whatnot. It's sort of more something you did on your own and then we shared it at the Writers' Workshop. We had this teacher who would throw out a question and we'd all get mad at him and all of the sudden we're all talking. (*laughs*) It was a way of just really moving it around fast. So there was feedback there because of the way that Tony Friesen operated, and the way we variously fought or declared whatever.* We were discovering things.

DF: What about Stan [Persky]? Did you send drafts of your writing to him?

GH: I wrote all those letters to Stan when I was in Wisconsin, but I didn't say, "What do you think of this?" or anything like that.

DF: But he read it, though? He read the stuff you were working on?

GH: I don't know if I sent a story to him or not. I think I might've, but I don't recall. I'd have to read his correspondence to see if he was actually commenting. But if you went to Stan and said,

---

* Tony Friesen was a creative writing professor at UBC in the 1960s who led the Writers' Workshop.

"Read this and tell me what you think," he would tell you. I'd do the same thing, too.

**DF:** Yeah.

**GH:** No, I suppose I don't have that many interlocutors. It didn't seem much of an issue when I think of it. Really, I don't think I'm different in that when I imagine George telling Frank something about his writing, or Frank telling George something. They would do the bravado thing over something else, but…

**DF:** However, there are lots of drafts of people's work in your archive, things that people sent you. In our last interview, you were telling me about giving Roy Kiyooka feedback on *Kyoto Airs*\* and saying that there was like this jokeyness that was getting in the way.

**GH:** But, see, Roy came to me through the Vancouver Poetry Conference, basically, and by sitting there through those things, so we talked. At that point, he was just starting to write, so he came and asked me for feedback. So that's different than seeing something and saying, "Oh, by the way, such and such." So I would say there's relatively little of that. Maybe people do it more often in other groups or at other times, but we like being together, there's no doubt about that.

**DF:** Why do you like being together?

**GH:** We just had a lot of fun and felt just full of life. George and Lionel [Kearns] and I took many drives, often with Kenny Tallman present, cuz he was not yet in school. We just had a lot of fun together. The trips might be short, but they might be two hours. We liked to do that.

(*pause*)

**DF:** Okay. So, switching gears, I can't believe you told me you went and visited Olson for a couple of weeks or something.

**GH:** Well, neither can I. Something that I read recently said a week. It felt like it was three weeks. I mean, he literally told me most of his life story with the exception of Frances Boldereff, about whom he did not mention a word in that entire time.† He would just get up and start talking, and talking, and talking, and talking,

---

\*  Roy Kiyooka, *Kyoto Airs,* (Vancouver: Periwinkle Press, 1964).

†  See Charles Olson and Frances Boldereff, *Charles Olson and Frances Boldereff: A Modern Correspondence,* eds. Ralph Maud and Sharon Thesen (Hanover and London: Wesleyan University Press, 1999).

and eventually if we were going to get some food to have for supper, we had better get to the store, which closed maybe at six o'clock or something. We'd better get down there by 5:30 p.m. and pick up the mail at the same time. I really enjoyed that time, but it was a hard time, too, because he was going through a lot, and had a lot of regrets and was expressing them. But then we'd get on to something else. He was negative about a number of people that I know and I just took it in and didn't fight it at all.

**DF:** Sidestepping, kind of?

**GH:** Yeah, you know. He would say of Creeley, "Domesticity," sort of barking, "with curtains! Do you think I would want curtains?" That sort of remark. I like Creeley. I like his wife, Bobbi [Louise Hawkins], too. But he would tell me stories and anything I wanted to ask, I could. And of course, occasionally, he would fish and say something like "the Feminine Mistake" – he could not say *Feminine Mystique*. He had to keep fumbling on that, but he was probably just trying to get a rise out of me. He hadn't read the book or anything like that. Then we had an argument about Hawthorne or D.H. Lawrence, and he'd stop in the middle of a bridge. I'd say (*laughing*), "Can't we just walk on it?" "No, no! We have to settle this right now!" It was sort of like – was I twenty, twenty-two? What year was that? '63, '64. Yeah, '64. Yeah, so he's sixty-four. So there I am, twenty-four years old, this man is three years older than my father, and everybody just loves him. The earth that he walks on, you could kiss, or something like that. Which is not a good, healthy thing. I mean, he could read well, but I never got to hear him read well. I was at Berkeley [Conference, 1965], I was in Vancouver [Conference, 1963], and he just was not – evidently, we read the Tom Clark book, and this is what he did at almost every reading, stall and stall, and this and that.*

**DF:** You said in the interview it was probably very uncomfortable at that Berkeley reading for most of the people who were there.

**GH:** It was horrible. Ralph Maud thought it was one of the greatest things, and when I read it, I thought, "Hey, it's much more interesting than you ever thought at the time."† We were scared.

---

\*  See Tom Clark, *Charles Olson: The Allegory of a Poet's Life* (New York: Norton, 1991).

†  See Charles Olson, *The Berkeley Reading*, ed. Ralph Maud, trans. Zoe Brown (Berkeley, CA: Coyote, 1966).

He had things on almost everybody in that room, so he could hurt someone like Creeley if he wanted to, or Duncan. He probably had hurt Duncan at times. Nobody could feel easy in that situation. And the fire marshall was telling you, "You have to get out!" and this and that, and Charles is just sort of going on – he'd had drugs, I think. I mean, not just alcohol but drugs combined. No, nobody was easy that I know of in that entire room. There may have been somebody who knew nothing about anything of that sort and came in and felt easy. (*laughs*)

**KS:** Blissful ignorance. (*laughs*)

**GH:** They might've actually have their ears open and not have any fear. But there were several people in there, and many people left, too. I mean, a four-hour event. When did it start, at eight, or seven? It's approaching midnight, and we're being told we've got to get out, and he's just not gonna do it. We just wanted him to read. We'd say, "Read a poem! Read a poem!" He'd say, "Yes, I will." But when I read it, I thought, "Amazing!" All these things were being said, and I wasn't listening to this the whole time.

**DF:** Interesting. So what was the occasion for you going down to visit him?

**GH:** He called. I think he wanted Ellen. He was calling the Tallmans, I was out on the boat, and when I got back in, they said, "Charles would really like you to call him." When he was at the Vancouver Conference, Ellen took total care of him, and I think he really wanted Ellen to go to Buffalo, New York – well, not Buffalo, but around there, get to where he was.* But he did ask for me, and somebody had come out prior to me whom he had met at the conference, and it hadn't worked out very smoothly or something. I'm not sure what happened.

**DF:** You said it was it because he was in a bad way, that he wanted something?

**GH:** Well, his wife had died about two months prior, and he didn't know whether there was any physical ailment.† He didn't think so, he saw it as suicide. So it was hard for him to take. Plus the fact that he has a boy in grade one, and he's not even paying any attention to him. He probably never paid any much attention

---

\* Olson was actually living in a small village called Wyoming, NY.

† Augusta Elizabeth (Betty) Kaiser (November 3, 1925–March 28, 1964), Olson's second wife.

to that boy. Charles Peter. They were isolated out there. The Hooker Chemical people had let him stay rent-free in this estate. Yeah, he was stuck, really stuck, and he needed a boot to either move or do something.

**DF:** And you were the boot? (*laughs*)

**GH:** Yes, I was. Well, eventually. I thought it was a longer time, but somewhere I read it was one week, ten days, or whatever. In order to go there, I didn't have much money, just the money from that one trip, and so I went to the Union Hall to see if I could work in the lakes, if a shipping boat would be good for the lakes, from the American side, and they said, "Well, probably, you're going to have to go across the border to Canada to get on. But it may be that we'll be able to write you a letter, a note, so you could show them that." If you got on the shipping boat, they can see it; they'd write a note that I could give to their union rep. This is if I wanted to ship out of Buffalo and be on the lakes for the summer.

**DF:** And so you did that?

**GH:** No, I didn't. But I prepared. I thought, "My money's gonna run out shortly." I didn't have any money, being at school all year, and then this is just sort of one trip.

**KS:** Did you drive there?

**GH:** No, I took the train. I got this call when the train arrived, paging me. It was Charles saying, "Fly to Rochester, New York." I said, "What?" He said, "Just get a flight." Well, I had enough money to get to Rochester, but that would further reduce what little funds I had, in case I wanted to get out of New York. (*laughs*)

**DF:** And so, other than listening to him talk endlessly about things, what else did you do while you were there? Do you have any specific memories?

**GH:** Well, one time we went out and got some ice cream, stopped at a soda bar, American soda bar, in some little nearby village. He didn't get up until noon, or one, or maybe eleven, but I was always up a lot earlier. He stayed up all night, too. One time we went out into this cornfield, and just lay and watched all the stars, talking and whatnot. It was kind of fun. But the only social thing we did was when Ed Dorn and Amiri Baraka came, who was LeRoi Jones at that point. They came and they were all excited, and I was all excited about them coming, too.

**DF:** So why do you think that so many people are drawn to Olson as this almost kind of cult following? What do you think it is about either him or his work that people find so magnetic?

**GH:** Well, I guess he's our Pound, the Pound of the other generation, where there was one person who just felt more strongly at the centre for a number of the others. I would choose Williams over Pound any day, but it's Pound who was the real sort of main force of attention there. Olson's entirely different from Pound, but he visited Pound many times when he was in St. Elizabeths. This is the type of thing we talk about, and then there'll be another revelation. Oh, God, it would be great to have a tape of that!

**KS:** No kidding!

**GH:** It just kept coming and coming. Olson's willing to be more prescriptive than some of the other writers. You know, "Do this, don't do that," that sort of thing. He was in drama and he was a great dancer, and he was so tall. So there was a way in which people were drawn to him, and then other people are drawn to those people who are drawn to him. I mean, Duncan was on the edge of Black Mountain, too. But would you say Duncan's a Black Mountain–ite? I would not. So, yes, he taught there a little bit, but Charles was sort of the main force. He's magnetic, too. He does have a type of larger appeal. I don't know why there are so many, but there are, and then they become obsessed with every single word... (*laughs*) He was magnetic, yeah, it's just a very strong personality.

**DF:** My sense is that it had a lot to do with him as a person, as a personality, as a sort of larger-than-life persona.

**GH:** There's definitely a larger-than-life figure, and in a sense, larger than Allen Ginsberg, but Allen Ginsberg's the more worldly figure. Like, certainly the newspapers would not know anything of Charles Olson, but Allen Ginsberg coming to town was sort of a different thing.

**KS:** Really like the people's poet versus the poet's poet.

**GH:** Yeah.

**DF:** So the first time you met Charles was at the '63 conference? And you said that Ellen was hosting both Charles and Allen and did so very gracefully, given the circumstances? (*laughs*)

**GH:** Yeah.

**DF:** We've talked about this off the record, but some of the challenges of that event seemed to be just barely finding enough space for everybody to stay.

**GH:** Well, Ellen and Warren had to get out of their beds so Charles could have the bed. He was a big man.

**KS:** 6'8"?

**GH:** Yeah. Well, I don't know. I've heard 6'8", 6'10". And so that takes care of that room. So Ellen and Warren have to sleep somewhere, so that probably displaces Karen, and Karen couldn't be sleeping with her brother Kenny. There was also Philip Whalen who came up and stayed there, so I don't know how all the arrangements worked, but…

**KS:** And you were living there at the time, too?

**GH:** No. I had left, in the beginning of the same year. '63? Yeah, probably. I found a place in Kitsilano in January '63, and then we didn't know the Poetry Conference was about to happen until February. Yes, that makes sense.

**DF:** Is that the place with Leni?*

**GH:** By myself, and then Leni used it when I was out on the boats. Then we got a place where the landlady booted us out after Allen Ginsberg was out there on the front lawn, chanting. (*laughs*) This was around the '63 conference. We went to something that evening and afterward, for whatever reason, Creeley says, "Could we come to your apartment?" He had never been there. And so all these men with beards came up the steps, and the landlady had a door that faced the outer door. She always managed to leave it open, so she could see all of this, but she didn't like us to know that she was watching us. We were making noise, but it was before eleven o'clock, and at that point you're not supposed to have anybody in your place but the person who's renting it. But she calls at, say, ten o'clock, or quarter to ten, and asks if everybody could leave. But she gets my mom on the phone – Mom had come to this reading, and or whatever this event was – and my mom answers the phone and says, "Oh yes, she's here. But you don't understand, these are very important poets. (*laughs*) No, I will not tell her to tell them to leave." But they all overheard this, and so Allen goes and says, "Oh, I'll make her go…" and so goes down the stairs and sits on their lawn and starts Om-ing. (*laughs*)

**DF:** Did you talk to her afterward?

**GH:** Oh, I mean, she said we had to move out at the end of the month. We said, "Fine. We've had enough." We had a beautiful

---

\* Leni Hoover, Hindmarch's sister.

view from Point Atkinson all the way to Simon Fraser. It was gorgeous. I'd go out there on the roof, which probably you're not supposed to do. I'd go through the little sunroom and sit on the roof with my tea and look out. I really just loved that.

KS: That was the end of that?

GH: Yes.

DF: That's interesting, though, that your mom came up for the reading.

GH: My mom had to finish summer school. She finally decided to get a degree. They tried to upgrade teachers those years and there's something about that that I've seen recently. My poor mom. She went to grade thirteen, senior matric, because it's cheaper than going to university. Then she goes to UVic, to what they call "Normal School." From Normal School, you can get a certificate to teach, but you must take summer school courses every year for a number of years to eventually get an education degree. But the very year that she teaches, they then decide that all teachers needed upgrading. Well, she just finished all those courses on how to teach, she just needed more real courses, not sort of a how-to that the teachers had just gone through with then. But no, the government in its wisdom doesn't say, "Well, anybody who's been to Normal School in the last two years doesn't have to do this." They're teaching identical things to what she just learned the previous year, but she had to take the courses anyhow. So eventually she took English 200 in Nanaimo by going to night school as she was teaching this and that. Eventually she reached the point where she had to get some university – she needed one more course to get her education degree. That was the year that she turned fifty. So she was in Vancouver at Acadia Camp, and was a don so she didn't have to pay any board so she could do this. And of course, her daughters were going out with these guys from Texas, and from Harvard, and flitting around and swirling in all this sort of energy. (*laughs*) So she went to whatever reading she could.

DF: Like the poetry course, the '63 one.

GH: Yeah, sure, yeah. They were open to the public. You had to pay for them, but she would go. Leni would have been at the readings too, cuz she went to all of them. So I'm not sure how that all happened, but she definitely handled it on the phone. (*laughs*)

DF: No kidding. So what did she think of all that, of the readings? Was she keen on them?

**GH:** Yeah, yeah, yeah. Mom always liked whatever is "in." If she could see what's in and coming up, she could just grab it and snap it up. She was relatively stylish in her choice of dress. Our Grandma Grey was a really good seamstress, so she could take things and make my mom – Well, I showed you that picture. (*shuffling*) Here, I'll get it out. (*shuffling*) Oh, you don't see much. This is her at about eighteen, but you can just see from the top of that dress, you can imagine it was probably quite fitted. I don't mean fitted tight, tight, but, yeah.

**KS:** Wow.

**GH:** Yeah.

**DF:** She's beautiful. So she wasn't fazed by all these radical poets?

**GH:** Oh, no, she loved it! She thought, "Oh, that's great, Allen Ginsberg! Oh, what a nice man!"

**KS:** That's awesome.

**DF:** Oh, that's really great.

**GH:** She was not fazed by much.

**DF:** Meanwhile, the landlady seemed quite fazed.

**GH:** Oh, she was very British.

**KS:** So we talked a little bit last night about Ellen's role in the '63 Poetry Conference, and I wonder if you could maybe take us back through Ellen's work during the conference.

**GH:** Well, prior to the conference, she would be making connections. Warren made connections, too, but between Duncan and Allen, she was there. To open your household in that way, and have as many parties, and to sort of choose among the people who perhaps had a big enough place ... They didn't want to exclude people, but there were a lot of people coming to the readings that weren't part of the lectures or seminars and she wanted to make sure the people who came to the seminars were included. So she was very strong and gracious in that way. But she had her hands full because she was really looking after Charles and making sure that he got to things. There were three weeks of seminars with three different groups, and she had to make sure that he got there on time rather than an hour late, and she managed. She had two young kids running around, too, but she did it. She had a great time. There was a fair amount of booze involved, and you're getting that and getting the food in and out. I made a big shrimp chowder, and of course they had no space in the refrigerator to put this, and it was a warm day, and

I said, "Oh, my God, how is this going to work?" Well, I won't be able to put the shrimp in there until we're steaming it. It's already pre-cooked in wine anyway. Those have got to go in the fridge, but the pots will just have to sit there all day, like for four or six hours, and hope that it's not eighty, ninety degrees out because there's no room to do anything. But I made two large containers. There's gonna be forty or fifty people, you can't just give everybody a tablespoon. (*all laugh*)

**KS:** Industrial-sized soup pots.

**DF:** You cooked it at Ellen and Warren's place? Or you cooked it at home and brought it?

**GH:** I must have got the pots from her. I mean, I couldn't borrow from the boat or anything like that. I don't know who else would've given them to me. Even just as simple as that, if you're gonna make something for that amount of people, you've got to have a space to make it. But then you have to have a space to store it while whatever is going on. There were a number of hours, and I was worried. And I said, "Well, the shrimp will not go in. It'll have to be put in and stirred. It has to be throughout the thing, we can't have it so that some people get a whole bunch and others get none." But even just that, that was another logistic thing that would be minor compared to people arriving by plane and by train and …

**DF:** Picking people up and dropping people off.

**GH:** Picking up, and assuming that there's a drugstore around the corner, and all those things, yeah.

**KS:** It seems to me that this kind of work is so infrequently talked about. I mean, Pauline Butling talks about it in *Writing in Our Time*, which is one of the first times I've seen someone be attentive to that kind of labour that mostly women were doing. When you hear people talk about the conference they're obviously interested in the poetics – that's a huge part of it – but they also always want to talk about the parties.

**GH:** Oh, they were great parties.

**KS:** Yeah, it's kind of social fuel at that event. It's what made it not just a conference.

**DF:** And not just an academic course.

**KS:** Yes. Something that was so much more memorable and dynamic. The work that Ellen did, that work that so many women did –

**DF:** Pauline, too.

**KS:** Yes, Pauline. That aspect of the event seems just as important as the writers' discussion.

**GH:** Oh, I think so, I think so. But people don't tend to think that in academia. It's too bad that they miss the opportunity to really get into some things in that way. (*pause*) No, there were a lot of people who were doing things like that, yeah.

**DF:** Is there anybody else, notably, that you can think of who was important to that side of the social aspect?

**GH:** Well, Sam Perry, who had been my lover for a couple years prior to this, his parents have a lovely place out near Horseshoe Bay, so one of the things Ellen asked was, "Do you think Sam could have something at his place?" I said I was pretty sure that he could, but I'd ask. So he arranged something. It wasn't everybody, but there were quite a few of the people. We went swimming and had a salmon barbeque, and hamburgers, and whatnot. That was a lovely time. So that would be one of the social events that probably just people who were involved in the conference attended. Jamie and Carol Reid were not yet a couple. They were just becoming a couple at that point. But they had a place that Sam Perry had rented and it became Jamie's place, right at the foot of Georgia Street. There's a street that goes into Stanley Park, and say Graham Street is here, there's a place called Melville Street, just on the edge above the railway track. There was an old house there, and that was filmed by Bobbie Louise Hawkins, I think. So there's a film with us all outside talking. A number of people had parties at their places, but the bulk of them were at the Tallmans'. But it wasn't something that she had to do every single night of the week.

**DF:** For three weeks. (*laughs*)

**GH:** But she had to feed Charles his cinnamon toast every single day. (*laughs*) His prodigious appetite. And get him there by 1 p.m.

**DF:** So just to go back for a little bit, can you tell us a little bit about what the parties were like? The '63 parties?

**GH:** They really were great parties. A lot of this is happening prior to the Beatles, and they even became greater because there was dancing. We always had records or whatever we were using. Must've been all records. The music would go on and we'd start dancing, and dancing, and dancing, and talking and dancing, and drinking beer and dancing. A lot of fun, a lot of energy, and full. Big parties. It's nice to have a small party where everybody gets to talk with each other, but it's also great to have a really big party. It's sort of clearing the spirit and when you have a really big party, especially if everybody's really enjoying themselves.

**DF:** Did you say "clearing the spirit"?

**GH:** Yeah.

**DF:** (*laughs*) I like that.

**GH:** I like to clean up the house, have a party, and then there's the next day of re-putting, repositioning the house again. But saying, "Hey, yeah, I remember what so-and-so over there was doing. He was sort of smiling and laughing and whatever." No matter what the size of the party is. So I liked those social events, and I thought, "Well, maybe people don't have parties anymore. Why am I not invited to parties? Well, maybe there aren't any parties anymore!" (*laughter*) It could easily be that that's the case. No, they were a special time, a lot of fun, and sometimes wild. I had one in our apartment once. This would happen almost every Friday night, somebody would buy a gallon of Calona Red. I can't think of the name, but everybody else would remember the brand. It's just like a gallon of red from the cheapest wine that Calona could make. (*all laugh*) So this would happen every Friday for quite a while. One time in the summer, every single room in my apartment was packed. There were drums in one room, a conversation in the other, and a record player that somebody had brought – cuz I didn't have one – in another, where there was dancing. Finally I said, "Jesus, awfully noisy in here," and I went for a walk. I was three blocks away, I said, "What is that noise? (*laughing*) Oh, that noise is coming from my place." Well, I mean, that's what sort of took over. One of my students two or three years later said, "Oh, I've got a confession to make." I said, "Oh, a confession." And she said, "I was at your place once." (*laughs*) "We were just walking up the street and thought, 'That looks like a lot of fun,' and we joined it, and it was a lot of fun." (*all laugh*)

**KS:** So I was reflecting recently on how very structured readings today can be, especially in universities. Thinking back to the sixties and to Warren's way of organizing things, it feels a bit more organic, improvisational.

**GH:** Yes.

**KS:** I can remember him on one of the tapes. He's in a classroom and he's just addressing the class, saying, "Take this pamphlet and give it to anyone that you think is true to poetry, or is a true fan, and tonight at 7 p.m., this poet" – I can't remember who. It's some American poet – "is gonna be here ..."

GH: Welch? Could be.

KS: I can't remember. Someone from San Francisco. But Warren says, "This poet's going to be here, and I don't know what's going to happen, and he doesn't know what's going to happen, but it's going to be great." And so, I was interested in that sort of spontaneous, unplanned *happening* kind of aspect. It's planned, but it's not hyper-structured. Do you think there was some element of that in the sixties around spontaneous readings, or spontaneity in general?

GH: In the readings. But when you knew somebody was coming, even just two days in advance, you made a choice. You were going to go there or not. Certainly, there could be just somebody reading out on the lawn, and then all of a sudden there's a reading happening, too. But I won't blame the Canada Council for that. I do blame them for the insistence of having two or three readings in an area. It's not like the difference of saying, okay, one in Edmonton and one in Calgary – that makes sense. But to say you have to have two in Edmonton to have even one reading approved, that can be a mistake, in terms of those people from the various institutions came to mix with their peer group and meet some others. I do think that's not being well handled.

DF: What else aligns with Merce Cunningham, and John Cage, and lots of the people in the UBC Festival of the Arts, who are thinking about the happening in this sort of multimedia arts way? This seems to maybe carry over, at least nominally, into how poetry readings are being imagined at the time, too. That they're unstructured and spontaneous.

GH: Well, they're not all spontaneous, because if you're bringing in somebody, then that's something you know ahead of time, as compared to a group wanting to present something.

DF: Yeah. But the idea that the content can be really unstructured in the same way that a John Cage piece can be unstructured ...

GH: That's right, yeah.

KS: Like in the time-length of the reading. It seems to me that readings were much longer.

GH: There were quite a few long readings.

DF: Okay. So I did want to ask you a little bit more about the commune. I know we talked about it last night, but now that we're on the record, I'd like to ask you how it came to be that you all decided on this communal mode of living in the York Street commune.

**GH:** Okay. So Cliff [Andstein] and I needed a place. Stan [Persky] and Brian [DeBeck] had a place very close to Cliff's and to my own place. This is just after returning from Madison, Wisconsin. We went out to Still Creek and looked at a house and we all said, "Ooh, I want to be out here," and went back and then said, "Why not your [i.e., Stan and Brian's] place? Why not the house that you're in? It's right near the beach, the location's good." So at that point it would just be the four of us. Lanny [Beckman] had married, he left with Martha, his wife, and within a month he was back. I don't know why he got married. He was back and he wanted to be with us, and asked if there was another bedroom. There were three bedrooms. Actually, there were four, because there was the writing room ... We were renting this. The landlord said that we had to move because he's going to sell. I think I told you this last night, but if I didn't, we want to put in on tape, so I'll go through it again. So Brian has fed the reindeer out at UBC, his summer job. Along with another Brian, Loomes, they're out there. He was bicycling back, and where he turned was within three blocks of where we lived. There was this house for sale. So he came in all excited and said, "There's a house that's for sale." Because we were saying, "Where are we gonna live? What are we gonna do now? We don't wanna go to Still Creek or equivalent. We want to stay in this area if we can." So we quickly – well, it wasn't that quickly, but we decided we would like to stay together and we put an offer in. This is where we got screwed up, because I went to the Teachers' Federation and tried to get a mortgage. It took them three weeks to say no, and then one day to tell me why when I went back, one hour or forty-five minutes. This lovely, point-by-point list. I just was quiet, just wrote it down. Then I thought, "Okay, now if we try to get money again, we know what to emphasize and what to not say anything about." In the meantime, the realtor said, "Why don't you try VanCity?" So when I got home, we wrote this letter. Stan got this smashing letter and then made an appointment. Now we've got this letter to support that we could afford it. And we could. We were able to do it. It wasn't easy, but anyways. But we had not really talked about how the work is distributed within the commune. At one point, another commune invites us over to have dinner. That's unusual, when you've got five people, that you're invited out to dinner. People are always coming over to your place, but seldom are you invited as a group. They wanted to talk about the labour within the commune. And I thought, "Good conversation." So we go back home, and I thought, well, this would be a perfect time to have this discussion about the work in the commune, to work out some things. My ex-husband, who wasn't ex at that time, he and Brian DeBeck were doing all the, quote, "manly" things. Stan was just sort of, "Oh, Brian, I need a ride somewhere." Wouldn't get his driver's licence. "I need a ride," that sort of thing. And Lanny didn't get up till one o'clock in the afternoon, and the mental patients were calling me all the time.* But there would be more things, like couldn't we dust once a week, and couldn't the floors, especially in the kitchen, be washed every second day, or as needed? Maybe it would be once a week, but not just sort of leave it all up to who notices. Cliff took the stance that if you notice it then you do it. (*all laugh*) Well, that was totally unhelpful. And Stan, of course, didn't want this discussion because he knows that he's gonna have to do something. So, of course, it all fizzled out. I was pissed off and feeling resentment. Brian, next to myself, was the caretaker of Lars. Brian loves kids, but that doesn't mean that you have to always be on. Lanny's job was supposedly to fold the diapers once we stopped the diaper service. We should've stayed with it. We stopped it right away. He said, "I'll fold them, but I can only fold them after I come back from work." So you wash the diapers in the morning … (*laughs*)

**DF:** I know, what are you supposed to do the whole day?

**GH:** After the dryer they're as crinkled as can be. "Why do you have to fold them this way?" I said, "Well, this is the only way I know how to fold, but you could learn to fold as long as they'll work. If they're not gonna stay on, they're not working." "Well, why can't we use these plastic ones?" "Cuz they end up in the landfill. I just refuse that we should be sending more to the landfill. Do you really know what's happening in the landfills in North America

---

\* The York Commune was the home of Vancouver's first mental-health crisis line (Vancouver Mental Patients' Association), for which Hindmarch volunteered while she lived there. See below.

right now? It's full of plastic, and poop, and pee. Do we really need this, because it's convenient?" Well, of course, everybody's gone that way anyway, it's continuous. They have things that the kids are now wearing for a whole day. You used to change the diaper every time the kid went. Certainly every time the kid pooped, you changed the diaper. Just imagine this. There's hundreds and thousands of them. So, that was me, I refused.

**KS:** Absolutely.

**GH:** It would've been easier for Lanny if we were willing to pay and just continue on with the damn diaper service. They were clean, they would take them away, and they'd come back. Anyway, this was the only job that Lanny had to do, and that's how it is. (*laughs*) So I really wanted discussion when the other commune asked, "How do you solve your problems over there?" "Oh, we don't have any." (*all laugh*) This attitude. "Oh, no problem for me." That's what you do. Something's broken? "Okay, Cliff! Brian, plumbing!" Then Jeremy Prynne comes to visit with the Dorns,* and when the Dorns were staying here with their two kids, Jeremy Prynne wanted to come. So suddenly now it's Jeremy, Cliff, and Brian replacing a toilet. (*laughs*) You've got a number of people living in this place. You have to either be able to fix it, or it's got to go. And you have to have the money for something like that. Well, they did it. They were able to do a good job on it. But it was constant. But I really thought it was a good time to have a discussion without screaming away. But it was just a void.

**DF:** It never happened.

**GH:** Yeah. Then, within about a month Cliff left, so I'm going through other things, and I'm just like, "How in the world did I get here?" I love this house. I love it. I would just love to just stay in it. It was lovely. It was really quite a special place. And we got it for only $40,000. The real estate person who wanted to purchase from us six weeks later offered us $60,000.

**KS:** Wow.

**GH:** Yeah, I just said, "Hell no." I didn't even wait for the commune to get back together. I said, "I'll take your card in case there's another decision from the commune." But I knew there wouldn't be.

**DF:** So, can I just rewind a little bit and just ask how you met Stan, Brian, and Lanny in the first place?

---

\*      Ed Dorn and his second wife, Jennifer Dunbar Dorn.

**GH:** Okay. Well, Lanny lived down the street from me for quite a while before. I don't know when Stan moved in there. Stan moved in there at some point, but Lanny would've been there first. Then Brian moved in. I'm not sure, could ask Brian if he was with Stan at that point or not. But I knew Stan before I knew Brian. I met them all prior to going to Madison, so probably sometime in the mid-sixties. I knew Stan from San Francisco.

**DF:** And everybody else is just sort of around from the social scene?

**GH:** Yeah, they're right on it. Lanny was extremely attractive, and he was in films and whatnot, a lot of films. He went to Buffalo, too, I think, somewhere in the state of New York to get his Ph.D., but he didn't finish it. He came back, and he was depressed. Everybody liked Lanny. He could organize if he wanted to, when he wanted to, but he was always troubled. There are probably some films of his that you could see on my TV. Canadian films that he's in. So, it wasn't like a conscious decision. I knew them a year or two before we asked if we could perhaps live together.

**DF:** You got on well enough.

**GH:** It was great at first, yeah. My only rule was that everybody had to cook. This was difficult, because Lanny didn't want to learn to cook. Stan said he would teach him, and he managed to teach him two meals ... (*laughs*)

**KS:** So you knew what you were getting on his nights. (*laughs*)

**GH:** You always knew it was one or the other, yeah. And he really wanted – "Well, why can't we just get pizza in from Olympia?" There's no cooking on Friday, unless somebody wants to. Often Stan and I took turns on the Friday. "Oh, yeah, well I'll do it." The idea was there's not cooking on that night, but it always worked out.

**KS:** And was it breakfast and dinner? Or just dinner?

**GH:** Just dinner, yeah. Everybody looked after their own breakfast and lunch. And when Barb and Steve joined the commune, they did all the shopping at Woodward's. I kind of liked food shopping in a way, so I missed that, but they wanted to do it and take over and were willing to lug all those things and whatnot, so they did that. Which is part of the labour of the household.

**DF:** Oh, for sure. Huge.

**GH:** Lanny could've said, "Well, I'll do the shopping," or Stan could've, but it was "Oh, no, I can't because I don't drive." (*laughs*)

**DF:** So who was doing it before Barbara and Steve?

**GH:** Whoever was cooking the meal that night. There was a butcher store nearby, and a bakery nearby, and a Safeway up on 4th, and I think we had delivery of milk – maybe eggs, I don't know. I don't remember yogourt coming in. I mean, yogourt was still big. I used to make yogourt, so I'm not sure whether that came with milk or not. It makes sense that it would. I guess we must've had milk delivery.

**DF:** And so was all the food communally purchased, too? Was it from a fund?

**GH:** Lanny was in charge of the money and made sure the rent was paid and the taxes and all those things all along. Then we had a jar that we kept money in. If it was running low, either he would fill it, or somebody else would put it in, but then take it out, and let him know that it had gone short – say, if we had to get ten pounds of flour or whatnot. That seemed very smooth. And the fact was that we were paying off the mortgage and were able to pay back our parents, to start paying them back quite shortly. We thought it was gonna be really hard, and it wasn't as hard as we thought it would be.

**DF:** When you decided to do this together was it more of a convenience thing, that everybody needed a place to live and it was cheaper to do it, or was there a sense that you were doing something kind of politically oppositional?

**GH:** I think there was that sense it was politically oppositional, but… Stan was constantly, "The communal kid, the communal car, the communal child …" (*all laugh*) I sort of resisted that part, because he'd run out to the campus, pack up Lars, show him all off for half an hour and come back. (*laughs*) See, the fathers nowadays, a lot of them are the caretakers of their kids. It's quite a different attitude. Much more observant and totally aware of the kids in a way that was all the mother's role before. I mean, it's just super, what has happened.

**DF:** Agreed. And then, above and beyond that, there's a huge amount of communal or collective activity happening in all these different ways, right?

**GH:** The Mental Patients' Association. The Food Co-op. New Star Books. And then the forming of the Food Co-op, which I believe is now this East End Food Co-op. I'm not positive, I don't know how to find that out. And the NDP was being elected at the

same time, so we had the coffee klatches for Rosemary Brown.*
She got in. So, all of this was all happening while Jeremy Prynne,
Ed Dorn, and Jenny Dorn, and the two little Dorns arrived for
a three-week stay. I mean, it's and, and, and ... (*laughs*)

**DF:** Can you walk me through your involvement in each of those three
groups – the Food Co-op, New Star, and the Mental Patients'
Association?

**GH:** I had nothing to do with the Food Co-op. Cliff's brother, Bob,
was the mover on that. He must've asked at some point if they
could have meetings at our place. I wasn't there to say, "I think
we have enough meetings. Find another place." (*laughs*) But
we started having them. And, of course, as they got revved up,
there were more and more of them. Like, you literally just clear
off the supper table, and then there's another meeting occurring.

**DF:** But you were involved with the Mental Patients' Association,
with the crisis line, right? Taking the calls?

**GH:** Well, taking the calls until we finally got a second phone line.

**DF:** And was that phone line for crisis relief?

**GH:** Yes, it is. And we weren't trained. I wasn't trained, I'd be holding
the baby, and you might have a suicidal woman on the other
line, on the telephone. And you're holding an infant and then
you think (*sighs*) "I can't." "I'm awfully sorry you feel like killing
yourself and hang on, you can't do that." You know, it was too
much. I mean, it really was too much.

**DF:** But the idea that it was for a community of people who were
working with mental health issues and support for those people
from within that community?

**GH:** Well, you see, it was found that the mental patients had no rights
up until that point, no rights whatsoever. And so Lanny said this
recently – it may be recorded or not – but he said, "The gays are
organizing, the women are organizing, what's happening with
the nuts? We have nothing." So then they got T-shirts, "Nuts to
You," you know? And then, fortunately or unfortunately, one
way or the other, the columnist in *The Sun,* Robert Hunter, puts
in the paper, "If you're interested in joining the Mental Patients'
Association ..." and publishes our telephone number. So this is

---

\* The first Black Canadian woman to be elected to a Canadian provincial legislature, Rosemary Brown served as a New Democratic Party Member of the British Columbia Legislative Assembly from 1972 to 1986.

the same month that Lars is born. You're not gonna get much sleep anyway, and then you've got this reporter – there were only three people for the first meeting, but then the next meeting, guess where it's held? At our place. So the Mental Patients' Association decided they have some rights, too. They needed things. So eventually they were able to rent a place, and then almost because Lanny learned how well it works, how money works, that a society works in a different way until you get a mortgage, you start to understand it. And he said, "We should get LIP [Local Initiatives Projects] grants and everybody will give 25 percent of their LIP grant into a fund to get a down payment, and we'll be able to do this within four months," or whatever.* This is exactly what happened, that they got it. They had a rule that you must take your medication, and you couldn't smoke dope in the house. They probably were still drinking in the house, but they had to have some simple rules. But they did organize, and that's part of why we got the Pine Street Clinic, and a number of things came out of that grassroots organizing.† With the Liberal government's LIP grants, if you came up with a good project, they gave money for it. You had to be accountable in terms of the money that you spent, and it worked out really well for the Mental Patients' Association. They got to then own a number of places all over the city. That was Lanny perceiving that it could be done, and we all supported him in that because it made sense. But what didn't make sense to me was that our phone was tied up for hours from people who needed help. And we were not trained for this or anything. Lanny was, even though he quit his degree and everything, he had the training to figure things out smartly and smooth things down and disperse a crisis, of which there were several, and he handled all that. He did a good job.

---

\* LIP grants were from a federally funded program 1971–1979 (with major cutbacks to the program in 1973) aimed at reducing unemployment by having community organizations, municipalities, and First Nations come up with "imaginative" projects that would result in "community betterment," at which unemployed people could work to get enough weeks of employment to then go on Unemployment Insurance.

† The Pine Street Clinic was a grassroots public healthcare clinic in Kitsilano that opened in 1972 and provided services to those without provincial medicare (many people lacked the permanent mailing address and length of residency in B.C. to qualify for medicare).

**DF:** And what about your involvement with New Star Books?

**GH:** Very little, except for Daphne's book, *Rings*.* It was just a week or so after Lars was born, I was going around and round the table, collating. Finally thought, "God, I'm getting dizzy," and I said, "I'd better lie down." I should not have been doing that because I was still bleeding a bit. Here I was, "Oh, yes, of course, yes, we'd better get this book together." This needed a little bit more labour. (*laughs*)

**DF:** Yeah. (*laughs*) Who was the moving force behind New Star Books?

**GH:** Stan at first. Rolf [Maurer] came into it fairly early. Stan and Dennis Wheeler helped set it up in the basement at the commune building that we ended up owning. Dennis built all the shelves and got stuff so there was a good space to work there.

**DF:** Did they print stuff in-house?

**GH:** Yeah, yeah, at that point.

**DF:** In the basement?

**GH:** I think they were. That'd be a good question to ask Brian DeBeck. He would probably know. Or Stan would definitely know. I don't remember hearing the Gestetner churning over or anything like that. I think at first they were all probably in-house, but I don't know.

**DF:** So you've got this big household into which you're putting a lot of labour, and you're answering the phone, you've got a new baby, you have people visiting all the time. So how did you manage, period, with all that stuff going on?

**GH:** I don't know, you know. (*laughs*) I do know that I said that I'm not going to go to any of those Food Co-op meetings. Plus, the NDP. Yes, we were very excited. We wanted change, but I didn't realize that this was going to take a lot, too. All happening in the same time period.

**DF:** Yeah, so I guess the question is how did you manage, and furthermore, how did you manage to write through all that?

**GH:** Well, I just got up every day, I fed the kid, and in the first three months of life, you sleep quite a bit. So burp, feed, burp, check the diaper, put to bed. And then put him out in the porch. So I'd be in here and he was just out on the porch in the pram. Somebody lent us a pram, and so he would just be right there. I didn't

---

\* Daphne Marlatt, *Rings* (Vancouver: Georgia Straight, 1971).

|       | see him because there was a wall in between, but I could hear. If he made a squeak, I could've heard it. |
|-------|---|
| KS:   | Is that so he could have fresh air? |
| GH:   | Yeah, out in the fresh air, and on the porch. A high porch, so if somebody steps on the steps, you'd be able to hear them. You'd know somebody has come. |
| DF:   | So you did manage to get some writing done in that period, even though you now had this new son? |
| GH:   | Yeah, I wrote the whole of *A Birth Account*. We moved into the house in June, and I think there's just a week later when I'm starting to write the labour account. So I wrote it quite quickly. It was finished before Cliff left, and before I went to a family reunion August 18, 1971. There's been very little change. One of the things was to try to get the breathing right. So I announce in the front of the book, "Thanks to Lionel Kearns," because I could not figure out how to indicate that it's coming in and going out without being cumbersome. And how long it is. Nobody's going to read it, to get that, the sense of endurance. |
| DF:   | What do you remember most fondly about your time from the commune? |
| GH:   | I think the dinners. I really liked them. We were very scheduled. Six o'clock, everybody was there. They just all arrived all at once. We didn't drink beer or wine or anything there. We could have, but it was not our norm at all. Then by quarter to seven, or seven o'clock, the dinner was over and somebody had been assigned to wash the dishes, and the pots, and whatnot. Some cooks are pretty messy, and some clean up as they go along. But there were no disputes over that. Nobody said, "I can't do the dishes," or "If I'm not there, the dishes are always dirty," or anything. There were never any arguments about these things. Or even about money. It's pretty good to have that group for quite a while. In some instances, people would be really upset over various things, and that wasn't happening. |
| DF:   | And it was a nice time to gather? For dinner? |
| GH:   | It was, yeah. And on the whole, good conversations. You know, "What'd you do today?" Basically, like, "Where are you in *A Birth Account*?" Dennis Wheeler would drop by quite often, and Brian Loomes, who became a lawyer, and Barbara Coward were there all the time, but they didn't speak much. I found that a bit disconcerting. They kept saying, "Well, can we cook? Or can |

we do something?" They were trying – But we didn't want to say, "Move in." (*laughs*)

**KS:** Did the commune eventually come apart?

**GH:** It took a long time, and in the end it was just Stan and Lanny. (*laughs*) The least competent of the works. How did this all happen?

**DF:** Maybe that's why. (*laughs*)

**KS:** Was it collectively sold, then?

**GH:** No. After I left, at a certain point, my parents hadn't been paid back yet. My dad wanted to get their money back. They were building a house. Money became available to give to my parents, so I was free of that debt. But then when they wanted me to sign off a few years later, because somebody else wanted to move in, I said, "Well, I will, but this is what it was valued at when we got it, and you have to know the value today. I don't care whether you divide it by the number seven, which would be with Barb and Steve and the originals, or six, cuz Cliff would be out, or eight, the new person, but I would want a share, that share of the difference between that." Cliff tried to talk to me about this, so they had obviously spoken to Cliff, and I said, "I'm firm on this." So he had to tell them no, that she's not gonna budge. They got him over to talk, they thought, okay, well, he's the best person to talk to her about this. Well, he was not the best person. So then they sent Steve over to take me to the coach house, which I live close to, on a night that they knew that Cliff was taking Lars. He said, "We'll have a drink and we'll talk about it." I said, "No, Steve. I'm firm. I'm entitled to that. Yes, the money went back to my parents, but look at the difference between what it was valued at and what it was valued at less than six weeks after we got it." We got half the gain on it. And then Robin Blaser heard this, cuz by this point, Robin and Ellen [Tallman] had moved to a building at the end of the same street. He said, "Be careful to just stick with what you've said, Gladys, just stick to it and you'll see." He says, "You're gonna lead to where the next exit is." And of course I didn't know, but Barb and Steve decided to leave. So I was the template for how you get out. Well, in the end, Lanny Beckman's mother had to keep putting money into this thing to make it work. Stan by then was teaching quite a bit at Capilano College, so he was earning money. There were no longer any LIP grants, but whatever Lanny was managing went

**KS:** up. They managed to stay there a long time, without doing any maintenance.

**KS:** So in the end, they bought you out.

**GH:** Yes.

**DF:** And what would you say was the most challenging part of communal living?

**GH:** Cliff and I didn't get to be alone enough. That was a challenge, but I didn't take up the challenge and try to sort of fight that. You get quite tired in early pregnancy, and then you get a huge amount of energy, and then near the end, it's more how can you manage. You need more sleep than you normally do. So we didn't try to create more alone time. There were so many things that had to be done. Like when you're first moving into a place, whether you're a couple, or single, or a commune, and it's a place that has not been cleaned properly for a long while, and you decide to paint the whole thing, then there's labour, there's all this labour involved. So you're not really paying attention to your psyches. You're happy, but whether you're pulling out the morning glories or whatever, you're moving on. (*laughs*) I don't know if I accepted any real challenges. I mean, I reached the point where I just got tired of political discussions, discussions under Barb and Steve. They were being courted by the Communist Party, I think. It happened with Jamie [Reid], too. But anyway, there's a whole line, there's a whole way they do it, and then all of the sudden it becomes relentless and whatnot. So, suddenly Stan would be arguing with Steve, and Barbara started chipping in now, and that's good, she's talking, but it just didn't engage me, and I was no longer connected in that way. Luckily I was able to work part-time at the Vancouver City College program – general programs division or something. But I didn't earn as much money as you do as a college teacher, and when I was offered a full-time job at Cap, I applied for half-time and they interviewed me wanting me for full-time, and it took me a while into the interview to figure out this is why they were willing to see me late Friday afternoon at this strange hour, and went on and asked me about my psychic something or other. (*laughs*)

**DF:** Moving on, I was wondering if you could tell me a little bit more about the women's lib group. Would you talk a bit about that?

**GH:** I got this call from somebody from UBC who wanted me to come to this meeting, and I went, and it was a large meeting. Then they asked if I would run a group, a small group, and there were eighteen or something in this small group in the old cafeteria. What was decided before the next meeting was that you could pick between a political or a more consciousness-raising group. And I chose consciousness-raising over political. I went, and only two people turned up. One was a nurse and the other was a sociologist whose husband was a biologist with a job at UBC, but she didn't have a job at this point because she moved to be with him. As it turns out, she was pregnant, too. She said, "I don't know what happens, but this happens to me every time there's a group of something. No one shows up." She was New York, strong accent, Jewish, and just sort of like, not "poor me" but "this happens." And I said, "Well, what are we gonna do?" I said, "What if we each find somebody and bring them next time?" We got Sheila Day, and it was such a great collection of people. Then there were two more added. So we had a group of eight. It lasted for two and a half years, I guess, and we met weekly. It was really, really good. Then we had all these requests to join our group, and I was quite insistent that we stay under ten members, so another group formed. Because it reaches a point that then some people will just be quiet. Seven or eight is the optimum number for a group like that.

**DF:** Yeah.

**GH:** And so Barb Coward, Daphne Marlatt, Judy Copithorne, Angela Bowering, and Thekkie Cuff and three other people were interested. Angela refused to go to the new group. She had been visiting. Her dad died in January, and she had come to my group two or three weeks in a row. And she said, "I have to come back because it's really important to me." I said, "the other group will be equally good. It will become equally good." She said, "No, I must be in this group." And Pauline [Butling] came to my group, and several people from Malaspina came over. We had a number of visitors, but there was a core group, and it was really a very good experience to be able to talk things through.

**DF:** When you say you had to decide whether you were political or consciousness-raising, what did those two terms mean?

**GH:** Well, political was for people who really wanted to change things – change the world, change the community, the city, and whatnot. They were more interested in political activism than personal growth or exploration. Now, someone like Sheila Day could have easily been in the political group, but she wanted to take some time with what was happening with her personally and came into this group.

**DF:** So that's what consciousness-raising was, talking about personal things?

**GH:** Yes. For some reason, the men always thought we were talking about them ... (*all laugh*) And it wasn't happening! It was our chance to talk about our attitude toward, say, money – and that may lead to a whole bunch of discussions. There was nothing barred from discussion.

**DF:** What sort of topics?

**GH:** We didn't have to pick a topic for the night, we would just get together and we all had plenty to talk about.

**DF:** And did you find that there was a good balance with the eight of you? That there wasn't one person who dominated the group?

**GH:** Well, Angela was a very strong voice, and Sheila was very strong too, that way, so ... and Renee [Kasinski], she was a sociologist, and pretty savvy. She went back to teaching in a women's university somewhere on the eastern seaboard. So she was very aware of root behaviour and would point things out quite readily. Her husband was working with Dave Suzuki, and things weren't working out – different problems and things. It seemed to me we were talking about everything but we would get on one subject and we would be there for a good time, and into another one, so probably talked about two things in each night. Or if you'd just been reading a good book, probably you'd talk about your book or something. So it had a really nice flow to it.

**KS:** How would you describe your contribution to the group, or your voice within the group? Were you a facilitator?

**GH:** I don't know if I was a facilitator. I just felt like I was an equal member of the group.

**DF:** It lasted a really long time, on a weekly basis. So what sort of purpose did that group fulfill in your life? Why was it important to have that on a weekly basis?

**GH:** Well, it certainly gave me some balance from the commune. It was sort of the male commune and the female group. And Judy Williams's aesthetic was similar to mine. It's different, but there are similarities. And with Judith Lodge, there was this proposal for a women's magazine, *The Women's Monthly*. I mean, we didn't call it that, it ended up being called that. But anyway, we put in this proposal for a grant and we didn't get it. And they chose me to be the editor and I wasn't sure I wanted to do that anyway, so I'm just as glad that it did not go through. But the whole editor thing, I wanted to share the type of things that we had been doing and discussing. (*pause*) It was just a free flow. We'd talk about political events, too, we'd talk about the things we cared about the most and what was important that week.

**KS:** And this was before Women and Words, right?*

**GH:** Yes, quite a bit before.

**KS:** Did it last? I mean, did it end well before Women and Words? I mean, Women and Words was '83.

**GH:** Let's see, okay, when would that be? It would be formed in '71, so that was late fall that first meeting. But there must've been a couple meetings before, in November, December. So '71 to '72. I moved out in October '72. I don't remember going to the meetings after that. So maybe it was just a year and a half. I don't know. I'll try to figure that out by reading my diaries. In my head it was two or three years, but maybe it was less than that. Merrilyn [Payne], one of my closest friends, was in that group. Her family owned the Avalon Dairy, but it was not highly successful the way it's become in the last twenty years. The father gave it to the youngest son. She has a sharp business sense, so she was the business person of the group. That's who I invited next. At that point, she wasn't a friend, she was married to Gordon, who did the paintings, and lived in the studio underneath me.

**DF:** Oh, maybe just for my completionist tendencies, can you just one more time name the women who were in the women's discussion group? The eight of you?

**GH:** Okay. Renee Kasinski was the one who said, "It happens to me all the time." Nina the nurse, whose last name I can't remember right now, Merrilyn Farquhar, who is Merrilyn Payne at that point, Sheila Day, Judith Lodge, and Judy Williams, both artists. Oh, now I'm seeing this image of a person with curly, dark brown hair. I forget her name right now. And Lise Selman, whose husband worked in fibreglass. And Leith somebody. One was Lise and the other one Leith, so I'm already up to nine, yeah. There may have been times where one wasn't there, but eight was the max. And then Angela joined us.

---

\* Women and Words was a conference of feminist writing held at Simon Fraser University in Vancouver in 1983.

**DF:** Maybe one more question: How's the dynamic different in discussion when you're a group of women as opposed to, say, a mixed-gender group?

**GH:** If the group is not too large, everybody can talk. And if somebody isn't talking at all, we try to encourage them to jump in in some way or other. But I think because we all had such different work, it was really neat knowing people who were doing different things other than what you were doing, but were encountering the same problems. So they liked being on problems somehow more than on joys. (*all laugh*) The problem of how you're trying to solve this and come to it and whatnot. So there was no formal order and when the people from Malaspina came, they said, "Oh, we just love it! It's so free-flowing! How do you do this? We're getting into arguments all the time." I said, "What?" "Well, we just seem to get on to one thing, then all of a sudden, we're arguing about something."

**DF:** And when did the group decide to stop meeting, or why?

**GH:** Well, that's what I'm wondering – why? When I moved out of the commune, I was teaching part-time at night. Then I shifted to day teaching. I'd like to know from somebody else in the group when it actually ended, because I don't recall going out to the group, either taking Lars or making arrangements for Lars so I could go to the group.

**DF:** Right.

**GH:** Whereas before, at the commune, it was very easy. Lars always fell asleep early, and I would go, and be fully confident that somebody would hear him cry if he did wake up. Because by that point we moved down to the room right near the kitchen, right near the bathroom. So all those meetings on the main floor, they're using the bathroom and the kitchen. They for sure would've heard him. A kid could sleep through anything.

**DF:** So you don't remember why the group stopped meeting?

**GH:** No, no. And I also am, for the first time, thinking it may have just been a year and a half, but a very intense year and a half.

Deanna Fong, Karis Shearer, and Maria Hindmarch, Vancouver, 2019.

# Occasional Writings

FROM

# Women and Words Workshop

## *Writing and the Erotic**

1983, PREVIOUSLY UNPUBLISHED

## Writing and the Erotic

Originally I was to share this workshop with Betty Lambert and we were to workshop (whatever that is in this context: to me it indicates a place where you take work and everybody gets to use the tools that are present and for writing the tools are all the experiences we've had with language up to the moment that we hear and read a new piece of work, but I've also heard the term used at folk music festivals where it means simply a smaller stage and that players who might not ordinarily play together perform or fool around if one can fool around in front of two or three hundred people: small in this case a relative term), but back into the mainstream of this sentence: we were to share a workshop on Writing and Eros. Now Eros, the god of love, the child of Chaos or of Aphrodite by Ares (war) or of Hermes, is present if we care about writing, about another human being, about our sweet world at all: it is at the centre of our creative power and move toward order or wholeness or harmony.

    I am going to assume, before we get into the erotic, that there is not a woman present today who has not been deeply affected by the Eros of Death and Violence, which pervades the thinking of the men (and a few women) who form the governments who fill the boardrooms who create the irreligious plan for our planet. I take it we all desire to live freely on an earth where violence and destruction, the possibility of total destruction, are not at the core of what country or group owns what. In this Chaos that the powerful have helped to create and the powerless have worked to perpetuate – it is, afterall, a job, isn't it? I get paid for it, or, if I didn't work on this (fill in missile,

---

\*    The materials Hindmarch created for the workshop she gave at Women and Words, in 1983.

discovery, film, ad, weapon) someone else would – several millions live in fear and pain and impoverishment (fear of total destruction, actual physical torture, and mutilation, and starvation) and several million have lost the ability to feel or fear or care at all: include here the Hollow Children and Adults of an all-too-impoverished culture living on a continent that appears to value ignorance above all. If the Eros of Life were dominant, everyone on earth could drink clean water, could eat nourishing food, could work and sleep without fear of abuse or violation: our energies and resources (again sources) would be used for distribution, not retribution. Out of Chaos or Aphrodite would be born the creative not the destructive, a sense of sharing and play between equals, a dance of language and intellect and selves, a collective dance that includes and does not exclude the body/bodies.

# Workshop Survey

1. What is the most erotic passage you've read or written? (If you can't choose quickly, name two or three.)
2. What do you recall of the context?
3. In my passage (check which are applicable):
    a. I identify with both lovers
    b. I stand outside their bodies at about the same position the author does which is
    c. I feel I inhabit someone else's body which becomes my body or my body becomes the other person's
    d. there is one person plus bees, a bear, pigs, fish, horses, or a horse
    e. smells are clear
    f. there are no smells
    g. colours are clear
    h. there are no colours I can recall
    i. shapes are not surface only (visual) but have substance
    j. there is laughter
    k. the words dance somehow
    l. there is a multi-focus on the whole: the emphasis keeps shifting
    m. there is one main person and just a part of another – fingers, clitoris, eyes, cock, tongue
    n. I feel skin/breath/hair/muscle/the movement of/the shape of
    o. there is surprise
    p. there is no surprise: it is all expected
    q. there is an equality of power: no hierarchies here
    r. do the lovers utter?
    s. is language a central energy?
    >a foreplay energy?
    >a loveplay energy?
    >an afterplay energy?
    >of both?
    >of only one?

# For Warren

FROM *WARREN'S BOOK**

1987

Warren
I have so many memories
of huts, of parties, of readings, of talking
windstorm Buchanan penthouse Kerouac saxophone prose
snowy sad walks
sheets of yellow paper written in pencil fall onto the carpet
windshield wipers click punctuate your sentences
chalk in one hand cigarette in the other
a blackboard of possibilities
a diagram of our
perceptions

you never forced
one of us to go your way
yet you insisted, oh, how you insisted
and one Sunday
when you were arguing with a number of us in your living room
you had three cigarettes going at once

summer Spicer evenings of talk and reading
lights on/lights off (Warren this is all wrong)
parties for Duncan, Creeley, Olson, Ginsberg, Ferlinghetti
(the TISH boys all hiding in the kitchen/Bowering's fist punching
a baseball mitt – not wanting to be part of the crowd around F.)
you taught us a type of arrogance which you denied along with a
trust in our own ways of seeing for which we are forever
grateful

---

\*   Written on the occasion of Warren Tallman's retirement, this piece was originally published in *Warren's Book*, edited and published by Peter Quartermain and republished in *Line* 9 (Spring 1987).

you are in each of us
who became more ourselves through you
you are with each as we enter a classroom as we answer
or ask an interesting question
you are in each of us in part of how we read
you are in each of us in part of how we write

sometimes I'd love to be back in Buchanan Building
with you at the front
Barry Hale, Frank Davey, Lionel Kearns
near me at the back
the board covered in language and signals
Mary Haig-Brown answering a question
Bob Davis listening intently

sometimes I'd love to enter a Tallman party
living room full of dancers
kitchen full of smoke
people pushing up the stairs on their way to the bathroom
your writing table covered in food
McClure or Creeley or Welch or Dorn around the corner
and always the excitement
the young-kid-with-bag-full-of-candy type of excitement of
simply being present, right there: a whole world

# Pauline and Fred

## *Friends, Parties, Community*

OPEN LETTER 12.2 (2004)

I met Pauline and Fred through the essays each had written for Warren Tallman's poetry class in the Spring of 1961. I recall Pauline wrote on "A Poem Beginning with a Line by Pindar" by Duncan and Fred on hands in either a Williams or Wieners poem. I was knocked out by their original compositions in different ways: Pauline's was smooth, structured, and flawlessly elegant as she opened perception after perception; Fred's was staccato, blunt, and full of attitude – get it? So, before we met, I already knew we had something in common about the way we saw and responded to poetry.

By then I was twenty-one and was in a circle of writers that included George Bowering, Frank Davey, Lionel Kearns, David Dawson, Daphne Marlatt, Jamie Reid, Carol Bolt, Bob Hogg, Ginni Smith, and David Cull, along with many others. What drew us together is that we liked to write and wanted to share our work. Despite the fact that Frank twice got better marks than I did writing by writing parodies of my works in our creative writing class, we became friends and set up a booth together in the armories on clubs' day hoping to get enough students to form a Writers' Workshop and enough money to pay for paper and stencils. In 1960, the Writers' Workshop began meeting every second week at UBC professor Tony Friedson's house and was lubricated by gallons of Frank's sake (most of us were under the legal drinking age of twenty-one). So first came words and syntax, a sense of a person's voice coming through – such as I had when reading a Bowering story then introducing myself at his table in the old cafeteria on a rainy February afternoon. Then came that quick recognition that we had a common interest in writing, and that we wanted to talk. We didnt yet have a vocabulary for our aesthetics, but we did have places to gather: classes, hallways, the library, the Heidelberg, the Cellar, the Friedsons' for workshops, and the Tallmans' for parties.

Several of us came from small towns where everybody knew everybody and where, as Ed Dorn once said, "Every person is a member of the constabulary." We were delighted to be free to meet each other and our city kin (Jamie Reid and Davids Dawson and Cull) at UBC where friendships were choices. I had no idea then that more than forty years later we would still connect as we do. There's a feeling of coming home to the familiar in friendship, a sense that it's safe to differ and be different, to explore perceptions, to share ups and downs, to speak one's mind. In friendships that last decades, there are the delights of being with others who were there shortly after a child was born and witnessing her or him (and them) through the tangles and accomplishments of growing up. There's also the ease with which one can speak of loss and death. Pauline and I walked through Stanley Park as she told me in detail about the death of her mother. I felt honoured to be there with her. Frank was there for George through the days immediately after Angela's death, and George for Frank after Linda's.

For me friendships are there right from the start. When I met Pauline and Fred at that Tallman party near the end of the spring 1961 semester, I had this immediate and familiar sense. I have no idea what we talked about but since I always asked "Where are you from?" we probably did establish they were from Nelson in the Interior and I from Ladysmith on the Island. I remember reaching far outside of self and our smiles. Fred, especially, has a big grin that lights up wherever he is. Community comes from *communitas*: fellowship, people with shared interests, work, or neighbourhood; it is connected with communication, the giving and exchanging of information, ideas, messages, signals, feelings. Communities have centres both formal (school, town hall, community centre) and informal (someone's kitchen, the general store, a garage, a café). Here the *real* exchanges of the day take place and sometimes the most important decisions are made before they are put into motion. This is how polis works: several eyes, I & I & I & I become a we through exchanges leading to common ground and hopefully consensus. That summer of 1961 was formative for many of us. Twenty or more students from the Writers' Workshop and Warren's poetry class tried, along with three professors, to get a handle on "Projective Verse." God did we try. We were inside for three sunny Sunday afternoons arguing about "sprawl," "form is never more than an extension of content," and "kinetics." We were getting nowhere. We needed help. We asked for it. We put in $5.00

each ($50 or more nowadays) and got Robert Duncan to come up from San Francisco by bus to give us three three-hour talks at the Tallmans'. Fred and two of his friends were working cutting peat at Burn's Bog that summer. He always had his hands in so to speak, to dig in, to push things along, to get them done. Pauline was listening quietly like I was and taking a summer course? Or was she, with her powerful shoulders and eyes that survey everything, lifeguarding? I was working as a stewardess-cashier on a downtown Vancouver to downtown Nanaimo ferry boat that no longer exists, but I made it to most of those talks and some more (Duncan extended his stay, a pattern Spicer was to follow) that were simply fabulous and unlike any lectures any of us had ever heard before.

It may have been then that we first heard about *Kenkyusha*. Jess Collins, a marvelous collagist and Duncan's lover had drawn phrases from a Japanese–English dictionary and placed three in each envelope. Duncan opened the envelopes in front of us then began talking using the given words or phrases as departure points. Everybody Duncan talked about seemed to be connected with everybody else. We may not have made it any further into "Projective Verse" but we heard about H.D., Ezra Pound, Charles Olson, Robert Creeley, Denise Levertov, Robin Blaser, Jack Spicer, Gary Snyder, Joanne Kyger, and Michael McClure. We heard about "COMPOSITION BY FIELD," resemblance and disresemblance of sound, tone leading. There were circles and circles of people out there who were writing, talking, interconnecting, seeing anew, and living on very little money. Fred, Frank, George, David, and Jamie, listening to Duncan, felt they wanted to connect to the outside too. We had our places to meet, to exchange ideas, but now these young men wanted to publish ("publish" comes from *publicare*: to make public). In August of 1961 I heard grumblings about beginning a magazine, with Duncan arguing for it and Tallman resisting. I missed most of the discussion because I was working and sleeping on the ferry except for my days off. Come mid-September, everybody was back at school and the first issue of *TISH* was out. The original five editors didn't call it a collective or an editorial board but their structure was simple, two pages to do what they wanted. All the editors, including some of those who weren't, such as Lionel, Pauline, Bob Hogg, Carol Bolt, Sam Perry, David Cull, Daphne, and myself, enjoyed arguing about lines, words, what got in, how good or bad it was. I can't remember a course I took that fall other than Ron Baker's linguistics, but I do remember the feeling of being deeply connected as we talked and talked at parties, in hallways, in the cafeteria under the auditorium, and in a new gathering spot: the old army hut where George, Frank, Lionel, and Pauline had their TA offices and where the Gestetner machine resided.

Our circle kept expanding as more and more people declared themselves poets, e.g., Dan McLeod, George's English 100 student who was later to correspond with Olson and to start the *Georgia Straight* which he still runs. Our collective enthusiasm and energy had one person who always knew what to do with the old Gestetner to keep it going: Fred. Every month in the middle of the month, a new issue of *TISH* came out. Through the printed word, *TISH*ites argued, began to clarify their aesthetics, and reached out to Vancouver and beyond.

Duncan put a word in for us that brought part of the Black Mountain circle to Vancouver. In February of 1962, Robert Creeley came and gave an amazing reading of poems from the yet unpublished *For Love* in a large and full lecture hall in the old mathematics building. The audience was blown away by how new and different his work was, and we heard every word, every line break. After an hour of reading, we clapped so much he had to do an encore for another half hour starting after five o'clock. Then he answered questions for another half hour. This in February darkness where so many people would take long bus rides through the rain home. Scarcely anyone left. I've heard Creeley live many times in my life, but this one was the best ever. He had us all laughing, listening closely, at moments totally silent. He thanked us and thanked us, and we were totally grateful that he had come up the coast to read for us. That night there was a party at the Tallmans' and unlike the party after the Ferlinghetti reading the week before when the *TISH* boys, as I called them, sulked in the kitchen and wouldn't come out to talk, we were all totally animated, expansive, and excited beyond belief. Creeley's reading set another phase into swing. Warren and Bob became immediate friends that weekend. By Monday, Warren was strategizing and negotiating to get Creeley a job offer from UBC. It wasn't easy, for Bob's M.A. was from Black Mountain which made him marginal in academic circles. I have no idea how he did it but Warren was the most insistent man I've ever encountered. Creeley came to Vancouver for the 1962–1963 academic year that led to the Vancouver Poetry Conference of summer '63 (a three-week course) and a full-time professor offer from the University of New Mexico: in a sense, having a position at UBC legitimized his credentials enough to make it possible for that American university to offer Creeley a full-time job. Likewise, the fact that Charles Olson had a summer position at UBC in 1963 made it possible for Albert Cook of the University of Buffalo to offer him a full professorship even though he had an M.A., not a Ph.D., from Harvard. Suddenly, two of our penniless literary heroes would no longer be poor. Most of us had already absorbed an unspoken lesson: get a further degree.

The year Creeley taught in Vancouver, I was working on coastal freighters as a relief cook or mess girl: it's on these experiences that my boat stories, later called *The Watery Part of the World*, were based. I was now part of a shipping community where mess tables, union halls, and beer parlours were centres. I remember taking pots and pans to Pauline and Fred's as a wedding gift. I kept in touch with all my newly married friends through phone calls, letters, visits, readings, and listening to Duncan tapes in Pauline and Fred's tiny living room. I also visited the Tallmans, and often Bob was there talking with Warren in the little kitchen nook – I remember making fudge for his birthday as they yakked and drank coffee. When the 1963 Poetry Conference was announced, there was no doubt that I would sign up.

After Ginsberg's reading at the conference, more than a hundred people showed up at the Wahs' second-storey apartment that was right next to the RCMP station on campus. Their place was no more than eleven feet wide with the staircase coming up the centre. It had a kitchen built in a closet and narrow living room at the front, a bathroom in the middle, a bedroom to the right of the hallway, and a tiny study adjacent to the bathroom on the left. The living room held, at most, twenty people standing close. I went down the crowded hallway to the bedroom where Duncan was resting on Fred and Pauline's bed. I flopped down next to him and was patting his belly when Ellen Tallman floated into the room. "Me too," she said, and lay on his other side. He hugged us both laughing and giggling and just feeling free and good. Charles, beaming and full, then entered the room and gracefully dove onto the bed next to me (though heavy he moved lightly – his thighs and feet were a dancer's). Pauline followed, and all five of us played moving sculptures like kids sometimes do.

"There's room, there's room," one or several of us called to Creeley and Barbara Joseph, Duncan's friend from Berkeley. We touched (how could we help but) and felt each other and laughed a lot and told secrets (none of which I remember) and generally encouraged others to join the moving bed. Perhaps Daphne Marlatt and Karen Johnson were two of the female others Olson refers to in Tom Clark's book?

I was called away but Olson didnt want me to leave and insisted he would save my place on the bed. By then several others, including Alan Graves who was almost Olson's height and weight had landed on top. I also absolutely *had* to go to the washroom. I crawled out from under six or more bodies to get off the bed and into the long lineup for the bathroom. I watched Ginsberg kissing Hardial Bains – this is 1963, remember, and it was certainly the first time I saw a man kiss another man fully on the mouth. I was fascinated. Bains was later to become head of the Marxist–Leninist Party of Canada and to help organize the farm workers so that they could have much better living conditions. I saw Bob there also waiting. I don't know who got the idea, but we both went outside past the cops past the garage to some long grass and separated, he to the pavement, me to earth, and came back feeling better. By this point, the party had been going on for hours and over two hundred guests were crowding the staircase, hallway, and rooms. The RCMP were looking for a reason to enter the Wahs' place and check people's IDs. Their excuse was, "We have found minors in possession." The minors were my sister and Tom Webster from Harvard who were out necking in my mom's car where I had stored a case of beer in the trunk. "But the case isnt opened," I argued with the young, blond officer who was scared.

The older officer came over and argued, "It doesn't matter that it is not open. They have control over it." End of party. We had many great parties that summer at Carol and Jamie's, Sam Perry's, and at the Tallmans', but the party of all parties for me and for Roy Kiyooka was that one at the Wahs'. In fact, Roy and I became friends talking about that conference and party for the next four months.

When the conference was over, the guests and the *TISH* editors, with the exception of David Dawson, left the city: Frank to Victoria where he later began *Open Letter* (another magazine formed on a non-hierarchical, non-institutional basis); George and Angela to Calgary where he wrote *Rocky Mountain Foot*; Lionel and Dolly to England. Fred and Pauline were going to visit San Francisco on their way to attend the University of New Mexico where Creeley would be, and the Tallmans asked me to join them on a trip to Berkeley. Once we made it through the border where an official tried to stop Fred from entering even though he had a student visa and a letter saying he had funding from the University of New Mexico, we had a great time driving down, switching cars so we could talk to each other about the conference.

One morning, Fred decided he wanted to buy a *Kenkyusha* and he found one at a second hand store. He flipped the pages and put his hand down and got, "Bring a friend." He needed money so he came back to the house to get some from Pauline, and I was there.

"Where are you going, Fred?" He was evasive. "A bookstore? Let me come along." I did.

When he got there, he held the *Kenkyusha* he wanted. He flipped it open to "Speak to another."

"Where?" he asked.

"Beside you."

I flipped it open and asked it, "Will you talk to me?" The answer had "everlasting" as one of its words.

Fred shook his head and said, "It's yours. I'll have to go back to the one in the University bookstore which said, 'Steal me.'" I don't think he did. When he needed a name for the magazine he was starting in New Mexico, he had me consult the *Kenkyusha* and I got *Sum*.

When Tom Wayman wrote me a note about participating on a panel for this conference, I consulted my *Kenkyusha* and the first phrase I touched thinking of Pauline and Fred was "adhesive power." Individually and as a couple, they have this quality. They knew early they wanted to marry, that their lives would be surrounded by poets and other artists, and that they would take on the tasks necessary to make things happen. On that trip down to San Francisco, I overheard Ellen telling Pauline, "I married Warren because I knew life with him might be difficult, but it would always be interesting." I think life has been interesting for both: they are constantly evolving and growing together within the communities they joined and helped to develop.

They created space in their homes, no matter where they were, that was/is somewhat like the Tallmans' – places where people come to gather, gab, drink, eat, exchange the news, and sometimes listen to visiting writers read. I came to visit them many times at their place in South Slocan and remember eating bowls of borscht with crusty homemade bread, turkey dinners with all the trimmings plus pumpkin pies, fresh fish with spring greens, tomatoes right out of Pauline's garden. I loved to cook and felt at ease helping in their kitchen as they did in mine. From Fred's study, I saw a black bear about twelve feet away shaking the apples off a tree. From my place, they saw a whole street in mauve-pink light of Japanese cherry blossoms with the port, city, and Stanley Park beyond.

However, Pauline had to tolerate a lot on both the public and private fronts. First there was the problem of getting a job: she had plenty of work to do with two kids and garden in a house that was forever being added to, but she wanted to participate equally with men in the college community and needed to be part of the discourse. I thought it totally unfair that Pauline, with an M.A., and having passed the Ph.D. comprehensive exams, which Fred hadn't, wasn't able to get a full-time job, for we all knew several couples who worked at Capilano College, Malaspina College, Simon Fraser University, and UBC, which were all part of British Columbia's post-secondary system. When she did get her job in 1974 by fighting for it, I cheered.

During part of the time when Karen Tallman was living there, they had a calendar on which both of them marked each project Fred said he wanted to start. The month I visited had almost every day marked with a new one. The two previous months, likewise. In the meantime, the toilets were an issue. On the main floor, the bathroom just off the kitchen went for close to a decade with a partially complete wall. I remember Brian DeBeck regaling me shortly after Lars's birth by describing sitting on the pot with the door closed yet still hearing every word of a nearby conversation between Stan Persky and Fred. On the upper floor, a Swedish toilet that made compost and that previously hadn't worked out on the main floor was installed on a platform and was too high for the girls to use easily with a roof a little too low so people my size and taller had to duck and lean forward while sitting. I've seldom seen Pauline give up or even express irritation – but I would like to have heard her the day Fred started to tear down the chimney starting at the bottom.

As I said earlier, communities have gathering places, and the Wah–Butling residence was certainly one of these. I'll give you an example from one of my favourite gatherings at their South Slocan place: I was up there to read at Selkirk College or David Thompson University Centre. I have a blurry impression of a reading and talking about my boat stories in Pauline's Canadian literature class. They asked if I would be willing to read my birth account to a small group on Sunday. "But it's two hours long." Fifteen or so people gathered in their living room. The fire was going. We had tea and beer to quench our thirst. By the end, Fred had a headache. So did the other men. They were scrunched into fetal positions. We women were smiling, sitting with our legs wide open, glad that the pushing and breathing were finally over and that Lars was born. Caught in our poses, the whole group of us laughed and laughed.

Pauline and Fred realized that creating a space to publish work that reflected their sense of poetics was a necessity, a service to the literary community so to speak. They were instrumental in so many little mags: *TISH, Sum, Niagara Frontier Review,* the *Magazine of Further Studies, Scree, Writing, Open Letter, Swift Current,* etc. Like *TISH,* they had not one but several editors: people willing to work and share to make things happen; people who resist hierarchical models. No matter where they live, a writing community forms – Vancouver, Albuquerque, outside Buffalo, South Slocan, Calgary. They have had guests to hundreds of dinners and have hosted well over two hundred writers. Pauline has written articles on works by me, Audrey Thomas, Paulette Giles, Jeff Derksen, Phyllis Webb, and *Seeing in the Dark: The Poetry of Phyllis Webb*. Fred, as we all know, has so many books (*Mountain* is my favourite of the earlier works – he read the whole once in what felt like one breath), but he was also instrumental in creating a writing program at David Thompson University Centre, a Professional Writing Program at Selkirk College, and the non-funded cooperative along with Tom Wayman and Colin Browne, the Kootenay School of Writing in Vancouver and Nelson. And he was willing to take on the responsibility of being Chair of The Writers' Union of Canada, a full-time unpaid job of its own. Like Warren Tallman before him, Fred has done hundreds of unseen tasks in order to make something new work. The something always reflects his literary community's aesthetics and polis. Like Ellen Tallman before her, Pauline taught as the children grew up, stood her ground when she had to, and was/is a presence wherever the couple abide.

Pauline Butling and Fred Wah have, as do several attending this conference, "adhesive power." Even when facing adversity, neither of them gave up doing what has to be done, getting their hands in, digging deep. And both of them still dance.

# For George

*71(+) FOR GB: AN ANTHOLOGY FOR GEORGE BOWERING ON THE OCCASION OF HIS 70TH BIRTHDAY*

2005

You can hear George everywhere. Go to a ballpark, he's shouting at the umpire; go to a pub, he announces TFP (Traditional First Piss); go to a party or a reading, he's the loudest man in the room. No kidding. You cant miss hearing him even if you're a whole block away, or you're driving by Nat Bailey Stadium with your windows down.

You know what that loudmouth side of him does? It creates space around him so he can write his heart out. He jokes off his worst so he can write his best. He can hit a poem out of the park, slam a paragraph over the infield, and land a chapter that looks so easy that the outfielder catches it with grace.

No one can strike his writing out. There's a George rhythm to his work and play. Friends and readers sometimes have to stretch to catch a joke, but there's no doubt Bowering has balanced his life so he can compose books. More books than he's had birthdays – not bad, eh? He catches phrases and creates lines or sentences with glee. Deep love and consciousness also. "Consciousness is how it is composed."

Happy, happy 70th.

# For Sharon

THE CAPILANO REVIEW 3.05, SPRING 2008

Sharon and I met sometime in the mid-sixties through my sister Leni, brother-in-law Neap, Sharon's first husband, Brian Fawcett, and my then-husband, Cliff Andstein. I don't recall the moment, but she was suddenly there with those sky-blue eyes, sharp wit, and swinging dark hair. She worked as a secretary while Brian went to SFU, but after two or three semesters she enrolled too.

•

Sharon and Brian were always on the move – it seemed every six months or so – and Cliff and Neap and others drove out to Port Moody or walked over to their new pad in Kitsilano to paint their walls, white of course. Every rented place was quickly transformed from salmon pink and institutional green (landlords' colours those days) to white.

•

Shortly after everyone moved them into a place in Fairview, she and Brian started a Shakespeare reading group. Various of us, including Stan Persky, Brian DeBeck, Tom Grieve, Michael Boughn, Dennis Wheeler, and Alban and Julia Goulden took parts in whatever play we were assigned. We read through rainy winter Sunday afternoons to backyard balmy midsummer's eves.

•

I have known Sharon through her various husbands, cats, dogs, and son Jesse, as she has known me through my various men, dogs, and son Lars. We even managed to escape to Parksville one weekend when the boys were under two; but when we returned Brian and Sharon got in a fight about essays they had both written on Coleridge – who had done the best one.

In 1974 and in 1975, I and then Sharon joined Capilano College where we both worked into the 2000s. Over the years we've discussed what works in the classroom or how we escaped from a dreadful class – with both of us laughing at our fumbles and foibles.

•

Sharon and I participated in a women's group for two years or so and, later on, a New French Feminisms reading group that ended abruptly. We read Simone de Beauvoir, Benoîte Groult, Annie Leclerc, Hélène Cixous, Luce Irigaray, Marguerite Duras, Julia Kristeva. Other members of the group were Daphne Marlatt, Eleanor Wachtel, and Kathy Mezei, maybe Percilla Groves too, maybe even Betsy Warland. Daphne and Sharon were always at the centre of the argument.

•

In the mid-seventies, when I just couldn't face retyping my *The Peter Stories* for bpNichol at Coach House, Sharon did it for me. In 1987, after Coach House published *The Beginning of the Long Dash*, I wrote a review that was published in *Brick* and she wrote a comment on my *Watery Part of the World*. Neither of us read what the other had written until it was in print.

•

Until she left for Kelowna, we'd drink tea in each other's kitchens, and eat suppers at each other's tables. Sharon can make a cherry pie or chocolate cake without a recipe and do each faster than anyone else I know. We would talk as she cooked or as I made a salad in my kitchen on Parker where I've lived for twenty-eight years – just a few blocks from her last Vancouver place on Kitchener Street near Commercial Drive.

•

Since we both had dogs, we often walked them together. Our walk/talks took in the whole range from Writers and Company to vet visits, from GG and BC Book Awards to breast-cancer treatments, from hairdos and good cuts to Charles Olson and Frances Boldereff's relationship.

# Hey, Pierre

*ONE MORE: FOR PIERRE COUPEY'S 70TH*
*CAPILANO UNIVERSITY EDITIONS, 2012*

Hey, Pierre
French Finnish English
painter poet teacher editor
founder of *The Georgia Straight* and
*The Capilano Review*

good eyes good ears
clear sense of design
contemporary all ways

I met you in the mid '60s

in Warren Tallman's living room
when you took a graduate seminar
on Pound and Williams
you were quick and smart
still are

taught with you and others at Cap in '70s '80s '90s

and three of the '00s
so even though you are just turning 70
we've met for hours in classrooms
greeted in hallways
drunk in kitchens and living rooms and tavernas
in six different decades

We've partied many times
after readings and openings
my places yours (once everyone wore
white) Bill's Penny's Jean's Sharon's

and Robin's too when Yevtushenko came
and the RCMP lurked outside
in Blaser's perfect garden

had a marvelous late morning–all afternoon–all evening
talking and drinking time with Al Purdy
at the Sylvia Hotel & English Bay Pub
the day after he read at Cap
partied past 1 a.m. then
spent the rest of the night
reading my entire copy of
Bid Me to Live by H.D. and called me at 10 a.m.
I couldn't believe it – he seemed so much older
than we were yet didnt sleep at all
but he was younger then than we are now

We've fought cutbacks together
protest marched with 15,000 others
in downtown Vancouver against the
actions of the Socred government
and we went out on strike two or was it three times
for what we believed

You've always known the right
thing to do and say
whether in public or private
and when I was
diagnosed with inflammatory breast
cancer you sent me one
Finnish word
sisu
that means courage
deep-in-the-gut courage
and focus
it meant so much to me

Thank you Pierre
you too Patti
for being out there
on the edge of my life

Hey, Pierre
welcome to your 70s
let's celebrate and
have moments of
fun each day

# Untitled

*for George Woodcock*

2012, PREVIOUSLY UNPUBLISHED

UBC in the late '50s: crowded. Classes were in army huts and permanent buildings six days a week because there was not enough space to run them in five. Every year I was there, UBC had the biggest enrollment, with '57–'58 surpassing '46–'47 for the first time. That's when the vets returned from World War II were offered free education and filled the campus from '46–'49.

English 100 was a compulsory year-long course with compulsory curriculum set by the department for all students, and English 200 for all arts, science, and education students. I dont know what the failure or dropout rates were then, but it was not unusual for people to repeat 100 two times or even three times or to enroll in 200 three or four times (during the regular session or at summer school) before they could pass and receive their education, science, or arts degrees.

UBC February 1958
English 100 in an army hut
radiators hiss
rain blasts the windows

Warren Tallman who teaches my
8:30 morning class
reads from Yeats's "The Second Coming"
(a compulsory poem in a compulsory course)
Warren whose voice is feathery anyway
can barely be heard

"Things fall apart; the centre cannot hold;
Mere anarchy is loosed upon the world,
The blood-dimmed tide is loosed ..."

"Anarchy."
I dont know that word
just like I didnt know "gyre"
in the first line
and I wish these guys behind
me would stop laughing
about the title because
I want to borrow Dave's dictionary.

"Miss Hindmarch, do you have a question?"

"Yes, Dr. Tallman, what is 'anarchy'?"

The class stops chatting and most pick up
pens (ink pens in the '50s) or pencils to write a note.

"Chaos. Lack of order. (us)
Forces beyond control: the
centre – the structures of governments, militaries,
economies, nations, churches 'cannot hold' cannot contain
nothing can stop the carnage and destruction and change
throughout post-WWI world:
'the blood-dimmed tide is loosed.'"
My impression of anarchy becomes chaos and the worst of
WWI/WWII combined.

A couple of years later in
Ellen Tallman's kitchen,
Ellen refers to
George Woodcock
as an anarchist
(that quiet man with such
a warm voice
who dashed in here a
moment ago to
pick up Warren's
review of Richler's *Duddy Kravitz*
for *Canadian Literature*).
Anarchist? I cant believe that.
"He's no threat at all," I say.

"Do you think anarchists are threats?"
"I do."
"I'm an anarchist," she says, "if I am anything."
"You are?"
"I have no political allegiance – here or there [meaning California].
I dont trust leaders in either country or Supreme Court Justices to
do what is best."
"What do you believe in?"
"Freedom, choice, love, free expression of ideas and self, no exploitation,
no class structure, a classless society – no power of any sort over others."
Ellen and I talked about this for quite a while.
Her closest friend Marthe
was married to Kenneth Rexroth
and I had met them in San Francisco.
"He's an anarchist too.
I think many intellectuals are."
My sense of "anarchist"
utterly changes.

My impression of Woodcock at that time:
a true intellectual – perhaps
European –
arms full of books and paper.
He's not squinched in like some profs are
but open to ideas.
He's not tall – close to my height
and wears soft suit jackets.
I often pass him dashing
into a Buchanan Building
classroom just after
the starting bell rings
on Tuesdays and Thursdays.
He looks eager, excited.
He seems just the opposite of a
full professor who once said to me:
"I never have nor will I ever read a
novel written in the twentieth century."

Lionel Kearns took
European Literature in Translation from Woodcock in that classroom.

They studied Dostoevsky, Turgenev,
Chekhov, Tolstoy, Stendhal, Kafka,
Pirandello, Céline, Brecht, and more.
When I interviewed him for this talk
Lionel said
"He's the opposite of Warren.
He read his lectures
which were written out
on paper and appeared to be
articles or essays or chapters in
process of composition,
of something soon to be
published.

Our class could interrupt with a
question or statement if
we wanted to but
most of us didnt."

He hated committee work
and complained about it
but he was doing literary and journalistic
work all the time –
book after book after book after book.
He was an activist for the Tibetan refugees –
both of them were, his wife Inge and George.
He didnt participate in the literary
scene here, had no children, and was
busy with his own stuff – that's my main impression:
busy writing, busy editing, busy teaching,
busy as an activist.

I saw him as open and generous, I say to Lionel.
Yes, he was, very.

George Bowering
who attended Woodcock's
class on Saturdays
to take notes for Angela
who worked at Purdys Saturdays

said
"Woodcock spoke better
than anybody I ever met.
He could talk
in complete and complex
sentences for fifty minutes without one 'er' 'tthh' or 'eh'
like the radio
as if he were on CBC
all the time.
His classes were just the opposite
of Warren's."

He also recalled
watching Inge
pick Woodcock up
at the N.E. corner of Buchanan Building
right after class.
She'd get out of her car
lovingly wrap a scarf around
George's neck and help
him settle in
then return to the
driver's side and drive
off.

# Kitsilano (1963–1969)

*for Judith Williams**

THE CAPILANO REVIEW 3.39 (FALL 2019)

1963–'69 I lived on
the corner of Yew & York
on the 2nd floor
above a corner store
with my sister Leni & soon her boyfriend (husband-to-be) Neap Hoover
her friend Jo-Ann Huffman and soon her boyfriend Mike Sawyer
then Elsa Young (just left Robert who was with Maxine)
who met her lover painter Jack Wise next door

then my sister Mary
and my boyfriend soon to be (later to unbe) husband Cliff Andstein
below us
bill bissett & martina & oolya then painter-runner Gordon Payne
& Merrilyn (who becomes my friend in the '70s) then bill again then
Gordon again
next to us:
Bing Thom, Jay Bancroft, & often Marian Penner
across the landing:
John and Susan Newlove & children sired by Gerry Gilbert
later the Ridgeways
and next to them directly opposite us:
Gerry Geisler (New Design Gallery)
and Helen Sturdy & children

our kitchen faced theirs
apple pies in my oven & stew or toast in theirs
we cd smell everything like the time Cliff and I fell asleep as pork hocks
simmered in my big red pot (Joan cleaning them for an art project)

---

\*   Based on notes written for *Walking to Water*, an installation by Judith Williams at the Vancouver Art Gallery in 1996. Revised in 2018–2019.

charred and burned almost caught on fire
would have if Gerry hadnt woken us up
and that building a total tinderbox
always worried bill wd start one

my bedroom/study faced east
to the Molson Brewery and the Burrard Street Bridge
and I could watch the West End and high-rises grow
and across Yew Street white sheets on a clothesline dry
as I'd sit at my bay window
and write and mark
on a smooth board cut to fit exactly the sill

I'd glance up and see
people like Judy & Bobo & Carol & Jamie & the Trumans
walking down Yew to Kits Beach
open the window & shout
drop by on your way back

dropping by
everybody did it
days filled with coffee, tea, poetry, cigarette smoke
crises, trips, talkedy talk talk

during and after the Vancouver Poetry Conference –
Olson, Creeley, Duncan, Levertov, Avison, Whalen, Ginsberg –
Roy Kiyooka and I became friends
and there were readings in my bedroom
every second Sunday
red cast iron pot full of bean soup or corn chowder or spicy meatball
vegetable stew
simmering and cheese scones baking
people would come and read new work one week
and the next week there'd be a TISH meeting
with Daphne Marlatt, Dan MacLeod, Pete Auxier, David Dawson,
and David Cull

painting hard-edge strong coloured
also intricate silver-point mandalas
and collages

a gallon of Calona Red
one warm October night
became a party
of one hundred or even more
dancing in my bedroom to music on a tape recorder
dancing in the other to records
two bongo drummers drumming in the kitchen
talking in the room with the blue-tile fireplace
so many bodies I couldnt hear the music
from inside our hallway
just saw the taller heads
moving together to different beats
in almost darkness

similar to that crazy night at the Wahs' place
during the conference
everybody landing on one bed
everybody kissing everybody in the hallway
something to do with space
so tight that everybody had to rub other
bodies simply to go anywhere
gorgeous

someone was always being followed
someone was always writing a poem or beginning a painting
or working all night

in the spring of '64
Roy said he had a painting he wanted to give me
but it was big and heavy (hardboard not canvas)
he borrowed a truck and someone perhaps Dallas Selman helped him
up the dusty always-dirty long stairs with *Hoarfrost*
which we hung on a wall in a room just big enough to hold
my round oak table (used to be Bowerings' – they bought a whole
household of furniture for $80 and when they moved to Calgary
they gave it to Joan and then when she moved she stored it with me)

months later Elsa and I tore apart the wall on which *Hoarfrost* first
hung with our screwdriver and hammer and Gerry's crowbar
we were shouting angry hexes at Robert all the way

and *Hoarfrost* got the prime wall in our now-bigger living
room with the blue-tile fireplace

rent $60 a month didnt change
and some years the wind was so cold on the side facing the North Shore
and that wall froze behind my pillows
utilities in winter: $60 a month

the police were something else
the narcs had a right to question anybody anywhere so
Cliff was up at the laundromat on 4th and they burst in: what are you doing?
Ray from Ladysmith was stopped nearly every second time he dropped by to visit: where are you going? and what is your purpose? and how long will you be?

someone was always getting busted
someone was always tripping out
someone was always going to Europe or Japan or Tibet

here is my journal entry on June 9, 1968:
(the evening of the first-ever National Leaders' Debate on TV)
"I am looking forward to seeing Pierre Trudeau – hope he gets pushed into/onto answering more directly than he has in the past. I, like many others including every gay man I know, do have a crush on him: he has much more style than any Canadian politician so far. I mean style in the true sense of the word, it is him, not affected ... Cliff, of course, doesn't trust him at all and thinks he's a sellout. I dont go that far, yet. But I do think that compromising is the only way a politician can work this country and I do not like all the PR, razzmatazz, fundraising, and allegiances that go into just getting elected: our system seems to be based on gullibility ..."

coming home at night up Yew Street
whether from downtown or Kits Beach or Paul the butcher's or Elsie the baker's
I loved looking up at my north-facing windows
goldy gold mesh curtains
light filtering through
so warm and so inviting

*Waiting for Gladys*, James Blake, reproduced with permission.

# Unpublished Prose

FROM

# Third Person Singular

PREVIOUSLY UNPUBLISHED

## She Was a Talky Child

She was talkative. "Comes by it honestly," her dad said referring to her mother's compulsive talking and his need to bait others into arguing. In elementary school, her teachers used various strategies to shut her up: her grade-one and -two teachers, Miss Hill and Miss Ferguson, chose her to be the king in *The King Who Never Smiled* because her voice was so much louder than all the boys', and because she would have only six lines at the end of the play, so she would have to be silent for the several weeks of rehearsal for the Christmas concert. Her grade-four teacher, Mr. Weeks, made her be the princess in *Sleeping Beauty* for much the same reasons. And her grade-five teacher (in a rural school in a place called The Diamond) used to let her help other kids in grade four and five with arithmetic and reading, and by January had her helping the some of the grade sixes who had difficulties understanding what the problems were they were being asked to solve for math. She helped them at the back of the room near a pot-bellied stove: "Quiet," Mr. Wilson would shout, "Keep it quiet or you'll have to return to your seats."

She knew she wasn't quite the same as other kids, but neither were they all the same so that didnt bother her except that sometimes even *she* knew she was talking too much and just could not seem to stop. By the time she was in grade eight, she was used to her role of answering questions and asking them – both the ones she had and the ones others wanted to ask but were afraid to so they asked her to ask for them. Sometimes she was able to get Mr. Webster off track for twenty minutes or so, and her class loved it and they all probably listened more during these times than at others, e.g., an anecdote about the French Revolution and the Tennis Court Oath or a piece of an account with Métis leaders Gabriel Dumont (an amazing strategist) and Louis Riel gleaned from biographies and articles he had read. Grade eight was also the year she began playing sax for hours each week: a sure way to stop her voice, but now both the school and marching band conductors kept signalling the saxophone section to quiet down or to mute it.

By grade ten, she was tired of asking, answering, bating her breath, waylaying, and making requests. She was tired because it was expected, so she did it less. It was around then her teachers began shouting at her along with some others. Their homeroom teacher, Mr. Nicholson, once came flying into their room shouting, "Hindmarch" (her name) and "Hlady" the name of the boy in the seat behind hers. Everyone had been talking, but their voices, *their* voices could be heard down on the first floor at the other end of the building just outside the principal's office. Mr. Nicholson told *them*, "Shut up now or you will spend the rest of today down there."

But it wasn't until grade twelve that she was dared to be silent. Hlady wrote her a note during English which was intercepted by Mr. Nicholson and read out loud to the whole class.

"Bet you cant shut up for a whole period." The whole class laughed.

"How much?" she asked.

"Two-bits," he replied.

She nodded her head in agreement and addressed Mr. Nicholson, "Sir, I wont be answering any more questions today."

"That's fine," he said, "it means everybody else will have to work harder." And they did.

At the end of the period, Mr. Nicholson said, "It certainly is different when she doesn't talk, but it is not unpleasant."

That did it. In the break, Hlady didnt pay up but dared her.

"Bet you couldn't do it for lunch hour."

"Of course I could."

"Bet you couldn't do it for a whole day."

"Of course I could."

"Bet you a dollar you cant."

"Sure I can."

"Cant."

"Can."

By the end of that noon hour, the whole school knew about it. Hlady would collect all bets – many of which were pennies and nickels. She got him to agree that she would pay nothing if she lost. In the 1950s, within a day and a half, Hlady had collected almost eighteen dollars in pledges: this was the amount that a female clerk working at Knight's Hardware Store earned working forty-four hours a week, so it was a considerable sum. Their history teacher even contributed two whole dollars saying he was tired of only three people speaking in class and he would pay another dollar to keep Hlady shut up for just the history class as long as it was the same day.

Friday came, and the bet began. Boys greeted her at the bus stop by whistling. Others, almost all boys, in the hallways at school whistled and made handsigns and sucking noises. One girl almost tripped her, but it might not have been deliberate. She made it through both English and Math without problems, but it was much more difficult than she thought it would be. Difficult to not answer when others could not. Difficult to sit and listen to others complain that they had to answer too many questions and didnt realize how much she normally spoke. Lunch hour was going to be the hardest, next to history. She made it through by eating slowly while sitting quietly in the grass listening to four other girls.

In history, Mr. Eliot decided to have unprecedented and unprepared-for debates. He explained the rules, divided the class into groups, and gave each group only four minutes to prepare. She gave her written answers to yesterday's homework to others in her group – a boy who has since become a federal prison warden, a quiet girl who married at eighteen and had three children by twenty-one, and a boy who is now an army officer in Kingston. She found it hard, even in her small group, not to butt in. When the first debate began, she could hardly stand it. But she remained silent. And then there was the next one. She disagreed with both sides. What could she do? Mr. Eliot was doing this deliberately, so she just focused on keeping her mouth shut and so did Hlady. Mr. Eliot kept looking at her – as if he could tell when she was about to burst, to give up. But she didnt.

At the end of the period, he said, "I had no idea that this class relied so much for its flow on you – you've earned every penny – your silence and Hlady's was worth it."

Physical education was last. Volleyball today. She was on a team which was two people short but she preferred it that way so she wasn't stumbling over other players. She found the hardest of all was to not shout when they scored. They were five points ahead when Miss Crehan stopped the game.

"Did you brush the net?" she asked.

"Nn –" she said before she stopped.

Miss Crehan laughed. Had she forced her to break the silence? No. All the girls agreed that they had heard an "Nn" but nothing more: a sound, but not a word. Miss Crehan, reluctantly, agreed also. She played the rest of the match extremely carefully and afterwards showered and changed in silence. By this time, most of the girls were saying they knew she could do it all along.

After the dismissal bell had rung, she met Hlady outside at the back entrance to the school where the buses all came to pick up the rural and Chemainus kids. In front of students from all grades and boyfriends who had driven up to the school to pick up their girlfriends, he paid her off counting each coin and bill aloud. The students clapped with each piece:

"$17.10, $17.20, $17.25, $17.35, all the way up to $17.87." This was not a bad price for one day's silence from a boisterous and vocal young woman who just wanted to prove to Hlady that she could shut up.

## Sentences

She is sitting at her table in East Vancouver drinking coffee and trying to think of something, *any*thing, to write for the David Thompson University Centre reading at the Western Front eleven days from now. As a fiction writer, a ten- or seven- or five-minute limit is so ridiculous that, well, why *not* read a third of a story? or two pages, or one fat paragraph? One sentence: that's it, a reading where the whole audience gets to read and each person can read only one sentence from any source – that would cut the crap, wouldn't it? Of course some writers would be assigned a handicap for they can write a continuous sentence in the continuous present that is longer than a page. Perhaps a judge: Colin Browne could ring a bell the second his attention was lost.

There could be prizes too: one for the sentence that conveyed the most in the least syllables (perhaps a DTUC calendar edited by Fred Wah with a poem for each month and Fred would be the judge); one for the person who guessed most closely and wrote or audiotaped the guess down ahead of time what the largest numbers of others would choose before they read it (a Smartass Trophy with George Bowering as judge); one for the sentence that made the audience laugh the loudest (Calvin Wharton judge); one for the sentence that caused the most surprise to be measured by the silence of the audience before it breathes again (Pauline Butling judge); one for the most lyrical (Daphne Marlatt judge); one for the sentence that most clearly articulates work (Tom Wayman judge); one for the most fun, the most lusty, the most snarly, most postmodern, etc. – like a kids' party with prizes for all.

Anyway, she didnt mean to get off onto that tangent anymore than she did to follow through on an image which came to her when she wrote the word *anything* way up above – but prose works that way and following one thought through eliminates another thread for a paragraph at least. *Any*thing made her think of Sharon Thesen's "Sleeping Beauty" remark and that led her to see Sleeping Beauty in a blue silk dress lying on a table. A hard, varnished table. She had not thought of that for years. In grade four, she (a tomboy and chatterbox and not nearly as attractive or feminine – those two meant the same then) was chosen (by whom?) to be Sleeping Beauty in a fundraising event for the Red Cross. It was nothing she had wanted, and she suspected Mr. Weeks (to whom she had once said, "If you really want us to be more quiet, sir, maybe you should whisper instead of shouting") had decided to do it to shut her up briefly.

 The prince was Brian Grant, the only boy in Ladysmith Elementary who had to wear short pants throughout winter and who never played with the other boys at recess, just as she didnt play with the other girls – up until then. Everyone – all the grade fours at least – knew he had to kiss her at the end, and even though they never DID IT at rehearsals (which were held during class time and lunch hours). She soon stopped playing fort and chase at recess because she was afraid of the teasing and all because of Sleeping Beauty and her curiosity which led her to a hundred years of silence and more importantly, that stupid kiss.

The kiss itself was no problem at rehearsals, for Brian didnt have to do it then. But not talking and not giggling were a problem, for she had to lie there on that hard table and wait and wait, a pudgy curly-headed wiggly Beauty in ordinary clothes imagining how it might feel when it really happened and listening to the bad fairies and good fairies stumbling through their lines. She'd start to giggle and all the fairies and the king would giggle and soon Brian would forget his lines and Mr. Weeks would be furious. She resented Beauty. She resented what she did by taking away her noon hours and making her put up with looks and teasing on the school bus and playgrounds where she used to play chase. She resented her right up to the day that their neighbour lent her mother a blue silk dress for her to wear. Then, suddenly, she wanted to be Beauty. She looked so grown-up that she tried to be graceful. She walked around our house balancing and holding books on her head.

She took the dress to school the next day and the grade-six teacher said she could make it fit with a bit of basting and safety pins. Two days later, she pinned her into the long dress and put on her makeup then took her to the principal's office where all the fairies and Brian were getting made up. When they walked into a stinky classroom where all the grade fives and sixes had gathered, she *was* Sleeping Beauty. Her lines, all their lines, were clear and straight. She lay on the table for almost all of the play waiting, waiting, concentrating on the one line she had to say after the Prince DID IT, listening to the fairies and all their wishes, lying in her long blue silk dress. Their Prince was simply marvellous, no longer Brian, but a PRINCE, and the jammed-in audience was silent. She almost went into a trance as he glided over and around her. She could feel the audience building up for THE MOMENT, but she did not care. She didnt care if they laughed. What's a kiss anyway? It could not be worse than Grandpa's porridgy breath. It could not be worse than teasing and stares, and besides that, as her mom said, it would be over in a second. Brian paused. Maybe he wasn't going to do it. Then his wet lips touched hers and with the audience cheering, he really kissed her. She didnt like it. His teeth were hard. But since no one was laughing, it wasn't so bad. They each said their last line and nobody giggled. They cheered. And all the teachers who were standing at the back of the room, including Mr. Weeks and the principal, clapped and clapped.

She hasn't thought of Sleeping Beauty for years. She doesn't know how she can be related to DTUC or even to her own silence in relationships with men or at union meetings. Beauty, after all, didnt have to fight for anything like they do. A hundred-year sleep is an enormous sentence to pay for curiosity. Those who sleep now will have no good fairies, no classroom or college in the east interior of B.C. that is a real place for studying the arts where there is time to develop and play with interesting lines and sentences and forms – without punishment for curiosity.

## Face It, Mom

In the middle of writing, she is interrupted. Her son, fourteen, wants her to take him to a motocross race on Vancouver Island. For him, this *is* the world. For her, writing isnt.

The boy cannot go with his dad because *he* wiped out and is now in a body cast. The boy cannot go with others, although he tried and phoned several, because their vans and trailers are full. It will be his first big race in the A-class: he might come in last but he wants to, he wants to race real bad.

He runs upstairs to his mom's study every hour. He reads what she has written. "Face it, Mom, face it: you'll never make it. Eight pages in six hours, you have to do fifty a day for the 3-Day Novel Contest, and *you* cant even *type* that fast!"

She knows this is so, but she is in the middle of writing. She wants to go on. But her desire is not as strong as his insistence. She tells him she will take him, but she wants to write for just one more hour. In that hour he makes arrangements for Boss at the dog kennel, packs, gets all the gear ready including an air mattress for her. She continues typing.

While they drive Boss to the kennel, she tries to tell her son how she feels. She says, "Writing has got to be as important to me as racing is to you." But does she mean become? For fourteen years, he has come first, her full-time work second, her home third: even the stating of this is difficult and she questions the order, the accuracy of it.

## Write Woman

Write Woman: a form yet to be developed with fragments that create an open complexity and directness where a woman resides. Stories that complete themselves in their incomplete sentences yet are not categorized as postmodernsemioticproprioceptivenonnarratives. The sentences go on and on, and the gossip, the work, the child, even noisy crows, the laundry interrupt as the whole continues. Not the same whole of the modern story where we enter the world and leave it intact. But a patch quilt of multiple perceptions as real and there as the geranium on my windowsill is.

## A Mother's Form

Why was that difficult to write? Is it that she doesn't want to publicly admit how she reacts to her ex-husband or that her son usually out-manoeuvres her on housework and money? Or is it that it isnt writing writing? Fiction and poetry remove all that clutter, give clear essences of. Our most realistic fiction scarcely includes housework. There is no room for mother's form – her elbows bent scrubbing or lifting wet laundry or packing bags of groceries through the rain or steering a vehicle through morning rush hour to get the child to the orthodontist and back to school before she goes to work. Tallman once told her she would have to invent a mother's form: something flexible, full of fragments, pieces she could write in twenty minutes, bent paragraphs. She didnt do it. She tried instead to write graceful sentences in shapely paragraphs making stories that had structures which weren't immediately perceived. These paragraphs held the present out. Even the paragraphs about the here and now were so concrete that most of the actual was filtered out.

## She Knows

She knows that we each make up our own definition of love and then fight to have it our way even if our way is being miserable. She knows that her sexuality is central to loving and that for others this is not so. She knows she can be hurt. She knows she can hurt. She wonders about writing a story about love, all those permutations: a story with the form of Arnason's *50 Stories and a Piece of Advice*. How can she create time to write? What will she not do in order to do it? Today she watched her son play soccer after driving him to the field miles away. When he assisted in a goal, she and his dad and he and his teammates all smiled; then when he scored – he who has never scored in ten years as defence – his face couldnt contain his smile. She felt such pride/love then. Last night while making love with J, making love, not fucking, not screwing, but making love, she wanted to say I love you, but didnt. Happy Birthday, she said after, Happy Birthday. Their four eyes touched almost, heads held ten inches or so apart – just enough to see into each other at that moment not other.

## Listen

10:30 p.m. Listen to the train. Listen to the docks. Screen door. Evening air. Echoes of train whistle. Car starts. Not her car – her car is still getting fixed. For the past two hours or so she has been printing this journal. Odd to dip into the past year after weeks of being with boat stories which she began writing in 1967: presents and past intertwine. The noises from the docks get louder and louder as vehicle traffic in the city lessens. She can hear voices from two and three blocks away: this neighbourhood is a contradiction, quiet and full of people noises. She is a contradiction, both passive at times almost sleeping and then move move move wanting to talk wanting to love wanting to eat wanting to write wanting to have everything in a day of her life.

## Eyes Tired

Eyes tired. She has just been on the boat for six hours – first at the end of the trip and after lunch near the beginning. Strange sensation. To have the book emerging as book – to feel part of the shape of it and then to have another part of it slip through her fingers like a jellyfish. She knows it was sunnier earlier in the day because she felt it through the skylight, but she is almost unaware of weather when she is at her computer. She looks up after the mini-story and sees all the grey clouds. Feels odd to have six hours just disappear off the screen. Yes, words and sentences are on a disk, but the experience is that the lines just scroll over and go away – like the day.

## Today She Is on Strike

Today she is on strike. She sits at her computer and feels good for the first time in weeks. She knows she has no money in the credit union. She knows this might take more than a month. She knows how strongly she feels about teaching nine sections a year: enough is enough, too much is too much, to mark nine times thirty times five thousand words and to prepare lectures for nine times eighteen times fourteen classes, and to attend three to five hours a week of meetings on top of that is crazy, just crazy. She has not been here doing any of her own work since September began. She has, however, written reports, letters, grammar exercises, outlines, etc.: not the same energy as journal writing or writing writing at all, not the freedom, not the grace, not the flexibility. College writing is like hopscotch: she must stay within the lines. Writing writing touches those lines from the outside and inside of the outside. In writing writing a whole world can become present in a gesture or sentence or shift of rhythm. Eh? Huh? You know.

## Scrolling Amber

She was in a line up at the Food Co-op when an anthropologist asked her, "How is your computer?" This was not the day to ask. She had had a story over twenty pages up when her cursor got stuck and would not move anywhere. Nothing would move up or anywhere until, eventually, FATAL ERROR covered her whole screen.

"Right now," she said, "I'm mad at it – unfriendly in computerese." "Do you normally think of it as a he or a she?" "It hasn't any gender, if it had I guess it's a she. Actually I dont think of it as a machine or object at all – the words or lines that used to appear inside my head simply appear in amber on an outside screen. I am part of it, or it is part of me. Lines disappear off the top and sometimes I scroll them back. I cant even remember where something is – I can be five or six screenfuls off – all spatial perception disappears. I love it, I really do, except when it speaks to me or gets stuck. That FATAL ERROR got to me." "I guess," she said, "it was just trying to let you know."

## Name Me a Truly Monogamous Man

"Name me a truly monogamous man," Roy says as she pours water through a Melitta filter held in a red container perched on a clear plastic measuring cup.

"Is there one?" she asks and they both laugh as she describes an ex-lover's attempts not to touch her in someone else's kitchen.

They discuss what few men they each know who are monogamous, but the question is, "Truly?"

"I know, I know," she says and names one they both know who is. They share everything each knows about his love life and they qualify each other's ignorances until they agree he must be the one truly monogamous man they know.

"I dont know how he'd take this," Roy chuckles, "but why dont you send him a postcard: you're my number-one truly monogamous man."

## the day before

the day before she is to read at malaspina college, she sits at her desk to revise a piece from this journal. since the typewriter ribbon is almost worn out, she changes it to an old one which is darker than the one put in by the serviceman just six weeks ago, but she doesnt do it properly. it scrunches every time she hits the shift key, so she has no capitals or questions or parentheses as she writes this. she wonders why anyone who has typed for twenty-five years cant put in a ribbon. she usually lugs her typewriter to the repair shop but changing always looks so easy that she feels foolish. she tries it again.

does something wrong again. she wonders if the same type of simple things are happening with her and the computer she seldom uses cuz something is always wrong. at first it might have been the choice of programs but then it was the printer itself but of course she didnt know that. that it was simply the printer card and not her machine. after it was replaced free of charge twice, she switched to wordstar and was just beginning to feel friendly toward her machine when something went wrong with the automatic paper feed which her friend fred suggested might just be the weight of her paper, so she went out and bought new paper and then when it wouldnt work lost all patience with her userunfriendlyfrustratingexpensiveexasperating machine, so of course now she is back at a typewriter which is falling apart and that she doesnt want to pay to get fixed because she has already paid 140 dollars in servicing to have the same thing fixed but not permanently fixed three times since 1985.

## Image of a Corner

She sits at her computer to revise a story she wrote nineteen summers ago. Some of the words seem childish. Other images are strong and she knows when they are not conveyed clearly. Stick with the image. The image of a corner. She can see the disbalance in her head, but it is not there on paper. It takes too many words, and she wants it short. She tries to convey the perception of an unbalanced corner accurately while keeping the language precise and rhythmical: the two buildings on the west side of Main are wooden, one has two storeys, the other is single, the buildings on the east side are more substantial, one was made in 1910 of stone while the other is concrete and faced with stone. The disbalance is not caused simply by substance but also by the fact that stone and single-storey buildings have glass doors which face into the corner. She spends more than two hours trying to get this image right and it is still not accurate.

FROM

# Swimming with Cancer

PREVIOUSLY UNPUBLISHED*

## Imaginary Valentines

My fingers and thumbs press each other to form a peak. I breathe deeply, place my head underwater and begin to slowly exhale as my scrunched-up legs spring open to make a frog kick and my arms shoot straight forward forming the point of an imaginary valentine. I glide through the water a second or two before I stretch my arms into the outer sides of a plump valentine as my hands and fingers start to meet again below then above my breasts to form another stroke.

I love breaststroke – so graceful and easy. I am weightless and my muscles and lungs know what to do. I don't think. I don't worry. I don't mull over my day. I simply breathe and glide forward forming valentine after valentine.

After twenty-five metres of breaststroke (the length of our pool), I switch to the crawl and my breathing changes to quick and deep. Loud bubbles rush past my ear when an arm lifts before it extends as far as it can before plunging down in about a forty-five-degree angle: I am. My legs flutter-kick continuously creating hardly a splash: I am. After four strokes exhaling all the way, I turn and inhale in a tiny air trough formed by my left arm that's about to shoot out and slightly up before plunging down again. My body does the crawl for three lengths, seventy-five metres, before it switches back to breast and gliding.

When I swim lengths I focus only on my breathing and the upcoming number one, two, three ... fifteen, sixteen ... twenty-eight, twenty-nine until forty which is a kilometre ... forty-two, forty-three ... forty-eight. That's when I begin a cool down by alternating breast one length, crawl the next length, up to sixty-four which is a mile. When I finish, I turn over in the shallow end and float. My hands become my pillow, my legs

---

\* The following sections of *Swimming with Cancer* were previously published in *The Capilano Review* 3.01/3.02 (Winter–Spring 2007): "Core Needle Biopsy," "Who's There?," "What's That?," "I Want to Swim," "Swimming Again," "And Again," "Damn Blister," and "A Visit with My GP."

bob up to surface, my bum tucks in as I lift my pelvis, ankles cross. I bob and float there until my breathing slows down to normal and even slower. Sometimes, I feel the water rocking me to the edge of sleep.

## Signs

Five months before I heard the words *inflammatory breast cancer*, I had several signs that I did not register as signs:

1. DEPRESSED (INVERTED) NIPPLE. One December night, my lover was cold so he popped himself entirely under my quilt. He could not see, missed my left nipple and surrounding areola, and sucked beneath it instead. I pawed him off because it hurt.

2. REDNESS OF BREAST SKIN OR INFLAMMATION. The next morning, I saw a bright red spot and concluded it was a hickey. A few days later, I saw a slight but larger redness under the skin of my left breast after I climbed out of the pool after swimming a mile. I thought my suit, just three months old and chlorine resistant, was already wearing out. Damn it. No time to shop. Have to mark over fifty research papers and finals. I also noticed that my right breast was not as reddish, but no signal went off in my head about a difference even though I had in my top dresser drawer right next to my bed a breast cancer pamphlet that stressed changes.

3. HEAT. Menopause is no pause for any woman. I often awoke to a hot flash. I could not sleep for more than three hours at a time. About once a week, I would find an arm or leg dead and could not move it for minutes. Often I had to change my nightie or pyjamas (and pillow slip too) because they were soaked through with sweat. Almost every week, I had nights when I stopped breathing as I heard someone on my porch or inside my hallway or on the staircase close to my bed. I woke up to a familiar voice calling my name as my heart pounded. Enough is enough. I made an appointment for after Christmas to raise the level of the dosage of my hormone replacement pills – from the lowest to medium.

4. CRUMPLED SKIN OR *PEAU D'ORANGE*. My left areola had an area of puckered skin but this was intermittent. I only saw puckering once a week.

5. ITCHY AND PAINFUL NIPPLE. Both nipples hurt and were itchy for three hours. The left hurt more than the right.

## Lost Girl

When the autumn semester was over, I took the ferry to Victoria to cook Christmas dinner for ten of us. When I arrived at my mom's condo the afternoon of December 24, I heard from a full-time homecare worker that Taimi (pronounced "TIE-me") had pulled an underground fire alarm in the building's basement/parking area at 5:30 a.m. The parking area door locked behind her and she did not have her key. She was wearing only her nightie in an unheated lot. Mom said to me, "I was looking for a lost girl. I looked everywhere. I couldn't find her." Mom had no way of getting out, so she pulled the fire alarm.

Before Lars and I had even unpacked the groceries, the condo resident who lived next to Mom knocked on the door. She told me in the hallway that all the residents and guests who were in two six-storey condo towers were forced to evacuate. When two fire trucks and a fire chief arrived in less than four minutes, most residents were not outside their buildings. The chief noted some people took twenty-seven minutes to get out, that some refused to help others who needed assistance, that some people didn't let others into the elevators and passed by their floors, and that no one knew how many people were away from their premises for the holidays or how many guests were present. He promised a surprise drill in the near future. If they did not pass it, their fire insurance would be void.

We needed to get our mother into a twenty-four-hour care facility as soon as possible. This became our focus. I didn't ask my sisters to see my breast when both nipples were itchy. I scratched them. I had Hindmarch Christmas stuffing to make. (Smitty our neighbour when we lived north of Ladysmith taught my dad how to make it: mashed potatoes, back bacon, onions, bread torn into small pieces, an egg or two, sage, garlic, pepper, salt, poultry-stuffing spice.)

## Locum

December 29, 1998. A pleasant woman calls my name. I assume she is a new nurse until she introduces herself as a locum filling in for my doctor. She might be right out of medical school.

"I'm here to get my hormone replacement prescription renewed, but I'd also like you to look at my breast because the nipples have been hurting me."

She asks me to sit down and lean over for her exam. She lightly chops each breast with both hands – a technique I had not experienced before. Nothing hurt. Both of my breasts are a light pink.

"Everything is fine," she says, "but you should call the B.C. Screening Mammography Program for a mammogram."

"I'm really hot at night. Could you please increase my hormone replacement dosage to the medium level?"

She writes the prescription, and I drop it off at London Drugs on my rainy way home. As soon as I am in the door, I call the Breast Screening for a mammogram. This day begins my four months of waiting.

Waiting to get an appointment. "The first available one is March 30."

"Can I get a cancellation should there be one? I can come any time on Fridays because this semester I don't teach any Friday classes. There are moments my left breast goes red but not as red as Rudolph's nose."

Within an hour, the receptionist calls me back: "January 22 at noon."

"Thank you so much."

## Where Can Taimi Live?

Before the spring semester begins, I go over to Victoria to view six care homes that my sisters have made appointments for us to see. We are appalled by three – no privacy, two single beds squished in a room that once held a double or queen bed, no space to turn around, narrow halls filled with wheelchairs making it almost impossible to navigate through, plus one place that had lemon and pine disinfectant smells in the hallways and every room we visited. The two we like the most have waitlists close to three years long. One of them has to stop with medium-level care whereas Mom, according to her doctor, needs a place that includes long-term care because she has Lewy body dementia. With Victoria attracting seniors from all over Canada, the government (municipal or provincial) decided each person was allowed to be waitlisted for only one in Victoria.

Lars and I make an appointment to view the Finnish Home in Vancouver which has long-term care when needed. It is better than any I had seen in Victoria. It is so good (clean, uncluttered, wide hallways, warm, good food, a range of daily and special activities) that there is no sense looking elsewhere if she were to come to the mainland. For one thing, she would be able to speak Finnish and English to all the staff and 70 percent of the residents speak Finnish. If she became like her dad in the end, that would be the only language she would have. For another, decades ago she told Leni if she ever needed to be placed in an old-age home, she wanted it to be the Finnish Home. After phoning Leni and Mary, I put her on the list which was in the upper forties. I was told it might take up to a year to get in.

Normally, I swim Friday afternoons and Sunday mornings – not this weekend.

## Screening Mammography

January 22, 1999. Waiting in the waiting room after filling out a form. Waiting with two other women ahead of me and construction noises including a compressor close by. I begin reading Elizabeth Hay's *Captivity Tales – not the best choice for today*. After half an hour, my name is called and I am led through a construction zone to a temporary booth made of plywood with a cloth curtain for a door. The air temperature is the same as outside. Inside the booth is a handwritten sign: "We suggest you remove your bra but not use the provided gowns – street clothes are okay." I take off my bra and pull my woollen, black sweater back on. I try to read, but power saws saw and hammers hammer.

When I pull off my sweater in the temporary room where the mammography machine is, my left breast is a bright red. I ask the technician to look at it first. She does and writes something down. After we do all the adjusting we need to do for her machine to get the right picture, I wait for the pressure of the glass squeezing each breast which usually hurts a lot but it does not hurt as much as usual – either this tech knows how to do a good mammogram or she is sensitive to bumpy breasts and knows how to spread big ones out.

## Dr. A Examines Me

January 26. Waiting for results. Waiting to see Dr. A for the first time in a year since all visits last year were with his replacements. He examines my breast, but it is pink, not tinged with red. I tell him about it and the occasional puckering. His office makes an appointment for me at Johnson and Associates while I wait. I will take the first available one this time no matter what day it is. This is the only time in thirty-five years that I've cancelled a class for a dental or medical appointment.

## To Victoria

January 29–31. Friday morning, I go to Victoria to join Leni and Mary to get Mom ready to move into a lovely private facility. We are lucky they had an opening. It costs several thousand a month and is not set up for long-term care. She will be there until a space comes up either in Victoria or Vancouver. As we were instructed to do, we mark and iron the tags with her name onto each piece of her clothing including socks. We help her choose items from her walls that will make her room feel homey: a photograph of her mother, of her father, and of herself (each in big oval, wooden frames), a favourite colourful wall hanging, plus a comfortable chair. We laugh and talk and have fun then go out together for dinner at her favourite Greek restaurant. On Sunday we set up her room then I head to the ferry with essays to mark while I wait in line and sail across to the mainland.

## No Diagnosis Today

February 2. "Why did you go for screening instead of coming here in the first place?" Dr. B, the diagnostician, asks me.

It's not my fault, but he makes me feel it is. "Dr. A's locum told me to call Screening."

He mutters his reply. He observes a small blip of darkness on the sonogram screen and I see it too before it slips off the screen. He orders the tech to get a clear view. She tries several times but cannot. He gets mad. He takes over her wand and comes at it from other angles and levels – he tries at least ten times. He can't find the tiny black bit either. The tech then tries again while the doctor, somewhat subdued, watches.

After about three or four minutes, he says to me, "I don't want to aspirate because I might miss the very area we are trying to reach." This is when I hear he's been asked to do a fine needle aspiration. I know what that is because I had a doctor try to do one before. I decide to tell him.

"Years ago, the partner of my breast surgeon tried to aspirate a cyst on my right breast. He took this long thin needle and without anaesthetic of any kind pushed it in nine times in the course of three weeks. When the surgeon returned from Hawai'i and saw my breast for his first time, he said, 'That type of cyst I never aspirate – it's like hunting for a pea in a washing machine full of golf balls.'"

Dr. B laughs. He tells me that my sonogram is "inconclusive," so I should go around the corner for a close-up mammogram of a particular area.

Each squeeze hurts. I have dense, 40D breasts. She tries to get close-ups of my lower inner quarter at several angles. The glass compresses down as tightly as she can make it toward the bottom piece of glass five or six times. My breast is flattened like a large pancake five or six times until the second the top glass is lifted.

I wait several minutes for Dr. B to come in to tell me to stay for more or to go. He doesn't. Am I to assume that what is "inconclusive" is nothing to worry much about? (If he had taken just thirty seconds to explain to me that he was recommending someone else do a biopsy, I would have been in Dr. A's office within two working days just as I was after the first report was received.) One of his assistants finally comes in to tell me I can leave. I cancelled today's class of thirty-eight first-year fiction students to find out nothing?

## No Swim Today

February 5. Damn it. No swim again today. My swim bag is ready in the car and I want to swim, but first I attend a Friday afternoon information session at the college for people who began teaching in the mid-'60s to early '70s. Our room is windowless and tiny. Everybody looks pale. There is no air circulating. I cannot concentrate on numbers and what our administrator is saying about an early buy-out of $60,000 if we stop teaching at sixty or do teach a single section a semester. The buyout would be one-fifth less for each year we were older. The only question I want to ask is, Why does a new building with a view from almost every angle have this windowless room? And why, since it is Friday afternoon (our college has scarcely any classes in that time slot) aren't we gathered in a classroom?

When the session is over, the rain is so dense and pounds so hard that I offer to drive our German instructor to the Fir Building where our offices are. Once she gets out, I look at myself in the rear-view mirror. I am flushed right up through my cheekbones on both sides. I feel awful. No swim today. I drive home, make a pot of tea, take it upstairs, and crawl into bed. Of course, I don't call Dr. A. Yes, it is Friday. If I am going to get sick, it seems it is always a weekend or a holiday.

It was the worst cold-flu I've ever had.

## No Results

March 1. I call my doctor's office because I still have not heard the results of my visit to Dr. B. By now, I've marked the third set of essays for my English 100 students and two sets from my first- and second-year fiction courses.

## A Flip-Flop

March 2. I enter Dr. A's office and wait. When he comes in, he tells me, "Everything is okay." Then he turns to page two of the report and says, "I would like you to see a breast surgeon. We had one here this morning – I should have given you an appointment."

He tells me Dr. C, a dermatologist I've seen off and on over the '80s and '90s for scalp eczema (always in the spring – pollen), will be in his office this Saturday. Because I know him, I ask for an appointment. Perhaps this occasional redness in my breast is contact dermatitis. Somehow this seems better than waiting weeks to see a breast surgeon I have not met before.

"Sometimes my upper-left breast looks dead, " I tell Dr. A. "The area around the nipple gets white and hard." White and bloodless.

## Dr. C Stalls for Time

March 6. I greet Dr. C and tell him how crumpled my areola gets (which it is not right now). He examines it gently with a gloved hand and directs a comment to a medical resident he addresses as doctor. At this moment, both breasts look perfectly normal.

He says to me, "I dont think it's cancer."

"While you are here, could you please look at these scars caused by, I think, insect bites?" On either side of my belly button are recent marks half the size of a dime and there's another one below my right breast plus scar tissue formed under my nose when my flu became a cold. "Scar tissue appears and doesn't fade away."

"The pigment has thickened," he says. "There's nothing much you can do about age. Call my office Monday. I'll do a biopsy just to make certain. Tell them you want a B appointment. Because of doctors' reduced activity days and spring break, you'll have to wait three weeks."

When I called his receptionist, she says, "You'll have to wait until April 16."

Six weeks not three. "But Dr. C said three weeks." I want it over. I don't want to wait this long. "Could you give me any cancellation that comes available? If you contact me at home or at work, I can be there in forty-five minutes."

"I don't think that's likely," she says, "because you have a longer appointment."

I am just part of one of many queues: patients on dialysis waiting for a transplant until they are almost dead, cancer patients waiting weeks not days for radiation, hip- and knee-replacement patients waiting years not months while they move less and less.

## Teach Mark Teach

During March, I feel easy because nobody is worried about breast cancer, but uneasy because I don't like the activity inside my left breast. Off and on. Sometimes, the deeper layers of skin turn red. Sometimes, chunks of flesh on the upper-inner breaBoth nipples hurt and were itchy for three hours. The left hurt more than the right.st turn white. Sometimes, I wake up to my heart pounding and if I turn on the light, my arm and breast look dead. I don't know how I twist myself into peculiar positions, but sometimes I sleep with my whole body scrunched over my left breast.

I teach and mark, mark and teach. My life is flat. Nothing much appeals to me. Usually, I enjoy teaching and often get excited in classes, but even when my second-year fiction class is having a good discussion, I am somewhat removed. I swim a mile two times each week but it doesn't make me feel as good as usual. My left arm feels heavy. It seems to drag rather than lift when I crawl. I enjoy making love yet it's not as intense nor playful. My lover scarcely touches either breast now and I bet I know why – his memory is so bad that he avoids both rather than caress the wrong one but that's okay with me – they are both useless, numb, thick, lumpy, heavy, in the way. I am not going out to parties or dinners nor inviting people over. And without Boss (our long-haired white-and-tan Great Pyrenees–golden retriever cross who died at sixteen last summer) I don't walk as much as I did last year.

I can't even seem to make a financial decision about retirement. I sought advice from an accountant and can't decide. (Less than two years ago, I bought the house next door to me and it took only ten days from my offer to possession – that decisive, that fast.)

Easter comes and goes. I don't do or eat anything special. Sometimes my breast skin goes red and sometimes white. If I knew it would stay steady, I'd go to a doctor, but in ten minutes it usually changes back to normal. I might as well stay here tied to my green chair and mark.

## Punch Biopsy

April 16. I wait in Dr. C's office only a moment. His receptionist takes me to an examining room where I remove my bra and put on a gown. Dr. C comes in with a senior dermatology resident in tow who will watch him perform a punch biopsy.

"Did you know that a dermatologist developed the first punch biopsy over a hundred years ago?" he addresses the resident.

"I am going to freeze you so it wont hurt," he says to me. He does it quickly and chats with his resident. Then he tests it.

"I can feel that." He gives me more freezing. They talk. I wait.

He tests again after a few moments then takes a core of flesh out of my areola and stitches me up.

"I really don't think this is cancer – I've done it fifty or so times. Not one has been cancer."

I wait for results: one week, two weeks. Classes are over. I mark essays and exams. I meet with two students who plagiarized. This is an aspect of my work I could do without. I once had a young man scream at me, "Why are you so uptight about quotation marks?"

## Running Close to Empty

April 29. This morning I am in a classroom where my second-year fiction class writes the closed-book portion of their exams while I mark three late essays. There is absolutely no noise other than paper turning over. After an hour, I start grading their short paragraph answers while they write essays. I can see some of them smiling and can feel the whole class is confident and concentrating.

When I get home, I go immediately to my green chair and finish their short paragraph answers (five each); then, I begin the essay section.

Before midnight, I almost finish the set – just ten to go. In one day, I read and evaluated over 55, 000 handwritten words. I am running too close to empty.

## This Is It

April 30. I finish marking and start adding up the grades in the morning, leaving just enough time to shower and make a sandwich before my 1 p.m. appointment. As I drive west toward the Fairmont Medical Building, I don't prepare myself one way or the other. After I park my ten-year-old Mazda on the top deck of the Holiday Inn parking lot, I take a couple of minutes to enjoy the view of False Creek, Burrard Inlet, and the North Shore mountains. As I walk across Broadway to the medical building, I tell myself I probably have nothing to worry about. In a few minutes, I will know for certain and that will be better than all this waiting and not knowing.

Shortly after I enter the office, the receptionist takes me into an examining room. I sit there in clean blue jeans and a striped blue chenille top with a zipper down the middle, the same top I wore on the biopsy day two weeks ago because it is easy to remove and soft and comfy to cover myself with which I have done. I close my eyes, place my hands on my knees, and breathe while I wait.

Dr. C knocks lightly before he comes in. He begins talking before he reaches me.

"Have you spoken to J?" he asks.

"J?"

"Dr. A."

"No. I have not."

He starts to approach me but is still some distance away.

"I am sorry to be the one to tell you this, but you have cancer."

He stops about five feet from me. His lips move.

"J was supposed to tell you. I checked with the pathologist and even had a second pathologist check over the results because I did not believe them myself: you have inflammatory breast cancer. I am so sorry."

## A Piece of Glass or Sheet of Ice

I can scarcely hear him. It's as if a piece of glass or thin sheet of ice is between us. Cancer. Cancer?

"You will probably have to have radiation and chemotherapy."

I am pissed off. I stand up. "It is unconscionable that I have had to wait from the end of December until now to find this out."

He steps back. "Could I take some pictures to show my students?"

"Sure," I snap. "Go ahead."

He asks me to sit on the examining table. I hide the bite scars beneath my right breast with my hand. I want to stand up so the fat between my ribs and hips won't look so bad. I know he is taking pictures to show students how healthy an unhealthy breast can look, but here I am feeling self-conscious about this shit while I'm pissed off about the delay of my biopsy caused by this very man snapping pictures. I try to take in the news. This is it. Cancer. Inflammatory breast cancer. This is what I was waiting to hear.

Before I leave, Dr. C says, "I am sorry. Let me know how you are doing." He sounds sincere, but I don't believe he cares.

## No More Waiting

As I drive home, I concentrate on traffic. I am in shock and don't want to cause or be in an accident. I heard chemotherapy *and* radiation not *or*. As soon as I am in the door, I call for the first available appointment at Dr. A's.

"You can be fitted in at four."

"I have just found out I have breast cancer, and I don't want to wait in the waiting room. If he is going to be late, please call me by 3:45."

"You won't have to wait," she says.

I have just enough time to finish adding up and recording the rest of my grades. I don't call anyone. I just get my work done. At fifteen to four, I drive to his office and park. When I enter at exactly four, I do not have to wait. The nurse escorts me straight to an examining room. Dr. A enters right away but doesn't look me in the eye.

"I've been trying to get through to the Cancer Agency all week. I haven't made contact."

I don't believe him.

He quickly shuffles each doctor's report as he is putting them into chronological order. I feel disconnected from him and from my own feelings. He comments on something he reads. I can't hear what he's saying. He asks me two questions about dates – he's getting ready to fill out a form the Cancer Agency requires.

"I've only seen this type of cancer once before while I was in training."

"What happened to her?"

"That was different," he says. "Her skin was so red and everything so advanced – yours doesn't look like hers did at all."

"Did she die?" (Why is he not looking at me? Why can't he look me in the eye?) He doesn't answer.

"How long am I going to have to wait to get to the Cancer Agency?"
No answer.

"Will you tell them how long I've waited to get this news?"

He doesn't have any answers. He seems sombre and distant, but I know him to be a kind man.

"You may have to have surgery," he says. "We won't know until you see an oncologist, but you may have to have a mastectomy before or after chemotherapy. When will be up to the oncologist."

This whole visit is a blur. I feel flat when I walk through the waiting room. This is it.

## Before I Knew and Now

I climb into my blue Mazda with its loud muffler and head to Capilano College. Hastings to Renfrew left at Cassiar and onto the Ironworkers Memorial Bridge to move over to the North Shore in the midst of Friday rush-hour traffic. Questions fly into and out of my head: cancer? mastectomy? Why didn't I get the biopsy in February when Dr. B recommended it? When am I going to get into the cancer clinic? Why has this happened? Why? And why am I insistent on getting these marks in now? I want the term to be over, that's all. Done with. I want to be able to get back home and crawl into bed. I want the weekend to be what I thought it would be this morning.

This morning and this afternoon divide: before I knew, now. Before, I could imagine the summer stretching out before me. Now, I have breast cancer. I'll tell Lars the moment we see each other. Here is another birthday – he was born on May Day – we won't celebrate. Marianne, his stepmother, died of liver cancer in April when he turned nineteen. He, his dad, and stepbrothers took a trip to Lasqueti Island to bury her ashes on the weekend before May 1. Hugh, one of his closest friends, died around midnight May 1 the year Lars turned twenty-one. He has faced seven deaths since 1989, including three boys his own age. Now this.

Parking at Capilano College is easy because it is almost five on a Friday and there are no classes at the end of term, so I find a spot next to the Fir Building where the Humanities Division and my office are.

When I walk in, no one else is here. I have to have someone check my marks. I see Alan Morris at the far end of the hall in the Social Sciences Division and go there to ask him if he'll be able to help me – a five-minute job at the most since all my other grades are in, but an imposition because he probably just wants to leave. He tells me he will meet me in the Division entrance in ten minutes.

While I wait, I pick up my mail to distract myself and read a note that was received in our Divisional Assistance's email this morning from a student I taught a decade ago. I had no idea that Greg Gowe, now a lawyer, counted me as such an influence:

> Through the years I've written many, many papers and have always received good grades and positive comments about my writing style. My writing has been my strength and has, for the most part, got me where I am.
>
> I have always felt like I owed it all to you. You taught us the fundamentals of writing so well and went over our papers in such detail, forcing us to learn how to structure an argument. As I've become aware over the years, that is something that so few students are taught or are taught properly.
>
> I was devastated when my high-school grades weren't good enough to get into UBC right away, but in hindsight I feel extremely fortunate to have ended up in your class.

Greg has no idea how much at this moment I need to feel good about what I've spent most of my adult life doing. His spirit calls out to my spirit and I feel grateful. It's as if he speaks for himself and others also.

Alan comes and we go through the marks to make certain that the letter grades in my grade book are identical to the ones on the grade sheet to be sent to the Registrar's Office. He signs. I sign. I don't tell him what's happening with me. I don't want to say cancer or see his response or have him feel he has to do something. I want everything to be normal, but it can't be. I don't want to cry here. I want to be home. Maybe this is just a dream. Maybe I'll wake up.

When I get in my Mazda, I have trouble buckling the seat belt that crosses over the top of my left breast. I've been having this trouble for weeks but thought nothing of it but now I know – breast cancer. I drive above the Upper Levels and take the clover leaf down to merge into it and merge to move with the slow Friday rush-hour traffic over the Ironworkers Memorial Bridge, whip along McGill till it slows at Nanaimo, right at Pender, left at Victoria, cross Hastings, right at Parker, left at Salisbury, down the alley to home.

While I am walking up the steps of my back porch, I hear Lars's van in the alley. I drop my book bag and purse on the landing and go back down. He steps outside smiling. He can see right away that something is wrong. I walk toward him and get caught by our overgrown rose bush near the back fence.

"Lars, I have breast cancer."

He hugs me and I hug him and we hug for several moments then let go.

"I was wondering why they were taking so long," he says. "I wish I had pushed you."

I've nothing to say. I can't kiss his hurt away. Nor cry. Usually, we chatter, but now words are inadequate. Cancer took Marianne away. She died just one month and three days after she got her diagnosis of liver cancer. It took her months to get that diagnosis. She knew something was wrong, but her doctors could not see it. She had only one chemotherapy treatment, and Lars visited her during part of it. I know he is scared for me and himself. He just wants to be alone now.

## First Visit to the Vancouver Cancer Agency

May 6. Sharon picks me up in her Pathfinder and drives me to the Cancer Agency next to Vancouver General Hospital. We talk about normal things like work to be done, money to be spent, her dog Oreo, and a vet she has found who does house visits to put pets down when it's time. (Just last summer and for three or four years before that, we used to talk and walk around our neighbourhood with Boss and Oreo once or twice a week.) By the time our conversation gets to our recent encounters with men, we are both laughing at ourselves.

Just as we emerge from the Cancer Agency Parking and open a door to the building, I say, "I'm really glad I'm starting to get help and that you are with me."

The first thing that strikes us about the Cancer Agency is how tranquil it is. No rushing. No shouting. No antiseptic smells. Several people are sitting in chairs but scarcely anyone is talking. A receptionist tells us where to wait and we do, briefly. A woman calls my name and directs me to someone who is sitting in front of a computer.

"May I see your CareCard? Where were you born?"

"Ladysmith, B.C."

"Where do you work?"

"Capilano College."

"Have you ever been treated for cancer before in the Agency?"

"Yes, but it wasn't here."

"Where?"

"In Vancouver General Hospital in 1981."

She pauses and on a computer finds my number beginning with 81, then goes to another machine which gives her a blue plastic card with my British Columbia Cancer Agency number on top, name, birthdate, and CareCard number on the bottom.

"Keep this to use whenever you come to this Agency."

We wait only a couple of minutes before the nurse escorts us to an examining room (a sink, an examining table, two chairs, a stool, scales) where we meet both Dr. D, an attractive, intelligent woman of around forty with shoulder-length curly gold-brown hair, and resident-oncology training, Dr. E, a man in his twenties with jet black hair.

"What took you so long?" is her first question.

"Everybody made mistakes," I answer, "Everybody. Have you ever seen inflammatory breast cancer before?"

Her arms reach out and her hands touch both my knees, "Yes, I have."

"How many people have you treated with this type?"

"We, in the Agency, see ten to thirteen patients with it a year, and I might treat two or three of them."

"I see." I don't see anything, but that's what I say. Thank god. I had been beginning to think I was imagining the whole thing or that I was stuck in one of my tangled nightmares.

"Dr. E, our resident-in-training, will examine you and take your background information, then I'll return to examine you also."

I put on a blue soft cotton gown that ties at the back, and Dr. E comes in.

"Could you please tell me when you were admitted to the hospital in the past, for what reason, how long you were there, and what type of anaesthetic was used?" His voice is confident and gentle.

"Every time?"

"Yes."

"I had my tonsils removed in 1944 at age four. They used ether. It was at the Ladysmith Hospital and I stayed two nights."

"I had my appendix removed in 1948 at age eight and they used ether. It was at Ladysmith Hospital and I think I was there ten days."

"I got a piece of dirt in my knee during a frosh initiation at high school in 1953, age thirteen, and it became infected. I went to the Ladysmith Hospital where they steamed it for a week. Then the doctor tapped it and a cup of yellow stuff the width of toothpaste came squirting out all over the canopy."

"In 1965, age twenty-five, I had a cyst that had to be removed. I don't know what general anaesthetic Dr. Herstein used. I believe I was there two nights." I hated this. I was in such pain I could scarcely walk.

"In 1970, age thirty, I had what is known as a missed abortion in my nineteenth week of pregnancy, but the pathology report said the fetus stopped growing at eleven weeks. We were living in Madison, Wisconsin, and the doctor gave me a general anaesthetic to do a D&C."

"In 1971, at thirty-one, I gave birth to my son, Lars, at VGH. Although my labour was short, Dr. Herstein had to use forceps so he froze me down there with a local so he could grab my baby who was slipping up and down the birth canal."

"In 1981, age forty-one, I had cervical cancer determined by a punch biopsy. I had a general anaesthetic two days in a row. The first day, Dr. L removed a cyst from my right breast and the cyst turned out to be benign plus Dr. Herstein removed the cervical cancer which was in situ and he had a pathologist look at it. The next day, Dr. Herstein did a hysterectomy. I don't know what anaesthetic was used."

"Has anyone in your immediate family had cancer?"

"My mom had uterine cancer shortly after fifty and had radiation plus surgery. Her mother, my grandmother Lempi, died of breast cancer at thirty-three."

"What treatment did she receive?"

"My grandma? She lived in Nanaimo where a vet was posing as a doctor. He told her not to worry about the lump. My grandpa took her on the ferry to Vancouver to see a specialist who wanted to remove the whole breast, but Lempi refused. She died without treatment."

"What symptoms did you have?" he asks in a voice that gives no hint of his own reactions.

"In December, an itchy nipple that was painful for three days right around Christmas, a little crumpled skin on the areola, a slight redness like a rash. In January, I twice saw my breast flush redder. Then it went back to normal, but my doctors never got to see it go red."

"In February, I had this horrible flu. I felt the heat right up to my cheekbones and there it stopped. I was extremely hot, but my thermometer said I was close to normal."

Dr. E then unties my gown to examine me. He palpates both breasts carefully and gently. His touch is not firm like Dr. A's or erotic yet firm like Nik's. Maybe he is afraid he will hurt me, or maybe he has only touched three or four breasts in his life. I can feel him thinking as his fingers make little circles as he goes around each portion of each large breast. He asks me to lift one arm and then the other. Touching much more firmly, he examines my underarms both open and partially closed.

As soon as he leaves, Sharon says, "I didn't know it looked so bad. I wish I had asked to see it when you were wondering about it."

"Don't feel bad, Sharon, please, I spent the weekend wishing this and that. I am just so glad you're here with me now. It means a lot."

"How do you remember all those dates?"

"I've always associated events with my age and where we lived. Since I was born on New Year's Day at the beginning of a decade, my age is really easy to keep straight."

Dr. D zips in and opens my gown so she can examine me. Instantly, I feel her fingers know exactly what to do. She closes her eyes to concentrate and palpates each area of my breast completely. She makes little circles and presses firmly against the chest wall when she can. She feels all the layers and bumps. She gets me to raise one arm then examines the armpit. Then I lower the arm and pull it inward for her. It takes her about seven minutes to do the complete examination. She doesn't say anything other than give me instructions.

"What are my chances?" I ask her.

"They'd be much better if you had got here when the signs first presented themselves." (Her lips tighten. She looks mad. Her skin is white. Sharon and I both notice.)

"When did I get this?"

"That's hard to tell, typically two or three years ago but it could be more. The mammograms I do have tell a story, but I'll have a clearer picture when I see the ones from years ago."

"Are you staying with Dr. A?" she asks.

"For now," I say, "but I don't know. I'll have to think about it."

She brings out two sets of stapled sheets on standard and trial treatments. She explains each to us and writes what she has observed on the back of page three of the standard one.

"You have Stage III cancer. Your nipple contains extra fluid, is edematous. The blood vessels in the deep layer of skin contain cancer. You have *peau d'orange*. Together this means you have an aggressive tumour and invasive cancer. The cancer is not in the ducts where it belongs. It is not in situ like your cervical cancer was. Inflammatory cancer typically spreads widely, so we use systemic treatment first, chemotherapy, to try to stop the spread; then we use local treatments, surgery and radiation. We call this multi-modality."

"Has it spread elsewhere already?"

"Not likely, but we don't know. We will be giving you tests to see what can be detected, but our tests cant detect microcells. I want you to stop taking estrogen pills today."

She explains both sets of treatments to both of us.

"With the standard treatment, you'll have six cycles of chemo, of about one and a half hours each. With the Taxol trial, you'll have eight cycles, taking five or more hours for each of the first four and seven hours or more for each of the second. The weakness and fatigue might be worse, and there's a higher risk for infection but only a little bit. You can withdraw from the trial at any time, or I can withdraw you if I feel it is necessary."

"What is the difference in outcome?" I ask.

"We don't know yet. But we do know you'll do as well on this as you would on standard drugs. Otherwise, we would not offer it to you. It has worked well on shrinking some metastatic breast cancer tumours."

She leaves the room. Sharon and I discuss the choice.

"Yes, I want to be on the trial. I'll get most of the same tests, but I'll have a couple of extra ones."

"You'll be monitored even more closely."

"The closer the better."

Sharon pulls out her pen and I sign and she signs as my witness. I quickly get dressed and we go next door to give the form to Dr. D who is looking at my mammograms through a light board.

"You can keep that copy, sign this one." We both do. "Now go back to the side waiting room until they book a series of appointments for the tests before chemotherapy can begin."

"Her fingers have intelligence," I say to Sharon. "She has knowledge right there in the tips – just like Dr. Herstein did. She has the touch."

"I think she's smart," says Sharon. "I feel safe with her looking after you."

"I do too."

We go to the side room and wait for another ten or fifteen minutes during which my nurse comes back with all sorts of pamphlets. She holds up one on Wigs and Scarfs, but I don't particularly want it.

"You might consider getting your hair cut shorter before you begin chemotherapy," she says. "Many people do and I think they find it easier because they take control."

At this moment, I could not care less about losing my hair. I just want to live.

We wait another fifteen minutes before my nurse returns and presents me with a schedule the size of a credit card:

| | | |
|---|---|---|
| May 10 | Bone Scan   VGH | 9:00 |
| | Mammo 3rd floor | 1:40 |
| May 12 | MUGA VGH | 12:00 |
| May 13 | Organs/Ultrasound 3rd floor | 1:00 |
| May 17 | Biopsy/Ultrasound | 1:00 |
| May 19 | Doctor | 11:30 |
| May 20 | Chemo 6th floor | 9:30 |

"A map of my immediate future," I say to Sharon. "Let's go."

## MUGA

May 12. Sounds like a dance – mambo, tango, samba – but means Multigated Acquisition Scan. Sounds like fun. They have to do this in order to know if my heart can take the heavy-duty chemo I need.

Sharon Thesen and I go to VGH, park in the lot, then take the elevator down to the basement. We walk the long hallway passing Lung and Heart Disease to Nuclear Medicine where some people are sitting on chairs outside of regular waiting rooms. I give a receptionist my card five minutes before my appointment time of noon and she tells me to wait until I hear someone call my name.

We chat about superficial things which is not our usual way of talking. Twenty minutes. Thirty minutes. I go to the receptionist to ask about the delay. She's not the person who was here before. She looks befuddled. She moves my file to her left. We hear people having a party of some sort – bursts of laughter – retirement or birthday? Wait another fifteen minutes.

"Gladys Hindmarch," a nurse calls my name.

"Have you been busy?" I ask.

"No. We've been waiting."

"Me too."

She takes me to a little broom-closet-size room and wraps an amber hose around my right arm. "Make a fist ... Hold it ... Let go." She injects a dye of sorts into the vein in the crease of my elbow. "Now go out there and wait thirty minutes and we will call you."

Sharon and I flip magazine pages and continue to talk quietly about things we dont mind others hearing. I see all sorts of sick people and dont identify with them and wonder if I will soon be like them. After twenty minutes, my left arm starts to tingle. I raise it. It stops. When a male technician comes to get me, I am holding it above my head.

"We will be taking pictures of your heart pumping from different angles. When we have them all done, we will put images together to make a more complete image."

"Can I see it?"

"Only if there is time. Now, just sit there and be as still as still as possible. The camera will move and during one ten-minute period it will be very close to your chest, but dont worry."

Hums. Clicks. After ten minutes, he comes and adjusts or moves part of it to my left side almost touching my breast. Hums. Clicks.

"You're so still – I thought you were asleep," he says.

Hums. Clicks. Ten minutes later, he moves the camera again.

When he finishes, he lets me see the screen. He focuses in on a valve pumping away: three gentle triangles opening and closing – like inside an open barnacle. That's my heart. That's inside my heart.

## Core Needle Biopsy

May 17. Before Penny Connell comes to pick me up, I call my dentist's receptionist to ask the name of the freezing my dentist no longer uses on me – so I can tell it to the doctor who will be performing my core needle biopsy.

"It's on the front of my record," I say to her. "NO EPI is printed in red."

My dentist comes on the line. "Tell them to use Isocaine," he says. "Say no epinephrine." He explains to me, "Most locals have some adrenalin in them even if it is very little; that is most likely what you react to."

Penny and I enter the Cancer Agency and take the elevator. This seems odd to us because at Capilano College (where we both teach English) the elevators are slow and the stairs clearly visible. The last time I was here, I looked at the emergency map and was surprised that the staircases appear to be hidden away from the core. No wonder we cant see doors or signs that indicate stairways.

After we check in at reception, we follow blue lines to the sonogram and mammogram waiting area where I slip my appointment card into a Plexiglas container. We chat about how different this journey is from our May adventures in Greece years ago. We talk about where we'll go for lunch: Italian, Japanese, Lebanese, or a new soup and sandwich spot called Beetnix. It's only eleven o'clock, but I'm hungry.

The technician who scanned my organs last week appears and shows me to the booth which is closest to her sonogram machine. I remove my upper clothing and put a gown on.

"Can my friend come in to watch?"

"No," she says, "there isn't enough room because we have an extra doctor today."

I hand Penny my purse, and my upper clothing stays in the booth. The tech brings me to the room I was in for organ scans. I climb onto the table and she quickly positions me and locates on the sonogram a particular area in my left breast she found last week. This time, I can look up at an angle and see her screen. That's me. That little black wiggly spider leg thingamabob is cancer.

I am introduced to two doctors, but I don't catch their names.

"Could you please not use freezing with adrenalin in it?" I ask. "My dentist uses Isocaine."

"Why?"

"Adrenalin makes my heart beat rapidly."

The older doctor flusters.

"I've had extensive dental work. I don't mind taking extra shots. Dr. Hupfau gives me extra ones whenever he needs to."

She accepts this and goes away. I close my eyes when the doctors return so I don't have to see the hypodermic needle. The injection is soon over and doesn't hurt at all.

Once the doctors are certain the anaesthetic is working, one of them makes a quick, small incision and sticks in something that on the screen looks like a white tiny triangle attached to a long thin white tail or a loose thread that floats and bobs. On the screen everything moves – depths shift, no horizon on top, no fixed end to bottom or the sides. Everything is fluid. Helped by the tech, the younger doctor starts to fish with the white point for a particular image. A piece of black no bigger than a thin hyphen appears and bobs away from where the white point is. The black thing slips off the screen.

"Dorsal," says the tech. She adjusts the image so a tiny spidery black nest appears higher up the screen. Both the technician and I seem to have a clearer view than the doctors do. The white triangle emerges further to the right. The young doctor moves it as she tries to get close to the bobbing black which has now transformed into something like a tiny jellyfish – edges undefined – slippery.

"There," she says.

"Got a purchase?" I ask.

"You are going to hear a shot."

I wait. I can see the loose tail tighten and arc – like a tiny harpoon about to descend. My eyes shut as I hear the shot – sounds like a single bang from a nail gun. When my eyes open, the catch has disappeared. The doctor takes her instrument to a container and empties it into a tube of liquid. The two doctors mutter to each other.

The younger doctor tries again. Closer. The cancer slips to the right. The technician brings it back and almost to the centre of the screen.

"There it is – at nine o'clock."

The white point lowers to about eight. I focus on keeping my eyes open, but again they close just as she shoots. She removes a second core.

"Fishtailed," says the older doctor. "I will do the next one."

I can see the needle or triangular point as quickly as the tech.

"Bottom left."

"Over there now. There. Turn forty degrees right."

The doctors can't see well. It's ridiculous that they don't have a second screen facing the doctor at the correct angle so she doesn't have to turn her body at the same time as she explores and tries to locate the correct layer of my breast.

"I'm going to try to centre it. Just keep the needle steady," says the tech, "steady."

A black slippery thing slips down to the centre of the screen as the technician scrolls upwards and brings it closer to the surface. The doctor shoots it.

The younger doctor does the fourth. They examine it.

"May I do another one – just to make certain?"

"Yes."

Five core needle biopsies in all. By the time they are finished, almost two hours have passed.

"You were brilliant," says the tech.

"Yes," says a doctor as she bandages me. "Quick."

The tech gives me a bag of ice plus a white washcloth to apply pressure to my breast which I am supposed to do continuously for two hours. By the time I pull my bra and top on using only one hand in a tiny booth, I don't care where or what Penny and I eat. Just something warm and comforting that takes just one hand.

Weeks later, I read that the needle shoots at seventy-eight miles per hour.

## Visit with Dr. D the Afternoon before First Chemo

May 19. I am ready to ask Dr. D questions. But first, Penny and I go into a little examining room where I am weighed then introduced to a study nurse who thanks me for signing up for the Taxol trial.

"How are you doing?" Dr. E asks me when he comes in.

"I'm anxious about my first chemo tomorrow and can't wait to get started."

"How are you feeling?"

"Fine." Not so fine. "I noticed an immediate softening of my breasts when I stopped the estrogen. My left arm is swollen and drags a bit when I swim. I am waking up to my heart pounding two or three times each night." Of course I am scared, but I don't say so.

Dr. E examines my breast and underarms. His touch is gentle but firmer than the first time. "Your breast *is* softer but there's hardening around the nipple and in the biopsy areas. I don't feel anything in the lymph nodes but Dr. D might."

"What are the results of the biopsy?"

"The biopsy? The results aren't here yet. Do you have any other questions?"

"Yes – I want to know if I can swim between treatments if I'm up to it."

"Dr. D will answer that."

Moments later Dr. D comes in and tells me, "Yes, you can swim between treatments."

"I don't just paddle around. I swim a mile. There's no danger of causing my cancer to spread?"

"None whatsoever. All your tests – skeleton, chest, heart, organs – came out clear. That's good – it doesn't mean there aren't microcells out there, but so far there are no visible growths."

She carefully examines my breast again. Her fingers carefully aim for places between my purple and yellow bruises.

"Now raise your left arm, that's it. A node here is about one and a half centimetres, not a classic but it might be cancerous," she says to me looking straight into my eyes. "Do you have any questions?"

"Tell me if you think it might have spread."

"It is hard to know. Individual strands might have escaped to somewhere. The risk is high enough to warrant chemo."

"I've read in a passage from *Dr. Susan Love's Breast Book* that only 40 percent survive five years." Dr. D's face tightens. "What are my odds for complete recovery and for recurrence?"

"We don't think in those terms. You have only one option: to embark on rigorous treatment. Your positive attitude helps. Believe you'll be okay. Manage the side effects. Make your use of information and reading constructive. Don't reinforce bad news. Ask yourself, what do I need to know in order to believe in the treatment?"

"Are there things I can do to build my immune system? Some friends are giving advice about complementary medicine and taking large doses of vitamin C. What's yours?"

"The main risk is bacterial infection. Don't try any alternative medicine until after the first four cycles, so we'll know how it's doing. Don't take vitamins of any sort, not even vitamin C without telling me. The key is a low-fat, high-fibre diet."

"What can I eat tomorrow morning?"

"Anything light and not fatty – toast is fine."

"Cream of wheat?"

"Certainly."

"Coffee?"

"Go ahead. In general, after chemo, expect to eat frequently, small portions, light."

"I'm up in the middle of the night with a pounding heart. Sometimes I hear my doorbell ringing. Sometimes I hear people on my front porch. I think I am not breathing before I wake up to breathe and that my brain perhaps makes these noises to wake up."

"I'm not too concerned about that – it won't affect the cancer or its treatment. If you can swim a mile, your heart's well." She smiles. Her curls bounce. I can visualize her at recess skipping on a playground in grade three or four.

"What are you going to do about your GP?" she asks.

"I'm not certain. I have asked friends and created a list of possible new ones. If I read you their names, could you recommend one?" I can see she does not like to be put in this position but I name three anyway – she's heard positively or knows two, and she gives me the names of two others.

"I'm not ready to leave Dr. A, yet. He's kind and knows me."

What I don't say is, if I am going to die, I'd rather stay with him.

She doesn't respond for a moment then says, "But does he have visiting privileges at Vancouver General?"

"St. Paul's and Burnaby," I answer.

"It might be easier if you could find a doctor who does," she says, "but it might be difficult because many GPs, particularly newer or less established ones, do not have admitting privileges at Vancouver General. It's becoming a crisis. It's certainly a problem you both could write about."

Neither Penny nor I say we will or won't. At this point, I just want my chemotherapy to begin. My sense of future is immediate – tomorrow, not even next week.

With her hand on the door, Dr. D says, "Prepare yourself emotionally for a mastectomy." That's months away. Let me get through tomorrow first.

## Chemo Hats and a Kind Stranger

Before we leave the agency, Penny and I take the elevator down to the main floor, walk across the entrance to the side room where I was first admitted, and pick up a box of cancer hats – little scarf-like bonnets that somehow tie at the back in every possible colour, sewn by volunteers. We sit down while I try on several. I choose a bright red-and-white one and a more muted mauve with tiny pink flowers. I take that one off just as an animated couple comes through the door. The woman looks over to us, checks in at the receptionist, steps back.

"I have a wig with hair like yours, " she says. "You can have it. I don't need it. I didn't lose mine."

"I will lose mine," I say. "100 percent chance for one drug and 100 percent chance for another."

"Well, I've just had my last radiation," she says delightedly and flips her head to show both of us that she's lost a third of her hair. "If you don't use it, pass it on to someone else."

She gives me her business card so we can make arrangements. She lives in Nanaimo and has had to come to Vancouver for radiation treatments because there's no space in Victoria General Hospital. The couple go off holding hands as if they were heading out for a date. Penny and I smile and laugh. Synchronicity. Friendship. Moments to feel good.

# First Chemo

May 20. I am so excited I hardly slept. When I get up, I pack my red bag: the *Vancouver Sun*, Kleenex, red lipstick, red notebook, a banana, an orange, an apple, plain crackers, gum, hard candies, three prescriptions. I dress: jeans, a salmon-coloured T-shirt with colourful appliqué, a soft sweater, sandals with socks on because it's not a warm day but that could change in minutes. I eat breakfast: cream of wheat, orange juice, two bites of toast. I set the alarm and lock the front door. I sit on my front steps sipping a big mug of latte and reading a section of the *Sun* as I wait for Sharon to pick me up.

We chat as we drive along 1st Avenue and across the viaduct over what used to be the head of False Creek onto Terminal Avenue, *Terminal,* over Main, up Quebec (part of the Indy route), along 2nd, up Ash, *Ash,* to 10th Avenue. Everyone is being wonderful: Melanie is teaching Sharon's four-hour summer class this morning so Sharon can be with me for as long as I need her. My sister, Leni, who has arranged for two days off work, is going to catch a ferry from Victoria to come here and stay with me for two or three nights to make certain I'm okay. My neighbours have offered to cook soups, water plants, pick up groceries and run to the drugstore – anything you need, we mean it, anything.

"What can we do?"

"Just hug me when you see me."

I've told my colleagues who offered to drive me to appointments or be with me through a chemo, "once I know what it's like for me, I'll make a schedule." (For the first one or two, I want Sharon, Penny, Leni – if I'm going to puke or want to sleep, I want to feel totally free. I also have Karen Tallman's pager number in my little red book. I can call her at Vancouver General just a long block away if I need her.)

As Sharon pulls her Pathfinder into the Agency parking lot and winds her way up three levels, I feel like we're at an airport about to depart to a beyond. We take the elevator up to the sixth floor and go past two full chemo rooms on our way to the nursing station and check in, then on to the waiting room where people in clumps of twos and threes sit on armchairs and stand. There's a pair of knitting needles with several colourful rows begun on the table next to where we sit and a thousand-piece puzzle with lots of sky partially completed on a table and a TV (thankfully off).

We wait ten minutes. Fifteen. Twenty. Sharon glances at two or three of the magazines then pulls out her new *Vogue* while I read the *Sun*. I get up to use a washroom and to fetch more water. A member of my healing circle told me to drink lots of water for two days before each chemo to get fully hydrated so it's easier to stick the IV in. I did it.

Iris comes to the door of our waiting room and says with a big smile, "I'm going to be your nurse for today. I'll be back to get you in ten minutes. Did you bring your medication?"

"Yes," I say happily (happy I have Iris).

"Let me see." She checks the three containers, drops one back in the bag. "Take one yellow and one white."

Ten minutes later, she is back. Instead of starting at 9:30, we begin at 10:00. She leads me to a room with two vacant chairs and sits me down in one which is still warm from the last occupant.

"What is your birthdate?"

"January 1, 1940."

On the counter behind Iris, I see several bags of liquid marked with "Hindmarch" in black felt pen. She wraps an electric heating pad around my lower right arm and then reads my chart and sits down to check the calculations made by a doctor or pharmacist. She then wheels an IV pole next to me which has an almost car-size battery on it just above at my arm level and sets up a litre-size bag ready to drip.

"How does that arm feel?"

"Getting hot."

She touches it then smiles, "Good."

A middle-aged woman's machine beep beep beeps. Iris goes to her to remove the needle from her arm and quickly rolls up the tubes before discarding them into a large container marked "Hazardous Waste." The woman's husband appears in the doorway holding a winter jacket open for her. He gently helps her put each arm into it then does up the zipper. So sweet, so caring.

Sharon and I try to make small talk, but what can we say? We don't have a vocabulary for this. What's the etiquette of chemo? Just do whatever feels best for you – light distractions for me until that needle is in.

Iris comes and touches my arm once more then taps the vein she's chosen – the one that runs from my thumb and crosses my wrist. I keep talking and looking right in Sharon's eyes, but when I know Iris is ready, I close mine.

"You'll feel a little nick," Iris says, "That's it."

She got it just like that. My tension level drops in half as she tapes my needle into place with a specially designed bandage that makes it secure, then wraps my arm in the heating pad again.

"The first liquid will feel cool and in a few moments your feet might feel like dancing. We begin with an anti-allergy drug, Dexamethasone, so your body will be ready to accept the chemo."

I start sucking ice. Leni told me her brother-in-law who is recovering from stomach cancer said, "Ice stops sores from forming in the mouth."

Within a few minutes, I have to get up to use the washroom.

"Wait a moment until I unplug you," Iris says from across the room. She explains when she does it. "This machine operates on batteries when it's not plugged in. Feel free to walk about."

I hold the tubes and thick electric cord with just the fingertips of my right hand (the rest encased in bandage and tube) and with my left push the IV trolley causing my drip bag to swing slightly. The cubicle has a thick heavy door and is in the corner of the room. In order to open it, I have to reposition the trolley with my left hand. I back in by positioning the trolley so it's on my right facing out. Then I try to zip my jeans open using only my left – these jeans are a mistake. Someone like Lucille Ball or Carol Burnett could do a great three–four minute routine with this. I wore the jeans because they are familiar and thin enough to be cool if the temperature suddenly changes. Pulling them down over both hips with just my left hand and then pulling them up and zipping up is awkward and impossibly slow. Washing with only my left hand, soaping, is not easy. My first washroom visit takes ten or more minutes.

When I come out, there's a red-haired mid-thirties woman sitting in the chair right next to the bathroom. She has a romance novel with her and her arm is wrapped in a heating pad.

"Hello, I'm Maria.* That's my friend, Sharon."

"I'm Lucy," she says. "I came in for a checkup yesterday and now I'm here starting over again."

The three of us talk while Iris puts two bags of drips on my machine and works it so they feed simultaneously.

"You are now getting anti-nausea drugs. One of these might make you sleepy," she says.

"I'm still dancey."

"You can get up and walk around the unit," Iris informs me, "but be back in fifteen minutes."

I turn my head away as Iris begins to insert Lucy's needle. She

---

\* Gladys Hindmarch began using her middle name, Maria, *circa* 1995.

has two young children and wants to be with them at least until they grow up. I feel grateful to have had these years already. Lucy gets a drip, but it's only a little bag compared with mine.

When Lucy says, "It is only my faith in the Lord Jesus Christ that has kept me alive so far," Sharon is more engaged than I am. I get up and start circling the Chemo Ward anticlockwise with chemo rooms like mine on my right, then chemo rooms with hospital beds, north-facing offices, and more chemo rooms plus the water/fridge room and the waiting room on my right. The nursing stations and service elevators (to move the fragile in their beds) back to back with three regular elevators on my left.

I use the phone at my nursing station to call Lars on his cell.

"How's it going, Mom?"

"Good so far. I got Iris. She had no trouble getting the needle into the centre of my vein."

"You do feel good?"

"Speedy right now. I cant sit still. "I'm circling the halls but I'd rather be swimming laps."

"Lots of love."

"Lots of love."

After four or five circles, I go back into my room. Sharon and Lucy have finished their conversation and Iris is injecting a red drug in a syringe thicker than a large toothpaste tube into Lucy. Again I go to the washroom. Stupid jeans. Right weight for today's temperature but next time I'll wear something with a wide elastic or loose cotton waist.

Iris gives Sharon a larger container to fetch me more ice and water, and Sharon brings some for Lucy too. I am incredibly thirsty. And Sharon and I move over so a fit man, wearing khaki shorts, can get his arm wrapped up to begin.

"I'm Maria," I say once Iris has him set up, "and this is Sharon, and that is Lucy."

"Jack," he says.

"We teach at Capilano College," I say, "What do you do?"

"Policeman."

He looks so healthy. I don't ask what type of cancer he has but we talk about shift work, B&Es, and prostitution. There's a kiddie strip a few blocks from where I live and almost every morning I see men in SUVs, some with children's car seats in the back, circling the area and making arrangements with what appear to be teenagers as I drive by on my way to work.

Iris has two large syringes of a red drug for me.

"What is that?"

"Doxorubicin." Later I find out the brand name is Adriamycin and some patients call it the Red Devil.

She injects it into one of the tubes above a Y. I watch it travel through the tube to my arm. The vein smarts. Heats up. I chat on and hardly notice. I don't feel sleepy at all. I am stoned. I can see Sharon's lips move and Lucy's. I can follow what they are saying, but I have to concentrate much more than usual and I don't fully understand or even hold a whole thought together. There's no back-and-forth flow from me. Am I having trouble just thinking?

Lucy's already finished. Iris frees her and welcomes someone else in. Lucy slides her arms slowly into her white sweater just as her mother arrives to pick her up.

"I'm going to go to London Drugs to find new magazines and pick up a drink at Starbucks. Do you want anything?" asks Sharon.

"A latte and something light to eat."

I have no idea how things will taste, but once Sharon's gone, I nibble the apple from my bag and it seems pasty. I don't want my perfect banana that now smells sickly sweet. My orange would be simply too drippy even if it were peeled for me.

Suddenly, Jack is finished.

"That was short," I say.

"I come every day this week," he says.

"Do you go back to work?"

"Only if necessary. Not today. I'll take a cab home and nap."

"Good luck," I say as he leaves.

"Hi, I'm Maria."

"I'm Ann."

"Inflammatory breast cancer."

"Breast cancer – I don't know what type."

I hear the noon horns from downtown. I am already on my fourth bag of liquid. Did Iris say something about saline to clear the veins? She checks the tubes and resets my machine.

"How long does this one take, Iris?"

"An hour."

I go to the washroom: my pee is rosy.

When I come out, Iris looks at me quizzically.

"My pee's pink," I whisper as I pass her at her station.

After I settle in, Ann and her husband, Robert, and I talk about how long it took us to get here in the first place.

"I saw my GP one day. The next morning I was in a breast surgeon's office. Three days later, I met my oncologist. We haven't had one week to even think yet. We own a business on Granville Island and we can't afford help, so we just shut down while we go to appointments and open up as soon as we get back. Everything changes so fast."

I tell them about my slow start. "It took four months from my first visit to diagnosis. I had four doctors and each of them made one mistake or another. They didn't think I had cancer because there wasn't a tumour there that the doctors could distinguish, but my oncologist certainly knew what it was and that it's in the deeper layers of skin too. In fact, she asked me 'What took you so long?'"

Next a man enters and takes the seat Lucy vacated. Iris starts Ann's drip and turns to Herb to wrap his arm. Soon we are all laughing.

"This is the party room today," says Iris.

Sharon arrives with some Japanese noodles and vegetables that I try but are too salty for me, plus a latte, and a bowl of cut honeydew and cantaloupe that isnt ripe. She bought a little terry-cloth hat on impulse – trying to make summer begin – and models it for us.

We all laugh away with Ann and Robert and Herb all making us laugh more as Iris adjust something from behind me. Between laughs, I am wondering about the Taxol. I turn away when Iris puts the IV into Herb which she does so quickly. I go to the washroom again. Now my pee has only a tinge of pink. Iris looks at me when I come out.

"Iris, when will the Taxol begin?" I ask after I am settled.

"You've been having it for half an hour already."

"I have?"

"You have."

This pleases me. Sharon and I giggle. She could see Iris's face when she did it, but Iris indicated for her to not tell me but to keep me distracted. Finally, I am getting the juice of the western yew tree or the stuff that is an exact chemical derivative of it. Each treatment in an article my neighbour Phil found on an internet source gets the chemical equivalent of the juice from the bark of one entire yew tree.

A moment later, Leni arrives with a present, the second edition, fully revised of *Dr. Susan Love's Breast Book*. (The Cancer Agency librarian had Xeroxed the partial page on inflammatory breast cancer from this for me.) I gulp. Mom would have been here if she could be. That's exactly the type of gift she would have bought a year or two ago. We haven't told her. She would not understand. We know she would focus on the fact her mother died of breast cancer and stay in that loop of that crying that never releases or eases her. We don't want to have to support her through that again right now. I am so glad I have Leni, an angel. And Mary my youngest sister too.

Leni and Sharon and I talk about how it's been going and how good Iris is. My head isn't clear and I am speedy, but I greet the juice, the Taxol that drips into my veins from one to almost three. It doesn't hurt me at all. There's no pressure in my hand or arm even though I've had four or five litres of liquid infused in that little vein I normally don't see. Sharon leaves a room full of warm goodbyes. I keep drinking water, chewing ice, talking, going to the bathroom. Maybe my pee is now a tiny bit green. I'm tired. Stoned. I want to be home. I want to be on my sofa or in my bed.

At 2:30, a couple in their fifties or sixties come in. The woman sits in the chair next to mine with a window behind her and Iris wraps her arm in a heating pad.

"I'm Maria," I say. "This is my sister, Leni. I have inflammatory breast cancer."

"I'm April," she says, "and my husband's name is Mike."

"Did you have trouble parking?" I ask him as Iris sets up April.

"No," he says, "we're only here half an hour so we just park on the street."

"Half an hour?"

"I have colorectal cancer," April says, "Mike brings me in daily – only one more treatment after this."

"The oncologist says it's for insurance," Mike says. "Things look clear now."

"Do you get sick from chemo?" I ask.

"No," April says. "We go out for supper close to home, and I eat almost anything. But I do drink ginger and hot water if I feel queasy."

Once Iris injects the needle, April's therapy takes only three minutes.

After they've gone, Iris starts my post-chemo hydration bag. It's just as big as the Taxol bags: one litre. I'm ready to head home. Have to do this. Leni turns up the music. I'd rather dance or sleep. She brings me a blanket. I can't settle. All wound up but winding down. Want to be home. Want to leave. Finally, after 3:30, we do.

## Heading Home

Wobbly. My legs are okay, but my feet seem quilted and out of sync. Leni and I walk slowly to the elevator, go down to the second floor, then along a darkish corridor to the door Sharon and I entered what seems like yesterday not six hours ago. My head buzzes. We have to take an outside elevator up to wherever the top of the parking lot is – fourth or fifth of the inside floor level. I am glad chemo's over. I flop into the passenger's seat. Leni circles and winds our way down five or so levels to the entrance/exit where she pays the attendant and, finally, we're out.

"What's the best way to go?"

"In rush hour? They're all slow – that's what Lars called it when he was six, the slow hour. Hey, Broadway doesn't look choked, turn right."

I chew gum all the way home as Leni and I talk about Mom and Sally, Leni's daughter who's handling a tough separation from a threatening husband.

Home again, home again, jiggity jig. As soon as I'm in the back door, I head straight for a tap to drink water in my own kitchen. Then I go to my TV room to snuggle on my sofa under my duvet. Leni makes us a pot of tea. I've hardly had two sips when we hear the basement door bang open and loud, male voices.

Lars is home with someone. Several feet run up basement stairs. I turn left to see him and Eliot, Marianne's eldest son, just as their heads lean into my room. They are braced against what might be. When they see my face, theirs open up into big smiles. They don't ask anything about chemo. They just want to see that I'm okay and head for the kitchen to get cold beer. Better than okay. I intend to be here in this world for as long as possible, here in this house too.

Leni and I watch the early news and chat about this and that. She decides to make Spanish rice because I have leftover basmati in my fridge and fresh tomatoes on my counter and there's tomato paste, onion, and cheddar cheese to grate for the top. Shortly after six, she brings me two pills – a Zofran (twenty dollars each) and Dexamethasone (the dancing one) to help me not vomit. Every twelve hours for the next three days, I'll be taking them. When Leni's Spanish rice comes out of the oven, the topping is golden and crispy just like I love it.

At eleven o'clock, I'm still speedy. Some women clean house just before they go into labour – their urge to is overwhelming. I use this energy so while Leni is talking on the phone with her husband and daughter, I find myself on the top floor where my study is filing away and creating piles of this and that but I need scissors for something and they are in the kitchen which is downstairs so suddenly I am tidying a cupboard down there before returning upstairs. In the meantime, rain falls on grape leaves (one of my favourite sounds) and Leni takes a bath in my old-fashioned bathtub.

When I do climb into bed, I feel like a child listening to rain on the roof and skylight. I snuggle under my duvet and Leni comes in to sit on the bed and chat. We talk well into the dark hours until I fall asleep and she goes off into the guest room adjacent to mine.

## Itchy Head

June 4. I am watching a Russian movie on Bravo when a spot on the upper back of my scalp starts to itch. I pull out a clump of hair about the size of a mouse and wait for a commercial. It turns out there are no commercials between five and seven because, I guess, most people are watching the news or sports on other channels or they are eating, so advertisers don't want to advertise here. I keep waiting for a break, but none comes.

Another spot right on top starts to itch and zing. Several individual hairs lift one by one. I can't stand it. I leave the movie (no PVR) to shampoo my hair in the kitchen sink – so I don't have to bend too far down. I dampen my head and clumps start falling out, so I tug my hair lightly before I shampoo. Most of it falls out onto stainless steel. I have about a quarter of an inch left in various places. I use only a pea size of shampoo to clean my entire head. I throw my hair into the kitchen garbage as if it were carrot or potato peelings. Then I rush back to the movie without even looking in a mirror.

## Who's There?

June 18, 3 a.m. I get up to pee and for a second don't recognize who's there in the mirror: a ridged bald head, high cheekbones, distinct yet balanced face, neither male nor female, a little scar on the right side.

## What's That?

June 18, 6 a.m. Grey West-Coast morning. I go down to the lower floor to make coffee and pick up the *Vancouver Sun* from my front porch. I come back upstairs to bed holding orange juice, coffee, thermos, and paper. Then I snuggle under my duvet and read the first page. When I turn it, I see something moving on top of Gordon Payne's painting of Ford Creek on Hornby Island. Startled, I shake my head and see black glass frames sliding slowly on top of curved sandstone. So many shapes. Simple yet intricate. That skull behind the glasses is me? I love Gordon's painting which a few years ago I got from him when I traded a Josef Albers print both he and Mary had borrowed from me for a year or two and just loved.

## Buzz Off

June 5. The next morning, I get up and go straight to a seven-dollar haircut place below my doctor's office and have a woman buzz off what little is left. I like my head. Its shape is much more attractive than I expected, more of a peak. My hairline has always been low, so now I have a real forehead. I pull on the red cancer scarf-bonnet I chose from a box at the Cancer Agency and trot upstairs in the same building to pick up an insurance form from my doctor's office then drive to the Trout Lake Farmers Market to get fruit and vegetables before it's impossible to park.

## Electric

June 8. I arrange to see Keith who shaves his head and always looks good because I want to know how he does it. Minutes after consulting with him, I am in a nearby shop buying a Braun electric trimmer that has a top that will move to fit the contours of my head. Cost? Ninety dollars with tax. Within three months, I'm going to be saving money.

## Getting Ready for Second Chemo

Clothing: I go to The Dressing Room for the third time in a month to buy a flared, black cotton skirt and a black-and-white striped top with short sleeves (better for IV and lab needles). This time, I'll pee more easily and look fine too.

Food and Drinks: I go to Superstore to buy things I might be able to eat and drink: frozen juice bars, raspberry-cranberry cocktail, peach-mango punch, graham crackers, Stoned Wheat Thins, arrowroot cookies, plain crackers, vanilla ice cream. I go to Santa Barbara Market to load up on fruit: pineapple, watermelon, bananas, grapes, B.C. blueberries.

## Bloodwork and Bruising

June 9. Bloodwork is easy when the nurse gets you on her first stab, but I get one who misses and creates a bruise on the inner side of my right elbow the size of a quarter.

Last time I waited forty minutes past my appointment time before someone took my blood, but this time I'm finished right away. I go to the cafeteria for coffee and a blueberry muffin and sit in a seat where I can look out for Renee Rodin. When she comes to the Cancer Agency's entrance, I wave and signal to meet in the lobby. We take the elevator up to a large waiting room so crowded that there are no two empty seats together. A woman around my age sees what we're trying to do and moves to another seat to create an opening for us. We smile our thanks. She smiles.

## Yew Amulets

Renee reaches into her bag and gives me a small branch of her yew – an amulet for the start of my second chemo. She then pulls out a Ziploc bag with a piece of slightly purple bark from her yew tree.

"Talismen or would it be talismans?"

We laugh and chat quietly for forty-five minutes until a nurse, not Maureen, calls my name. Renee and I hug goodbye before she goes off to work at MacLeod's Books.

## Visit to Nurse and Doctor Prior to Second Chemo

The nurse weighs me, asks about side effects, and I read her my list while she writes notes.

"Little pings inside my left arm twice during chemo and my left lung bottom at the back. Also, my right leg below the knee. Slight burning in my thyroid – three times during the fourth and fifth days. Nausea for eight days. Thrush on the sixth day – my mouth went furry. Almost no joint pain except for my little toe of my left foot. Hair loss on the fifteenth or sixteenth day. Couldn't eat greens until the tenth day – they smelled too gassy. "

"Did you have any pain in your breast?"

"Just once. About a minute."

"Remove your top and put on this gown."

I sit in the cubicle for another forty-five minutes waiting for Dr. D. By this time I am angry. Twenty minutes off schedule, anyone can understand. Even thirty. Beyond that, there's something wrong. Over an hour and a half off schedule is ridiculous.

"I've just been having a long talk with Dr. A on the phone," Dr. D says when she comes in. "I think maybe you should stay with him."

I don't know what to say. I wiggle the yew tree branch at her. I don't tell her how I feel about waiting for her. I want to ask her when and why she changed her attitude.

Instead, I say only one word, "Yew."

"He'll be your best advocate," she says.

(He's scared I'll sue. Probably he is afraid I'll report him and the others to the College of Physicians and Surgeons.)

"He's received a letter I've written to all four doctors about the time they took causing delays in my getting a diagnosis. I have a copy for you and Dr. E."

"Dr. E's not with us," she says in a slightly angry tone. "You can take the letter to the receptionist on the fourth floor just before the library, and she'll pass it on. What were your side effects?"

I give her the whole list including "too much speed from the pre-Taxol drug."

"You can take less Dexamethasone tomorrow," she says. "You don't have to have the evening one, but do take the morning ones for two days or more. Use the Apo-Metoclop for nausea when you are through with the Zofran."

"Got it."

She examines me quickly and with her head facing her notes she asks, "Do you have a breast surgeon in mind?"

"No ... yes. My friend, Merrilyn, was pleased with Dr. F, so I think I'd like her."

"She's good. Make an appointment when you get home. You want to get on her surgery list early so there's absolutely no delay after your eight rounds of chemotherapy are complete."

Here it is just a day before my second of eight chemos and we're already talking about an end. We're talking about lopping off my breast as casually as pulling out a tooth that cant be repaired. I can hardly think. I am surprised Dr. D didn't get mad at Dr. A. I wonder what they really said. I'd love to be a fly on that wall!

## Second Chemo

June 10, 10:45 a.m. November-like sky. Rain about to begin. I didn't dress in my new black skirt and black-and-white top I bought for today – too chilly, more like November than eleven days until summer. I pulled on my comfortable brown velour pants with an elastic waist, a rust-coloured velour top with long loose sleeves, and my grey winter jacket. In my red bag I have the *Vancouver Sun*, a yew tree branch, yew bark, eyeglass cleaner, grapes, plums, frozen juice bars, two plain ham sandwiches I made on fresh French bread from Andy's. Whole-wheat bread might be too heavy; mustard, too hot or metallic.

After Penny and I check in with Lynn, we put the juice bars in the freezer and sit in the waiting room which now has real botanical watercolours, not prints, on the wall. They are slightly stiff. No fluency of line or space. Yet there is much more texture and life in them than prints have. There is also an incomplete two-thousand-piece puzzle of a sailing ship that three family members are working on.

"I guess the puzzle's there so people can do something when there's no more words to say to each other," I say quietly.

"Do we always need to distract rather than face pain?" asks Penny.

"Maybe they've spoken of their love for each other as much as possible."

"Maybe it's there so nurses and social workers don't have to deal with them."

There's a large TV (off again) and on the table next to ours are knitting needles with several rows already complete. Penny picks them up and quickly knits a row.

"Do you think someone unravels these at night to reuse the wool?" asks Penny.

"No. I bet they make little lap blankets out of squares."

11:20 a.m. No Iris Today. A nurse calls my name and introduces herself as Sally. I notice her hand shake as we follow her to my room for the day that is right next to the one I had last time. So does Penny. Parkinson's? She looks over sixty-five. Maybe the nursing shortage has hit our Cancer Agency, or there aren't many who can take the stress, or they need experienced personnel so others can take vacation time. I wish I had Iris, but I'll make the best of it.

11:30 a.m. "Hello," I say to the woman who found another seat yesterday so Renee and I could sit together. Her chemo seat is the one closest to the washroom. She smiles at me and points to her left breast.

I point to my left. "My mom doesn't speak English," her son explains.

"Could you please thank her for me? She found another seat yesterday so my friend and I could sit together."

He translates as I sit in the empty chemo chair still warm from the last occupant. I am kitty-corner to her and her son, and we nod and smile then smile some more.

Penny pulls up an unused chair from near a silver-haired woman who is wearing an ocean-blue sweatsuit and is in the chemo chair on my immediate left. Sally adjusts my right chair arm to the correct height, then wraps my right arm in a heating pad.

"I'm Maria," I say to a woman who looks like a model. "This is my friend, Penny."

"Ruth," she says as she looks up from her book. "I'm lucky they let me in here."

"Why?"

"They don't usually let people over seventy have chemo. I'm fit, want it, need it, and my oncologist said yes."

"How long have you had cancer?" I ask.

"I've lived with cancer twenty years already, and I hope to live at least another ten."

"Wow."

While the three of us chat about being positive, my arm warms up under a heating pad. My nurse checks the calculations on the medication. I'll get more bags than anyone else does again today, each marked "Hindmarch."

11:50 a.m. ID for IV. Before she begins my drip, Sally asks, "When were you born?"

"January 1, 1940. Out of curiosity, why does everyone ask?"

"With a surname like Hindmarch, there's almost no room for confusion, but a name like Campbell, Johnson, Wong, Lee, Smith, it's possible, and it has happened to me several times, that two of them come for treatment on the same day and in the same room. One day, I had three Wongs, two with the same type of cancer."

Sally taps today's chosen vein lightly. I close my eyes and take a deep breath. She inserts the IV into a vein in my right hand and it hurts. I then watch her check to see that it's working by having the blood come up the tube slightly. She bandages the needle into position. Then the Dexamethasone (the dancing drug) in a one-litre bag starts to drip into me.

Penny and Ruth and I continue to chat about eating well and

exercise while Sally adjusts something in the woman's IV.

"Doctors can't get rid of my cancer, but treatments keep it from growing."

"They can do that?"

"Sometimes, not all types – I'm lucky."

"You're finished," Sally says to Ruth.

"Over until next week," Ruth says to us.

"Goodbye. Good luck." Good attitude. Good people.

"Penny – let's stroll around the chemo wing. I'm antsy."

Sally unplugs my IV from the wall outlet. Now the metal box (almost the size of a car battery) will run on it. I hold all the wires in my IV hand with my right fingers while with my left I push the pole and its machine out the door Penny has opened.

"Did you see Sally's hand shake?" I ask when we are far enough away she can't hear.

"Yes," says Penny, "but it didn't shake when she put the needle in. I looked very carefully. She didn't shake one bit."

My legs stretch out as we move more quickly.

"Too fast," Penny says as we circle past Lynn the second time. "We're almost running."

I laugh and slow down. My legs are longer than most men's and Penny is five inches shorter than me. I was paying no attention to pace. After five or six loops around the centre of the ward, we go back to my chemo room and I go to the washroom before I get into my seat. Not easy but so much easier than last time. When I get out, Penny is talking with the new patient who took Ruth's spot. I drink water and meet Eddie, a handsome man in his sixties who's flown down from the Northwest Territories. I drink more water.

12:05 p.m. Adria. The red stuff, 109 mg of Adriamycin (doxorubicin) in the two toothpaste-thick syringes, smarts as it enters my blood through the intravenous tube.

"That hurts a bit," I say, "I feel it half way up my arm." Sally adjusts the needle.

Adria, Adria, kill cancer cells. Do your stuff. Stop them. Stop them replicating now.

We find out that Eddie is an engineer who has just retired. His positive attitude is totally evident despite the bad news he keeps getting from his oncologist. Happy to be alive. Happy to have lived in the north. Happy to stay there. "The doctors can't get rid of the cancer, but treatments every three months keep me floating." He takes a slug of

Gatorade – "This increases the electrolytes. You might want to try one."

12:45 p.m. A Neglected Garden. With the Taxol started and Eddie about to leave, Penny and I and my IV machine walk to the fridge to pick up the ham sandwiches and then take the elevator down to the fifth floor where there's a large outside garden off the waiting room. Even though it is chilly, we both want to be outside. But first, we have to get through the two glass doors that open in rather than slide. Penny holds one of the doors, but my left hand can't push the pole and open the left door at the same time because my right is encumbered with the machine, so I used my right hip to open the door – rather awkward. Once we get outside in the chilly air, immediately I feel drainage gaps in the bricks as the narrow wheels of my IV machine bounce. Also the wooden sidewalks with spaces between the planks (after all we live in a rain forest – rain does have to drain) are not made for upright machines with tiny wheels, so we only circle once. There might as well be a sign: NO INTRAVENOUS PATIENTS HERE. The flowers and other plants aren't cared for. There are dead begonia and dead ivy, but not one live flower, not even a morning glory which most West Coasters consider a nasty weed. The planters are full of various weeds, too full. Neglect. Maybe no one is paid to care for flowers due to cutbacks. Maybe no volunteers want this job because it is the only smoking area the Agency has. Not exactly a tranquil outdoor space to relax in on a cool summer day or stretch out in the sun.

When we get back to where we began, we sit at a table near the rain/wind shelter and where hospital staff, visitors, and even a cancer patient have come to smoke. Penny and I roll our eyes and laugh then her expression changes.

"It's not dripping," Penny says.

"What?"

"It's stopped dripping." She tries to read the numbers on the machine. "I'm afraid of air going into your vein."

Within two seconds, we're up and racing – as much as I can race given that the pole is taller than I am. The bags swing and jiggle due to the bumps over the bricks and wood. We make it through the door quickly because somebody coming out holds one side open while Penny grabs the other. We zip to the elevator which, thankfully, is right there and almost empty.

"Sally, Sally," Penny calls running ahead of me.

"It's okay," Sally says as she checks my needle. "These machines are virtually foolproof." She resets mine.

"Enough adventure for today," I say. "Maybe we should try meditating."

## First Few Days after Second Chemo

Almost no nausea this time. I even ate a mean Sunday: pork, mashed potatoes, carrots, cauliflower, no greens. Less speedy than last chemo. I get tired suddenly and rest. I then get up and buzz around.

Distractions. My brain lacks focus. I pay attention to one thing and flit to another. I forget why I am in a room. I walk up the Drive and a beaded curtain lures me inside Beckwoman's – I have to buy it right now. Rainbow colours shift in light as I walk down the hill toward home. I nail it up over our back door. Lars looks at me as if I flipped back to the sixties. Every time I see it, my belly smiles.

## I Stumble

June 12. While watering my front lawn, I stumble and fall backwards onto the grass and moss. Why? I've lost some feeling in my feet and my balance is now off. My chemo does that to fingers and toes. I won't be able to go for walks unaccompanied.

## Strolling in a Storm

June 15. Rick Pelletier, a neighbour of twenty years, lives on the upper floor directly across my street in a house as old as mine (1908) or even older. He teaches graphic arts at Delta Secondary School and is now into the windup phase: school annual at the print shop, final projects coming in, reports to do.

Rick and I arrange to take a short stroll about the neighbourhood after the Dallas–Colorado hockey playoff game finished. As we chat about what's going on with our lives, I am astonished how little we really know about ourselves and why we do what we do.

"How's chemo going?" he asks.

"Okay so far. I hope these crazy cancer cells can be zapped by it, stopped from dividing. I pray chemo's killing them so I might live."

"How about the side effects?"

"Tolerable so far. My fingers have lost their sense of touch. I can't tell when hot is hot or cold cold so I have to be careful. The funny thing is I can't eat romaine lettuce – one of my favourite things – because it smells so gassy – I also can't drink giger ale or beer unless I let them flatten a day or two."

"Hair loss?"

"Compared to life – a small deal."

We are between Victoria and Nanaimo Streets close to Lord Nelson Elementary (about ten blocks away), when we hear thunder and turn back (hip hop, talky talk) through rain which suddenly stops, so we add blocks to get more stretch and air and yakkity yak. Just as we are heading north toward the mountains and only three blocks from home, lightning cracks close by. Holding arms, we skip and run through pelting rain to my porch to get under cover and to watch the light show over our city. (Unlike elsewhere, Vancouver seldom gets lightning storms especially ones that last more than three minutes, so of course we are gleeful and kid-like and want to stay out to see.)

A young father staying out late, Phil Djwa, arrives home on his red Yamaha and runs through rain to join us. When the lightning ends and thunder stops, we watch rain bounce on concrete and car hoods then the water becomes so thick that our street looks like a man-made river and sidewalks like creeks. The whole city feels wonderfully wild and alive with sirens from ambulances and fire trucks and every dog everywhere yowls. We are giddy, warm, wet. We linger like kids did last night when I overheard: "Not yet ... not now ... we'll come in ten minutes ... we promise, we will." When the rain lightens and Commercial Drive grows quiet, we return to the insides of our three comfy old homes.

## I Want to Swim

I want to swim. I haven't for a whole month. My muscles miss toning. My heart and lungs miss working out. My bones and joints miss being surrounded by water. I especially love the stretches, the extensions of arms and legs that only come after twenty-five or thirty lengths when my reach seems to increase an inch or so. I usually swim a mile, sixty-four lengths: three lengths of crawl, one length of breast up until fifty. Then crawl and breast alternate. Today, I'll be happy if I can do half of that.

I call Rae Nickolichuk, a young Capilano College English instructor who used to be a lifeguard. I want her to be with me in case anything should happen. Bad news for today – she has to mark English placement tests for someone else. We arrange to meet tomorrow at Ron Andrews Pool over in North Vancouver. Ten minutes later, I want to go right away. Stop behaving like a three-year-old, I say to myself. Go to

Templeton Pool (only seven or eight blocks away). Tell the lifeguard. Drive there just in case you are too weak to walk back.

When I get to the pool's changing room, I hesitate about pulling on my bathing cap. Certainly don't need one. I pull it on anyway so I won't have to put up with stares.

"I'm in week two of a chemo cycle," I tell the young, blond lifeguard. "Can you watch out for me?"

"Certainly." He gives me a big smile, and I am off.

I decide I'm going to do forty, a kilometre, no more. The first six lengths are easy and feel good – just like they usually do. I love water. Always have. My arm stretch out: belly, back, and bottom float higher than almost all men's do. It's as if I plane just inches under the water's surface. After ten lengths, I wave over to the guard to indicate I'm okay. After twenty, I'm into a faster swim. At thirty, I start alternating breast and crawl lengths.

Then I float at the shallow end of an empty lane for a few minutes.

## Swimming Again

June 19. Rae Nickolichuk and I swim at Ron Andrews Pool. I don't wear my bathing cap this time because I've no hair to keep from the pool, the cap's protecting nothing but my scalp. We each have a lane to ourselves: my idea of heaven. Every so often, I look over at Rae who glides along much faster than I do. I swim sixty-four lengths, no problem, feels good. My fingertips and toes vibrate.

## And Again

June 20. Swim again with Rae. Sixty-four lengths again.

## Damn Blister

June 21. "I have a blister from my nose to my lip," I say to Jennifer, Dr.D's receptionist at the Cancer Agency.

"Dr.D is on duty this afternoon," she says. "I'll speak with her and call you back."

An hour later, during my normal nap time, I am in a waiting room and almost falling asleep on the only hot day we've had all June. Opposite me, a Japanese Canadian man in his early twenties falls asleep sitting up. Another patient and I get up and lift the young man's legs onto his bench so that he can be more comfortable.

When I see Dr.D, she gives me a prescription. "Without nostril hairs, you can expect your nose to run."

## A Visit with My GP

June 23. When I do get to see Dr.A, we're both uneasy. I don't say anything about the letter I wrote him and my other doctors, but neither does he. We hesitate.

"How are your treatments going?" he asks.

"Fine, so far. I've lost my taste buds this time, my sense of touch both times, my hair the first time. Chemo is so powerful. Just look at this cordy vein." I stick my right arm out at him. "I also get lights inside my head from one of the drugs."

"You have to have surgery?"

"Yes – a total mastectomy." Pause.

"Have you a surgeon?"

"Yes – but I haven't seen her yet."

"You never know," he says. "Nowadays with reconstruction and with doctors who want to conserve, you might not need a mastectomy."

Pause. This is awkward. "Do you use the internet?" he asks. "There's all sorts of information there that you might read – there are even cancer chatrooms."

"Not yet – but I do have dial-up access through the college."

"Do you visualize?"

"I'm not tranquil enough."

"It works well for children."

"I just run around saying, 'Zap it, kill, kill, kill!'" I am startled by the power of my voice.

He laughs lightly. Is he scared?

"Why did it take you from Monday until Friday to give me my diagnosis?"

"My wife was mad at me for that too," he says.

"Why? You knew it wasn't going to go away by itself."

"I wanted to have an appointment for you at the Cancer Agency."

"So you could pass me on." Too bad he didn't do that at the beginning of February not May.

"Little microcells," I say to myself as I drive home, "I want to kill you. Go. Fly. Drop. Starve. Disappear." I also identify with the cancer. Those cells want to live just as much as I do.

(This was my final visit with him but I didn't know that.)

## I Practice Saying Goodbye to My Breast

October 9. When I wake up, my left eyeball is stuck to its half-open lid and my mouth is full of blood. Aftermath of last chemo. I grab a Kleenex and apply pressure inside my lower lip. Last night I bit it (partially because the ends of my nerves are non-existent so my sense of touch everywhere in my body is spongy) and cut myself where there's a small vein. I applied pressure to it for fifteen minutes before the bleeding stopped. Now, pressing my lip with my right hand, I go to the bathroom to splash water into my eye so I can open and close it.

An hour later, I am scared. I know I'll get through surgery, but I do not want to go under. I do not want a mastectomy. All the accounts on the inflammatory breast cancer website certainly convinced me that this form of cancer comes back and most women die. Dr. F and Dr. D's offhand remarks make more sense to me than what I've read in books: "When this cancer comes back, it spreads like wildfire, wildfire." "No case of inflammatory breast cancer in this hospital has been treated with a partial removal."

I work on saying goodbye to my breast just like I said goodbye to my uterus years ago.

"Goodbye, sweet breast, goodbye. We had such fun. Your sister will miss you too."

Saying goodbye to my uterus really did help me, but that was invisible, and this is so visible. One thing I think about is how I will miss the sensations that run through my nipple and breast, the softenings and hardenings, the erotic responses.

You'll still have the other, I tell myself. You know that the best thing is to get this breast off so you won't have to worry about cancer starting there again. You know it can begin in the scar tissues, the chest wall, and that is why you must take the radiation, and that is why the breast must go. All this knowing doesn't help much. Saying goodbye might.

"Goodbye. Goodbye."

## Love All

October 10. I know my time may be limited. I enjoy each of my friends right now. I love them as they are. I love my son, sisters, mom, nieces, and nephew. You too, Nik.

I am not putting on a face. If I feel bad, I say so. If I have to stop, I do it. I can't push myself now as I did a year ago. I feel stress in my skin. Both chemo and hot flashes make me pink and red. I stop right away: sit down, lie down. I hope all this activity means the poisons are working.

Poisons change every cell in my body.

Last night with Nik, I came, then four or five seconds later a shock (a rush of chemo?) burned right up my spine and I screamed. If I had hair anywhere to stand on end, it would have been sticking right out for at least five minutes.

## Last Acts before Surgery

October 20. I drop off a letter at my lawyer's in the Il Mercato building at 1st and Commercial. I seek out the North Health Unit in the same building and tell the receptionist who I am so the community nurse will know when St. Vincent's Hospital calls her. Also while there, I take out enough money from Vancity Credit Union to last two weeks. After that, I cross Commercial Drive to another building to make an appointment with a physiotherapist one week from tomorrow which I can cancel in advance if need be. I pick up oranges, salad greens, tomatoes, and apples at Santa Barbara Market. Then I go home to make a supper of roast chicken, carrots mashed with turnip, baked potato, and salad. Then I go to my healing circle.

"We ask for special care for Maria tomorrow when she has her surgery. We ask that her surgeon encounters no obstacles and that Maria heals quickly."

## Surgery Thursday

October 21. I get up early and Nik arrives before 7:30 a.m. to drive me to St. Vincent's Hospital.

"Off with my breast!" I shout from porch to a neighbour. "I'm ready," I say to Nik as I get in. "It's time."

Nik drives easily through morning traffic and up to 33rd just off Cambie and Heather. We are greeted by a Sister who takes me up to a little room to change, shows me where to place my belongings (including glasses when I am through with them) in a metal locker, and tells us the nurse will be with us shortly. Nik and I chat as if nothing unusual is happening as I undress and slip on a blue hospital gown.

A pleasant nurse enters and asks, "When did you last eat or drink?"

"Nothing since last night."

"Do I detect a New Zealand accent?" Nik asks her.

"Yes," she smiles. "After thirty-two years in Vancouver, it is still faintly present."

She checks my chart, takes my blood pressure, and tells me to wash myself using the antiseptic. Because I have no hair, I don't have to use the razor to shave my underarm.

I am acutely aware this is the last time I will wash her. Nik looks at me and at her and says nothing.

"Goodbye, goodbye," I say.

He comes toward me and helps place my hospital gown back on.

"It might be an hour or so," I say. "Maybe you should go?"

"I have a lot of work to do," he says, "but I would stay if you want me to."

We kiss a long, wet-on-his-part and dry-on-mine kiss. Nothing tentative or pecky about either of us even here.

The nurse comes in just as we finish. She places a pill under my tongue.

"Let it dissolve on its own – don't bite it."

Minutes later, I am in the prep room. A young nurse comes to give me an IV, takes one look at my right arm and leaves. I hear three people talking about intercepting a particular surgeon whose surgery is just over and might still be here. I assume she has a reputation for being good at finding difficult veins. She will have to use the right because they are operating on the left. Even the chemo IV nurses had to use the left the last three sessions because the right veins were shot. She assesses for two minutes or even more and then gets the needle into a vein on her first stab. They set up the pre-anaesthetic and it begins to drip into me.

I meet the anesthetist, an ebullient man, who checks on my mouth.

"The pill is totally intact."

"I don't have any saliva to dissolve it," I say. "I haven't drunk a drop since eight last night."

He bounces away to fetch me a tablespoon of water in a folded paper pill cup.

"Hindmarch," he says. "Are you related to Peter and Pat Hindmarch Watson?"

"He's my cousin. Gladys was Peter's mother's name."

"He lives just up the alley from me," he says. "We will be seeing each other on Pender Island this weekend."

We both laugh. The coincidence seems funny. I dont know why.

"Now, do you have any questions about the anaesthetic?"

"I do. If you can go very lightly on the epinephrine, I would appreciate it."

"I saw that in the notes. Yes, we can. I'll also give you a painkiller so you'll have fewer after-effects. You'll find there's a big difference between the drugs they used in 1981 and now."

Dr. E comes in with her head covered in a green hat. She has a great smile. She looks at least fifteen times happier here than in her office. Her whole face is lit up. She's excited. She loves surgery more than anything. She takes a felt pen and draws an ellipse around a lump I have on my lower left rib and then makes a much bigger drawing all over the outer edge of my left breast.

Someone then wheels me to the operating room and helps me onto the chair/table. A green hat is placed over my head even though there's no hair to fall out.

"Me too," says the anaesthetist, placing a green cover on his head. "Now all of us are the same."

This seems incredibly funny to us, and we all laugh. That's the last I remember.

• • •

I wake up in a hospital room and then fall back to sleep.

• • •

Sometime in the afternoon, Lars comes in. "How are you doing?" he asks.

"Lars, my cancer is gone. It is gone now. " I say and fall back asleep after he kisses me.

An hour or so later, I need to pee. It is still light out. A nurse comes to help me get up and move with the IV pole still attached. She then helps me back into bed. Gone are the days of bedpans and such.

I sleep again until supper arrives – braised meat that smells good.

"Dorothy Jantzen has called and asked if you'd like a brief visit," says a worker noticing me plow through my food.

"Yes," I say. "Tell her to come."

This meat smells better than any I have eaten in the past three months. I eat the potatoes and everything.

An hour later, I get myself up and go to the washroom pushing the IV pole with my right hand. I then take it on a stroll through corridors. Just as I get close to washroom, I feel I am going to vomit. I make it through the heavy entrance door tethered to the IV machine and the door to a toilet stall before I upchuck. By the time I wash up, I feel fine, but weak. I decide to turn back and get into bed where I should have stayed.

I am asleep or almost asleep when Dorothy comes in. She is dressed in a marvelous Vogue jacket she sewed herself. She is holding flowers shaped like rooster's combs – some scarlet, some white. I have never seen these before nor has she. They are soft and scalloped. The long stems are covered in narrow but large green leaves. We talk for a minute or so before an attendant brings her a large vase to put them in. Dorothy fills it with water and is putting the flowers in the vase when I am suddenly sick again. This time, I can't contain it. Parts of my supper land on the floor, on my gown, on my bedding, and on Dorothy's sleeve.

It is only 8 p.m. when I go back to sleep. For the first time in months, I sleep through the night.

## Discharged Friday

October 22. Before eight the next morning, Dr. E comes in to see me.
  She asks me a few questions then says, "You are discharged."
"What?"
"You can go home."
"Lars."
"Mom."
"Lars, can you come and get me?"
"What?"
"You heard me. They're letting me go. They want me out."
"I'll be there in twenty minutes, but I have an important meeting at eleven. Who is going to look after you?"
"I'll figure that out. Just come get me."
  I call Jean Clifford and explain.
"What? You had a mastectomy yesterday and you're discharged the next morning?"
"Yes."
"It would be an honour, my friend."
"Bring your marking. I'll probably sleep the whole time."
"I will."
  I then call Bill Schermbrucker and ask if he can be with me after Jean.
"Yes."
  I'm getting dressed when a physiotherapist arrives. She was supposed to have half an hour with me so I could learn what to do, but

she gets only five minutes before Lars barges in. She does each exercise so fast in front of us and I am so doped I know I won't remember but hope Lars will.

At home, I go straight to my bedroom to pull on my pink satin pajamas. I am wearing a soft bra that was put on in the operating or recovery room. There's a gauze dressing where my left breast was and under my entire armpit. The dressing is not nearly as thick as I imagined it would be. I feel sore where the tube comes out on my rib cage, but that's about all. They gave me a prescription bottle of Tylenol 3s and told me to take one or two every three hours if I needed to. I don't. I fiddle around my sewing basket to find a diaper pin (much safer than a safety) to pin the tube and hockey puck–sized Hemovac drain to the left side of my pajamas.

I plunk myself down in my TV room and pull up a duvet. Lars makes me tea and then waits for Jean to arrive before he goes to his meeting.

She comes in and sits with me to chat for thirty or so minutes to calm me down. Actually, I am quite calm. I am shocked that they discharged me so fast.

A couple of hours later, Bill arrives wearing shorts. It's late October but to a man from Kenya that means nothing. We talk briefly and I fall back asleep.

That evening, Brian and Karen arrive with a cotton jacket I can wear in bed or out and a bottle of wine. We open it.

"To my beloved left breast," I say, "I hope to hell your death was totally necessary."

## Bad News

November 5. Merrilyn offers to come with me to Dr. F just in case the pathology report is bad. Dr. F greets both in an examining room.

"Your cancer was throughout your breast. Of the thirteen lymph nodes I was able to retrieve, seven contained cancer."

"Oh." That's all I can say for a moment. "Could I please have a copy of the report?"

"Of course," she says. "I have a copy for you. I am going to write you a prescription for a prosthesis and two bras."

"Bras?"

"You pay for them, but they are tax free. If you have extended health benefits, you might even be reimbursed for two each year."

Half an hour later at John and Merrilyn's condo on the edge of Granville Island with a view of False Creek and the Burrard Street Bridge, John and Merrilyn make sandwiches and soup while I read the report:

Three containers, each labelled by name. Specimen A is an ovoid mass measuring 5 × 2.5 × 1.2 cm. [This is a lump on my rib I've had for more than a decade that I asked Dr. F to remove.]

Specimen B consists of a mastectomy weighing 1005 g. [A kilogram? My breast weighed more than 2.2 pounds? Wow!] The breast measures 23 × 19 × 5 cm. It is surfaced by an ellipse of skin measuring 28 × 14.5 cm. There are no obvious skin scars. [Despite all my biopsies – eleven chunks in all.] The centrally located nipple is slightly depressed. The posterior margin is intact and painted with silver nitrate.

On serial sectioning, the breast is composed of approximately 75 percent fat and 25 percent firm white tissue. Within the latter tissue are several palpably firm areas which are suspicious for malignancy. These masses tend to be located centrally and in the lower quadrant. [This is where I first felt something.] None of these masses come close to the skin or the posterior margin. These masses vary in size from .5 to 2.5 cm.

Specimen B was divided into A through Z. A and B were the nipple. It shows no evidence of Paget's disease or invasive malignancy.

C through to I from both inner and outer central breast show that the palpably firm areas are all foci of infiltrating mammary carcinoma. Each focus shows an irregular area of stromal fibrosis [cushion-like hardnesses] infiltrated by nests and cords of malignant cells with marked tubular and rare mitoses [dividing cells – means the chemo was working in the last half.] On the glass slide these foci vary in size from .2 cm up to 1.5 cm in diameter. Calcifications are associated with some of the foci. There is minimal lymphocytic host response. [Sounds good to me – in other words it isnt spreading through the lymph glands, but it was until chemo hit it?] No vascular or lymphatic invasion is noted.

M, O, and Q from other areas of the breast show additional invasive foci.

R from the lateral [side] end of the breast shows a lymph node with some vascular congestion. No evidence of metastatic malignancy. [That lymph node is not spreading it.]

S consists of seven lymph nodes. These show partial replacement metastatic malignancy is associated with fibroelastotic stroma and calcifications. Section S shows a tumour deposit within axillary adipose [fatty] malignancy. Y and Z show three more tiny lymph nodes with no evidence of metastatic malignancy.

At the end, Dr. X wrote a summary:

1. Mass, abdominal wall – lipoma. [Just fat.]
2. Mastectomy with axillary contents:
   a. Grade I multifocal infiltrating mammary duct carcinoma. [To me, this confirms the chemo did its work. Instead of grade III or IV, the cancer was now only I.]
   b. No tumour involvement in nipple skin, or posterior margin.
   c. Estrogen receptor positive.
   d. Seven of ten axillary lymph nodes positive for metastatic carcinoma (apical nodes positive).
3. Three additional lymph nodes negative for malignancy.

This news is both positive and horrible: seven out of thirteen lymph nodes had cancer. They may be encapsulated, but, nevertheless, the cancer was there waiting to spread. John looks up "pleomorphism" in the dictionary and finds out it means "the occurrence of two or more forms in one life cycle."

"Does this mean the tentacles or nests coexisted with fibrous tissue?" I ask him.

"I think that's what it means."

## First Radiation

November 30, 2:00 p.m. I arrive at the Cancer Agency fifteen minutes early as arranged because I have to locate Linac 7 (short for Linear Accelerator) to get set up for my first radiation. As I walk through a maze of hallways, I steer to the right and notice that some of the waiting areas are packed full with close to twenty people waiting while others are nearly empty.

Linac 7 is the unit furthest away from the main radiation reception area. It has only two patients in its waiting room – one with apricot-coloured hair and the other with a silvery toque.

An attendant or nurse enters with someone who has just finished a treatment and hands me a pink cotton gown and a orange-green-navy plaid rectangular bag.

"Undress from the waist up. Leave your shoes on for now. Put your top and outer stuff in this bag and hang it here. When you finish your treatment, and are dressed, I want you to return the bag with your gown and hang it there for tomorrow." She points to a metal rack on which several other bags of various colours and patterns such as polka dots and zigzags are hanging. They are all different so each person can identify her or his. How practical. Why have a clean gown for each daily treatment since most last only a few minutes?

I get into the small cubicle with an awkward accordion door that's hard to shut. I can't turn around and I'm only 5'6", about average weight. A man or woman just a little bit bigger than me wouldn't be able to change in here. I can't get this tiny gown on and it's certainly not the room's fault. The whole thing gets stuck on my neck and naked head. It must be made for a six- or seven-year-old. I open the cubicle accordion.

"I need help," I shout.

The patient with apricot hair goes to find the attendant for me.

When the nurse opens the cubicle, she laughs.

"That one won't work. We don't have any today that will. How do you feel about wearing your clothes to the treatment room and then removing them quickly? We'll give you a sheet for cover. That will be easier all around as long as you are quick."

"I'll be quick."

She leads me down a corridor to a little reception area for Linacs 6 and 7.

"Put your card here."

Linac 7's plexiglass container has three other ingoing cards.

"Next time, put your card there when you arrive, then go back to the waiting room until we call you."

Moments later, I hear my name. The nurse quickly leads me to a room that feels like thick black velvet. I can't see a wall or ceiling or anything. I put my right hand out to feel where I will sit, then place my folded outer jacket on it and push my boots with socks in under it so no one will trip on them. Then I pull off my sweater and soft silk warm undershirt – glad I bought it for my naked skin where my left breast once was.

"Here's cover," the nurse says as she drapes a sheet over my naked front then leads me to a black table where I can see more. She guides me one step up, and I lie down on it. Behind me will be the giant metal washer-looking machine like the one I was measured on during radiation-simulation just five days ago.

"Today will take a little longer than your other treatments because we will be checking several things and making a film to check against the simulator film. Now, move up further."

A young man joins her and four hands adjust me.

"No. Too far. Come back."

"To your left," says the man. "You're an inch too far to the right." Once I move just a tad, he places a triangular foam under my knees and adjusts it so I can totally relax my whole legs.

"Board angle, nineteen degrees," the woman says. "Headrest B, position one, medium. Arm holder, B. Height, medium. Elbow rest, one and seven."

"One is off the chart."

"That's what Dr. W's instructions state: one and seven."

"Okay."

"Foot rest, 103 centimetres."

It takes them about eight minutes fiddling to get where my left breast used to be into the right place. I don't mind a second of it because I want them to get it exactly right. Then they remove my cotton sheet and place a plastic cover about a centimetre thick over my whole chest.

"What's this?"

"It's a bolus. Because you have no breast tissue on your left side, we use this as if it were your flesh. Move up just a touch." The bolus slides off to the right and lands on the floor.

"I'll fix that," she says.

She uses wide masking tape to hold it into position. Seconds later, it slides off again.

"Holy moly." She leaves the room to get another roll.

"This should fix that," she says when she returns. "We'll use a lot before you're through." She uses several feet of it to tape the bolus to my right hip and to my shoulder.

"A mummified right breast," I say. On my left, the bolus just drapes loosely like it was always meant to do.

"We'll be leaving now," says the young man.

"We'll be watching you," says the woman. "You can stop us if you need to. We will hear you."

"Be absolutely still when we tell you," he says. "Just relax."

Relax? He's got to be kidding. I hear some Bach through the speaker, but because of nerve damage to my right ear caused by chemo the brass section sounds like it is underwater.

"Can you turn up the sound before you leave?"

"Certainly."

"Enough?"

"Yes, that's it."

I am now alone in a black room that has glass I can't see through beyond my feet slightly to the right and Glenn Gould is playing the Goldberg Variations. The technicians are on the other side of that glass.

"Maria, we will just test the angles on the wall before we begin your first section."

Suddenly, there are hundreds of red and white dots forming lines on the ceilings and walls. They float between me and the room's edges. They seem to move with the music.

"Okay, Maria. We are ready. Do not move until we tell you. Breathe normally. First session will be two minutes."

I pick out a spot on the ceiling to look at. There's a clicking sound as the Linac starts to radiate me. I feel nothing, yet I know it is doing what it is made for. Two minutes is a long time – much longer than I ever think it is. Kill those cells. Kill cancer cells. Glenn Gould's fingertips seem to touch my chest. The lights keep dancing.

Dr. W instructed them to radiate my left chest and underarm from four angles. Each angle takes a minute or two. My nurse comes in before my third position to put a plastic thing into the muzzle of the machine, then she places a lead wedge made especially for me into the plastic so my throat will be protected. I hope it doesn't fall out.

The machine is close to me in that third position and in the fourth it seems far away. It is easier and seems faster but I can't really tell.

When I leave, I dress quickly. I can see much more easily. I'll buckle my boots when I am out in the hallway, so that the room can be set up for the next patient who is bound to be waiting.

All told, I've been almost an hour. It wasn't bad. It didn't hurt at all.

There's only one thing I want to do and I do it. I drive to Freedman to buy a large grey felt bag that I saw when I bought my boots. It is large enough to hold my winter jacket, sweater, teddy, bra, wallet, and glasses when I change for radiation. That way, I can wear my teddy there and pack my prosthesis/bra if I want to meet someone after or stop for groceries on my way home.

## What's My Prognosis Now?

December 1. A week or so ago, I asked Nik if he would come with me to be my extra ears for my appointment with Dr. B, my oncologist. I haven't seen her since September, so after visiting my breast surgeon, I called the Cancer Agency to make an appointment.

She is almost on time for the first time.

"Dr. B, I'd like you to meet Nik Cuff. Nik this is Dr. B."

"What can I do for you today?" she asks me.

"When do I begin tamoxifen or one of the newer drugs my breast surgeon recommended?"

"You are an ideal candidate for tamoxifen," she says as she locates something in her file. "Your estrogen receptor level is 3+, the highest rating we have. Tamoxifen will block the estrogen and starve any cancer cell that feeds on it. We might use some of the other drugs later on. You will begin today. Next?"

"My future seems to be one big question mark. I can see only a week or so ahead. Anything after two months seems grey. I can't even imagine a year. Can you give me your prognosis? I want you to be straight with me."

"First," she says with her hands on my knees, "what have you read about the future in general for inflammatory breast cancer patients?"

"Mostly, it's bad news. The stories I've read are dreadful. Dr. Love gives the only statistic I have seen: 40 percent survive five years; 60 percent do not. Since mine was in seven out of thirteen lymph nodes, I am worried about how much time I have left."

"What would you do differently if you knew you had only a year to live?"

"I'd probably wouldn't go back teaching. I do love it, but not enough to spend the last year of my life marking stacks of essays."

"What would you do if you had two or four?"

"I'd travel more – at least to see Saint Petersburg and Turkey, maybe Crete. Write. Read. If I knew I had four years, I'd teach one or two. Probably part-time. I just want my life to be more normal again. Teaching is normal for me."

"If I were you, I'd plan as if life is short and enjoy each day by living to the fullest. I'd make short term plans and longer ones."

Pause. Double pause. I don't know what to say. My head is mush. "Do you have any suggestions of books to read?"

"Yes, I do. They're both written by people who have had recurrences and there are several patients' stories in each. One is called *Dancing in Limbo* and the other had a previous title, *Holding Tight, Letting Go*, but is now called *Advanced Breast Cancer*. I can't recall who wrote or published them, but the titles should be enough. Read them awhile from now – not this month or next – but read them before you have a recurrence so you had a sense of what to expect."

"Do you have a prognosis?"

"Without a complete remission," she says, "it's hard to guess, but you will have a year for sure. If it comes back in less than six months, then you will probably have just a year. The longer you go between now and recurrence, the better your chances of fighting recurrence will be."

"Thank you for being honest," I say. "I appreciate it."

She nods to Nik when she says goodbye to us.

"You didn't say anything," I say as we walk to his van.

"You were doing well on your own," he says, "and you are clearly her patient."

"Do you like her?" I ask.

"Yes. She seems really bright and caring. Her advice has me thinking."

Nik drives me home through heavy rain and parks his van in my driveway leaving his noisy motor and windshield wipers on.

"Are you okay?" he asks.

"I'm feeling sad, Nik. The cancer was there throughout the breast and in the lymph nodes. There's nothing I can do about that now but accept it – I do – as fact. I put so much stake on chemo working and it did. Quite a bit. Not completely. It reversed the growth, shrunk it, but new cancer cells didn't disappear. I hope like hell that radiation and tamoxifen will get rid of it for me."

"I'll tell you what I've been thinking," he says as the wipers and motor continue banging away. "Live life to the fullest. Enjoy each day. Make short- and long-term plans. Everybody should live that way."

"We should but most don't."

"Are you sure you are okay to be alone?"

"I am," I say. "Got to be ready for my radiation at three. I think I'll nap a little right now."

# Postprose

# Postprose

PARAGRAPH 13, NO. 1 (1991)

She was writing something about her relationship with her lover and instead of "postpone" (they once postponed a talk for three months) the word "postprose" appeared on her screen. Postprose: what comes after, after what? After intricate structures she admires but never did learn to write? Or is this a message from her muse: post-the-prose? Prose – an outpost of heart and an inpost of consciousness.

Sometimes her mind dissolves as she marks. She knows this happens to other teachers too, as they disappear into a muddle of essays with occasional clear sentences or phrases or unusual errors to wake them from monotony: "Her lips are very sexy-looking and I sometimes feel like kissing her for a long, long time like a tapeworm attached in the intestine." She imagines kissing her own lover for a long, long time. They are standing near a door and the room is full of winter sunlight. Attached. When they separate, she sees green shining bamboo. Her student wasn't thinking about what he wrote, but he was there, right there, so inside the kiss he didn't visualize his simile but entered the closeness, duration, postponed the end of.

Should she post this piece to *paragraph*? She loves the name and the editor did send her a letter which she cannot at this moment find or reconstruct. What she wants to know is, do they publish only single paragraphs? A composition in a paragraph: *para-*, beside, alongside, beyond, aside; also to shield and to defend and to protect from; *-graph*, to write.

She no longer thinks of paragraphs as she writes, but she knows when one ends and another begins in a different way than her students do. Why? Because in grade eight she loved them and started to notice their structures and the way some writers break them early and others compose wildly or fully; some tuck their perceptions in, or defend a thought completely, or protect the whatever within the paragraph's shape or form. Mostly she composes paragraphs from the inside out. She never feels she's making a huge jump from one to another as some of her students do – as if there is a line or border there; but she has a confidence, an utter confidence, that this is the place to begin and this is the place to end.

Postprose/postpone. The end of the relationship, or the end of any expectation? It cannot be anything more than what it is, which is erotic, deeply erotic. In all other ways, she and he do not speak the same language. They translate the other. Present tense. Past also. The bamboo, which was covered in snow, now gleams again, and she walks through January slush to post the prose.

# Bibliography

## WORKS BY GLADYS HINDMARCH

Hindmarch, G. Maria. "From Swimming with Cancer." *The Capilano Review* 3, nos. 1–2 (Winter–Spring 2007): 78–83.

———. "Kitsilano (1963–69)." *The Capilano Review* 3, no. 39 (Fall 2019): 88–92.

———. "Untitled." In *71(+) for GB: An Anthology for George Bowering on the Occasion of his 70th Birthday*. Edited by Jean Baird, David W. McFadden, and George Stanley, 114. 2005.

Hindmarch, Gladys. "Before TISH." Interview by Brad Robinson. *Open Letter* 2, no. 1 (Winter 1971–1972): 30–36.

———. *A Birth Account*. Vancouver, BC: New Star, 1976.

———. "Cradles as coffins, coffins as cradles, a womb sometimes as both." *The Vancouver Sun*, July 7, 1981.

———. "Dear Roy." *The Bulletin: a Journal for and about the Nikkei Community* (February 1994): 27.

———. "Fair Harbour My Eye." *The Capilano Review* 12 (1977): 57–64.

———. "The Fifth Peter Story." *Imago* 20 (1974): 81–84.

———. "Had a wife." *Prism* 3, no. 2 (Winter 1962): 50–52.

———. "I Gotta Get Outta Here." *Iron* 2, no. 4 (November 1976): 5–7.

———. "Improsements." *Beyond Tish*. Edmonton, AB: NeWest, 1991. 55–59.

———. "Just Because These Words." *The Capilano Review* 11 (1977): 76–80.

———. "No Cheese." *NMFG* 4 (May 1976): unpaginated.

———. "Nothing Is Simple." *The Georgia Straight*. Supplement, *Writing* 9 (September 3–7, 1971): 10–11.

———. "Other Men Make The." *The Georgia Straight*, September 30–October 6, 1970. Page numbers unknown.

———. *The Peter Stories*. Toronto: Coach House Press, 1976.

———. "Postprose." *paragraph* 13, no. 1 (1991): 16.

———. "Review of *HERmione* by H.D.," *The Reader* 1, no. 4 (August 1982): 25–26.

———. "A Single Scrambled." *The Georgia Straight*. Supplement, *Writing* 5 (September 30–October 6, 1970): 13.

———. *Sketches*. Montréal: Beaver Kosmos Folio. 1971.

———. "Something's Going On." *The Capilano Review* 4 (Fall–Winter 1973): 5–7.

———. "Some Trip This Is Going to Be." *The Georgia Straight*. Supplement, *Writing* 7 (May 4–7, 1971): 2–3.

———. "Such as It Is." *The Georgia Straight*. Supplement, *Writing* 1 (October 29–November 5, 1969): 26.

———. "Thesen's Long Dash." *Brick* 32 (Winter 1988): 40–44.
———. "They Know What They're Doing." *The Georgia Straight*. Supplement, *Writing* 3 (April 1–8, 1970): 15.
———. "This Job's Been Good to Me." *Periodics* 2 (1977): 8–12.
———. "To Be Here." *Periodics* 7–8 (Winter 1981): 35–39
———. *The Watery Part of the World*. Vancouver, BC: Douglas & McIntyre, 1988.
———. "What Can I Do? Germaine Greer Slashes Myths." *The Ubyssey* September 24, 1971: 2.
———. "Where They Are." *The Georgia Straight*. Supplement, *Writing* 1 (October 29–November 5, 1969): 26–27.
———. "Which Way to Go." *Iron* 8–9 (1970): 39–42.
———. "Writers Forgotten." *The Vancouver Sun*, date and page numbers unknown.
———. "The Wrong Place." *Iron* 5 (1969): 37–46.
———. "You Wouldn't Want To." *The Capilano Review* 15 (1979): 128–134.
———. "Zeballos, B.C.," *The Capilano Review* 4 (Fall–Winter 1973): 8–15.
Hindmarch, Maria. "Hey, Pierre." In *One More: For Pierre Coupey's 70th*. Edited by Jenny Penberthy and compiled by Patti Kernaghan. North Vancouver, BC: Capilano University Editions (CUE), 2012. 39–41.
———. "Pauline and Fred: Friends, Parties, Community." *Open Letter* 12, no. 2 (Spring 2004): 14–24.
———. "Three Prose Pieces" In "New Writing, Critical Essays, Photography on the Work of Roy Kiyooka." Edited by Jill Hartman and derek beaulieu. Special issue, *Dandelion* 29, no. 1 (2003): 168–170.

## CRITICISM AND REVIEWS

Butling, Pauline. "*A Birth Account* Re Viewed." In *Women and Words: The Anthology / Les femmes et les mots: une anthologie*. Vancouver, BC: Harbour Publishing, 1984. 133–37.
———. "Gladys Hindmarch: Pointillist Prose." *Essays on Canadian Writing* 32 (1986): 70–91.
Fong, Deanna, Erín Moure, Karis Shearer, and Al Filreis. "In Conversation: A Corner Is Never a Firm Divide." *The Capilano Review* 3, no. 39 (Fall 2019): 93–98.
Fong, Deanna, and Karis Shearer. "Gender, Affective Labour, and Community-Building Through Literary Audio Artifacts." *No More Potlucks* 50 (May 2018). Online.
Stannard, Claire. "Hindmarch's Best Stories: Sensuous, Strong, and Authentic." *Room of One's Own* 12, nos. 2–3 (1988): 196–198.
Thesen, Sharon. "Writing the Continuing Short Story: Gladys Hindmarch's *The Watery Part of the World*." *West Coast Line* 25, no. 1 (1991): 166–170.

# Acknowledgments

The editors of this volume would like to thank the following people for their contributions to bringing this work to fruition: Catriona Strang and Kevin Williams at Talonbooks; Daphne Marlatt and Frank Davey for their consultation on the oral history interviews and correspondence; George Bowering for the photograph of Gladys Hindmarch; Karen Tallman for kind permission to reproduce the "Westcoast with Gladys" conversation with Warren Tallman; Erín Moure for her ongoing encouragement, as well as her generous proofread of and commentary on the manuscript; Tony Power for his assistance with locating materials and other rare books in SFU Special Collections; Mathieu Aubin and Jason Wiens for alerting us to documents discovered in their archival research; Jason Camlot for offering us the space in which we did our first "feminist close listening" that generated the idea of this book; Dayna McLeod for the invitation to write about the Hindmarch–Tallman conversations for the final issue of the feminist publication *No More Potlucks*. Every effort was made to seek permissions from original publishers; we acknowledge *Brick*, *The Capilano Review*, *Open Letter*, *paragraph*, *TISH*, and *The Reader* for works included in this volume. Deanna would like to thank Justin Fragapane and "Little Max" for their support and inspiration, for bringing her life into even closer orbit with this work. Karis would like to thank Alison Conway for being there for all the miles and all the finish lines, including this one.

The publisher has made a concerted effort to trace and contact the copyright holder of "Before *TISH*: from *Oral History of Vancouver*" (interview by Brad Robinson, 1971–1972). We ask anyone with information relating to the rights holder of this material to contact us.

# Biographies

**Deanna Fong** is a postdoctoral fellow in English and History at Concordia University in Montréal, Québec, where her research focuses on the intersections of auditory media, ethics, and listening. She is a member of the federally funded SpokenWeb team, who have developed a web-based archive of digitized sound recordings for literary study. With Ryan Fitzpatrick and Janey Dodd, she co-directs the audio/multimedia archive of Canadian poet Fred Wah, and has done substantial cataloguing and critical work on the audio archives of Japanese Canadian poet and painter Roy Kiyooka. She is the author of chapters in *CanLit Across Media: Unarchiving the Literary Event* (McGill-Queens University Press, 2019) and the forthcoming *Pictura: Essays on the Works of Roy Kiyooka* (Guernica Editions, 2020).

**Karis Shearer** is an associate professor in English and Cultural Studies at the University of British Columbia's Okanagan campus. Her research and teaching focus on literary audio, the literary event, the digital archive, material culture, and women's labour within poetry communities. She has published on a range of cultural production, including Sina Queyras's feminist website Lemon Hound, George Bowering's little magazine *Imago*, and Michael Ondaatje's *The Long Poem Anthology*. At UBC Okanagan, she directs the AMP Lab and leads the UBCO team within the SpokenWeb Partnership.

Born in 1940 to parents Taimi (Aho) and Robert Hindmarch, **Gladys Maria Hindmarch** became known as a central figure in the TISH community and the Vancouver literary scene in the 1960s and 1970s. As an editor, she was involved in the little magazine *Motion* (a prose companion to *TISH*); the second editorial phase of *TISH*, which she co-edited with Peter Auxier, David Cull, David Dawson, Daphne Marlatt, and Dan McLeod; and issues 7–9 of *The Capilano Review*. She attended and participated in major literary events including the Vancouver Poetry Conference (1963), the Berkeley Poetry Conference (1965), and Women & Words (1983). Her writing has appeared in a number of local and national journals and little magazines dedicated to innovative prose, Canadian literature, and women's writing, including *Iron, Imago, Periodics, boundary 2, Writing,* and *The Capilano Review* and anthologies *Cradle and All: Women Writers on Pregnancy and Birth* (1989), *Words We Call Home* (1990), and *Islands West: Stories from the Coast* (2001). She is the author of three books of prose: *A Birth Account* (New Star, 1976), *The Peter Stories* (Coach House, 1976) and *The Watery Part of the World* (Douglas & McIntyre, 1988). An active member of Vancouver's literary, academic, and activist communities, Hindmarch taught English at Vancouver Community College from 1965 to 1969 and 1972 to 1974, and then at Capilano College from 1974 to 2002. Until the late 1990s she wrote under the name Gladys Hindmarch, but since then prefers to use her middle name, Maria, pronounced the Finnish way with emphasis on the first syllable.